Alexander Mackenzie

The Life and Speeches of Hon. George Brown

Alexander Mackenzie

The Life and Speeches of Hon. George Brown

ISBN/EAN: 9783337141134

Printed in Europe, USA, Canada, Australia, Japan

Cover: Foto ©Raphael Reischuk / pixelio.de

More available books at **www.hansebooks.com**

THE
LIFE AND SPEECHES

OF

HON. GEORGE BROWN

BY

ALEX. MACKENZIE.

Toronto:
THE GLOBE PRINTING COMPANY
1882.

PREFACE.

In undertaking to prepare a memoir of the late Hon. George Brown, the writer desired to present to the public a faithful representation of his character in a personal and public sense, but mainly to show his position as a representative of the people.

It was naturally supposed at the time of Mr. Brown's death that abundant material for this purpose would be found amongst his papers. This belief was not sustained when an examination was made. He had given little attention to the preservation of papers affecting himself, though of the utmost interest respecting many public events in which he had borne a leading part; many reminiscences of a more personal character were also lost which would have thrown light on his private life. Mr. Brown seems not to have given a thought to the systematic preservation of documents which would have been of material use in presenting a perfectly faithful representation of what he really was as a public man and a private citizen. A somewhat intimate personal acquaintance, and a political connection of more than a quarter of a century, have enabled the writer to supply to some extent what was found to be wanting; if the information available on some subjects is not quite as exact as would be desirable, no opinions are expressed or conclusions arrived at which are not fully justified by what is known. No attempt has been made to record, in Boswellian style, petty incidents and events in which Mr. Brown bore some part; the intention was rather to present such a general view of his character, and the public events in which he figured so prominently, as would be reasonably satisfactory to the public generally, but especially to those with whom he was personally popular.

Mr. Brown's eventful life, and his position in Canada as a political leader, made it almost indispensable that some one should place on record the share he had in securing constitutional changes which made Canada a home of civil and religious equality and liberty, in such a manner as would do some measure of justice to his character as a true patriot. The writer regrets that this duty did not fall into more competent hands, and that a more graphic picture should not be presented of one, who was so deservedly popular, and who gave so much of his life and strength, as a journalist and politician, to combating public wrongs, and establishing a new constitution embodying just principles of government.

It is always a difficult task to write contemporary history. That difficulty had to be encountered in the present work. Other actors in the events described, who are still before the public, may be unwilling to accept the position assigned them. The writer would regret exceedingly if any of his remarks should, by any such persons, be considered offensive or out of place. The duty of the biographer of Mr. Brown is, however, while dealing fairly with others whose names or acts must be mentioned, to present a faithful picture of him as he was, and his services as they were, and deserved to be estimated by the public, uncaring whether this course should lead to censure or approval on the part of those whose paths were crossed by the departed statesman during his lifetime.

The asperities engendered amongst public men in Canada, strong as they have been, are not so bitter but that it may be assumed that Mr. Brown's contemporary opponents will be disposed to look kindly on the record of one who was always an honourable foe and a faithful personal friend.

A long continuance of ill health, which necessitated many months' enforced absence from any labour, has alone delayed the completion of this memoir, which at first the writer hoped to accomplish within a few months.

TORONTO, August, 1882.

CONTENTS.

IN MEMORIAM—*continued:*

CORRESPONDENCE—*continued:*

INTRODUCTION.

It is impossible to present any fair estimate of Mr. Brown's life
and character, or to do justice to his merits as a public man, without
dealing to a certain extent with the public questions in the discussion of which he was engaged for thirty-six years.

When Mr. Brown first appeared in Canada the country had not
recovered from the shock and confusion caused by the ill-advised
insurrectionary movements of 1837-9. These movements were brought
about by a quarter of a century's misgovernment at the hands of a
small but compact body of men, whose professed excessive loyalty to
king and church, though marred by an abhorrence of popular rights,
had generally secured to them the support of the British Government,
then also controlled to a great extent by the same unjust and anti-
progressive spirit.

The leaders of the popular party were almost exclusively engaged
in a battle with the powers of the day on specific grievances complained of, and consequently gave comparatively little attention to
the advocacy of fundamental principles of government which, left to
operate freely, would have removed all grievances by due course of law.
Mr. Lindsey, in his life of Wm. Lyon Mackenzie, says : " The people
"complained of the government, when they ought to have struck a blow
" at the system which rendered it possible for a party who could com-
" mand only a small minority in the popular branch of the legislature
" to continue their grasp on the reins of power." Wild attacks on the
leaders of the Canadian oligarchy (sometimes embracing the Governor),
and petitions to the Secretary of State for the colonies, on subjects
which the Canadian people, left to themselves, would have immediately
put right, were perhaps to be expected ; nor would it be just now to
severely blame, or to blame at all, that mode of procedure ; but such
a course only anticipated some temporary relief in some specific cases
of injustice caused by a bad system of government, rather than looked
for a radical cure.

The initiation of a system of partially responsible government with
the union of the two Canadas did not rapidly tend to produce perfect
contentment, for the simple reason that the name existed without the

possession of the substance.   The earlier governors sent from England hesitated about giving full effect to the principles of free parliamentary government, and were all much disposed to retain an undue control of public affairs in their own hands.   Even as late as 1854 Lord Derby made use of the following language while discussing proposed reforms in the Canadian constitution :

" Nothing like a free and well regulated monarchy could exist for a single moment under such a constitution as that which is now proposed for Canada. From the moment that you pass this constitution the progress must be rapid towards republicanism, if anything could be more really republican than this bill."

In 1850 Lord Elgin felt himself obliged to give a liberal Minister in England his views in the following terms :

" You must renounce the habit of telling the colonies that the colonial is a provisional existence.   You must allow them to believe that, without severing the bonds which unite them to Great Britain, they may attain the degree of perfection, and of social and political development, to which organized communities have a right to aspire.   .   .   .   There is nothing which makes the colonial statesman so jealous as rescripts from the Colonial Office suggested by the representations of provincial cliques or interests, who ought, as he contends, to bow before the authorities of Government House, Montreal, rather than those of Downing Street."

Lord Sydenham, notwithstanding his English Whig training, formed an administration of men who had never acted together, and who could not honestly do so in the future.   The sole bond of union was the personal influence of the Governor-General himself, who hoped in this way to retain in his own hands an amount of power and influence wholly inconsistent with a system of responsible government.

No vigorous effort was put forth anywhere to demand the inauguration of the new system by a full recognition of its principles.   The presence of Robert Baldwin and R. B. Sullivan in company with Wm. H. Draper, in an ordinary administration, sufficiently indicated the compromise character of the principles which would govern it in its administrative capacity, and also in its legislative programme.

The attempt to maintain the old system under a new and attractive name was continued with varying success until the final rupture with Sir Charles Metcalfe, a few months after his arrival in Canada, by the proper action of his then ministers, who formed the first Liberal or Reform administration of Canada, although at least some of them showed by their subsequent action that they held their principles of popular government very lightly.   It is hazarding little to say that the principles of responsible government were not well understood by the people, nor much insisted upon by their leaders up to this period, while the representatives of the Crown were either hostile to them or believed them inapplicable in their fulness to Canada.   Lord John Russell announced at the time Mr. Poulett Thomson went out as

governor, that " The principal offices in the colony would not be con-
" sidered as being held by a tenure equivalent to one during good
" behaviour, but that the holders would be liable to be called upon to
" retire whenever, from motives of public policy or for other reasons,
" this should be found expedient." This practically left it discre-
tionary with the Governor, not with a parliamentary majority, to
terminate the official life of a minister. It is probable that Sir Charles
Bagot would, had he lived, have taken a more constitutional course,
and governed by a parliamentary majority. No one now attempts to
defend Lord Metcalfe as having rightfully exercised the functions of a
constitutional governor. Mr. Walrond says of him that " Lord Met-
" calfe with great difficulty formed a conservative administration, and
" immediately dissolved his parliament. The new elections gave a
" small majority to the conservatives, chiefly due, it was said, to the
" exertion of his personal influence ; but the success was purchased at
" a ruinous cost, for he was now in the position, fatal to a Governor,
" of a party man." Lord Elgin was the first Governor-General who
determined to govern through his constitutional advisers having the
confidence of parliament, and even in his case it was not difficult
sometimes to discern traces of his influence over his council; but that
influence, though greater than usual, was a legitimate influence. " I
" believe . . . that there is more room for the exercise of influence
" on the part of the Governor under my system than under any that ever
" was before devised. On certain questions of public policy, especi-
" ally with regard to church matters, views are propounded which do
" not square with my preconceived opinions, and which I acquiesce in
" so long as they do not contravene the fundamental principles of
" morality."—(*Vide* letter to Mr. C. Bruce). Lord Elgin did materially influence his council on the settlement of the clergy reserve
question.

Mr. Brown arrived in Canada in time to participate in the renewed
battle for popular rights. This battle had, in a sense, been fought,
and in a manner won, but the enemy had not been followed up. They
were allowed to rally and again get possession of the defences. The
fruits of victory were only partially realized by the victors, and now
their opponents were in the field headed by the Governor-General
in person. He had by his unconstitutional conduct made himself a
mere party leader. Hitherto, under the name of the new system,
leading men among reformers did not hesitate about accepting office
with men belonging to the opposite party without any security that
their responsibility to parliament should take precedence of their
obligations to the representative of the Crown. The untimely death of
Lord Sydenham, and the illness and short reign of Sir Charles Bagot,
left them little time for ascertaining the views of the people or their

capacity for complete self-government, far less to put in operation the only principles upon which a free and intelligent people could be successfully governed. Lord Metcalfe, who succeeded them, was wholly unsuited for the duties of a constitutional governor, from the natural bent of his mind, as well as from the nature of his experience in public life in India and Jamaica. Although an English Whig by his British party connections, he was an autocrat in spirit, and almost immediately on his arrival in Canada he showed his determination to practise what he believed. Apart altogether from the question of right, there was something almost ludicrous in the assumption of this average Englishman that he was better informed and more capable of understanding Canadian affairs, and judging of the persons to be appointed to offices, than were the able Canadian public men he had as ministers. So it was, however; he boldly defied ministers and parliament ; a crisis had come which must be met, and the struggle restored to active political life much of the acerbity which had characterized pre-union conflicts, and which it was undoubtedly the desire of Lord Sydenham and Sir Charles Bagot to extinguish.

The bitterness of a previous dominant faction whose governing power had been necessarily destroyed by the new, though imperfect, system established after Lord Durham's visit, was as yet by no means uprooted. The remnants of this faction immediately attached themselves to the skirts of the despotic Governor : they felt that they had now a potential leader. They recalled former times when they "sat by the flesh pots" and "did eat bread to the full," and lamented the evil days and principles which brought them "forth into this "wilderness, to kill the whole assembly with hunger." This class were very zealous and, perhaps, in their own estimation, patriotic ; defenders of the usurpation of authority by His Excellency, they saw much to gain and nothing to lose by vigorously taking up his cause.

At this time the restrictions which surrounded the exercise of the franchise limited very much the political power of the people, and correspondingly increased that of the governing authority. Ecclesiastical questions occupied much of the public mind, and assumed proportions of greater or less magnitude in connection with popular rights and the recognition of perfect religious equality, as the ruling party were for or against legislation required to place all churches on an equality in the eye of the law. The champions of the *quasi* church establishment which had seized the national university and held the greater part of the clergy reserve lands, exhibited as bold and self-asserting a tone as ever. Combinations of clerical magnates and prominent lay disciples sitting in high places, striving to secure denominational superiority, if not supremacy, were constantly witnessed, and challenged the attention of all liberal patriots.

The struggle for freedom in religious questions from state control, which had been many years maintained by the majority in the Scottish national church, had just terminated in the secession of that majority from the establishment. The conflict extended itself to the Canadian presbyterian body, some members of which had accepted a share of the clergy reserve funds, and had supplied a strong detachment to give a vigorous support to the Family Compact oligarchy. It was very important that so influential and numerous a body should range itself on the side of perfect religious equality. A considerable number of its adherents strove to maintain the then existing state of affairs, and naturally ranged themselves on the Governor's side, though the vast majority held and acted on anti-state church principles, so far as related to this colony, whatever may have been their abstract views as to establishments. All the retrogressive elements of society were called into active life in order to sustain the reactionary Governor-General. There was a sudden resurrection of evil principles of government which were supposed to have been buried too deep to be restored. The barricade of vice-regal power was deemed sufficient to shelter those who aided him in degrading the true legitimate representation of legislative power and the fountain of administrative authority to a secondary place in the government of the country.

Mr. Brown's advent to Canada at this juncture was, under the existing circumstances, a great accession to the liberal ranks; he was the means, to a great extent, of precipitating an inevitable discussion on all the questions involved, in a manner not previously known, and to an extent not anticipated by the leaders of either party. Some very prominent liberals in political life were more or less conservative on Church questions, and evidently doubted the right or at least the wisdom of removing an injustice which had the sanction of the law for its existence. So far as this remark applies to certain prominent individuals, it will be dealt with in another place. The field of political life was open to any enterprising publicist bold enough to do battle for the great mass of the people against a most dangerous usurpation. The ministers, whose responsibility to parliament had been treated so lightly by the Governor-General, were not themselves fully united on any course of action; some of them openly sided with that functionary. The press was feeble and ineffective, and therefore rendered but little support to the ministers who did understand the true nature of the crisis, and the necessity of at once meeting the issue challenged by the highest authority in the land. The field so invitingly open for press and orator was at once taken possession of by the new-comer; and very soon the name of George Brown was identified with the most vigorous action and the most powerful newspaper writing ever known in Canada. That action and advocacy very soon commanded an influence more powerful than had ever been evoked by any one man, and remains to this day strongly impressed on Canadian public life. At this day it seems strange that so much vigour and laboured effort should have been necessary to resist an unconstitutional exercise of power by the representative of the Crown in Canada ; but we must remember that this was precisely the kind of action which up to a very late period commanded the support of English ministers. So late as 1873 we find Lord Kimberley gravely telling Lord Dufferin that he was to act without the advice of his ministers when he deemed it necessary. Mr. Brown did not commit the opposite fault of denouncing the fountain of authority because of the wrong exercise of power by the representative of the Crown in Canada, but opposed his action by a strictly constitutional appeal to the people, seconding in an effective manner the action of the expelled ministers.

While there could be no doubt as to the final issue in the unseemly struggle which the Governor-General forced upon the country, there remained much anxiety as to the duration of the interregnum during which constitutional authority would practically be suspended. The final disposal of great measures of reform, such as the clergy reserves and King's College questions, which had agitated the country so long, were necessarily delayed. The struggle for irresponsible power absorbed all the attention and exhausted the mental resources of the Governor-General and the imbecile administration which succeeded the government that resigned on September 30th, 1843. For over two months there was no minister but Mr. Dominick Daly, who agreed with his late colleagues in all their acts and measures, until they gave effect to their principles by resigning, when he determined to remain in office. For the succeeding nine months the ministry consisted of Messrs. Viger, Daly and Draper. Practically there was no government until after the general election in the autumn of 1844. The Governor-General in the meantime defended himself as best he could by means of letters and pamphlets, some of which were written by one gentleman who had once been a liberal M.P., and who found his well known inordinate vanity gratified by defending the usurping Governor. Some were written by a reverend gentleman whom few would have suspected of a willingness to defend conduct like Lord Metcalfe's. Both gentlemen had in early days been warm defenders of popular rights, though now enlisted in the ranks of the defenders of absolutism. One was shortly afterwards appointed to a highly lucrative office, and though it was vehemently asserted that the office was not the price of the advocate, the public could not avoid connecting the one with the other, to the great disadvantage of the appointee. The lay apostle made himself friends in the ranks of his former opponents. The works of both in controversy have neither literary nor political merit; one only wonders on reading them how they ever attracted any attention. By such aid, and the personal influence of the Governor-General, the conservative government succeeded in obtaining a majority of two at the general election, and were thus enabled to maintain a precarious and turbulent existence. But it was utterly powerless to promote useful legislation; nor did it seriously attempt the task. That government expired, in a manner worthy of its existence, in March, 1848. It was the offspring of the revolutionary act of the chief executive; the members, whatever might have been their personal excellences, were politically the mere creatures of the partisan Governor. As such they assumed office, though they knew that their predecessors refused to remain there on such humiliating terms.

The chaotic state of political life was aggravated by the sectarian and denominational discussions brought on by the determination of the temporary beneficiaries of the clergy reserve funds to ignore the settlement which had been made under the Imperial Clergy Reserve Act of 1840, and secure the right to divide the land itself and lease portions, to form permanent endowments. Sir Francis Hincks says "that for the re-agitation of the question the bishops and clergy of the "Church of England were chiefly, if not wholly, responsible." This naturally provoked counter action on the part of the reformers and voluntaries, who declared, through Mr. Price, that "vesting the land "in ecclesiastical bodies was an infliction that the country could not "and would not bear." The "infliction," however, seemed for a time to be imminent. The agitation from the first was conducted with great zeal and skill by the veteran Bishop of Toronto, whose great talents commanded respect, and, although he failed in his original plan to some extent, he had not, as now became manifest, given up the hope of securing some sort of ecclesiastical supremacy for himself and his clergy, though keenly opposed by many of his own communion. The time seemed favourable to accomplish his object. A reactionary Governor was at the head of affairs; prominent men in the Church of Scotland supported the Governor; the beneficiaries in that church from the clergy reserve lands were willing to uphold the demands of the sturdy Bishop.

Events afterwards proved that the public mind was not so quiescent as the agitators had calculated on, for although Lord Metcalfe proposed to vest the lands in the several sects, Mr. Sherwood failed to get an address passed to procure a new Imperial Act to authorize a division of the land.

While the agitation provoked by the ecclesiastical dignitaries referred to greatly embittered public discussion, it also had this effect— it aided the advocates of perfect religious equality and the voluntary principle in giving shape to their demands for the repeal of the Imperial Act, and the restoration to Canada of the right to deal with the whole question of religious endowments.

Many able writers were engaged in the *Examiner* and other newspapers in combating the advocates of exclusive rights ; but it is doing them no injustice to say, that the Messrs. Brown, senior and junior, were the most trenchant and accomplished writers who had yet appeared on the questions involved.

The entire population of Canada West, in 1844, did not exceed 600,000. In one respect it was much easier reaching them, as the population was generally congregated in districts comparatively easily reached by water. The large population now in the counties of Grey, Bruce and Simcoe, fill a region then almost without an inhabitant. It was therefore much easier for a vigorous public man, by personal contact or through the press, to reach the mass of the people than it is now even with the aid of railways. When Mr. Baldwin led the reform party he knew, more or less, nearly every man who took an active part in political discussion, and in an emergency—such as preparing for a sudden general election—he could communicate with most of them personally. Mr. Brown, as the chief journalist of the time and the coming leader, enjoyed the same advantage ; and it may be doubted whether at a later period, when the country was practically larger, even his indomitable energy could have resulted in accomplishing in so short a period the secularization of the clergy reserves, and later in securing representation by population and the adoption of the federal system. It will be admitted by his warmest friends that the times favoured him as a great popular advocate ; and his bitterest enemies will equally admit that he made a most admirable use of his abilities and influence ; by which he left his mark in ineffaceable lines on the history of his adopted country.

BIOGRAPHY.

CHAPTER I.

Mr. Brown's Early History.—Establishment of the "Globe" Newspaper.

Mr. Brown was a native of Edinburgh, in which city he was born on the 29th of November, 1818. He was the son of the late Peter Brown, who lived many years in Toronto ; his mother was a daughter of Mr. George Mackenzie, of Stornoway, in the Island of Lewis. Lord Brougham, in his autobiography, tells us that he believes he was indebted to the Celtic blood inherited from his mother (who was a Robertson) for the energy and power of his character. He says : " If " Mary Whelpdale had been my mother, she would, no doubt, have " enriched the Saxon blood I derived from my father ; but I should " have remained in the state of respectable mediocrity which seems " to have been that of my many ancestors. . . . I at least owe " much to the Celtic blood which my mother brought from the clans " of Struan and Kinloch Moidart." Similarly we may assume that Mr. Brown derived much of his energy, power and religious zeal from his half Celtic origin ; these qualities he possessed in an eminent degree, united with the proverbial caution and prudence of the Lowlander. Young Brown received his education at the High School and Southern Academy, in Edinburgh, where we know he made such progress as justified his family and teachers in anticipating for the young student a successful career in the race of life. Dr. Gunn, of the latter institution, when introducing him to the audience at a closing examination, to declaim an exercise, said : " This young gentleman is not " only endowed with high enthusiasm, but possesses the faculty of " creating enthusiasm in others."

It does not appear that he ever desired to engage in any of what are called the professions, though his father desired that he should enter the University with that view. Shortly after his leaving the Academy, Mr. Brown, senior, became involved in pecuniary difficulties, through the misconduct of an agent. This circumstance, after a time, induced Mr. Brown to emigrate to America, to retrieve his fortunes on a wider field. In 1838, the final determination was reached, when

Mr. George Brown accompanied his father to New York, leaving the other members of the family in Edinburgh for a time.

Mr. Brown, senior, was a highly cultivated man, an accomplished writer, and a keen politician on the side of liberalism. Probably no man in his day had a better knowledge of history, civil and religious, or a more correct opinion respecting popular government. An intense hater of slavery, and a keen defender of the British constitutional system, no man was better adapted to shine as a newspaper editor or contributor. As a writer in the *Albion*, he soon became known, and acquired such a knowledge of the country and the feelings of British residents, as justified him in commencing the publication of a newspaper of his own, under the name of the *British Chronicle*, and Mr. George Brown first became known to the public as its publisher.

The new journal first appeared in the month of December, 1842. It professed to have the same general character as the *Albion*, but it was doubtful if there was room for two papers of the same class. The *Chronicle* was probably looked upon more as an organ of the Scottish population than the *Albion*, but both journals had necessarily to take, in a general way, the same line in regard to British and United States' affairs, and appeal for support to the same constituency. The necessity for advertising and obtaining support for the *Chronicle*, led Mr. Brown to visit Canada in 1843, as well as most of the northern States. At this time the agitation in the Presbyterian church, in Scotland, which led to that grand politico-religious movement termed "The Disruption," had extended itself to Canada. The Messrs. Brown, father and son, were ardent adherents of the "Non-intrusion" party, but were also much in advance of the bulk of the Free Church party in the matter of church establishments. The greater part of the Presbyterians in Canada deeply sympathized with the popular party in Scotland, and were considering the necessity of formulating their views, even if it should split the church here. The arrangement made some years previously with the Tory oligarchy ruling Canada, by which certain Presbyterian ministers received a share of the clergy reserves, and thereupon ceased the agitation against the pensioning of English Church ministers from the national lands, was never approved by the mass of their people. The articles in the *Chronicle* suited the majority, and paved the way for Mr. Brown's favourable reception when he came to Canada in the interests of his journal. It was therefore natural that some anxiety should be felt to procure the establishment of the paper in the province where such important movements were on foot, and where there was no adequate representative of right opinion in the press. Conferences with leading men in the church resulted in Mr. Brown's accepting proposals to circulate the *Chronicle* extensively in Canada, as the organ of the new movement.   During his visit he was also brought into contact with leading public men of the liberal party of Upper Canada, then destitute of any leading newspaper capable of directing or controlling public opinion. The liberal party was in power, but liberal principles could hardly be said to be in the ascendancy, while the obstinate resistance to the principles of responsible government of the Governor-General, Sir Charles Metcalfe (soon to cause an open rupture with his ministers), made progress with measures of reform difficult, if not utterly impossible.   There can be no doubt that at the time of Mr. Brown's visit to Canada, ministers must have had a taste of Sir Charles Metcalfe's hostility to popular government, and even then were anticipating open war from the Governor-General.

Some of the ministers were noble, devoted men ; some others were able men, who would carry out reform measures, if they conveniently could ; others were mere time-servers, ready to serve on either side, as some did.   At the time of Mr. Brown's visit there was an undercurrent of belief that an open rupture with Sir Charles Metcalfe could not be long avoided, unless responsible government was, with the consent of ministers, to be trampled underfoot.   Although there was no formal agreement or understanding arrived at between Mr. Brown and Mr. Baldwin and others about publishing a paper in Canada in the interests of the liberal party, there is no doubt but what Mr. Brown left for New York impressed with the belief that he should move permanently to the British Provinces, and that the liberal leaders would like to have his services as a journalist to aid them.   The biographical sketch published in the *Globe* says : " Young Mr. Brown " made a decided impression on the members of the administration, " and had given them the idea that he would be a potent ally of any " political cause to which he might attach himself.   .   .   . And " when he left Kingston, he must have felt that, in the event of his " taking up his abode in this country, he could count on a pretty " strong support from the government."

As the result of deliberations on the subject, and of further overtures from Canada, the publication of the *British Chronicle* in New York was given up, and Mr. Brown, with his father and family, moved to Toronto, where the *Banner* made its appearance on the 18th of August, 1843, as a weekly paper, as an organ of the Free Church party, and partly as a paper strongly supporting the liberal party and the existing administration.   The anticipated rupture with Sir Charles Metcalfe occurred a few weeks after the *Banner* appeared.   His ministers resigned on his refusal to accept their advice respecting appointments.   It was clear that the battle for responsible government had to be fought over again, before much attention could be devoted to internal and detailed reforms, however important.

Mr. Brown, through the columns of the *Banner*, threw himself into the conflict with all his immense energy, but it soon became apparent, to himself and others, that this journal could not carry on the war with the Erastian party in the church, and fight Lord Metcalfe and his clerical and lay supporters at the same time. The necessity for a purely political paper was urgent, and the leading men of the party pressed Mr. Brown on the subject. The result was that the publication of the *Globe* was undertaken, and the first number was issued on the 5th of March, 1844. The *Globe* prospectus had the following paragraph: "The wide circulation of the *Banner* has brought its " political views generally before the public, but in a paper in which " so large a part is devoted to religious and ecclesiastical information, " it was impossible to do justice to these views. The same political " opinions will be maintained in the *Globe*, and a wider field afforded " for the expression of them, as it will be entirely devoted to secular " subjects." The *Banner* was published by Mr. Brown, senior, for several years after the first publication of the *Globe*, and rendered great service in its own peculiar field of newspaper life, but also having much influence as a newspaper, independent of its ecclesiastical character.

While there is no doubt that existing circumstances were favourable to the enterprise, there is equally little doubt that the immediate success of the new journal was owing chiefly to the great ability and immense energy of the editor-in-chief. At this time, Sir Chas. Metcalfe was conducting the government in defiance of parliament and parliamentary government, having a skeleton administration, consisting of Hon. Mr. Draper, Hon. D. Viger, and Hon. Dominic Daly, the latter gentleman having retained his office when his colleagues resigned a few months before, although he agreed with his colleagues' policy, up to the resigning portion of it. An early dissolution was inevitable. The articles in the *Globe* were directed towards preparing for the coming struggle, and to the exposure of the autocratic and unconstitutional conduct of the Governor-General, with his aiders and abettors. Trucklers on the liberal side, and the resurrected Tory oligarchy, were alike assailed with a vehemence and power which left nothing to be desired on the part of those who demanded a vigorous, able management in the new paper. The articles produced a great effect on the country, but the Governor-General had many advantages on his side, which rendered the issue somewhat doubtful for a time. The state of the franchise and of the election law gave the Governor a great advantage in a parliamentary election. Writers were also found who were willing to uphold Sir Charles Metcalfe in his struggle against parliamentary government. One reverend gentleman, Dr. Ryerson, who had in earlier days rendered good service on behalf of religious equality and popular rights, was induced to undertake the defence of the new assailant of the rights and privileges he had formerly so well defended. The means taken by the government resulted in a partial, but not honourable, success on their side ; but the general impression was so strong against the Governor-General and his apologists, that they must have felt that such a course could never be attempted again, and that a return to sound constitutional principle was inevitable.

The services rendered by Mr. Brown in the columns of the *Globe* were so well appreciated, that he was pressed to become a candidate at the general election of November, 1844. This he wisely declined, for personal and political reasons. He felt then, as he did on a later occasion, to which reference will be made, that he could more effectually aid the liberal party by influencing public opinion through the press. The *Globe* was not wholly a political journal ; its reputation as a newspaper, though high, had yet to be fully established ; it would therefore necessarily be much injured at that time by its chief editor devoting himself to the legislative work of the province. The Draper administration managed to obtain a bare majority, and maintained a precarious existence until the general election in 1847. The country was, in the meantime, being much agitated by the tactics and policy of the government. Mr. Brown was a chief instrument in working up a public opinion, which was gradually becoming extremely hostile to the ministry. From 1844 to 1847 he travelled over a great portion of the country, and soon established intimate relations with leading men in all quarters, and also a correspondence, which gave him more accurate information than could be obtained by any one else of the drift of public opinion. The circulation of the *Globe* was greatly extended ; a semi-weekly issue was commenced in 1846, soon to be succeeded by a tri-weekly in 1849 ; and a branch paper, under the name of the *Western Globe*, was established in London. In 1849, Mr. Brown was prosecuted at London for libel, by the late Judge Prince, at that time member for Essex. Mr. Prince, though only partially successful in the suit, admired Mr. Brown's ability, and became his fast friend, as the following sympathetic letter will abundantly show :

THE PARK FARM, 6th March, 1858.

MY DEAR SIR,—I cannot refrain from writing a few lines to congratulate you upon the course you have taken to protect yourself against the infamous conduct of that . . . Attorney-General Macdonald towards you, and to bring him to condign censure and disgrace. As a Briton, I am proud to witness your manly conduct, and that you so stoutly resisted the tenders of some puny legislators to give way. Every one of the charges brought against you are, in point of law, gross slanders, and I have no doubt but a jury would mulct him in heavy damages, because his language (though uttered where it was and upon the occasion it was) cannot be called privileged. It was gross, wilful, false, malicious slander, and I trust the committee will do you justice. I think they will, and I am glad my friend John Wilson is one of them. You have acquitted yourself admirably in the matter. Go on, and the country will sustain you ; and Macdonald could not promote your popularity more than by taking the course he has.

I remain, my Dear Sir, sincerely yours,

JOHN PRINCE.

To GEORGE BROWN, Esq., M.P.P., Toronto.

When the general election took place late in 1847 and in January, 1848, Mr. Brown devoted all his efforts as a speaker and writer towards the defeat of the ministry. Many of his speeches delivered then on behalf of liberal candidates, are still remembered by those who heard them as being the most effective they had ever listened to. He had a singular power in rousing enthusiasm in a popular assembly, and very few cared to encounter the tremendous tide of his rhetoric. This election campaign fully established his reputation as one of the foremost men in Canada both as a speaker and writer, and then and ever afterwards he could have obtained a seat in parliament for many of the constituencies. Up to the triumph of the liberals at this election, Mr. Brown and the regular liberal leaders worked generally harmoniously together. They were all engaged in an ardent attempt to secure, not the form alone, but the essence and spirit of responsible government. There could be no question as to the condemnation of Lord Metcalfe's acts and policy with any reformers (unless, indeed, we except those who went over to the enemy, but who affected to defend it as liberals, to whom allusion has already been made). Points of disagreement, which subsequently became vital, had as yet no existence. A common danger to the first principles of representative government kept all reformers together. All were supposed to be agreed on certain great reforms as yet untouched, especially the secularization of the clergy reserves and King's College, Toronto.

CHAPTER II.

REFORM MINISTRY OF 1848.—MR. BROWN PROSECUTED FOR LIBEL.

Mr. Brown and the country were soon to learn that some of the leaders had not courage to carry out their convictions, that some others hesitated about the policy and would not step over the Rubicon, and that some were actually hostile. Seldom had any country before witnessed the spectacle of party leaders being returned to power by the people by a large majority, to carry out certain specific reforms and to give effect to certain principles, and such leaders hesitating or refusing to introduce the measures they were bound by their principles and pledges to carry, as they could carry, in a friendly parliament. They seemed to forget that the ante-electoral battle was not fought to place Mr. Baldwin, Mr. Lafontaine, and their subsequent associates, in power, but as means to a great public end ; the end being the passage of measures in parliament which would restore to the people property which had been seized by a sect or sects, and to abolish every appearance of a dominant church. Other fundamental reforms relating to the franchise and electoral laws, municipal government, the marriage laws and other more or less important measures, were also reasonably expected by the people. On such questions the mass of the people would have no compromise ; there could be no compromise with honest men. Either it was right or it was wrong that certain sects should have a supremacy by law ; if wrong, it must be put an end to ; and few but the beneficiaries were disposed to defend the absurd and wicked policy which sought to impose an established church on Canada, and so introduce the discord and constant agitation which prevailed in the mother land.

Parliament was summoned to meet on the 25th day of February, being about a month after the return of the writs. Of course, every one knew that although the conservative government determined to meet parliament, they were ignominiously beaten at the polls.* The liberal leaders knew equally well that they would have to assume the responsibilities of office, and that this carried with it the responsibility, to the people who placed them there, of carrying into effect

---

* The conservative press and leaders, in 1878, joined in vigorous denunciation of Mr. Mackenzie's government remaining in office from the polling day, Sept. 18th, to October 10th, a period sufficiently short to finish up business ; but in this case, the spectacle o conservatives retaining office for three months, after sustaining a decisive defeat at the polls, attracted no censure.

the measures already alluded to, as containing the just and proper demands of the nation, the advocacy of which was to give them power and authority. It appeared, however, from the first that no agreement had been arrived at for a decisive policy.

The new reform ministry was formed on the 10th of March, and consisted of Messrs. Lafontaine, Baldwin, Sullivan, Hincks, Aylwin, Lesslie, Caron, Price, Viger, Taché and Cameron.

While much important legislation was accomplished in this session, none of the burning questions alluded to were touched. The great mass of ministerial supporters were, however, disposed to consider it as not very unreasonable that ministers should have time during the first recess to consider their measures, and therefore waited patiently.

In 1849 Mr. Brown accepted an appointment as one of the commissioners instructed to inquire into the management of the Provincial Penitentiary, also acting as secretary. This institution had been left almost entirely to the care of Mr. Smith, the warden, without a sufficient inspection by some competent officer. It was charged that many prisoners were cruelly used ; that extensive transactions in the business affairs had been grossly mismanaged ; that the institution had been made a comfortable resort for relatives of the warden ; and that the funds placed at his disposal for the accounts had, to a greater or less extent, been improperly applied to other objects. The result of the inquiry was to establish the truth of many of the charges, if not all, and the consequent removal of the warden. The son of that gentleman (Sir Henry Smith) sat in parliament as member for Frontenac. He bitterly resented the exposure made, and laid the report chiefly at the door of the active secretary, whom he never ceased to attack when opportunity offered. The report, however, was looked upon by the public as an able and exhaustive one, and the conclusions and recommendations as the just and inevitable outcome of facts elicited during the inquiry. Many years afterwards this report was made the occasion of a scandalous attack on Mr. Brown, to which reference will be made elsewhere.

Mr. Brown's journalistic career was signalized in May, 1849, by the famous libel suit, at the instance of Col. Prince, to which reference has been made, who swore out a criminal information against him for copying some injurious comments on him in the capacity of Crown counsel, and for some criticisms afterwards indulged in at the Colonel's expense. The offensive articles appeared in an edition of the *Globe* published in London as the *Western Globe*, late in 1847. He was indicted in 1848, but it was not until May 1849 that he was brought to trial. On this as on subsequent occasions he defended himself. His cross-examination of the gallant Colonel was one of the most amusing court scenes ever witnessed in Canada. At that time the law of libel in Canada was most unjust, and behind that of England. A defendant was not allowed to plead the truth of the libellous allegations as a justification, nor was he allowed to examine the prosecutor or plaintiff on matters of difference which may have led up to the motive for commencing the prosecution. In this case the indictment was in three counts. The first was having published evidence at some trial which reflected on the Colonel ; the second and third counts were grounded on criticisms on Mr. Prince's conduct in a subsequent paper. Mr. Brown boldly threw away all technical grounds of defence, admitting the publication, and defended himself on the merits of his case, a perilous course to pursue in the then state of the law. He derived no benefit from proving his case. He was stopped by the Judge when he ventured to broaden his defensive ground by examining the prosecutor as to the differences of opinion which led him to seek satisfaction in a libel suit. Colonel Prince had been elected by the reformers as a reformer in 1847, but soon went to the other side, for which action the *Globe* had paid him some unwelcome attention. This was probably the real cause of the offence. Mr. Brown conducted his case with great ability for a layman, and addressed the jury in a speech of great power. The jury acquitted him on the first count, but found him guilty on the second and third counts, as they were compelled to do by the charge of the Judge. He was sentenced to pay a fine of £30. Some of the audience wished to pay it for him on the spot, but he declined to allow them. It may be questioned whether he then pursued a wise course in defending himself in person, if he looked only to the obtaining of advantages in the course of the trial ; but if he looked to the public effect only, he was undoubtedly correct in determining to defend himself. If he was less successful with a Judge than a professional advocate, he was probably more successful with the jury. In this case the leading barrister in London, the late John Wilson, congratulated him warmly, and volunteered to become his surety before leaving the court room.

CHAPTER III.

The Rebellion Losses Bill.—Mr. Brown Defends Lord Elgin.

In the second session of this parliament the government brought in a bill to provide for the payment of losses sustained by the loyal inhabitants of Lower Canada during the rebellion. The principle of the measure was just, and therefore defensible as explained by its promoters, though it was quite possible that some disloyal persons might be able to secure some advantages from it. Mr. Draper's administration had three years before appointed a commission to inquire into the losses sustained by the insurrectionary movements. This commission reported in April, 1846, that the claims for losses amounted in the aggregate to £241,965 10s. 6d., but that a sum of £100,000 might be considered sufficient to meet the claims which ought to be paid. No further action was taken by that government. Upper Canadian losses had been arranged for by the Act of 1840 and 1842, and the Assembly, in 1845, had unanimously passed an address, asking His Excellency the Governor-General to take measures " to insure to the " inhabitants of that portion of the Province, formerly Lower Canada, " indemnity for just losses by them sustained during the rebellion of " 1837 and 1838." The estimate given was, under instructions to the commission, a " general " one, " the particulars of which must form " the subject of more minute inquiry hereafter."

The measure introduced to give effect to the report was, as Lord Elgin remarked, " nothing more than a strict logical following out of " their own acts [meaning the late ministry's acts] ; though," he added, " it is not altogether free from objection," but " their predecessors " had already gone more than half way in the same direction, though " they had stopped short, and now tell us they never intended to go " further." No legislative Act passed during the existence of the union provoked so keen a controversy or gave rise to so much violence and agitation. The loss of the election fifteen months previous to this time would seem to have embittered the Tories to an intense degree. Acts of lawless violence against prominent reformers and the property of the state were almost invited by the speeches of these leaders ; and at last they inflicted lasting disgrace on themselves and the country by a violent attack on the Governor-General and the outpouring of a continuous torrent of abuse upon him, although he confined himself strictly to the performance of his duty in giving the royal assent to the bill, which had passed both Houses. Lord Elgin

wrote : " The Tory party are doing what they can by menace, intimi-
" dation and appeals to passion, to drive me to a *coup d'état.* . . .
" If I had dissolved parliament I might have produced a rebellion,
" but most assuredly I should not have procured a change of ministry.
" The leaders of the party know that as well as I do, and were it
" possible to play tricks in such grave concerns, it would have been
" easy to throw them into utter confusion by merely calling upon them
"to form a government." At this trying time Mr. Brown, in the *Globe*
and at public meetings, threw himself into the thick of the fight in
defence of the Governor-General and the government, not wholly
because he fully approved of the manner in which the measure was
promoted, for he did not—so important a measure, he felt, should have
been mentioned in the speech from the throne, and should have been
previously foreshadowed, and time given to its careful consideration
before introducing it—but he thought that the constitutional course
of Lord Elgin, in giving his entire support to his advisers on a subject
which had already been partially dealt with by the opposite party,
should be as vigorously defended as the unconstitutional course of Lord
Metcalfe, in refusing to take advice from responsible ministers, was
denounced. The utmost energy was shown by the *Globe* in calling on
the people to support the Governor-General. Every number was filled
with articles, letters and addresses, from all quarters, supporting Lord
Elgin's action. The insane fury of the Tories against him only
diverted public discussion from the merits of the bill and towards the
defence of the representative of the Queen, so unjustly assailed. The
general result was that addresses were sent to the Governor-General
signed by nearly 150,000 people, while a petition got up by the Opposition praying for his recall was signed by about 25,000 to 30,000.

When the bill passed the House early in the session a disgraceful
riot took place in Toronto, when the Tory mob expressed their opinions
by attacking the private houses of Messrs. Baldwin, the Premier, Mr.
Blake, Solicitor-General, Mr. Brown, Mr. Wm. Lyon Mackenzie, and
others, and burning them in effigy. Happily no very serious damage
was done to property, and no life was lost. An attack was threatened
on the *Globe* office, but the chivalrous rioters were content with
smashing the doors and windows of Mr. Brown's private residence on
Church Street. The Montreal riots occurred some time afterwards on
the occasions of Lord Elgin giving the royal assent to the bill, and
his visit to the city to receive the address from parliament. On both
occasions he was pelted with missiles of the foulest kind. This abomi-
nable conduct, as well as the burning of the parliament building, was
the work of well-dressed persons, not of the lowest class of the population, as might be expected. Amongst the numerous deputations
from the Province of Ontario sent to the Governor-General with

addresses, were those from Toronto, Kingston and Cobourg. The members of these deputations were entertained at Tetu's Hotel by some of the ministers on May 12th. In the course of the evening a violent mob of the opposite party surrounded the hotel, smashed all the windows of the dining-room and some of the doors, and tried to set the house on fire. At the same time a desperate attempt was made to force their way into the dining-room. At this juncture one of the ministers fired on the mob ; the shot took effect in the neck of one of the assailants, after which the attack was abandoned. An attack was also made on Mr. Lafontaine's house, which was partially destroyed by fire, when one of the assailants was killed. This violence was attempted to be excused on the ground that it was very offensive to be obliged to divert public money to reward rebels. The real reason was Lord Elgin's refusal to make himself, as his predecessor had done, the tool of the Tory party, and this bill was selected as the most profitable to raise an issue upon, as its scope could be so easily misrepresented. Mr. Brown's share in encountering the riotous obstructionists was a large and prominent one. His chivalrous nature would at once lead him to defend the person of the Governor-General, but he felt that a far more important interest was at stake. The question whether a constitutional system of government, with ministers responsible to parliament, could exist in Canada or not, came up. "The first really efficient and "working government that Canada had had since the Union" (to use Lord Elgin's words) was assailed by force. The most seditious language was used towards the Governor. No greater crisis could have arisen. The party who then assailed Governor and ministers with violence, who defied the solemn decision of parliament, had succeeded six years before, with a Governor-General who was a suitable instrument, in destroying parliamentary government for a time before there had been time to fairly develop its principles. Had they succeeded in securing the recall of Lord Elgin, and, as a necessary consequence, the disallowance of the Rebellion Losses Bill, another severe blow would be struck at parliamentary or responsible government. As Mr. Brown stated at the time, "all such attempts to damage the new system "must be put down with a strong hand, and free action be accorded "to it." The violence and insults offered to the Queen's representative were to be at once resented and deplored. But the "ark of "the constitution" had to be defended first of all, as the peace and happiness of the whole people depended on its preservation, especially as the defence of the one implied and necessitated the defence of the other.

The Montreal disturbances ultimately gave birth to a new organization under the name of "The British North American League." This association was a queer mixture of Tories and Annexationists, and comprised all the disappointed items. Like King David's famous army at the Cave of Adullam, " Every one that was in distress, and " every one that was in debt, and every one that was discontented, " gathered themselves " to the meetings of the League. The *Globe*, and liberal journals generally, greeted the new political mongrel with a storm of ridicule. They were dubbed " Children of the Sun." After one brief attempt to effect something by their meeting at Kingston, the concern collapsed from the sheer rottenness of its material. They advocated extreme Toryism, extreme disloyalty, and finally threatened to drive the French into the sea.

The clumsy attempt at revolution had failed. The Governor-General had proved himself a true constitutional ruler. By his moderation, firmness and prudence, he had averted serious dangers while giving full effect to the new system of government. Long before the close of the year many of his opponents showed they were ashamed of their conduct towards him ; and he ultimately left Canada one of the most popular Governors that ever held sway over it, and probably the ablest of them all.

CHAPTER IV.

Mr. Brown Denounces the Ministry.—Letters to Mr. Hincks.

Mr. Brown, in the *Globe* articles, also took this view of the ministerial position respecting the non-introduction of measures to settle the questions discussed at the elections in 1847, that some more time should have been allowed, but at the same time kept up the fire of agitation on these questions, which at no distant day bore fruit, in forcing legislation upon them, though at the expense of the disruption of the liberal party. The writer thinks Mr. Brown showed too much indulgence in this matter. There is no doubt but that the supineness of the liberal leaders at this time laid the foundation of the dissensions which were to rend the party asunder at no distant day. It would be too much to say that their inaction was due to treachery, but it is impossible to avoid the conclusion that their course had all the effect, on public questions to which the party were committed and on the party itself, which deliberate treachery would produce. Some of the leaders subsequently went over bodily to the conservative party, softening their action by dubbing the party they acceded to as a coalition. The smaller minds slipped backward into the Tory lines, with the words "Baldwin Reformer" pinned on their breasts or painted on their backs. These people had none of the high character belonging to Mr. Baldwin ; they were not actuated by his unselfish spirit and devotion to the public interests generally ; but they grasped his political blunders, and considered themselves sufficiently clothed therewith. Probably they were right.

Some important sections of the party, however, notably the *Examiner* newspaper, refused to endorse or condone the passive attitude of ministers, and bitterly assailed them as being untrue to their promises. Mr. Brown, for a considerable time, defended ministers, no doubt believing that the delay was caused by unforeseen obstacles, and having faith in the men individually who composed the ministry. This defence, mild as it was, drew, not unreasonably, some censure on Mr. Brown from many reformers, who could not and would not excuse the apparently needless delay ; and Mr. Brown never entirely regained the confidence of some of the discontents, who thought he defended the ministry too long.

Before the second session was over, it became evident that a serious break would soon take place in the reform ranks, unless the government should adopt a bold and vigorous policy—should, in a word, fulfil their promises. It became known also, that one of the difficulties lay in the determination of the leading French liberals not to assent to the secularization of the clergy reserves. This was a most unexpected obstacle, and naturally had to be seriously considered by the government and the newspapers supporting them. It has been claimed that this alone was a sufficient reason for ministerial delays. While this cannot be admitted, it must be allowed that so unexpected an embarrassment naturally would have postponed action for the first session, but only that. At the same time, it was impossible for the liberals of Canada West to consent to any compromise on this question which would admit of any church, with the national sanction, express or implied, assuming the status of an established or dominant church. The demand was imperative that all denominations of Christians must stand equal in the eye of the law. It was, however, the duty of leading men, not only in the interest of the liberal party but also in the general interests, to avoid, if possible, a split, which would have the effect of restoring the Tory party to power, and so retarding for a time the triumph of the voluntary principle, and the adoption of liberal measures generally. The reluctance of Mr. Brown to break with the government was sufficiently shown by the attacks made upon him in some liberal journals for supporting the ministry, notwithstanding their apparent infidelity to professed principles, while he was endeavouring to influence the ministers to a right course without an open rupture. The accusation was, however, enough to cause his defeat in Haldimand, where he became a candidate at a special election early in 1851. The state of feeling in the country and in the House is well given, as follows, in one of Mr. Brown's letters, published in September, 1851, and addressed to Mr. Hincks :

Sir,—At the close of the Session of 1850, there existed much dissatisfaction with the proceedings of the administration, and strong suspicions of your integrity on important questions. These feelings were entertained by your supporters in parliament as well as out of it ; and a letter, signed by nearly all the Upper Canada adherents of government in the House of Assembly, was addressed to the leader, expressing the general dissatisfaction, and the inevitable consequences, unless a more progressive policy and greater deference to public sentiment were immediately exhibited. No attention whatever was paid to that letter ; and the marked contempt thereby shown towards its authors, coupled with the singular good understanding seen to exist between you and several leading conservatives, strongly confirmed the prevailing rumours that a coalition ministry, to embrace moderate reformers, moderate conservatives, and moderate French Canadians, was seriously contemplated. Many things combined to lead well-informed persons to this conclusion, and so early as the 8th October, 1850, the *Globe* denounced the project in the following language :

" We see constant allusions to a coming Coalition Ministry, which, in the opinion of many, the position of parties naturally points to. We sincerely trust that, so far as the ministerialist party are concerned, no such movement is in any way contemplated. The constitutional reform party of Upper Canada needs no assistance, and we are very sure that any attempt at coalition with Toryism would be fatal to all who touched it. That a reorganization of the liberal party is necessary few will deny ; but that a more progressive policy, a firmer step, and more sympathy within the party than heretofore, would reunite the constitutional portion more heartily than ever, and carry it triumphantly through the elections of 1851, we feel perfectly confident."

Six months after this article appeared in the *Globe*, **Mr.** Brown accepted the nomination of the Liberal Convention for the representation of Haldimand. The following extracts from his address show the grounds on which he sought election :

I adhere to the liberal party because I think that the principles and measures of that party are best adapted to advance the interests of our country. To the reformers, Canada is indebted for the thorough control now exercised by the people over the executive government. To them we owe the enjoyment of religious equality ; a national system of education free from sectarian bias ; municipal institutions, simple and efficient ; public works, unsurpassed in any country. We are indebted to the liberal party for an amended jury law, an improved assessment system, cheap postage, and many other valuable measures. In matters of commerce and finance they have ever been in advance. To them we are indebted for the present high standing of our public securities, and through their exertions the trade of Canada was freed from British navigation laws and differential duties. During the few years the reform party have enjoyed power very much good has been effected. But there is much to be done ; and I doubt if there ever has been a time when men holding liberal sentiments were more loudly called upon to sink minor differences and stand together on the great questions before the country. I mean not that any one should sacrifice principle for the sake of party, but that in matters of expediency we are bound to yield our opinions to secure the combined action of those holding the same general views.

I am opposed to any connection between church and state, and desire to see all denominations placed on a footing of perfect equality. I am opposed to grants of public money for sectarian purposes, and I desire to see the clergy reserve lands withdrawn from the object to which they are now applied, and devoted to the general purposes of the province or to education.

I am in favour of national school education free from sectarian teaching, and available without charge to every child in the province. I desire to see efficient grammar schools established in each county ; and that the fees of these institutions and of the national university should be placed on such a scale as will bring a high literary and scientific education within the reach of men of talent in any rank of life.

I believe that the material interests of Canada would be best advanced by the adoption of the free trade principle as our commercial policy. By close economy, the judicious management of the public lands, and the rapidly increasing revenue from the canals, the point, it is to be hoped, may be reached when Canada will be enabled to dispense with the whole customs department : and to that end our efforts should, I think, be turned ; meanwhile, I advocate commercial reciprocity with the United States and the British West Indies, and that the trade arrangements now existing between Canada and the other British North American provinces should be sustained and extended.

The usury laws I deem seriously injurious to the best interests of the province, and requiring extensive alteration. Money can seldom be had in Canada on bond at the legal rate of interest; and the borrower is too often forced to evade the law and pay a much higher rate than the market value of money, as an indemnification to the lender for the risk he runs in taking over six per cent.

I advocate the abolition of the law of primogeniture, and think that the property of a person dying intestate should be equally divided among all his children.

The divisions in the liberal ranks caused his defeat. William Lyon Mackenzie was his principal opponent, but another candidate divided the liberal ranks. There can be no doubt that Mr. Brown was weakened by the support he had almost up to that time given to the liberal administration, though it failed to carry out the policy of the party. There was also a certain amount of sympathy manifested, not unnaturally, with Mr. Mackenzie because of his sufferings in exile, however unwise his ultimate action was in raising the flag of insurrection. It must also be stated that some liberal journals opposed Mr. Brown for no other reason than a feeling of jealousy. The new candidate had overtopped them all as journalist and popular orator, and seemed destined to rise higher, while they, who had borne the burden and heat of the day, were to be left behind. Rather than see Mr. Brown succeed, this class was willing to see the success of the party jeopardized by division. The discussion on the subject of Roman Catholic separate schools and religious corporations also alienated the Roman Catholics from Mr. Brown. It is probably, also, not incorrect to say that the ministers did him what injury they could, notwithstanding his services, as they had no desire to see such a man obtain more influence and power by obtaining a seat in Parliament. The regular nomination he received as the party candidate was not sufficient to save him from defeat, with so many adverse influences ranged against him.

Shortly after this Mr. Brown made up his mind to publicly denounce the ministry as the only course left. The following reasons appeared in an article in the *Globe* of March 11th, 1851:

The *Globe* came into existence when the reform party were out of office —when the prospect was black, and the temptations of profit all on the other side. From March, 1844, to March, 1848, while the party were out of power, we "battled the watch" with an earnest zeal not surpassed, we think, by any of our contemporaries, and we believe contributed our full *quota* to the change of feeling which sent the reform leaders back to power with overwhelming majorities. The success of his party might have been supposed to give the editor of the *Globe* some influence with the new government. Did he abuse that possible claim—did he assert it at all? Of the many lucrative and permanent offices which fell to the disposal of the late government while in power, was he ever an applicant for one for himself, or relative, or personal friend? Not in one instance : he was too fully alive to the danger of such favours. . . Let our contemporaries leave vague vituperation for once, and show from facts, if they can, wherein we did wrong as the organ of the late administration. We were not ignorant of their errors, we were not blind to their foibles ; but we are bound to say, now that we are in opposition to most of its members, that our differences with the late government were on matters of high public principle and expediency, and that we know of no jobs, no trickery, which were chargeable upon it. The high personal integrity of Messrs. Baldwin, Lafontaine, Price and Leslie, was ever a protection against such things. Let us hope that one behind the scenes for the next four years, when parted from the actors upon the stage and in opposition to them, may be able to say as much of the present ministry. There were mistakes, there were blunders, there were wrong acts on the part of the Baldwin-Lafontaine ministry, but we are prepared to vindicate them against all comers from the charge of corruption. Nay, more, for all their public acts during the sessions of 1848, 1849 and 1850, while we supported them, we are quite willing to bear full responsibility. Some things we thought wrong, and we said so at the time; others we doubted and held our peace; but their course as a whole we justified then, and we justify now. The causes of our separation from the late government are to be found in the parliamentary proceedings of the session of 1851. . . .

But what caused the change in 1851? Why did we leave the ministry? Why did we join the combinations? Why do we not support the present government? We now go to these points.

The great difficulty in the way of the late ministry and of every liberal ministry in Canada, is the fact that the reformers of Upper Canada have no large party in the Lower Province thoroughly with them. The great causes of political difference in Upper Canada hang upon the question of state-churchism. The Upper Canada reformers are entirely opposed to it in every shape, their allies in Lower Canada are in favour of it. For some time after the government was formed, it was hoped that the French Canadians would give us their aid in the settlement of the ecclesiastical grievances of Upper Canada, but when the trial came in the session of 1850, it was too evident that our allies were not to be relied upon on these questions. In the debate on Mr. Price's clergy reserve resolutions, Mr. Lafontaine, the leader and exponent of the views of the Lower Canada members, used the following language :

" At last a decision was given by the law officers of the Crown in England. The true meaning of the Act of 1791 was declared to be that the churches of England and Scotland were entitled to share in the reserves, but no other bodies whatever. That division was kept secret, he had reason to believe, from the members of the Church of Scotland, which was another mistake, as it might have gone far to allay the excitement then prevalent in the province. The two bodies might have shared the lands between them, and set the question at rest. . . In 1840, the year in which the Act was passed, the opinion of the judges of England was given to the effect that the words 'protestant clergy' in the Constitutional Act, did not mean the Church of England or the Church of Scotland, but all the protestant denominations. This was the decision upon the matter by the judges, and *he held that the endowments of that Act must be held sacred, and be carried into effect if practicable.* . . . If some sects refused to take their share, it might be given to others. . ." The French Canadians joined us in the application to the Home Government asking for full power over the reserves, but what they would do with them when that power was received, they had not declared. There was hope yet, and we stuck to the ministry on the strength of that hope. We saw that the reformers of Upper Canada could get their vital question settled more easily and quickly by the assistance of the French if they could be carried right, than by any other process ; and we saw clearly that the policy of the Upper Canada reformers was not to cast loose from them while there was a hope, but to use every means to carry them with us, to use their assistance while we had it, in obtaining other measures necessary to strengthen us in Upper Canada in the event of a separation ; and when that separation was inevitable, that it should be made on the clearly defined question of the abolition of all connection between church and state. Again and again, in public and in private, the editor of the *Globe*, from June, 1850, up to the meeting of parliament in 1851, pressed this policy on the Upper Canada leaders. He insisted with pertinacious earnestness on such a change of the constituencies as would give justice to the large counties, and consequently to the reform party, and on a thorough reform of the franchise ; and, this done, he urged that the Upper Canada members of the government should come to a clear understanding with their Lower Canada colleagues, that they should take their stand on thorough anti-state church principles, and in case of refusal, come out of the government and appeal to the people at the coming election. . . Occurrences at the time of the Haldimand election and immediately after prepared us for the infidelity of the administration, but certainly not to the extent which we afterwards witnessed. From the commencement of the session, it became too apparent that Mr. Hincks and his colleagues had succumbed to French Canadian influence, and that the ministerial policy was to be in open hostility to the views of the reform party of Upper Canada on the ecclesiastical questions. No bill was proposed to rearrange the constituencies, none to equalize the suffrage ; no action was proposed on the reserves; ecclesiastical corporations were increased; and on the retirement of Mr. Baldwin, and the accession of Mr. Hincks to the leadership, that gentleman announced that he had taken his stand with the French Canadians, and if his Upper Canadian supporters did not cease their grumbling, he and his Lower Canada friends would coalesce with the Tories ! He said : "I regret to say there have been indications given by a section (the anti-state churchmen) of the party to which I belong, that it will be difficult indeed, unless they change their policy, to preserve the union. I will tell these persons (the anti-state church reformers of Upper Canada) that if the union is not preserved by them, that, as a necessary consequence, other combinations must be formed by which the union may be preserved. I am ready to give my cordial support to any combination of parties by which the union shall be maintained. . . ." On this we left the ministry openly and decidedly. We denounced the infidelity of Mr. Hincks and his Upper Canada colleagues, and his indecent attempt to sell the power entrusted to him by the reformers into the hands of the high churchmen. And to show that this was his intention, let us quote an authority which will not now be disputed ; the *North American* of 27th June, 1851, says : " However much old friends of the ministry may be disinclined to credit it, we solemnly assert our belief in movements afoot for the formation of a coalition ministry, and we think that few men who have scanned the political horizon closely for the past three months will doubt the truth of our conjectures."

We spoke out our suspicions plainly, and demanded from the organ of the combination a full explanation of the grounds, the principles, the measures, on which this "consolidation" had been so "successfully and satisfactorily carried out." But we got no satisfaction. What then was our course? We saw all the danger to the anti-state church cause, which, in fact, is the main cause in jeopardy ; we saw that if Mr. Hincks as Prime Minister carried his own election, and the elections of those who had gone with him through all the passages of 1851, with the strength of the French Canadians and the disposition of the conservatives to coalesce with him, the voluntaries of Upper Canada would be completely at his mercy for four years; that he could turn out Dr. Rolph and Mr. Cameron at any time, and laugh at them. We therefore turned all our strength towards this point. We insisted that the country should be told ere the election what ground the ministry took and were prepared to stand by on the ecclesiastical questions, and we urged on the electors the absolute necessity of their knowing this ere giving their votes. The combination papers denounced us for asking their principles, called us traitor, and cried " Peace, peace," but not one word of explanation was obtained. . . . All this added force to our fears and suspicions; but the danger of division in the ranks stared us in the face on the eve of an election, and we saw it our duty to support cordially all the reform candidates in the field, with the exception of the ministers, and to endeavour to force them into declarations on the vital questions from which they could not afterwards retract.

Later in the year 1851, he published the series of letters addressed to Mr. Hincks, already quoted from. In the first letter, the following arraignment of ministers was presented : " At last election (1847) the " reform party occupied a noble position. The country had long " groaned under an irresponsible system of government, from which the " most grave abuses had resulted. The reformers promised to replace " that system by one of strict accountability to the people. They " enunciated that the ministry, for the time being, are responsible for " the executive administration of public affairs—that it is the duty " of the ministry to take in hand and carry out all great legislative " measures affecting the body politic—and that when they fail to carry " any such measures through Parliament, or when the opposition carries " any vital measure not by them deemed to be demanded by the neces- " sities of the country, it is their duty to resign office and transfer the " reins of government to other hands ; and by this rule they promised " to be guided. The country had long suffered from a most iniquitous " and injurious system of class legislation and executive favouritism, " and especially so in matters of a sectarian character. The reformers " promised that they would remove every ground for contention on " this score, by sweeping away all state endowments for ecclesiastical " purposes, by placing all denominations on an equal footing, and " regarding no man or sect in the light of their religious views. " The country had long suffered from the old theory, faithfully reduced " to practice, that colonists were not entitled to self-government, and " that their rulers, whether of imperial or provincial appointment, " were the best judges of what was requisite for the good of the " land. The reformers utterly repudiated such doctrine : they de- " clared that the people of Canada knew best what the necessities of " the country required, and they promised that the popular will " should rule the government while they held power, that legislation " should progress with public opinion and never do violence to it. The " country had deeply suffered from the existence in our midst of two " distinct races, with different languages and institutions, and from " the corrupt and injurious system which had grown up of appealing " to the local prejudices and feelings of the two sections for political " ends. The reformers denounced this policy as evil in the extreme ; " declared they would carry out the union of the provinces in its in- " tegrity, and would seek to assimilate the laws and institutions of the " two divisions, and to knit the population together by the bonds of " sympathy and interest. The liberal party had long suffered from the

" unfair distribution of the parliamentary representation—by which
" one-third of the population, living in boroughs and small counties,
" enjoyed a larger share of representation than the remaining two-
" thirds ; and the country had suffered as deeply from the corruption
" and infidelity entailed, when parties were nearly balanced, by the
" small number of representatives. The reformers pledged themselves
" to increase the number of representatives, and to distribute them
" more fairly. On these principles, and the measures which neces-
" sarily flowed from them, the liberal party sought the suffrages of the
" electors at last general election, and they met a hearty response
" from the intelligence of the country. And not less popular than the
" measures were the leading men of the party. Mr. Sullivan and you
" had not passed unscathed through your previous political careers,
" but the good services you had both rendered had regained for you
" the confidence of your party ; and Mr. Baldwin, Mr. Price, Mr.
" Cameron and Mr. Merritt, enjoyed the unbounded confidence and
" respect of the liberals of Upper Canada. Never did a party go to
" the polls with a better cause or more united ; and, as a natural re-
" sult, the most triumphant success rewarded them.

" The reform party, by their success at the polls, obtained office—
" four years have they now held office—three sessions of Parliament,
" with overwhelming majorities, have placed them in a position to ful-
" fil the just expectations of the country. Have they done so? Is
" the legislation of the last session such that the reform press can
" point to it with confidence as consistent with the promises of 1847,
" or as the pledge of a wholesome administration for the future ? *You*
" *dare not, on your conscience, say it is either.* You and your colleagues
" have trampled under foot your constitutional responsibility as minis-
" ters of the Crown.'

CHAPTER V.

CLERGY RESERVES, RECTORY ENDOWMENT, AND SEPARATE SCHOOL
QUESTIONS.—THE "GLOBE'S" ATTITUDE.

From this time Mr. Brown and the *Globe* were ranged in opposition
to the ministry, which, on Mr. Baldwin's resignation, was led by Mr.
Hincks.   Mr. Lafontaine retired at the same time.   The latter gentleman was probably the greatest obstacle to progress.   Mr. Baldwin was
timid ; Mr. Lafontaine was hostile ; and it is not improbable that if
the ministry had proceeded with the necessary measures for secularizing the clergy reserves, that he would have seceded.

It is impossible to avoid charging him with something like deception or treachery.   He knew the principles avowed at the general
election : he knew this carried the country ; he accepted office with
the cry for justice ringing in his ears, yet he retained office from
April 1848 to October 1851, ostensibly as a liberal minister practically
pledged to carry out the electoral programme, though he must have
known that the course he pursued was not altogether what would be
expected from an honourable high-minded man, and must result in the
disruption of the party whose policy and principles he was bound to
sustain and promote.   That Mr. Lafontaine's friends may have something to say for him is very probable.   That many, indeed all, of
the people loved Mr. Baldwin for his high personal qualities, is very
true ; but nothing can excuse the course pursued by them when they
were placed in power for a specific purpose and then failed to attempt
the accomplishment of that purpose.   Sir Francis Hincks long afterwards wrote concerning Mr. Lafontaine as follows :

"The French Canadians as a party were extremely unwilling to
" commit themselves on the clergy reserves or rectory questions . . .
" Mr. Lafontaine himself had a strong conservative bias, and two of
" his colleagues, Colonel Taché and L. M. Viger, fully shared his
" sentiments . . . Mr. Lafontaine went cordially with his col-
" leagues for the repeal of the Imperial Act, but there is great reason
" to doubt whether the Lafontaine-Baldwin ministry could have agreed
" to a bill for settling the clergy reserve question."   Messrs. Lafontaine and Viger voted against the resolution moved by Mr. Price (then
a member of the government), which declares "that the appropriation
" of the revenues derived from the investment of the proceeds of the
" public lands of Canada, by the Imperial Parliament, will never cease

" to be a source of discontent to your Majesty's loyal subjects in this
" province, and that when all the circumstances are taken into consid-
" eration, no religious denomination can be held to have such vested
" interest in the revenue derived from the said clergy reserves, as
" should prevent further legislation with reference to the disposal of
" them." Their votes on this occasion were the more remarkable, as
the resolution provided for the payments of the stipends then derived
by certain clergymen from said lands.

In 1851 one element of discord was found in the prevailing feeling
respecting the endowment of the rectories founded by Sir John Col-
borne from public lands. The popular opinion was undoubtedly not
only hostile to that step, but that the act of establishing the rectories
was not legal.

The law officers of the Crown in London gave an opinion in 1837
that the endowments of the 57 rectories were not valid and lawful acts.
The same officers reconsidered this decision, having obtained certain
other documents, and gave another opinion that they were legal and
valid acts. This last opinion, dated January 24th, 1838, contains the
following words in addition to the opinion that the act was lawful ;
" We are of opinion that the rectors of the parishes so erected and
" endowed, have the same ecclesiastical authority within their respec-
" tive limits as is vested in the rector of a parish in England." The
difference in the two opinions was altogether based on the interpretation given to the royal instructions, and the terms of the royal commission issued to Sir Patrick Maitland in 1825, so that the rectories
were established simply by virtue of a royal permission, and not on
any legislative authority. The Act of 1851 practically settled the
question in favour of the incumbents on the condition that the patents
had been validly issued. The English opinion obtained was hostile,
but the Court of Chancery decided that they were valid.

The following extracts from *Globe* editorials of January 15th, 1852,
and March 9th, will show the view taken immediately after the general
elections :

Had the reformers of Upper Canada been rallied to the polls upon
clearly-defined principles and measures—on issues framed to meet the
difficulties encountered in the previous parliament ; had the ground of
" union " been in full accordance with those principles and not the support
of Dr. Rolph and Mr. Hincks, the dissensions and apathy in the ranks
would have been removed, and the victory at the polls the most triumphant ever witnessed. . . .

The reformers have been greatly injured as a party by these proceedings ; they have no acknowledged leaders, no avowed policy, no great
defined aims as a party. The premier of our government was returned by
a Tory constituency, which, if true to his party, he must stand ready to
disfranchise ; and in his own county, one of the most decidedly reform
constituencies in Upper Canada, he owed his election to men who but a
day before were denouncing him, and only gave him their votes under

the pressure of circumstances which they deplored. But if the injury to the reform party has been great, how much more serious has been the evil of breaking down those constitutional bulwarks which our system of government requires, and permitting the public men of our country to shirk the avowal of their opinions and policy, and to obtain the reins of government, not by virtue of their principles, but by the cleverness of their *finesse!* There is nothing more vital to the safe working of British constitutional government than the open declaration by each political party, previous to a general election, of the measures and principles it will carry out if successful at the polls. It makes the people the final arbiter in all political strife; and the knowledge that these pledges must be carried out under the penalty of losing office makes politicians guarded in the avowal of their views. Public men think seriously ere committing themselves to new principles, but once committed, their political success is linked with the fate of those principles, and a protection is established at once against mere electioneering professions and infidelity to the public cause. Break down the barrier; let men go into power uncommitted to any special course, and once seated they will care not for the success of their principles, but cut and carve their measures to suit the humour of the day and the retention of office. All men are honest men when they are well watched, and human nature in all ages and climes has needed watching. The tendency of office is to corrupt the incumbent. We do not believe there was ever a more upright body of men combined in an administration than the late government; but they were found wanting under every constitutional check. And were the present men so politically irreproachable that the bonds could be safely relaxed towards them which were found too weak for their predecessors? With all the experience we had obtained, the fences should have been built higher and stronger than ever; but they were not, and we have four years' further experience before us.

He recollects that when the want of principle manifested in the combinations, and its injurious tendency on the anti-state church cause, was insisted on, the answer was: "What else can be done? we "will go divided to the polls; ministerial reformers will be opposed "by anti-ministerial reformers, and the Tories will gain power." We think that at this point Mr. Brown stated something like this: "Well, let them; better that they should prevail than that we should "sacrifice our principles by helping an alliance founded on deceit "and formed between men utterly opposed on principle. If we are "out of power four years our principles will gather strength, and we "will return with unity of aim and increased force." But that he ever expressed an unqualified wish for the success of the Tories is not only without foundation, but so palpably absurd as to require no contradiction.

The alienation of the Roman Catholic vote in Haldimand was the immediate result of a sharp controversy in the *Globe* on the subject of separate schools and the legislation creating ecclesiastical corporations. The feeling was doubtless much intensified by the introduction of many matters which form a standing subject of controversy between the Roman Catholic and reformed churches. The memoir in the *Globe* gives the following account of the origin of the articles in the news-

paper: "In 1850 the Pope had put forth a bull, creating, or profess-
"ing to create, a papal hierarchy in Great Britain, and had sent over
"a cardinal to England with the title of Archbishop of Westminster.
"The English protestants resented the Pope's action, and the senti-
"ment was re-echoed with increased fervour in Canada. Mr. Brown
"for some time gave no special prominence to the subject in the *Globe*,
"although he entertained strong feelings about it. Cardinal Wiseman
"had put forth a pronunciamento, in which the argument on the
"Roman Catholic side of the question was presented with much clear-
"ness and force. A copy of this document was handed to Mr. Brown
"by the Hon. Sir E. P. Taché, who half jocularly challenged him to
"publish it in the *Globe*. Mr. Brown expressed his willingness to
"publish the pronunciamento, but not unreasonably stipulated that,
"in case of his doing so, he should publish a reply, to be written by
"himself. To this Sir E. P. Taché assented, and accordingly both
"the pronunciamento and the reply appeared at full length in the
"*Globe*. In replying to the Cardinal's arguments, the writer was
"compelled to present the matter from the protestant point of view,
"and in a light which was far from being acceptable to Roman
"Catholics. The question was taken up by the entire press of the
"country, and was argued with great bitterness on both sides.
"Mr. Brown thus came to be regarded as the Canadian champion of
"protestantism. This circumstance, it will readily be understood,
"answered admirably for an election cry, and was made the most of
"by his opponents in Haldimand." Like all religious or semi-
religious controversies, this one developed hard words and harder
feelings, which eventuated in some injury to the political party led by
Mr. Brown. Apart altogether from the special controversy on the
subject of what was called the papal aggression in England, there
was much agitation in Canada West over the demands for separate
schools for Roman Catholics. It was generally felt that if one church
obtained special rights it would be difficult to refuse them to any
church. The fact that the non-catholic churches were generally
agreed on the subject of a secular system of education was not much
dwelt upon; though it might be used to show that the Roman
Catholic element was not precisely on the same footing. Mr. Brown
undoubtedly had the whole reform party, with few exceptions,
sustaining him in resisting the disruption of our school system, and
the multiplication of corporations managed by ecclesiastics, and holding real estate for other than the purposes of the society. It must not
be supposed that all Roman Catholics were entirely agreed on the
attitude of the clergy in relation to these subjects; on the contrary,
many of them adhered to the views of the liberal party, and supported

the reform candidates as before.   The fact that many Roman Catholic
countries held similar views was, of course, not without its weight in
determining their course of action.   On the other hand, it is not to
be denied that deep offence was taken at many articles in the *Globe*
and other papers by a large majority of the Roman Catholics, who did
not come into personal contact with Mr. Brown personally, and appreciate his kindly and honest nature.   Looking back, it is impossible to
deny that many harsh words were written which had better not have
been written ; but no one article ever appeared which bore the character of intolerance.   No warmer advocate of equal rights ever lived
than Mr. Brown proved himself to be, and, right or wrong, he
believed he was writing in defence of religious equality during the
period which that controversy covered.   Unscrupulous politicians, of
little or no standing as public men, for years filled their scrap-books
with garbled extracts, torn from their context, and used them as electioneering weapons, mixing with these extracts much offensive
matter which had never appeared in the *Globe*.   When all other means
failed in combating. Mr. Brown and his friends in political contests,
these forged passages were made to do duty, until the public were disgusted with the forgeries, as well as the resuscitation of statements
and arguments which had no relation to new questions and a new
state of political life.   The bulk of the anti-Catholic element, and
particularly the Orange society, was always violently opposed to Mr.
Brown, though a very small section of the Orange party were politically agreed with him, and at some elections gave effective support.
The mass of the Roman Catholics, on the other hand, had supported
the liberals, and joined heartily in the long struggle for religious
equality and parliamentary government.

There was therefore no reason why Mr. Brown should hate Roman
Catholics, as he was represented to have done by parties who were
interested in making such misrepresentations.   Many of Mr. Brown's
most devoted friends, in and out of parliament, were staunch Roman
Catholics.   During Mr. Brown's first parliamentary session the Rev.
Mr. Gavazzi, a Roman Catholic priest who had refused to acknowledge
the papal supremacy, made his appearance in Canada.   Early in June
he attempted to lecture in Chalmers' Free Church, Quebec.   The
church was assailed by a mob, the doors and windows were smashed
in, and a portion of the rioters rushed in and attacked the lecturer in
the pulpit.   He succeeded, after a brief struggle, in effecting his
escape uninjured.   The mob then marched direct to the parliament
buildings, apparently determined to reach Mr. Brown, even if they
should attack the House for that purpose.   He did not respond to
their calls to come out, and they were finally persuaded by some of
the members to disperse.   This demonstration of the catholic element

against Mr. Brown was doubtless the outcome of the somewhat bitter controversy which had prevailed for some time respecting separate schools and religious corporations, in which discussion Mr. Brown had taken a very prominent part. He was designated by his opponents as the leader or head of a protestant political party, though in fact he had never advocated or favoured the formation of a political party based on religious distinctions. Indeed, it would have been entirely foreign to his conceptions of the constitution of political parties. His advocacy was incessant for a complete separation of church and state, so as to remove discussions on religious subjects from the domain of politics, and when this separation was completed in Canada these polemical discussions also ceased in political circles. As the editor-in-chief of a leading newspaper, it was manifestly impossible to wholly avoid subjects of discussion which involved the consideration of the church polity of several denominations in respect to matters affecting the general public. When Mr. Brown formed his cabinet in 1858 it was upon an agreement that the separate school question should be dealt with after a full inquiry should be made into the school systems in other countries, catholic and protestant; and there is no reason to doubt that, had his ministry been permitted to go on, means would have been found to harmonize the various views held by himself and his political associates. The Amended Separate School Act of 1863, and the immediately succeeding arrangement effected in the Confederation Act, removed this question from the field of controversy, but even before then nearly all irritation had ceased in Ontario, though it still continued in other provinces, where Mr. Brown had never pretended to possess any special influence, and where the separate school question was raised long after it was set at rest in old Canada.

Apart altogether from the questions at issue between Roman Catholics and protestants, Mr. Brown rendered great service to the country by his advocacy of a non-denominational system of education. There were not wanting signs of an attempt being made by some other churchmen to introduce the sectarian element in the management of our schools; and an open effort was made to ruin Toronto University by the appropriation of its revenues to sustain sectarian colleges.

CHAPTER VI.

MR. BROWN ENTERS PARLIAMENT.—HIS RELATIONS TO THE REFORM PARTY.

After Mr. Brown's defeat in Haldimand he received communications from several constituencies offering to procure his nomination ; amongst others the reformers of the then united counties of Kent and Lambton offered to nominate him in the interest of the wing of the liberal party to which he belonged, and with considerable difficulty induced him to accede to their request. Mr. Brown afterward wrote of the Haldimand contest as follows : " Had I known that the battle " of religious equality would have been fought, as it has been by " Messrs. Mackenzie, Morrison and Notman, and you (Mr. Hincks) " and your colleagues brought to book as you have been, I never " would have put my foot in Haldimand as an aspirant for political " honours." Mr. Brown was at this time generally supposed to be very anxious to get into parliament. It was not unnatural that this should be the case. He had much to do with the parliamentary work of the previous seven years. As the leading political writer on the reform side, he knew all that was passing in political life. He also knew that under existing leadership there was great danger that the liberal ranks would be shattered to pieces. He had every motive for entering parliament which could actuate a patriotic mind ; besides, it was natural that he should feel an honourable ambition urging him to accept a seat in the parliament of his country.

The truth was, however, that he was very reluctant to come forward as a candidate at this time. He was yet a young man ; the *Globe* required all his time ; and he felt that he could accomplish more by zealously working, through his journal, on the public mind of the whole country, than by conquering his opponents in one constituency. The following letter was written by him to the secretary of the Reform Association of Lambton, giving his views privately to that gentleman :

[Private].

TORONTO, 13th Sept., 1851.

MY DEAR SIR,—I am in receipt of your letter of 11th inst., and am very much indebted to you and my other friends for your kindness. I shall give you a frank answer to your question. There is no constituency I would feel so gratified to represent, were I in parliament, as Kent. I have many friends in it ; it is a large rising county, capable of much improvement, and therefore a good field for an energetic representative ; and moreover, I own some seven or eight hundred acres of valuable land in it.

But I am not anxious to go into parliament. I tried for Haldimand with the one object of settling, if I could, or at any rate pushing to test votes before the general election, the representation, reserves, rectory, sectarian schools, sectarian money grants, marriage and suffrage questions. This was, however, done by others, with so sorry a result as must have convinced all true friends of the cause that a hard battle has yet to be fought. Into that battle I shall throw myself with all my strength; and there is reason to believe that the *Globe* is exercising considerable influence throughout the country in awaking the public mind to the importance of making the voluntary principle in all its length and breadth the great issue at the coming election. But while earnestly striving for the return of men of my own principles, I have refrained from offering for any county, and have left unimproved several opportunities presented to me, from the fear that my seeking personal advancement might hurt the cause I espouse, might weaken my testimony on behalf of great principles. Moreover, I have spent nearly two months this year already in an election contest; and having been long enough behind the scenes to lose all sublime ideas of parliamentary life, it needs all one's patriotism to think, without quailing, of a second contest and a three months' residence yearly at Quebec for four years, leaving business to take care of itself.

Notwithstanding all this, it would be a high honour to sit for Kent, and it would be a loud testimony in favour of the cause in which I am enlisted were the convention to give me the nomination without solicitation on my part. I fear I could not refuse such an offer were there a likelihood of success.

I am, my Dear Sir,
Very truly yours,
GEO. BROWN.

A few days after this letter was written, the Reform Convention met at Dresden and nominated Mr. Brown. In reply to the letter informing him of the result, Mr. Brown wrote as follows:

TORONTO, Oct. 2, 1851.

MY DEAR SIR,—I duly received your letter announcing the result of the Dresden Convention, which, I assure you, very much surprised me. I had not the least expectation of such a result. I am much obliged to you and other friends for your exertions in my favour. With yours I received a letter from Chatham stating that I had no friends there, that I had not the ghost of a chance, that some prominent reformers will vote against me, and that the Roman Catholics will to a man go against me. Of course I take all this *cum grano*, but I am the last man to divide the party interest. I have no personal object to gratify in the matter, and unless the electors generally want me, I assure you I don't want to trouble them. I am ready to do anything for the cause, but I am sure I can be better employed here, firing away in the *Globe* and perhaps affecting several counties, than canvassing Kent with a divided party supporting me. I am entirely in your hands. Your committee, of course, know the county and could not be deceived as to public feeling on the subject. Unless all go with the movement it would be wrong to proceed; wrong in any one, but doubly wrong in me, who must preach union to others many times ere the elections are over. Write me fully, and believe me

Yours truly,
GEO. BROWN.

Such were the views he entertained at that time regarding the acquisition of a seat in parliament. The unselfish spirit shown in that correspondence only increased the determination of the electors of

Kent and Lambton to elect him as their representative. Mr. Brown ultimately accepted the nomination, with the understanding that he was not to spend more than two weeks in the county. A few weeks after the action of the convention, Messrs. Baldwin and Lafontaine retired from the Government. Mr. Hincks was entrusted with the formation of the new administration, and succeeded in getting two of the most demonstrative reformers against the policy of the Baldwin Lafontaine government, in the persons of Hon. Mr. Cameron and Dr. Rolph, to join his government. Mr. Cameron and Caleb Hopkins were among the earliest to manifest their discontent with the do-nothing policy of Mr. Baldwin at a time when Mr. Brown and the *Globe* were freely supporting that government. These two gentlemen were attacked with great vigour by the *Globe*, and sarcastically dubbed the "clear grit" party, a term which has since then found a permanent place in our political nomenclature, embracing in its more extensive application the originator of the appellation. Mr. Cameron deeply resented the attacks made upon him, and immediately after Mr. Brown's nomination intimated his intention to oppose him. Mr. Cameron was at that time the sitting member for Kent, but had publicly informed the electors that he intended to contest Huron at the coming election, thus leaving them free to make another choice. Mr. Cameron was personally popular in the county, and believed he could easily defeat Mr. Brown with some candidate of his own. He accordingly brought out Mr. Arthur Rankin, of Sandwich, as a reform candidate, while Mr. Larwill entered the field as a straight Tory. Mr. Cameron had miscalculated his own strength in the county as well as the influence of the *Globe*. He attended a few of Mr. Brown's meetings, and finding an almost universal determination on the part of the liberals to support Mr. Brown, he abandoned the county and all hope of electing Mr. Rankin. Mr. Brown, by his eloquence, but above all by his evident earnestness, made a most favourable impression wherever he spoke.

Mr. Cameron at one or two meetings promised to support Mr. Brown, if he would pledge himself to support the new administration. This Mr. Brown declined to do, unless the ministry avowed their intention to deal with the great question of the clergy reserves, rectories, representation, sectarian schools and money grants. Mr. Cameron not being in a position to make any promises, demanded the candidate's support purely on the ground that the government was a liberal one, and therefore entitled to the support of all liberals. The electors, however, were not disposed to forget that four years ago Mr. Hincks and his colleagues had been elected on a distinct policy, and that many of the most important measures embraced in that policy had not been dealt with, though essential to the peace of the country and the existence of the liberal party.

When Mr. Cameron left Toronto to attend Mr. Brown's meetings, much was expected from his efforts, and the *North American* modestly announced that Mr. Brown had gone to Kent, but that "one was after him mightier than he, whose shoe latchets he was unworthy to unloose."

Though a few good reformers did not support Mr. Brown, it was soon evident that nearly the whole party would cast their votes for him. The Hinck's administration considered, and properly considered, that Mr. Brown's election would necessarily be considered as a condemnation of the government by their own party. Mr. Rankin was therefore kept in the field solely and purely to divide the reform vote, and thereby to secure Mr. Brown's defeat by electing the Tory candidate. Some, however, of the warmest followers of Mr. Cameron declined to be placed in that position, and voted for Mr. Brown when all hope of electing Mr. Rankin was abandoned.

Another effort indeed was made of a very clumsy character to divide the party. A Mr. Wilkes appeared suddenly as a third reform candidate. His supporters and Mr. Rankin's supporters made this proposal to Mr. Brown's committee: That each of the candidates or their friends should nominate a committee of six, and that the eighteen so selected should designate the candidate as a kind of arbitration board. Of course all was supposed to be done in the party interests. Mr. A. McKellar, the chairman of Mr. Brown's committee, agreed to the arbitration, but said that as many of the electors were as much interested as the proposed committee could be, he proposed that the decision should be referred to the whole body of the electorate, and that the vote should be taken on the 13th and 14th of December (the regular polling days). This concluded the negotiations, and all parties prepared for the struggle. The result was Mr. Brown's election by a fair majority. Although he was forced into a position of hostility to the government by the logic of events, there was no reason to fear his opposition if reform measures were honestly brought forward. The new administration doubtless desired to do all they comfortably could to meet the just expectations of the country, without imperilling their own position. But it contained a reactionary element; one gentleman was there who, instead of meeting western reformers by argument, designated them as "Pharisaical brawlers." The truth is, that Mr. Taché (afterwards Sir E. P. Taché) was not a reformer; his appropriate place was in the conservative ranks, to which he drifted by easy gradations, and where he filled a respectable position for many years.

Mr. Brown expressed himself as follows immediately after the contest, respecting the principles involved in it:

State-churchism has been the great pivot on which the election has turned, and there is no misunderstanding the public feeling upon it here.

Mr. Rankin **and** myself were the **avowed** advocates of total separation of church and state—of sweeping away reserves, rectories, money-grants, and every shadow of connection, and together we obtained an immense majority of the suffrages.   Even Mr. Larwill, the high church candidate, did not dare to avow the usual pretensions of his party ; he talked of a more "equitable arrangement" than the present—of the *difficulty*, not the "injustice" of upsetting the whole system—and hundreds of his voters, to my personal knowledge, strange as it may appear, would sweep away at once every vestige of state-churchism were the power in their hands. They had been so often appealed to on the same question that they despaired of any good being effected, and voted from old party associations ; but their hearts were with the voluntaries.   And who that cares for the prosperity of his country would not be with them ?   Look back as far as you can recollect, and tell me if all the other causes of discord and strife and bad feeling in the province put together have entailed such aggravated evils upon us as this one question of church endowments ?   Church has been **set** against church, family against family, sectarian hatred has been fostered, religion has been brought into contempt by the scramble for public plunder, and infidelity has been in no small degree promoted by the sight of men preaching one day the worthlessness of lucre, and battling on the next to clutch a little of that same commodity, though gained by the grossest partiality and injustice.   And all this to serve the cause of religion !   Men do not quarrel about **religion.**

A VOICE : It's all about the *bawbees !*

MR. BROWN : Yes ; it is all about the *bawbees*—take away the cash, and our sectarian animosities will be **at an end.**   Settle, and settle finally, this question of endowments to churches, and I know not where **we** shall find a country with lighter grievances than Canada ; religion will prosper better by the voluntary gifts of the Christian people, and our political differences will be stript of an element so hurtful. .   .   .

There is another point on which the result of this election is to me most satisfactory.   The disagreements between the late and present ministry **and** myself have been made prominent issues in the contest. .   .   .

The merits of this antagonism have been fully brought out at this election, and you by your votes have decided that the late ministry betrayed the reform cause in the last session of parliament ; that the present ministry was not formed in **a** satisfactory manner ; that it had no right to claim public confidence on the mere character of its members, but should have explained fairly and fully to the electors the principles and measures by which it was prepared to stand or fall ; and that any confidence it may win **must** be by its measuress and its measnres alone. .   .   .

As far as I am concerned, I have no personal hostility to the present **ministry.**   Our differences are on public principles ; they have the power in their hands yet to redeem their character with the Upper Canada Reformers ; and if they act firmly and honestly on the great questions of the day, they shall have no opposition from me.   But if they do not act satisfactorily on these questions, they may depend **upon it** that no bugbear fear to "new combinations" will deter me **from giving** them earnest opposition.

Mr. **Brown,** on taking **his seat in the new** parliament, **took the** ground **ever afterwards** held, that there could be **no** compromise **with** principles, however much he might be disposed to make allowances, as he had already done to too great an extent, for delays occasioned **by** unforeseen circumstances.

Mr. Cameron at some of the Lambton meetings said that Mr. Brown **was** angry because he **was not asked to** join the **government, and be-**

cause the *Globe* was not now continued as the organ of the ministry. As to the latter charge, it is well known that the *Globe* declined to follow the government, not that the ministry abandoned the *Globe.* Mr. Brown's own reply to such insinuations was as follows, addressed to Mr. Hincks : " I am accused by your new allies of being actuated in my " present course by selfish pecuniary motives. They allege that I was " the pliant instrument of your government while I enjoyed its patron- " age, and only spoke independently when that patronage was with- " drawn. You well know, sir, how utterly unfounded is such a charge, " and that from the beginning to the end of my connection with the " government, you have had 'and have made a very different com- " plaint ; you know that I have been at open issue with you throughout " in regard to your systematic disregard of the feelings and wishes of " your supporters, and the disastrous effects on the party thereby pro- " duced. . . . I am also charged with acting as I now do from " ambition, mortified ambition. As for the mortification, I am not " aware of any ground for it in the progress of seven years ; and if I " were unduly ambitious, I might have conciliated the French Cana- " dian phalanx, soothed the Tories, and finessed with the Rolphites, as " you have done. I have sense enough to see that plain words help " not the ambitious, but I have denounced without scruple all these " in turn when duty to the public required it."

On the 10th day of June, 1851, Mr. Hincks spoke as follows on the occasion of the *Globe* denouncing a Religious Corporation Bill, which gave extraordinary powers to hold property : " I am ready to " give my cordial support to any combination of parties by which the " union shall be maintained. I would refer more particularly to the " course lately pursued by what is considered the organ of the party " with which I act. Attempts are being made to damage my in- " fluence." So it seems the *Globe* was " damaging Mr. Hincks' influ- " ence," while it was yet considered the organ of the party with which he acted !

It is of course a question for argument whether Mr. Brown's course was right or wrong ; whether he was chiefly responsible for breaking up the reform party by the non-recognition of leaders who had been unfaithful, or whether Mr. Hincks, who avoided the introduction of promised and needful reforms rather than offend his opponents, and who coquetted with enemies, was the really responsible party. In the light of events no one can be at a loss to discover upon whom the blame must be cast. Every person who is conversant with the current political movements from 1844 to 1848, will readily recall the questions which were submitted to the electors in the autumn of 1847, and will also keep in view the policy of the reform party always. Was the policy of the liberal party on which the elections were carried acted upon by

the reform administration ? This question must be answered in the
negative so far as most of the great questions are concerned. It is
true that Mr. Hincks pled that Mr. Brown defended all the acts of
the administration until a few weeks before the general election of
1851. Were this literally true, it would neither palliate nor excuse
the inaction, to use a mild term, of the government. The government
had undoubtedly passed some good measures, for which Mr. Brown
gave them ample credit, as shown by the extracts from his Haldimand
address already given. Mr. Hincks, the new leader of the government,
had resented certain articles in the *Globe*, which paper, he says, " was
" considered the organ of the party with which he acted," and in his
wrath openly declared his readiness to support " any combination of
" parties " to oppose the *Globe's* views. He also stated that " no wise
" statesman would attempt to carry on this union upon any other prin-
" ciple than that of equal representation to both sections."

He was also to " oppose all organic changes in the constitution."
He little thought that thirteen years after making this unwise speech,
every statesman in both sections admitted that equal representation
was not just, and therefore gave unequal representation, which now
stands as 92 to 65. He evidently did not then dream that within two
years he would himself propose another " organic change in the con-
" stitution." It would be easy to multiply to any extent extracts from
speeches, and to give votes, and cite cases of manifest omissions of
duty in the liberal leader, which would show that he was then conscious of having lost the confidence of a large portion—the largest
portion—of the reform party, and was plainly offering himself as a
component part of a new combination, made up of all classes of politicians who would join the ministerial omnibus. The miserable pretence of maintaining the union was too shallow ; no one knew better
than Mr. Hincks that the only danger to the union arose from wrong
legislation, which created new abuses, and the want of legislation to
remove old grievances. That Mr. Hincks' personal views were wholly
in favour of perfect religious equality, and the justice of the other
measures sought by reformers, probably few will be disposed to doubt.
That he lamentably failed at a critical time to show that he had the
courage of his convictions, no one will deny. If he had changed his
opinions he should have frankly avowed it, and resigned the position
he had attained by liberal votes. It was no answer to the reproaches
heaped upon him by those whose aid he obtained at the elections to
fly into a passion, and threaten to join his political adversaries.

CHAPTER VII.

ATTITUDE TOWARDS THE MINISTRY.—MAIDEN SPEECH IN PARLIAMENT.

Mr. Brown's appearance in parliament justified the expectations of his friends who had hoped so much from his great knowledge of public affairs, political and commercial, and his ability as a speaker. It is very seldom that a new member is able, at the very start of his political career, to take rank as a leading man. He was tacitly acknowledged at once as the leader of reformers, who did not give Mr. Hincks and the government a regular support, though he was not regularly selected to occupy that post. Parliament was not called together until late in the summer, but Mr. Brown did not wait for the meeting of parliament to promulgate his views on matters of great concern to the state and to the liberal party. He had been elected for Kent and Lambton on a thoroughly independent platform as regards Mr. Hincks' government, and pledged only to promote the well understood policy of the reform party, either with or without the action of the government. Some reformers undoubtedly did desire to pursue a mild policy, and hoped for decided action from Mr. Hincks. That gentleman, however, repelled those who were disposed to still trust in him, and who urged him to adopt a policy which would unite the party and at the same time benefit the country, by passing measures of reform urgently demanded. To remonstrance or threats his reply was, that if pressed, he would form other combinations which would maintain the *status quo.* In the meantime Mr. Brown continued his pungent writing in the *Globe* in the most direct hostility to the government. But every member of the government knew that he would support them, if haply they would introduce the measures demanded by the country.

In January the following piquant description of the ministry was given in the *Globe :*

" In this remarkable collection of heterogeneous elements was to
" be found the cautious conservative and the fierce republican; the
" ardent admirer of Andrew Marvel and the meek subject of Pio
" Nono ; the model constitution monger and the haughty scorner of
" ' all organic changes;' the unswerving voluntary and the high estab-
" lishment man ; the panegyrist of Baldwin and the devotee of Rolph ;
" the Roman priesthood of Lower Canada, and the evangelical minis-

" try of Upper Canada. . . We have clergy reserve men and anti-
" clergy reserve men ; rectory bill men and rectory lawsuit men ;
" sectarian school men and secular school men ; sixteen million Trunk
" Railway men, and the bitter foes of that precious scheme ; . . in
" short, the advocates of every conceivable change, and the advocates
" of their antipodes. No party supports the ministry . . . its sup-
" porters are units from all parties, and they are suspicious of their
" leaders, but hope they may go right."

Mr. Brown did not, however, then or at the general election just over, oppose any reformer who was a candidate. The ministry started candidates against himself, Mr. Price and Mr. Morrison, who then sympathized with Mr. Brown's views more or less. In May the Hon. Malcolm Cameron, who had accepted office as President of the Council, appeared in Huron for re-election. He was opposed by Mr. James Brown, and the secretary of that gentleman's committee wrote to Mr. Brown to ask his assistance in the county.

This invitation he declined. In his letter to the secretary, after referring to some objectionable portions of Mr. Cameron's career, he said : " But notwithstanding all this, Mr. Cameron is so pledged on the
" voluntary question that he cannot escape from it. This is probably
" the only question on which parties will be in any degree tested in
" the present parliament, and if the voluntaries of Huron see proper
" to take Mr. Cameron as their candidate, I cannot do anything to
" injure the cause which has my warmest sympathy."

The speech from the throne, on August 21st, was singularly barren of committal or reference even to controverted questions, a bare reference to the treatment of the clergy reserve matter in England alone excepted. No promise of any action even on that subject was made. Mr. Brown made his maiden parliamentary speech on the address. It consisted largely of a review of the position of the reform party, and a criticism on the position of ministers in regard to the great questions of the day ; in other words, the questions relating to what Mr. Brown was wont to term " state-churchism." He spoke from the ministerial side, but had no hesitation in attacking ministers, especially the Premier and Messrs. Cameron and Rolph, for not boldly moving in these questions as a ministry. It was taken for granted that, as Mr. Brown had denounced ministers at the elections, he would also vote against them in the House. He had, however, to consider who would take their places, before going into an out-and-out opposition ; nor did he even then despair of the government taking such action as would enable all reformers to give them a full support. He took advantage of the occasion to lay down the sound constitutional principles on which the ministry were bound to act in regard to great questions which agitated the whole country, if they intended to follow a proper course in carrying out responsible government.

He pointed out that ministers had no right to rely for parliamentary support on mere general declarations of their liberality, instead of specific statements of their policy on certain great measures on which the people had made up their minds long before. This, however, was precisely what the ministry did, and Mr. Brown dealt plainly and boldly with them and the principles at stake, as he was bound to do by his promises to the electors.

The following extracts from his speech on this occasion, will give some idea of the position of the ministry as well as of Mr. Brown's capacity as a parliamentary orator and leader. In this, his first appearance in parliament, he demonstrated his power as a speaker and thinker, notwithstanding Dr. Rolph's pedantic sneer when he referred to Mr. Brown as "a person of tolerable education." The new minister was soon to learn that the new member must be met, if met at all, with something more than an ill-mannered sneer, as untrue as it was unfair.

Mr. Brown, after referring to various incidents which became public in regard to the formation of the government, said:

But it is in regard to the principles on which the ministry was formed that the total absence of satisfactory explanation must be felt more deeply by the House. The Inspector-General tells us the administration is formed on progressive principles. . . . He said there had been divisions in the reform party, and it was necessary to secure the co-operation of both sections. . . . I was more than surprised to hear the Inspector-General say there had been "no serious differences of opinion." What can possibly be a serious difference of opinion in the eyes of the honorable gentleman?

There is not one principle of constitutional government, not one prominent measure before the country, on which they were not wide as the poles asunder. In the whole history of free institutions, where will a parallel be found for the bitter unscrupulous opposition waged for two years by the present President of the Council and his allies, or the Inspector-General and his colleagues? . . . When parliament last sat they were ranged against each other in fierce battle array; a few months pass, and lo, they sit together in sweetest harmony. . . .

He glanced at the leading incidents of the Metcalfe parliament, acknowledging the firm manner in which Mr. Lafontaine and many members now in the house had stuck to their Upper Canada allies in spite of the seductions of office, and showed how closely the alliance had been cemented by the events of that period. The result of the elections of 1847-8 was the triumphant success of the reform party at the polls, and consequent accession to power of the Baldwin-Lafontaine ministry.

From the very foundation of that ministry, a principle of separation began to show itself in the liberal party, which gradually forced a breach in their ranks, and finally broke up the ministry. That principle of separation was found in the difference of opinion as to the employment of public money for sectarian purposes. Our allies in Lower Canada are in favour of a close connection between church and state, while Upper Canada reformers are opposed to it in every shape. We not only oppose the payment of public money for sectarian purposes, but we say that religion is a matter between each man and his Maker, and that the government has no right to determine for the country what is the truth, but ought to leave a matter so sacred to the conscience of each member of the community. . . . Honourable gentlemen opposite knew well that the division in the reform camp alone gave them a chance at last election ; and I hesitate not to affirm that if an appeal should ever be made to the people of Upper Canada on the question of state endowments to the church, it will leave the benches opposite almost vacant. Who could seek a better evidence of the state of feeling in Upper Canada than the election addresses of gentlemen opposite ? Did one of them dare to avow the old claim of monopoly for the Church of England ?

Will the gallant knight who leads the high church party venture to say that even he could have been returned for the city of Hamilton had his declarations on these questions been of the same old stamp? Will the honourable member for Middlesex say that he could have obtained his seat on high church principles ? . . . The people of Upper Canada feel intensely on this question. It has been the grievance of the country for 30 years. And if the gentlemen from Lower Canada could understand how the bitterness which flows from it affects every relation of life, whether social or political, they would not wonder at the eagerness to have it settled for ever.

In this county (Quebec) a large proportion of the people are of one faith, and it appears not so odious to give that church a preference ; but I ask them if a sect or two sects, forming a small minority, a mere fraction of the community, engrossed all the honours and emoluments of the state, and asserted a position of dominancy over the majority, whether they would not have united as one man for the overthrow of such a system. This, then, was the question of Upper Canada, and the reform party fully expected that the first act of the Baldwin-Lafontaine ministry would have been to settle it for ever. Unhappily the Rebellion Losses Bill obtained the preference, and the reserve question was set adrift for the session. That bill was introduced into parliament, I am well convinced, without the knowledge or consent of one member of the Upper Canada reform party not in the government. Every one knows the convulsion it produced in the country, and that in standing by their Lower Canada allies upon it, the reformers of Upper Canada were well nigh upset.

I have no doubt whatever, that at that time, and for many months afterwards, the Upper Canada section of the ministry believed, and entertained no doubt, that their Lower Canada colleagues would give them a cordial support, when the day of trial came, on the reserve question. I think it was not until just before the session of 1850 that they found their mistake ; and I entertain not the slightest doubt that Messrs. Baldwin, Price and Hincks strove to have the settlement made a ministerial question. When parliament met in May, 1850, it was announced that it was to be an open question, and it was apparent that the other ecclesiastical subjects of dispute in the western province were to be sacrificed to the Lower Canada allies. It might have been a question whether the Upper Canada ministers should not then have resigned, and cast themselves on the country. I confess I was one who then thought that it was not their duty to resign at that moment.

The French Canadians were willing to vote for an address to the Crown, asking the transfer of the control over the reserves to the provincial parliament, and it was well to take their help even to this extent.

But far beyond this was the consideration that if they then resigned and new parties were formed, the unjust arrangement of the constituencies of Upper Canada would be a strong bar in our way at the coming general election. It was the obvious duty, then, of the Upper Canada ministers to seize the opportunity and prepare for any event by reforming the parliamentary representation; and their neglecting to introduce a bill extinguishing some of the small boroughs and rearranging the counties—which they had full power to do by a majority vote—excited the first doubt in my mind as to the firmness of the Hon. Inspector-General and his colleagues on these vital questions. . . . Is it to be wondered at that the country was becoming dissatisfied, and that a new party was arising who denounced the ministry as faithless to their trust and to their principles? It matters not now to inquire the motives which originally actuated those who commenced the agitation within the reform party against the leaders of that party. "They saw everything with distorted vision, and denounced without measure."

The passage which follows recounted the divergence of views of the advanced wing—Cameron, Hopkirk, and others—from those held by Mr. Hincks and his friends, until they united. Reciting extracts from the journals of the House and other documents, Mr. Brown then proceeded:

Here, then, we have an unimpeachable record of the views of the two sections of the reform party; and in the face of all this the Hon. Inspector-General ventures to tell this House that there was no "serious difference of opinion" between them; and, sir, the discordance between them was no less violent than the disagreement as to principles and measures. I hold in my hand extracts from the organs of the new allies of the Inspector-General showing the bitter, the savage hostility with which they regarded that gentleman and his colleagues, . . . using terms towards them which I cannot bring myself to utter. However lax may be the political morality of the Hon. Inspector-General, I gladly disclaim sympathy with such insinuations, and have always been ready to defend him from attacks on his personal integrity, which I believe beyond reproach.

It may be contended that only one member of the administration is identified with the ultra views recorded in our journals; but I contend that to every one of these views the Hon. Commissioner of Crown Lands (Dr. Rolph) is as fully committed as his colleagues. He was the silent instigator and counsel of the new party in its conception—he was in public and in private recognized as the leader of that party—as the representative of that party he was elected by the people, and as the representative of these views he was forced into the government. It is true the hon. gentleman has managed with wondrous skill to cover his real sentiments with an impenetrable mask, and to this moment we know nothing of his sentiments; but silence gives consent; and if the hon. gentleman does not hold the views of the member for Huron (Mr. Cameron), the country has been shamefully deceived.

Thus opened the session of 1851, the ministerialists hoping against hope that their leaders would be true to their party and their principles on the great questions of Upper Canada, and the secessionists eager for war. The ministerial policy was too soon developed, and it became apparent that the western members of the ministry had succumbed to their French Canadian allies, and that reserves, rectories—everything—was to be sacrificed to their demands. How the Inspector-General meant to go to the country in the face of such a course was a mystery to every one, but on the retirement of Mr. Baldwin after the Chancery Court division, the secret was discovered.

That event placed the Inspector-General in the leadership of this House, and on the night of his inauguration he used the following language: "I regret to say there have been indications given by a section of the party to which I belong, that it will be difficult indeed, unless they change their policy, to preserve the union. I will tell these persons (the anti-state church reformers of Upper Canada) that if the union is not preserved by them, as a necessary consequence other combinations must be formed by which the union may be preserved. *I am ready to give my cordial support to any combination of parties by which the union shall be maintained.*"

The gallant knight (Sir A. N. McNab) who leads the opposition replied to this overture : " I will only say, and I want it to go over the country, that I will do all I can to prevent a clear grit party rising through the land, and will support any party to prevent that."

Sir Allan N. McNab : That is correct.

Mr. Brown : Of course it is correct, and the most amiable understanding existed then as now between the high contracting parties.

Sir A. N. McNab denied that he had held on any occasion any political conversations with any members of the government at any time except in the House.

Mr. Brown continued : From that day to this not one word of explanation had been given as to the terms of the compromise. Before the general election we strove to get at the secret ; not even at the contest was any satisfactory explanation attempted to be offered. The Hon. Inspector-General assured his constituents that the composition of the government should be sufficient guarantee to them for the policy to be followed ; the Chief Commissioner of Public Works told his constituents that the character of his colleagues must be the guarantee for their measures ; and the organ of the union told the country generally that the presence of the members for Norfolk and Huron in the ministry was sufficient guarantee for anything. We were told last session, when we asked for explanations, wait until Mr. Lafontaine resigns ; after that event we were told, wait until a full cabinet has met and measures have been discussed ; a little later we were told, wait until parliament assembles ; and now that parliament has met, we are without a word of explanation.

Sir, I think we should not have been obliged to extort explanation in this way from gentlemen on the treasury benches. I think they should have given them fully and freely long ere this, and I cannot doubt that they will do so without further delay. We have a right to clear information on two points ; first, how did two sections from Upper Canada harmonize their antagonistic opinions on so many constitutional questions? and, second, how did these gentlemen overcome the difficulty which the state church principles of the provincial secretary and his country presented to a settlement of the ecclesiastical questions of Upper Canada ? Are we to have new constitutions, elective governors, universal suffrage and the political gamut of the hon. member for Huron, or have he and his colleagues sent all these to the winds ? Have the lower Canadian portion of the ministry yielded to the just demands of Upper Canada, and agreed to remove every vestige of state-churchism ? Or was the assertion that they had done so a delusion, and the position of our allies in this parliament precisely what it was in the last ? The country has a right to a clear, unequivocal reply. Such exhibitions as this strike at the root of public morality.

Mr. Cameron : And virtue !

Mr. Brown : Sir, the gentleman may sneer if he likes it, but this is not a matter to be met in such a spirit. If a public man may resign his post in an administration at the risk of breaking up the government ; if he can protest before the country that his conscience would not allow him to remain while a useless officer existed ; and if he can but a few months later eat up all he said, and that very office, with impunity, the public morals are indeed concerned. If, sir, a public man can avow certain opinions, agitate the country on those opinions, attempt to destroy the government by the influence of those opinions, and the moment office is in his reach can laugh at his professions and sends all his principles to the winds, it strikes at the root of public morality. And, sir, if a member of a responsible ministry can forget the confidential relations in which he stands to his colleagues, and secretly plot their removal and his own aggrandisement, where shall we look for good faith among men? . . . Our constitutional system is placed in jeopardy by exhibitions so improper.

There is no principle in the theory of responsible government more vital to its right working than that parties shall take their stand on the prominent questions of the day, and mount to office or resign it through the success or failure of principles to which they are attached. This is the great safeguard for the public against clap-trap professions, and when strictly enforced it makes men seriously consider ere they commit themselves on leading questions. The conduct of gentlemen on the treasury benches in this view strikes a serious blow at our constitutional system. If a public man can hold one set of principles out of office, another set in office, responsible government is a farce. I readily acknowledge the good service rendered in past years to the cause of ministerial responsibility by the Inspector-General and the Provincial Secretary. But so much the more blamable is their conduct in these transactions. To their hands it was given to guard over it, and they have betrayed that trust. A few such blows and how shall it be upheld? There are two systems of government now being tested on this continent: the United States system of checks and fetters, which no official can overstep, and the British system of balanced power, with little check but that of public opinion. I believe our own system is the best, but high personal honour and a watchful opposition are necessary to its working; and if such things as we have recently witnessed are to be repeated, we will be driven in self-defence to the severe restraints of republican institutions. Either the present ministers came together without any definite understanding, with the single tie of office, or else there is a mystery yet to be explained. The Inspector-General sees nothing strange in the matter; he says "We are advocates of progressive reform, and that is enough." Where shall we look for proofs of their progression? Shall we find it in the votes of last session after the consummation of the union? Do we find it in the speech from the throne, now under discussion? I agree with the honourable member for Frontenac that the suffrage is the only question on which any advance has been made; and even the suffrage movement, as I understand it, is no change of principle but only an extension of the existing system, by which certain classes now unjustly deprived of the franchise shall have it conveyed to them. It may be that details of measures promised may exhibit evidence of progression, but it is not found in the speech. It may be that the ministerial measures, like the ministerial principles, are in a state of progression, and that this debate will help to liberalize them. But on the great question of Upper Canada there is no progression whatever, and there is no likelihood of any.

The Honourable the Inspector-General made an eloquent appeal on the subject of the reserves. He told us he was the warm friend of their secularization, that for twelve years he had always been so, that he had *never* varied in his views. I believe every word uttered by the honourable gentleman; but of what avail are his sentiments if we don't get his votes? How can he reconcile such views with the dark record of last session?

But perhaps the hon. gentleman can see no discrepancy in the case, for he says he has *never* varied. Are we then to have this session a repetition of the scenes of the last? But even if the Inspector-General should have changed his views, and be prepared to reverse his votes, what will it avail? The difficulty in the way of the ecclesiastical question was not with him or his Upper Canada colleagues, but with the gentlemen from Lower Canada. And after all the loud trumpetings of harmony in the cabinet, and promises of united actions on the reserves, what are we told by the Provincial Secretary? That he thinks the present decision of the reserves unfair; that he thinks the present settlement should be broken up; that he will aid us in getting the control transferred to the provincial parliament; but—and I pray the House to mark it well—*he will not say how the lands should be appropriated.* And this was coupled with the declaration that he would never interfere with "acquired rights." What, then, have these combinations gained for us? Are not the sentiments of Mr Morin precisely those of Mr. Lafontaine? Was it not for taking this very position that the late government was "ostracized?" Was it not for denouncing the faithlessness of the Upper Canadian ministers, in holding office after such a declaration by their colleague, that the members for Norfolk and Huron forced themselves into power. I call on the honourable gentlemen on the treasury benches to tell us now, if they can, in what manner their combinations have benefited the cause of ecclesiastical reform. I challenge them to show that they have advanced one step beyond the ground of the late administration. . . .

I would have been unjust to my party, faithless to responsible government, and false to the highest interests of the country, had I sat silent on this occasion. The vote that I shall give may appear strange to many. If I rightly understand the practice, by voting against the ministerial address, we declare that we desire to see the cabinet ejected from office. Highly improper as I view their proceedings, I confess I am not prepared to say that I would like to see the present ministry out, and the gentlemen opposite in their places. I would try them by their measures. It may be they will take warning by this debate, and yet justify by their action their claim to be advocates of progression. But if they do not—if they trifle with the great questions of Upper Canada—I will not hesitate to prefer an open enemy in power to a faithless friend. . . . I regretted to hear from gentlemen opposite the allusions to the salary of the highest authority in this province. The appointment of that high authority is the only power which Great Britain yet retains. Frankly and generously she has one by one surrendered all the rights which were once held necessary to the condition of a colony—the patronage of the Crown, the right over the public domain, the civil list, the customs, the post office, have all been relinquished, and the control over the reserves will soon follow with the rest. She guards our coasts, she maintains our troops, she builds our forts, she spends hundreds of thousands among us yearly, and yet the paltry payment to her representative is made a topic of grumbling and popular agitation. I know nothing so contemptible. However gentlemen opposite may view the matter, I am sure I speak the sentiments of the entire reform party when I say, that as long as we have such governors as the present there would be no grumbling from this side of the House were the tribute double what it is. Unlike other governors whom we have had, the distinguished nobleman who now graces the vice-regal throne has confined himself to the legitimate exercise of his authority, and respected the rights and privileges of the people; and for the stability which his wise rule has given to our constitutional system, when he and those who now bear rule have long passed away from the stage of life, His Excellency will live in the grateful affections of the Canadian people.

CHAPTER VIII.

INCREASING INFLUENCE.—THE "GLOBE" AS A DAILY.—THE COALITION.

After Mr. Brown's success in parliament, his influence in the country generally increased very much, while the power and influence of the *Globe* was constantly growing. The ministry was nominally a liberal ministry, though three of its members, besides the premier, never again acted with the reform party. It was still largely supported by western Canada liberals, though very few had any confidence in it. Indeed, Mr. Brown himself, while freely exposing their course to blame, did not feel at liberty to take the position of a regular opposition member.

In a letter, written to a friend just before the election of 1851, he says : " The ministry is formed. I have no confidence in it, but of " course prefer it to the Tories, and if returned will vote with it when- " ever I can, but against it on bad measures, and strive to have it " reconstructed on more out-and-out principles. This may change " your ideas in regard to my canditature, and if so, I hope you will " speak plainly." That reconstruction never came. Three years afterwards there was a reconstruction, but not of reform materials. The Premier and a few of his followers had been consciously drifting to the Tory side during the life of that parliament, and when the election of 1854 developed his weakness in the county, like Burke, he "quit the " camp," and from thenceforth was identified as having his sympathies with the conservative side. The threatened combinations were made, and when Mr. Hincks (now Sir Francis) returned to Canada, after some years' absence, he found that the union was not "maintained ;" on the contrary, it was broken up as the result of the triumph of principles he refused to acknowledge, and a fresh union established on a foundation more just to his own province. Sir Francis Hincks appeared again as a colleague of Sir John Macdonald, and curiously enough, issued an address as leader of the reform section of the government appointed by Sir John Macdonald, for which he got well laughed at.

The exigencies of commercial no less than political reasons necessitated the issue of the *Globe* as a daily paper, and in the autumn of 1853 the publication of the *Daily Globe* was commenced. A vigorous agitation was maintained in favour of the secularization of the clergy reserves, representation by population, and other measures long demanded by reformers, and the effect of the trenchant articles on these subjects was very great on the public mind.

No progress had been made with the clergy reserve question. In 1850 Mr. Price moved his resolution, and an address founded thereon, praying the passage of an Act by the Imperial Parliament to authorize the Canadian Parliament to deal with the question conditionally. Earl Grey in a formal despatch, early in 1851, advised Lord Elgin that the ministry was compelled to postpone this bill to next session.

A conservative government which succeeded declined to pass the necessary Act, and it was only in the winter of 1853 that the Imperial Act was finally passed. In the meantime a bill had been passed by the Canadian parliament, increasing the number of representatives from 84 to 130, and in this prospective increase the ministers found an excuse for not proceeding with the Clergy Reserve Bill. At the beginning of the session of 1854, a motion was carried by a majority of 13, condemning the government for not introducing a measure for the settlement of the clergy reserves. The conservatives had not obtained a sufficient share in the good things to keep them quiet, and therefore they united with the reformers against the government, and secured its overthrow.

A general election immediately followed the ministerial defeat. Mr. Brown became a candidate for Lambton, which county, under the new law, had a member for itself. He was opposed by the Hon. Malcolm Cameron, Postmaster-General, whom he defeated by a majority of about 200. Many other prominent supporters were defeated, making it tolerably certain that the government could not live. Mr. Brown gave his support in certain cases to candidates of the conservative type, on the ground that there was nothing to be hoped for from the ministry, and conservatives doubtless led some to believe that they would agree to an immediate settlement of the clergy reserves. Supporting conservative candidates was a perilous experiment which could hardly produce any good, though of course in this case it secured the defeat of the government, and also secured the final settlement of the clergy reserve question, though not exactly as it should have been settled. Mr. Brown was entitled to the chief credit for the anti-ministerial success at the elections ; Mr. Hincks was entitled to the discredit of forming a new combination with the Tories for no apparent reason but to wreak his vengeance on reform opponents. Mr. Hincks did not himself form one of the new government, but he narrates that Sir Allan N. McNab, the new Premier, " opened a negotiation with him, the result of which " was that two of the Upper Canada supporters of the late govern- " ment became members of the new ministry," Messrs. John Ross and Robert Spence being the two members. Mr. Ross had been a member of Mr. Hincks' government for over a year. These gentlemen and some other western reformers who supported the new government never returned to their allegiance to the liberal party. The Lower Canadian members of Mr. Hincks' government, who joined the so-called coalition government, were Messrs. Taché, Morin, Chabot, Chaveau, and Drummond ; the latter gentleman afterwards acted with the liberal party, and became a member of the Brown-Dorion administration. The other four had been for some time leaning to the conservative camp, and now made it their permanent home. Indeed, Sir Francis Hincks does not refer to those French gentlemen as parties to the coalition, as he does of the two Upper Canadians ; their adhesion was treated of as a matter of course.

The new government was savagely assailed by the *Globe.* No one could expect that a government in which the names of J. A. Macdonald, Sir Allan McNab, and Mr. Cayley appeared, could be other than hostile to the determined demands of the Upper Canadian people. They had all declared by speech and vote against any measure secularizing the clergy reserves, and by those who did not know them intimately, it was believed that their principles would compel them to resist any interference with the appropriation of these lands. The possession of office had a mollifying effect on their political consciences, and they yielded their views of public questions or principles to the demands of office and public clamour, as some of them have often done since then. Several conservative candidates had, however, promised at the elections to aid in procuring a settlement of the clergy reserve question according to the popular view. It is not the intention of the writer to discuss the settlement here further than to say that though Mr. Brown and other reformers opposed some provisions of the bill, all were glad to have a troublesome question disposed of. The principle long advocated by him, that no church should have any connection with, or support from, the state, was by that settlement conceded. The concession was largely due to Mr. Brown's exertions in the *Globe* and his advocacy on the platform. The amount of labour he undertook could be accomplished by few men. His own articles were easily recognized from their trenchant, free, off-hand style. His influence as a popular speaker has never been equalled in Canada. The *Globe* no doubt circulated largely amongst the presbyterian population, from the very fact that it displaced the *Banner*, which was a presbyterian organ, but the management of the paper and its views on all ecclesiastical questions also commended it to the intelligence of the Free Church element, whose views harmonized with Mr. Brown's. The high moral tone of the paper, and its growing excellence as a newspaper, did much for its circulation among all classes of the population. George Brown and the *Globe* became, in fact, convertible terms. Both editor and paper had many opponents, some might be called enemies, but no man ever had so large a portion of the population ranged on his side as warm devoted friends as had Mr. Brown. Nevertheless, the schism in the reform ranks continued, though events were maturing a feeling in favour of united action and formal organization. Mr. Brown had in several constituencies supported conservative candidates who pledged themselves thoroughly in favour of representation by population and secularization of the clergy reserves ; this, in several instances, accomplished the defeat of liberal candidates who were more or less unwilling to commit themselves to out-and-out measures. It may fairly be questioned whether this course was the best party movement for a leader to take, even under the peculiar circumstances then existing ; but if the triumph of righteous principles was the right thing to aim at, there can be no doubt that Mr. Brown's policy was successful. A comparatively good government might be had under a vicious system for a time, but for permanency in good government it was necessary that the English population of Upper Canada must be put on terms of perfect equality with the Lower Canadians, and that legislative enactments which brought certain churches in close relationship to the state, thus giving them an exceptional standing, must be swept away, and all denominations of Christians be placed on terms of perfect equality in the eye of the law. To the advocacy of such measures Mr. Brown applied himself in this parliament with untiring zeal and indomitable energy. If others fell out by the way wearied with the march, he held on his way, making light of all obstacles; and looking forward with a hope that was never dimmed to the objects to be reached, he never allowed himself to doubt of ultimate success.

The work he performed in the sessions of 1854, 1855, 1856, and 1857, was far more than any man should attempt. He had noble supporters in the toil in William Lyon Mackenzie and others, whose patriotic efforts for good government will never be forgotten.

CHAPTER IX.

ATTACKED BY MR. J. A. MACDONALD.—REPORT OF COMMITTEE OF INVESTIGATION.

In proportion to the vigour of Mr. Brown and the opposition in opposing bad measures and promoting the reverse, did the bitterness of Tory and coalitionist in the government increase. This bitterness at last took shape in the session of 1856 in a concerted attack on Mr. Brown by the government in connection with the Penitentiary Commission, which they hoped would banish him from parliament. Mr. John A. Macdonald made a violent speech in relation to this subject in the House on the 26th day of February, in which Mr. Brown was accused of falsifying the evidence, suborning witnesses, procuring pardons for murderers at the price of evidence to be given against the then management of the institution. The pitiable spectacle of the chief law officer af the Crown indulging in such violence and perpetrating such injustice, created unusual astonishment. If he believed Mr. Brown guilty of such conduct he should have brought him to trial for the specified offences. Mr. Brown rose immediately, and said there was not a vestige of truth in the charges made, and that he would next day move for a committee, and compel Mr. Macdonald to prove his statements.

Next day Mr. Brown made the following motion : " That the " Honourable John A. Macdonald having, in the course of a debate on " last evening, charged Mr. George Brown, a member of this House, " while acting, in 1848, as a member and secretary of a commission " appointed by the government to inquire into the condition of the " provincial penitentiary :—First, with having recorded falsely the " evidence of witnesses examined before the said commission ; second, " with having altered the written testimony given by witnesses after " their evidence was closed and subscribed ; third, with having " suborned convicts to commit perjury ; fourth, with having obtained " the pardon of murderers confined to the penitentiary, to induce " them to give false evidence, or in words substantially to the same " effect ; and the said Honourable John A. Macdonald having pledged " himself to substantiate these charges, a special committee of seven " members be appointed to inquire and report with all convenient " speed as to the truth of the said charges, with power to send for " persons, papers and records."

This motion, singularly enough, was opposed by some ministerialists, who were unwilling to afford to the accused an immediate opportunity of disproving the infamous charges. Some called for delay, others for amendment. Mr. Macdonald would neither admit nor deny that the language in the motion quoted as his was uttered by him, but he demanded that the committee should be required to find out what he did say, and then *investigate the conduct of Mr. Brown on the commission.* Mr. Cayley put these extraordinary views in writing in amendment to Mr. Brown's motion. He moved " that a committee " of seven members be appointed to inquire into and report with all " convenient speed as to the *nature of the charges* made by the Attorney- " General against Mr. George Brown, a member of this House, and as " to their truth, and that this committee be struck to-morrow." Mr. Loranger, Mr. Cameron, and others on the ministerial side, urged the immediate appointment of the committee to have the charges gone into. Indeed the accuser, in making his charges, was bound in honour to make his charges good at once, as he alleged he could do, while the accuser was not bound, by law or custom, to prove a negative. Mr. Brown, however, at once waived his right and determined to disprove the charges, yet some ministerialists desired that he should not be allowed to do so, but that he should lie under the accusation as long as possible. An overwhelming majority were, however, determined that a committee should at once be granted, the Speaker also ruling that the committee, if granted, must be struck that day, and the motion was carried by a vote of 94 to 12. The report of this committee was presented on the 16th of June, every effort having been made by the ministerial majority in the committee to delay its production until it should be too late to act upon it during the session. The minority report was also produced on the 16th of June. The ministerialists on the committee acted throughout in the most partisan manner. Instead of finding whether the charges were true—yes or no—they entered on a prolonged discussion as to the mode in which Mr. Brown and his co-commissioners had conducted the penitentiary inquiry. They assumed that the condensed evidence reported was the actual detailed evidence, and affected to find discrepancies, and so reported. The report cunningly implied blame to Mr. Brown, and finally blamed Mr. Macdonald for having allowed himself to *reiterate* charges. It was coolly assumed that such charges had been made before, whereas the matter alluded to was on a general charge against the commission which Mr. Macdonald had made some years before.

When the report was presented, on the motion " that the report " be received," Mr. Wilson moved in amendment, seconded by Mr. Holton, " That all the words after *that* be left out, and the following

" words substituted: ' The evidence adduced before the said commit-
" ' tee completely fails to substantiate any of the charges against Mr.
" Brown.' "

Mr. Felton (a government supporter) moved, in amendment to the amendment, that the words following be inserted before the words " the evidence : " " While Attorney-General Macdonald appears to " have acted under a firm conviction of the truth of the charges made " against Mr. Brown, and to have been justified in doing so by all the " evidence within his reach." The effect of the amendment would have been solely and simply to fully exonerate Mr. Brown; the effect of the amendment to the amendment would have been to exonerate John A. Macdonald from malice in his attack.

It was supposed and generally believed that the original report of the penitentiary commission was burned in the parliamentary buildings at Montreal in 1849. On this belief the attack was planned. It is said that at one of the first meetings of the committee, Mr. Vankoughnet, counsel for Mr. Macdonald, in moving for an order to examine certain convicts in the penitentiary, stated that unfortunately it was found that the report of the penitentiary commissioners was destroyed in the Montreal fire. He said he regretted this, as, if that report were extant, he would be able to prove his case without calling such witnesses as he now proposed to put in the box. Mr. Brown was in the committee room sitting with his overcoat on waiting for the proceedings to commence, and on hearing Mr. Vankoughnet's speech, he unbuttoned his coat, and drawing from it the original report of the commission, said he was happy to hear that that document was all that was wanted, and throwing it on the table, said, " There it is." Mr. Vankoughnet immediately left the room, and meeting Mr. Macdonald, said to him, " Your case is dished." The committee was most unfairly constituted of five ministerialists, some the least scrupulous of any, and two opposition ministers. Mr. Brown took no exception to this, however, knowing that no man could avoid declaring the charges to be without foundation. It was remarkable that one of Mr. Macdonald's colleagues, Attorney-General Drummond, was candid enough to declare that there was no evidence criminating Mr. Brown. Sir Allan McNab and other conservatives took similar ground, and boldly stated their views. Had a division taken place on the report, it is all but certain that the government would have been defeated. The utmost sympathy was manifested for Mr. Brown, as may have been observed, by many still in active life, from the newspapers of the day of all political shades. Some indeed, while condemning the attack, said Mr. Brown had, by his violent attacks on his adversaries, provoked retort. Probably he did provoke some retaliation in kind, but this was not that, but a personal attack of the vilest character, and peculiarly out of place, coming from the head of the government.

The ultimate effect of the attack was that Mr. Brown stood higher than ever in the national affections. Many people very naturally believed that when such charges were made by the leading man in the government, there must be some truth in them; and when an investigation, by a committee of Mr. Macdonald's own choosing, could not find a particle of evidence to establish one single charge, the reaction in the public mind was complete.

CHAPTER X.

CALLED ON TO FORM MINISTRY.—CORRESPONDENCE WITH SIR EDMUND HEAD.

The next general election took place late in the autumn of 1857. Mr. Brown did not again offer himself for the county of Lambton. This was a great disappointment to the electors of that county. Mr. Brown was, unwisely, persuaded to offer himself for the city of Toronto, with a fair prospect, no doubt, of carrying the metropolitan constituency, but it withdrew his active efforts necessarily from other places, and enabled him to win one important place probably at the expense of the loss of several other counties. The uncertainty always more or less felt as to city elections induced Mr. Brown's friends to secure a seat elsewhere. He was accordingly elected for North Oxford. When parliament met he decided to sit for Toronto, and induced Oxford, with some difficulty, to elect Mr. Wm. McDougall. The old issues of 1851 and 1854 respecting ecclesiastical corporations, sectarian schools, the course pursued by ministers and representation by population, formed the most engrossing subjects of discussion at the elections.

The new parliament met on the 25th February. The ministry had a majority varying from ten to thirty in their favour, although on the representation question they could only command a majority of twelve. On the following motion, respecting the selection of Ottawa for the seat of government, on the 28th day of July: "That in the "opinion of this House the city of Ottawa ought not to be the "permanent seat of government for the provinces," the ministry were defeated by a majority of fourteen. Ministers at once placed their resignations in the hands of the Governor-General, who promptly accepted them. He at once sent for Mr. Brown, "as the most promi-"nent member of the opposition." In order that the circumstances connected with Mr. Brown's acceptance of office may be thoroughly understood, the official correspondence between the Governor-General and Mr. Brown is here inserted.

On Thursday, 29th July, the following note was received by Mr. Brown :

(Copy.)

TORONTO, Thursday, 29th July, 1858

The members of the Executive Council have tendered their resignation to His Excellency the Governor-General, and they now retain their several offices only till their successors shall be appointed.

Under these circumstances, His Excellency feels it right to have recourse to you as the most prominent member of the opposition, and he hereby offers you a seat in the council as the leader of a new administration. In the event of your accepting this offer, His Excellency requests you to signify such acceptance to him in writing, in order that he may be at once in a position to confer with you as one of his responsible advisers.

His Excellency's first object will be to consult you as to the names of your future colleagues, and as to the assignment of the offices about to be vacated, to the men most capable of filling them.

(Signed,)   EDMUND HEAD.

GEORGE BROWN, Esq., M.P.P.

Immediately on the receipt of this document, Mr. Brown waited on the Governor-General, and asked time to consult his friends.

On Friday morning Mr. Brown waited on the Governor-General by appointment, and stated that he was engaged consulting his friends, but would next morning give His Excellency a final answer.

On Saturday morning Mr. Brown waited on His Excellency with the following acceptance of the trust proposed to him :

(Copy.)

Mr. Brown has the honour to inform His Excellency the Governor-General, that he accepts the duty proposed to him in His Excellency's communication of 29th inst., and undertakes the formation of a new administration.

CHURCH STREET, 31st July, 1858.

On Sunday night at ten o'clock, Mr. Brown was waited on by the Governor-General's secretary, and presented with the following memorandum :

His Excellency the Governor-General forwards the enclosed memorandum to Mr. Brown to-night, because it may be convenient for him to have it in his hand in good time to-morrow morning.

The part which relates to a dissolution is in substance a repetition of what His Excellency said yesterday at his interview with Mr. Brown.

The portion having reference to the prorogation or adjournment of parliament is important in determining the propriety of the course to be pursued.

His Excellency therefore requests Mr. Brown to communicate the memorandum to his future colleagues, in order to avoid all misapprehension hereafter.

GOVERNMENT HOUSE, TORONTO,
    August 1, 1858.

(MEMORANDUM.)

His Excellency the Governor-General wishes Mr. Brown to consider this memorandum, and to communicate it to the gentlemen whose names he proposes to submit to His Excellency as members of the new government.

The Governor-General gives *no pledge or promise, express or implied, with reference to dissolving parliament.* When advice is tendered to His Excellency on this subject, he will make up his mind according to the circumstances then existing, and the reasons then laid before him.

The Governor-General has no objection to prorogue the parliament without the members of the new administration taking their seats in the present session. But if he does so, it ought, His Excellency thinks, to be on an express understanding that parliament shall meet again as soon as possible—say in November or December. Until the new ministers meet parliament, His Excellency has no assurance that they possess the confidence of the majority of the House.

The business transacted in the interval ought, in his opinion, to be confined to matters necessary for the ordinary administration of the government of the province.

If Parliament is prorogued, His Excellency would think it very desirable that the Bill for the Registration of Voters, and that containing the prohibition of fraudulent assignments and gifts by traders, should be proceeded with and become law—subject, of course, to such modifications as the wisdom of either House may suggest. Besides this, any item of supply absolutely necessary should be provided for by a vote of credit, and the money for repairs of the canals, which cannot be postponed, should be voted.

His Excellency can hardly prorogue until these necessary steps are taken. If parliament merely adjourns until after the re-election of the members of the government, the case is different, and the responsibility is on the House itself. A prorogation is the act of His Excellency; and, in this particular case, such act would be performed without the advice of ministers who had already received the confidence of parliament. His Excellency's own opinion would be in favour of proroguing, if the conditions above specified can be fulfilled, and if Mr. Brown and his colleagues see no objection.

(Signed,)   EDMUND HEAD.

GOVERNMENT HOUSE, Toronto,
    July 31, 1858.

Early on Monday morning Mr. Brown, on his own personal responsibility, and without consulting his proposed colleagues, sent the following note to the Governor-General :

Mr. Brown has the honour to acknowledge receipt of His Excellency the Governor-General's note of last night, with accompanying memorandum.

Before receiving His Excellency's note, Mr. Brown had successfully fulfilled the duty entrusted to him by the Governor-General, and will be prepared, at the appointed hour this morning, to submit for His Excellency's approval the names of the gentlemen whom he proposes to be associated with himself in the new government.

Mr. Brown respectfully submits that, until they have assumed the functions of constitutional advisers of the Crown, he and his proposed colleagues will not be in a position to discuss the important measures and questions of public policy referred to in His Excellency's memorandum.

CHURCH STREET, 2nd August.

On Monday morning at half-past ten, Mr. Brown waited on His Excellency, and submitted for his approval the names of the proposed government. At noon, on the same day, the members of the government took the oaths of office. On Monday night adverse votes were given against the administration in both Houses. On Tuesday Mr. Brown waited on His Excellency, and informed him that the cabinet advised a prorogation of parliament with a view to a dissolution. The Governor-General requested the grounds of this advice to be put in writing. In compliance with His Excellency's request, the following memorandum was communicated to the Governor-General:

MEMORANDUM FOR THE CONSIDERATION OF HIS EXCELLENCY THE
GOVERNOR-GENERAL.

His Excellency's present advisers having accepted office on His Excellency's invitation, after the late administration had, by their resignation, admitted their inability successfully to conduct the affairs of the country in a parliament summoned under their own advice, and being unanimously of opinion that the constitutional recourse of an appeal to the people affords the best if not the only solution of existing difficulties, respectfully advise His Excellency to prorogue parliament immediately with a view to a dissolution.

When His Excellency's present advisers accepted office, they did not conceal from themselves the probability that they would be unable to carry on the government with the present House of Assembly. The House, they believe, does not possess the confidence of the country; and the public dissatisfaction has been greatly increased by the numerous and glaring acts of corruption and fraud by which many seats were obtained at the last general election, and for which acts the House, though earnestly petitioned so to do, has failed to afford a remedy.

For some years past strong sectional feelings have arisen in the country, which, especially during the present session, have seriously impeded the carrying on of the administrative and legislative functions of the government. The late administration made no attempt to meet these difficulties, or to suggest a remedy for them, and thereby the evil has been greatly aggravated. His Excellency's present advisers have entered the government with the fixed determination to propose constitutional measures for the establishment of that harmony between Upper and Lower Canada which is essential to the prosperity of the Province. They respectfully submit that they have a right to claim all the support which His Excellency can constitutionally extend to them in the prosecution of this all-important object.

The unprecedented and unparliamentary course pursued by the House of Assembly—which, immediately after having by their vote compelled the late ministry to retire, proceeded to pass a vote of want of confidence in the present administration, without notice, within a few hours of their appointment, in their absence from the House, and before their policy had been announced—affords the most convincing proof that the affairs of the country cannot be efficiently conducted under the control of the House as now constituted.

At two o'clock this day the following memorandum was received from the Governor-General :

(MEMORANDUM.)

His Excellency the Governor-General has received the advice of the Executive Council to the effect that a dissolution of parliament should take place.

His Excellency is no doubt bound to deal fairly with all political parties ; but he has a duty to perform to the Queen and the people of Canada paramount to that which he owes to any one party, or to all parties whatsoever.

The question for His Excellency to decide is not, " What is advantageous or fair for a particular party ?" but what, upon the whole, is the most advantageous and fair for the people of the province.

The resignation of the late government was tendered in consequence of a vote of the House which did not assert directly any want of confidence in them.

The vote on Monday was a direct vote of want of confidence on the part of both Houses. It was carried in the assembly by a majority of forty, in a house of a hundred and two, out of one hundred and thirty members, consequently by a majority of the whole house, even if every seat had been full at the time of the vote.

In addition to this a similar vote was carried in the upper House by sixteen against eight, and an address founded on the same was adopted.

It is clear that, under such circumstances, a dissolution, to be of any avail, must be immediate. His Excellency the Governor-General cannot do any act other than that of dissolving parliament by the advice of a ministry who possess the confidence of neither branch of the legislature.

It is not the duty of the Governor-General to decide whether the action of the two Houses on Monday night was or was not in accordance with the usual courtesy of parliament towards an incoming administration. The two Houses are the judges of the propriety of their own proceedings. His Excellency has to do with the conclusions at which they arrive, provided only that the forms observed are such as to give legal and constitutional force to their votes.

There are many points which require careful consideration with reference to a dissolution at the present time. Amongst these are the following:

1. It has been alleged that the present House may be assumed not to represent the people. If such were the case, there was no sufficient reason why, on being in a minority in that house, the late government should have given place to the present. His Excellency cannot constitutionally adopt this view.

2. An election took place only last winter. This fact is not conclusive against a second election now, but the costs and inconvenience of such a proceeding are so great, that they ought not to be incurred a second time without very strong grounds.

3. The business before parliament is not yet finished. It is perhaps true that very little which is absolutely essential for the country remains to be done. A portion, however, of the estimates, and two bills at least, of great importance, are still before the Legislative Assembly, irrespective of the private business.

In addition to this, the resolutions respecting the Hudson Bay Territory have not been considered, and no answer on that subject can be given to the British Government.

4. The time of year and state of affairs would make a general election at this moment peculiarly inconvenient and burthensome, inasmuch as the harvest is now going on in a large portion of the country, and the pressure of the late money crisis has not passed away.

5. The following considerations are strongly pressed by His Excellency's present advisers as reasons why he should authorize an appeal to the people, and thereby retain their services in the council.

(1.) The corruption and bribery alleged to have been practised at the last election, and the taint which on that account is said to attach to the present Legislative Assembly.

(2.) The existence of a bitter sectional feeling between Upper and Lower Canada, and the ultimate danger to the union as at present constituted, which is likely to arise from such feeling.

If the first of these points be assumed as true, it must be asked what assurance can His Excellency have that a new election, under precisely the same laws, held within six or eight months of the last, will differ in its character from that which then took place?

If the facts are as they are stated to be, they might be urged as a reason why a general election should be avoided as long as possible; at any rate until the laws are made more stringent, and the precautions against such evils shall have been increased by the wisdom of parliament. Until this is done, the speedy recurrence of the opportunity of practising such abuses would be likely to aggravate their character, and confirm the habit of resorting to them.

The second consideration, as to the feeling between Upper and Lower Canada, and the ultimate danger of such feelings to the union, is one of a very grave kind. It would furnish to His Excellency the strongest possible

motive for a dissolution of parliament, and for the retention of the present
government at all hazards, if the two points were only conclusively established, that is to say, if it could be shown that the measures likely to be
adopted by Mr. Brown and his colleagues were a specific, and that the only
specific, for these evils, and that the members of the present council were
the only men to allay the jealousies so unhappily existing. It may be that
both these propositions are true, but, unless they are established to His
Excellency's complete satisfaction, the mere existence of the mischief is not
in itself decisive as to the propriety of resorting to a general election at the
present moment. The certainty, or at any rate the great probability, of
the cure by the course proposed, and by that alone, would require to be also
proved. Without this, a great present evil would be voluntarily incurred
for the chance of a remote good.

6. It would seem to be the duty of His Excellency to exhaust every
possible alternative before subjecting the province for the second time in
the same year to the cost, the inconvenience, and the demoralization of such a
proceeding.

The Governor-General is by no means satisfied that every alternative has
been thus exhausted, or that it would be impossible for him to secure a
ministry who would close the business of this session, and carry on the administration of the government during the recess with the confidence of a
majority of the Legislative Assembly.

After full and mature deliberation on the arguments submitted to him
by word of mouth, and in writing, and with every respect for the opinion of
the council, His Excellency declines to dissolve parliament at the present
time.

(Signed,)   EDMUND HEAD.

GOVERNMENT HOUSE, TORONTO, C.W.,
    Aug. 4., 1858.

Immediately on the receipt of this document, Mr. Brown proceeded
to the Government House, and placed in the hands of His Excellency
the resignations of himself and colleagues in the following terms :

Mr. Brown has the honour to inform His Excellency the Governor-
General that, in consequence of His Excellency's memorandum of this afternoon, declining the advice of the council to prorogue parliament with a view
to a dissolution, he has now, on behalf of himself and colleagues, to tender
their resignations.

EXECUTIVE COUNCIL CHAMBER, TORONTO,
    4th August, 1858.

The course taken by the Governor-General, in accepting the resignation of his ministers and sending for the leader of the opposition to
form a new administration, beyond all question did commit him to
give Mr. Brown his full confidence. It was open to His Excellency to
assume that the vote against the late government was not strictly a
party vote, as he afterwards did assume ; and that their resignation
did not call for his sending for the opposite party leader. He might
at once have sent for some other member of the ministerial party, as
he afterwards did ; or he might have declined to accept the resignation of ministers, on the ground that they still possessed the confidence
of the House on general grounds. He chose the other course, and
thereby gave Mr. Brown to understand, as plainly as if he had said it

in so many words, that whatever he, Mr. Brown, found it necessary to do he should have his support. No consultation was invited as to the terms on which Mr. Brown would accept the trust imposed upon him. He was simply asked, in His Excellency's letter of Thursday, to " signify such acceptance to him (the Governor-General) in writing, in " order that he may be at once in a position to confer with you as one " of his responsible advisers ;" and further, " His Excellency's first " object will be to consult you as to the names of your future " colleagues, and as to the assignment of the offices." In reply, Mr. Brown asked for time to consult his friends. On Saturday, two days after the Governor-General wrote the first letter to Mr. Brown, that gentleman waited on His Excellency with his written acceptance of the offer made him. He had in the meantime seen his friends, and made such arrangements as enabled him to accept the trust. The members of his government were Hon. James Morris, Hon. A. A. Dorion, Hon. O. Mowat, Hon. M. H. Foley, Hon. J. S. Macdonald, Hon. L. T. Drummond, Hon. M. Thibadeau, Hon. L. H. Holton, Hon. M. Laberge, Hon. Dr. Connor and Hon. George Brown.

Then His Excellency informed Mr. Brown that he gave no pledge to dissolve parliament. Hostile writers have assumed that Mr. Brown at his interview attempted to make a bargain with Sir Edmund Head as to granting a dissolution. That this was not the case is perfectly clear, not only from Mr. Brown's narrative but from the Governor's own memorandum, sent to Mr. Brown on Saturday night. Others state that when Mr. Brown was called in the Governor " warned him " that a dissolution would not be granted him."* This is doubly wrong. Mr. Brown was not " warned " until two days after he was called in—until, in fact, he had made his arrangements—and then he was simply told that His Excellency would give no pledge to dissolve. No one asked him to give a pledge of any sort, but every one naturally thought that he would, as a constitutional ruler, give his ministers all his confidence and assistance after inviting them to come to his assistance. Either the Governor had back stairs advisers, whom he had consulted and whose advice he followed, between the time when he invited Mr. Brown to undertake the formation of a government on Thursday and the interview of Saturday, or he had determined from the first that if Mr. Brown should undertake the task imposed upon him he (the Governor) would prevent him fulfilling the duty, and therefore, two days after his first communication he made the gratuitous statement to Mr. Brown, hoping that it would prevent that gentleman going any further in forming his government. On either ground

---

* " Scot " in British North America, page 509.

the action of the Governor was disgraceful, and manifestly the proceeding of a shameless partisan.

The memorandum sent to Mr. Brown on Sunday evening was seemingly written under the impression that it was desirable to supplement the conversation relative to a dissolution by other conditions, in case Mr. Brown should advise a prorogation. In the memorandum he then proceeds to build up an effectual barrier against prorogation, as follows: "The Governor-General has no objection to " prorogue the parliament," but "if parliament is prorogued, His " Excellency would think it very desirable that the Bill for the " Registration of Voters, and that containing the prohibition of fraudu- " lent assignments and gifts by traders, should be proceeded with " and become law.   Besides this, any item of supply absolutely neces- " sary should be provided for by a vote of credit, and the money for " repairs of the canals, which cannot be postponed, should be voted." His Excellency afterwards incautiously admitted that "very little " which is absolutely essential for the country remains to be done in " the House." His Excellency can hardly "prorogue until these " necessary steps are taken."

Sir Edmund Head knew perfectly well that his ministers could not be in their places in parliament for three weeks ; that a majority existed hostile to them in the lower House, which would make it impossible for them, not having a seat in the House, to conduct legislation and vote supplies. Yet these conditions were imposed as the price of prorogation. Every step betrays the head and heart of the conspirator.

On Monday morning Mr. Brown informed the Governor that he had, before receiving his memorandum, "fulfilled the duty entrusted "to him," and would at the appointed hour submit the names of his colleagues. He also informed His Excellency that until they were sworn in as his councillors they would not be in a position to discuss the important matters referred to in his memorandum. It would have been difficult to have given a more correct and dignified rebuke.

At noon on Monday the members of the cabinet were sworn in, and the same evening votes of want of confidence were passed in both Houses. The government at once advised a prorogation, with a view to a dissolution. This was refused after a demand for reasons from the ministers. The reasons given embrace, as will be seen, statements relating to various matters of public policy which called for immediate action, especially some relating to sectional disturbances between Upper and Lower Canada ; but the strong reasons urged were, that they accepted office "on His Excellency's invitation after the late "administration had admitted their inability to conduct the affairs "of the country ;" that they had a right to claim all the "support

" which His Excellency could constitutionally extend to them." The memorandum concluded with a reference to the " unprecedented and " unparliamentary" course of the House in voting want of confidence in the absence of newly created ministers.

The Governor in his reply enumerates all the reasons he can with the diligence of an extreme party man. He admits being "bound to " deal fairly with all political parties." He was, however, only called to deal with the men he had himself called to his aid. They were more than a "political party," they were his constitutional advisers. The mere fact that the vote against late ministers did not, as he says, " assert directly any want of confidence in them," was no reason why he should refuse his confidence to the men he had called to fill their places. It might, as has been stated, be a reason why he should call on some one else to form a government. He might have known, and did know, that the elements hostile to Mr. Brown when he asked him to assume the duties of office were strong enough to vote want of confidence in him. It was the duty of His Excellency to see that the action of the House towards the man who had accepted the trust at his hands was contrary to " parliamentary courtesy." He was bound, as a ruler and as an honest man, to see that no impediment should be thrown in the way of his new advisers getting fair play in submitting their policy to the country through the medium of a new election. He does not in a single paragraph discuss his duty as a constitutional governor towards his ministers. On the contrary, he urges that the business is not finished yet; that items of the estimates are not passed; that the Hudson Bay resolutions were not passed ; the time of the year inconvenient ; pressure of money crisis not passed away ; that an election took place only last winter ; and the cost and inconvenience of an election.

He then devotes the remainder of his paper to a carping criticism of the ministerial paper. What assurance could he have, he asks, that a new election would in its results differ from the last? He asserts that a general election should be avoided until more stringent laws are made. If it could be " conclusively established," he says, that Mr. Brown's measures respecting the sectional difficulties "between Upper "and Lower Canada would prove a specific." He also wished it conclusively established that the members of the present council were the only men to allay the jealousies so unhappily existing! Imagine a demand from the Crown to " *conclusively establish*" the exact result of some amendment to the law or constitution at a moment when there was no time to do more than indicate the line to be taken. To be more emphatic, he gravely adds that "the certainty, or at any rate " the great probability, of the cure by the course proposed, and by that "alone, would require to be proved!"   Mr. Brown's reply to this gubernatorial tirade was simple, short, and dignified; he resigned for the reason that the advice of the council was refused.

Many of Mr. Brown's friends considered that the Governor's paper should have been answered in detail, so as to place him clearly and at once in the wrong.   There was a great temptation to do so, for a more vulnerable and scandalous state paper it would be difficult to find in modern times.   It was not necessary, so far as public opinion was concerned, for the minister to criticise this paper.   His Excellency's conduct provoked a feeling of great indignation amongst liberals and lovers of fair play of all shades of opinion, and it was only defended by rabid party organs on his own political side.   The transaction will be ever remembered as a shameful violation of constitutional usage on the part of a Governor-General, apparently entered upon for the benefit of the Tory party.   The following extract from the *Globe* of August 5th gives a fair view of the feeling of the people generally regarding the Governor-General's conduct:

Sir Edmund Head has chosen deliberately to place himself in an attitude of hostility towards his advisers and the people.   Influenced by the secret counsels of a cabal, he has openly insulted the men to whom he had entrusted the administration of affairs; he has preferred obedience to back stairs dictation to the constitutional requirements of his ministers. . . . The convenient veil of executive neutrality is thrown off at last; and he stands revealed the active and unscrupulous partisan of men who are the convicted apologists of frauds the most gross. . . . The demeanour of His Excellency throughout the ministerial crisis is unintelligible, except on the hypothesis that his determination was to play into the hands of the Macdonald-Cartier alliance. . . . Mr. Macdonald was allowed to patch a cabinet and dissolve: Mr. Brown is not permitted to appeal to the people for judgment on a cabinet and a policy entirely new . . He has displayed a contempt for the decency common to gentlemen. . . We refer to the observance of the sincerity and frankness which are the main strata of honourable conduct. . . . Examine point after point in the transactions of the last eight days, and say whether any other conclusion can be arrived at than that the resignation of Mr. J. A. Macdonald, the sending for Mr. Brown, the refusal of Mr. Brown's constitutional demand, and the final resort to Mr. Galt, are not all parts of a deep laid plot. . . . We think that we are safe in prophesying that the result will be most damaging to the Governor and his allies. . . . Do Sir Edmund Head and his closet conspirators believe that they have strengthened themselves in any respect by the plot they have apparently ended?

It was commonly alleged that Sir Edmund Head was, during these two eventful days, consulting with leading men on the Tory side of party politics.   There may be no proof of this available, but it would not be difficult to believe that the man who could act with such perfidy to his own ministers would not hesitate to perpetrate the further crime of consulting their enemies as to the best means of destroying them.

CHAPTER XI.

The "Double Shuffle."—Liberal Convention of 1859.

By the unconstitutional course pursued by parliament, and the unfair course of the Governor-General, Mr. Brown and his colleagues were at once out of office and out of parliament. Mr. Brown again appealed to his Toronto constituents for re-election, where he was opposed by the Hon. J. H. Cameron, supported by the whole influence of the government and Government House, and such influences with a city constituency were very great. In the meantime, the old government were recalled, when the political trick known as the "double "shuffle" was performed, whereby the ministers were enabled to avoid going to their constituencies for re-election. The Independence of Parliament Act provided that a minister resigning one office and accepting another within one month would not require re-election. In this case all the ministers accepted other offices than those held before their resignation, and again changed to those they were to keep. It was said at the time that before midnight they were all sworn in to the changed offices with all due solemnity, and at the same sitting, after midnight, resigned such offices and were sworn into the others. Ministerial oaths are administered by the Governor-General in person. It must have been a melancholy sight to see the Governor winking at what was a violation of the spirit of the law, and—until a judgment was delivered affirming its legality—was believed to be contrary to its letter, and contrasting his conduct then towards his own political friends with the treatment he had given to Mr. Brown. It need only be added that, except with extreme partisans, his conduct found no defenders, while the liberals held his conduct and memory in execration, and few, if any of them, again accepted any invitation to Government House until a new incumbent reached it. How different was Lord Dufferin's conduct towards Mr. Mackenzie in 1873, under precisely similar circumstances.

The Toronto election was fought with great bitterness on both sides: ministers thought they were sure of defeating Mr. Brown, and made desperate efforts to accomplish this, while his supporters were naturally indignant at the action of the Governor and his ministers, and worked all the harder on that account. Mr. Brown succeeded, however, in carrying the day, and sat for Toronto until the dissolution in 1861.

The conspirators had failed in one important part of their programme. Mr. Brown continued his agitation for representation by population, having already impressed the public mind so thoroughly with its justice and reasonableness, that much of the discussion after this period was devoted to the plan by which it could be carried out. The members of the Brown-Dorion government were pledged to propound a plan for dealing with the question, but of course had no time to mature the scheme. Mr. Laberge, his Solicitor-General (east), had afterwards some misunderstanding with Mr. Brown as to the extent of the agreement, and some correspondence ensued on the subject.

Mr. Brown has been frequently assailed because of an alleged hostility to Mr. Baldwin by the small class of conservatives who call themselves Baldwin reformers. In fact, there was no hostility existing. There was not a sentence or word in Mr. Brown's articles or speeches which could be complained of by that gentleman or his friends. Criticisms on his public course on subjects of great importance to the country were undoubtedly indulged in towards the end of his parliamentary life. Such criticisms were not only just and fair, but —in the public interest, in the interest of the reform party—they were unavoidable. He was at the time, in that sense, public property, and had he continued to sit in parliament after 1851, he must necessarily have taken his share of censure from reformers in common with Mr. Hincks and others. In this year Mr. Baldwin was persuaded to emerge from his retirement and become a candidate for the Legislative Council. He failed to announce any views of public policy, or in any way to show his sympathy with the late reform ministry, which had a few weeks before been made the victims of an unconstitutional exercise of gubernatorial power. Mr. John Hillyard Cameron had barely finished his contest with Mr. Brown in East Toronto, when he signed a requisition to Mr. Baldwin to bring him out as a candidate for the upper House. In this Mr. Cameron was joined by several other leading conservatives. The following extracts on the subject are from an article in the *Globe* of September 3rd, 1858 :

We would not willingly utter a sentence depreciatory of Mr. Baldwin. Recognizing the value of much of his public service, estimating highly the integrity of his character and the excellence of his private life, according to him most sincerely credit for fidelity to his convictions, whatever they may be, we have no inclination to say a word that can be construed into personal suspicion or personal disrespect. And though of late years we have worked in opposition to the party with whom Mr. Baldwin is understood to have sympathized, we have never entertained any opinion derogatory to his personal worth. We differed from him politically ; as a man we never mentioned him without respect. . . .

If, then, Mr. Baldwin desires success as a candidate for the council, it is due to the public, due to himself, that he should afford the means of determining his position in regard to the existing position of public affairs. This is rendered the more necessary, since we find amongst his advertised requisitionists names that are certainly not entitled to confidence. Despite of inclination, we are constrained to seek information of a practical character when he reappears associated with Mr. John Hillyard Cameron, Mr. George Platt, Mr. James Beaty, Mr. John Crawford, and other representatives of the same school, all gentlemen whose political affinities are such that no reformer can consistently co-operate with them for the accomplishment of any party object. Under any circumstances, this contest will assume a party complexion. . . . .

In what light, moreover, does he view the recent ministerial crisis? Does he approve of the course pursued by the Governor-General in his dealings with the Brown-Dorion administration? Does he hold that His Excellency violated the spirit of the constitution when he rejected the reasonable counsel of his sworn advisers, and attempted to dictate the action of parliament on questions before it? Does he approve or condemn the unlawful and unconstitutional proceedings of the Cartier-Macdonald government in accepting and transferring offices without appealing to their constituents for re-election?

On the appearance of this article Mr. Baldwin withdrew from the contest, and the same parties who brought him out brought out the Hon. George Allan, and elected him as the conservative candidate. No person can be justly blamed for declining to allow personal excellences to atone for political error. It is sufficient to recognize such excellences, but the political failings must be exposed after such recognition. This was done by Mr. Brown as a journalist, and nothing more. The veteran statesman made no complaint himself of ill treatment, and doubtless he felt less offended by fair criticisms on his public acts than at the use made of his name by men who shared all his mistaken views, but who possessed none of his strict integrity.

The population of western Canada in 1858 was estimated as being 1,300,000, while that of Lower Canada was only estimated at 1,000,000, showing practically that 300,000 were without representation. It was also shown that the most important legislation regarding Upper Canadian matters was forced on the latter by a Lower Canadian majority. This state of affairs could not possibly last, and the treatment given by Governor and parliament to the only ministry which had determined to grapple with the evil intensified the demand for some constitutional changes. This demand was thenceforth scarcely opposed even by conservatives.

Mr. Brown called a meeting of the reform members of both Houses for the 23rd of September, 1859, to consider the state of affairs. This meeting decided to call a convention of the liberal party on the 9th of November. In response to this call 570 delegates met on the appointed day and discussed very fully the mode of remedying the existent evils. The result was the passage of certain resolutions affirming the failure of the existing union, the non-remedial character of the double majority plan, and that the true remedy lay in a federal union of the provinces, with "*some joint authority*" charged with "such matters as are necessarily common to both sections of the "province." An elaborate address of an exhaustive character was issued setting forth the great evils suffered by Upper Canada under the existing union. This document was chiefly the work of Mr. Brown, and bore ample testimony to his untiring zeal and industry. This convention, held under his auspices as leader, presented in their resolutions and address the principles and policy upon which the liberal party made their appeal to the country in 1861, and which was predestined to prevail in the parliament elected in 1863.

Resolutions embodying the policy adopted at this convention were submitted to parliament at the next session of parliament in the following resolution: "That the existing legislative union between "Upper and Lower Canada has failed to realize the anticipations of "its promoters; has resulted in a heavy debt, burdensome taxation, "great political abuses, and universal dissatisfaction; and it is the "matured conviction of this assembly, from the antagonisms de- "veloped through difference of origin, local interests and other causes, "that the union in its present form can be no longer continued with "advantage to the people." Mr. John Sandfield Macdonald, of course, opposed the policy because he clung to the double majority plan, but Messrs. Connor and Foley strongly opposed the policy of proceeding in parliament on the convention resolutions, because they hoped for some advantageous ministerial changes under the existing circumstances; in this course they were supported by several other members in the caucus meeting. Only Patrick and Wallbridge, of all those who usually followed the liberal leader, ultimately voted against the resolutions. Mr. Brown was undoubtedly right in proceeding as he did. He was bound, as the leader of the party, to carry into effect the policy decided on at the great party gathering called together for the express purpose of adopting and formulating a decisive policy. He had for some time been convinced that representation according to population pure and simple would long be resisted, and that the exigencies of the country no less than those of political party life called for some alternative policy which might be acceptable in Lower Canada. He did not, nor did his followers, intend for a moment to stay the agitation for the just principle of representation, which he had conducted from small beginnings until it had forced nearly every public man in the ranks of both parties in Upper Canada to pledge themselves to it. He did, however, intend to say in Lower Canada, "If you determine to resist our just "demand for representation in the present union, let us dissolve the "union and form a new federal system which will leave each province "free to manage its own affairs, and have some central authority for

" matters of common concern." The subject had indeed been once
discussed, on a motion of Mr. Galt, in parliament, but until 1860 no
political party had been as such committed to such a policy. From
this time until the final triumph in 1864, Mr. Brown kept this alternative policy prominently before the public without for a moment
abandoning the demand for reform under the existing constitution.

CHAPTER XII

REPUTATION ATTACKED.—BRILLIANT AND SUCCESSFUL DEFENCE.—ILLNESS.

The bitterness of the party warfare towards Mr. Brown at this time found a fitting illustration in the attack made upon him by a Mr. Powell, the then member for Carleton, who had the baseness to attack Mr. Brown through the person of his aged father, a gentleman who had made no enemies personal or political, though given to a plain expression of his views on all passing subjects. Mr. Brown, senior, had a business failure in Edinburgh, in which he was not subject to moral blame, but was rather the victim of misplaced confidence. Even assuming there had been some blame attached to that incident of his life, none could attach to the son, who was a boy at the time. Nevertheless, it had been the occasion of mean inuendo, or bold insolent attack, from unscrupulous opponents who could find no vulnerable point in Mr..Brown's Canadian public life. The member for Carleton on this occasion made an attack on this subject in the most offensive manner, disgusting every respectable member on both sides of the House. Up to this time Mr. Brown had never noticed the gross attacks made outside the House, but now that he was assailed in the chamber, he dealt with the accusation, and showed its falsity and its uncharitable character, with a power, pathos and dignity never surpassed. A few extracts may be given. He referred for a moment to the tactics of the ministerialists in attempting to meet public accusations of misgovernment by private or personal attack, and then said :

I hesitate not to affirm that the assault the hon. member has just made is but the well understood climax of the scenes lately witnessed, that was to crush me forever as a public man. . . . This is not the first time that the insinuation has been made that I was a public defaulter in my native city. It has been echoed before now from the organs of the ministry. And at many an election contest have I been compelled to sit patiently and hear the tale recounted. For fifteen years I have been content to bear in silence these imputations. I would that I could yet refrain from the painful theme, but the pointed and public manner in which the charge has now been made, and the fear that the public cause with which I am identified might suffer by my silence, alike tell me that the moment has come when I ought to explain the transaction, as I have always been able to explain it, and to cast back the vile charge of dishonesty on those who dared to make it. That my father was a merchant in the city of Edinburgh, and that he engaged in disastrous business speculations commencing in the inflated times of 1825 and 1826, terminating ten years afterwards in his failure, is undoubtedly true.   And it is, unhappily, also true, that he did hold a public office, and that funds connected with that office were, at the moment of his sequestration, mixed up with his private funds, to the extent, I believe. of £2,800.   For this sum four relatives and friends were sureties, and they paid the money.   Part of that money has been repaid ; every sixpence of it will be paid, and paid shortly. . . . It happened in 1836; I was at that time but 17 years of age.   I was totally unacquainted with it; but young as I was, I felt then, as I feel now, the obligation it laid upon me, and I vowed I should never rest until every penny had been paid. There are those present who have known my every action since I set foot in this country ; they know I have not eaten the bread of idleness; but they did not know the great object of my labour, the one end of my desire for wealth, was that I might discharge those debts of my father's. . . . I have been accused of being ambitious ; I have been charged with aspiring to the office of Prime Minister of this great country, . . . but I only wish I could make my opponents understand how infinitely surpassing all this, how utterly petty and contemptible, in my thoughts, have been all such considerations in comparison with the one longing desire to discharge those debts of honour, and vindicate those Scottish principles that have been instilled into me since my youth. . . . But why, asked the person who made the charge, has he sat silent under it? Why, if the thing is false, has he endured it for so many years? What, sir! free myself from blame by inculpating one so dear! Say, " It was not I who was in fault ; it was my father!" Rather would I have lost my right arm than utter such a word. No, sir ; I waited the time when the charge could be met as it only might be fittingly met ; and my only regret, even now, is that I have been compelled to speak before these debts have been entirely liquidated. But it is due to my aged father that I explain that it has not been with his will that these imputations have been so long pointed at me, and that it has only been by earnest remonstrance I have prevented him vindicating me in public long ere now. . . . The member for Carleton now pretends that he did not mean to insinuate anything against my father ; that he has a high respect for his character. I thank him not for the acknowledgment. No man in Toronto, perhaps, is more generally known in the community, and I think I could appeal even to his political opponents to say if there is a citizen of Toronto at this day more thoroughly respected and esteemed. With a full knowledge of all that has passed, and all the consequences that have flowed from a day of weakness, I will say that an honester man does not breathe the air of heaven ; that no son feels prouder of his father than I do to-day : and that I would have submitted to the obloquy and reproach of his every act, not fifteen years, but fifty—ay, have gone down to my grave with the cold shade of the world upon me—rather than that one of his gray hairs should be injured.

Of this speech a leading conservative journal said :

The entire address forms the most refreshing episode which the records of the Canadian House of Commons present. Every true-hearted man must feel proud of one who has thus chivalrously done battle for his gray-haired sire. We speak deliberately when asserting that George Brown's position in the country is at this moment immeasurably higher than it ever previously has been. And though our political creed be diametrically antipodal to his own, we shall ever hail him as a credit to the land we love so well.

This was the general feeling over the whole country   The nobility of his reply was everywhere contrasted with the meanness and brutality of the attack.

When the general election took place in 1861, Mr. Brown was urged to take some county constituency where his election would be certain, especially as such an arrangement would leave his hands free to aid in other quarters. He declined this advice with his usual self-denial, believing that he could carry Toronto East.

In the early part of this year Mr. Brown had a long and dangerous illness, which incapacitated him for months from giving any attendance on his parliamentary and other duties. Although his brother, Mr. Gordon Brown, kept the *Globe* up to its usual vigour and excellence, yet the multifarious other duties devolving on a political leader naturally suffered much neglect. More especially was this felt in the preparations for, and the management of, the elections. His defeat in Toronto and the loss of some other constituencies may not unreasonably be attributed to his physical inability to perform his usual work. One thing was very noticeable at this election. The candidates in Upper Canada generally pledged themselves to advocate constitutional changes almost as a matter of course. There was no further need to fight a battle to prove the wisdom and necessity for such changes. In this respect the work of the defeated leader and his coadjutors was practically complete, and the ten years' conflict was about to end in a complete vindication of the policy pursued by Mr. Brown since his entrance into parliament. It might be that the wonderful power of Canadian Tories to adapt themselves to existing circumstances would again place them in a condition to give effect to principles they had steadily and vehemently opposed as long as their advocates were comparatively few, or it might be that the true friends of the proposed changes would unite in giving legislative effect to their views; but at any rate changes had now become inevitable. It was nevertheless a great misfortune to the liberal party that the leader should be defeated at such a critical period. This was so generally felt, that immediately several of the newly elected members offered to resign their seats in his favour. He resolutely declined any and all of the offers made, having made up his mind to stay out of parliament, though not out of public life. He formally resigned the leadership and gave himself entirely to the management of the *Globe*. It is quite probable that he viewed the attempt at leadership by Messrs. Foley, McDougall and Connor, with a grim satisfaction. These gentlemen and others had often expressed the opinion that the party would do better without Mr. Brown, because of his very decided opinions and his mode of expressing them. Some of them were only waiting to get Mr. Brown out of the way to form other combinations. The work of the opposition side of the House, so far as Upper Canada was concerned, was entirely in their hands for the sessions of 1861 and 1862, and it was only characterized by the want of vim, earnestness and power, the possession of which always distinguished Mr. Brown's leadership. In 1862, an informal vote was taken in the reform caucus for the leadership, in which Mr. Foley got eleven votes, being one more than anyone else. The leadership resulting was only a farce which was ended two years afterwards by his joining the conservatives, a step he deeply regretted afterwards. In a letter to a friend, Mr. Brown remarked :

"I confess I do chuckle a little occasionally at the gentlemen who were so keen to get me out of the way, ' were it only for a week.' ' Why, sir,' they would say, ' this government would not stand a day were Brown out of the way ;' and now they have had a whole session to themselves, with opportunities never enjoyed by men before, and they are just where I left them. . . . In the eight years in which I led the opposition there were many to doubt the ultimate success of my policy, and many in consequence to condemn it ; but I recollect of no instance in which I was charged with want of vigilance, or grave blundering or incapacity. I don't think the gentlemen who were so anxious to thrust me aside can say so much for their one session " [1861].

Mr. Brown contemplated retiring from the leadership, if not from parliament, a year before this. Towards the close of 1860 he addressed a letter to Mr. Mowat, from which we give an extract :

"I need not remind you of my determination to retire from parliamentary life at the earliest possible moment, and that for the last two years nothing has prevented me from doing so except the fears that new combinations might result from my retirement highly injurious to the cause we have so much at heart. I think, however, the moment has come when I may retire not only without fear of that danger, but with the probability that my doing so may largely conduce to secure the great ends we have been fighting for. You must have observed that throughout their whole tour in Upper Canada the members of the administration have tried to excite personal hostility against myself, and revive the feelings inspired by the fierce party contests of the past. There has been no question whether representation by population is just and should be adopted, but whether by false colouring George Brown can be made to appear to have abandoned it. There has been no attempt to argue from or for principle. . . . It may be that some other person who would excite less personal hostility might be more successful at this moment."

A few months after this he was stricken down by a long and severe illness, which incapacitated him from attending in his place in parliament during the whole session of 1861, or indeed to take a very active part in the general election of that year. The vast amount of labour he had undertaken as a political leader and as editor-in-chief of the *Globe* was more than any man could bear. He however, for some years previous to this time, commenced farming on an extensive scale on a tract of land he owned in the county of Kent. He also erected extensive saw and grist mills and a cabinet factory in the village of Bothwell, which was built on the property mentioned. The attempt to do the work of four or five men resulted in the dangerous illness which laid him prostrate so long. Mr. Brown was a candidate again for Toronto East, where he had been twice elected. He was opposed by the late John Crawford, and defeated by a majority of 191. He took advantage of this defeat to retire for a time from the toils of parliamentary life. Many members would have gladly made way for him, but he declined to take any of the seats offered. From a letter written to a prominent member of the liberal party the following extract is given :

"As I shall not be in Quebec at the opening of parliament, I want you to do me the favour of communicating to our political friends, at their first meeting, my formal resignation of the leadership of the Upper Canada opposition. Failing health for many months, terminating in serious illness last spring, satisfied me that complete relief for a time from the pressure of public responsibility was necessary to the restoration of my health, and my private affairs requiring personal attention, I became earnestly desirous of retiring, at least for a time, from parliamentary life at the earliest favourable moment. The result of the contest for the representation of the city of Toronto at the general election has given that opportunity ; and I have declined to avail myself of the kind offers of friends to secure me a seat in the early part of the session."

CHAPTER XIII.

TESTIMONIAL FROM POLITICAL FRIENDS.—MARRIAGE.—DEATH OF
MR. BROWN, SENIOR.

In 1858 a movement was commenced to present Mr. Brown with
some kind of testimonial in token of the appreciation of the services
rendered to the liberal party for many years. After the proposal had
been partly acted upon in the city and in some parts of the country
districts, a meeting of the promoters was held in the city of Toronto,
when the following resolutions were passed:

1. That the fund collected, and the moneys which may be hereafter received for the proposed testimonial, shall be appropriated to the erection
of a suitable building for a publishing office, to be presented to the Hon.
George Brown as a mark of the high sense entertained by his political friends
of the long, faithful, and important services which he has rendered to the
people of Canada.
2. That Messrs. William McMaster, John McMurrich, W. P. Howland,
John Macdonald, Samuel Spreull, and William Henderson form a committee to select a site for the erection of such building, to make purchase
thereof or procure an advantageous lease for that purpose, and carry out
all necessary arrangements for the completion of the testimonial; and the
treasurer is herby empowered to pay over the moneys collected upon the
order of the chairman and any two members of the committee.

In accordance with these resolutions, the subscriptions were devoted
to the erection of the part of the *Globe* structure fronting on King Street,
containing the counting rooms, offices and editorial rooms, and formally
presented to Mr. Brown. This recognition of his disinterested zealous
labours on behalf of popular rights was peculiarly pleasing to him, not
because of the amount of money required or contributed—for he deprecated any laboured effort to bring the scheme extensively before the
public—but because so many leading reformers in this way fully acknowledged their obligations as a party to his active labours, at a time
when so many leading men had failed to recognize the duties and
responsibility devolving upon them as public men, trusted by the
people on account of their professions.

Early in July, 1862, Mr. Brown left Canada for a lengthened sojourn in Europe to recruit his strength and obtain some relaxation from
the cares and anxieties of his arduous labours. While on his visit to
Scotland, one of the great events of his life happened. On the 27th
of November of that year he was joined in marriage to Miss Anne
Nelson, daughter of the late well known publisher, Mr. Thomas Nelson,
and sister of the present publishers, Thomas, William and James, and

of the late Rev. Dr. John Nelson, of Greenock. He shortly afterwards returned to Canada with greatly improved health, but rather averse to again entering parliament.

When the new parliament met in March, 1862, Mr. Brown was without a seat, having declined all the seats offered him. The Cartier-Macdonald government was tottering to its fall. Vigorous attacks were made by the opposition on several questions, and at last they fell on a vote respecting the militia. At the time of their defeat Mr. Foley was nominally leader of the Ontario opposition. Practically the leadership was in commission. The Governor-General did not send for Mr. Foley, but for Mr. John Sandfield Macdonald, although that gentleman had adopted views hostile to the main plank of the reform platform, representation by population, substituting therefor his plan of government by having a majority in each half of the province. Mr. Brown strongly opposed the formation of any government that did not provide for a reform of the representation. The liberal members at their caucus declined to support the government on the double majority principle, but agreed on all things else to support it. This qualified support, Mr. Brown's opposition, and Mr. Dorion's early resignation, weakened it so much that it became necessary in 1863 to make some changes, which gradually brought it into greater harmony with the party generally. When reconstructed in 1863, Mr. Brown gave the government his active support. Early in May Dr. Connor, member for South Oxford, was appointed Judge, and Mr. Brown, at the urgent solicitation of his friends, consented to re-enter parliament as member for that county. The reconstruction of the ministry by the introduction of Messrs. Holton, Mowat, Dorion, Letellier and Thibaudeau was largely the work of Mr. Brown, and as the representation question was to be an open question with the government, the double majority scheme being tacitly abandoned, he gave his influence in parliament and in the *Globe* strongly in its favour. Merely making the representation question an open one was not considered a sufficient advance on Mr. Sandfield Macdonald's previous policy, but it was clear to Mr. Brown that nothing could then be obtained in advance of that at this time, though various indications might be seen that concessions on the representation question might be proposed by more than one party in the House at no distant day. The Lower Canada leaders could not go further, and the Premier was believed to be ready to make propositions to other quarters unless his proposals were accepted. The weakness, however, was incurable, and the elections of 1863 added no perceptible strength to the government. The fall session of 1863 was got through with some difficulty ; but in 1864 it became clear that the government could not effectively conduct the legislation and business

of the country with only a majority of one or two, and rather than
continue such a struggle, the ministry resigned on the 21st of March.

Mr. Brown, senior, died in 1863. He was a noble old man, and
universally beloved wherever he was known. Dr. Burns, of Halifax, says of him: "He was a fine-looking old man as I remember
" him, and wielded a trenchant, vigorous pen ; his acquaintance with
" ecclesiastical and general subjects was extensive and accurate."
He always took a very active part in discussions on church matters,
and occasionally took part in public meetings called to discuss the
affairs of King's College or the clergy reserves, in which subjects he,
as an anti-state churchman, took an active interest. He took a prominent part in inducing the elder Dr. Burns to settle in Toronto in
1845. The doctor and Mr. Brown were not, however, always able to
agree on church questions, or, perhaps it might with more propriety
be said, they were very seldom able to agree. Both had very decided
views ; neither were slow to give their views expression by voice or
pen, and even on such questions the layman would not yield to the
churchman. The result was that some amusing controversies took place
between the two, in which the minister was not always the victor.
On one occasion Mr. Brown presided over some social gathering connected with church affairs, after experiencing some trouble from his
clerical friend, when he alluded to Dr. Burns' first visit to Canada
as a Free Church deputy, and to a similar gathering in Dr. Burns'
honour. On that occasion, said Mr. Brown, "we accompanied him to
" the ship, sorrowing most of all that we should see his face no more :"
adding in an undertone, "we did, however, see his face again."
The doctor's quick ear heard these words, and he called out, "Ay, did
" you, to your sorrow." When Mr. Brown was very ill a warm personal friend called to see him, and after a little conversation he asked
the invalid if his mind was at peace with God, and what were the
grounds of his hope. Mr. Brown shaded his face with his hand, and,
after a short pause, repeated Cowper's beautiful lines :

> "Since the dear hour which brought me to Thy foot,
> And cut up all my follies by the root,
> I never trusted in an arm but Thine,
> Nor hoped but in Thy righteousness divine ;
> My prayers and alms, imperfect and defiled,
> Were but the feeble efforts of a child ;
> Howe'er performed, it was their brightest part
> That they proceeded from a grateful heart ;
> Cleansed in Thine own all purifying blood,
> Forgive their evil and accept their good.
> I cast them at Thy feet ; my only plea
> Is what it was—dependence upon Thee ;
> While struggling in the vale of tears below,
> That never failed, nor shall it fail me now."

This was the only answer he made to the all-important question. What need for more ? Few men were more missed by a large circle of devoted friends, personal and political.   His health had been seriously impaired by the loss of a beloved daughter, Miss Catherine Brown, who was killed a few years before in a railway accident at Syracuse, when on a journey from New York with her father.   This tragic event touched father and mother very deeply, and saddened their declining years.   His habitual cheerfulness, nevertheless, brightened his face and warmed his manner to the last.   Mr. George Brown's chivalric devotion to his father has been already referred to ; his tenderness towards him might be daily witnessed.   Father and son might be seen any day going to or returning from the office to the home on Church Street, the father leaning heavily on the son's arm ; attention was often called to the care taken by the stalwart son of the aged father.

The elder Mr. Brown's general information, his genial humour, and his fund of anecdote, made his company of an evening very delightful, and of course caused him to be all the more missed in the office and the home.

CHAPTER XIV.

CORRESPONDENCE CONCERNING THE RECIPROCITY TREATY. — CONSTITUTIONAL CHANGES PROPOSED.

Towards the close of Mr. Sandfield Macdonald's official life as Premier, the reciprocity treaty with the United States excited much attention, as notice had been given, or was about to be given, by the United States to terminate it as soon as its terms permitted. Mr. Macdonald asked Mr. Brown to visit Washington, and see the public men there respecting the continuance of the treaty. Mr. Sandfield Macdonald addressed the following letter to Mr. Brown:

QUEBEC, January 7th, 1864.

MY DEAR BROWN,—The agitation in congress, as well as the action of some of the northern states, point unmistakably to the termination of the reciprocity treaty. You can well imagine this has not escaped the attention of the government. If we have abstained thus far from indicating by any public announcement the policy to be adopted, or from taking steps either by representing the anxiety we feel to the home government, or to the British minister at Washington, with a view to imperial action, it is because we were waiting the result of events which we could not control. The aspect in which the matter now presents itself admonishes us to prepare for the fight. We have considered that the first movement to be made is to select a competent individual who could be entrusted to deal with the subject at Washington, and who by his position could approach all parties at that capital. By the freedom of the intercourse thus afforded, it is conjectured that much of the existing prejudice against the treaty would be greatly modified.

I need scarcely tell you that one and all of my colleagues point to you as possessing all the qualifications required for that highly important mission. I am authorized to bespeak your co-operation in any way you may feel disposed to lend it towards maintaining the treaty as it is; or, if that should be impracticable, to promote the best terms that can be secured in any new arrangement that may be agreed upon as the basis of a fresh treaty. I may add that it will be a source of regret to me to learn that anything should stand in the way of your accepting this important mission, connected with which there would be an amount of responsibility which you are eminently fitted to assume, and for which the Canadian people would feel grateful in proportion to the magnitude of the task imposed on you. I shall be glad to hear from you at your earliest convenience.

Believe me, yours faithfully,
(Signed), J. S. MACDONALD.

HON. GEORGE BROWN, Toronto.

P.S.—I may mention that during an interview I had with Mr. Seward in New York, he strongly recommended this course to be taken early—namely, having a *quasi* political agent to remain at Washington for some months, with whom he and Lord Lyons could confer informally from time to time on matters concerning Canada.

J. S. M

To this letter Mr. Brown sent the following reply:

TORONTO, January 25, 1864.

MY DEAR MACDONALD,—Your letter of the 7th on the subject of the American reciprocity treaty reached me on Saturday, and, late though it be, I am very glad to learn that you intend now to take action in regard to it. It appears to me that the importance to Canada of maintaining the treaty can hardly be overrated; and that to secure its renewal we should be prepared to discuss all reasonable suggestions for its modification. I think that the clamour against the treaty has been allowed to go too long unchecked, and that no further time should be lost in communicating the views of the Canadian government not only to the executive at Washington, but to the present members of the senate and house of representatives, in whose hands the fate of the treaty now apparently rests.

I think that the working of the treaty in all its relations should be clearly brought out, and placed under the attention of all the members of congress, and especially that the committees of both chambers charged with the subject should be frankly told that while the people of the United States have profited by the treaty quite as much as the people of Canada, we are desirous for its renewal, and are prepared to discuss any modifications they may propose.

It might not be without advantage, moreover, to have the Canadian view of the whole subject placed clearly before the Boards of Trade of New York, Boston, Chicago, and other places. But there is a difficulty in doing all this. The renewal or modification of the treaty is an imperial matter; the negotiations must be carried on through the imperial authorities, and no doubt Lord Lyons will desire to conduct them in his own way and according to his own ideas. Unless his views have recently undergone a change, I believe he thinks we should not move in the matter at all. I know that was his opinion very recently. But even if his views have undergone a change, and he is prepared to move in the matter, the negotiation must be in his hands. All that we can do here, I apprehend, is to place before Lord Lyons the wishes of the Canadian government, and co-operate with him in his efforts to give them effect.

It appears to me Mr. Holton is the man best fitted to do this. From his commercial training and his knowledge of the subject, and the men he would have to deal with, Mr. Holton would be of the greatest service in the negotiations, and his official position as Minister of Finance would give him a standing at Washington that no unofficial person could possibly have. He would be in a position to speak officially the views of the government, and to say at once what modifications could or could not be assented to.

The matter is of such vast importance to the province that I think no consideration should prevent Mr. Holton assuming this duty at once and carrying it through. As regards myself, I do not doubt that in some respects I could be of service in the negotiations. But, in the first place, Mr. Holton is the proper person to be sent to Washington; in the second place, I do not see how any unofficial person could be placed in a position at Washington that he could accept; and in the third place, it would be exceedingly inconvenient for me to be absent from home for any length of time at present. I purpose going to Europe early in the approaching summer, and it will require every spare hour before leaving to arrange my affairs for a lengthened absence. But while I cannot see my way to undertake the duty you proffered to me, I feel more deeply anxious on the subject of the reciprocity treaty, and if Mr. Holton goes to Washington, I will gladly lend him all the aid, personally and otherwise, that I possibly can.

Faithfully yours,

GEORGE BROWN.

HON. J. S. MACDONALD, Quebec.

The proposed negotiations at this time never assumed any shape. They were proceeded with eighteen months afterwards under other auspices, and proved abortive. In the eventful session of the Canadian parliament about to open, Mr. Sandfield Macdonald's government received the full support of Mr. Brown. The conservative opposition showed their usual disregard of everything but what would most embarrass the government. The government again got tired of neverending senseless discussion involving little but the ascendancy of the one side or the other, and though it might have survived the session, it is doubtful if any useful legislation could have been passed. Their resignation was not universally approved by the liberal party, and it may be doubted whether it was in a tactical sense a wise movement. It did, however, lead at once to the event which precipitated the constitutional changes which were so soon to be concreted in the British North America Act forming the present federal union of all the provinces. On the 30th of March a new conservative government was formed under Sir E. P. Taché. This administration had a very precarious existence; indeed, only succeeded in living a day by the purchase of two members of the liberal party by office. In the meantime Mr. Brown obtained a committee of the leading members of both sides of the House to "consider the best means of settling the "constitutional changes which might be recommended, to avoid "trouble." The committee consisted of Messrs. John A. Macdonald, Galt, Cartier, Chapais, Street, J. H. Cameron, Turcotte and McGee, from the conservative side; and Messrs. J. S. Macdonald, Mowat, Holton, McKellar, Scoble, McDougall and Brown, from the liberal side. The report was presented at the opening of the House on the 14th.

Mr. Brown—from the select committee appointed to inquire into the important subjects embraced in a dispatch to the colonial minister addressed to him on the 2nd day of February, 1859, by the Hon. G. E. Cartier, the Hon. A. T. Galt, and the Hon. John Ross, then members of the executive council of this province, while in London acting on behalf of the government of which they were members, in which they declared that "very grave difficulties now present themselves in conducting the government of Canada in such a manner as to show due regard to the wishes of its numerous population." That "differences exist to an extent which prevents any perfect and complete assimilation of the views of the two sections." That " the progress of population has been more rapid on the western section, and claims are now made on behalf of its inhabitants for giving them representation in the legislature in proportion to their numbers." That " the result is shown by an agitation fraught with great danger to the peaceful and harmonious working of our constitutional system, and consequently detrimental to the progress of the province;" and that " the necessity of providing a remedy for a state of things that is yearly becoming worse, and of allaying feelings that are daily being aggravated by the contentions of political parties," has impressed the advisers of Her Majesty's representative in Canada with the importance of seeking for such a mode of dealing with these difficulties as may forever remove them, and the best means of remedying the evils therein set forth—presented to the House the report of the said committee, which was read as followeth :

That the committee have held eight sittings and have endeavoured to find some solution for existing difficulties likely to receive the assent of both sections of the province. A strong feeling was found to exist among the members of the committee in favour of changes in the direction of a federative system, applied either to Canada alone, or to the whole British North American provinces, and such progress has been made as to warrant the committee in recommending that the subject be again referred to a committee at the next session of parliament.

The whole respectfully submitted.

GEO. BROWN, *Chairman.*

The Hon. John A. Macdonald, John S. Macdonald and John Scoble, alone opposed the adoption of this report.

The day after the committee came to the decision to make this report, the government was defeated on a motion of want of confidence, moved by Mr. Dorion. Mr. John A. Macdonald had on the previous day recorded his vote against the conclusion reached by the committee in favour of a solution of the constitutional crisis as one which both sections might agree to. The want of confidence motion in the government, of which he was a prominent member, quickened his perceptions, and a few hours sufficed to induce him to acknowledge the existence of a serious crisis, and the wisdom of meeting it by the very plan suggested by the committee, but which was promulgated by the reform convention in 1859 as an alternative to representation by population with the existing union.

The first use made of the victory by Mr. Brown, as the western leader, was to consider how to turn the defeat to account in securing the constitutional changes required. He consulted some of his most intimate friends and supporters with a view of ascertaining whether they would be disposed to abate the ordinary party advantages now in their grasp in order to achieve a more signal triumph in securing such constitutional changes as would effectually do justice to Upper Canada. Finding a general disposition prevailing to adopt his view, he next addressed himself to some government supporters—notably Mr. Morris, member for Lanark—suggesting that they should press on their leaders the wisdom of trying to come to some agreement on constitutional changes which could be accepted by east and west. The Lower Canadian liberals declined to be parties to any arrangement with the conservative government, preferring to allow the ordinary course to be pursued which must follow the defeat of a government. During the negotiations which succeeded the conversations alluded to, Mr. Brown was pained to have to act without the countenance or aid of his trusty allies from Lower Canada—a band of noble men under the lead of Messrs. Dorion and Holton ; but he made every effort to induce them to join in the scheme to obtain a final settlement of sectional troubles, and when they failed to respond, he could only go on without them; indeed, he was bound to do so in the interests of his own province. Many of the Upper Canadian members agreed, with much reluctance, to the negotiations, partly because they feared treachery on the part of the conservatives, and partly because it seemed probable that a separation from their Lower Canadian allies would be the result.

CHAPTER XV.

A Coalition Proposed.—Mr. Brown Urged to Enter the Ministry.—A Federal Union Resolved on.

Mr. Morris having reported to the conservative leaders Mr. Brown's conversations, on the following day, June 16th, Mr. John A. Macdonald asked if Mr. Brown would meet Mr. Galt and himself to discuss the situation and the proposed remedy. This was at once assented to, and a preliminary meeting was held next morning, at which Messrs. Macdonald and Galt appeared as a delegation from the defeated administration, authorized to invite Mr. Brown to strengthen them, with a view to their carrying on the government for the purpose of settling the sectional difficulties between Upper and Lower Canada. When this proposal was made Mr. Brown at once informed them that nothing but the extreme urgency of the present crisis, and the hope of settling the sectional troubles of the province for ever, could, in his opinion, justify their meeting together with a view to common political action. . . . Mr. Brown then stated, on grounds purely personal, that it was quite impossible that he could be a member of any administration at present, and that even had this been otherwise, he would have conceived it highly objectionable that parties who had been so long and so strongly opposed to each other, as he and some members of the administration had been, should enter the same cabinet. He thought the public mind would be shocked by such an arrangement, but he felt very strongly that the present crisis presented an opportunity of dealing with this question that might never occur again. Both political parties had tried in turn to govern the country, but without success; and repeated elections only arrayed sectional majorities against each other more strongly than before. Another general election at this moment presented little hope of a much altered result; and he believed that both parties were far better prepared than they had ever been before to look the true cause of all the difficulties firmly in the face, and endeavour to settle the representation question on an equitable and permanent basis. Mr. Brown added that if the administration were prepared to do this, and would pledge themselves clearly and publicly to bring in a measure next session that would be acceptable to Upper Canada, the basis to be now settled and announced to parliament, he would heartily co-operate with them, and try to induce his friends—in which he hoped to be successful—to sustain them until they had an opportunity of presenting their measure next session.

Mr. Macdonald replied that he considered it would be essential that Mr. Brown himself should become a member of the cabinet, with a view to give guarantees to the opposition and to the country for the earnestness of the government.

Mr. Brown rejoined that other members of the opposition could, equally with himself, give that guarantee to their party and the country by entering the government in the event of a satisfactory basis being arrived at. He felt that his position had been such for many years as to place a greater bar in the way of his entering the government than in that of any other member of the opposition.

Mr. Macdonald then said he thought it would be necessary that Mr. Brown himself should, in any case, be identified with the negotiations that would necessarily have to take place, and that if he did not himself enter the cabinet he might undertake a mission to the Lower Provinces, or to England, or both, in order to identify himself with the action of the Canadian government in carrying out the measure agreed upon.

It was then suggested by Mr. Brown, and agreed to, that all questions of a personal character, and the necessary guarantees, should be waived for the present, and the discussion conducted with a view of ascertaining if a satisfactory solution of the sectional difficulty could be agreed upon.

Mr. Brown asked what the government proposed as a remedy for the injustice complained of by Upper Canada, and as a settlement of the sectional troubles. Mr. Macdonald and Mr. Galt replied that their remedy was a federal union of all the British North American provinces ; local matters being committed to local bodies, and matters common to all to a general legislature, constituted on the well understood principles of federal government.

Mr. Brown objected that this was uncertain and remote, as there were so many bodies to be consulted, and stated that the measure acceptable to Upper Canada would be parliamentary reform based on population, without regard to a separating line between Upper and Lower Canada.

Messrs. Macdonald and Galt said it would be impossible for them to accede to or for any government to carry such a measure, and that unless a basis could be framed on the federative principle suggested by the report of Mr. Brown's committee, it did not appear to them that anything could be settled.

Ultimately it was found that a compromise might probably be had in the adoption of the federal principle for all the provinces as the larger question, or for Canada alone, with provision for the admission of the Maritime Provinces and the North-West Territory.

Mr. Brown contended that the Canadian confederation should be constituted first, in order that such securities might be taken in regard to the position of Upper Canada as would satisfy that section of the country, and that in the negotiations with the Lower Provinces, the interests of Upper Canada would in no case be overlooked.

It was then agreed to communicate to parliament that day, June 17th, a statement that the state of the negotiations warranted a hope of an ultimate understanding.

On the 19th, a general accord was reached, "that . . . as the " views of Upper Canada could not be met under our present system, " the remedy must be sought in the adoption of the federal principle."

At this stage of the negotiations Mr. Brown requested to have the views of the government in writing. This was done that same afternoon, Mr. Brown in the meantime seeing the Governor-General. The following memorandum, approved by the government and the Governor-General, was then given to him :

MEMORANDUM.—CONFIDENTIAL.

The government are prepared to state that immediately after the prorogation they will address themselves in the most earnest manner to the negotiations for a confederation of all the British North American provinces.

That, failing a successful issue to such negotiations, they are prepared to pledge themselves to legislation during next session of parliament for the purpose of remedying existing difficulties, by introducing the federal principle for Canada alone, coupled with such provisions as will permit the Maritime Provinces and the North-West Territory to be hereafter incorporated into the Canadian system.

That, for the purpose of carrying on the negotiations, and settling the details of the proposed legislation, a royal commission shall be issued, composed of three members of the government and three members of the opposition, of whom Mr. Brown shall be one, and the government pledge themselves to give all the influence of the administration to secure to the said commission the means of advancing the great object in view.

That, subject to the House permitting the government to carry through the public business, no dissolution of parliament shall take place, but the administration will again meet the present House.

Shortly after six the parties met at the same place, when Mr. Brown stated that . . . he had seen a sufficient number of his friends to warrant him in expressing the belief that the bulk of them would accept a measure for the federative union of the Canadas, with provision for admitting the Maritime Provinces and the North-West Territory. The proposal was then formally agreed to in the following terms, subject to the approval of His Excellency :

The government are prepared to pledge themselves to bring in a measure next session, for the purpose of removing existing difficulties by introducing the federal principle into Canada, coupled with such provision as will permit the Maritime Provinces and the North-West Territory to be incorporated into the same system of government.

And the government will seek, by sending representatives to the Lower Provinces and England, to secure the assent of those interests which are beyond the control of our own legislation, to such a measure as may enable all British North America to be united under a general legislature based upon the federal principle.

Mr. Brown then stated that, having arrived at a basis which he believed would be generally acceptable to the great mass of his political friends, he had to add, that as the proposition was so general in its terms, and the advantages of the measure depended on the details that might finally be adopted, it was the very general feeling of his friends that security must be given for the fairness of those details, and the good faith with which the whole movement would be prosecuted, by the introduction into the cabinet of a fair representation of his political friends.

Mr. Brown stated that he had not put this question directly to his friends, but that he perceived very clearly that this was the strong opinion of a large majority of them, and that his own personal opinion on this (to which he still adhered) was participated in by only a small number. Messrs. Macdonald, Cartier and Galt, replied that they had of course understood, in proposing that Mr. Brown should enter the government, that he would not come alone, but that the number of seats at his disposal had not been considered by their colleagues. Mr. Brown was requested to state his views on this point, and he replied that the opposition were half of the House, and ought to have an equal influence in the government.

On Monday, June 21st, at 10.30 a.m., Messrs. Macdonald, Cartier and Galt, called on Mr. Brown, and they went together to the secretary's office ; when Mr. Brown, having been asked how he proposed to arrange equal representation in the cabinet, replied that he desired to be understood as meaning four members for Upper Canada and two for Lower Canada, to be chosen by the opposition.

In reply, Messrs.' Cartier and Galt stated that, so far as related to the constitution of the cabinet for Lower Canada, they believed it already afforded ample guarantees for their sincerity, and that a change in its *personnel* would be more likely to produce embarrassment than assistance, as the majority of the people of Lower Canada, both French Canadians and English, had implicit confidence in their leaders, which it would not be desirable to shake in any way. That in approaching the important question of settling the sectional difficulties, it appeared to them essential that the party led by Sir E. P. Taché should have ample assurance that their interests would be protected, which, it was feared, would not be strengthened by the introduction into the cabinet of the Lower Canada opposition.

Mr. Macdonald stated that, as regards Upper Canada, in his opinion the reduction to two of the number of the gentlemen in the cabinet who now represent Upper Canada would involve the withdrawal of the confidence of those who now support them in the House of Assembly, but that he would be prepared for the admission into the cabinet of three gentlemen of the opposition, on its being ascertained that they would bring with them a support equal to that now enjoyed by the government from Upper Canada.

Mr. Brown asked in what manner it was proposed the six Upper Canada ministers should be selected. Was each party to have *carte blanche* in suggesting to the head of the government the names to be chosen? To which Mr. Macdonald replied, that as a matter of course he would expect Mr. Brown himself to be a member of the administration, as affording the best if not the only guarantee for the adhesion of his friends. That Mr. Macdonald, on Mr. Brown giving his assent, would confer with him as to the selection of the Upper Canada colleagues from both sides, who would be the most acceptable to their respective friends, and most likely to work harmoniously for the great object which alone could justify the arrangement proposed.

Mr. Brown then inquired what Mr. Macdonald proposed in regard to the Upper Canada leadership. Mr. Macdonald said that, as far as he was concerned, he could not with propriety, or without diminishing his usefulness, alter his position, but that he was, as he had been for some time, anxious to retire from the government, and would be quite ready to facilitate arrangements for doing so. Of course, he could not retire from the government without Sir E. P. Taché's consent.

Mr. Brown then stated that, without discussing the propriety or reasonableness of the proposition, he would consult his friends and give an early reply.

Immediately after this meeting Mr. Brown summoned a meeting of the Upper Canada opposition members, to whom he fully detailed all that had taken place between himself and the members of the government, and then invited them to consider what course the party would pursue. The following minutes give the proceedings, though not the discussion at length :

QUEBEC, June 21st, 1864.

A meeting of the Upper Canada opposition was held this day in the Kent House. Robert Bell, Esq., M.P.P., of Lanark, was called to occupy the chair.

Mr. Brown then gave a statement of the negotiation he had for some days carried on with the government respecting the reconstruction of the government, with a view to accomplish a settlement of the constitutional difficulties between Upper and Lower Canada.

It was moved by Mr. Hope F. Mackenzie, seconded by Mr. McGivern, "That we approve of the course which has been pursued by Mr. Brown in the negotiations with the government, and that we approve of the project of a federal union of the Canadas, with provision for its extension to the Maritime Provinces and the North-West Territory, as one basis on which the constitutional difficulties now existing could be settled."—Carried. Thirty-four voted for the motion, namely : Messrs. Ault, Bell (Lanark), Bowman, Brown, Burwell, Cowan, Dickson, Dunsford, Howland, McFarlane, McIntyre, Mackenzie (Lambton), Mackenzie (Oxford), McConkey, McDougall, McGivern, McKellar, Mowat, Munro, Notman, Parker, Ross (Prince Edward), Rankin, Rymal, Scoble, Smith (Durham), Smith (Toronto), Stirton, Thompson, Wallbridge (Speaker), Wallbridge (N. Hastings), Wells, White and Wright. The following members declined to vote either yea or nay, namely : Messrs. Biggar, MacDonald (Glengarry), MacDonald (Cornwall), Macdonald (Toronto), and Scatcherd.

It was moved by the Hon. J. S. Macdonald, "That the proposition for at least three members of the opposition entering the government be accepted."

Mr. Mackenzie (of Lambton) moved in amendment, "That the proposition for three members entering the cabinet be rejected, and that the proposition for the settlement of sectional difficulties receive an outside support."

Mr. Mowat suggested that a division be taken on the understanding that those voting " yea " were in favour of the first proposition, and those voting " nay " were in favour of the second proposition.—Agreed to.

The yeas and nays were then taken as follows : Yeas—Messrs. Ault, Bell, Dunsford, Howland, Macdonald (Glengarry), MacDonald (Cornwall), McFarlane, McConkey, McDougall, McGivern, McIntyre, Munro, Notman, Parker, Rankin, Ross (Prince Edward), Rymal, Smith (Toronto), Smith (Durham), Stirton, Thompson, Wallbridge (Speaker), Wallbridge (N. Hastings), Wells, White and Wright—26. Nays—Messrs. Bowman, Brown, Burwell, Cowan, Dickson, Mackenzie (Lambton), Mackenzie (Oxford), McKellar, Mowat, Scatcherd and Scoble—11. Mr. Macdonald (Toronto) declined to vote.

Moved by Hon. Mr. MacDonald, of Cornwall, " That it is all important that Mr. Brown should be one of the 'party' to enter the cabinet." —Carried unanimously, with the exception of Mr. Scatcherd, Mr. Brown, and Mr. Burwell.

Moved by Mr. White, and carried unanimously, " That Mr. Brown be requested to continue the negotiations with the government."

R. BELL, Chairman.

Another meeting was held on Tuesday, 22nd, by Mr. Brown and the Messrs. Taché, Macdonald, Cartier, and Galt, when Mr. Brown informed these gentlemen that his friends had authorized him to continue the negotiations.

A further meeting was held at 8.30 p.m., at which the details of the arrangements, in case Mr. Brown and his friends accepted office, were discussed at great length.

Mr. Brown contended strongly that the reformers should have a larger representation in the cabinet than three members. To which it was replied that the administration believed it was quite impossible to satisfy their own friends with a different arrangement.

Mr. Brown then asked if he could be sworn in as an executive councillor, without department or salary, in addition to the three departmental offices to be filled by his friends. Mr. Macdonald replied that the principle of equality would in this case be destroyed, and he was satisfied that it could not be done.

Mr. Brown asked if it was a *sine quâ non* that he himself should enter the cabinet ? To which it was replied, that to secure a successful issue to the attempt to settle the sectional difficulties, it was considered that Mr. Brown's acceptance of office was indispensable.

Mr. Brown then stated that it was now for him to consider what course he should pursue, entertaining as he still did the strongest repugnance to accepting office.

On Wednesday Mr. Brown met the same ministers, and informed them of his final decision, that he would consent to the reconstruction of the cabinet as proposed; but inasmuch as he did not wish to assume the responsibility of the government business before the House, he preferred leaving till after the prorogation the consideration of the acceptance of office by himself and the two gentlemen who might be ultimately selected to enter the administration with him.

Sir E. P. Taché and Mr. Macdonald thereon stated that after the prorogation they would be prepared to place three seats in the cabinet at the disposal of Mr. Brown.

The preceding narrative of the negotiations of Mr. Brown with the conservative leaders is nearly *verbatim* from the memoranda published at the time.

CHAPTER XVI.

PROGRESS OF THE CONFEDERATION SCHEME.—DEATH OF SIR E. P.
TACHE.—NEGOTIATIONS FOR THE RECONSTRUCTION OF THE
CABINET.

In the wisdom of Mr. Brown entering the coalition government
the writer never concurred, but he yielded his opinion to the great
majority who held otherwise.   Mr. Brown himself also had misgivings
of coming trouble, which were realized within eighteen months of the
consummation of the coalition.   In the meantime Mr. Brown was, on
June 30th, sworn in as President of the Council, with Messrs. Mowat
and McDougall as his colleagues (the latter being a selection very few
desired), and devoted himself with great zeal to the promotion of the
great scheme of political reform, or revolution, to which he and his
friends committed themselves.

With other members of the government he visited the Lower Provinces during the summer, where he addressed meetings at Charlotte.
town, Halifax, and St. John.   He returned in time to take part in
the convention of the provincial delegates that assembled in Quebec
on the 10th of October, where he took an active part in preparing the
resolutions which formed the basis of the Confederation Act.   Parliament met early in 1865, and as soon as the usual formalities could
be disposed of, the scheme for reconstructing the government of the
North American Provinces was brought up for discussion.   The debate
was a memorable one, for the ability which characterized it as much
as for the importance of the questions which it decided.   Mr. Brown's
speech was a most able and exhaustive one.   To him, as leader of the
liberals, the position was a painful one.   He was opposed by a large
portion of his own friends from Lower Canada.   Among all the sacrifices he made on public grounds, none were so great as the necessity
laid upon him to be compelled to stand upon the opposite side to his
old colleagues Messrs. Dorion, Holton, and their friends.   The result
of the debate was that the federal resolutions were carried by a vote
of 91 to 33.   Of the minority only eight were from Upper Canada,
and of these eight, it will be observed that the names of several members are recorded who voted at the caucus of 1864 for Mr. Brown's
scheme, and who asked him to enter the coalition cabinet.

It was no secret that His Excellency, Lord Monck, took a very
lively interest in the proposed constitutional changes, and did all he

properly could do to secure the proposed unification of the British provinces under a federal system. During the interregnum—for it could hardly be said that there was a government in existence after the hostile vote—Lord Monck had several interviews with Mr. Brown with a view to induce him to set aside his scruples and act as a minister in securing the acceptance of the new system. Lord Monck was a thoroughly honest man, an upright Governor-General, and an enthusiastic lover of Canada. He was also in British politics a well-known liberal. The opinions of such a man very naturally had much weight with public men generally. It may be too soon to discuss the full share he had in bringing influence to bear on the governments of some of the provinces, and possibly on individuals, but it may be accepted as incontrovertible that the means used and the influence exerted were such only as he was justified in using in a great crisis.

The following letter was written by His Excellency to Mr. Brown on the same day on which the liberal caucus was held, and materially influenced him in assuming the responsibilty which the liberal party from Ontario wished him to take on his shoulders.

QUEBEC, June 21, 1864.

MY DEAR MR. BROWN,—I think the success or failure of the negotiations which have been going on for some days, with a view to the formation of a strong government on a broad basis, depends very much on your consenting to come into the cabinet.

Under these circumstances, I must again take the liberty of pressing upon you by this note, as I have already often done verbally, my opinion of the grave responsibility which you will take upon yourself if you should refuse to do so.

Those who have hitherto opposed your views have consented to join with you in good faith for the purpose of extricating the province from what appears to me a very dangerous position.

They have frankly offered to take up and endeavour to settle, on principles satisfactory to all, the great constitutional question which you, by your energy and ability, have made your own.

The details of that settlement must necessarily be the subject of grave debate in the cabinet, and I confess I cannot see how you are to take part in that discussion, or how your opinions can be brought to bear on the arrangement of the question, unless you occupy a place at the council table.

I hope I may, without impropriety, ask you to take these opinions into consideration before you arrive at a final decision as to your own course.

Believe me to be, yours very truly,

(Signed,) MONCK.

HON. GEORGE BROWN.

At the close of the first session of 1865 Mr. Brown, with Mr. John A. Macdonald, Mr. Cartier and Mr. Galt, visited England to confer with the Imperial government on the proposed constitutional changes, commercial treaties and legislation, the consideration of the defences of Canada, arrangements for settlement of North-West Territory and Hudson Bay Company claims, and generally upon the critical state of affairs by which Canada was at that time most seriously affected. The Canadian ministers were received with great cordiality in Britain, and especially by the Queen and royal family. The project of a federal union of the colonies was highly approved of by the Imperial authorities, "as (to use Mr. Cardwell's words) an object much to be " desired, that all the British North American colonies should agree " to unite in one government." The Lower Provinces had manifested strong objections to the union, though the Nova Scotia legislature had formally approved of it; and the British government undertook to press the wisdom of the measure upon them. However desirable it might be to embrace all the provinces, it was not right to apply any pressure. This was undoubtedly done by Mr. Cardwell, and doubtless at his instance Mr. Arthur Gordon, governor of New Brunswick, applied all the pressure in his power, and not very fairly. He succeeded, but at the expense of some keen feeling, in the expression of which by some Mr. Brown was unjustly blamed.

On the 30th day of July Mr. Taché, the Premier of the coalition government, died, and negotiations for the continuance or reconstruction of the government were commenced with Mr. Brown by Mr. Macdonald, who was the senior member. He desired to be Premier himself, but failing that, he was willing Mr. Cartier should be placed in that position. Mr. Brown, as leader of the liberal section, was bound to see that neither the reform party nor the policy agreed on were jeopardized by the new arrangements to be made. The following correspondence will best show the ground he took, supported by his two colleagues :

MINISTERIAL NEGOTIATIONS FOR THE RECONSTRUCTION OF THE GOVERNMENT CONSEQUENT ON THE DEATH OF SIR E. P. TACHÉ.

No. 1.—*Memorandum made 4th August, 1865, of Conversation held on the preceding day between Messrs. Macdonald and Brown.*

Mr. Macdonald, yesterday, sought an interview with Mr. Brown and informed him that His Excellency the Governor-General had sent for him that morning, and had stated his desire that the administration, as it was formed in 1864, should continue in office, with as few changes as possible, in order to carry out the policy announced by the government on its formation ; that, with that view, His Excellency had expressed the opinion that the most obvious mode of supplying the place, vacated by the death of Sir Etienne Taché, would be for Mr. Macdonald to assume the position of First Minister, as being the senior member of the ministry ; and that Mr. Cartier would, on the same principle, become the leader of the Lower Canadian section of the government ; and that, for the purpose of carrying those views into effect, he had commissioned Mr. Macdonald to take the post of First Minister, at the same time requesting all the other ministers to retain their offices. Mr. Macdonald further informed Mr. Brown that he had assented to this proposition of His Excellency, and had seen Mr.

Cartier, who at once agreed to it. He then invited Mr. Brown to accede to the proposal of His Excellency.

Mr. Brown replied that he was quite prepared to enter into arrangements for the continuance of the government in the same position it occupied previous to the death of Sir Étienne Taché ; but that the proposal now made involved a grave departure from that position. The government, heretofore, had been a coalition of three political parties, each represented by an active party leader, but all acting under one chief, who had ceased to be actuated by strong party feelings or personal ambitions, and who was well fitted to give confidence to all the three sections of the coalition that the conditions which united them would be carried out in good faith to the very letter. Mr. Macdonald, Mr. Cartier, and himself (Mr. Brown) were, on the contrary, regarded as party leaders, with party feelings and aspirations ; and to place any one of them in an attitude of superiority over the others, with the vast advantage of the premiership, would, in the public mind, lessen the security of good faith, and seriously endanger the existence of the coalition. It would be an entire change of the situation. Whichever of the three was so preferred, the act would amount to an abandonment of the coalition basis and a reconstruction of the government on ordinary party principles, under a party leader unacceptable to a large portion of those on whose support the existence of the ministry depended. Mr. Brown reminded Mr. Macdonald that when the coalition was formed, the liberal party in opposition constituted a majority of the House of Assembly; that, solely for the accomplishment of a great measure of reform essential to the peace and progress of the country, they had laid aside, for the time, party considerations, and consented to form a coalition with their opponents, on conditions which nothing but the strongest sense of public duty could have induced them to accept. He reminded Mr. Macdonald of the disadvantageous and embarrassing position he (Mr. Brown) and his colleagues, Mr. McDougall and Mr. Howland, had occupied during the past year, united as they were with nine political opponents who held all the important departments of state ; and he asked him to reflect in what light the liberal party must regard this new proposition to abandon their distinctive position, and place one of their chief opponents in the premiership, though his conservative supporters in parliament were much inferior, numerically, to the reform supporters of the coalition. Mr. Brown stated his conviction that the right mode of settling the question would be to invite some gentleman, of good position in the legislative council, under whom all the three great parties to the coalition could act with confidence, to become the successor of Colonel Taché. In no other way, he thought, could the position heretofore existing be continued. Mr. Brown concluded by saying that the proposal of Mr. Macdonald was palpably one for the construction of a new government, and that if the aid of the reform party of Upper Canada in the assembly were desired in its formation, a distinct statement of the policy of the new government must be made, and a definite proposition submitted. Speaking, however, for himself alone, he (Mr. Brown) occupied now precisely the ground that he had held in the negotiations of 1864 ; he stood prepared to give an outside but frank and earnest support to any administration that might be formed, pledged, like the coalition government, to carry through parliament, in the spring session of next year, either a measure for the final completion of the confederation scheme of the Quebec conference, or one for removing existing difficulties in Canada, by the introduction of the federal principle into the system of government, coupled with such provisions as will permit the Maritime Provinces and the North-West Territory to be incorporated into the system.

Mr. Macdonald stated in answer that at the time the coalition was effected in 1864, Sir Étienne Taché held the position of Premier, with him (Mr. Macdonald) as leader of the Lower House, and of the Upper Canadian section of the government. That on reference to the memorandum containing the basis of coalition, it will be seen that Mr. Brown at first preferred to support the government in its policy as then settled without entering the government, but that it was afterwards agreed, in deference to the wishes of his supporters and at the pressing instance of Mr. Macdonald, that he and two of his political friends should enter the government. These terms were acceded to, the offices that happened to be then vacant placed at Mr. Brown's disposal, and the coalition was completed. Mr. Macdonald further stated that Sir Etienne Taché was not selected at the time of the coalition, or as a part of the agreement for the coalition, as First Minister, but he had been previously and was then the head of the conservative government, and was accepted with all his Lower Canadian colleagues without change. That on the lamented decease of Sir Etienne, His Excellency had, without any previous communication of his opinion to him or (as he understood) to any one else, come to the conclusion that the best mode of carrying on the government was (as already stated) for Mr. Macdonald to take one step upward; that Mr. Cartier, as next in seniority, should do so also, and that the other arrangements should remain as before. That he (Mr. Macdonald) thought with His Excellency that this was the best solution of the matter, and could not but accede to it; that, however, he had no personal feeling in the matter, and that if he had, he thought it his duty to set aside such feeling for the sake of carrying out the great scheme, so happily commenced, to a successful issue. He therefore would readily stand aside and waive his pretensions, so that some other party than himself might be appointed to the premiership; that he thought Mr. Cartier should be that party; that after the death of Colonel Taché, Mr. Cartier, beyond a doubt, was the most influential man in his section of the country, and would be selected by the Lower Canadian supporters of the government as their leader; that neither Mr. Brown nor Mr. Macdonald could dictate to Lower Canada as to their selection of leader; that the Premier must be, according to usage, the leader or senior member either from Upper or Lower Canada; and that as he (Mr. Macdonald) had, in consequence of the position taken by Mr. Brown, waived his own pretensions, it followed that Mr. Cartier should be appointed as Prime Minister. Mr. Macdonald stated in conclusion that although he had no reason to suppose that His Excellency would object to the selection of Mr. Cartier, yet he must of course submit the proposition to him, and obtain His Excellency's assent to it.

Mr. Brown replied that in some of the views suggested by Mr. Macdonald, there was a difference between this proposition and the original one; but still that this, like the other, would be a proposal for the construction of a new government, in a manner seriously affecting the security held by the liberal party. Before saying anything upon such a proposition, however, were it formally made, he would desire to consult his friends, Mr. McDougall and Mr. Howland.

The interview then terminated, and the following correspondence took place:

No. 2.—Hon. John A. Macdonald to Hon. George Brown.

QUEBEC, August 4, 1865.

MY DEAR SIR,—Immediately after our conversation, the heads of which we have reduced to writing, I obtained His Excellency's permission to propose to you that Mr. Cartier, as being the leader of the ministerial majority of Lower Canada in parliament, should assume the position of Prime Minister, vacated by the death of Sir Etienne Taché, the other members of the administration continuing to hold their position and offices as before. All the Lower Canadian members of the council assent to this proposition, so do Mr. Campbell and myself; and I am sure I can also speak for Mr. Solicitor-General Cockburn, who is now absent.

May I request the favour of an early reply.

Believe me, my Dear Sir, yours faithfully,

HON. GEO. BROWN. JOHN A. MACDONALD.

No. 3.—*Hon. George Brown to Hon. John A. Macdonald.*

QUEBEC, August 4, 1865.

MY DEAR SIR,—I have received your letter of this afternoon, inviting me to retain my present position in a government to be formed under the premiership of Mr. Cartier. In reply I have now to state, after consultation with Messrs. Howland and McDougall, that we can only regard this proposition as one for the construction of a new government, in a manner seriously affecting the security heretofore held by the liberal party. Anxiously desirous as we are, however, that nothing should occur at this moment to jeopardize the plans of the coalition government on the constitutional question, we cannot assume the responsibility of either accepting or rejecting it without consultation with our political friends. This I am prepared to do without any delay, and to that end it will be necessary that I have clearly stated in writing the basis on which Mr. Cartier proposes to construct the new government.

I am, my Dear Sir, yours truly,
GEO. BROWN.

HON. JOHN A. MACDONALD.

No. 4.—*Hon. John A. Macdonald to Hon. George Brown.*

QUEBEC, Saturday, 5th August, 1865.

MY DEAR SIR,—I regret to learn from your note of yesterday that you cannot assume the responsibility, without first consulting your political friends, of either accepting or rejecting the proposition that Mr. Cartier should be placed at the head of the government in the stead of the late Sir Etienne Taché, with the understanding that the rest of the council should retain their present offices and positions under him. I have conferred with Mr. Cartier on the subject, and we agree that, at this late hour, it would be highly inexpedient to wait for the result of this consultation.

Parliament is to assemble on Tuesday next, and in our opinion it would greatly prejudice the position of the government as well as the future prospects of the great scheme in which we are all engaged, if we met parliament with the administration in an incomplete state, and therefore with no fixed policy.

I have His Excellency's permission to state his concurrence in this view, and his opinion that the public interests require the immediate reconstruction of the ministry.

Under these circumstances, and to prevent the possibility of the scheme for the confederation of British North America receiving any injury from the appearance of disunion among those who coalesced for the purpose of carrying it into effect, Mr. Cartier and I, without admitting that there are any sufficient grounds for setting either of us aside, have agreed to propose that Sir Narcisse Belleau shall assume the position of First Minister and Receiver-General, *vice* Sir Etienne Taché ; that the position and offices of the other members of the executive council shall remain as before ; and that the policy of the government shall be the same as was laid before parliament in July, 1864, as the basis of the coalition which was then formed. His Excellency authorizes me to make this proposition, and expresses his desire for an early answer.

Believe me, my Dear Sir, yours faithfully,
JOHN A. MACDONALD.

HON. GEORGE BROWN.

No. 5.—*Hon. George Brown to Hon. John A. Macdonald.*

QUEBEC, 5th August, 1865.

MY DEAR SIR,—Your note of this afternoon was handed to me by Col. Bernard, and having communicated its contents to my colleagues, I now beg to state the conclusions at which we have arrived.

Without intending the slightest discourtesy to Sir Narcisse Belleau, we deem it right to remind you that we would not have selected that gentleman as successor to Sir Etienne Taché ; but as he is the selection of Mr. Cartier and yourself, and as we are, equally with you, desirous of preventing the scheme for the confederation of British America receiving injury from the appearance of disunion among us, we shall offer no objection to his appointment.

I think, however, it will be necessary that Sir Narcisse Belleau shall have stated to him, and shall accept, in more distinct terms than you have indicated, the policy on which our coalition now rests. It is quite right that the basis of June, 1864, should be stated as the basis still, but he should also clearly understand the modification of that agreement, rendered necessary by succeeding events, and which was ratified by Sir Etienne Taché in March, 1865. The agreement of June, 1864, was as follows : " The government are prepared to pledge themselves to bring in a measure next session for the purpose of removing existing difficulties by introducing the federal principle into Canada, coupled with such provisions as will permit the Maritime Provinces and the North-West Territory to be incorporated into the same system of government. And the government will seek, by sending representatives to the Lower Provinces and to England, to secure the assent of those interests which are beyond the control of our own legislation, to such a measure as may enable all British North America to be united under a general legislature based upon the federal principle."

Sir Narcisse Belleau should understand that occurrences in the Maritime Provinces unfortunately prevented this agreement from being carried out, so far as regards time ; that it became necessary to consider what course ought to be pursued in consequence of these occurrences ; and that we came to an agreement that we should earnestly strive for the adoption of the scheme of the Quebec conference, but should we be unable to remove the objections of the Maritime Provinces in time to present a measure at the opening of the session of 1866 for the completion of the confederation scheme, we would then present to parliament, and press with all the influence of government, a measure for the reform of the constitutional system of Canada, as set forth in the above agreement of June, 1864.

I remain, my Dear Sir, yours truly,

GEO. BROWN.

HON. JOHN A. MACDONALD.

No. 6.—*Hon. John A. Macdonald to Hon. George Brown.*

QUEBEC, August 7, 1865.

MY DEAR SIR,—Sir Narcisse Belleau returned from the country yesterday, and I am happy to inform you that he has, though with great reluctance, acceded to the request of Mr. Cartier and myself, and accepted the position of First Minister, with the office of Receiver-General.

He accepts the policy of the late government, as stated in your note of Saturday to me, and adopts it as that which will govern his administration.

This policy will of course be announced in both Houses of parliament as soon as possible.

Believe me, faithfully yours,

JOHN A. MACDONALD.

HON. GEO. BROWN.

CHAPTER XVII.

Mr. Brown Advocates the Acquisition of the North-West Territory.—Withdrawal from the Government.—Confederation Accomplished.

Parliament met the day after the ministerial negotiations were completed for a brief session, or half session, of forty-one days. At the beginning of the session the report of the deputation of ministers to England, already alluded to, was submitted, with accompanying dispatches from Mr. Cardwell. Next to the all-absorbing question of confederation, Mr. Brown placed the annexation of the North-West Territory to Canada. An arrangement was finally made to accomplish this purpose, which was afterwards carried out. For twenty years he had steadily urged the vast importance to Canada of the acquisition of the northern and western territories, so long held in the hands of a grasping monopoly. For many years a portion of the Canadian press made light of the representations of Mr. Brown and the *Globe*. The company industriously circulated the impression that these territories were valuable chiefly as a hunting ground, and comparatively few people had any knowledge of the country. Fewer still had any faith in it as a valuable one, for actual and close settlement, beyond the banks of the Red River. For many years the late Sir George Cartier and his friends resolutely opposed all attempts to open up these regions for settlement, on the pitiful plea that its development would add to the political power of Ontario. The adoption of the federal system at once removed all petty objections to the immediate acquirement of these western lands, which are yet to add so much to the wealth of Canada. Mr. Brown, all through his agitation for the opening up of the North-West, derived much assistance from Mr. Isbester, of London, formerly of the North-West, to whom Canada is largely indebted for assistance in this matter. On the day parliament was prorogued Mr. Brown met with the other members of what was called the " confederate council," formed at the instance of the Imperial government, of delegates from all the provinces, for the consideration of commercial treaties. At this meeting certain resolutions were passed relating to trade with the West Indies and South America, the appointment of a commission to these countries, and another to Washngton, all abortive in the end.

From the period when the discussions in this council terminated, there is no doubt that Mr. Brown felt his position irksome. The dispute regarding Sir E. P. Taché's successor had not improved the feeling of latent hostility towards Mr. Brown, which existed with Mr. Macdonald and some other members of the cabinet. The new Premier was a weak and vain man, totally unfit to hold the balance between men much his superior in mental power and political experience. Sir N. Belleau was, in fact, quite ignored by Mr. Macdonald. When Mr. Brown resigned it was Mr. Macdonald, not the Premier, who invited Mr. Howland to take Mr. Brown's place, so the nominally Tory leader nominated the new reform leader, as he after nominated Sir Francis Hincks to succeed Mr. Howland. Mr. Macdonald was not an ardent advocate for the constitutional changes soon to be inaugurated, and he adopted the new policy, not because he loved it, but because it afforded the most convenient, if not the only, method of retaining office, and the most likely to break the power of the liberal party by the gradual absorption of its members who might, for strictly coalition purposes, enter the spider's "parlour." There was no hope of influencing Mr. Brown, but something might be hoped from the other members, and, as a matter of fact, the other members were swallowed up and remained in the Tory family. The constant effort to obtain party advantages on the one side had to be borne by the other and weaker side, necessarily with impatience. "As streams "their channels deeper wear" so, in this instance, did the steady political attrition daily render his position more unpleasant. It was therefore with a sense of relief that he felt bound, a few weeks after the confederate council adjourned, to adopt such decided views on the question of reciprocity with the United States, against the views of his colleagues, as to render his resignation necessary. This was the immediate cause of his resignation. During Mr. Brown's absence from Ottawa on public business, Messrs. Galt and Howland were sent to Washington, and were negotiating there with the committee of ways and means. The ministers subsequently agreed to accept a scheme of concurrent legislation for the interchange of commodities instead of a treaty. Commercial intercourse by reciprocal legislation would inevitably derange our trade relations with the United States. Stability is an element that cannot be dispensed with in commerce, and so Mr. Brown considered. There can be no doubt, however, that Mr. Brown felt a personal slight was offered him when Mr. Howland was sent with Mr. Galt on a mission to promote reciprocity—when Mr. Howland, who was not a member of the confederate council on commercial treaties, was sent on such a mission, although Mr. Brown and Mr. Galt were the members of that council.

Mr. Brown felt that in leaving the government then he was not jeopardizing the confederation scheme. To use his own words, he thought "that confederation had even then reached that point where "no danger of its failure need be apprehended." It was true the great question had reached such a stage, but it is equally true that some important changes were afterwards made, and action in other matters adverse to the liberal party taken, which his presence would probably have prevented. Still, the resignation was not only justifiable but unavoidable. Strenuous efforts were made by some of his colleagues to induce him to remain. The following letter was sent by Mr. Cartier :

EXECUTIVE COUNCIL CHAMBER,
OTTAWA, 19th Dec., 1865.

MY DEAR BROWN,—I have just called at your hotel with Campbell), with a view to have with you a friendly interview. We were very sorry and much disappointed to find that you were out. Both of us left our cards. We intend calling again this afternoon in the hope of being more successful. If perchance you happen to be in when this note reaches you, be kind enough to send me word that you are at your hotel. I hope, and every one of your colleagues hope, that after a friendly interview you will be induced to reconsider your present intention.

Believe me, my dear Brown, your devoted colleague,
(Signed),   G. E. C.

HON. GEO. BROWN.

To this letter Mr. Brown sent the following reply :

RUSSELL HOUSE, 19th Dec.

MY DEAR CARTIER,—I have received your kind note, and think it right to state frankly at once that the step I have taken cannot be revoked. The interests involved are too great. I think a very great blunder has been committed in a matter involving the most important interests of the country, and that the Order in Council you have passed endorses that blunder and authorizes persistence in it . . . I confess I was much annoyed at the personal affront offered me, but that feeling has passed away in view of the serious character of the matters at issue, which casts all personal feeling aside.

I desire to leave you in perfect harmony. I shall, of course, place in writing my grounds of resignation, but seeing the prejudicial effect their present publication might have on the negotiations, I propose that no reason be given for my resignation until the reciprocity question is settled one way or other. I propose to state in to-morrow's *Globe* that my resignation has occurred from a grave difference in the cabinet, in which I stand alone on an important public question ; that the explanations will be given in parliament in due time, and that it would be inexpedient for the public interests that they should be given sooner. I make this suggestion believing it the best thing for the public interest, *and on that ground alone ;* but any other proper course of procedure I am ready to adopt at the wish of my late colleagues.

In conclusion, let me say that if you stick to the compact you made with me when Sir Narcisse came into the government, my being out of the government will not change my course in the slightest, and that you will have my best aid in carrying out the constitutional changes we were pledged to.

Believe me, my dear Cartier, faithfully yours,

GEO. BROWN.

HON. G. E. CARTIER.

OTTAWA, 19th Dec., 1865.

MY DEAR BROWN,—I feel very sorry at your telling me that this step you have taken cannot be revoked. Whatever might be, at this moment, the strength of your determination, I flatter myself that after a friendly interview with you, Campbell and myself, this evening, you might be induced to change your mind. Mr. Campbell happens to be at the same hotel with you; arrange with him the time and place at which we may meet after dinner; Campbell will let me know when and where, and I will not fail to hasten to the rendezvous. Until we see you try and bring your mind to a listening mood. I must frankly say, that if unfortunately you cannot be induced to retrace the step you have taken, the terms and mode you suggest to make known your resignation, by a telegram to the *Globe*, are the most consistent with the public interests. The same announcement will have to be made by us. Allow me to say to you that whatever may be the result of our interview this evening, I will always feel very thankful to you for the patriotic and generous sentiments you are so kind to express in your note to me.

Believe me, my dear Brown, yours very truly,

GEORGE ET. CARTIER.

HON. GEO. BROWN.

The personal interview with Messrs. Cartier and Campbell did not affect the decision Mr. Brown had arrived at. To use his own words, he stood alone; Mr. McDougall was not in Canada, and even had he been it is more than probable he would not have stood by his leader in resignation; Mr. Howland had committed himself to the policy of the government on the reciprocity question, and there was a possible danger ahead of his getting himself committed to a perpetuation of the coalition after the cause and justification for its existence had passed away.

As already stated, Mr. Brown entered the coalition government reluctantly, and only on the urgent representation of a party caucus. That the circumstances were such as justified a coalition of political parties no one will doubt, unless indeed it be affirmed that no circumstances will justify such a movement. That there were strong reasons to be urged for his entering the government as leader of the Upper Canada liberals cannot be denied. He was the originator of the revolutionary movement just commenced. The strongest man in the cabinet, Mr. John A. Macdonald, only accepted the proposed policy as an immediate political necessity. He was opposed to a federal union, and made no secret of his preference for a legislative union. It was therefore feared that, if Mr. Brown, with two strong colleagues, were not in the cabinet, the opposing power would render the federative system about to be adopted more or less incomplete, with a view to an early return to the other system, which was then abandoned. He felt himself the greatest repugnance to joining the government, and this feeling was shared by his most intimate friends, but the force of the reasons on the opposite side were at last admitted and acted upon. One prominent member of the assembly, now dead, wrote to Mr. Brown

as follows : "How can you hope to secure the settlement of the con-
"stitutional questions without your own personal participation in the
"preliminary and advanced stages of the negotiation. The negotia-
"tion must go on during recess and session, 'hail, rain, or shine.'
"But you, unless a minister, cannot be on the spot, cannot enter the
"council chamber—cannot, in short, speak, think or act for yourself,
"unless you are a member of the government."

The general feeling amongst liberals was one of pleasure that their
leader had retired from a position which was by them regarded with
more or less dislike from the first. The promise made by Mr. Brown
to Mr. Cartier, to give the government his "best aid in carrying out
"the constitutional changes" if they adhered to the compact, was religiously kept. He gave the ministry his full support in getting the address
through the House.

The government did not, however, adhere to the determination
formerly arrived at, to avoid any unnecessary legislation which could
place any section of the combined forces in a false position, or force
them to divide. Legislation on banking, the tariff, and other questions, which forced Mr. Brown to oppose the government, was proposed at the ensuing session. His intention was that as soon as the
Confederation Act became law the two parties should resume their
normal position, and that the general election which must be held
would determine which party should succeed to power for the first
parliamentary term. The existing administration of Canada would
necessarily, so far as the provinces of Quebec and Ontario were concerned, have the organization of the local governments in their hands,
as well as the provisional arrangements for the Dominion, though nominally all this might be supposed to be done after the first day of July,
1867. That administration might now be said to be conservative,
though there was a nominal representation of the reform side still
in it, and the determination of these representatives to remain in
Sir John Macdonald's government only realized previous apprehensions. Some reformers thought that Mr. Brown should have made an
effort to remain in the government until the time came for the inauguration of the new system, to guard the interests of his political
friends. Much might be said in favour of his doing so, since he had
consented at all to enter a coalition government by those who urged
that step. Those who were behind the scenes knew that this would
have been a matter of extreme difficulty, and the great mass of the
liberal party never liked the coalition even for the special purpose in
view, and were glad when Mr. Brown was constrained to leave it by a
difference with his colleagues on another subject. Had his reform
colleagues left it promptly when its work was done, probably little
harm would have been done by their remaining after he left. As

it was, they became members of Mr. Macdonald's ministry, thereby owning his leadership, making the pitiful and sham plea, that they remained to secure the safety of the union and set the "new machine" working ; and the little influence they possessed, when thrown into the Tory scales, sufficed to cost the liberal party a number of constituencies. The first day of July, 1867, saw the great reform accomplished for which Mr. Brown had toiled so many years, and saw also the conservatives who opposed it to the last now reaping the fruit of their opponent's labour.   Thenceforward Mr. Macdonald would be able to boast that he was the father of confederation, on the same ground that he boasted of carrying the measure to secularize the clergy reserve lands.   He strongly opposed both measures, on principle, as long as it was possible to do so, and then joined the men who initiated and carried forward the movement of both, and declared the work was all his own. Having no great work of his own to boast about, he bravely plucks the laurel from the brows of the actual combatants and real victors, and fastens it on his own head.

CHAPTER XVIII.

MR. BROWN'S WORK IN ACHIEVING RELIGIOUS EQUALITY AND COLONIAL UNION.—CORRESPONDENCE WITH DR. RYERSON.

Although not in office, no one rejoiced more over the accomplishment of confederation than Mr. Brown. No political objects lay nearer his heart than the union of all the British provinces and perfect religious equality. Both objects were now accomplished. No church could lay claim to any superiority in the eye of the law ; no man could say that he was not represented in parliament. Every one could feel proud of being a citizen of a new colonial nation, about to work out its destiny in copartnership with the motherland. To use Mr. Brown's eloquent words : " The history of old Canada, with its contracted " bounds and limited divisions of Upper and Lower, East and West, " has been completed, and this day a new volume has been opened ; " New Brunswick and Nova Scotia uniting with Ontario and Quebec " to make the history of a greater Canada, already extending from the " ocean to the head waters of the great lakes, and destined ere long to " embrace the larger half of the North American continent from the " Atlantic to the Pacific. Let us gratefully acknowledge the hand of " the Almighty disposer of events in bringing about this result, preg- " nant with so important an influence on the conditions and destinies " of the inhabitants of these provinces, and of the teeming millions " who in ages to come will people the Dominion from ocean to ocean, " and give it its character in the annals of time. Let us acknowledge " too, the sagacity, the patriotism, the forgetfulness of selfish and " partisan considerations, on the part of our statesmen, to which under " Providence are due the inception of a project of a British American " confederation, and the carrying of it to a successsful issue. Without " much patient labour, a disposition to make mutual concessions, and " an earnest large minded willingness to subordinate all party interests to " the attainment of what would be for the lasting welfare of the whole " people of British America, the result we celebrate this day would " never have been achieved. It has taken just three years to accom- " plish, not certainly an unreasonable period of time for a work of such " magnitude."

Mr. Brown might indeed say that, chiefly by his own labour, the work of his life had been accomplished. Deeply attached to the mother country as a matter of interest as well as sentiment, neither the blunders of British governors or colonial ministers, nor the ridiculous assumptions of leaders of the governing class at home, that colonists were unequal to the task of working responsible government, for a moment shook his ardour for the continuance of good relations with the empire, or his faith in the possibility of the permanence of a union mutually beneficial. He felt that, with a central government possessing wider powers and more extensive application, the chances of any collision were more remote ; that the desire to interfere in strictly American business, not involving the interests of the empire, would be reduced to a minimum. As an Ontario citizen he frequently referred with great satisfaction to the freedom of action obtained by the provinces. Ontario could now, unhampered by the less progressive province, take an independent course in developing the vast resources of the country, and adjust taxation to suit its own interests. The immediate acquisition of the North-West Territories, to attain which he had done so much, he looked forward to with great pleasure, as affording a large and almost limitless field for the enterprise of Canadians to fully develop. The removal of matters relating to education from the domain of Dominion political discussion, and the limitation of the powers of local governments to maintain the systems of education as they existed at the time of the union, so far as sectarian schools were concerned, was peculiarly welcome to Mr. Brown, who had at one time incurred some odium in one quarter for the strong ground he had always taken in favour of a non-sectarian system. This was one of the questions he was bound to deal with and settle when he formed his government in 1858. It was one of the difficult points which had to be dealt with in the confederation compact. The settlement might not be exactly all that he desired, or that his opponents on the education question demanded, but it was loyally accepted by all at the time as a fair compromise. The effects of the long and sometimes bitter controversy did not, however, at once disappear. Some disputes were afterwards brought before the Dominion parliament, and some local irritation prevailed for a time in some provinces. In Ontario the last incident in that connection occurred in a correspondence between Mr. Brown and Dr. Ryerson. The controversy respecting Lord Metcalfe's struggle for absolutism necessarily involved sharp comment from the *Globe* on Dr. Ryerson's course as his principal—we will not say defender, but apologist. The disputes concerning the establishment of separate schools, which continued for many years, also resulted, ultimately, in the *Globe* blaming Dr. Ryerson for allowing himself to be made the instrument in ministers' hands in extending and perpetuating a system which he had frequently denounced as unsound ; and charging him with being substantially rewarded by the minister for yielding when principle, opinions and duty counselled him to resist. An article in the *Globe* of December 8th, 1858, reviewing the question and the superintendent's various opinions on it, provoked a lengthy reply from Dr. Ryerson, addressed to Mr. Brown personally. Mr. Brown, while not admitting the authorship of the article, replied in person ; both letters were published in the same number of the *Globe*. This reply was a severe one, but as the severity consisted chiefly in references to former expressions of opinions by Dr. Ryerson, and in references to questions of fact which had transpired in the committees of parliament, the doctor had no special ground of complaint. This was the only occasion on which Mr. Brown was personally brought into contact with Dr. Ryerson, and that was caused by the doctor addressing him in person, and introducing matter which had no connection with the subject of separate schools, such as accusing Mr. Brown with forming a political alliance with Thomas D'Arcy McGee. The chief superintendent was bold enough, while at the head of the school system, to express himself freely on political topics and even to publish electioneering pamphlets. He was a hard hitter, but preferred to give blows rather than take them; he was never known to turn the other cheek to the smiter. Nevertheless, o impatient was he of contradiction, that he was disposed to regard those who did controvert his opinions, and did so in decided and severe terms, as personal enemies. An acknowledgment of his admitted services in the cause of education, to use the language of Mr. Brown's letter, would not alone satisfy the pugnacious superintendent. An amusing proof of this disposition was shown in the terms of a letter he wrote to Mr. Brown in 1868; which, however, while showing the disposition referred to, was tempered by an offer of forgiveness. The following are copies of the letter and Mr. Brown's reply, which are published to show the views held by Mr. Brown of the *Globe's* battles with Dr. Ryerson :

Toronto, March 24, 1868.

To the Hon. George Brown.

Dear Sir,—I desire on this, the 65th anniversary of my birth, to assure you of my hearty forgiveness of the personal wrongs which I think you have done me in past years, and of my forgetfulness of them, so far at least as involves the least unkindness or unfriendliness of feeling.

To express free and independent opinions on the public acts of public men ; to animadvert severely upon them, when considered unavoidable, is both the right and duty of the press ; nor have I ever been discourteous or felt any animosity towards those who have condemned my official acts or denounced my opinions. Had I considered that you had done nothing worse in regard to myself, I should have felt and acted differently from what I have done in regard to you—the only public man in Canada with whom I have not been on speaking and personally friendly terms. But while I wish in no way to influence your judgment or proceedings in relation to myself, I beg to say that I cherish no other than those feelings of good-will towards you with which I hope to—as I soon must—stand before the Judge of all the earth, imploring as well as granting forgiveness for all the wrong deeds done in the flesh.

Yours very sincerely.
(Signed,)   E. RYERSON.

The following reply was sent by Mr. Brown. The writer is not aware whether it was followed up by any further correspondence.

TORONTO, 24th March, 1868.

SIR,—I have received your letter of this day and note its contents. I am entirely unconscious of any "personal wrong" ever done you by me, and had no thought of receiving "forgiveness" at your hands. What I have said or written of your public conduct or writings has been dictated solely by a sense of public duty, and has never, I feel confident, exceeded the bounds of legitimate criticism, in view of all attendant circumstances. What has been written of you by others in the columns of the *Globe* has been always restrained within the limits of fair criticism towards one holding a position of public trust.

As to your personal attacks upon myself—those who pursue the fearless course of a public journalist and politician, as I have done for a quarter of a century, cannot expect to escape abuse and misrepresentation, and assuredly your assaults on me have never affected my course towards you in the slightest degree. Your series of letters printed in the *Leader* newspaper some years ago were not, I am told, conceived in a very Christian spirit. But I was ill at the time they were published, and have never read them. Your dragging my name into your controversy with the Messrs. Campbell, in a matter with which I had no concern whatever, was one of those devices unhappily too often resorted to in political squabbles to be capable of exciting more than momentary indignation.

I am, Sir,
Your most obedient servant,
GEORGE BROWN.

REV. DR. RYERSON, Toronto.

CHAPTER XIX.

The Reform Convention of 1867.—Resolution of Thanks to Mr. Brown.—Mr. Brown's Reply.

The near approach of the day on which the new system was to be put in operation necessarily caused some anxiety in Mr. Brown's mind. As leader of the liberal party, he was desirous of securing joint, harmonious action at the coming elections. As on two former occasions, he desired to accomplish this object by full consultation with the party. He accordingly issued a call for a convention of reformers, through the Reform Association Committee, on the 13th June, 1867, to meet at Toronto on the 27th June; the executive committee first communicating with and obtaining the approval of members of parliament and candidates, as well as other local associations.

The object to be attained was briefly stated: "To rejoice over the "great success attending their past labours, and to adopt measures "for securing the correction of the abuses so long deplored by the "reform party, and for the infusion of those sound reform principles "into the daily administration of public affairs, to secure which the "constitutional changes now achieved were so long and earnestly "laboured for. . . . For consultation and friendly intercourse "amongst prominent men of the party; and to afford an opportunity "of consolidating the party and harmonizing the views of those who "were temporarily estranged by the events of late years."

The response to the proposal was cordial all over Ontario, and on the appointed day about 650 leading men from all quarters met in Toronto. In this magnificent gathering Mr. Brown took the greatest possible interest, though he made no attempt to control its proceedings. It was his desire at this time to retire from Parliament, if this could be accomplished. One gentleman, in a brief speech at the convention, expressed a fear that it was called "to make one man the leader of the "reform party without consideration." Mr. Brown, in presenting the report of a committee, of which he was chairman, a few minutes afterwards, alluded to that remark as follows: He said "he scorned "the imputation. He stood here at the end of twenty-five years "service to the reform party, and he defied any man to show the first "act of selfishness of which he had ever been guilty with reference "to that party. He defied any man to show one word that had ever "crossed his lips, as the representative of the people—one motion

" he ever made—one speech he ever delivered—one vote he ever
" gave—which was not in harmony with the principles of the reform
" party of Upper Canada. So far from there being any ground for
" that imputation, one great cause of this convention being called was
" that he might deliver up his trust to the members of the reform
" party of Upper Canada, and that they should start with the new
" machinery in a position, in respect of unanimity and distinctiveness
" of purpose, at least equal to that it occupied when he first took the
" responsibility of leading the reform ranks. It was unfortunate that
" there were some reformers who took up these ideas of the conserva-
" tive press who, when they could not attack a man because of his
" votes and speeches, took hold of these flimsy things, ' Oh! George
" ' Brown wants to be the dictator of his party.' And it seemed as
" if some reformers, by hearing this so constantly repeated in the
" Tory press, really fancied there was some foundation for it. He
" thought if any answer were necessary to be given to all this trash,
" it was to be found in the fact that he gave his vote in the executive
" council that there should be a meeting of the representatives of the
" people throughout the country, to take the responsibility off the
" hands of individuals of declaring what were the principles and
" measures on which the party should go to the country." These
remarks were received with the greatest applause and evidences of
sympathy. The silly and stale accusation implied in the speech that
Mr. Brown replied to had the effect of evoking their enthusiam for
and confidence in him which all popular gatherings manifested as occasions occurred.

At a subsequent stage of the proceedings this feeling was more
strongly shown, when Mr. Currie moved the following resolution, with
a view to induce Mr. Brown to withdraw from his declared purpose
of not entering parliament again : " That this convention cannot sepa-
" rate without expressing to the Hon. George Brown the gratitude of
" the reform party, of which he has been so long the able leader, for
" his services to the people of Canada, and also the earnest hope that
" he will reconsider his intention of retiring from parliamentary life,
" and accept a position in the legislature of the country."

When the chairman put this motion to the meeting all the people
sprang to their feet and gave utterance to their feelings by prolonged
cheering, showing how very heartily the whole convention appreciated
Mr. Brown's past labours and desired their continuance in parliament.
He replied briefly, apparently being taken by surprise, and so over-
powered by emotion, as to be unable for some time to control his
feelings. The following extracts from his speech have some public
interest, apart even from their connection with himself :

I hope the members of the convention will grant me their indulgence in the position in which I find myself. I have had but little sleep for several successive nights, and was totally unprepared for the high honour you have done me by the passing of this resolution. But I think it is due to you, and an act of justice to myself, that I should explain the reasons which induced me to decide on retiring from parliamentary life. There were many reasons which, in my opinion, made it desirable, not only on personal but on public grounds, that I should adopt this course. One of these was very strong, and was the reason on which I mainly based it. I entered parliamentary life, in 1851, strongly against my will, inasmuch as I entertained the conviction that the editorship of a leading party journal was, to some extent, incompatible with holding a leading position as a member of the legislature. And I have since learned by many years' experience that the incompatibility is vastly stronger then I had conceived. So strongly have I felt this, that years ago I would have resigned my position in parliament, but that I feared that my doing so might have injured the cause of constitutional reform for which I had struggled so long. As a general rule. the sentiments of the leader of a party are only known from his public utterances on public occasions. If a wrong act is committed by an opponent, or by a friend, he may simply shrug his shoulders and say it is very bad, but no one need know his opinion of the transaction unless it is forced on the consideration of the legislature. But this is not the case with the public journalist. If true to his country, and true to his position, he must speak out, and say wrong is wrong and right is right, no matter whether it offends friend or foe. You have often seen attacks on myself, even by some portions of the reform press, for my having acted firmly in this way. They say, " Mr. Brown has fiercely assailed public men ;" but I tell you, if the daily thoughts and the words daily uttered by other public men were written in a book, as mine have been, and circulated all over the country, there would have been a very different comparison from what now exists as between them and myself. I have been in the peculiar position of having a double duty to perform. If I had been simply the leader of a party, and had not controlled a public journal, such things would not have been left on record. I might have passed my observations in the confidence of private life, and nothing more would have been heard of them. But. as a journalist, it was necessary I should speak the truth before the people, no matter whether it helped my party or not ; and this, of course. reflected on the position of the party. How. often have I had several political friends candidates for the same office—all equally urgent for the support of the journal under my control—and totally unwilling to believe that the candidate supported was the right man in the right place, and best entitled to the office. Frequently, when I have seen a man doing a wrong thing, I may have felt sorry for him as an individual ; I may have known the circumstances of temptation under which he was placed, and as a man have felt deeply for him. But as a journalist, I had but one duty to the public to discharge, and that was to maintain a high standard of political morality. And I do not doubt that, when the political history of this country comes to be written, and justice is done to me, as I am sure it will be, it will be seen that when I have been compelled to denounce the conduct of public men, it was because the public interests were at stake— and that the verdict of public opinion has sustained me in every case. Consequently, I have long felt very strongly that I had to choose one position or the other—that of a leader in parliamentary life, or that of a monitor in the public press. And the latter has been my choice, being probably more in consonance with my ardent temperament, and at the same time, in my opinion, more influential ; for I am free to say that, in view of all the grand offices that are now talked of—governorships, premierships, and the like—I would rather be editor of the *Globe*, with the hearty confidence of the great mass of the people of Upper Canada, than have the choice of them all. No one will fancy that I claim for a moment that in my long career there have not been many mistakes. Human nature is liable to err, and I have a full share of human frailties. But of this I am quite sure, that when the twenty-five volumes of the *Globe* are examined to find what has been the political history of this country during the last quarter of a century—and a better record of that history does not exist than is to be found in those volumes—it will be found that fair play between man and man, justice and earnestness with regard to all public questions, and an ardent desire to serve the people of Canada, have marked that record from the beginning to the end. In this resolution which has been read to me, I find the confirmation of that which has been my stay and comfort during many years of arduous political contest, when we were hoping almost against hope, when we hardly dared to hope that we would be able to accomplish our great ends within any reasonable period. During those contests, it was this which sustained the gallant band of reformers who so long struggled for popular rights, that, abused as we might be, subjected to reproach and slander as we might be, we had this consolation, that we could not go anywhere among our fellow-countrymen from one end of the country to the other—in Tory constituencies as well as in reform constituencies—without the certainty of receiving from the honest, intelligent yeomanry of the country—from the true, right-hearted, right-thinking people of Upper Canada who came out to meet us—the hearty grasp of the hand, and the heartfelt greeting that amply repaid the labour we had expended in their behalf. That is the highest reward I have hoped for in public life, and I am sure that no man who earns that reward will ever in Upper Canada have occasion to speak of the ingratitude of the people. I have received, at the hands of the yeomen of Upper Canada, far more kindness than my services deserved, and far more than any public man could have a right to expect. But I had another urgent cause for retiring from parliamentary life. You are aware that daily journalism is no light task. A daily journalist has to consume the midnight oil, not only from year to year and from month to month, but from day to day. Seldom does he lay his head upon the pillow until the late hours of the morning ; and, with a near relative—who has for a number of years greatly lessened my labours, and taken many responsibilities off my hands—now in infirm health, it seemed to me impossible that I should think of continuing the burden of the two positions. I had looked forward to the triumph of representation by population as the day of my emancipation from parliamentary life, and now that it has come, I resolved to take advantage of it. But I am free to admit that what has now taken place—the announcement of this new coalition—this secession from our party—somewhat alters the case. Where work is to be done for the reformers of Canada, and for the people of Canada, I shall not shrink from it. And I am free to state what is the course I now intend to pursue. I think it is desirable that the members of parliament, and the candidates, who are present, as well as those not here who agree generally with the resolutions we have passed, should have communication together at the earliest moment, and that we should arrange for the political campaign on which we are about to enter. And if it shall be found, in the course of this communication among ourselves, that my services for a short while in parliamentary life can be of use to the party, I shall not refuse. At the same time, I repeat that my determination is not in the slightest degree altered. There is this further difficulty that I encounter in going into parliamentary life, and if my doing so can be dispensed with, I strongly desire that it should be. It is absolutely impossible that I could in any way take upon me an official position —and this was one of the reasons which made me think it exceedingly desirable that I should retire at once—that I might not sit in parliament in the way of those who would become leaders of the party when it assumed office. I thought it would not be just or generous to stand there as the leader of a party in opposition, taking, perhaps, some popularity away from others who might be called upon to assume the reins of office. But if there is work to be done, and a hard fight to be gone through, probably this can be arranged. We will have a communication with the representative men of the party, and whatever decision is arrived at, I am prepared to bow to their judgment. I again heartily thank the convention for the great compliment they have paid me. I value it above all the testimonials I have received in my public life.

CHAPTER XX.

MR. BROWN CONTESTS SOUTH ONTARIO.—HIS BOW PARK FARM.— HIS INTEREST IN CONFEDERATION.

As the foregoing extracts show, Mr. Brown promised to reconsider his expressed intention of retiring from parliament. Several constituencies were at once offered for his acceptance, where the seat would be perfectly safe. His chivalric disposition was shown in his acceptance of an invitation to contest the riding of South Ontario. This county, for various reasons, which need not be here discussed, had politically degenerated from being a strong reform constituency to be a very doubtful one. Mr. Brown's opponent was a strong local man, who had previously been elected on some pretensions to be more or less in sympathy with the liberals. He had now the full support of the government and the whole Tory party, as well as the local support which he would naturally command where he carried on an extensive business. The contest was a keen one on both sides, and resulted in Mr. Brown's defeat by a majority of 69.

His best friends strongly objected to his acceptance of the candidature in any weak constituency when perfectly safe ones were at his command ; but their remonstrances were overborne by his enthusiastic confidence in his ability to carry the contest to a successful issue. His exclusion from the first parliament of the Dominion was a public loss, and was deplored by not only his own political friends and followers, but by many who did not claim to be either. On the other hand, it afforded great satisfaction to the Tory leaders and the Tory press. One gentleman, aspiring to be a historian, and who occupied a seat in the House of Commons for a time as a member enjoying an official salary but having no cabinet office, had the bad taste, in his work on Confederation, to speak of Mr. Brown's defeat as "his suicide," and also wrote that "throughout the vast province of Ontario, in which he "had been wont to be a moving power, no constituency returned him." Mr. Gray knew—every one knew—that Mr. Brown could have made a selection from twenty constituencies had he so desired ; with his wonted bravery and patriotism he left the safe counties to be won by weaker men, and devoted himself to a brilliant attempt to win a county from the enemy. Mr. Gladstone pursued precisely the same course in accepting a nomination for Midlothian, a notoriously dangerous county for a liberal candidate ; he succeeded, Mr. Brown failed. Both leaders were bold, and both were imprudent, though Mr. Gladstone's friends took the precaution of electing him for another constituency; Mr. Brown's friends insisted on adopting the same course, but he refused his assent. There is no doubt Mr. Brown considered his parliamentary career teminated by this defeat, and equally little doubt that he intended, out of parliament, to take that part in public life for which he was so eminently fitted, in support of the principles he had so long struggled to maintain, and of the party he had so long led. The leadership which he had resigned in 1861 had never really been committed to other hands, and when he again appeared in parliament in 1863, he was tacitly acknowledged to be leader. After the election of 1867 no one was for some years formally chosen as leader, not indeed until after the general election of 1872, when Mr. Mackenzie was chosen to fill the vacant place. Mr. Brown very properly refrained from expressing any opinion, either personally or in the press, as to the choice of his successor, his opinion being that the selection rested in the hands of members of parliament.

After the general election in 1867, Mr. Brown, with his family, paid a visit of some months duration to Europe, but made no public appearance anywhere except at a reunion of the old students of his academical time, at the High School, Edinburgh. At this meeting he met many of his old college companions from all parts of the world. Some were in prominent positions in Australia; some were filling high offices in India; and many were amongst the prominent men of their native country. Mr. Brown afterwards often spoke with delight of this meeting, and the personal pleasure it afforded him; also of the healthy influence of the thorough, though severe, educational system of the school in which he had been trained for the active duties of life.

After his return to Canada Mr. Brown devoted much of his time to his Bow Park farm, where he had made great improvements, and commenced the formation of the short-horn herd of cattle which in latter years became so famous, and was deemed one of the finest in the world.

As in 1861, when defeated in Toronto, Mr. Brown had offers of several constituencies. He was not, however, desirous of remaining in parliament, and therefore resolved firmly, as he was defeated, to decline election elsewhere, at least for a time, or until circumstances should show an urgent reason or necessity for his reappearance there.

In a letter to a friend shortly after the election, he wrote as follows: " I am not a bit discouraged by the result of the elections, and " did not feel two minutes' chagrin at my own defeat. Our friends " behaved very generously to me. I had at once several offers to " make way for me—even Mr. —— and Mr. ——, on whom I had no " particular claim, wrote me—but I was too glad to be a free man " to think of accepting these kind offers. But if out of parliament

" definitively, I don't by any means intend to be out of public life,
" and will work for the ascendancy of my friends, federal and local,
" as cordially and enthusiastically as ever ; indeed, far more so, as I
" shall be entirely free from official responsibility."   Two years later
there was an opportunity afforded of obtaining a seat in the Commons.
In response to an inquiry whether he would allow his name to be used,
he wrote : " I have in no manner changed the views I expressed to
" you on a former occasion ; I have not the slightest desire or inten-
" tion of re-entering parliamentary life, and nothing but the most
" imperative party necessity would induce me to do so."   No further
effort was made to induce him to change his views and re-enter parliament.   Nor did he ever in after years attempt to control or influence
parliamentary proceedings as conducted by the liberals in opposition,
or in the government ; while always willing to give his opinion when
asked on any particular question, he never volunteered his advice.
His opinions of course received free utterance in the *Globe*, which was
more unfettered by reason of his absence from parliamentary leadership, though even there it was rare indeed that any articles were published which were calculated to inconvenience or discomfort those
who occupied his former position.

In farming generally he took great delight ; no recreation was to
him equal to a ramble over his magnificent farm, examining the crops
and animals.   The cultivation of high bred stock was to him a novel
undertaking, lacking, as he necessarily was, in the knowledge of the
breeds of animals, and the excellences of each class or family.   This
knowledge he soon acquired by his perseverance.   The steadily improving character of the farm at Bow Park and the stock of all kinds,
gave abundant evidence of the intimate knowledge the proprietor had
of the science of farming.   With all this, however, it took many years
to bring his fine short-horn herd to perfection, and of course it involved a heavy expenditure which could only be very gradually realized
again.   The farm, which he commenced to operate more as a recreation than as a serious business, gradually developed into a very large
undertaking, which it was evidently impossible for Mr. Brown to
manage alone, considering the extent of other business engagements.
This led to the formation, in 1875, of a joint stock company, under
the auspices of which the business has since then been conducted,
though Mr. Brown retained a large portion of the stock, and was
president of the company until his death.   No more enthusiastic
farmer could be found in Canada.   He was always delighted to meet
farmers at Bow Park, and go over it with them to see all that could be
seen ; many availed themselves of the privilege of examining freely
his system of farming and feeding, as well as the fine animals with
which he had stocked the now famous farm at very great expense.

The minutiæ of scientific farming was doubtless more attended to at the government model farm, but farming on an extensive scale, and thorough-bred stock-raising, could only be seen at Bow Park. That this was a public benefit of a large character no one can doubt; that it was not productive, in his time, of any adequate return to the enterprising projector, every one will regret. It is to be hoped, however, from recent appearances, that the company will now reap a golden harvest, as the result of embarking in an enterprise which has been so beneficial to Canada.

Mr. Brown, as the enthusiastic advocate of a political union of all the British American provinces and the consolidation of British power on the continent, was, very naturally, much pleased at the prospect of British Columbia, Prince Edward Island, and Newfoundland joining the confederate provinces, and he worked hard, by correspondence and personal intercourse with public men, from the two latter provinces especially, to promote their accession to the union. On one occasion he had a long interview with two Newfoundland public men which pleased him much, as he considered all obstacles to the union practically removed; meeting the writer shortly afterwards, he asked, "What " is the public event desired that would give you most satisfaction at " the present time ?" Not receiving an immediate reply, he asked if the complete consolidation of the confederacy, by the acquisition of Newfoundland at an early date, would not be the most pleasant event that could be looked for? On being answered that the pleasure would be qualified by the attendant conditions, he said scarcely any conditions could prevent him rejoicing over such a consummation. Similarly on another occasion, when some one suggested the expense of building the Intercolonial Railway as a serious condition to the union of the provinces, Mr. Brown replied that he would rather build six Intercolonial Railways than fail in the project. Of course this was only an exaggerated form of expression to convey his hearty advocacy of the new political movement. He fully believed that the time had come when political changes of some serious kind were inevitable; that concerted action from all the provinces in relation to colonial office management, and the foreign relations of the empire, where the North American colonies were chiefly or wholly concerned, would be difficult without a union of these provinces. He believed that the public men of the colonies were more likely to negotiate, under the Crown, in their own interests with certain foreign powers, and that the union of all the provinces would naturally carry with it an accession of power which could not be disregarded by any colonial secretary sitting in Downing Street, and therefore lessen the probabilities of any serious complications occurring between the imperial and colonial authorities. He, in common with all colonial statesmen who have had to arrange colonial business in

Downing Street, knew how incapable the average colonial secretary is to comprehend nice colonial questions, and how satisfied he is of the superiority of British ministers, even in matters where the colonist must necessarily be better informed. The North American colonies had now reached a stage of maturity which forbade any administration of their affairs from the colonial office other than that involved in its being the channel of communication between the provinces and the supreme authority. Their consolidation into one dominion, with a federal constitution and central authority, would, in Mr. Brown's opinion, add to their importance, and relieve all anxiety at home as to the course of events on this continent. Mr. Brown, in his speech on the confederation project, after pointing out its effects on general industrial pursuits and political importance, said : " I ask any member " of the House to say whether we will not, when thus united, occupy " a position in the eyes of the world, and command a degree of respect " and influence, that we never can enjoy as separate provinces ? . . . . " I am persuaded that this union will inspire new confidence in our " stability . . . it will raise the value of our public securities, it " will draw capital to our shores." His closing words in that memorable debate contained the following passage : " The future destiny of " these great provinces may be affected by the decision we are about " to give to an extent which, at this moment, we may be unable to " estimate ; but assuredly the welfare, for many years, of four mil- " lions of people hangs on our decision. Shall we then rise equal to " the occasion ? Shall we approach this discussion without partisan- " ship, and free from every personal feeling but the earnest resolution " to discharge conscientiously the duty which an overruling Providence " has placed upon us ? It may be that some among us will live to see " the day when, as the result of this measure, a great and powerful " people may have grown up in these lands—when the boundless " forests shall have given way to smiling fields and thriving towns— " and when one united government under the British flag shall extend " from shore to shore."

Mr. Brown himself lived to see the day he longed for. He saw the work of union all but fully accomplished ; only one colony, and that one the least important, choosing to maintain its isolated position. This was a measure of success which he scarcely ventured to hope for in 1864, when it seemed probable that federal relations would be established at first only between Upper and Lower Canada. It might be said that he was too enthusiastic in his anticipations of benefits from the new system. He had, however, an abiding faith in the capacity of the Canadian people for self-government, and, in common with political thinkers, he knew that union meant an increase of moral strength, and believed that the measure of success was prospectively greatly increased by the hearty adherence of all the provinces.

CHAPTER XXI.

LETTER TO THE ROMAN CATHOLIC COMMITTEE.

Early in 1871 Mr. Brown had some correspondence with prominent Roman Catholics in relation to their position politically in the province of Ontario. The controversies respecting separate schools and ecclesiastical corporations had resulted in a serious secession of Roman Catholics from the ranks of the reform party. Now that these matters of difference were all removed by the new constitution, many of both sides were desirous of reaching an understanding. The following letter was published on the 9th March, 1871, in response to a paper laid before Mr. Brown by the Roman Catholic committee to whom it was addressed :

To John O'Donohue, Patrick Hughes, J. D. Merrick, and Thomas Mc-Crosson, Esquires, a Committee acting on behalf of a Meeting of Prominent Catholics from all Sections of Ontario.

GENTLEMEN,—I have read with care the paper you have been good enough to place in my hands, with the request that I should reply to it in writing.

I am in no manner entitled to speak officially for the reformers of Ontario. At the convention of 1867 I voluntarily resigned the leadership of that party, and have not since then taken any action in that capacity. Mr. Alexander Mackenzie is now leader of the liberal party from Ontario in the House of Commons, and Mr Edward Blake is leader in the Ontario Assembly ; they have my most cordial confidence and support, and to them I refer you for an official answer to your questions.

I explained this verbally to you when you did me the honour to call upon me, but you still thought it desirable to have a reply from me, as one who took a prominent part in the agitation which in past years separated the great mass of the Roman Catholic body from the liberal ranks, and who has reliable personal knowledge of the feelings and sentiments of the reformers of Ontario. From this stand-point I have no objection to answer your queries. Indeed, I am glad you have given me an opportunity of doing so, and at the same time of vindicating the policy which the party I had so long the privilege of leading in parliament felt it their duty to inaugurate, and carried to a successful termination.

In what I shall say I trust no offence will be taken if I speak frankly and plainly as to matters of past history and the present situation. The action you and your co-religionists now take may affect most materially the future stability and prosperity of our young Dominion ; and it would be but petty statesmanship to conceal from ourselves either the prejudices that have been created in the past, or the principles of justice and equality on which alone a lasting reunion of all sections of the liberal party can be formed.

Will you pardon me for making another preliminary observation ? I am sure you did not mean to convey that it was either possible or desirable that the whole catholic vote of Ontario could be transferred to one political party. God, for His own wise purposes, has created us of different minds, so that, with equal intelligence and equal honesty of purpose, different men will come to totally different conclusions from the same premises ; and assuredly it would be most unwise and unjust to constrain catholics, or any others, to cast their votes in a manner contrary to their conscientious convictions. I quite understand that the entire scope of your present application is to enable you to lay before your catholic fellow-countrymen the principles and policy to be maintained by the liberal party of Ontario in the future, so that the large portion of them who hold reform principles, as contra-distinguished from conservative principles, may judge whether it is expedient for them to cast in their lot with the great liberal party.

In the early days of the political history of Upper Canada, the great mass of the Roman Catholics were earnest and reliable members of the reform party. They suffered from Downing Street rule, from family compactism, from a dominant Anglican church establishment, and from clergy reserves, rectories, and ecclesiastical disabilities, in common with the numerous protestant bodies who with them were insolently styled "dissenters ;" and they fought the battle of civil and religious liberty and equality side by side with their protestant fellow-reformers. And had Upper Canada remained as it then was, a separate province, they would, I doubt not, have fought the same battle up to the hour of its final triumph. The union of Upper and Lower Canada in 1841 was the commencement of a change. · The French Canadian element then came into the political field and gave the catholics a position of dominance they had not previously held. From 1843 (when Mr. Baldwin as leader of the Upper Canada reformers formed a political alliance with Mr. Lafontaine as leader of the French Canadians), up to the year 1850, the protestant and catholic reformers continued to act together harmoniously. The *Globe* was the recognized organ of the party in Upper Canada, and I remember with pleasure the intelligent and cordial manner in which the Irish catholics through these years sustained all liberal and progressive measures. We were then fighting the battle for responsible government in opposition to Sir Charles Metcalfe and his conservative advisers—which was closed triumphantly in the winter of 1847-48 by a grand success at the polls, and the complete establishment of the great reform for which we had so long and so earnestly contended.

Messrs. Baldwin and Lafontaine came into office in March, 1848 ; the reform party was all-powerful in both houses of parliament : and the reformers of Upper Canada had the right to expect that the principles and measures they (protestant and catholic alike) had contended for, and been taught by their leaders to expect, would now be carried into full operation. The French Canadian members of the cabinet and their supporters in parliament blocked the way. Not only were reformers refused that which had been promised for years, but principles and measures were urged or endorsed by the reform government in direct hostility to the views and feelings of the reformers of Upper Canada. A large section of the liberal party becamed alarmed, and remonstrated ; but without effect. Indignation and estrangement followed. The French Canadians felt their power and used it relentlessly ; a section of the Upper Canada reformers went into opposition, while another section adhered to the government, and the party became thoroughly disorganized.

Need I remind you of what followed? Although much less numerous than the people of Upper Canada, and contributing to the common purse hardly a fourth of the annual revenue of the united provinces, the Lower Canadians sent an equal number of representatives with the Upper Canadians to parliament, and by their unity of action obtained complete dominancy in the management of public affairs. Acting on the well-known adage

"*Nous avons l'avantage, profitons-en !*" the French Canadians turned the divisions among Upper Canadians to their own advantage in every possible way. Unjust and injurious legislation, waste and extravagance in every public department, increased debt and heavier taxation, were the speedy consequences, until the credit of the country was seriously imperilled.

A remedy had to be applied to this state of things ; and it had to be such a remedy as would overthrow the unjust dominancy of the Lower Canadians over Upper Canada affairs, and remove from the public arena as far as possible all such questions as excited strife and heartburning among our own people. That remedy was believed to be found, first, in the adoption of population as the basis of parliamentary representation, thereby securing to Upper Canada her just influence in the legislature ; and, second, in the entire separation of church and state, placing all denominations on a like footing, and leaving each to support its own religious establishments from the funds of its own people. The reform party became strongly impressed with the conviction that until these measures of reform were obtained, good government was impossible, and sectional and sectarian strife would continue to afflict the country. They as heartily believed that if legislation and the control over the public expenditures were placed by just representation in the hands of those who paid the taxes, and if the state were debarred from regarding the people in their sectarian character, but treated all alike without regard to their religious opinions, a day of solid prosperity and internal peace would dawn on Canada such as had not before been witnessed.

Acting on these strong convictions, and in the conscientious belief (rightly or wrongly entertained) that by no other measures could the end sought be permanently secured—the reform party entered on an organized agitation for a reformed system of representation, and for the sweeping away from the public arena of all sectarian issues. The men who led in that agitation fully comprehended the gravity of the responsibility they assumed, and the painful separations that it must entail ; but they were upheld by earnest belief in the absolute necessity of the course they were taking : and they looked forward with hope and pleasure to the day when their policy would be vindicated by the results it would achieve. In parliament and out of it, the agitation was prosecuted with all vigour. The injustice of the existing system of representation was attacked on all occasions, and the practical evils flowing from it were pressed on the public mind ; petitions for its reform were poured into parliament, and at every election throughout the land the hustings was made a battle-field for the promotion of the great end sought. At the same time, the most determined efforts were put forth for the final but just settlement of all those vexed questions by which religious sects were arrayed against each other, clergymen dragged as combatants into the political arena, religion brought into contempt, and opportunity presented to our French Canadian friends to rule us through our own dissensions. The clergy reserve injustice was assailed, the 57 rectories were exposed, the impolicy of separating the youth of our country, and studding the land with sectarian schools, was strongly enforced ; and the waste and impolicy of using the public funds for sectarian uses was firmly maintained and enforced. On all these and many similar questions we were met by the French Canadian phalanx in hostile array ; our whole policy was denounced in language of the strongest character, and the men who upheld it were assailed as the basest of mankind. We on our side were not slow in returning blow for blow, and feelings were excited among the catholics of Upper Canada that estranged the great bulk of them from our ranks.

But the cause advanced. Our annual motions for reformed representation got a stronger support every session, until hardly a candidate dared present himself for election without pledging himself to go for it. Our anti-sectarian motions were still more successful. The justice of them commended itself to the public mind, and one after another all these vexed questions found permanent solution and disappeared from parliamentary discussion. And I call your attention to this fact, that settled though some of these questions were in a very unsatisfactory fashion, the day of their settlement was the last of their existence as topics of debate. Not in a single instance was it proposed to rake their ashes from the tomb, or make the mode of their settlement, after the event, the subject of party warfare.

Need I remind you how, year after year. the reform party stuck to their great purpose ; and how, at last, by a party sacrifice having few parallels in party history, they won for the people of Upper Canada— protestant and catholic alike—that great measure of justice embodied in the Act of 1867. Under that Act the people of Ontario enjoy representation according to population ; they have entire control over their own local affairs ; and the last remnant of the sectarian warfare—the separate school question—was settled forever by a compromise that was accepted as final by all parties concerned.

I deny not that in this protracted contest words were spoken and lines were penned that had been better clothed in more courteous guise. But when men go to war they are apt to take their gloves off ; and assuredly if one side struck hard blows the other was not slow in returning them. And looking back on the whole contest, and the ends it has already accomplished, I do think every dispassionate person must confess that had the battle been ten times fiercer than it was, and the words spoken ten times more bitter than they were, the triumphant success that has attended the long agitation would have sunk all the evils attending it into utter insignificance. We have obtained our just share in the administration of the affairs of the Dominion ; we have obtained exclusive control over our provincial affairs ; we have banished sectarian discord from our legislative and executive chambers ; and we enjoy a degree of material prosperity, and have a degree of consideration for the religious views and feelings of each other, that no living man ever witnessed in Canada till now.

I claim that to accomplish these great ends was, all through our agitation, the avowed object for which we fought. I claim that the principles involved in our agitation were precisely those that the catholics of Canada held and firmly contended for in the olden time when they worked cordially in the liberal ranks. I repeat my conviction that, had it not been for the intrusion of French Canadian dictation in our affairs, the reform party might have remained intact until this day. And I ask those of you who can do so, to carry your minds back to the position held by catholics in times gone by, and say whether any other section of the people of Upper Canada has such good reason to rejoice in the banishment of sectarian issues from the political arena, and the perfect equality of all denominations now so firmly and so happily enjoyed, as have the catholics of Ontario.

There are tens of thousands of catholics throughout the province who can well remember the days when protestant and catholic reformers acted cordially together. They have had fifteen years trial of alliance with our opponents, and I ask them to say frankly how the position they have held, as hewers of wood and drawers of water for the high church and state Anglican party, compares with the just consideration they received when allied with us ? How many Irish catholics have been elected for conservative constituencies ? How much of the enormous patronage of the Crown in the past fifteen years has fallen into catholic hands ? What pretence of consideration has been shown to the prominent catholics of the province, except the honour of marching up to the polls and voting for Tory candidates ? Ay, and what disadvantages might not the catholics to this hour have been labouring under, had protestant reformers left them to the tender mercies of the men whom they are now striving to bolster up ?

As I have already said, I am in no official position to entitle me to speak for the reformers of Ontario ; but thirty years of journalism in close connection with that party, and many years of leadership in parliament, have given me a thorough knowledge of their principles, and feelings, and opinions; and I am persuaded I shall not err when I say that protestant reformers, with very trifling exceptions, would welcome with gladness the return of catholic reformers to their party, and that as they were treated in the olden time, so they would be treated now.   All the vexed questions that caused the separation have been settled and swept away, and now all are free to act together for the advancement and prosperity of our country, and to treat all men alike, without regard to their religious opinions.

I believe it is the universal feeling of protestant reformers throughout Ontario, now that French Canadian interference in our affairs has been brought to an end—now that the protestant majority is completely dominant in our province, and the catholics placed by their scattered position at disadvantage—that it is the incumbent duty of the reform party, dictated as well by their most cherished principles as by justice and good policy, that a full share of parliamentary representation according to their numbers, and generous consideration in all public matters, should be awarded to the catholic minority.   And they have shown their sincerity by placing Irish catholic reformers—not because they are catholics, but because they are good men and true all of them—as candidates for seats in the assembly in four most important constituencies, and with every prospect of success --with certainty of success should their fellow-catholic electors cast their votes in their favour.   This the reform party has done voluntarily, gladly, without condition, although a vast preponderance of the catholic electors will in all probability cast their votes in the coming contest in favour of our opponents and against our candidates.   I leave you to judge from this, how different your position as catholics would have been to-day, had we been able to bring forward liberal candidates in other constituencies where, from the strength of the catholic vote and its opposition to our candidates, we have been unable to make a move.   In the position you now occupy, you get but the little you can extort from the fears of those you serve ; but as members of the liberal party you would have all the influence and all the advantages that perfect equality and common interests can secure.

Now, don't mistake the drift of this paper.   I am not assuming to advise catholic reformers as to the course they should pursue in public affairs.   That is for them alone to judge and decide.   Neither am I seeking to cloak over past feuds or apologize for past occurrences.   The principles and measures my party contended for in the past I contend for still.   I glory in the justice and soundness of those principles and measures.   I am proud of the men who, amid long and bitter discouragement, stuck to the good cause until they carried it to victory—and I point with glad thankfulness to the banishment of religious jealousy and discord that so long rent our country, and to the peace and prosperity that now reign amongst us, as the undeniable fruits of the twenty years' conflict of the great reform party of Upper Canada.

I have written as I have done simply to show catholic reformers in plain language, from a reform point of view, how the separation between protestant and catholic liberals arose ; the great ends for which the agitation was carried on ; the signal success that has attended it ; and the entire settlement and removal by it of all these questions that barred the way to a reunion of the old reform party.   All I ask is that they shall forget for a few minutes whose name is attached to this paper, and read calmly what is written.   Let them blaze away at George Brown afterwards as vigorously as they please, but let not their old feuds with him close their eyes to the interests of their country, and their own interests as a powerful section of the body politic.   I am no longer in parliamentary life, and have no public favours to ask of anybody ; but I confess it is with no slight satisfaction I entertain the conviction that the day is near at hand, if indeed it has not already come, when even our catholic fellow-citizens will be ready to admit that the wisdom and patriotism of the policy of the reform party from 1854 to 1867 has been amply justified by the great results it has brought about.

I remain, Gentlemen, yours truly,

GEO. BROWN.

GLOBE OFFICE, Toronto, 9th March, 1871.

CHAPTER XXII.

Mr. Sandfield Macdonald's " Patent Combination."—The Elections of 1872.—Mr. Brown and Mr. Justice Wilson.

At the general election for the Ontario House of Assembly in March, 1871, as well as in the election for the Dominion in 1872, Mr. Brown devoted himself by pen and voice to advancing the interests of the liberal party with great success. The result of the election for the Ontario House was the defeat of the coalition government under Mr. Sandfield Macdonald, in spite of the strenuous support given that gentleman from his allies at Ottawa. It may here be stated that when Mr. Sandfield Macdonald was intrusted with the formation of the first Ontario administration Mr. Brown waited on him and assured him of the hearty support of the liberals if he formed a liberal government. It would appear he was not at liberty to do this by his Ottawa arrangements. Mr. Brown and the *Globe* therefore very properly vigorously opposed the small coalition as he opposed the larger one. The same principle was at stake in the existence of the one as in the other.

At no time was there any personal feeling existing between Mr. Brown and Mr. Macdonald, although the latter gentleman, to use his own words, had a crow to pluck with Mr. Brown because he had opposed the Macdonald-Dorion government in 1862. Mr. Macdonald imagined that he had, by taking conservatives into his government, for ever secured the adherence of that party to his standard. He was soon to be undeceived ; immediately after the first decisive vote was recorded against him in the assembly, "they all forsook him and " fled." This ingratitude touched the fallen minister to the quick. Without him they never could have held the government ; by adhering to him in his adversity they would have shown they had more than office in view ; instead of this, "they all began with one consent " to make excuse." Mr. Brown, like many another opponent of Mr. Macdonald's, had a liking for his brusque and honest character, and many a set-to they had at chance meetings, half in jest half in earnest, about current events, and particularly about Mr. Macdonald becoming a Tory, as Mr. Brown would put it. The Ontario Premier invariably denied vehemently that he joined the Tories, and claimed that they joined him to form not a coalition but a " patent combina- " tion." (The phrase belonged to Mr. Hincks.)

The Dominion elections in 1872 were fiercely contested by the liberals, and with every prospect of winning a large majority. Into this contest Mr. Brown threw himself with characteristic ardour, and his efforts were crowned with great success. Indeed, the success was greater than at first appeared, for the country was ignorant for a time of the great advantages enjoyed by the conservatives in the expenditure by their leaders of hundreds of thousands of dollars to carry the election. Shortly after the new House met rumours of the dark transaction reached the public ear; these were increased from time to time until the month of July, when the *Globe* appeared one morning with a "full, true and particular account" of the great election bribery. At no time in the history of the *Globe* did it show more power and ability than during the summer and autumn of 1873. Many of its articles were directed to the course of the Governor-General, and denounced his action in proroguing parliament, and agreeing to the appointment of a commission by his ministers to try themselves. It is said that some of these articles were never quite forgotten in vice-regal quarters. In addition to the specific acts complained of, the tone of the despatches to the English minister was such as invited comment, and the sending of the famous dispatch to parliament on the eve of an important discussion, so well calculated to aid the accused ministers, confirmed Mr. Brown in the opinion that vice-regal influence was used to an unjustifiable extent, considering the nature of the revelations which had then already been made. Time was to show that Lord Dufferin at least intended only to give his ministers as full an opportunity as possible to make good their "solemn assurances " that they were absolutely innocent of the things laid to their " charge." In the following five years of Lord Dufferin's term no paper did him fuller justice than the *Globe*, and Mr. Brown was among the first always to give him credit for being, what he undoubtedly was, a fair and constitutional Governor, though many continued to doubt the wisdom of all he did at the time when the shadow of the Pacific scandal hung over the land. Efforts were made by the Tory press to get a small offset to the notorious Pacific scandal revelations by bringing into great prominence a copy of a letter written by Mr. Brown towards the close of the election campaign to three or four friends, asking for a contribution towards meeting expenses of some elections yet to come off. Mr. Mackenzie stated publicly, when this letter was first published by the party who stole it from Mr. John Simpson's office, that the entire expenditure of the central authorities for election expenses in 1872 was only $3,750, all of which was expended for legitimate purposes, chiefly for printing documents and payment of travelling expenses, but he disclaimed any knowledge of what individual candidates might have spent on their own responsibility.

9

Early in 1876 a local paper made violent attacks upon Senator Simpson in connection with certain elections, and for having received and responded favourably to Mr. Brown's letter of August 15, 1872. Mr. Simpson applied for a rule to show cause why a criminal information should not issue against the editor of the paper in question on three counts. On the 29th of June the application came before Chief Justice Harrison, Justice Morrison and Justice Wilson. The Chief Justice delivered the judgment of the court, which was in brief that a criminal information should be filed against the editor for two of the offences mentioned ; the third was refused on the ground that a sufficient case had not been made out. Mr. Justice Wilson was not content with the Chief Justice's unobjectionable statement of the opinion of the court, but availed himself of his technical right to enter into a long account of his reasons for concurrence in that judgment. In this extra-judicial speech—it would be an abuse of terms to call it a judgment—he had the bad taste to assail Mr. Brown, who was not in any way before the court, on the ground that the letter referred to " was written with a corrupt intent, to interfere with the freedom of " elections." Mr. Simpson was similarly assailed, because he was *supposed* to have received this letter and had contributed money for the purpose asked. The Judge knew that the fact of such a letter being in existence was not legally ascertained, and was not in any way before the court. If he read the public journals—and he read some very diligently as his speech showed—he must have read Mr. Brown's statement, published months before this, respecting the now famous letter, which was as follows : " I have, then, to state " that the party subscription in question was got up to aid in defray- " ing the legal and necessary expenses of candidates unable to bear " the whole cost of hotly contested elections, or fighting for the liberal " cause in constituencies hopeless at the moment ; and in defraying " the expenses of public speakers, circulating political documents, " and other similar legal and proper expenses of a great electoral con- " test. I believe that the whole of the money subscribed was applied " strictly to these purposes. I further state that the entire amount " so raised and so expended was $3,700, or the trumpery sum of $45 " to each of the eighty-two constituencies, had they all participated " in it. And I state still further that there was no general reform " fund but this for election purposes at the election of 1872, and, had " there been any other, I think I must have heard of it." Judge Wilson also had before him Mr. Simpson's statement that he " had " no recollection of having received or having seen any such letter ; " and that he is quite certain he contributed no money to the fund " referred to."

Clearly Mr. Justice Wilson had no right to refer to a letter not in any way before him ; had no right to assume guilt to attach to the writer of the letter until it was proven. Nay, he was bound to accept the reasonable and true statement of its author respecting it, until he had legal evidence controverting it. Similarly he had no right to assume moral or political wrong in connection with Mr. Simpson's letter to the Finance Minister, for there was none ; nor was there a particle of evidence to sustain such a contention. He propounded the extraordinary doctrine that because Mr. Simpson made no statement about a letter not in his possession, when it was not incumbent on him to make any, therefore "it must be assumed that "he cannot make any satisfactory explanation to the court concerning "it." There actually was, however, an explicit denial under oath by Senator Simpson, in his original affidavit making the application for the rule, in the following words : "I say that the statements, charges, "and imputations therein contained against me, are false, malicious, "and without foundation in fact. . . . I further say, that the "imputations against me of political intriguing, and of procuring "substantial aid for corrupt purposes, and that I have paid out money "for the purpose of bribery at elections, and that I used the money "of others corruptly, are untrue, false and malicious." He then proceeded, nevertheless, to give the letter a meaning of his own, and upon that interpretation, which was wholly unsupported by any evidence, to impute corrupt motives to Mr. Simpson. The only justification Justice Wilson gave for his political deliverance from the high seat he occupied was that he "might take notice of those matters "which every person of ordinary intelligence is acquainted with." It was an unfortunate circumstance that his "acquaintance" was wholly with what he thought would tell against the two senators.

It was no wonder that, a few days after Justice Wilson made this speech on the bench, an article appeared in the *Globe* from Mr. Brown's pen, headed "Justice Wilson on the War Path," in which the Judge was handled roughly. The article was a very long and able one, and was a complete answer to the ill-advised attack of the Judge. After a careful and critical analysis of the deliverance of Justice Wilson, combined with statements of fact to set himself right, the article proceeds : "According to Mr. Justice Wilson's new doctrine, that the "court may properly 'take notice of those matters which every person "'of ordinary intelligence is acquainted with,' whatever the matter may "be, and whether before the court or not at the moment, we suppose "we must accustom ourselves to such outrages from the bench. But "this Mr. Justice Wilson may rest assured of : that such slanders "and insults shall not go unanswered, and if the dignity of the bench "is ruffled in the tussle, on his folly shall rest the blame. We cast "back on Mr. Wilson his insolent and slanderous interpretation. The

" letter was *not* written for corrupt purposes—it was *not* written to
" interfere with the freedom of elections—it was *not* an invitation to
" anybody to concur in committing bribery and corruption at the
" polls ; and be he Judge or not who says so, the statement is
" false.

" Does Mr. Wilson mean to say that no party fund for proper pur-
" poses in election contests can exist—that there are no expenditures of
" money in keenly contested elections which are absolutely necessary,
" perfectly moral and legitimate, and highly conducive to good govern-
" ment ? Was there no such fund when Mr. Justice Wilson was in
" public life ? When the hat went round in his contests for the
" mayoralty of Toronto, was that, or was it not, a concurrence in
" bribery and corruption at the polls ?

" Probably there never was another general election in Ontario, or
" Upper Canada, that on either side of politics cost so small a sum for
" general party purposes as the reform expenditure of \$3,700 at the
" election of 1872 ; and assuredly there was at it neither the design
" that a penny of it should be spent for corrupt purposes, nor was
" there a shilling to spare from the legitimate and necessary expendi-
" tures for any such purpose. How could Mr. Justice Wilson, in his
" hunt for things that ‘ every person of ordinary intelligence is ac-
" ‘ quainted with,’ omit to state that while the entire general election
" of the liberal party for that year (1872) was but \$3,700, raised by
" subscription from a few private individuals, the conservative fund
" on the same occasion amounted to the enormous sum of \$200,000—
" raised by the flagitious sale of the Pacific Railway contract to a
" band of speculators on terms disastrous to the interests of the
" country ?

" The law has been greatly changed since the election of 1872.
" Every known method of spending money, under which even the
" suspicion of corrupting the electors could lurk, has been most pro-
" perly forbidden under severe penalties, and successfully enforced.
" But do election contests even now cost nothing ? Are there no pure,
" legitimate, and legal modes of expenditure still remaining ? Of
" course there are. In Ontario, official returns on oath are made of
" the total expenditure by each candidate in every contest for a seat
" in the provincial chamber. And what do these show ? Why, that
" in the last electoral contest the declared cost of Mr. John Robin-
" son's election for West Toronto was \$893.75 ; of Mr. Platt's contest
" in East Toronto, \$972.76 ; of Mr. M. C. Cameron's contest in East
" Toronto, \$944.59 ; and of that of Mr. Crooks in East Toronto,
" \$957.10 ; or in all, for the expenses of these four gentlemen alone,
" \$3,778.20—more than the entire amount of the fund of 1872 for
" the general conduct of the entire Dominion elections of Ontario.

"It is in the face of these facts that Mr. Justice Wilson had the
"audacity—without any evidence that such a letter ever was written,
"or sent, or received, or acted upon, and without the slightest evi-
"dence as to the circumstances under which it might have been writ-
"ten, or the special purpose to which the money was to be applied
"—to denounce as a thing of monstrous depravity a request by one
"reformer to another for a subscription to a general election fund of
"probably $50, but at most $100.

"We deeply regret being compelled to write of the conduct of any
"member of the Ontario bench in the tone of this article, but the
"offence was so rank, so reckless, so utterly unjustifiable, that soft
"words would but have poorly discharged our duty to the public."

The court or Judge so vigorously assailed did not take any formal
notice of the article; and severe as it was, the general verdict of the
country was that no man had a right to shield himself behind the
judicial bench, the seat of justice, to make such assaults, and that if
made they must be met.

Some months afterwards the editor against whom Mr. Simpson
proceeded obtained a rule calling on Mr. Brown to show cause why
a writ of attachment should not issue against him, or why he should
not be committed for contempt of "this honourable court" for printing the said article. The case was tried before Chief Justice Harrison
and Judge Morrison. Mr. Brown appeared in person and claimed,
1st, that the party obtaining the rule had no rights in the matter—
that he was not charged with protecting the dignity of the court ;
2nd, that five months had passed since the publication of the article,
during which time the court was silent, and that Justice Wilson's
judgment and the *Globe's* criticism were the subject of violent discussion *pro* or *con* over the whole Dominion; and that the time had elapsed
within which the court could by any rule or usage call him to account
for any offence against its dignity.

Mr. Brown then boldly justified the publication of the article, on
the ground that he had suffered just provocation, and quoting one
passage as follows : "No sooner had the Chief Justice finished than
"Mr. Justice Wilson availed himself of the occasion to express his
"views on the matter, with a freedom of speech and an indifference to
"the evidence before the court, and an indulgence in assumptions,
"surmises and insinuations, that we believe to be totally unparalleled
"in the judicial proceedings of any Canadian court."

Then proceeding, he said : "I wrote so then, I say so now. I
"have searched the law books in vain to find a case parallel to this,
"and I defy the learned counsel on the other side to show any language
"ever used in the last half of the nineteenth century by any British or

"British colonial Judge, that for indiscretion and injustice bears the
" slightest parallel to that of Mr. Justice Wilson, for commenting on
" which this complaint is made." . . . Mr. Brown further pleaded
" that the article was written under compulsion ; that it was absolutely
" necessary to meet the bitter attacks on the government, on the
" reform party, on public men on the reform side, and on himself,
" by the conservative press, based on the official judgment of a Judge
" of the court." He claimed that the ground could hardly be taken
that a Judge could do no wrong—that he might say what he pleased of
anybody, and if strong remonstrance were made, to summarily fine and
imprison the offender without question or appeal. The speech was an
able and eloquent one, and practically it justified the whole article.

Chief Justice Harrison decided against Mr. Brown on all the points.
Judge Morrison decided, 1st, that the complaint was too late in point
of time ; 2nd, that the applicant failed to sustain the constructive contempt ; and lastly, that the applicant, having failed to sustain his own
complaint, was not entitled, under the colour of such a complaint, to
ask the court to punish, at his suggestion, the publisher of the article,
upon the ground that it contains a direct contempt of the court
itself.

The motion, being supported by one Judge and opposed by another
of the two present, fell to the ground. Mr. Brown, by his boldness
and skill, succeeded in what he desired to do at the commencement of
the case, to vindicate his right to defend himself against a gross attack
made upon him by a Judge in court, where he was not present as a
party to a suit or as a witness. In his day Mr. Brown had many a
fight for popular rights and justice. In his journal he never hesitated
to expose wrong-doing by high or low. In no case did he do such
service as when he vigorously opposed and denounced the injustice of
a Judge gravely attacking individuals apparently to gratify some personal feeling of hostility or political prejudice.

Mr. Justice Wilson had for years been supported by the *Globe* in
municipal and parliamentary contests ; he had, in fact, been made by
the *Globe*, so far as his public life was concerned, and it is difficult to
say what could have led to such an attack on his former patron. It
is, however, charitable to suppose that he must have been labouring
under some hallucination, and did not see the great wrong he had committed.

CHAPTER XXIII.

Mr. Brown made Senator.—Appointed Joint Plenipotentiary to Washington.—Declines the Lieutenant-Governorship of Ontario, and the Title of K. C. M. G.

A few weeks after Mr. Mackenzie's accession to office Mr. Brown was offered a seat in the senate, which offer he accepted. He was not anxious to take this position, or to enter at all upon parliamentary life again, but was induced to accept a seat in the body which he did so much to create under the new political system. At that time many of those who had sustained the proposal to have an upper House nominated by the Crown became convinced they had made a mistake. Mr. Brown, however, was firmly convinced still that if a second House existed at all it should not be elective. It was therefore peculiarly fitting that he should accept a nomination as senator. Other events prevented Mr. Brown taking his seat or performing any senatorial duties during the first session. Nothing had been done by the Canadian or British governments with the fishery clauses of the Washington treaty of 1871. Mr. Brown was asked by the government early in February, 1874, to proceed to Washington and ascertain what prospects there were of negotiating a commercial treaty which would also embrace a settlement of the fishery question. Mr. Brown was long and favourably known to prominent public men in the United States. The course he pursued as editor-in-chief of the *Globe* during the civil war in that country in upholding the national government and the anti-slavery party made him popular wherever his name was known. Mr. Brown from the first, as well as his brother, looked upon the struggle in the United States as one of vast interest to humanity—as involving the general interests of freedom all over the world. To him it seemed most revolting to see any Britons committing themselves to a support of the south, as that meant building up a slave power. The north might in some respects be wrong, but their cause was the cause of liberty. These views found eloquent advocacy in the columns of the *Globe* day after day until the battle was over. He was therefore peculiarly well qualified to act in this *quasi* ambassadorial capacity, apart from his possession of talents and tact to manage such inquiries. He met with a very cordial reception from the United States government and from many public men, including the lamented President Garfield, then a member of congress. He accordingly reported to the government at Ottawa that he believed a very general desire existed in that country "for the establishment of better " commercial relations with Canada." The government at once determined to ask the Imperial government to accredit Mr. Brown to the Washington government as joint plenipotentiary with the resident minister. This step was taken in connection with the determination of Mr. Mackenzie's administration to have all questions of Canadian diplomacy dealt with by Canadians : of course acting under general arrangements with Her Majesty's Imperial government, and subject to their approval. Canada, to be sure, was represented by the presence of one Canadian amongst the six high commissioners who negotiated the treaty of Washington. The humiliating conditions of that treaty to Canada showed only too clearly that the Canadian representative was either utterly powerless to accomplish anything or utterly incompetent to point out the true line which should be adhered to. Some years after the negotiation of this treaty a Canadian gentleman was discussing its terms with Mr. Disraeli, then Prime Minister, and remarked to that gentleman, "I do not know what you think, Mr. " Disraeli, of that treaty, but in Canada it was looked upon as a great " humiliation." Mr. Disraeli, holding up both hands, replied, " It was " one of the most shameful things in our history." The Canadian remarked, "You never attacked it in public in that way, Mr. Disraeli." The response was, " How could I ; Mr. Gladstone put North- " cote on the commission." The Tory leader had a just conception of what was wrong in the treaty, but Sir Stafford Northcote's presence on the commission sealed his mouth. Previous blunders of English diplomats respecting the Maine boundary and the North-West boundaries, were of a character which inflicted irreparable injury on British America, and could hardly have occurred if the negotiations had been conducted by an experienced Canadian statesman. So far as the determination of boundaries was concerned, all the mischief was done already that could be done ; but questions respecting navigation, fisheries and commercial relations might be of vast importance still.

In this case the Imperial government, after a brief delay, assented to the request of the Canadian government, and appointed Mr. Brown joint plenipotentiary with Sir Edward Thornton. On no other terms would the Canadian government or Mr. Brown have entered upon the negotiations.

The negotiations were formally commenced late in the month of March, and terminated about the end of June. During this time Mr. Brown had to maintain a very heavy correspondence with the government at Ottawa, much of it by cipher telegraph. He also placed himself in communication with a large number of the editors of leading newspapers in the United States, and obtained their co-operation.

Excellent articles in favour of greater freedom in commercial intercourse with Canada were published in all the large cities in the principal newspapers. The " Memorandum on the Commercial Relations " Past and Present of the British North American Provinces with the " United States of America," published by the plenipotentiaries, was the work of Mr. Brown. It contained able summaries of the trade statistics of the two countries bearing on reciprocal trade, the figures of which were extensively published and produced a good effect. To use the official description of this paper by Sir Edward Thornton in his despatch to Lord Derby : " The greater part of this document is " occupied with the history of the past fifty years of the trade relations " between Canada and the United States, and shows the advantage " the United States, as well as Canada, would derive from greater " liberality in those relations." A draft treaty was ultimately agreed to by Sir Edward Thornton and Mr. Brown, also by Mr. Fish, on the part of the United States, on June 17th, and submitted by that minister to the United States senate for approval a few days afterwards. That body postponed action until the next session, for the ostensible reason that the time was too short for consideration. The United States government approved of the draft treaty, but did not exercise any of its legitimate influence in their submission of it to the senate for approval. Apart altogether from the attempt to negotiate a treaty of commerce, Mr. Brown's sojourn in Washington was highly beneficial to Canada. For reasons already stated, he was everywhere popular in the states, while he was equally well known as a devoted British American subject of Her Majesty. His presence helped materially to dissipate the feeling of irritation which existed during and after the war at the (erroneously) supposed sympathy of Canadians with southern rebels, and to produce a more kindly feeling towards Canada than had existed for many years. Mr. Brown's exposition and defence of the treaty submitted to the senate of the United States by Mr. Fish will be found in his speech delivered in the senate on the 5th of March, 1875. (*See* " SPEECHES.") . The proposed convention received the assent of the Imperial government, though wholly negotiated under the auspices of the Canadian administration. Its failure necessitated proceeding with the arbitration, provided by the treaty of Washington, to ascertain the value of the Canadian fisheries to citizens of the United States. This was, with much difficulty, reached two years afterwards, when Lord Carnarvon desired to name an English gentleman as commissioner. This Mr. Mackenzie declined to assent to, and he insisted that the Canadian government should nominate the commissioner to be formally appointed by Her Majesty's government, and also control the procedure of the commission. This demand was ultimately conceded. Mr. Brown was offered the appointment, but declined it for private reasons, principally that he could not devote his whole time to the work so far from home.

Mr. Brown had, at great personal inconvenience, given four months of his time to the work at Washington, without making any charge against the government, or accepting remuneration of any kind, for the vast amount of labour he had undertaken and accomplished. Although Sir Ed. Thornton was joint plenipotentiary with Mr. Brown, the labour of preparing the tables of trade statistics, and placing the information into proper shape for publication, devolved naturally and necessarily on Mr. Brown. A sum of $10,000 was placed in the estimates to meet the necessary expenditure at Washington. Some time afterwards, when an attack was made by the opposition on the government and on Mr. Brown in connection with this vote, it transpired that the whole expenditure had only been $4,000 ; that all payments had been made by Sir Edward Thornton, and that the plenipotentiaries had not received one dollar of it for their own purposes or expenses. Any one who chooses can compare the Washington expenses of 1854 with those of 1874. More work was done in the latter year, but more *influences* (a mild term) were brought to bear in the former year.

It is not proposed to discuss here the effect this treaty, if ratified, would have had on Canadian commerce ; that, of course, would be a matter of opinion. Up to a very recent period it was assumed by all that much benefit would necessarily be derived from participation in the trade of foreign countries. The wonderful development of British trade in consequence of the removal of all shackles on the intercourse with foreign nations, so far as Britain could remove them, and the retrogressive progress of the merchants of the United States, where efforts had been made for twenty years, by severe customs restrictive laws, to force business into the hands of their own citizens, seemed to be sufficient to satisfy any one of the evil effects of a system of " pro-" tection," so called.

The resurrection in Canada of a system of this nature, which Cobden and Bright buried thirty years before in Britain, was however, as it turned out, imminent. The singular belief in a democratic country that it is desirable to discourage the very existence of foreign trade, in order that the wealth of the nation may be concentrated in the hands of the few at the cost of removing it from the hands of the mass of the people, is a craze which cannot last long. When the country returns to an enlightened commercial policy the efforts of Mr. Brown and the late administration to promote international intercourse between the great nation on our southern border will be better understood and appreciated. Mr. Brown was a firm advocate of perfect freedom of purchase and sale, as well as of personal movements. He was the firm opponent of attempts to compel the people to purchase from and trade with certain persons only, or classes of persons—of all monopolies created for individuals—of all taxes imposed for any purpose except to meet the necessities of the state.

He had already, with others, encountered an oligarchy which monopolized political power. He was the principal opponent of an ecclesiastical oligarchy that insisted on being established as the sole guardians of the religious life of the nation. The result of the conflict in both cases was that power remains vested in the hands of the people, and that every church is equally protected by the state, and none have special privileges. If trade monopolies are of a different character they are not the less dangerous, and no one appreciated that danger more thoroughly. In neither speeches nor writings was an uncertain sound ever given on this subject, so important to a nation's welfare.

In the month of May, 1875, the Hon. John Crawford, Lieutenant-Governor of Ontario, died. Mr. Brown was known to entertain very strong views of the course pursued by the conservative government in appointing Mr. Crawford after they ceased to command the confidence of parliament and they had, in fact, resigned office, and of Mr. Crawford's course in accepting that office under the circumstances. He was invited to the inaugural ceremonies at Government House, but declined to accept the invitation for the reasons given in the following letter :

TORONTO, 11th Nov., 1873.

MY DEAR MR. CRAWFORD,—A note has been sent me requesting my attendance at Government House to-morrow on the occasion of your being sworn in as Lieutenant-Governor.

It would have afforded me great pleasure to be present on the occasion, could I have done so consistently with my views of the manner of your appointment. I hold that the Lieutenant-Governor should be regarded by all parties from a non-political stand-point, without reference to the side of the political arena on which he was ranged before his appointment ; and there is no member of the conservative party whose appointment by his own political friends to the office would have been more agreeable to me than your own. But the circumstances attending your appointment appear to me so unconstitutional, so much to be deprecated, that it would be worse than inconsistent were I to attend the ceremony to-morrow.

While I feel thus in regard to the official ceremony of your inauguration, I trust you will believe that no change has occurred in our personal relations, and that when you are duly installed in your high office, no political feeling will stand in the way of those marks of respect and consideration to which you will be entitled socially and in public.

I am, my Dear Sir, yours faithfully,

GEORGE BROWN.

JOHN CRAWFORD, ESQ., Toronto.

The position was at once offered to Mr. Brown, and he was urged by many friends to accept it. While the offer of the chief office under the Crown in his own province was peculiarly gratifying to him, he declined the honour after one day's consideration, but without assigning any reason for his determination. There is, however, no reason to doubt that he felt he could not, with his strict notions of propriety, be the principal proprietor, and, nominally at least, editor-in-chief of the leading political journal, and at the same time Lieutenant-Governor of the province. It was, however, as gratifying to his friends everywhere as it could be to himself, that his political friends at Ottawa had given him the offer of the highest place in the province for which he had done so much. Chiefly to his long labours was it due that it was possible to have such a position to place at his disposal, and there can be no doubt that had he accepted it the appointment would have been acceptable to all classes of the population. With this offer he had either received, or might have received, all the honours his fellow-countrymen could bestow. He had been many years in parliament as one of Ontario's representatives; he was Prime Minister of old Canada, and a senator of the Dominion ; the Queen had already honoured him by appointing him a joint plenipotentiary at Washington; and a year afterwards he might have been elevated to the rank of knighthood as a K. C. M. G., had he consented to accept that honour.

There was no more attached adherent of the British monarchy—no more devoted admirer of Her Majesty as Queen of Britain—than Mr. Brown, and he was not disposed to regard with indifference the honours dispensed by the Crown, however much he might blame ministers for their distribution. Under appropriate circumstances he might, and no doubt would, have accepted a title of honour. In 1879 he was again proffered a title as K. C. M. G. For some reason it was then fully expected that he would accept it, and his name was actually gazetted on that assumption. His Excellency the Governor-General was commissioned by Her Majesty to confer the title, and he appointed a meeting at Montreal for the purpose of formally investing Mr. Brown and some others with the insignia of the order. He went to Montreal to meet His Excellency, but only to thank him in person for the offer and to give a formal declinature in writing. It was known that Mr. Brown was strongly urged by many liberals of the most pronounced character, such as the late Mr. Holton, to accept this second offer, but these influences failed to convince him that the circumstances would justify him in accepting the title which some men are so anxious to obtain and honour so little.

CHAPTER XXIV.

Mr. Brown's Assassination.—Universal Sympathy and Sorrow.—
The Funeral Obsequies.

On the 25th of March, 1880, George Bennett, an employé in the *Globe* office, who had just been discharged by the foreman for habitual tippling and gross neglect of his duties, went to Mr. Brown's office to demand a certificate of character.

When Bennett was invited by Mr. Brown to come in he did so, and proceeded to shut the door behind him. Mr. Brown thinking his movements singular, stopped him and asked what he wanted. The man seemed to hesitate, but at last presented a paper and asked Mr. Brown to sign it, remarking that it was a statement that he had been employed in the *Globe* office for five years. Mr. Brown said he should apply to the head of his department for the certificate, as he (Mr. Brown) was not aware of the length of his services. Bennett replied that the head of the department would not give it to him. Mr. Brown then told him to apply to Mr. Henning, the treasurer of the company, who had the books, and could tell how long he had been employed. Bennett made no reply, but insisted upon Mr. Brown signing his paper with much vehemence.

On Mr. Brown continuing to refuse, Bennett began fumbling apparently at his pistol pocket, whereupon it passed through Mr. Brown's mind, as he himself said, "that the little wretch might be meaning "to shoot me." He got his pistol out, however, and then Mr. Brown seized him by the wrist and turned his hand downward. He had got the weapon cocked before his hand was seized, and at once pulled the trigger, the muzzle being pointed downwards. The ball struck Mr. Brown on the outer side of the left thigh, taking a slanting direction, and passing through four inches below and towards the back of the leg. Mr. Brown, to prevent more firing, closed with his assailant, and in the struggle they got outside the door of the office on the stair landing. Mr. Brown got Bennett firmly pressed against the partition wall of the waiting room and called for assistance. By this time the alarm was given in the office, and a number of employés rushed to Mr. Brown's aid and seized the assassin. It would appear that Mr. Brown himself took the pistol from him, while Mr. A. Thompson and Mr. Ewan held him fast. Mr. Brown walked back into the office, carrying the weapon, apparently not seriously hurt. There is little doubt that Mr. Brown's struggle with the wretch alone prevented him finishing his work, as he tried repeatedly to fire off his pistol after Mr. Brown seized him.

The shock to the system from the shot, and the intense nervous excitement consequent on the struggle with the armed assassin, had a very injurious effect, and materially retarded his hoped-for recovery. Mr. Brown was removed at once to his private residence, and medical aid summoned. A fatal result was not anticipated by any one. Mr. Brown himself made light of the wound, and firmly believed that a few days' rest and care would set him all right again. His restless energy was probably quickened afresh by the nervous excitement, which never left him, as shown by his determination to transact business in his room. There was indeed no reason for apprehensions of evil, though the possibilty of a serious turn was clear to every one ; he was still in the fulness of his strength, and his cheerful, hopeful, sanguine nature must have been a favourable element looking to recovery.

The excitement through the country was very great as soon as the murderous assault was made known. This was particularly the case at Ottawa, where so many of his old political friends were gathered together for their parliamentary duties. When it was ascertained that, though the wound was serious, there was no likelihood of the danger proving very great, a great sense of relief was felt by every one on both sides of the House. When two weeks passed with no improvement, an uneasy feeling again became predominant ; and one evening, when evil tidings respecting the patient's condition reached the House, there was no disposition among his friends to pursue their ordinary legislative duties.

The next morning telegrams were received which stated that the former report was not warranted, and that his early recovery was confidently anticipated. The writer well remembers the feeling of unalloyed pleasure which was expressed on all faces by the reassuring messages. The hope and pleasure so inspired were soon to be dashed to the earth, not suddenly, but slowly, steadily and gradually. Bright intervals occurred, and seeming progress made now and then, only to be succeeded with deeper gloom. Like the descending of the sun in a cloudy evening, while passing behind a cloud, the earth is enveloped in gloom ; presently an opening appears in the cloudy pall, and the light streams out lighting up glen and mountain. Nearing the horizon, the greater compactness of the vapoury shade makes the glimpses of sunshine more and more brief, while the waning daylight shows the inevitable and near approach of night. So with the invalid : day after day developed some new sign of possible progress ; physician and friend thought, as some fresh display of reserved physical strength and mental power was made, that there might be—there would be—a slow restoration. But soon the symptoms of increasing exhaustion would reappear, and close observers saw with sorrow that each day on the whole left him weaker than he was on the preceding one; and unless this continuous uniform loss of strength could be arrested, it was apparent to all that there could be but one result, though his own sanguine temperament and the illusive hopes of near friends buoyed the spirits of all inquirers to a belief that the probabilities were in favour of his recovery.

Hopes were entertained by the attendant physicians of his ultimate recovery up to within a few days of his death. His natural energy asserted itself in his illness, overcoming in the desperate struggle for life the nervous exhaustion and the waste of the system caused by the wound. The members of his family, who were in constant attendance upon him, were less sanguine as to the final result for the greater part of the time of his illness. Except for the first eight or ten days, he was afflicted by delirium and such clouding of his mental powers as made it unadvisable to add to his weakness by interviews with any but his medical attendants and members of the family. Throughout he hoped he would recover, but at the same time he felt that the chances were even, if not against him. Often in the stillness of his bed-chamber he was heard, when he thought that none but God was near, praying earnestly for recovery in order to finish his work, but always expressing his resignation to God's will if it should be otherwise ordered. About two weeks before his death, at a time when his family and medical attendants entertained the most serious apprehensions, he had a long conversation with Dr. Greig, his old pastor, and members of his family, all of whom he had gathered round his bed. In that conversation he spoke freely to them of his faith and hope, and, we are told, poured out his soul in a full and fervent prayer. He then asked them to sing some psalms or hymns, and in particular the well-known one, " Rock of Ages," in the singing of which he warmly joined. It was evident that his mind dwelt much on the future, and that while he desired that his life might be spared for his family, the hopes of the Christian burnt brightly within, and enabled him to look forward without fear to a possible unsuccessful issue of his illness. For about a week previous to his death it could scarcely be said that any one expected his recovery, though some of his physicians still thought it possible. The intervals of consciousness were gradually becoming less frequent and also more brief, but during their continuance they were characterized by inexpressible tenderness and love to the members of his family, all of whom he recognized almost to the last, even when, through growing weakness, the tongue refused its office of communicating to them his thoughts, hopes and desires. No doubt the knowledge that he was walking very near towards the verge of the unseen world drew his mind away from all other things ; his physical strength was also steadily waning and indisposing him to further exertion. The writer had the melancholy pleasure of seeing him on the Wednesday morning preceding his death, but the invalid was not conscious of the presence of any one. From this time forward he sank rapidly. He made no complaint, and no one could tell what his sufferings were. He lay quite still most of the time, neither inviting nor refusing the nourishment forced upon him, or conscious of the attempts made to minister to his comfort.

On Thursday and Friday there were still gleams of intelligence lighting up his countenance, and some hopes were even then entertained, soon to be clouded over, for on Friday evening the physicians ceased to press upon him nourishment or stimulants, as it became manifest any further effort would only do harm. After consultation the medical attendants were obliged to confess that the resources of their art were exhausted. Thenceforward all that could be done was to soothe the patient by the kindness of the grief-stricken but loving members of his family. On Saturday it was quite evident to all that the end was very near. The long struggle was at an end. The once strong frame became weak as an infant's. The massive head and expressive features indicated as much as ever the gigantic intellect and the warm heart, but the wasted form told at once the severity of the battle for life and the nearness of its close. The Angel of Death had entered the room and taken possession, and in the stillness of the quiet chamber his presence could be felt. Everything recalled Hood's description of a death-bed :

> "Our very hopes belied our fears,
>   Our fears our hopes belied ;
> We thought her dying when she slept,
>   And sleeping when she died."

Early on Sunday, a beautiful May morning, shortly before the break of day, the sad scene closed. The Angel of the Covenant had come to convey the spirit home, and, to use Longfellow's words, "Two angels came out where only one went in," leaving in the room only that still, inanimate form to represent him who, but a few weeks before, strode through the rooms and halls of the happy home in all the vigour of matured manhood, rejoicing in his domestic peace and happiness. Many friends calling, as usual during his illness, on Sabbath morning learned of the sad event and spread the tidings through the city. Though a fatal ending was fully expected, yet it created the most painful and profound impression. In most if not all the churches, his death was referred to in solemn and touching terms. All felt that a great man had passed away, and that a great calamity had overtaken the country. The tragic circumstances attendant on his death, and the high personal character of the lamented statesman, combined to evoke the most profound expressions of sympathy, and caused a feeling of deep gloom to pervade the city. Many eyes were suffused with tears in the several churches where reference was made to his character and death. Political and even personal differences were forgotten in the general desire to show kindness and sympathy. Every person showed themselves only anxious to say and do what could be said and done to assuage the grief and comfort the hearts of those who had been so suddenly and cruelly bereft of a tender husband and loving father.

Other cities, and the towns and villages, were informed by telegraph of his decease almost as soon as it was known in Toronto, and everywhere the same touching sympathetic feeling was shown. In many churches prayer had been publicly made for his recovery from the moment that danger was apprehended, while hope justified an expectation of recovery. The constant inquiries from all quarters could not be all answered, but the telegraph companies were good enough to give an extensive circulation to the physicians' reports from day to day. This in a large measure kept the country informed of the hopes and fears entertained. It should also be stated that the leading conservative journals showed the utmost kindness and good feeling throughout. A man so pronounced in opinion, and so energetic in expressing and giving effect to his views on all public questions, could scarcely be expected to escape much personal antagonism, more or less bitter and intense, but in the hour of his extremity few if any had the disposition to remember past feuds ; while hosts of warm personal and political friends all over Canada felt a grief at his tragic death second only to that felt for intimate and near blood relations.

The arrangements for the funeral were made with the simple understanding that the friends of the deceased would themselves provide for order and regularity in paying the last mark of respect to his remains. Arrangements were made in many distant towns and villages to send deputations to represent the respective communities. The vast multitude that attended showed that the people of the nearer towns and country very generally attended. Many of Mr. Brown's old associates and opponents in public life were present. His old personal and political friends, Sir Antoine Dorion and Hon. Alexander Mackenzie, were placed at his head in the procession ; the other pall-bearers were Hon. Edward Blake, Sir Alexander Campbell, Sir Richard J. Cartwright, Hon. Archibald McKellar, Professor Wilson, Judge Morrison, Hon. G. W. Allan, Hon. L. S. Huntington, Hon. David Christie, Hon. Wm. McMaster and Sir W. P. Howland.

The day was a beautiful May morning, and all without seemed bright and gay as the sad procession was formed. The streets in the vicinity of his late residence were so densely crowded by people from city and country that it seemed impossible to clear a way, yet a few moments sufficed to form into regular order. The various delegations promptly fell into line—that from the county of Lambton, led by Rev. Mr. Thompson of Sarnia, taking the lead, as the first county that had given Mr. Brown a seat in parliament. The streets by which the procession moved to reach the Necropolis Cemetery were lined the whole way by a multitude of sympathetic people, who reverently uncovered as the cortege passed.

With these manifestations of universal sorrow and regard all that was mortal of George Brown was laid to rest beside a revered father and mother. Canada mourned for her accomplished son. The voice which had swayed popular assemblies so long and so powerfully was hushed in the silence of the tomb. The commanding figure and kindly impressive face disappeared from public view. No one could be more missed from the social and political life of the country. The place he occupied in all relations of the citizen and statesman must remain vacant for the present. His death in the ordinary course of nature would have evoked much feeling and sympathy, but the violent and sudden rupture of all the ties of social, business, and political life made the bereaved home, the business office, and the council of the political party he was identified with, miss all the more the genial hearty face and the commanding intellect which had long been so well known and appreciated in almost every county in Ontario.

CHAPTER XXV.

MR. BROWN'S SERVICES TO LIBERALISM IN CANADA.—ESTIMATE OF HIS PUBLIC AND PRIVATE CHARACTER.

Mr. Brown's Canadian career extended over a period of thirty-six years. He came to the country in early manhood with little or no influence or fortune, depending entirely on his personal exertions. In one year he established his reputation as a journalist, and obtained the confidence of the leading men in the liberal ranks. All felt that in him the party had secured a potent ally, and his newspaper within a year became its recognized organ. At that time newspaper literature had not any special influence. The seat of government was in a small city, and the administration itself was not hampered or strengthened by keen criticism or warm support from the press. Political life was in a changing uncertain condition. The new constitution was yet in its infancy. The promoters of reform in former days were more concerned in the exposure of grievances than in the construction of a new political edifice broad enough to embrace all desirable reforms. Popular rights and religious equality had to a great extent been conceded, but much remained to be accomplished. A class of reformers, becoming less numerous every day, remained, who devoted themselves and their newspapers to fighting past battles, rehearsing old grievances, and denouncing the Family Compact. This class had a goodly portion of the " know-nothing" element ; its members seemed to resent the coming from other lands of sterling reformers as almost an intrusion, and their advocacy of a building up, broad policy, establishing a really responsible government, was often met by carping criticism and personal attack.

Mr. Baldwin and some other leaders of the liberal party were, to say the least, timorous and undecided in their course, and the Governor-General exercised an improper influence in the administration of affairs. Into such elements the new candidate for popular favour precipitated himself with all his characteristic energy, sweeping aside the cobwebs of the past, taking his stand on the unassailable ground that all classes and creeds must enjoy equality in the eye of the law, and that all the class legislation of the past must be speedily repealed. The result was that he soon obtained an influence in the country generally which was unparalleled.

Liberal statesmen felt that they had a powerful supporter in the new journalist, but some of them also felt that a new power was put in motion which would compel them to move on or subject them to be trampled over in the inevitable onward movement. The journal commenced by the young Scotchman became immediately the recognized organ of the liberal party, and in little more than eight years after he became a resident of Canada, he was elected a member of the legislature for one of the largest counties. This success was partly owing to his great energy, partly to his power as a speaker, but mainly to the influence he wielded as editor of the *Globe*. The intense earnestness and vigour he displayed as a speaker at popular meetings, enhanced greatly by his fine presence, enabled him to communicate an enthusiasm to his audience which seldom failed to carry him through triumphantly.

His information on public questions of the day, and on historical facts bearing upon them, was very extensive ; while his skill in debate, his rapid utterance and enthusiastic energy, often overwhelmed opponents who were themselves able men. There was no man amongst the public men of the past generation so effective as a political speaker ; but the very qualities and circumstances which gave him his influence and power with the masses, and constituted him a natural leader, also conduced to raise up many bitter enemies. He was often assailed by members of his own party, some of whom objected to the rigid code of political morality as to measures which he inculcated. His path as a reform journalist was often crossed by time-servers who were willing to compromise principles, or postpone action thereon, for the sake of office. Sooner or later this class came under the lash of the *Globe*, and some of them never quite forgot what they conceived to be an injury. In some cases the denunciatory language was undoubtedly too severe, and possibly sufficient allowance was not made for the initial difficulties to be overcome in getting into working order the system of parliamentary or responsible government. On the other hand, no political leader ever was more disposed to welcome back members of the party who had been temporarily alienated from their friends. It became his duty, in pursuance of the policy he adopted, to condemn the course of the reform leader, Robert Baldwin. Nothing need be said here as to what was involved in that act, as their relations have been already dealt with in this volume. There was undoubtedly a considerable portion of the liberal party that more or less sympathized with the timid policy of this statesman, or rather who admired his personal character so much that they looked more lightly than they should upon his failure to carry out the pledges made or programme understood or adopted before the general elections of 1844 and 1847, but who were quite loyal to the party generally. For a time this class blamed the *Globe* as having been needlessly severe to an able and upright but too dilatory public man. It is elsewhere demonstrated that there was no just ground for this opinion, and long ago all sections of the party were satisfied that the leading journal only discharged a plain duty in pointing out Mr. Baldwin's unfitness to lead in carrying out the reform policy.

There was another class which sought shelter from the consequences of treachery by hiding under Baldwin's name. This class moved to the Tory camp under the name of "Baldwin Reformers." It was insignificant in numbers and ability—too insignificant as a class to be attacked—but there were individuals in it who had some standing in the country. These men were vigorously assailed and their election opposed by Mr. Brown. In doing so he incurred some censure and subjected himself to much misrepresentation, which remained to some extent in the public mind to the last. His line at that time was, as a matter of course, strongly condemned by both these classes. He was characterized as a tyrant and dictator, just as he was in later times by men who vacillated between the two political camps, between free trade and protection, between British rule and annexation to the United States. The question naturally arises, what did he demand as the duty of public men when he first made known his discontent at the leaders' course? The reply must be, that after years of patient waiting for the fulfilment of pledges given, he refused, and properly refused, to defend further or wait longer, and denounced the conduct of Baldwin, Hincks and others as suicidal and calamitous morally and politically, besides being unfaithful to their promises, and to the anti-state church policy held as a sacred principle by the reform party. The strong ground taken by Mr. Brown led to such expressions of hostile opinion that he at one time spoke of himself, when replying to charges of personal ambition, as a "governmental impossibility." There can be no doubt that he assumed a grave responsibility in adopting a course which resulted in an alienation, more or less complete, of many liberals and many liberal newspapers. It must be remembered, however, that the course of the liberal ministry of 1848 was such that it made a disruption of the party inevitable, and that long before Mr. Brown turned from them, the Toronto *Examiner* had vigorously denounced them, and that a party had even appeared in the liberal ranks in parliament hostile to the government. When this opposition first appeared Mr. Brown vigorously attacked it, and humorously designated Caleb Hopkins and Malcolm Cameron as "*Clear Grits*," this being the first time the phrase, now commonly applied to the party generally, was used. He hoped at the time that the indications of discontent then apparent among ministerial supporters would have a salutary effect. When this appeared hopeless he at once determined to adhere to principle by proclaiming his views, let the consequences be what they might.

It is impossible to condemn such a course, if wisely conducted. It would be rash to say that this was always the case ; and, on the other hand, it would be unjust to say that Mr. Brown was not actuated by the best motives, and that success was not achieved at last for the principles he advocated mainly or very largely in consequence of his efforts at that early day. His course at that time, in vigorously opposing his own political friends when recreant to their principles, undoubtedly secured the complete triumph of those principles at a much earlier day than if he had allowed them to neglect these interests with impunity.

Every one will remember that he afterwards acted heartily with many public men of his own party whom he at one time opposed because they supported a policy of delay, thereby showing a proper but generous spirit, and a right appreciation of the necessities of political life. In no one thing did he sacrifice so much of his personal feeling as when he consented to serve in the same administration with Mr. John A. Macdonald : that gentleman had done him a grievous injury in making the charges he did concerning Mr. Brown's conduct while serving on the Kingston Penitentiary commission, which was never atoned for. Nothing could be more unpalatable than to have such a colleague, but Mr. Brown, at the request of his party, joined Sir E. Taché's government to carry out the confederation scheme. When he left the coalition government he resumed his former relations of non-intercourse with Mr. John A. Macdonald, though doubtless prepared at any time to accept in its right spirit any expression of regret for so unjustifiable an accusation as had been made. That expression never was uttered. It is known that Mr. Macdonald promised, when the coalition government was formed, to make a public retractation of the false charges he had brought against Mr. Brown in this matter. This promise he failed to fulfil, thereby lowering his own position, and justifying Mr. Brown in refusing any social recognition of him. Mr. Macdonald might possibly have pleaded, as many of his supporters did, that he had reason to believe the charges true when he made them ; but when, with a committee of his own choosing, he failed utterly in establishing a single charge, he should at once have risen to the dignity of the occasion, and admitted he had been deceived, and apologized for the attack.

Hot words and bitter expressions are often doubtless exchanged in political warfare by most leaders, and Mr. Brown was no exception to the rule, but he never transgressed by making a purely personal attack, and many with whom he had fierce struggles in the arena of politics became afterwards his warmest friends. A man of strong feeling and warm enthusiastic disposition, he conveyed sometimes to those who met him occasionally the idea that he was intolerant of other people's opinions, and resolved to have his own way. Those who thought so did not know him. He was often blamed by his close allies in the Liberal ranks for too readily admitting into political confidence men who had shown something very like a wilful abandonment of party and principle. In council he was always disposed to listen to others' arguments, and defer much to the opinions of those in whom he had confidence. As a political leader he was always considerate to his supporters, but he would not lead on any doubtful policy, and when once a policy was adopted by his party, none was so resolute in carrying it towards a conclusion. A notable instance occurred in 1860, when he moved certain resolutions in the House of Assembly, in pursuance of the conclusions at which the Reform Convention of September, 1859, had arrived. Several powerful members, including the late J. S. Macdonald, H. M. Foley, and Dr. Connor, objected to his proceeding with the resolutions, but he resolutely adhered to the policy adopted, and the recusants were obliged to submit.

It must be admitted that many of the objections to his thorough system in political life between 1850 and 1865 were based on the belief that it would keep the liberal party out of power. He cared chiefly for a straight advocacy of essential principles, with the belief that every struggle brought them nearer his reach. He saw no special benefit in having a government called by the name of reform, composed of men who called themselves reformers, if they were either unable or unwilling to give effect to reform measures and principles. His principal opponent in the reform ranks, on the other hand, did not hesitate to say openly in parliament that he was prepared to join any combination of parties which would prevent any disturbance of the then existing union, even so far as to grant representation by population. This policy doubtless kept Mr. Hincks in power for some years, and so far kept in the background reforms which were inevitable, and which an honest perseverance in pursuing a liberal policy on his part might have anticipated by some years. The one gravitated naturally to the Tory camp on the (political) broad road, and after many years he became a minister again after the reforms had been accomplished which he had determinately resolved to prevent by "any combina-"tions." The other had the proud satisfaction of knowing that to his efforts mainly was his party and his province indebted for the final triumph of the principles he had so long contended for. Long before he passed away there was no vestige of state-churchism in the land; all churches stood equal in the eye of the law. A just system of parliamentary representation had taken the place of one partial and unjust; and in addition to this, his long cherished hope of living to see a powerful British nationality in America was realized in connection with the reforms he had advocated. The "some joint authority" of the modest convention resolutions in 1859 had developed into a powerful federal government, exercising supreme authority from Cape Breton to Vancouver, within the bounds of the "federative" system quietly suggested by Mr. Brown in his report from the House committee in 1864, already referred to.

Mr. Brown often remarked in his speeches, when replying to charges of being ambitious, that few men who devoted themselves to a pressing advocacy of reform and change lived to benefit personally by them, and that assuredly he did not expect to be any exception. This in his case was literally true. He was for eighteen months a member of a coalition government formed to carry out his programme of political changes, but left that government as soon as the proposed reforms were safe. If being a member of a government be a political reward, his was a poor one—a minister for eighteen months out of thirty-six years of continuous service. He had, however, an honourable pride in contemplating his achievements, and his name will ever be associated with the federal union of the British provinces and the obtainment of justice for his own province.

In the early years of his journalistic life, when heading the assault against the endowment by the state of any church, he was looked upon as the enemy of the favoured sects. Every person now knows that a church does not prosper necessarily because the state aids it. In Canada it was shown that those churches prospered most which did not touch the money or lands of the state ; while the churches that did receive a share of the clergy reserve lands did not prosper so much. The sympathy of the masses was withheld, from college and church alike, as long as the injustice continued, and it was only after the lapse of years had sufficed to induce forgetfulness of the past that all the churches shared in the full sympathy and support of the people. Perhaps in nothing else did Mr. Brown rejoice so much in the latter years of his life as the settled state of public opinion as to the permanent nature of the relations of Canada and Great Britain. Twenty-five years before there was at least an uneasy feeling abroad; once or twice this feeling found expression in several parts of Canada ; its existence was referred to in despatches from Canada to the Imperial government. Some classes of British politicians seemed disposed to look upon the colonial possessions of the empire as a clog and hindrance—a source of danger and expense. This latter class seemed to have only one consideration before their political vision, "Will it pay?" One Governor-General at least went so far as to tell Canadians that they might cut the connection as soon as they pleased, so far as Great Britain was concerned. The school of commercial politicians had obtained so strong a footing in Britain that they felt able to instruct or influence the Queen's representative in Canada to make such a public declaration. Mr. Brown always maintained that perfect liberty and independence of action in everything of local concern was compatible with the colonial state of political existence. He felt an honest pride in the glory of the British empire, and he also felt that the cause of freedom over the world would be seriously injured by its disintegration, even so far as to sever any of its great colonies. It was with him both a matter of sound public policy and sentiment to remain a member of the great Anglo-Saxon power, to share in its growth and successes, and, if need be, to bear a share of its reverses.

Mr. Brown and the *Globe* did much to cultivate a national feeling, national in the broadest sense of the term, embracing Great Britain and all her colonies. He was, however, a true cosmopolitan in this sense, that he was a warm friend of the United States, Britain's child but also commercial rival, and of all other countries where the arm of the oppressor was broken. During the existence of the slave power in the United States there was no more outspoken friend of the poor slave than George Brown ; no more eloquent defender of the fugitive than he when the slave-driver dared to pursue his human chattel into Canada.

True to his Scottish instincts, he was a strong friend of Sabbath observance. Though a strong voluntary in principle, he deemed a public recognition of the Sabbath by individuals and governmental departments as a sacred duty—an essential one in the maintenance of public morality.

The cause of temperance and every moral reform found in Mr. Brown a warm friend and courageous advocate. The *Globe*, under the management of the brothers George and Gordon, had therefore a firm footing with the better classes of the Canadian people, as all felt that, whether its political preferences were at all times acceptable or not, it was the consistent friend of public morality.

Mr. Brown was a member of the presbyterian church, devotedly attached to what was, before the union, the Free Church section of that body. Had he lived in the time of the Stuart persecutions he would have been, from his nature, among the first to sign the Solemn League and Covenant—among the first to repudiate allegiance to an untruthful and persecuting monarch. As it was, he was a devoted admirer of the noble men who fought for religious liberty in Scotland and secured the same blessing for England.

As to his domestic relations, the biographer may have no right to do more than say that they were singularly happy. Whatever clouds might cross his path outside, he carried the utmost cheerfulness and geniality to his home ; a chief trait of character was his intense love of home. His meetings with wife and children, when the exacting day's duties and vexations were over, were perfect illustrations of

domestic happiness and enjoyment.   No man could be more beloved
than he was by his family ; no man deserved that love more.   It is
pleasant for them to look back to, but it made the parting all the
more painful.   He left two daughters and one son, named after himself (George Mackenzie Brown), to mourn a loss to them irreparable,
though Mrs. Brown, with her well-known excellent qualities of heart
and head, will nobly fulfil many of the duties the lamented father
would have discharged if he had been spared.

IN MEMORIAM.

" And when the stream
    Which overflowed the soul was passed away,
    A consciousness remained that it had left,
    Deposited upon the silent shore
    Of memory, images and precious thoughts
    That shall not die, and cannot be destroyed."
WORDSWORTH.

The brave, large-hearted statesman was now at rest. To use Dr. Cochrane's eloquent words, " There has been laid in the grave, since " last we assembled in the house of God, a kingly man ; one who for " many years has by unanimous consent been ranked among the " princes of the land. Over his grave the people have wept, and a " feeling of unfeigned sadness has possessed all hearts, because of his " untimely end." The voice of censure and detraction was hushed ; only what was generous and kindly in the nature of the departed was remembered. Tokens of universal sorrow were everywhere manifested, and found expression in the press of Canada and the United States ; in public meetings where all parties attended ; in church courts ; and in the resolutions passed by municipal corporations. In nearly all the churches of Toronto reference was made to the lamentable event on the Sabbath he died ; and on the succeeding Sabbath a very large number of sermons were preached in which his life and death were discoursed upon. Touching reference was made, in some of the ecclesiastical bodies of several churches at meetings held shortly afterwards, to the shocking occurrence by which one so prominent and generally beloved was stricken to the earth, and a family so harmonious and happy thrown into the deepest distress to which humanity is subject.

It was to be expected that the party he had led so long and so well in political warfare should in a special manner seek to do honour to the memory of the departed leader. This feeling naturally led to reform associations and clubs in all quarters calling meetings, at which resolutions were passed expressive of the deepest sorrow for his untimely fate, and kindly regard for his family in their grief. The sympathy for the family was genuine and hearty, and could public feeling have assuaged their grief, that grief had not lasted long. To that hour the domestic circle had been unbroken, and the genius of domestic peace presided over the household as if it never would be broken.   They were soon to learn that

> " There is no fireside, howsoe'er defended,
>   But has one vacant chair."

Could brilliant talents, a splendid record as politician and publicist, an unblemished reputation in private life, have detained him, he had not left ; but sometimes, as now, "Death loves a shining mark, a signal blow."

The manifestations of public sympathy were all that could be desired by Mr. Brown's warmest friends.   Extracts now given from some of the sermons and proceedings at public meetings, and a selection from the numerous addresses of condolence sent, will show better than any description the extent and character of these public manifestations.

Shortly after his death there was a general desire expressed in favour of the erection of a monument to his memory in some public place in the city of Toronto.   In accordance with this desire, a meeting was called in Shaftesbury Hall, which was attended by a large number of prominent citizens, including several members of the local government.   After a number of gentlemen had addressed the meeting, all in favour of the proposed monument, a committee was appointed to carry out the proposal made.   Subsequently the committee met and organized at the Board of Trade rooms, with John Macdonald, Esq., as chairman, James D. Edgar, Esq., as secretary, and David Blain, Esq., as treasurer.   Subscription lists were sent to various parts of the country, and, generally speaking, were well signed.   It was decided to erect a statue of Mr. Brown in the University Park, in a spot to be selected by the authorities.   Mr. Brodie, the celebrated sculptor of Edinburgh, was selected to execute the work, but unfortunately Mr. Brodie was taken ill before he had well commenced the statue, and, after a brief illness, expired.   There will not, however, be any serious delay in getting the work executed, as another artist has been engaged of equally high reputation.

It may well be said that no monument was needed to keep the name of George Brown in remembrance, even with those who did not always agree with him ; but there seemed to be a general desire to do honour to his memory in the manner chosen in all ages to commemorate the name of the chief citizens whose names were already linked with the history of their country.   His name and public labours will always occupy a large space in the history of Canada, and however men may differ as to the wisdom or unwisdom of his political views and the mode of giving them effect, all will admit that his record is an honourable one.   His friends can boast also that the principles he advocated from his first advent in Canada were crystallized in the statutes of the country before his death, very largely by his own efforts.

When the inscription on his marble monument will be worn away, the work he accomplished, the patriotism he manifested, will be held in grateful remembrance. The granite or marble will yield to the ravages of time, but the results of his labour will influence national life, stimulate individual effort, and exert a moral influence to the end of time.

CITY COUNCIL OF TORONTO.

At a meeting of the Council of the Corporation of the city of Toronto, held on Monday, the 10th day of May, 1880, the following resolution was unanimously adopted :

Moved by Alderman McMurrich, seconded by Alderman Close, and

Resolved,—That the death of the Honourable George Brown, senator of Canada, after a painful and lingering illness, caused by an attack by a mis-guided person on the 25th March, which, while not immediately fatal, has resulted in his demise on the 9th instant, is regarded by this Council with sentiments of no common emotion and sorrow.

That on an occasion such as the present all party feeling is hushed, and every dividing sentiment merged in the recognition of eminent talent, high patriotism, loyal citizenship, and a position proudly earned as one of the foremost of Canada's public and representative men.

That in the removal, under such appalling circumstances, in the full vigour of his commanding abilities, of one possessing so distinguished a hold on the sympathies of his fellow-countrymen and citizens, it is difficult to find words which will adequately express the profound feeling by which the Council are moved. They can but record a national loss of the gravest character, and a domestic bereavement of the most painful nature, and, while joining in the feeling of respect which pervades every class of society in contemplating the one, approach the other with still sadder feelings, in attempting to offer to his sorrowing widow and family an expression of heartfelt sympathy and condolence.

JAMES BEATY, Jr., *Mayor.*
ROBERT RODDY, *Clerk.*
SAMUEL B. HARMAN,
Treasurer, and Keeper of the Civic Seal.

COUNCIL CHAMBER, TORONTO,
   May 10th, 1880.

BUFFALO CITY COUNCIL.

CITY CLERK'S OFFICE, BUFFALO,
May 11th, 1880.

I, W. P. Burns, City Clerk of Buffalo, New York, hereby certify that at a meeting of the Common Council, held at the Council Chamber in the City and County Hall on the 10th day of May, A.D. 1880, a preamble and resolutions were adopted, of which the following is a true copy :

Whereas, God in His providence has removed from earth, in the fulness of his years, the Hon. George Brown, of Toronto, Ont.—a man strong in purpose, pure in heart and noble in life ; by whose death this country and the people of the world have lost a friend to the cause of freedom ; whose broad grasp and advanced ideas were ever exerted in the interests of liberty and humanity ; and as the Dominion of Canada in his death has lost a statesman and journalist who was wise in council and characterized for his courage and veracity, and who filled every position to which he was called with fidelity and honour—therefore, be it

Resolved,—That the Common Council of the city of Buffalo hereby record their tribute of respect to the memory of our deceased friend and the distinguished statesman, and with grief express in this feeble manner our sympathy with the bereaved family of the deceased, and with his country-men in this their hour of trial.

Resolved,—That His Honour the Mayor be requested to cause the flag on the City Hall to be placed at half mast on Wednesday, the day of the funeral, as a token of respect to the memory of the deceased.

Resolved,—That a copy of these resolutions be forwarded by the City Clerk to the family of the departed.

Adopted unanimously.

(Signed,)   W. P. BURNS, City Clerk.

[Seal.]
ALEX. BRUSH, Mayor.

UNIVERSITY OF TORONTO.

REGISTRAR'S OFFICE, May 13th, 1880.

DEAR MADAM,—I have the honour to enclose herewith copy of resolution of the Senate of the University, passed at a meeting held on Thursday, the 13th instant.

I have the honour to be, Madam,
Your obedient servant,

(Signed,)   W. G. FALCONBRIDGE, Registrar.

MRS. BROWN, Beverley Street, Toronto.

Moved by Dr. Wilson, and seconded by Professor Buckland, and

Resolved,—That the Senate of the University of Toronto, at this its first meeting after the death of the Honourable George Brown—a senator of the Dominion of Canada, a member of this senate, and throughout his long public career a consistent and faithful advocate of the highest interests of education and of the extension of its privileges to all, untrammelled by distinction of race or creed—record their profound sorrow at the loss which the university, in common with the province and the entire Dominion, sustains by his death.

Certified as a copy of a minute of a meeting of the senate, held the 13th May, A.D. 1880.

(Signed,)   W. G. FALCONBRIDGE, Registrar.

FROM CANADIANS IN CHICAGO.

CITY OF CHICAGO, COOK COUNTY, ILLINOIS,
May 13th, 1880.

To MRS. GEORGE BROWN, Toronto, Canada.

DEAR MADAM,—A large number of Canadian gentlemen, residing in this city, held a meeting in the exchange room of the Grand Pacific Hotel, on the evening of the 12th instant, to give expression to their feelings on the receipt of the news of the death of the late Hon. George Brown, your lamented husband ; and, as instructed by the meeting, we have the honour to convey to you a copy of the resolutions then adopted, with the assurance of our high regard and sympathy with yourself and family in the loss you have sustained.

We are, Dear Madam, very respectfully,

(Signed,)   ALEXANDER C. BELL, *Chairman.*
               CLEMENT D. GRASETT, *Secretary.*

Mr. C. R. Brooke, formerly of Toronto, after giving a *resumé* of the principal events connected with Canadian history during the last half century, moved the following memorial resolutions, which were seconded by Mr. Hugh Innis, and unanimously adopted :

Resolved,—That the Canadian residents in Chicago have heard with profound sorrow of the death, by the hands of an assassin, of the Hon. George Brown, of Toronto, the founder and editor-in-chief of the *Globe* newspaper, for nearly forty years one of the most prominent statesmen of the Dominion of Canada.

He was the indomitable advocate of many great reforms, and had the rare fortune, of living to see them all accomplished, and the country of his adoption finally united in a confederation, which will in future years enable her to rank among the most independent and happy nations of the world.

Resolved,—That so useful a life should be thus struck down is to the Dominion of Canada a national calamity, and to his numerous friends who have observed his political and literary life, a cause of the deepest regret.

Resolved,—That the meeting instructs its chairman and secretary to forward a copy of these resolutions to his bereaved family, with an expression of its sympathy with them in the great and irreparable loss they have sustained, and as a mark of respect entertained by the Canadian residents of Chicago for one whose name as a statesman has been so intimately connected with every movement for constitutional reform in a country which will remain endeared to them by early recollections.

Done at Chicago, Illinois, this 12th day of May, 1880.

(Signed,)   ALEXANDER C. BELL, *Chairman.*
               CLEMENT D. GRASETT, *Secretary.*

CITY COUNCIL, OTTAWA.

Moved by Alderman Scott, seconded by Alderman Jamieson,

That this Council hereby expresses its deep regret at the untimely death of the Hon. George Brown, senator, and to place upon record its appreciation of his services as a public man during the past quarter of a century.

Furthermore, this Council expresses deep and sincere condolence with the widow and relations of the deceased gentleman.

Resolved,—That a copy of this resolution, under seal, be sent to the widow of the late Hon. George Brown.

Certified true copy of a resolution of the Council of the Corporation of the city of Ottawa, passed on the 12th day of May, 1880.

W. P. LETT, *City Clerk.*

[Seal.]

CITY COUNCIL, GUELPH.

Moved by Alderman McLagan, and seconded by Alderman Chadwick,

That this Council, acting for and representing the citizens of Guelph, at this its first regular meeting after his death, expresses its great sorrow at the loss the country has sustained in the untimely death of the Hon. George Brown, so suddenly cut off in the prime of his manhood by the dastardly act of an assassin.

Senator Brown, for a period of upwards of a quarter of a century, occupied an exalted position as a statesman, journalist and citizen of his adopted country ; was an unflinching advocate for the political, social and religious liberties of the people ; British connection, equal rights to all classes, irrespective of nationality, creed or colour ; a sincere and devout Christian, who throughout his whole career was an upholder of truth and those great moral principles which enabled him to carry with him to the tomb the white lily of a blameless life ; whose services to his country will be handed down to generations yet unborn as those rendered by one of the greatest and best of our public men who have adorned our legislative halls and our country.

Be it resolved,—That a copy of the foregoing resolution be sent to the family of the late senator, tendering to his sorrowing widow, his fatherless children and his relatives, the deep and fervent sympathy of the citizens of Guelph in their sad bereavement.—*Adopted.*

Jno. Harvey, *City Clerk.*

[Seal.]

GALT TOWN COUNCIL.

May 12th, 1880.

It was moved by Mr. Richard Blain, and seconded by Mr. Hugh McCulloch,

That this Council desires publicly to express its deep regret at the tragic death of the Hon. George Brown, a gentleman whose name has been associated with the history of Canada for the past forty years, and whose name has been a "household word" with its people.

In his lamented death it is felt that the country has lost a sincere friend and devoted servant ; the profession of journalism one of its most vigorous and able writers ; his widow and family a loving husband and father ; and his friends and acquaintances a noble and generous man.

And, to give expression to these sentiments, this Council desires further to express to the widow and family of the deceased their heartfelt sympathy with them in the loss they have sustained, and to express the hope that He who doeth all things well will extend to them His consolation and support.

And that a copy of this resolution be engrossed, and forwarded to Mrs. Brown.

TORONTO PRESBYTERY.

Toronto, 90 Maitland Street, May 21st, 1880.

Mrs. George Brown.

Dear Madam,—The accompanying copy of a minute adopted by the Presbytery of Toronto—which came into my hands only to-day—I now transmit to you, as instructed by the Presbytery so to do. And I beg to say that with all that is contained in said minute I heartily concur.

I have the honour to be, Dear Madam,
Yours with respect and sympathy,

(Signed,)   R. MONTEATH,

Presbytery Clerk.

The Presbytery of Toronto agree to record their deep sorrow at the death of the Hon. George Brown.

In common with the entire community, they recognize his great intellectual abilities and pure character ; his uprightness and zeal for the public welfare ; his consistency, and indomitable perseverance and courage in the advocacy of all measures which approved themselves to his judgment ; and the great services which, thus endowed, he was enabled to render Canada. The healthful moral result of the manifold and earnest labours of Mr. Brown will now also be heartily recognized by all, and his powerful advocacy of interests dear to all who seek the good of society and have respect to the Divine law. To all well directed efforts made for the relief of the suffering and wronged, for the advancement of education, for the protection of the Sabbath, for the establishment and extension of Christianity, he devoted his powerful influence and generous aid. As a member of the presbyterian church, holding with strong conviction its characteristic principles, he did much both directly and indirectly to promote its work in the land ; especially was he honoured to illustrate and defend the freedom which the church of Christ, in all its branches, is entitled to enjoy, while at the same time he zealously guarded the civil prerogatives against all ecclesiastical encroachment. By his pure life and conversation he commended the religion of Christ ; and the Presbytery rejoice to know that he was sustained, during his last trying illness, by his trust in God and in the blood of the Redeemer, and was enabled calmly to submit himself to the will of the Almighty.

The Presbytery desire to express their deep and respectful sympathy with all the members of the bereaved family, and their earnest prayer that grace may be given to sustain them under the pressure of their great affliction, and to sanctify it to their spiritual and eternal welfare.

In name and by appointment of the Presbytery of Toronto,

(Signed,)   JNO. SMITH, *Moderator.*
R. MONTEATH, *Clerk.*

TORONTO, 11th May, 1880.

COLOURED CITIZENS OF TORONTO.

At a meeting held in the Baptist Chapel (corner of Victoria and Queen Streets) by the coloured citizens on this date, the following resolutions were ordered to be sent to the family of the late Hon. George Brown :

Resolved,—That the death of the Hon. George Brown, late senator of Canada, has caused another vacancy in the ranks of the noble and disinterested champions of freedom which can never be filled, and that we recognize that loss with the deepest and most heartfelt feelings of sorrow and regret, knowing that the Sumner of Canada has passed away, whose voice and pen was always ready, able and willing to do battle for the cause of the downtrodden and oppressed of all peoples.

11

That we tender our earnest and heartfelt sympathy to the bereaved family, and that we ever pray that the Divine blessing may comfort them in this their dire affliction.

HENRY LEWIS, *President.*
F. G. SIMPSON, *Secretary.*

TORONTO, May 11, 1880.

CONGREGATIONAL CHURCH.

TORONTO, May 12th, 1880.

MRS. GEORGE BROWN.

DEAR MADAM,—The Central Association of Congregational ministers—assembled this day in Zion Church, Toronto—passed the following resolution, and desired me to forward the same to you.

Moved by the Rev. John Burton, B.A., seconded by the Rev. J. J. Hindley, M.A., and unanimously

Resolved,—That this Association would record its deep sense of loss sustained by the country in the death of the late Hon. George Brown.

They would recognize with gratitude the important part he has taken in the formation of our Canadian nationality and liberties, his energy as a journalist, and his worth as a private citizen. They would express their deep sympathy with his bereaved widow and family, commending them to the consolation of a sympathizing Saviour, and the hope of the reunion hereafter.

May the God of all comfort comfort them in their deep affliction.

J. I. HINDLEY, *Secretary.*

COBDEN CLUB, ENGLAND.

At a meeting of the committee, held on the 22nd May, 1880, it was resolved that an expression of the great regret felt by the committee on hearing of the death of the Hon. George Brown, of Toronto, an honorary member of the club, should be placed on the minutes of the proceedings of the committee.

(Signed,)   RICHARD GOWING, *Secretary.*
THOS. B. POTTER, *Hon. Secretary.*

Extract from the Proceedings of the County Council of the County of Oxford.

COUNTY COUNCIL CHAMBER, WOODSTOCK,
18th June, 1880.

Moved by Mr. Wm. Peers, seconded by Mr. B. Hopkins, and

Resolved,—That this Council embrace the first opportunity to express their profound regret at the loss the Dominion of Canada has sustained by the death of the late Hon. George Brown, a gentleman who formerly represented this county in parliament, and has, as a journalist, statesman, agriculturalist and a man, for many years laboured with distinguished ability and zeal to serve his adopted country according to his best judgment.

And we desire also to express our deep disgust and horror at the crime which led to his death ; and our sincere sympathy with his widow and bereaved family and friends.

And that a copy of this resolution, signed by the Warden and Clerk, with the corporate seal attached, be forwarded to Mrs. Brown.

A. L. WILCOX, *Warden.*
[Seal.]   JAMES WHITE, *County Clerk.*

"CLUB NATIONALE," MONTREAL.

At a largely attended meeting of reformers and members of the "Club Nationale," held on Friday evening in the club's rooms, the following resolutions were passed on the sad death of the deceased senator :

It was moved by Messrs. R. Profontaine, M.P.P., Hon. J. R. Thibaudeau, Ald. Thomas Wilson, Joseph Duhamel. Q.C., Chs. Berger, J. N. Bieuvenu, Chs. Meunier and Raoul Dandurand,

That this meeting has learned with regret of the death of the Hon. George Brown, who, as a journalist, legislator and statesman, figured in the front rank of the defenders of the reform and progressive party of Canada.

That by his remarkable talents, his love of work and energy, Mr. Brown proved himself an honour to his adopted country, and his name will be perpetuated in its history during this century for elevating to its highest rank the Canadian press, procuring the secularization of the clergy reserves, and the abolition of certain privileges of caste.

That the friends of the liberal party leave to history all the weight of impartial judgment which it will carry on certain acts of Mr. Brown, and it will become recognized that this distinguished man was imbued with patriotic sentiments and ideas really in harmony with the liberalism and professions that we, as a party, know them under the British constitution.

It was moved by Messrs. Ernest Tremblay, N. W. Trenholme, Q.C., F. X. Archambault, Q.C., Euclide Roy, Chs. Ouide Perrault, H. Beaugrand, N. Lefebvre, A. P. Globensky, G. A. Morrison and P. R. Martineau,

That the name of Hon. George Brown will remain engraved on the national monument, which is called responsible government of Canada.

That Mr. Brown was one of those courageous men, one of those clear-minded patriots, who contributed to obtain for Canadians the fulness of responsible government, to acclimate it to Canada, to fight against the encroachments of the Crown, and to inspire the population with love and respect for the institutions which we have fully enjoyed since 1847.

It was moved by Messrs. A. E. Poirier, C. A. Geoffrion, Q.C., E. C. Monk, Ald. Robert, P. G. Martineau, P. H. Roy, A. P. Carriveau,

That this meeting offers its condolence to the family of the Hon. George Brown, fallen under the bullet of the cowardly assassin at the moment when his contemporaries, rising above political passions, were rendering just homage to the philanthropy, to the patriotism which was so greatly personified in the regretted deceased.

It was moved by Messrs. A. P. Morin, A. S. Mackay, Louis Perrault, F. O. Rinfret, L. Forget, P. Durandand, and J. D. Leduc,

That a copy of the present resolutions be transmitted to the family of the deceased, to the liberal press of the Province of Quebec, to the *Globe* of Toronto and the *Free Press* of Ottawa.

D. MESSIER, *President.*
P. R. MARTINEAU, *Secretary.*

BROCKVILLE TOWN COUNCIL.

BROCKVILLE COUNCIL CHAMBER,
17th May, 1880.

Moved by Mr. W. H. Cole, seconded by Mr. G. A. Dana, and

Resolved,—That we, the Town Council of Brockville, take the opportunity of this our first meeting to express our regret at the untimely death of the late Hon. George Brown, one of Canada's greatest statesmen, and whose name has been so long identified with the best interests of our country ; and whose death will be an irreparable loss to the Dominion.

And we would also express our horror at the dastardly act which caused his death, and we beg most respectfully to tender to his bereaved family our heartfelt sympathy with them in this their sad affliction ; and that the Clerk do forward a copy of this resolution, with the seal of this Corporation attached thereto, to the widow of the deceased.

WM. HENRY COMSTOCK, *Mayor.*
JOHN DARGAVEL, *Town Clerk.*

[Seal.]

PORT HOPE TOWN COUNCIL.

COUNCIL CHAMBER, PORT HOPE,
May 11th, 1880.

MRS. GEORGE BROWN, Toronto.

MADAM,—I am desired by the Mayor and Council of the Corporation of the Town of Port Hope to forward you a copy of the following resolution which was passed at the meeting held on Monday, the 10th May, 1880:

Moved by Councillor B. D. Deering, seconded by Councillor C A. Hagerman, and

Resolved,—That this Council having heard with regret of the death of the Hon. George Brown, and being deeply sensible of his great public services, desire to express its sincere sympathy with the widow and family of the deceased, and instructs the Clerk to forward to them this expression of condolence with them in their great affliction.

H. V. SANDERS, *Town Clerk.*

WOODSTOCK TOWN COUNCIL.

COUNCIL CHAMBER, WOODSTOCK,
May 10th, 1880.

Moved by Henry Parker, seconded by Warren Totten, and

Resolved,—That the members of the Council of the town of Woodstock avail themselves of this opportunity of expressing their profound sorrow at the demise on Sunday last of the Hon. George Brown, who has been at different times the representative in parliament of both ridings of this county. The occurrence which prostrated that hon. gentleman sent a thrill of horror throughout the length and breadth of the Dominion, and it was hoped, in the merciful dispensation of Providence, no disastrous effect would follow. It has been ordered otherwise, and one of Canada's greatest statesmen has fallen. We desire to extend to the bereaved widow and family of the deceased our heartfelt sympathy in their sore affliction, and we co-operate with our fellow-countrymen, of every political party and creed, in paying a tribute of respect to one whose energies were ever devoted to his country's good, and whose example will be ever remembered in the future of our country's progress ; and that this Council, as a token of respect to the memory of the lamented deceased, do now adjourn; and that a copy of this resolution, with the corporate seal affixed thereto, be transmitted by his Worship the Mayor to his family.

JAMES SUTHERLAND, Mayor.

[Seal.]

GAELIC SOCIETY, TORONTO.

TALLA SHAFTESBURY,
10mh latha d'on 5mh Mios, 1880.

Aig coinneamh mhiosail comunn Gailig Thoronto chaidh na ruintean a leanas a leughadh a's a dhaingneachadh le lan aonta :

Run I.—Gur h'ann le mulad annabarrach a chuala sinn mu bhas bronach an Urramaich Deorsa Brunn, duine uasal a bha re iomad bliadhna a saothrachadh gu misneachail, durachdach, agus gu bitheanta le mor shoir-bheachadh ann an aobhar na duthcha so s'an robh a chomhnuidh, agus a bha daonnan a nochdadh cairdeas blath do'n ghineal do'm buin sinne.

Run II.—Gum bheil sinn a co-mhothachadh gu trom domhain le teagh-lach an fhir-stata nach maireann, agus gur e ar dochas durachdach gum faigh iad am measg am bron diomhair a's an creach, solus agus furtachd anns an Ti as airde, far an robh an earaid aiumeil cliuiteach riamh a scall-tuinn airson cuideachadh agus treorachadh.

Run III.—Gun teid ath-sgriobhadh do na ruin so a chur a dh'ionnsuidh teaghlach an fhir a chaochail, agus mar an ceudna do'n Phaipeir-naigheachd ris an robh e an comh-cheangal.

DONULL MACEOCHAIN,
Run Chleireach.

(Translation).

At their monthly meeting, held at Shaftesbury Hall, on Monday, May 10th, 1880, the Gaelic Society of Toronto unanimously passed the following resolutions :

First,—"That it is with extreme sorrow we have heard of the tragic death of the Hon. George Brown, a gentleman who for so many years exerted himself strenuously and often successfully in the cause of his adopted country, and always showed a warm friendship for the race to which we belong."

Second,—"That we deeply sympathize with the bereaved family of the deceased statesman, and earnestly hope that they may find amid their profound grief consolation in that great Being to whom their distinguished relative ever looked for help and guidance."

Third,—"That a copy of these resolutions be sent to the family of the departed."

 LIFE AND SPEECHES OF

KINGSTON REFORM ASSOCIATION.

Moved by Mr. John Carruthers, seconded by Mr. William Ford, and

Resolved,—That the Reform Association of Kingston deplore the national loss sustained by his adopted country in the death of the Hon. George Brown—a great journalist, who founded and conducted to eminent success the leading organ of public opinion in Canada; a distinguished statesman, whose public life was devoted to the fearless advocacy of civil liberty; whose determined efforts contributed largely to the establishment of responsible government in this province; to whose lofty patriotism, rising above mere party considerations, the confederation of the British North American Provinces was mainly due; and one who unselfishly dedicated his tireless energies and great talents to the furtherance of the public good and the dissemination of the principles of the great reform party.

Moved by B. M. Britton, Esq., seconded by C. F. Gildersleeve, Esq., and

Resolved,—That this Association desire to express their deepest sympathy with the widow, family, and other relatives of the Hon. George Brown in the hour of their great grief, and to convey to them a heartfelt expression of profound sorrow that a life so blameless in all its domestic relations, and so eminent in its services to the state, should have had so sad and untimely an end.

Moved by Alexander Gunn, Esq., M.P., seconded by William Robinson, Esq., and

Resolved,—That a copy of the resolutions just moved be forwarded by the secretary to the widow of the Hon. George Brown.

ST. THOMAS REFORMERS.

St. Thomas, May 18, 1880.

Dear Madam,—I have been instructed to communicate to you the resolutions passed at a meeting of reformers held at this town on the 11th inst. A copy of the minutes of the meeting is accordingly subjoined. I have the honour to enclose herewith copies of the St. Thomas *Journal* of May 11th and May 14th, 1880, and to remain

Yours respectfully,

James H. Coyne, *Secretary.*

Mrs. G. Brown, Beverley Street, Toronto.

A meeting of reformers, which was attended by a large number of representative gentlemen belonging to the town and county, was held in the Town Hall this afternoon for the purpose of expressing their sympathy with the relatives of the late Mr. Brown in their sad bereavement, and to record their admiration of his great qualities.

Mr. Walter E. Murray, of Aylmer, was appointed chairman, and James H. Coyne, of St. Thomas, secretary.

A letter was read by the secretary from Mr. T. M. Nairn, M.P.P., regretting his inability to be present, and expressing his high regard and esteem for the deceased statesman, and his sorrow for the loss the party and country had sustained in his death.

It was intimated by the chairman that Dr. Wilson, ex-M.P.P., had been unexpectedly called away by telegram, and desired to express his sympathy with the objects of the meeting.

Moved by Rev. Mr. Fraser, and

Resolved,—That by the death of the Hon. George Brown Canada has lost a statesman, who perhaps more than any other has contributed to the upbuilding of our Canadian nationality in all that tends to make a great and noble people; a citizen who has always laboured for the advancement of every worthy and beneficent cause; a man who, throughout his career " wearing the white flower of a blameless life," has left a memory to his fellow-countrymen which they will always cherish as a most valued inheritance.

The motion was seconded by Rev. D. Rowland, and supported by Rev. R. C. Parsons and Rev. George Simpson.

Moved by Mr. Colin MacDougall, and

Resolved,—That whereas the late Senator Brown was for many years the trusted leader of reform principles in this province, and by his great ability, energy and eloquence, and by his lofty character, he won for himself the love and esteem of his party and the respect of his political opponents, the reformers of St. Thomas and county of Elgin desire on this sad occasion of his death to offer their tribute to the memory of their great statesman and leader, and to express their profound grief at the loss of a life so valuable to the reform party and to the state.

The resolution was seconded by Mr. Joel Lewis, of Yarmouth, and supported by Dr. McCarthy, ex-Mayor, and by Mr. Mayor Smith.

Wm. Coyne, J.P., then moved, seconded by Mr. James Stewart,

That we tender to the widow and children of the deceased our heartfelt sympathy in their great and irreparable loss.

It was then moved by Rev. J. E. Lancely, seconded by John Farley,

That a copy of the resolutions passed at this meeting be forwarded to Mrs. Brown by the secretary.

The several resolutions were carried unanimously.

It was announced that special arrangements had been made with the Great Western Railway on behalf of those who desired to attend the funeral of the Hon. Mr. Brown. A large number intimated their intention of being present to pay the last honours to the great reform leader.

JAMES H. COYNE, *Secretary.*
W. E. MURRAY, *Chairman.*

NORTH GREY REFORM ASSOCIATION.

Moved by A. Gifford, seconded by James Cleland,

That at this, the first meeting of this association since the death of the Hon. George Brown, we desire to place on record the regret we feel at the loss to the country of so able a statesman, so eminent a journalist and champion of liberty as the deceased gentleman was.

That this association deeply sympathize with his bereaved family and relatives; and that the secretary be instructed to forward a copy of this resolution to his family.

REFORM ASSOCIATION, WINDSOR.

WINDSOR, May, 1880.

At a meeting of the Reform Association of Windsor, Ont., held on Tuesday the 11th day of May, 1880, the following resolution was unanimously adopted :

Whereas, the Hon. George Brown has, after many weeks of suffering, yielded up his life a sacrifice to the diabolical act of an assassin, against whom he had committed no offence ;

Whereas, the deceased was for many years the regularly recognized, trusted and esteemed leader of the reform party of Canada, alike in and out of the legislature ;

Whereas, in George Brown we beheld the great champion of civil and religious liberty in Canada, and the genuine patriot through whose courageous advocacy, manly conduct and unflagging exertions, our fair land, after long struggling, attained to the full measure of freedom which the people of this vast Dominion happily now enjoy ;

Whereas, we utterly detest and abhor a resort to violence by individuals as a means of removing real or imaginary grievances ; more especially to that species of heartless crime which at once sacrifices human life and robs nations of their most worthy, useful and best honoured sons ;

Therefore be it Resolved,—That the liberals of Windsor tender their heartfelt sympathy to the widow and other relatives of that distinguished patriot, statesman and journalist, whose unprovoked murder we so deeply deplore.

That a deputation be appointed to represent us at the funeral of the deceased at Toronto, May the 12th.

That we severally wear for one month, upon the left arm, a badge of mourning to show how sensible we are of the great loss which we as members of the liberal party have sustained by the untimely death of Mr. Brown, and how thoroughly we venerate his memory.

That, guided wholly by a desire to see our public men shielded as far as possible from a calamitous end like that which overtook our lamented friend, and uninfluenced by a spirit of vindictiveness, we venture to express the hope that speedy justice may be meted out to the person whose act accomplished Mr. Brown's death.

That this resolution be immediately engrossed, signed by the secretary and chairman of this meeting, and transmitted to Mrs. Brown.

(Signed,) GEORGE E. KILLEN, *Secretary.*
JAMES DOUGALL, *Chairman.*

ST. ANDREW'S SOCIETY, TORONTO.

"Relieve the distressed."

At a meeting of the above society, held on Thursday, June 10th, 1880, the following resolution was unanimously adopted :

That the members of this society take this the earliest opportunity of recording in the minutes their deep sense of the loss they have sustained by and of the regret they feel at the removal by death of the late Honourable George Brown, who was for so many years a member of the society, and who twice filled the office of president of the society.

Mr. Brown by his many estimable qualities had gained the confidence of all nationalities, but was especially dear to those of his own nationality and the members of this society; and while bearing himself with dignity in office, he was ever willing to counsel those who sought his advice and to relieve the distressed where necessity required.

While the society express their own feelings, they also take occasion to offer their heartfelt sympathy to the bereaved members of the late Mr. Brown's family, and commend them to the care of Him who alone can give true comfort in their sore trial.

(Signed,)   WM. RAMSAY, *President.*
JOHN DAVIDSON, }
JAMES GRAHAM, } *Vice-Presidents.*
KENNETH A. MILLER, *Secretary.*

TORONTO, June, 1880.

WHITBY PUBLIC MEETING.

At a public meeting held at Whitby—Mr. James Holden in the chair—the following resolutions of sympathy and condolence were passed :

Moved by Mr. J. E. Farewell, seconded by Mr. D. Ormiston,

That this meeting has learned with deep regret of the death of Hon. Senator Brown from the effect of the wounds received by him on the 25th of March last. That by the dastardly outrage then committed, Canada has lost her foremost statesman and leading journalist—one who by his earnest and praiseworthy efforts to improve the agricultural and develop the commercial interests of the Dominion, has merited the esteem of its people, no less than by his earnest and powerful advocacy of all measures tending to improve the moral and social condition of the people of the Dominion.

Moved by Mr. W. H. Higgins, seconded by Mr. King,

That this meeting, in recording its sincere sorrow at the sad and untimely death of Mr. Brown, desires also to convey to his bereaved widow and family the profound expression of our deep sympathy at their irreparable loss, and that a copy of the proceedings of this meeting be forwarded to Mrs. Brown.

Moved by Mr. Higgins, seconded by Mr. Ferguson,

That all who from Whitby attend the funeral of the Hon. Geo. Brown, on Wednesday, be a delegation from the town, and that they join with those who attend from other parts of the county, so as to give the county of Ontario a representation in the funeral procession.

PUBLIC MEETING, BRANTFORD.

At a public meeting of the inhabitants of the city of Brantford, held in the City Hall on the fourteenth day of May, 1880—at which Dr. Henwood, Mayor, presided, and Allen Cleghorn, Esq., acted as secretary—the following resolutions were unanimously passed :

Moved by Alfred Watts, Esq., seconded by William Paterson, Esq., M.P., and

Resolved,—That the people of the city of Brantford, in the county of Brant, in public meeting assembled, irrespective of party, nationality or creed, do hereby give expression to their profound grief and heartfelt sorrow at the recent death of the Honourable George Brown, senator of this

Dominion. In the death of the honourable senator they feel that Canada has lost one of her most gifted public men—one noted for his patriotism, and for his earnest, conscientious and energetic advocacy of all measures and enterprises which he deemed calculated to promote the social and material interests of Canada, the land of his adoption. While they deeply mourn his early demise, they have the assurance that his name will ever be held in affectionate remembrance by the Canadian people, as he was one whose well-stored mind and indomitable energy were constantly exercised, according to his views, in promoting the welfare of his country, and in ameliorating the condition of humanity. They feel that to the honoured and departed gentleman Canada owes a debt of gratitude for his able and fearless advocacy of the rights of the people, both as a journalist and statesman, for a period of nearly forty years, and as a leader of one of the great political parties of the country.

Moved by H. McK. Wilson, Esq., seconded by Hon. A. S. Hardy, and

Resolved,—That in view of the irreparable loss sustained by the bereaved widow and children and relatives of the deceased statesman, the citizens of Brantford, in the county of Brant, here assembled, respectfully tender to Mrs. Brown, her children, and their relatives, their heartfelt sympathy in their severe affliction, and offer their most fervent prayer that they may be enabled, through divine aid, to endure the painfully sad and unexpected calamity which has befallen them, and in which they have the earnest assurance of the most sincere regret and condolence of all present.

Moved by Thomas McLean, Esq., seconded by William Watt, Jr., Esq., and

Resolved,—That the foregoing resolutions be properly engrossed and transmitted to the widow of the deceased senator.

REGINALD HENWOOD, *Mayor.*
ALLEN CLEGHORN, *Secretary.*

PUBLIC MEETING AT STRATHROY.

In response to a requisition presented to the Mayor, a public meeting was held in the Firemen's Hall, on Tuesday evening, May 11, composed of people of all shades of political opinion, to take into consideration resolutions of condolence to the family of the late George Brown. His Worship the Mayor acted as chairman, and Mr. J. B. Winlow as secretary.

The following resolution was moved by Col. John English, seconded by Dr. Thompson, and carried unanimously:

Resolved,—"That this meeting deeply deplores the great loss inflicted upon Canada by the sad and tragic death of the Hon. George Brown, who, both as a journalist and a statesman, devoted himself for over thirty-five years to the welfare of his country, and who, under all circumstances, was loyal to what he believed to be her best interests, ever anxious to see her enjoy in the fullest degree that constitutional liberty and natural dignity which are the peculiar birthright of a free people."

Besides the mover and seconder, Messrs. Jas. English, Robert Brown (of Metcalfe), and G. W. Ross, M.P., spoke on the resolution.

The following, moved by Mr. E. Rowland, seconded by Mr. Stevenson, was also unanimously adopted:

Resolved,—"That we express our deep sympathy with the family of the deceased, and trust that the memory of his usefulness will in some degree tend to soothe their sorrow, knowing that with them the whole country

weeps over the grave where lies a patriot, a statesman, and a public bene-
factor."

Messrs. D. M. Cameron, T. L. Armstrong, A. Auld, J. H. English,
D. W. Vary and G. W. Francis, also supported the resolution.

The meeting was unanimous in the expression of esteem for the late
Mr. Brown as a journalist, a statesman, and a patriot, as well as of sympathy with his family and friends.

COBOURG REFORM ASSOCIATION.

Cobourg, May 12th.

At a special meeting of the Cobourg Young Men's Reform Club, held at
their room yesterday, for the purpose of appointing a deputation to attend
the funeral of the late Hon. George Brown, the following resolutions were
adopted :

Resolved,—"That we feel deeply the irreparable void caused by the
demise of the Hon. George Brown, not only as a statesman, but as a journalist and leader of public opinion. We feel a useful life is closed. The
lifelong and earnest advocate of the liberal party in the Dominion, the
great promoter of liberal principles, the fearless upholder by voice and
pen of social progress and reform, the champion of civil and religious
liberty, one who had ever at heart the best interests of his country—the
great patriot is now no more. The music of his speech will be heard no
more in the halls of the living. He speaks now and henceforth only
through the past. In his hand truly the pen was mightier than the sword.
In this hour of our loss it behooves us to give expression to our feelings ;
therefore, be it

"*Resolved,*—That we deeply lament the tragic death of the Hon. George
Brown, the great representative of our liberal institutions, for whose
development and advancement his whole life was given with a zeal and
energy never surpassed in the history of any country. The duties in
which he was engaged, the high position he occupied in the councils of the
nation, his far-reaching judgment, his thorough knowledge of men and
principles, all unite in his death in making an irreparable loss to this
Dominion.

"*Resolved,*—While recognizing the greatness and extent of the services
rendered his country and party, and feeling the difficulty of adequately
filling his position, the great principles he advocated will ever be cherished
by all liberals, the fruits of his earnest and devoted life will live to perpetuate his memory, and the lessons of his noble character will ever remain
for our guidance and emulation.

"*Resolved,*—That we deeply sympathize with the family of the honoured
deceased, and assure them in this their hour of affliction that they have the
sincere condolence of every member of this club ; and that a copy of these
resolutions be transmitted to them."

REFORM ASSOCIATION, GODERICH.

At a special meeting of the Reform Association of the town of Goderich,
held on the 12th of May, 1880, the following resolutions were unanimously
adopted :

Moved by M. C. Cameron, Esq., M.P., seconded by A. M. Ross, Esq.,
M.P.P., and

Resolved,—That the members of the Reform Association of the county of Huron hereby desire to express their profound sorrow at the death of the Hon. George Brown, by whose demise Canada has lost one of her ablest, purest, and most patriotic statesmen; one whose powerful influence was always effectively used to further the moral, intellectual, and material interests of his adopted country, and to strengthen the bonds of union with the motherland; whose voice was ever raised in support of constitutional government and human freedom. His unswerving integrity of purpose commanding eloquence, and honest advocacy of everything he deemed for the welfare of his country and humanity, have won for him the love, respect and esteem of the whole people of the Dominion. In him the reform party has lost its most able and trusted guide and leader.

Moved by Mr. S. Sloan, seconded by Mr. Joseph Williams, and

Resolved,—That we tender to the bereaved widow and family our sincerest sympathy with them in their sad affliction, and that a copy of these resolutions be signed by the chairman, and sent to Mrs. Brown.

ELIJAH MARTIN, *President.*

GODERICH, May 12th, 1880.

HAMILTON REFORM ASSOCIATION.

At a meeting of the Reform Association, held in their rooms, May 11th, 1880, the following resolutions were unanimously adopted :

Moved by the Hon. Adam Hope, and seconded by A. T. Wood, Esq.,

That in the death of the Hon. George Brown, not only his family, but his party and his country, mourn the untimely end and the premature grave of one of the noblest men of his day and generation. His patriotic labours are written in the history of his country. He was at all times the unflinching friend of civil and religious liberty, and in that may be summed up his political faith. He was throughout life the warm and consistent supporter of British connection, and no uncertain sound ever escaped his lips on that subject, yet he was ever true to the interests of his adopted country, and fearlessly advocated all the rights and privileges due to a great and self-governed people. He laid the foundations broad and deep of that great confederation of provinces which stretches from the Atlantic to the Pacific, and proudly resting upon that great and essential cardinal principle of all Anglo-Saxon institutions, the local authority, and self-government of the various parts of the great confederacy. In life he was beloved by his friends, and in death he has not left an enemy behind him.

Moved by Mr. J. M. Gibson, M.P.P., and seconded by B. E. Charlton, Esq.,

That while deeply deploring the great public loss that has been sustained in the untimely removal of the distinguished statesman and journalist who has so long filled so prominent a position, and exerted so wide and useful an influence in this country, it is our desire to express, as an association, the feeling universally prevailing in the community of sincere sympathy for the widow and family of the deceased in the hour of their great affliction.

Moved by Charles Magill, Esq., and seconded by A. Copp, Esq.,

That the secretary is hereby instructed to forward a copy of the foregoing resolutions to the family of the deceased.

WM. E. SANFORD, *President.*
J. C. McKEAND, *Secretary.*

HAMILTON, Ont., May 12th, 1880.

BOTHWELL TOWN COUNCIL.

Moved by Councillor Swalwell, seconded by Councillor Johnson, and

Resolved,—That this Council, representing the residents of the town of Bothwell, beg to express their heartfelt sorrow at the lamentable death of the late Hon. George Brown, and our sincere regret that Canada has lost one of its most distinguished and able men. It adds to the grief of many when we recall the pleasant social intercourse and kindly aid rendered by him to us when he founded what is now this prosperous and important town.

PRIMITIVE METHODIST CHURCH—TORONTO DISTRICT.

QUEEN STREET PRIMITIVE METHODIST CHURCH,
TORONTO, May 12th, 1880.

We, the members of the Toronto District meeting of the Primitive Methodist Connection, being in annual meeting assembled, desire most respectfully to offer the widow and family of the late Hon. George Brown our heartfelt sympathy in this their season of sad bereavement.

While we do not wish to intrude on the privacy of their sorrow, we cannot refrain from expressing our high appreciation of the noble character of the deceased gentleman.

By the too early removal of Mr. Brown, we feel that Toronto has lost one of its most distinguished ornaments and most useful citizens; and the Dominion has lost a statesman whose unselfish patriotism and far-seeing sagacity have done not a little to shape its destiny.

We feel it is unnecessary to remind Mrs. Brown and her family that in seasons of trial God is a refuge and strength to His people; and we most sincerely pray that the God of all consolation will most graciously sustain them, so that they may be enabled to bow submissively to His wise though mysterious providence.

Signed on behalf of the District meeting,

WILLIAM BEE, *President.*
JAMES COOPER ANTLIFF, *Secretary.*

To MRS. GEORGE BROWN AND FAMILY,
154 Beverley Street, Toronto.

PORT ELGIN REFORM ASSOCIATION.

PORT ELGIN, May 12.

At a meeting of the Reform Association of the North Riding of Bruce, held at Port Elgin on the 11th inst., it was

Moved by Dr. Sinclair, seconded by M. F. Eby,

"That the Reform Association of the North Riding of Bruce take this opportunity to put on record how exceedingly they deplore the loss sustained not only by the great liberal party of this province, but the entire Dominion, in the death of t e Hon. George Brown, one of the most patriotic and distinguished statesmen and journalists of his adopted country, the great and unceasing advocate of civil and religious liberty, and also his untiring efforts for long years to secure responsible government; and that his death has left a void not easily filled in the hearts of all true patriots in this country."

Moved by A. H. Cannel, seconded by N. M. White,

"That this Association deeply sympathize with the bereaved wife and family of the distinguished statesman in the irreparable loss they have sustained, and would commend them to the care of Him who has promised to be the husband of the widow and the father of the fatherless."

TORONTO REFORM LITERARY AND DEBATING CLUB.

At a meeting of the Toronto Reform Literary and Debating Club, held on Monday the 17th May, 1880, the following resolutions were unanimously adopted :

It is with profound sorrow that this club is called upon to record a great national calamity. That under circumstances most painful and appalling, the Honourable George Brown, while in the full vigour of life, has been removed by death from the midst of our community.

With a knowledge of the man, we can with confidence point to a life nobly devoted to the service of his country ; to the advocacy of all the great reforms intended for the people's good for the last thirty-seven years ; to a heart pure and a character stainless, which in all the heat and temptations of a prominent public career never swerved from the line of stern, unflinching integrity ; to an energy and courage equal to the great occasions of which he formed a part; a mental power and breadth of thought attested by the results which he achieved ; a geniality and kindness of bearing which will make his form long missed from our streets. He was a man who deemed life's exertions best rewarded by a consciousness of having done right, who regarded a title to a place in the hearts of his countrymen as a Canadian's highest rank ; who encouraged in younger men the exercise and development of those talents and virtues so marked in himself.

Therefore, Resolved,—That the Toronto Reform Literary and Debating Club expresses its deep and sincere grief at the loss to his country, his fellow-townsmen and his family, of him who was at once a statesman and patriot, the respected neighbour and citizen, a kind husband and father; whose example has been an inspiration to so many of those who, following after him, have battled in the cause of justice and freedom.

Resolved,—That a copy of these resolutions be transmitted to the afflicted widow of the honoured dead, with an earnest expression of the hope that she and her family may be supported in this terrible hour of trial by that overruling Providence whose mercy, however mysteriously bestowed, is over all His works.

(Signed,)

G. B. SMITH, *President.*
W. MALLOY, *Secretary.*

TORONTO, May, 1880.
[Seal.]

CALEDONIAN SOCIETY, TORONTO.

At the regular monthly meeting of the Caledonian Society, held in their room at Shaftesbury Hall, on Tuesday, the first day of June, 1880, the following resolution was unanimously adopted :

This society mourns the loss of the Hon. George Brown, one of its most active members—one who held the office of president for several years ; who was intimately known to us all, and who always took a warm interest in everything connected with this society ; one who was always ready to assist the poor and needy, to give advice to strangers, to befriend the friendless, and to promote the well-being of all with whom he came in contact.

The members one and all desire to express their deep sympathy with Mrs. Brown and her family in their sad bereavement, and to commend them to the care of Him who has promised to be the husband of the widow and the father of the fatherless.

(Signed,) WM. ADAMSON, *President.*
A. G. HODGE, *Secretary.*

TORONTO, June, 1880.
[Seal.]

COUNTY COUNCIL, HALDIMAND.

Moved by Mr. Nelles, seconded by Mr. Montague, and

Resolved,—That the Council, at their first meeting since the sad event, the death of the late Honourable George Brown, desire to place on record their deep regret for the loss the country has sustained in the death of one of our leading statesmen and one of its ablest journalists, a friend of the agriculturalists, a true patriot and an honest man ; and also to express their deep sympathy for his bereaved family.

Resolved further,—That a copy of this resolution be signed by the Warden and Clerk and transmitted to Mrs. Brown.

ADAM A. DAVIS, *Warden of the County of Haldimand.*
F. S. STEVENSON, *County Clerk.*

CAYUGA, June 3rd, 1880.

BOARD OF TRADE, MONTREAL.

OFFICE BOARD OF TRADE, MONTREAL,
May 15th, 1880.

DEAR MADAM,—I have been desired by the President and Council of this Board, to communicate the accompanying extract from minutes of Council meeting of last Tuesday, the same being a resolution expressing sorrow at the untimely decease of the Honourable George Brown, and also sympathy for yourself and family.

To the official utterance of the Council, I beg respectfully to add my own regret for the sad event that occasions this communication, and my condolence with you and other relatives.

I am, Dear Madam, your obedient servant,

WM. J. PATTERSON, *Secretary.*

MRS. GEORGE BROWN, Toronto, Ont.

Extract from Minutes of Council meeting of the Montreal Board of Trade, held May 11th, 1880.

Moved by Mr. James P. Cleghorn, seconded by Mr. Thos. White, M.P., and unanimously

Resolved,—That the Council of the Montreal Board of Trade have learned with the most profound sorrow of the death of the Hon. George Brown, and avail themselves of this their first meeting after the sad event, to express, on the part of the Board, their sense of the great loss which the country has sustained through his death, and to convey to Mrs. Brown and the members of his family their condolence and sympathy in their terrible bereavement.

GALT REFORM CLUB.

At a large meeting of the Galt Reform Club, held on Monday evening, May 10th—James McFeiggan in the chair—the following resolutions were unanimously adopted :

Moved by James Young M.P.P., seconded by John Goldie, Esq.,

That the deplorable death of the Honourable George Brown is not simply a loss to the liberal party, but to the whole Dominion of Canada, whose architect he largely was, and whose interests, in union with those of Great Britain, ever found in him an able, patriotic and zealous advocate. The members of the Reform Club of Galt, therefore, in meeting assembled, take the earliest opportunity to place on record their high sense of his great and disinterested services to Canada as a statesman and journalist during the last thirty years; their exalted opinion of the good advanced by his unswerving advocacy of sound, moral and political principles; as well as their profound sorrow at the untimely death of one who was not only a sincere patriot, ever desirous of promoting the best interests of Canada and the mother country, but who possessed many noble qualities of head and heart, which endeared him as a public-spirited citizen and a generous warm-hearted friend.

Moved by J. G. Mowat, Esq., seconded by Gavin Hume, Esq.,

That whilst this meeting gives expression of sadness on this mournful occasion, they would not forget those related to the deceased statesman and patriot, who have been plunged into the deepest sorrow, but would request the president and secretary to send a copy of these resolutions to his afflicted family, conveying to them the assurance that they have the profound and heartfelt sympathy, not only of this association, but of all classes of this community in their sad and unexpected bereavement.

Signed on behalf of the club,

JAMES McFEIGGAN, President.
THOS. D. WARDLAW, Secretary.

GALT, May 10th, 1880.

MOUNT FOREST TOWN COUNCIL.

MOUNT FOREST, May 12th, 1880.

Moved by the Reeve, James McMullen, seconded by the Deputy-Reeve, Josiah Hampton, and

Resolved,—That we, the members of the Municipal Council of the town of Mount Forest, desire to express on behalf of ourselves, and also the residents of this corporation, our utter abhorrence of the dastardly act that has resulted in the untimely death of one of our most distinguished journalists and statesmen, the Hon. George Brown.

We regard the removal of the departed senator as a national calamity, knowing as we do his true patriotism and untiring zeal for the progress and prosperity of this his adopted land.

Be it further Resolved,—That the Mayor and Clerk convey to the departed senator's partner in life the entire sympathy of this corporation in her sad bereavement.

THOS. SWAN, Mayor.
WILLIAM C. PERRY, Clerk.

[Seal.]

PUBLIC MEETING, HARRISTON.

Town Hall, Harriston, May 17th, 1880.

A meeting of the citizens of the town of Harriston and township of Minto assembled in the Council Chamber this afternoon for the purpose of passing resolutions of condolence at the death of the Hon. George Brown, which, owing to the absence of the Mayor last week, and other uncontrollable circumstances, was not held until to-day—A. Meiklejohn, Mayor, in the chair, and M. P. Empey, Secretary. The following resolutions were passed :

Moved by Mr. Prain, Warden of the county of Wellington, seconded by Mr. S. Robertson,

That this meeting of citizens of the town of Harriston and township of Minto, hereby desires to express deep sorrow at the untimely death of the Hon. George Brown, senator of the Dominion, and the great regret felt by this community at large in the demise of one of Canada's most patriotic and distinguished statesmen. This meeting recognizing the greatness and extent of the services rendered by the deceased as a journalist and statesman, as well as the efforts put forth by him in advancing Canadian agriculture—giving his whole life with zeal and energy to the best interests of his adopted country, an unceasing advocate of civil and religious liberty of the people—Canada has, therefore, in the opinion of this meeting, lost one of its most able and talented public men, and looks upon the loss of the great senator as a national calamity.—*Carried.*

Moved by Mr. T. G. Lambert, seconded by Mr. George Preston,

That the mayor and secretary of this meeting convey to the widow and family of the deceased a copy of the resolution, expressing the warm sympathy felt by this meeting and of this community at large in their severe and trying affliction.—*Carried.*

A. Meiklejohn, *Mayor.*
M. P. Empey, *Secretary.*

ST. ANDREW'S SOCIETY, BARRIE.

Barrie, 18th May, 1880.

At the regular meeting of the St. Andrew's Society of Barrie, it was

Moved by Wm. Hunter, Esq., seconded by Wm. Milne, Esq., and

Resolved,—1st. That we, the members of the St. Andrew's Society of Barrie, have learned with profound regret of the death of our fellow-countryman, the Hon. George Brown—a man whose life has been an honour alike to the land of his birth and of his adoption. By the energy, consistency, and indomitable pluck with which he advocated every measure which he deemed calculated to advance the material interests of his country, by the hearty support which he gave to every cause tending to better mankind, his name has become among us a household word, and we feel that in his death Canada has suffered an almost irreparable loss.

2nd. That this Society desire to express their deepest sympathy with the widow and relatives of the deceased senator in the hour of their great grief, and to convey to them a heartfelt expression of profound sorrow that a life which had been spent so far above reproach, so kindly among his friends, and so eminently useful to his country, should have such a sad end.

3rd. That the secretary be instructed to send to the family a copy of these resolutions.

D. Farquharson, *President.*
G. McCuaig, *Secretary.*

WEST ELGIN REFORM ASSOCIATION.

Moved by Peter Stalker, seconded by Col. C. A. O'Malley,

That this association takes this the first available opportunity, to express regret at the sad and untimely death of the Honourable George Brown, the staunch advocate of reform principles during a most important era of Canada's history. His honest and unswerving advocacy of every measure he deemed for the welfare of his country and humanity won for him the love, esteem and respect of all classes in the community. We take this occasion to convey to those nearest and dearest friends of the deceased statesman our heartfelt sympathy in their affliction and bereavement.

Signed on behalf of the Reform Association of West Elgin by

JOHN McCALLUM, *President,*
THOS. URQUHART, *Secretary.*

COLLINGWOOD TOWN COUNCIL.

MAYOR'S OFFICE, May 11, 1880.

Moved by Mr. Burness, seconded by Mr. Lockerbie,

That this Council have heard with deep regret of the untimely end of the Hon. George Brown, who, as a patriot and statesman, has left his mark on the history of Canada.

That we sincerely lament his death, especially under the circumstances that has taken him from us, and that by it the Dominion has lost a true friend.

And that the Clerk be instructed to send a copy of this resolution to his afflicted family.

A. BLIGH, *Clerk.*

[Seal.]

FROM "*GRIP.*"

The varying noises cease,
And pitying men, jaded or jubilant before,
Pall 'neath the common grief.
The cortege passes now in princely circumstance,
'Mid quiet thousands in the city's streets,
While the aspiring throb of anxious hearts,
Busy and buffeted in life's rough way,
Is mute in conscious widowhood.
Ah! he was noble who lay coffined there—
A peer in Nature's aristocracy ;
Bearing the unction of that generous grace, which in the life
Wins love from toiling men,
And, dying, summons them like children round the tomb.
So pass away, great spirit,
But thy work, so well and truly done,
Shall stand a witness to thy goodness and thy gifts.
On that enduring pile a superscription,
Written in letters that shall ever glow,
May tell the rugged grandeur of his life
In simple narrative :
How homespun worth and royal honesty
Braved the distempers of ambition's path,
From youth of filial love and lofty thought,

To sterling manhood and vice-regal place ;
How on that height he bore a manly front,
Lending his pen to freedom's sacred cause—
Counselling wisely for the nation's weal,
And smiling down the ills that menaced her ;
Then how at eventide his light was quenched
By base assassination, and his star
Went down 'mid clouds of pain and weariness,
While in its fading rays, ere yet 'twas gone,
Sad-visaged friends, drawn by the bonds of love,
And generous foes who knew and prized his worth,
Paid, side by side, the tribute of their tears.
His faithful fight is o'er ; his work is done ;
He lived sublimely, and his footsteps mark
A noble course upon the sands of time.
" He was a man, take him for all in all,"
But only man, and therefore had his faults,—
Not weaknesses that rise from recreant heart,
But such as mark and mar the best of lives ;
He hated falsehood with a burning scorn,
But may have erred, mistaking true for false ;
His nature was a rushing mountain stream,
His faults but eddies which its swiftness bred.
Yes, carve his name on marble monument—
'Twill mark his resting place to reverent eyes
Perchance of generations, until Time,
The tireless sculptor, with relentless hand
Has written an inscription over it
In weird, grim characters of mildewed moss,—
A grander line upon life's fitful dream.
Yet is his name deep graven in our hearts,
A more abiding record, that will pass
From sire to son as proudly-guarded pearl,
So long as Canada shall have true men,
Who love the memory of the great and good.
And may that ever cease ?   Shall ages come
When man's frail memory is clouded o'er,
And history's page is shrivelled into dust ?
Comes there a day when all the lives of earth,
The thoughts and actions, yea, and earth itself
Shall vanish in eternal nothingness ?
So be it—yet our Statesman's name shall live !
There's an eternal tablet in the skies
Where names are written that shall never fade ;
Perish, then, record on ephemeral stone, —
Fade, trivial ink on human history's page,—
For with the blood of God's anointed Son,
'Mid all the names of humble, faithful ones,
His name is written in the BOOK OF LIFE.

FUNERAL SERMON.

Preached in St. James' Presbyterian Church—where Mr. Brown usually worshipped—on the Sabbath after the Funeral, by the Rev. Dr. John King.

Text : John xiii. 7 "Jesus answered and said unto him, What I do thou knowest not now ; but thou shalt know hereafter."

In these words of the Saviour, first spoken long ago, and often since re-called by dark and sorrowful experiences in human life—recalled very forcibly by the event which is present to all our minds this morning—we may find a theme of meditation not unsuitable to the occasion on which we are met. They recognize the inscrutable mystery which surrounds in the meantime many of the dealings of God with His people : they convey the assurance that one day this mystery shall be dispelled, and the meaning of the divine procedure towards them made plain : and they carry, at least by impli-cation, the promise of their entire satisfaction with this procedure. when its character and aim are fully understood. First, the words before us bear testimony to the mystery with which many of the dealings of God with His people are meanwhile invested. They assert their present igno-rance of the aim and the significance of much which befals them. On the occasion on which the words were spoken, the Saviour was about to leave in death the disciples whom He had attached to Himself by very strong and tender ties. With the distinct consciousness of His divine dignity, "knowing that the Father had given all things into His hands, and that He was come from God and went to God," and actuated by an affection for His own which knew no diminution as the appointed end drew near, "He began," previous to partaking of His last meal with them, "to wash the disciples' feet." To Peter this seemed an inversion of all that was proper, almost an indignity to which the Lord was subjecting Himself, and with characteristic warmth of feeling and forwardness of speech he remonstrated against the act being done in his case. "Lord, dost Thou wash my feet ?" Wouldst Thou, my adored Master and Lord, perform for me, Thy unworthy disciple, a service which only the humblest of men thinks of rendering to his fellows ? "Jesus answered and said unto him, What I do thou knowest not now." This act of mine, to which thou offerest opposition, has a meaning which thou dost not discern, which thou canst not now discern. It has a depth of condescension in it even greater than thou dost suppose. It possesses a moral instructiveness which it were too much to expect thee to perceive without my help. It has, moreover, a symbolical meaning, a meaning in relation to sin, and man's cleansing from its defilement, which only sufferings to be endured by Me, and illu-mination to be bestowed on thee as the fruit of these sufferings, can be expected to make plain. "What I do thou knowest not now."

The words spoken under these circumstances to the Apostle Peter have their application continually in human life. They find their application in events even which seem quite ordinary, which excite in us no surprise or wondering inquiry at the time of their occurrence, but which are after-wards seen to have wholly unexpected issues bound up with them. For let it be observed what the most proper force of the Saviour's words really is. It is not our ignorance of the motive of His action so much as of its significance that is affirmed in them. It is not why He does this, but what it is that He does, that the disciple is declared not now to know. And it is exactly here that our human ignorance is most affecting. It is not simply that we cannot descry the future or ascertain the purpose of God in refer-ence to events which have actually befallen us in life ; it is that we cannot give the exact significance to the most ordinary of these events. An acquaintance is made, a friendship is formed, a sphere of life is opened up to us in the providence of God, how often with results for good or for evil not only undiscerned but undreamt of at the time. The issue has shown that the act had a wholly unsuspected meaning. Much, indeed, of the pathos and the poetry of human life springs from this very circumstance, the unknown possibilites that lie bound up, as in a closed bud, in some providential change, the incapacity to discover in what colour it will open out and into what fruit it will ripen.

While the words of the text have their application to many events in life which seem at the time of their occurrence quite ordinary and unimportant, they are brought home to us with peculiar force by other events which at once strike us all as strange and exceptional : as when a career of eminent public service is suddenly terminated—like that, for example, of Sir Robert Peel, by what appeared a chance occurrence ; or as when a young man is cut down just as he is entering on a course of usefulness, for which long years of careful preparation had been fitting him ; or again, as when one on whose active brain and busy hands infirm age or helpless childhood is wholly dependent is stricken down by disease—when the strong support is removed, and the weak, tender, leaning wife or child is left alone, like a vine deprived of the stay to which it clung, to creep henceforth upon the ground ; most of all, when one who seemed to be the greatest earthly help to piety in another, husband, son, or friend ; one whose influence seemed necessary not for that other's happiness, but for his faith and his goodness, is taken away in death ; and the as yet only half-decided candidate for heaven is left to carry on the unequal struggle with the flesh, the world, and the devil without the one human presence which gave it visible support and promise of success. Then, indeed, in circumstances like these, the words of the text are forcibly recalled. He whose agency is as real and unmistakable in the world of human life as it was eighteen centuries ago in that guest-chamber, seems to say to us again, " What I do thou knowest not now."

The cloud of mystery, however, which in the meantime rests on so much of the divine procedure assumes the darkest form of all in connection with the power allowed to evil and the results which it is suffered to bring about. When we see sin permitted to assail weak virtue and to triumph in its fall ; when we see men without piety and without principle raised to positions of authority and influence ; when we see bad men permitted to become the oppressors of the weak and the wronged, or when we see evil allowed in the very wantonness of its folly to bring a life of great usefulness to a sudden close, and cover with desolation a once happy home, our inability to understand the nature and meaning of the dealings of God is most deeply felt. Then He may be said to throne Himself in thick darkness, and while defying our comprehension, to challenge simply our submission and our trust. There is, no doubt, an easy, off-hand solution of the difficulty which such cases raise offered to us, namely, the denial of any agency whatever of God in them, the tracing of all such occurrences to the operation of merely natural causes ; this solution is one which agrees well with the view which it is becoming so common, under the influence of the science of the age, to take of the universe ; but it is not one which the Holy Scriptures will allow, or which a mind at once wise and pious can accept. We cannot shut Him out from any phase of human experience without whom "a sparrow does not fall to the ground." If we find His will, as we are taught to do, in the crucifixion of the Saviour (Acts ii. 23), we can scarcely refuse to recognize it in the manifold and terrible, but surely less appalling, acts of violence and wrong which are happening in our own day and around ourselves.

And yet the mystery attending the power allowed to evil is very deep, and it has been very closely brought home to us in these sorrowful days.

A sudden arrest put by a mad act of violence on a course of unusual and beneficent activity; a public man cut down by such means in the midst of plans unmatured and enterprises unaccomplished; a life tenderly and widely loved, quenched, as we may say, in blood; a family stricken with sorrow. How should this have been permitted under the government of a righteous God? How is it consistent with justice and with mercy in Him who worketh all things after the counsel of His own will? What is its meaning, what ends are to be accomplished by it, what of grace is in it for the living or for the departed? Who shall tell? Here God acts, as so often in human life, as a God who hides Himself; One whose way is in the sea, and His path in the great waters, and His footsteps not known. Here He makes demands simply on our submission and our faith; disciplining us to humility and to trust, as He says out of the darkness in which He shrouds His dealings. "What I do thou knowest not now," and mercifully adds, "but thou shalt know hereafter."

This leads me to speak, second, of the assurance of light as to the divine procedure which shall one day be given us. We are permitted to believe on the authority of Christ that the mystery in which the providential dealings of God towards us are in the meantime involved shall not be perpetual, that the cloud which covers now so much which we would wish to know shall one day rise, and the purpose and meaning of events which try our faith and perplex our hearts be made plain. In Peter's case the explanation came almost as soon as the strange and perplexing action of the Lord was over. It was begun by the statement almost immediately thereafter made, "Know ye what I have done to you? Ye call me Master and Lord; and ye say well, for so I am. If I then, your Lord and Master, have washed your feet, ye also ought to wash one another's feet. For I leave you an example that ye should do as I have done unto you." The explanation was begun by this statement, and it was completed by the sacrifice offered on the cross, and by means of the closer fellowship into which thenceforth the Lord took His disciple through the Spirit. The meaning, literal and symbolical, of the Saviour's act became thereafter plain. It is thus no remote "hereafter" which is designated in the text, so far as the apostle's case is concerned, and hence some have proposed to translate the words, "Thou shalt soon, presently, know;" or to read them, as they would be literally read, "Thou shalt know after these things." In our case we must generally be content to wait longer for the light which is to clear away our perplexities in regard to the divine procedure. Sometimes, indeed, it is given us to see even in the present life the purport and the grace which belonged to some at first sight perplexing providence. We have all of us come to bless God for events which as they drew near awakened our apprehension and our sorrow, but which have developed into unsuspected issues of God, and in their light have learned the truth as well as beauty of the poet's words:

> "We see but darkly through the mists and vapours
>   Amid these earthly damps;
> What seem to us but sad funereal tapers
>   May be heaven's distant lamps."

More frequently, however, we must be content to wait for the light which is to resolve our doubts and our perplexities, and to walk even to the end of this earthly life by faith and not by sight. But the explanation is only delayed, and will without fail be given. When we come to stand at the close of this earthly course and look back upon life, not in the slow process of development, but in its completed form; when in the light of another world the missing links are supplied, and the subtle connections and far-off issues of things are discovered; when we come to know Him of whose wondrous plans the events which have perplexed us are the accomplishment, to "know even as we are known," and to be in possession of a sympathy with Him in His aims which even the holiest do not attain here—then the mystery which in the meantime rests on the divine procedure shall be cleared up; we shall know the meaning and the motive of providences which for the present sorely try our faith. We must hold fast by this hope at all hazards. We must maintain the conviction that as certain as is the present darkness, so certain is the future light; that as no part of the procedure of God towards His people is purposeless, so no doubt shall be left as to what the purpose of God was in every part of that procedure. This word of Christ to His disciple Peter will be fulfilled in the experience of all His own, and in relation to all that has befallen them, "What I do thou knowest not now, but thou shalt know hereafter."

There is, in the third place, the assurance, at least by implication, of the perfect satisfaction of God's people with His procedure towards them, when its purpose and meaning are made known. It is implied by the Saviour's words that the knowledge promised in them when it is imparted will remove all distrust of and dissatisfaction with the divine dealings; nay, that the dealings which now most perplex and try us will have our thankful acquiescence when their full meaning and far off issues are seen; that the purpose of God in the same will commend itself to us as equally wise and good, when that purpose is fully brought to light. The circumstance which seemed at first a discord in the life will be seen only to be a part of a higher and wider harmony, when the story of the whole life, and of other connected lives, is rehearsed. The change of view must be even greater than we can well conceive. As I have stood on the summit of a Swiss mountain, and looked down on a clear autumn morning on a floating sea of cloud covering the landscape for many miles, and marked its fleecy lightness, its distinct outline, its transparent purity, its fairy forms, etc., until the sun arose above the horizon, its motionless calm, an impression has been made and a memory left as of an object almost too wondrously beautiful to be a thing of earth. And yet to the dweller below, looking up at exactly the same object from his cottage door, it was only a thick, dark, gloomy mist, or perhaps a black and threatening cloud. Such difference does it make, from what side we view things, from above or from below, from the side which looks earthward or from the side which looks heavenward. Even so in life, circumstances which have filled us with apprehension or with gloom; events which have clouded our joy and tried our faith; may, or rather must, take on unexpected forms of grace and beauty to our life when they are looked at no longer from the earthward but from the heavenward side. And then, if not before, we shall be moved to exclaim in grateful adoration, "O the depth of the riches both of the wisdom and knowledge of God! How unsearchable are His judgments, and His ways past finding out. For of Him, and through Him, and to Him, are all things: to whom be glory for ever. Amen."

The application of the truths which have been now enunciated to the sorrowful event present to all our minds this morning is one which can be each made by any hearer, and which has no doubt been already made in thought by many.

It only remains for me to say a few words in regard to the personal character and public services of him who has been so suddenly and mysteriously removed from the scene in which he filled so large and so useful a place.

With the political principles and career of the deceased we have little to do in this place; we have to do with them at all only as they brought to light his moral qualities, or tended to promote the moral and religious well-being of the community. There is the less need of any attempt at a general characterization of the deceased; that testimony has been borne from so many different quarters, to the great vigour of his intellect, the kindling ardour of his enthusiasm, the force of his will, the largeness of his views, the honesty with which they were held, and the marked degree in which they have promoted the public good. From those more intimately associated with the departed, equally strong testimony has been borne to the warmth of his friendship, the generosity and frequency of his acts of kindness, and the integrity and purity of his private life. The attendance at his funeral of so many of the older men from almost every city and town in our province is the best proof of the strong hold which he had early taken, and which he to the end held, of the affections of a large portion, and that neither the least intelligent nor the least worthy of his countrymen. In his death our country has lost the citizen whose influence has been more potent than that of any other, and who has left his mark deepest on its history. It is surely a matter for thankfulness that the influence has been throughout a beneficial one, and that the mark speaks of liberties extended, and civil rights confirmed, and religious equality secured, and provinces consolidated. This result has not been reached without great, we may say indeed herculean, effort. Thrown into the stream of active life at an age when most young men are only entering on the last important stage of their education, and ever since engaged with an amount of public and private business under the weight of which most men would have sunk long ago, we may safely say that no more active, no busier life, no life which has undergone more of hard though not ungrateful toil and struggle, has been led in this land than that which closed so peacefully last Sabbath morning amid its hallowed calm and opening buds.

In many of the reforms, in the accomplishment of which deceased bore a leading part, religion among us had a direct interest, and has been a great gainer; by no more perhaps than by that change which swept away invidious and offensive distinctions between various branches of the Church of Christ, and set them all on terms of perfect equality. I do not know, however, that any service rendered by the departed to the moral well-being of our country is of equal value with the establishment and maintenance in this city of a widely circulated newspaper, which has throughout preserved a healthful, moral, and religious tone. When I see how easily in our day and in all lands the daily newspaper can become the apologist for, if not the propagator of, sceptical views, the vehicle of sneers at religion, the caricaturist of ecclesiastical bodies, or at least of their weaknesses, then I can only feel thankful, as I have often done, that through the enterprise of him who has been so mysteriously removed we have had among us a powerful organ of opinion, which has been the defender of the Sabbath, the upholder of the divine truth against prevailing error, the fearless rebuker of immorality and lawlessness, which has on all the more important questions of religion and morality, and in its general tone, reflected the sentiments of the best classes of the community. This is a service which I believe it would be difficult to overestimate.

Regarded in a moral point of view, the spirit in which a public man has done his work, the qualities he has evinced in doing it, are of even greater moment than the work itself. In this respect we may claim a very high place for the departed. Large in his views, sincere in his desire for his country's good, noble in his aims respecting it, honest in the convictions which he entertained, and fearless in maintaining and acting on them, adding the exercise of private virtues to the exhibition of public spirit, he has left an example which we may well wish were widely imitated. Granted that he may have sometimes asserted his will too strongly, we have more to fear both on patriotic and religious grounds from the suppleness and the selfishness which can pocket principles for power or pelf than from the assertion of individual conviction which may not be always so deferential as it ought to be to the opinions and feelings of others. The alliance of a life of public activity with the exercise of private virtues and attention to the duties of religion, while happily not singular, is nevertheless not so general that we may not find even in this an additional cause for thanksgiving on behalf of him who filled so large a place in the public eye, and whose example will have its influence for many years to come. These considerations, however, to which I have thought it right to call attention, are not the vital ones after all. The service which the departed rendered to his country may have been valuable, the qualities he evinced admirable, but the question still remains—and standing where I do I must pronounce it the most important of all—from what did this service, these qualities, spring? What was the sustaining principle? Had the life which we have described a Christian root? There is every reason to believe it had. I cannot doubt it. In the first place his faith in and attachment to the doctrines of grace were very strong and decided. The interest with which he listened from Sabbath to Sabbath to the statement of them is well known to the members of this congregation. The negative views that are afloat in our day had taken no effect on his mind, except to make his attachment more pronounced to the simple and positive truths in which he had been trained, and of which, it is believed, he had gained more than a theoretical knowledge many years ago. He was for himself a firm believer in the depravity of the race and in the sacrifice of the Lord Jesus Christ as the one hope of the sinner, even while he was tolerant of diversity of opinion and numbered among his personal friends some who were far enough from sharing his religious views. The extent to which his time and energies were taken up in the absorbing demands of public and private business left him little leisure—too little, let us say, for the service of Christ's Church; and he was living in the desire and hope, not to be realized, alas! that in his later years he would be free to serve it to an extent and in forms which had been found previously beyond his power. The readiness with which he agreed to address the annual missionary meeting of this congregation in February last may be accepted as an evidence of the sincerity of this desire, as the earnest and lofty spirit with which he spoke on that occasion—probably the last on which he addressed a public gathering—will be remembered as a proof of how much he might have done for the cause of Christ had he been spared and free to advocate its claims. This, however, was not to be. Nearer to him than any of us dreamed was even then the night, when one can no more work.

When it came, or when the shot was fired that was to bring it in a few short weeks, the doctrines of the Gospel, the sacrifice and the mercy which they reveal, were his only and sure trust. Resentment towards the poor, guilty instrument of all this suffering, there was none. His person was soon dismissed from thought, and not even amid the utterances of wandering reason was a single allusion made to the mad and merciless act. But, united with submission to the will of God, there was the deep sense of his own sinfulness, of the imperfections attaching even to his better acts, and at the same time most earnest and humble recourse, revealed in many a brief but touching prayer, to the Saviour, to Him "whom God hath set forth to be a propitiation through faith in his blood." "Erect before men, on his knees before God"—that is the description which a gifted writer has given us of the Christian. You who have seen the departed in public life do not need to be told how fully he was the one; those who knew him in the home, those especially who saw his exercise of spirit under this mysterious visitation, can testify how completely he was the other.

These details are not given to satisfy a vulgar curiosity. They are stated to the honour of that grace which had brought him to the cross, and by which alone we are saved. Our loss as a congregation is very great in his removal. His connection with us had not, indeed, been long, but it was very cordial from the first. We lose in him the largest contributor to our missionary and college funds: one, indeed, who was ever ready to help with his means or his powerful advocacy any good cause. The very endorsation, in his case so unmistakably given, by a mind of his grasp, of the views of truth stated from this desk was a source of strength which my brethren in the ministry present will readily understand. It has been the will of God that this should not be continued to us, and we bow to it, not without sorrow, but with a sorrow relieved by the thought that our loss is, as we trust, his gain.

Into the far more tender and sacred sorrow of the bereaved relatives, and especially of the desolate home, I would not venture to intrude farther than to give expression to the deep sympathy with it which you all feel. Here, where the prayer has often risen to God that if it were His will this loss might be averted, there can be no heart whose joy has not been sensibly clouded, none from which even now the prayer does not rise that God may be the light and the salvation of the bereaved in the night of their sorrow. For ourselves, let us hear in this, and so many other visitations of death among us since the year commenced, the summons of the Saviour to work "while it is day," as "the night cometh when no man can work." "Therefore gird up the loins of your mind ; be sober, and hope to the end for the grace that is to be brought unto you at the revelation of Jesus Christ." "Now, unto Him that is able to keep you from falling, and to present you faultless before the presence of His glory with exceeding joy, to the only wise God, our Saviour, be glory and majesty, dominion and power, both now and ever. Amen."

FUNERAL SERMON.

PREACHED IN ST. ANDREW'S CHURCH, SARNIA, ON SUNDAY MORNING, 9TH MAY, 1880, BY REV. MR. THOMPSON.

TEXT: Genesis xlix. 33 : "And when Jacob had made an end of commanding his sons, he gathered up his feet into the bed, and yielded up the ghost, and was gathered unto his people."

After some remarks explanatory of the event referred to in the text, Mr. Thompson proceeded as follows :

A week this morning one of our greatest and noblest men finished his earthly career, and on Wednesday his mortal remains were followed to the grave by such a multitude as no similar occasion in Canada ever brought together. The spontaneous outburst of sympathy and sorrow from all classes and creeds, and from every shade of political opinion, was truly marvellous, and told unmistakably how much the man was venerated and loved. His body was laid in the grave amid the sorrow of the nation, and the day was made sacred by a grief that covered the land. As the solemn procession wended its way to the city of the dead amid the assembled thousands, the look of reverence on every countenance, the audible stillness of the vast throng, the sober faces of the little children, the soft spoken word and silent tear, showed what a hold the man had on the affections of his fellow-countrymen, and how his character and work were valued by those who came from all parts of the country to pay the last tribute of respect to Mr. Brown's memory, and to show their appreciation of his life and labours.

And it was most fitting that thus it should be, for seldom have more valued services been rendered, and no country is more indebted to its leading statesmen than Canada is to Mr. Brown. This is not the place to discuss party questions in a party spirit, but it is both the place and the day to point to the life and labours of one of whom our country may well feel proud, and thankful for what has been done through his instrumentality.

He has been as a king among men, and has done the work of a giant. He was born to rule over men by the mastery of superior power. No one who has taken an intelligent interest in the shaping of our country's fortunes, or who is moderately acquainted with her past history, but will readily admit that Canada occupies a very different position to-day, politically and religiously, from what she did when, as a young man, he came forth into public life to do battle on her behalf. During those important years we have passed from feudalism to recognized citizenship. When a presumptuous oligarchy attempted to rule this country in their own family interests, as a family compact, unblushingly asserting that the many existed for the sake of the few ; when a dominant church, backed by the prestige of an establishment at home, attempted to trample on the liberties of other churches, and actually punished with imprisonment ministers of other churches for performing their religious functions ; when the bishop, in virtue of his office, took his seat in parliament and attempted to pass laws which made it a crime for Presbyterian or Methodist ministers to perform the marriage ceremony among those of their own flock ; when none of the young men of our country were allowed to attend the college that was supported by public funds without first signing the Thirty-nine Articles ; when a man was branded as a rebel if he dared to speak a word against these feudal enactments ; this illustrious statesman who has just left us, then as a young man beginning his public career, erected his battery on the foundation of popular rights and common justice, and opened fire with speech and pen, and almost single-handed broke down one wicked defence after another, and wrung from his opponents concession after concession, till to-day it is safe to affirm that all are glad to shelter themselves behind the defences which he has set up. It is most fitting that the country should be grateful for what he has done. It is, moreover, an interesting study to watch the political progress of our country from those days to this, and to feel that the very things that bring us honour and wise liberty and a brightening future, are quite recent blessings extorted from determined opponents in many a hard fought battle. For example, our municipal institutions, with all the valued principles of self-government (which one of our wise governors characterized as sucking republics, which were to work such ruin to our country if granted, and overthrow the throne of the nation) ; the throwing open the university of the country to the young men of the country, irrespective of creed ; the settlement of the clergy reserves ; a perfect equality of all churches in the eyes of the law ; representation according to population ; the unification of these scattered provinces into one grand confederation, with many other measures in which our country rejoices to-day, have all been contended for by him in the face of bitter opposition, as many a speech or article of his will show. He has been a tower of strength on behalf of popular rights and liberties, on behalf of morality, and religion, in the land he loved so well and served so nobly. But not as a politician on the floor of Parliament alone, but as a journalist his services to the country have been no less valuable and distinguished. The press and pulpit must be the two great agencies in moulding the future character of our people, and they must stand shoulder to shoulder. And when we know what a power the press wields, and what a direct and immediate bearing it must have on the shaping of national and individual life and character ; how it can both elevate and degrade, poison and nourish, the activities of human life, it is one of the greatest services rendered, that the leading journal of public opinion, controlled by him, has ever been pervaded by such a healthy tone, and has spoken so nobly on all questions where morality and religion were involved ; how he has guarded the spiritual interests of the Christian church ; how reverent towards God and all divine institutions ; how nobly he has spoken on public and private morality—the temperance question, the Sabbath question, the social evil ; how he has ever taken the side of truth against laxity of opinion and practice ; how steadfast and loyal he has been to the distinctive doctrines and polity of his own church, and how he has never hesitated to affirm and defend these no matter who might approve or dissent. When we consider these things, it must be admitted that he has been a tower of strength to the church as well as to his country : indeed, his first endeavours as a journalist were in connection with the church, and all through he has never ceased to view with joy her increasing prosperity. Always liberal, one of his last acts was the contribution of an additional $100 towards removing the deficit in the ordinary revenue of Knox College. Small men have often said he was dogmatic and domineering, while great men have greatly admired him for these traits of character that made him the man he was, and enabled him to do the work he did. He was a man of deep convictions, of intense individuality, of indomitable will, who never knew what it was to hesitate or fear in the presence of a foe; a man who put a great value on his convictions, as every noble man does, and like every man of great force of character and determination, who moves with heavy momentum along the line of his convictions, he was sure to have attached and ardent friends, as well as very decided opponents. But as the spontaneous outbursts of sympathy, and the sorrow of an afflicted people showed, he ever got credit, even from his opponents, for honesty of purpose, nobility of character, and the valued services he has rendered to his generation.

In my humble observations I have discovered that there are two great classes of public men : those who have convictions that mean something, and those who have none—men of expediency, who crawl into notice on the shoulders of other men as their parasites, and, as parasites, often feed on their large bounty ; men who never denounced a wrong in their life, or defended the right ; men who go as far as they think politic, and who turn back when the wind acts in their face ; men without conscience, who have nothing worth defending, and are ready to shift their ground as expediency requires ; men with no heart, but two faces, that look both ways at once. Such men have no *opponents*, nor have they *friends*, except what the exigencies of the hour call forth, and when they die, their names will rot, and those whom their false policy has blighted will rot with them, while the righteous will be held in everlasting remembrance. John Knox has also been blamed for the very same features of character. Men who measure him by their own little rule, have spoken of his domineering severity and dogged resolution. Little puppies have often scratched on his illustrious grave, and barked their little bark. But an enlightened Christian sentiment feels grateful for what Knox was, and for what he did. Much of the civil and religious liberty of our day has had its root in those very features of his character which the puppets of an hour have professed to deplore. At such great moral junctures of a nation's life, men needed moral muscle and a strong back-bone of conviction, while sneaks and vipers will crawl on their belly till the world ends. So was it with Mr. Brown ; while politicians and public men generally discuss his character—the supposed strong or weak points in it—and canvass the nature of the services rendered by him to his country, I wish to emphasize the fact that the great central principle that formed his character, the very trunk around which his nature grew and blossomed, was his faith in God ; the deepest of all his convictions was the fact of personal redemption through the blood of Jesus Christ : the strongest feeling of his heart was his feeling of loyalty to his Saviour, on whom he depended through life, and in whom he trusted at death. No man could be for any length of time in Mr. Brown's company without being convinced that he was not only a pure-minded man, but that he habitually lived under the power of the *world to come* ; and as he lived, so he died, trusting in the sacrifice which Christ had made for his sins, and in trustful submission to the will of God. In all his manifold duties and labours that were most exacting, he never forgot his duty to his God and

Saviour. After a day of toil and exciting debate in the olden time, it strengthened one's faith to hear him at the family altar, in earnest, simple, trustful language, plead with God for His blessing to rest on his family, the labours of the day, his country, and on the Church of Christ in all her branches. I have made these remarks for the purpose of pointing to Mr. Brown as a noble example to all our public men, and to show that a life of public labour and manifold cares is not only consistent with, but even helpful to, the growth of Christian sentiment ; that all the activities of our life may grow out of one root, and receive their noblest impulse from one centre, when Christ has laid His loving hand upon us, and we live as His servants, to do His will from the heart.

Public men require the prayers of God's people, for they are exposed to many and great dangers from which others escape who walk in the quieter paths of private duty. And political life especially makes such a great demand on men's time, and tends to engross the thoughts till the whole empire of feeling is swayed. And especially to men of ardent and impulsive temperaments, who pour out their life-forces on every undertaking, and work with both hands earnestly, the danger is great that the claims of the next world may be forgotten in the pursuits of this. And the world's work must be done, and it may be work sacred to Our Father in Heaven, who calls us to do it as loving service rendered to Him. It will be a day of unutterable ruin to our country if the conviction ever becomes general that politics must not be touched by Christian hands lest they be defiled, but must be left to the manipulations of those who have no conscience and no God. It is as much the duty of one man to be a politician as it is for another to be a missionary to China, nor is it a higher or lower kind of service, but simply different ; and as the labourers are sent forth, the Great Husbandman reminds each of his responsibilities. Our public offices require, and our representative men should be, our bravest and truest, the most devout towards God, and ready to honour the Gospel in all their public relations and duties.

Many statesmen have been examples of earnest Christians in the honoured discharge of high public duties. We need only mention the late Abraham Lincoln, whom his countrymen delight to honour, not more sagacious as a statesman than earnest as a believer in the Lord Jesus Christ. Or Guizot, the philosopher and illustrious statesman of France, recently departed amid the fond regrets of his countrymen ; or to Gladstone, the Premier of England ; or to him over whose new-formed grave our land mourns. All these are proofs that the Lord can be honoured in the most engrossing walks of public life. And Mr. Brown's name is all the dearer to us as a member of the Presbyterian church, a church which has had its own work and influence in moulding public sentiment, and in gaining those civil and religious rights for which we rejoice. Take away the religious history of Britain, or of the Anglo-Saxon race, and what have we left ? That which saved the nations of the Reformation was their faith in God ; that which made them brave, resolute, noble, was the religious atmosphere they breathed. Their religion formed their policy, framed their laws, fashioned their character, and shaped their after fortunes, and it ill becomes men whom a Christian public has entrusted with the discharge of high public duties to turn their backs upon all that has made our country what it is, and has been the chief distinction of those noble men that have rendered the truest public service. The great statesman whom we buried last week never hesitated to say that the hope of our country, as of all other countries, depended upon a sound Christian sentiment among our people, and it is a pity that some of the smaller of our statesmen would not learn to act accordingly, and not wound the Christian sensibilities of their best friends. I would not encourage persecution for opinions, but if these men are resolved to set the law of Christ at defiance, and act according to their supposed liberty, they must not complain if Christian people learn to act also according to their sense of propriety in not according political support to men whose example and influence tend to break down the institutions of God's appointment, and who systematically ignore all that is most vital in the judgment of Christ's loyal disciples.

But the grandeur of Mr. Brown's character is seen as much in the private relations and domestic duties of his life as in those that were more public. His personal friends were much prized, while the affection of his heart lit up the home, as sunshine resting amid spring blossoms. The life of Mr. Brown was a many-sided one. The general public think of him as a statesman and journalist. But Toronto will miss him who ever aimed at building up the interests of his adopted city ; the down-trodden slave remembers his noble advocacy on their behalf years ago ; the poor and friendless knew him as a sympathetic helper, for distress never appealed to him in vain ; while in his own home he was known as the faithful father, the loving husband and brother. His was a home full of domestic comfort —a true Christian home ; and now in these days of bereavement there is an air of quiet, subdued, chastened grief, a submissive, grateful yielding to the will of God, which is its chief glory. As I stood looking on the wasted features of the departed, and thought how still that brain was which once teemed with great resolves, I felt strongly what he himself said to his former pastor, on hearing of the death of his much-loved friend Mr. Holton : " How vain are all activities that are separated from the interests of our Redeemer, and how needful to keep the true aim of life constantly before us." For the last thirty-five years his name has been a household word, and like every man engaged in public affairs, he has met much severe criticism, but no stain has tarnished his honour, no cloud can rest upon his memory. He rests from his labours, and his works do follow him, while his record is before his God. It is a small matter to be judged by man's judgment ; He that judgeth every man is the Lord, and His judgments are according to truth. When high intellectual powers, true devotion to one's country, sound judgment, a large ripe experience, are all clasped by loyalty of heart to the Redeemer, it makes a rich, noble character, and one much needed. Such a man our country had in Mr. Brown. And it is unspeakably sad that one who had lived to such noble purpose should have been cut down by the hands of a miscreant ; a great national calamity, caused by what threatens to be a national curse. It is a mysterious providence that overhangs his departure, but we bow reverently to the disposals of an overruling hand ; and to the question, " Who will take his place ?" we reply, No man ever takes another man's place or does another man's work in the Master's vineyard ; the man and his place, the labour and the labourer, pass away together, while each man is called upon to occupy his own place and do his own work. And yet a good man lives in the future as much as in the past. The principles he has inculcated, the forces he has set in motion, the influences he has exerted, go down through the ages and modify the results of the waiting years.

His last days were full of weariness and suffering, but cheered by a sense of the Divine presence. Nor was his Christian character a thing of recent years ; he lived and died in the faith of Jesus Christ and in full reliance on His merits. During the later stages of his illness, when the cloud of delirium lifted from his mind for a brief period, it was unspeakable comfort to his sorrowing family and friends to hear his calm, clear, simple statement of his hope toward God and faith in the Lord Jesus Christ; his satisfaction that his labour should end if God so willed it. Such a statement from his lips is enough to baptise a nation's sorrow, and to assure us that the Lord hath taken another of His redeemed children from earth's day of toil into the rest where no strife of tongues can enter. As his life lay in the balance, we hoped the result would have been otherwise; and now the issue is determined, and George Brown is no more. But his memory will long remain green in the affections of his grateful countrymen, for he is one whom the nation will delight to honour. His name is his grandest monument, and as we laid his wasted body amid the cold clods of earth—dust to dust, and ashes to ashes—we said: "King of Terrors, do thy worst; we know the limits of thy power; it is not much you can do, it is not long." Christ hath gotten the victory and robbed death of its sting. By His resurrection and triumph He has shed a blessed light over the darkness of the grave.

The day of a believer's death is a great day, and one long to be remembered, for it is the final application to the redeemed soul of the ransom which Immanuel paid ; it is deliverance to the captive, it is joy in heaven and glory to God. The death of a believer is a great thing, but its greatness is turned toward eternity, and can neither be seen nor described by us ; we leave its greatness to *the day* to reveal that eternal weight of glory. And knowing that all the grandeur lies on the other side that looks into eternity, we make no attempt to decorate this side that looks into time. But one thing we do urge you to consider, that the solemn hour of dissolution awaits us all, and how blessed it is to have our faith resting in Him who is the resurrection and the life. "And I heard a voice from heaven saying unto me, write, Blessed are the dead that die in the Lord from henceforth ; yea, saith the Spirit, that they may rest from their labours ; and their works do follow them." "Therefore, my beloved brethren, be ye steadfast, unmovable, always abounding in the work of the Lord, for as much as ye know that your labour is not in vain in the Lord." Amen.

CORRESPONDENCE.

The following letters are given because of the interest they possess, in a political or personal sense, as illustrative of Mr. Brown's life. The greater portion of them were written to the late Mr. Holton, in whom Mr. Brown placed unlimited confidence, though occasionally obliged to differ with him in his view of public affairs. To many of Mr. Brown's old associates the incidents mentioned in this correspondence will doubtless be of much interest, as they necessarily recall many of the old battles preceding the constitutional changes effected during his active political life.

Their chief value, however, consists in their autobiographical character. Mr. Brown's outspoken, frank manner will at once be recognized, while his manifest disinterestedness will be apparent where he deals with the position of political friends, and especially with reference to his own position in the liberal party.

As the correspondence is fragmentary, it has not been considered wise or necessary to arrange it so as to connect certain periods and events. It is therefore printed in chronological order.

LETTER TO THE HON. JOHN SANDFIELD MACDONALD.

GLOBE OFFICE, TORONTO, August 16, 1854.

MY DEAR MACDONALD,—I congratulate you most heartily on the result of the elections. I had intended writing you for a fortnight past, but have been prevented by various causes from doing so. The loss of Cicero lessens your strength ; but you must admit that he deserved richly to lose his election. Moreover, your tail will, I imagine, be much longer in this parliament than it was in the last, and the orator will hardly be missed from it. From what I have heard there is no doubt of this. Many independent reformers look to you as leader, and if you take your stand firmly and wisely, and without delay, the game is in your own hands. You will have seen that the *Leader* endeavours to make bad blood between you and me by ranging you among my followers. I have not noticed the thing in the *Globe* for two reasons. First, it would be attracting additional attention to it ; and second, because I could not do so without defining my true position, which it would be inexpedient at this moment to do publicly. To you, however, I mean to speak plainly. Our long friendship entitles you to it, and your conduct to me in the Speaker's chair, and our compact at the breaking up of the House, also demand it. I tell you frankly then that, far from having any ambition to be the head of the party, I would not take office under any circumstances were it offered me. All I desire is the success of the principles to which I have attached myself ; and if you can form a government pledged to separation of church and state, representation by population, and non-sectarian schools, I will not only aid you in doing so, but will support your government with all my heart and vigour. I wish you to understand this, and to act upon it, as, with this knowledge, you may feel more at liberty to use my aid in carrying out your views. It is of course of much importance that an immediate understanding should be arrived at among independent reformers. If we go to the discussion on the address without previous concert, Hincks may frighten some reformers into voting for the government by the threat that they will lose their preserves. To meet this you must have it previously ascertained and shown that you can form a better and more thoroughgoing government, in which case nothing can save the government from defeat. If I were in your position, I would write to all the reformers I was on terms with, urging them to go down to Quebec by the Saturday evening boat, in order that the caucus might be held on the Monday before the meeting of parliament. In the meantime you should see Sicotte, Young, Dorion, and the other Lower Canadians you expect to act with, and to have matters thoroughly understood. They too should hold a meeting. I say nothing as to the speakership, taking it for granted that you will aim at higher game. One advantage of the course I suggest would be that you would thereby have an opportunity of judging beforehand as to the best mode of working the speakership vote. Of course, I think that in any case we must put you in as Speaker in order to show our approval of your closing speech last session. Your being in the chair would not, I suppose, interfere with your accepting the attorney-generalship, and forming a ministry in the event of a hostile reply to the address being carried. It is very clear that the present ministry are used up, even if they get over the hitch at the address. The new House will be far in advance of them. If Hincks, to please the Upper Canada members, should even change his position and liberalize his policy, he would thereby throw from him Moreau and the conservative section of the Lower Canadians. If, on the other hand, he plays as heretofore into the hands of his French friends, he will drive off from him the Upper Canada Radicals. It is clear that the natural allies of the reformers of Upper Canada are the Rouges, so called. Let me impress this on you in forming your alliance, that at this moment you can make any terms. Once your government is formed, there will be many difficulties found in the way of progressive measures. Let, then, the conditions of your accepting office be broad, and such as will secure credit to your government, if no more were done by it.

Yours ever truly,

GEORGE BROWN.

HON. J. S. MACDONALD.

LETTER TO MR. HOLTON.

GLOBE OFFICE, Jan. 29, 1858.

MY DEAR HOLTON,—I have to apologize for not sooner answering your note of last week, but absence from town and a crowd of engagements have prevented me from doing so before now.

I have since received yours of the 26th, which considerably relieved the disquiet produced by the other. I am very sorry our friends cannot feel themselves at liberty to take your clear view of our position, and resolve to cut their way out of it. No honest man can desire that we should remain as we are; and what other way out of our difficulties can be suggested but a genuine legislative union, with representation by population—a federal union—or a dissolution of the present union? I am sure that a dissolution cry would be as ruinous to any party as (in my opinion) it would be wrong. A federal union, it appears to me, cannot be entertained for Canada alone, but when agitated must include all British America. *We* will be past caring for politics when that measure is finally achieved. I can hardly conceive of a federal union for Canada alone. What powers should be given to the provincial legislatures, and what to the federal? Would you abolish county councils? And yet if you did not, what would the local parliaments have to control? Would Montreal like to be put under the generous rule of the Quebec politicians? Our friends here are prepared to consider dispassionately any scheme that may issue from your party in Lower Canada. They all feel keenly that something must be done. Their plan is representation by population and a fair trial for the present union in its integrity; failing this, they are prepared to go in for dissolution, I believe, but if you can suggest a federal or any other scheme that could be worked, it will have our most anxious examination. Can you sketch a plan of federation such as our friends below would agree to, and could carry? If so, pray let us have it as soon as you conveniently can. I perfectly agree with you in all you say about Sandfield. He has assuredly put his foot in it. I had a letter from his brother to say that whatever Sandfield did, he would be found right side up.

The Hastings dinner has had a good effect. The ministerialists calculated confidently on —— and ——, and were surprised to find they had made such a mistake. The truth is, I might say I feel alarmed at finding myself among so extreme a set of people!

Another day, and no government! We have strong rumours to-night that a government is formed, but I don't believe a word of it. Sidney Smith, Malcolm Cameron, and Cayley are the names of the hour, but very certainly neither of the first two can be returned, and where Cayley is to find a seat puzzles everyone. My own impression is that Mr. John A. Macdonald sees no further through the woods this night than he did a month ago, but I may be mistaken. John Hillyard Cameron says they will meet parliament with the offices unfilled so as to embarrass the opposition, and throw on us the responsibility of losing a session to the country. No doubt it would be much more difficult to arrange a new government with parliament in session than during a recess.

What say you to Bytown as the seat of government? I think it the second worst place in all Canada, and would a million times prefer Montreal.

Will it be possible to upset the decision? In our present position, with representation by population unsettled, I think the best move would be Toronto and Montreal alternately. With that conceded, I don't care much where the seat of government goes, provided Quebec and Bytown are not the places.

That was indeed a most amusing paragraph in the *Gazette*. How it got there I cannot conceive, but I am informed it has done me some good in Lower Canada, as people begin to hope that I am not so savage as I was supposed to be. No doubt the Starnes' conversation was the origin of the matter, but how that reached the proportions of a " proposal for political alliance " I cannot think. We were exercised here as to the best mode of opening communications with our friends in Lower Canada. Mr. Dorion and his friends have so frequently repudiated our policy, that we were unwilling to go direct to the mark by opening correspondence; your arrival here ended all difficulty as to communicating with the Rouges. While at Belleville I got a telegram from John Simpson, to say Starnes was with him, and he would like that I would wait over a night as I returned; this I had to decline. As the train came up Starnes and Simpson came to the station and went to the junction with us. Starnes said he and his friends (Sicotte, I suppose) were prepared to adopt the full anti-state church ticket, and admitted representation by population must come, and they were prepared to concede it, but how to do that and be returned for Lower Canadian constituencies they could not see. I endeavoured to put the measure in the most favourable light, and said that so long as we had the principle admitted, we were willing to have reasons concerning details. We parted before much had passed; the idea of forming any alliance was not even spoken of for a moment. So far as I was concerned, my effort was to make Starnes a convert to our views, and the folly of resisting them; I was not thinking of the men to carry them, but of the thing to be carried.

The only remark that went beyond this was an observation by Starnes that if I supposed he and his friends thought any more of the Upper Canada side of the government than I did it was a great mistake. He added that our views on the *ad valorem* duties were much more to their minds than the others' views. Thus you have the whole of this famous "negotiation." If Starnes had not mentioned it to you I would not have felt at liberty to repeat what passed, though the affair was not worth secrecy or publication, in itself.

I will be glad to hear from you as soon as convenient.

Yours faithfully,

GEORGE BROWN.

HON. L. H. HOLTON, Montreal.

LETTER TO MR. HOLTON.

TORONTO, Sept. 17, 1858.

MY DEAR HOLTON,—I am afraid you will never pardon my apparent carelessness—for it is only apparent.

I am out of health, worn out, driven to death, and cannot bring my mind to the most ordinary exertion. I ought to give up all business for a month at least, but it is very difficult to do so.

I entirely agree with you as to the necessity of sending a memorandum to the colonial office, and as to the propriety of the policy shadowed forth in your letter. I had arranged to go down to Montreal to discuss this matter; but I got so ill that I had to give it up and go to the St. Catharines baths.

I propose that we meet here before or after the great Hamilton demonstration, on Thursday next, to settle what we are to do. Dorion, McGee, and yourself, will of course be there, but it would be very desirable that Drummond and Lemieux should also be present. Drummond's defeat was very provoking, but cannot be helped. It is very important to have him returned. If you have not seen your way to a seat, I will talk with you when you come about one here. Your splendid victory in Montreal has greatly strengthened us, and will help much in the House.

We are in trouble here about the Upper House election. Our friends are much divided on personal grounds; for myself, I shall vote for Romaine. The run will be close, as neither candidate carries much enthusiasm with him.

You can have no idea how earnest and general the enthusiasm is for the Brown-Dorion government all over Western Canada, west of Kingston. I have never seen anything like it. Head and his fellow conspirators are proportionately condemned.

McGee's course has made him eminently popular. He is received like a prince in every direction.

Be sure and bring our friends to the Thursday dinner.

Yours faithfully,

GEORGE BROWN.

HON. L. H. HOLTON, Montreal.

LETTER TO MR. HOLTON.

GLOBE OFFICE, TORONTO, July 8, 1859.

MY DEAR HOLTON,—I trust the Laberge affair did us no harm in Lower Canada, and especially that it did not affect Dorion injuriously, for that would indeed grieve me. He has always acted so manfully and generously that it would pain me deeply to know that I should have been the means of compromising him. I could not help coming out on that unfortunate tenure business. The ill-advised speeches of some friends on the back benches rendered it absolutely necessary. I should have been greatly damaged had I not spoken as I did. Between ourselves, Laberge did me the best service in attacking me as he did. People were beginning to believe that I had sold Western Canada to Lower Canada for the sake of party success. I think some of the actors rue it already. They thought that I had committed a grand error in coming out for the constitutional changes, and some of them freely denounced me and the whole scheme. But already the wonderful success the movement has met with from all parties has effected a change. I had a letter from Foley on Tuesday, in which he refers to the whole affair at the close of the session and since, and winds up thus: "You may rely upon it, that henceforth you will not have the shadow of a cause of complaint."

My firm conviction is that we should merge all our questions in the one great issue of a change of constitution. It will elevate the tone of politics, cast aside petty vexatious issues, and be a tremendous card at next election, come when it may. I cannot see why it should be less successful below than here.

We propose having a Convention here in the fall, and if representatives from Lower Canada could attend it, the effect would be admirable.

There is an impression among ministerialists that Sir E. Head has had notice he will be retired, but how the change will now affect matters remains to be seen. The ministry was nearly finished on Lake Huron without the aid of the Clear Grits. Little as I owe them, I would not like them to go off in that way.

Will the Whig government last? Have not the Rads been cruelly sold? If Bright and Cobden work their hands well I really think Pam. has done them a service. Did you see much of Cobden? I hope he will not accept. It is the case of Rolph and Cameron precisely.

The crops are looking on the whole well. Frost has done much damage, but as there was a greater breadth sown the yield will be an average one. There is an unusual anxiety about the crops this year; we are made to feel our dependence on the farm very directly in such times as these. Business is very dull and money scarce, but the true elements of recovery are at work, hard labour and frugality.

I intend going to the sea coast for a few days, and will take Montreal n my way, as I much desire to have a long talk with you.

If the York vacancy occurs there will be no trouble in arranging for your return if you will accept a seat for a West Canada constituency.

Yours most truly,

GEORGE BROWN.

HON. L. H. HOLTON, Montreal.

LETTER TO MR. HOLTON.

TORONTO, May 2, 1861.

MY DEAR HOLTON,—Except a short note to D. A. Macdonald, thanking him for keeping F—— straight, this is the first time I have put pen to paper for nine weeks. I tried to write in ink, but it was like the scrawl of an old man of eighty. You must therefore be content with pencil. I have had a hard time of it. The disease had fastened upon me long before it became fully developed, and was undoubtedly caused by the great exertions I had to make to put my house in order, for there was no mercy. I thank Providence, I was not driven to my bed until the ship was safe inside the breakers in comparatively smoother water than it has known for years.

The paragraphs that appeared in the *Globe* about me were utterly absurd. When the inflammation of the pleura was overcome and the congestion of the liver reduced, I was to be well immediately, and I really felt I would bo astir in a few days. The feeling was only the buoyancy of fever; as it lowered, my utter prostration soon appeared. Then I had to take nourishing food; but the digestive powers were so sadly impaired, that stimulants alone could be used. At present I am greatly better, and am able to ride out for an hour. A frightful cough still hangs, and I suffered a slight return of the congestive attack. The doctors want me to be off the moment I can stand the fatigue of journeying. I have resolved to go to the water cure establishment at Clifton Springs, near Rochester. I think a week or two there will set me on my feet again.

I am ashamed of all this egotism, but I wanted to have some friends reconcile the statements of the *Globe* with my real condition.

May 8th.—So far I had written on the 2nd, when I had to stop from weariness. On Friday I had a consultation of physicians, which ended, I am sorry to say, unfavourably to my hopes of a speedy recovery. All concurred in saying I must consider myself laid aside from business for some months, and that the utmost care must be taken to avoid falling into a state of permanent ill health.

I need not say how distressed I am by all this for myself and the party, as ministers are sure to take advantage of it in their election arrangements. Well, there is no help for it—nothing but submission, with the determined resolution that nothing shall be wanting to secure as speedy a recovery as possible.

I need not tell you how disgusted I am that Galt's bundle of misstatements should have escaped scathless. Of all the scandalous productions I ever met with, his opening chapter to the Public Accounts and his speech in opening the Budget are the worst. Such downright deceit I never met with from any man in a high position. I dictated an article for the *Globe* on the true balance for 1860, and another on the amount of the public debt;

perhaps you noticed them. I intended following them up with a complete analysis of his other statements, but have not strength to go at it. Did you notice his division of the rise of the public debt into three epochs: the amount during Hincks' administration, the amount during Cayley's, and the amount during his own? By barefaced jugglery he makes his own show but $5,000,000, when in fact it has been $23,000,000. Observe he takes credit for the full amount of the Sydenham loan, though, in fact, more than one-half of it was lying in London when he took office, and so on. It is utterly scandalous that out of 128 men not one rose to cast his false statements in his teeth. That disclosure by Dorion is most frightful. In any well-governed country it would be enough to produce a revolution.

Yours ever faithfully,

GEORGE BROWN.

HON. L. H. HOLTON, Montreal.

LETTER TO MR. HOLTON.

TORONTO, Feb. 19, 1862.

MY DEAR HOLTON,—I congratulate you on the victory in the west. It really looked hopeless for some weeks, but now things promise well. There will be lots of northern men now; but, after all, have not the events of the last few months rather lowered your estimate of our neighbours? Has it not shown that there is something more needed to make up a great people than sharpness in business and agreeable social qualities? Has it not raised your estimate of the value of military power: of the faculty of commanding masses of men? Has it not proved the advantages of the people being taught to obey those placed in authority over them? I wish we had a chance to talk this over.

And so we are to have a session at last. What is to be the result of it? I am satisfied there is great disorganization in the ministerial camp. Vankoughnet has arrived by the *Asia*, and is expected to be gazetted Chancellor immediately. I greatly doubt his accepting it. If he does not Burns is to go into an equity court and Morris to become a puisne judge. John Ross openly declares he will not go to Quebec. He means to remain President of the Grand Trunk Railway Company, but he may lose that. Mr. Brydges is regularly installed in the Grand Trunk. He is trying to accomplish an increased postal subsidy by private arrangement with the members. I suspect the ministry have discovered they cannot carry it and are unwilling to risk trying it. What about the Intercolonial subsidy? The repudiation scheme, if they had one, has been fairly exploded. No one dreams here now that it can be touched, and even Hamilton is to cash up. I think the *Globe* has done good service to the state in that matter. The speakership is still subject of debate. I think Mr. Drummond the best man we can run, and I hope he will consent. What of Sicotte? Did you see or hear anything of him? I have seen a number of people from Waterloo county, and I feel confident he could be elected there without any trouble, should Foley elect to sit for Perth. I hear, however, that he talks of sitting for Waterloo. Singularly enough, I was strongly urging the necessity of having you in the House a few days ago among a party of our friends, when —— offered to resign for you. I have no doubt he means it, but we will see when the House meets if Foley comes to that determination. The Midland Division Convention gave Mr. McMaster the nomination, and I think he will accept. Mr. McGee was here some days, and I saw much of him; I was much pleased with him. He promised to see Dorion and you, and tell you all that is going on. What about the seat of government? Had our policy best be to stand by Ottawa? It has been suggested to refuse more money to this government. What do you think I should do about the opening? Go down or write a letter? I am not inclined to go down, as it might be said I went to influence the choice of a leader or the adoption of some party policy. Pray advise. I hope it is true that you cross the Atlantic with Mrs. Holton in the summer. It would be so pleasant to go together and compare notes occasionally as to men and things. The session, I conclude, will not last longer than June, and if you take your seat this session, of course you could not leave till the House rose, and I could not wait so late, having business waiting me in England.

Yours faithfully,

GEORGE BROWN.

HON. L. H. HOLTON, Montreal.

LETTER TO MR. HOLTON.

TORONTO, May 29, 1862.

MY DEAR HOLTON,—I was delighted beyond measure at the receipt of your letter. It is so refreshing to find that one of the old set at any rate sticks to the ship.

Believe me, that though I have not written, you have not been out of my mind for two consecutive hours in the last two weeks, and I have been more than once on the point of running down to consult you as to the course I should take. I was only deterred by fear of the construction that would be attached to my going east at such a moment. As it is, I would like much to have two hours with you, for who else to consult with I know not. My only reason for not writing was the necessity of sending a well-considered reply to that strange letter of McGee's. I am writing this at one o'clock in the morning, after a five hours' interview with Wilson and Foley. The conclusion I came to from all they have told me is that a greater set of incapables than the quartette was never got by accident into the government of any country. Would you believe it? They tell me their constitutional scheme is to be embodied in formal resolutions, and submitted for the adoption of parliament next session; that any modification of the plan will be adopted, and that they themselves will do their utmost to have representation by population made part of the scheme, and if necessary will resign, or take any other course the party desire! Foley says he will state the substance of this in his address, which he is to prepare to-morrow and submit to me for consideration. McDougall is to leave Quebec to-night, and will be here to-morrow night. Foley's address will be held over until he arrives and joins our consultation, so that it will not appear before Monday morning. I would do anything to have you here; is it not possible for you to come? It would be an immense relief if you did, it is so hard to tell how to act. There is no doubt that if I go into it, and stump the four counties, three of them at any rate will be beaten. But that would split the party, and bring on once more a most disagreeable personal warfare, which I wish to avoid of all things. I am keenly desirous of sticking to my business for a couple of years, and especially of getting myself off to England for a few months. To go into such a fight would knock everything on the head; but then, if we don't kill them their conduct may yet kill us as a party. If we could get the arrangement put before the public as an open question, and have it understood that resolutions (on which the whole relations of Upper and Lower Canada would come up) were to be presented to parliament next session, the complexion of affairs would be entirely changed. Only fancy the folly of these men telling the House and the public that the matter was closed, when they could with so much more advantage have told the truth, if indeed it is the truth.

Sicotte must have been very closely run on his side of the question, when he got the worst side proposed for his colleagues from Upper Canada, to strengthen himself in Lower Canada. I will write you from day to day to inform you of our negotiations, in case you don't come up. In the meantime, I need not tell you how much I would value any suggestions you have to make for the *Globe's* guidance.

Ever faithfully yours,

GEORGE BROWN.

Hon. L. H. HOLTON, Montreal.

LETTER TO MR. HOLTON.

TORONTO, June 2, 1862.

MY DEAR HOLTON,—I feel exceedingly obliged by your ready response to my unreasonable request, and only regret it was out of your power to come up. I cannot help feeling that the line of policy to be pursued by the *Globe* and by our staunch friends here was a question of no small difficulty and no light importance. Had I been able to discuss the whole matter with you, and we had arrived at a joint conclusion, all doubt would have been off my mind. The die is cast, however, and, right or wrong, I must stand by it.

Foley and Wilson, when with me first, both maintained they had sacrificed nothing, and were as ready to vote for representation by population now as ever. When I asked Wilson what he would do if a vote on it came up next session, he said he would vote for it unless it were put as a vote of want of confidence ; and that if a majority of the West Canada members would vote for it in the latter shape he would resign. Foley doubted how they would act in the former case, but was clear that if the motion in the latter case came from Tom Ferguson or J. H. Cameron, they would not regard it. However, they both agreed that resolutions embodying the new policy were to be laid before parliament next session ; that the whole question of the constitutional relations between Upper and Lower Canada would then come up; and that if an advance could then be obtained, or the party asked them to take a certain course, even at the risk of office, they would go heartily into it. I seized this declaration, and asked if they would put this in their addresses ? They both agreed to do so. Foley was to write his address out and show it to me on Friday forenoon, and when McDougall arrived that evening, to have a consultation as to the best means of putting matters in a more satisfactory shape.

Foley did bring me his address on Friday, but he found it very difficult to put his ideas in such a shape as would suit the purpose here and not offend his Lower Canada colleagues. After a good deal of debate we agreed to let the matter rest until McDougall arrived. He arrived on Friday night, as arranged, and was with me from half-past eleven till near three o'clock. After telling him my mind very plainly, we discussed the whole subject fully. He repeated all that Foley and Wilson said, and agreed to stand by it, but he refused positively to put it in his address, or to have it in any address.

Our discussion had evidently opened his eyes to the difficulty of putting the double majority delusion in formal resolutions, and made him shrink from pledging himself to submit them to the House.

Would it not be rich to have the whole constitution changed by the simple will of twelve gentlemen who happened for the time to hold the twelve state offices? McDougall evidently felt his oats, but Gordon caught a different impression. I was very candid with him and the others, but of course as courteous and friendly as the case would admit of.   Among other things, McDougall stated that Howland only held office temporarily, and that I was looked for as his successor. I scouted this suggestion, and asked him how it came that you were not made Minister of Finance, as we had all intended in the event of a crisis. He said because Sandfield and Sicotte were against it. He admitted the concern could not go on as it was, and that he looked on it as a mere make-shift.

The question now was what course should be taken? Start candidates against all four, and run out as many as possible? or permit them to go in unopposed, and hold them up to the mark under the stimulus of bit and spur? I had nobody to consult with but Gordon. We deliberated long, and finally concluded that the latter course was the best for the country and the party under all the circumstances. Friday's *Globe* contained no allusion to the matter, and Saturday's gave a gentle hint to the North York meeting that there were two sides to the question of rejecting them.   This morning's paper discussed the double majority humbug. We shall quietly fall into the attitude of independent but hearty support on all but the one question. I will ask no favours from them for anyone, and will stand ready heartily to aid them to the best of my ability, with the one reservation that on the constitutional question they are to be coerced on every occasion.

Now for the reasons that led me to this conclusion. To oppose the re-election of the new ministers would have been to split the party once more, not only in the five counties, but all over the province. The best men of the country would have gone with us, but a large section would have been estranged. It was no slight responsibility to face this result. Then, supposing that could be got over, where were the men to run? Several excellent men were available to run, but not such men as were necessary for the crisis. Suppose us successful at all the elections, who was there to carry out in the House the bold policy that such a result would render necessary? The worst of it is that nearly all our friends in the House had been committed to a partial support of the government, notwithstanding their retrograde policy, and might regard such success as a censure on themselves. I felt that to give effect to the movement I must run myself, and carry out in the House what had been begun in the country; this I was determined not to do. Then came the fear that our success might possibly kill the ministry, and bring back the corruptionists. I shrank from the responsibility of risking that. It could not be forgotten that the present men would certainly effect great practical reforms; and especially that while the old set would have been entirely beyond our reach if once reinstalled, the present men will always be less or more within reach if they stray from the right path. On the other hand, was there much chance of the present concern lasting long? And if it fell, would there not be a general election? With the party committed, partly, to this monstrous policy, would we not be swept from existence as a party? Moreover, was not the credit of the country and the honour of the liberal party at stake in the conduct of these four men and the reception given them by their constituents? And if returned unopposed, would it not be saying as plainly as possible that Upper Canada was quite content to set aside her claims for just representation and take a miserable delusion in its place? We weighed the whole matter seriously and maturely, and concluded to take the course I have already sketched. I hope our conclusion was right. Assuredly we arrived at it with a strong desire to do that which seemed best for the weal of the country.

Now, my dear Holton, the best news I have heard is that you are coming out for Huntingdon; I entreat you to do so; there could be no doubt of your success. If you come out, I promise that the moment you ask me to come back to Parliament, I will at once respond. The present ministry will not last long. From the strongest of them, with the best of our friends outside, a higher and better policy might be carried out for our country than what is in prospect for us now. Don't think of accepting the Upper House.

I hope to start across the Atlantic in about three weeks, but will try and see you before I go. Your candidature may interfere with your trip, but it would be pleasant to meet you in England. I would give much for that opportunity.

Ever faithfully yours,

GEORGE BROWN.

Hon. L. H. Holton, Montreal.

LETTER TO MR. HOLTON.

EDINBURGH, Sept. 3, 1862.

MY DEAR HOLTON,—I got here at a very interesting time—I mean to London. I was fortunate enough to be present at the great debate in the Commons and at the great Grand Trunk meeting. It would be hard to say which disappointed me most. The ignorance of English politicians about Canadian affairs is as astounding as the helpless dependence of the capitalists on the word of a few bell-wethers. I cannot tell you how glad I am at having had an opportunity of seeing how affairs are managed here. It is very curious and very instructive. I have met many people in the political and financial worlds, and have received the greatest kindness from all. The truths told in the *Globe* for the last ten years have not prevented the Barings and Glyns being very civil ; and those who escaped Grand Trunk benefits particularly so. I have a great deal to tell you when I see you. It would be absurd to attempt it in a letter.

I had a most satisfactory interview with the Duke of Newcastle at his request. His scruples about representation by population are entirely gone. It would have done even Sandfield good to hear his ideas on the absurdity of the double majority. Whatever small politicians and the London *Times* may say, you may depend upon this, that the government and the leaders of the opposition perfectly understand our position, and have no thought of changing the relations between Canada and the mother country. On the contrary, the members of the government (with the exception of Gladstone) are set upon the Intercolonial Railway and a grand transit route across the continent ! But for Mr. Gladstone's opposition, I have reason to believe that the scheme would have been announced by this time.

The meeting of the British North America Association, at which Mr. Galt spoke, was got up professedly to explain to the English public the present position of Canada and Canadian affairs, but in reality it was intended to force the Intercolonial Railway on public attention. I declined going because, in order to show our true position, I must have attacked some who were on the platform with me, and I did not think it fair to Sandfield and his colleagues to aid an agitation that might be embarrassing to them. So far I support the present government on everything else but the great constitutional issue and the school question ; and that I may have more to say on these two, I shall earnestly aid them on all other questions.

I am delighted to learn that your election for the Upper House is quite safe, though, of course, it is coupled with regret that you will not be in your proper sphere among the "Lords." Galt and I have made up the peace. By the way, he goes in now for constitutional changes stiff. He is to address the Manchester Chamber of Commerce on Canadian finances before he leaves. I have been asked to be present, and also to speak in several other quarters, but have steadily declined. I have no idea of *defending* Canada before the English people, and *defence* is the only possible attitude at this moment.

The bitterness against the United States here is remarkable, and the feeling is as senseless as it is bitter. The *Times* wields an astonishing influence over the length and breadth of the land. What it means by its present course I cannot conceive, and no one here can enlighten me. It seems to be meanly pandering to the passions of the people without regard to the inevitable hostile feeling that will arise in consequence of such writing in future years.

I got to this my native city a few days ago, and at once started off on an inspection of the old loved spots. I wandered from house to house and place to place where dear remembrances led me, and the mingled sensations were overwhelming. I have had many delightful meetings with old friends and cronies, but the sad, sad blanks tell the tale of twenty-five years.

Only one old friend recognized me, and he did so from having seen Gordon when here two or three years ago; all the others, though they had seen my brother and sister lately, failed to make me out.

I mean to stay here about a month, then, ho! for Canada. But for the sad thought that never more will I see my beloved mother ever recurring, my visit would have been one of intense pleasure throughout.

I needed nothing to "reconcile" me to Canada; but, after all I have seen, I say now as earnestly as ever, Canada for me!

Ever faithfully yours,

GEORGE BROWN.

HON. L. H. HOLTON, Montreal.

LETTER TO MR. HOLTON.

TORONTO, Jan. 5, 1863.

MY DEAR HOLTON,—Many thanks for your kind congratulations, and I assure you my friends may well congratulate me, for I am a new man in mind and body after my trip to England, and as happy as the day is long. I do not know when I may get down to Montreal, but whenever I do Mrs. Brown will accompany me, and I have promised her a great pleasure, and, I trust, the friendship of all your family circle. I quite weary to have a long talk with you on many subjects. I have much to tell. Is there any chance of your coming up? I may possibly be called to Montreal by business within three or four weeks, but it is not likely. I wish very much to have consultation also with Dorion. You would see an absurd article in the *Leader* of yesterday about new combinations. I need hardly say that, so far as I am concerned, there is not a shadow of truth in it. I never had any love for coalitionists, and certainly have as little now as I ever had. The *Leader* and its friends may rest assured that when I go to open war with the present ministry, it will be as a reformer and a party reformer, and that I shall take some small section of that party with me, sufficient at any rate to make war effectively for Upper Canada principles, whether the conservatives like it or not. But entirely re-established in health as I am, and free from nearly all business retardment, I have no desire whatever to re-enter parliamentary life, and would much rather accomplish through others what the country wants than be a prominent participant myself. I have thought out a course for myself pretty clearly, but shall make no sign or say anything until I see you and discuss our affairs fully. I regretted much you could not come to Great Britain this summer. You would have enjoyed it intensely. But I trust there is a good time coming. I am happy to know that I can now give you notes to many of the friends in England and Scotland who will welcome you heartily from the knowledge they already have of you. I met many Canadians in London.

Ever faithfully yours,

GEORGE BROWN.

HON. L. H. HOLTON, Montreal.

LETTER TO MR. ——.

TORONTO, Feb. 12, 1863.

MY DEAR ——,—I was greatly gratified by Dorion's refusal to join the present ministry. I fear that sooner or later we will be forced to part company with them, and it is a great relief to have Dorion out of it. Indeed, I cannot see how they are to get on with any comfort. The Intercolonial Railway matter stands in a very awkward position. If they were willing to face borrowing the money to build the road, and the annual deficit in running it, I think they need not have scrupled about the sinking fund. It strikes me it was a very small loop-hole to escape by; but let us rejoice the country is saved the burden threatened. The postal subsidy to the Grand Trunk is another rock ahead. I hear the government has been pledged to arbitration. I hope this is a mistake; but if not, it will create trouble. The school question, too, stands out in a threatening aspect, but perhaps that may be avoided as well as the *Credit Foncier;* but from what I hear, Sicotte's strength in Lower Canada is far from what was expected, and will prove the weakest spot of the administration. Sandfield, it seems, has promise of a dissolution; but so far as Upper Canada is concerned, I am persuaded that if he tries he will find himself mistaken. There will be unavoidable divisions in the reformers' ranks where conservatives will be united, and the result may easily be seen. If an election were to come now, I would not move hand or pen except for the individual whom I knew to be reliable from every point of view. I confess I view the position of our party with some degree of alarm—more alarm than I have felt for ten years. Ministers may get supporters to vote down representation by population, or they may treat their vote on that question with indifference; but the country will not do so, and any attempt to speak against it as the late minister did, will cause a burst of indignation over the country. Divisions will spring up. In every store and bar-room of Upper Canada the contest will be waged; the best of our men will be found where they were. One set will be pitted against the other; and when the election comes, the result will be seen. I have no desire to enter parliament; on the contrary, nothing but the strongest sense of duty would tempt me to enter it at present; but sometimes when I think of the gulf before us, I am almost tempted to wish myself once more in the House. A little reflection, however, soon brings me back stronger than ever for quiet and happiness. All you have seen—if, indeed, you have seen the trash which has been published—about Oxford and my connection with it, is entirely fabulous. Several prominent electors wrote offering support and urging me to stand. I declined, after thinking the matter seriously over. I know less of South Oxford than of any county west of Belleville. Were I desirous of going in I suppose I could do so by stumping the county, but I never was in the riding except at the village of Ingersoll. It is largely Hincksite, and has, I am told, nearly six hundred Roman Catholic electors. I would, however, get, besides many of the friends, a large number of Stephen Richards—and a little canvassing would, I dare say, make the thing sure enough. But I prefer keeping out. If the cabinet tumbled to pieces and I in the House—whatever I said or did—the doing of it would be thrown on my shoulders. Now, I do not want them to have any excuse for failure, but to stand or fall on their merits. I sincerely hope they will not fall this session ; but I hope still more earnestly that my friends in the House will not ruin themselves by giving bad votes on these questions to keep the government in office. I see John A. Macdonald is reported to have arrived by the *Europa*. What course he may take I do not know ; but whatever he does will very much affect the reliability or weakness of the ministry. Haultain, Cockburn, and others I wot of, in the event of the conservatives pursuing a different policy than what they have done, will not hesitate to act for themselves. Howland is still here. He seemed far from ill when I saw him a week ago, but they say he is not well enough to get through the work of the session. I hope you will write me from day to day your impressions of matters. On Monday I go back to the editorial chair, and mean to keep it during the session. I will be glad if you could have an opportunity of letting me know of Lord Monck as Governor-General. It is reported that the ministry and he had some difficulty in November, and that they had placed their resignations in his hands in the full expectation of being out ; but he thought better of it. The militia question is said to have been the cause of the trouble.

Ever faithfully yours,

GEORGE BROWN.

LETTER TO MR. ———.

TORONTO, March 7, 1863.

MY DEAR ———,—I got your telegram, and took your advice, and I am in. Had I consented to be a candidate three days earlier there would have been no contest, or, at least, nothing worth designating a contest. But the convention proceedings gave Bodwell something to talk about, and committed a great many people who regretted having to vote against me. South Oxford never was a constituency of my way of thinking exactly, and it was very gratifying to find how hearty and kind was the reception I got from men of all parties all over the riding, including those who voted against me. Not one harsh word passed during the contest ; and were the fight to be gone over again to-morrow, I think we could carry it by one thousand majority. It is not true that I got all the Tory vote. The Tories in South Oxford number between six and seven hundred, including the catholics, who generally voted against me. Of the protestant Tories I got perhaps from one-half to two-thirds, but by getting them I lost as many hard old Radicals. So that while I got many votes from the conservatives, I am not indebted to them for my return. I entirely agree with you about McDougall's speech. It was the most reckless as well as the most foolish speech ever made by a man in his position. I see, too, he goes in for sectarian schools, and the whole animal generally. Well, he had better look out for another constituency than North Oxford. I regret also to hear that Ferguson Blair has accepted the Receiver-Generalship *vice* Morris, but it does not take me by surprise. I suppose he will get returned, but it is because no earnest reformer will oppose him under the present circumstances. I do not intend going down for ten days unless you write me that there is necessity.

Ever faithfully yours,

GEORGE BROWN.

LETTER TO MR. HOLTON.

TORONTO, June 26, 1863.

MY DEAR HOLTON,—The elections are over. We have been as successful as we could hope to be, and now begins the real trouble. Were Sandfield a man of comprehensive mind and firm of purpose, all trouble would soon be overcome. But it is really sad to rejoice over victory at the polls as if we had nothing else to do but sit down and enjoy our spoils. I need not remind you that our very success in Upper Canada, and the complete rout of the old corruptionists, have rendered our future course more difficult than before. We cannot hold up the return of Sir John and Cartier as a scarecrow for those who insist on our carrying out our principles. We have men returned on our side firmly pledged to carry out our views, and what is more, all but two oppositionists returned are as earnest as we are in claiming the same reform. The vote for representation by population will be almost unanimous on the part of Upper Canada members, and the conservatives will now be most violent in their clamours for it, when they see that the country has completely adopted it. What is to be done—look the case fairly in the face, or wait the event? The former is very difficult after what occurred in Montreal, and the latter may throw the reform party into a defensive attitude not advantageous on such a question. It is impossible to make Sandfield think or speak seriously. Your own particular troubles are in no way light, though I confess they would g ve me no uneasiness if I occupied your shoes. I would just form my conclusions as to what was right, and carry them out firmly and boldly. Much is expected from you, and I am conscious that if you only carry out your own well-considered purposes, you will not go astray. I need not say that you can always rely on my sincere and earnest counsel whenever you think it worth while to ask it. An immense card, politically, would be the renewal of the United States reciprocity treaty. If you can fix that for twenty years you will give our party a hold on the farmers that would be very difficult to over-estimate. Sandfield spoke of my going down to Washington to see how the land lay. I would gladly do so were there any necessity for it, but of course you will attend to that yourself, and no doubt with as much influence as I could possibly exercise at the Washington Court. There seems less hurry about the matter now that the democratic party have had a check, but I am persuaded that President Lincoln is favourable, and while he is in power the thing should be attended to. I am strongly of opinion that you should summon parliament for the earliest possible day. Announce that it is for the Supplies and the Militia Bill alone. Push them through in ten days, and call us at the regular time—the end of January; this will give you a chance of feeling the temper of the House. It will enable you to discard troublesome matters in your Supply Bill on the score of time being needed to consider, and it will enable you to prepare your plans coolly and considerately before your session next winter.

Faithfully yours,

GEORGE BROWN.

HON. L. H. HOLTON, Montreal.

LETTER TO MR. HOLTON.

TORONTO, Oct. 23, 1863.

MY DEAR HOLTON,—I have this moment received your letter of yester day, and hasten to give you the reply you ask for. Of course, you are responsible for the financial steps to be taken at this moment. You and you alone will bear the burden if any error is made, and you have the credit if credit is won. It is therefore right that you should pursue the course that seems to your own mind the best; and in what I am about to write, therefore, you will understand that I am only giving you my own view of the situation at your request, and that I expect you will give it that influence, and no more, in making up your own mind, to which the arguments seem to be entitled. I understand your present inclination is to borrow from the Bank of Montreal a sufficient sum to secure your account with the English agents, and, in consideration of this accommodation, to transfer to the Bank of Montreal the government account. I admit that some advantage is to be gained from this arrangement. But on the other hand, there are very serious dangers that may arise from it. In the first place, you take from the commercial circles of the province a large portion of the capital of the Bank of Montreal that ought to be employed in developing the trade of the country. In the second place, you strike a blow at the Bank of Upper Canada that may be disastrous to that institution, and will certainly be most hurtful to the commercial interests of this section of the province. This bank is not in a condition to withstand a pressure, and a pressure will certainly come if you withdraw your government account. In turn they will press all their customers, and where that will end who can tell? I am led to believe that the board is gradually working through its difficulties, and that two years more would put it past serious trouble. If this is so, would it not be assuming a serious responsibility to take a step that may bring widespread ruin on Upper Canada? Let me add for myself, however, that I think the people of Upper Canada would have good cause to dread the accumulation of this great additional power in the hands of the directors of the Bank of Montreal. It is a Montreal institution, soul and body, and most hostile to Upper Canada interests. Its true spirit was displayed in the panic of 1857. I am persuaded that the removal of the government account to the Bank of Montreal at this moment, when the Bank of Upper Canada is struggling through its difficulties, would not only be an act of great injustice, but highly impolitic as regards the general interests of the country. It will certainly be viewed, coming from you, as a Montreal blow aimed at Upper Canada. I know well that no such feeling animates you, but assuredly this will be believed here, and it will very much surprise me if strong and excited feeling in Upper Canada does not flow from it. Frankly, the step would be a very grave one in my opinion, politically, financially, and every other way, and I would not like to have the responsibility of it on my shoulders. Nothing but absolute necessity could justify a step involving risks so serious, and I do not see the necessity. You are not responsible for the debt. No one will blame you for borrowing to secure accounts; and certainly, under better auspices, you can easily borrow in England. I have no doubt you can make what arrangements you like with Baring and Glyns. But failing them, you could get whatever you want in London, for any length of time you wish, by hypothecating debentures on moderate terms. All the Bank of Montreal proposes is to do with the money of Canadian merchants what you can do with the money of English capitalists. From an Upper Canada point of view, I could fancy few acts on the part of the present government more suicidal. I have written you my full mind in this matter, but of course with only partial knowledge of the subject. I am persuaded, however, I have expressed what will be the strong feeling of nine-tenths of the people of Upper Canada until the contrary is known.

Ever faithfully yours,

GEORGE BROWN.

HON. L. H. HOLTON, Montreal.

———————

LETTER TO MR. HOLTON.

————

TORONTO, Jan. 19, 1864.

MY DEAR HOLTON,—I dare say you are thinking you are not to hear from me again, and perhaps you think I am out of sorts about the bank matter; but you are wrong if such is your notion. I did think you wrong in that matter. I think so still; but it was your own affair, and had I been in your place, I would have carried out my own ideas. But I decline to discuss, for it is *au fait accompli.* I did not look at it from your point of view; I did not think your arguments were satisfactory. But what will it avail for us now to argue it out; the thing is done, and let it rest there.

I hope Richards will be re-elected for Leeds. Knowing nothing of the constituency, I cannot say anything as to the chances. The opposition are cock-a-hoop; but the minister seeking re-election is hard to beat. I think the appointment was a very wrong one. Notman should have been Solicitor-General; failing him, Shuter Smith, or Ferguson Blair, or Mowat should have taken it, and allowed a new man, not a lawyer, to come into the cabinet. I think the appointment of Richards was not in harmony with the arrangement under which the cabinet was formed. Richards holds, and did hold, all the views of the Macdonald-Sicotte ministry. Mowat and Wallbridge were taken in to give confidence to those who did not hold those views, and Wallbridge's successor should certainly have been of like opinions. Of course there was no bargain to that effect, but I think the government would have felt the benefit of it had this been done.

I am much concerned about the reciprocity treaty. It appears to me that none of us are sufficiently awake about it. I see very serious trouble ahead if notice of the repeal is given. Such a feeling will be manifested here as will determine the United States to repeal it. They will see then, if they do not now, how essential it is to our prosperity here in Canada, and what many here are prepared to do to secure its re-enactment. I do think you are taking on a very serious responsibility in not opening nego-tiations at Washington, as well with the committees of the House and the senate as with the executive. It would be a thousandfold easier to negotiate before notice than after; before members have committed them-selves, by speech or otherwise, than afterwards, I hear we are not to meet before Valentine Day. I am sorry, though it suits me personally much better than an earlier day.

But a truce to politics. Let me turn to more agreeable matters, and congratulate you heartily on the marriage of your daughter. Mr. and Mrs. Britton were here and spent an evening with us. They have all the prospects before them of as useful and happy a future as heart could wish, though it must have been a great trial to Mrs. Holton to part with her daughter. You would notice, perhaps, that Mrs. Brown had a little daughter a week ago. They are both doing well, and we regard it as a vast addition to our happiness.

Faithfully yours,

GEORGE BROWN.

Hon. L. H. HOLTON, Montreal.

LETTER TO MR. HOLTON.

TORONTO, January 29, 1864.

MY DEAR HOLTON,—Here's a pretty mess. Perhaps Sandfield will now have his eyes opened to the fact that it is only on the liberal constituencies the government can rely when the pinch comes, and that, convenient to him as it may be, and his friends in the ministry, it wants something more than his choice to get them there. I was astonished to hear that Sandfield had said I had consented to Richards' appointment. The very opposite is the fact. But both Gordon and I saw, as plainly as possible, that Sandfield was bent on making the appointment, and while I urged my views of the matter on him, I refrained from speaking against Richards. It was not for me to say that Richards' appointment would be a gross injustice and breach of faith, with the understanding at the formation of the government, while Sandfield was protesting all the time that he had no thought of appointing him and would do nothing without letting me know—a promise I had no wish for, and which was never thought of after it was uttered. What is to be done now? Can any single man in our party now fail to see that the policy you and I chalked out at the end of the session was the only safe one, and the only right one? If you come down with a weak speech, get defeated, and an election should follow, where would we be? And how about your tax scheme? Will you venture to go on with it in a House in which you are so weak as the present one? Don't you regret you had not made a stand before now? Sandfield will, I have no doubt, have shewn you my answer to his letter about the reciprocity matter. You are the only man to go there. You can go with authority. I have no idea of going to Washington as a lobby agent, to be snubbed by Lord Lyons for meddling in a matter he was sufficiently able to settle.

Faithfully yours,

GEORGE BROWN.

Hon. L. H. HOLTON, Montreal.

LETTER TO MR. HOLTON.

TORONTO, February 6, 1864.

MY DEAR HOLTON,—Your note of the 3rd has this moment reached me. I do not quite understand what you are driving at. Did my urging you to go into the government last May make me responsible, or impose on me the obligation of approving all that the government has done since? Did not you and I both see clearly at the end of last session that another such was not to be contemplated, but that a crisis during the recess was the wise and prudent mode of avoiding a great break-down in the coming session? Must I, whether I can honestly do so or not, approve of the course of the government on the bank matter, the seat of government matter, reciprocity, South Leeds, and the North-West business, on all of which I was consulted after the thing was done, or when it was too late to do anything; and

because I do not and cannot approve of the course of the government on
these points, does it follow that I will not stick to my party, and will not
aid to pull it through in spite of the course taken?   Have I ever shrank
from my share when the pinch came?   You speak of the men with whom
I cordially act as the main core of the party; but what one step has been
taken by the government to strengthen us, or even to please us?   No, not
one step, except the first move about the York roads, and there it hangs to
let a new government undo it.   I think Mowat and you should not have
allowed matters to get into the shape they have.   I have done my duty in
urging you both and warning you of coming troubles from my point of
view.   You have not seen proper to go upon it.   But I did not take the pet
on that account.   The question is not what I thought ought to have been
and might have been, but what is.   However, we up here will exert ourselves to get through the coming session.   I see you do not think a break-
up imminent.   Well, I sincerely hope you will prove right, for a break-up
now is not only to lose the reins, but to ruin the party west.   I don't want
that; and little respect as I have for a portion of the government, I cannot
separate them from the great reform party.   You ask why I did not write
to you, and you complain about Richards' appointment.   I answer because
Sandfield left me declaring it would not be made, and I heard not a word
more about it till I heard the deed was done.   I complained to Mowat;
but, in truth, what is the use of complaining?

Faithfully yours,

GEORGE BROWN.

HON. L. H. HOLTON, Montreal.

LETTER TO MR. HOLTON.

TORONTO, January 17, 1867.

MY DEAR HOLTON,—I agree with you in your suggestion that it might
not be a bad dodge for John A.'s purpose to shove off the confederation
settlement, and that it would be characteristic; but he cannot do it.
Nearly all the others consider it either now or never.   It is immediate or
political death certain.   Cartier perfectly understands his position, and
the sooner confederation comes the better.   I never was so confident as at
this moment that the movement was a right one, and will prove a great
boon to the province; and how any liberal politician could doubt that
any settlement of the constitutional question must place his party in the
ascendant and give a new face to the whole politics of the country. I never
could understand, and don't now.   Of course, you in Lower Canada have
a difficult card to play; but those who settle this question, it appears to
me, are playing your game for you.   Don't fancy there is any great change
in public opinion here.   There is a lull, a doubt, an uncertainty, but the
moment the right chord is struck, the response will be as of yore, only more
so, or I am no judge.   In great haste,

Faithfully yours,

GEORGE BROWN.

HON. L. H. HOLTON, Montreal.

LETTER TO MR. HOLTON.

TORONTO, May 13, 1867.

MY DEAR HOLTON,—Yours of the 25th came duly to hand, but being
busy since, I could not reply sooner.   I think the ground you take quite

consistent, truly patriotic, and one on which we can all meet. I hope you will have entire success in your effort to carry the Rouge party with you. I quite understood what you said about control. I had no objections to it from your point of view, but my fixed determination is to see the liberal party reunited and in the ascendant, and then make my bow as a politician. As a journalist and a citizen, I hope always to be found on the right side and heartily supporting my old friends. But I want to be free to write of men and things without control, beyond that which my conscientious convictions and the interests of the country demand. To be debarred by fear of injuring the party from saying that ——— is unfit to sit in parliament, and that ——— is very stupid, makes journalism a very small business. Party leadership and the conducting of a great journal do not harmonize.

I had an hour's talk with Mr. Howland. He tells me Lord Monck told him John A. Macdonald would form the new government, and urged him to take a seat in it, but that he absolutely refused to come to any decision until he got out to Canada. Mat. Cameron writes me that McDougall is quite undecided how to act; that he was intensely disgusted at the reception given to John A. on their joint arrival.

The list of senators was to be settled on Saturday and telegraphed to London; the proclamation is to be issued as soon as it reaches England, or rather as soon as the Queen returns from Balmoral. The union is to come into operation on the 1st July, and the elections are to follow as soon as possible thereafter. I have given you all the news I heard. Write me what you have. Good-by.

Faithfully yours,

GEORGE BROWN.

HON. L. H. HOLTON, Montreal.

LETTER TO MR. HOLTON.

TORONTO, July 5, 1867.

MY DEAR HOLTON,—Yours of yesterday reached me this afternoon. I was much amused at the life-like picture it presented of Sandfield's position. I have no doubt your surmises as to his expectations from the enemy are well grounded. I am not quite so sure that he will refuse their overtures. The question now is what to do about the eastern counties. Shall I take their case in hand myself, and make a raid through them, or leave them to the chance of Sandfield's moving? I have several very strong letters from M., urging action and promising cordial co-operation, but he failed to come to the convention. I am offered addresses and invitations from several counties of central Canada to visit them and speak on public affairs, and if I thought Macdonald would not move soon, and move vigorously, I would accept some of them, and stir up the dead bones. The Tories are in alarm about the movement. If Currie accepts the nomination from Peel, the Grand Master will certainly be beaten. We have had no communication whatever with the Roman Catholic clergy, but they, of course, know all about the position, and have probably determined not to interfere. The fact is, that there has not a word been passed, or a demand been made, or inducement sought or offered, that might not be cried from every housetop in the country; and the most interesting part of the business is that the most pronounced of them heretofore show a moderation, common sense, and confidence in our good faith exceedingly satisfactory. I observe a Mr. Roden by name is likely to oppose you in Chateauguay, but hope it will amount to nothing. Stories of all kinds are circulated here by ministerialists as to the utter overthrow of the liberal party in Lower Canada. Tilley told myself that fifteen was the outside number of liberals that could get in. He had better look to his own following. I have a letter from one of his strong men, speaking for himself and others, entirely approving of our course up here, and declaring that the reform party of New Brunswick will never ally themselves with the Tory party. If you do anything respectable in Lower Canada, out they must go, and if you don't, I go for sticking to you until you can do better. But of all this when we meet. As you have given me all the news that I could hope to obtain from Sandfield, I shall not go down to Montreal for some days—perhaps not for a fortnight, as there is much to do here. Do not believe one word about my being deceived by some of our candidates. I know more about that than anybody else, and think I know all the shaky fellows pretty well, though I don't tell everybody of it. Good-by.

Ever yours,
GEORGE BROWN.

HON. L. H. HOLTON, Montreal.

EXTRACTS FROM MR. BROWN'S PRIVATE LETTERS TO A RELATIVE, ON THE RECIPROCITY TREATY NEGOTIATIONS CONDUCTED BY HIM IN 1874.

WASHINGTON, Feb. 12, 1874.

It is really very hard work to see the leading spirits among 300 representatives, and carry on discussion with them. So far everything looks well, but one's heart sinks before the labour necessary to insure success. And after all the labour has been gone through, by some accident or whim the castle may be toppled over at the last moment. The government seems to be with us, and many of the most important men in congress. We know as yet of but few men who are bitterly against us. I saw General Butler, at his own request, on the subject, and I understand he will support us. Charles Sumner is heart and hand with us, and is most kind to me personally.

I shall try to get to the bottom of the general feeling as early as possible next week, and then return.

WASHINGTON, Feb. 14, 1874.

Everything has gone on as well as we could have hoped for. It is always difficult to say beforehand what any legislative body will do, and this legislature is one of the most uncertain on commercial questions ; but without overestimating the favourable symptoms, I feel confident that were a bill for the renewal of the reciprocity treaty (with some amendments) submitted to both Houses next week, it would be carried. Whether such a bill will get before congress, or what new influences may arise to affect its chances when it does, is a different thing.

On Monday I shall be able to get through all I can do at present, until the United States government take the initiative formally ; they have already agreed unofficially. Consent from England has also to be obtained before further advance is made. I therefore propose to leave on Monday night and go by New York direct to Ottawa.

WASHINGTON, May 10, 1874.

We have made a good deal of progress since I got back here. I had a long talk with Bancroft Davis, and he assures me they mean business, but do not feel they can deal with it without advice. I am informed they have called in Dr. Young. He went over the list with me, and showed me what we would probably get and what we would not get. We will probably accept such a compromise.

I have visited several prominent men whose views were doubtful, among others Senator Conkling, who goes heartily for a treaty, and will urge Mr. Fish to go ahead; I also saw General Garfield and Secretary Schurz, both of whom are favourable.

I shall go to New York for a day to obtain, if possible, the *Herald*, the *Times*, and the *Sun*. We have already had articles in the *World* and *Evening Post*. I have sent off our first despatch to the London *Times*.

WASHINGTON, May 15, 1874.

I was able to do good work in New York, having secured the support of the *Herald* and the *Times*. The enclosed article was published by the *Tribune*, with some trifling changes. The Chicago *Tribune* had a grand article, and so had many other papers that I heard of but have not seen. What a provoking thing it was that my manifesto, prepared at the request of the Associated Press people, was not sent, as promised, to all the papers. They only sent a small part to the press generally, and the whole to the New York press only. I could have done better without their aid.

Don't, I pray you, come to the conclusion that all is safe for the treaty. We know of not one thing more against us than we did when you were here, and we know of much that is favourable which has turned up since. But political matters are in such a mess here that it seems hopeless to get anything satisfactory done this session, unless Mr. Fish signs a treaty, and to do that he seems more and more unwilling. He is frightened at his shadow, and seems to have neither knowledge enough of the subject, nor breadth of grasp sufficient to cast his fears aside. If he had, the treaty would be carried without much trouble. On Monday we are to see him, when we hope to bring him to the point.

WASHINGTON, May 22, 1874.

I had a most pleasant interview with Mr. Fish on Monday. He promised to see us again in three or four days. We are making strength every day in the senate. I have issued a fly-sheet which, I think, will give us a hoist. Mr. Fish's four days are up, but we have not heard from him. I have just written him a note which, I hope, will bring him to the point. I hope now to know distinctly what he means to-morrow. Everything goes well meanwhile. The papers are coming out famously; the Chicago Board of Trade have passed excellent resolutions; the New York Board pass theirs to-morrow; the Boston Board of Trade on Tuesday; and the Detroit Board at the same time.

We had a cablegram to-day from Lord Derby, thanking us for our paper given to Mr. Fish, and declaring it an able document.

WASHINGTON, May 27, 1874.

We had a satisfactory meeting with Mr. Fish, who seems now to be thoroughly in earnest. I think we will get him to send the treaty to the senate for advice, as was done with the Washington treaty, and we think the senate will assent to it, but that is not certain. The bargain is not all we would like, but it will be a creditable treaty for us.

It looks very like winning. I had a long interview with Mr. Fish by myself at the state department, and settled everything as far as he is concerned.   I have telegraphed articles to Ottawa for approval.   The moment I hear from them I am to see Mr. Fish, and he is to call a cabinet council to have it approved and sent to the senate.   If it goes as we have it, it will be perfectly satisfactory to us and our people ; but we may find it broken up in the senate, or before it reaches there.   That will not, however, prevent our going at it again as long as the government endorses it.

WASHINGTON, May 30, 1874.

There is a hitch at Ottawa.   The articles sought to be introduced into the free list exceed the amount Mr. Mackenzie sees his way to relieve from paying duty.   I am going on to try and put the matter right, and I hope to accomplish it.

There seems to be no doubt that the treaty will go through if this difficulty at Ottawa is overcome.

WASHINGTON, June 7, 1874.

We had a long interview with Mr. Fish yesterday morning, when I made the suggestion necessary to meet the views of the Ottawa government.   The interview was, on the whole, pleasant, but he fought hard against any amendment.   Finally, he conceded all demands subject to three concessions by us : 1st, That we surrender for ever to the United States the right of passage through the Gut of Canso ; 2nd, That we make our canals 14 feet deep ; and 3rd, That the tolls on the Welland and St. Lawrence canals shall not discriminate by lighter charges on through vessels than on vessels going only part of the way down.   The second and third conditions, I suppose, can be arranged, but the first is a serious affair—in feeling.   There is no reason why we should not concede perpetual passage through the Gut of Canso.   The United States have always been allowed to use it, but not the right to fish therein ; and they will always have it in fact, though not in name.   It would, however, be a serious diplomatic concession.   I thought the matter over after we left, and hit on a plan for meeting his demand.   Sir Edward Thornton is enthusiastic about the suggestion.   It is to propose to-morrow, as a counter demand, the opening to Britain in perpetuity of the Rosario and Douglas channels on the Pacific coast, lately declared by the Emperor of Germany, as arbitrator under the Washington treaty, to be United States waters.

If I hear from Ottawa in time, the draft treaty is to go to the senate to-morrow ; appearances indicate a chance of success.   I saw yesterday Messrs. Butler, Boutwell, Dawes, Garfield, and others ; they are all willing to push it through this session.   The President speaks openly and strongly for it.

WASHINGTON, June 10, 1874.

I heard from Ottawa, two days ago, the difficulty there was arranged ; but three days are absolutely lost, because Lord Derby has not signified his assent to the draft treaty.   Sir Edward has in vain endeavoured to obtain from him an answer of yes or no !

Congress will certainly break up on the 22nd.   We have hardly a moment to spare, still we cannot move.   It is very provoking, but there is no remedy.   We have ascertained pretty accurately that if the treaty were now sent to the senate it would be carried.   Yesterday I saw Cameron, of Pennsylvania, our supposed great enemy, and had a long conversation with him.   I found him extremely friendly ; he told me he had read my pamphlet, and was much pleased with it.   He said he agreed with its reasoning, and if he opposed our measure, it would only be because he was attached to the protectionist party.   He thought I had made out an excellent case, and admitted the position of Canada was different from other countries.

WASHINGTON, June 12, 1874.

Lord Derby was "graciously pleased" yesterday to cable his approval, and that we might proceed ; so at it we went with Mr. Fish. Would you believe it? he was showing his timidity nearly as much as ever. "The difficulties were immense;" "the senate would certainly throw the draft treaty out." In short, there was no hope unless we made concessions now proposed for the first time. All this within ten days of the adjournment. We kept cool, made a memo. of his proposals, and retired to consider the situation. Sir Edward was downcast and angry ; my bump of hope, as usual, kept me up, and determined me to make one more attempt to bring Mr. Fish back to reason ; so it was determined I should go last night to see him at his house. I went, but found he was at the White House ; I therefore went to the state department this morning to see him. I expressed to him my regret that it was my painful duty to say that his propositions were entirely out of the question; that I would, if he desired, communicate them to the Canadian government, and Sir Edward would to the Imperial government ; but that, if they determined to accept them, they must find somebody else to act for them, for I would never sign a treaty that was not entirely reciprocal. I pointed out that the treaty he proposed would be entirely one-sided; that it would miss the end for which it was devised, and leave a strong feeling of dissatisfaction behind it. He seemed impressed by the argument. The people would not sustain his propositions. He asked me, after looking over his paper, "What I objected to so much." I told him—"The denial of the free navigation of Lake Michigan ;" "The demand of fishery rights on the Pacific coast ;" "The postponement of the free entry for lumber to the United States for three and a half years ;" "The striking out of ochres, seal oil, and salt ;" "The demand for 14 feet of water in our canals, that would cost millions ;" "The demand for free perpetual navigation of the Gut of Canso, without the accompanying concession of the same right to us in the Rosario channel :" and "The construction of the Caughnawaga canal, without any compensating advantage." These were the things I decidedly protested against, and would not assent to without equivalent. After a long tussle he agreed to give up all but one or two of the demands. I compromised for twenty-one years of Lake Michigan, and agreed to the construction of the Caughnawaga canal. At last he hesitatingly accepted that arrangement, because he felt certain if salt were left in, the treaty would be lost. He suggested that if salt was struck out of the free list by us, he would strike out something as an offset, and no doubt it would be all right, and he would see me again this afternoon. Some hours have elapsed, but yet no sign ; but I feel pretty certain it is all right, and if so, the bargain will be a good one for Canada.

June 13th.—I did not hear from Mr. Fish, as I expected, yesterday afternoon ; but this forenoon Sir Edward and I went to see him, and had two and a half hours with him. We occupied that long sederunt with a final revision of the treaty, improving the language and making the sense of each sentence as clear as possible. . Mr. Fish made no new demands, but made several sensible suggestions for the improvement of the paper, and was most courteous throughout. He hoped to get it completed and ready for the senate on Monday. The thought occurs to me that he means to throw us over the session ; I cannot believe it. He evidently had spent much time over the paper, and declared he had been at it till one o'clock this morning ; therefore, I think he means to sign the treaty.

WASHINGTON, June 18, 1874.

The treaty did not go to the senate on Tuesday, in consequence of a new demand for canal tolls uniformity. It really looked as if Mr. Fish were willing to throw us over for want of time.

I dined at the White House last night, and remained behind to speak to the President about the treaty. He spoke out most enthusiastically for it, and congratulated me on the great success that had been accomplished. He assured me he would take every means to have the senate endorse it. The treaty is now confidentially in the hands of the senate. It is being printed, and will be considered by the Foreign Relations Committee to-morrow morning.

WASHINGTON, June 20, 1874.

The President sent a message to the senate with the treaty, urging a decision before the adjournment of congress. I thought the message very good; but it has the defect of not speaking definitely of this particular measure as his own and his government's, and calling on the senate to sustain him. Had he done this the treaty would have been through now. But now, with a majority in its favour, there seems some considerable danger of its being thrown over until December. I told all this to Mr. Fish just as has happened, but he was quite set on having his own way. He may now have to regret it.

The first tussle in the congress was in our favour. Chandler tried to have the treaty sent to his committee. This the senate refused, and sent it to the Foreign Relations Committee. On that committee there are 7 to 2 in favour of a treaty. There were 6 present: 3 said to be for us; 1 against; and 2 for the measure personally, but wanted to hear from the country before acting. The committee adjourned without action. How it will end no one can tell. Had Mr. Fish signed the treaty and sent it down, it would have gone through without a doubt. *N'importe;* we have done all we could, and the United States Government must be responsible for what comes hereafter. If the senate concludes to throw it over till next session, I will leave soon; should an extra session be called, I may be delayed ten days.

Nothing, however, was done before the adjournment. The letters following have reference to what took place in the autumn of the same year:

WASHINGTON, December 15, 1874.

I found that on coming here Sir Edward's statements as to the treaty being dead and not having "ten supporters," rested wholly on Fish's bluff. The republicans are thoroughly demoralized, and know not what hand to turn to, and it looks as if they would continue not to know until the 5th of March arrives, with nothing done but talk and the democrats get to power. I find the democrats are stronger than ever with us, and will go for the treaty if the republicans propose it. The only grand scheme the republicans have is their transportation scheme, framed by Mr. Windom. The Caughnawaga Canal is its main feature. If they as a party go in for it, they will carry it; but they cannot separate the treaty from it; the two must go together. I did not see Mr. Fish to-day, as he was engaged with the King of the Sandwich Islands. I am to see him to-morrow; but I already know pretty well how the matter stands.

WASHINGTON, December 16, 1874.

I had a long interview with Mr. Fish this morning. He was kind and friendly. We discussed the whole matter in the best spirit, and while declaring his earnest desire that the treaty should pass, and his conviction that a treaty would be agreed to within a year or two, he confessed it seemed hopeless this session. "The money question occupied everyone's thoughts to the exclusion of every other subject. Parties were rent upon it. No one could see his way out of the woods; and what would be done he could not tell. There was no great hostility to the treaty, but utter apathy. To get a two-third majority was hopeless; to get a majority vote in the senate he did not believe possible. This was sure, that nothing would be done until Congress met after the holidays."

I have now got his views, and will try and learn what the democrats will do.

I have not yet seen the President, but will call to-morrow. I have an appointment with Carl Schurz to-morrow morning, to get the state of the case from him. To-night I see Allison and Dawes.

EXTRACTS FROM FAMILY CORRESPONDENCE.

The following extracts are wholly from letters addressed by Mr. Brown to members of his family, and are given separately on that account. Most of them contain matter of more or less public interest, while some are wholly of a domestic character, and delineate him in his relations to his family—with whom he had daily correspondence during his absence from home—better than any words of the writer can.

The first two letters have reference to his canvass for the representation of South Oxford. He was elected by a large majority.

Ingersoll, February 26, 1863.

Well, I am fairly into it, and I do assure you I wish I were once more quietly at home. I am persuaded that had I stayed out of it for a year longer I would never have returned, and I would have been right. However, I am into it for this struggle, however long I may remain in public life.

Norwich, February, 1863.

It is very pleasant to find how kind every one is to me—even those who are going strongest against me—not a harsh word, except for coming to drive out Bodwell, and Bodwell himself is compelled to say all sorts of kind things. I got to bed at 2 o'clock in the morning, and am off immediately to speak 8 miles from here at noon, and 8 miles further on at night. No one knows how an election will end. Bodwell is a strong candidate—a very strong candidate; but turn and twist it every way, I don't think it possible he can beat me. I don't feel the slightest doubt as to the result, but I am fighting for a good majority.

Bothwell, April 4, 1863.

We have had fine weather, and I have enjoyed my rambles over the fields immensely—especially going among the sheep and cattle. The flocks of sheep make at present a fine sight, with their heavy fleeces and their lambs skipping around them. The oil wells are a great fact. There seems no doubt that oil in any quantity will be had here. Many people arrive daily from different quarters to inquire into the prospects, and already three or four new companies have been formed to open wells. Every dwelling-house in the village is occupied.

Parliament was afterwards dissolved. Mr. Brown again ran for South Oxford. Mr. Hope Mackenzie was the liberal candidate in the North Riding. The following five letters have reference to the contest in these ridings:

INVERKIP, June 4, 1863.

I dropped you a line yesterday morning just before starting for Plattsville. We had a fine drive of 20 miles and a splendid meeting at Plattsville—carried all before us. In the evening we had a meeting in Drumbo, very large but not so favourable, one of our discontented candidates having opened out on us in a very scandalous manner. We got through the meeting at 2 o'clock in the morning, and then had 8 miles to drive. It was very cold, and we did not get to Chesterfield till broad day light. We came here this morning, and have had a grand meeting—swept all before us. I am sitting in the house of a substantial farmer ; have just had a good dinner, and am off for Embro immediately (16 miles), where we speak to-night. Mackenzie will carry the election, but not without effort.

EMBRO, June 5, 1863.

A man is just starting for Inverkip, and I seize the opportunity to send a line. We had a glorious meeting in the evening ; large hall crowded ; good speeches—great enthusiasm. This is the township that turns the tide in all North Riding contests, and Mackenzie is no doubt quite safe now. I am writing at 8 o'clock in the morning, and the horses are standing at the door waiting to carry us to Harrington, a distance of 10 miles, where we speak at 10 o'clock. From there we go to Thamesford, where we hold a meeting at night, which ends my work here. To-morrow is my nomination.

NORWICHVILLE, June 10, 1863.

Here I am in the centre of the Quaker country, and a most beautiful country it is. You could not fancy in a young country more substantial comfort than the people enjoy. After dinner we drove to East Oxford, where my first meeting was held. It was a very good meeting, and went unanimously for me. We left East Oxford about 3 o'clock and came on here, calling on one or two prominent people as we passed. We saw a sheep that weighed 350 lbs.—very interesting to you as a piece of intelligence. We had a splendid meeting at night. I find all my friends stanch, and a great many of my opponents turned into friends. There is literally no contest here, and it is too bad to be compelled to hold meetings.

SPRINGFIELD, June 11, 1863.

Another day gone. We came here in time for our meeting, which passed off very successfully. We went on in the evening from Springfield to Otterville, and there had a splendid meeting ; church crowded, and all perfectly unanimous. There was a majority against me in the township last time, but it will be very different indeed now. We came back to Springfield late last night, and I am staying with the principal farmer in this neighbourhood. He has been on this farm no less than 30 years. The country was an utter wilderness when he first settled. I had to get up to breakfast at 7 o'clock. I am writing this immediately after breakfast, and am half asleep now. I am going over the farm and dairy in a few minutes. I speak at Culloden at 10 o'clock, and in the evening at Tilsonburg. After that there will be but three meetings more, and then home.

TILSONBURG, June 12, 1863.

I have only a moment to send a line, as I start for Simcoe, county of Norfolk, in a few moments, to speak at the hustings to-day, and we have hardly time to get over. We had a capital meeting yesterday at Culloden, and a splendid one here last night. A deputation came here last night from Oxford and insisted on my going over to help them. My meetings here to-day are therefore to be taken by friends.

BOTHWELL, July 25, 1863.

I was up very early yesterday morning. Breakfasted at 7 o'clock, and off before the sun was hot to see a lot of outlying fields.

I have been very busy in the fields these two days—hard at work from 6 o'clock in the morning till 10 at night, examining the crops, the stock, and the buildings—planning new operations, arranging the fall work, settling with the hands, and making up the books. Lots to do. I could spend a fortnight here very profitably. Everything is looking well. The crops are very good—never so good before ; and the cattle are all in excellent condition. You would be delighted with a herd of 52 calves in one field—beautiful smooth coats, elegant shapes, and as lively as crickets. The rain has been coming down in torrents. It will do some damage to the hay, and a vast deal of good to the corn, roots, and peas. I have 350 tons of hay secured in beautiful order, and there is any quantity to come yet.

I got to London on Tuesday night, telegraphed to some friends that I was coming, and got through a lot of business before going to sleep at midnight. Up at 3.15 ; off to Detroit ; reached there at 8 o'clock. Beautiful morning ; most lovely view in crossing the river. Detroit is an active, stirring business place, built of brick very substantially, with a great deal of shipping at the wharves. I know no river so beautiful as the river that runs from Port Sarnia to Detroit.

QUEBEC, September 29, 1863.

I am writing in the parliamentary committee room, with a fierce discussion going on about a Grand Trunk Railway bill, in which all the magnates of the House are at work. I have been working hard since I wrote. We have lost the St. Hyacinthe election, and our strength will be greatly affected by it in the coming contest. As we stand now the vote will turn on the Speaker's vote. However it is to end, I hope it will be soon, and let me off home. I am wearying to be back.

QUEBEC, February 20, 1864.

Matters are very queer here. The government are very confident, but I doubt much if they have good reason for it. There are several members of the opposition who feel inclined to support them, but they feel rather shaky, and hardly know yet how they will go. The Ottawa members have a caucus to-day to determine how they will go ; and which way they may finally turn no one knows. The position of the ministry is very humiliating, trusting to the aid of men they utterly despise. For my part, I would a thousand times rather go out of public life for ever than be at the mercy of such people. I have been quite reserved with the government about the Bell matter, thinking it was their duty to speak first. But they have carefully avoided all reference to the subject. I have, however, spoken openly to others in strong condemnation, and it has no doubt reached their ears, as they have been excessively civil.

The "Bell matter" referred to was a rumour that Mr. Bell, the conservative member for Russell, was to be taken into the cabinet.

QUEBEC, February 22, 1864.

I have had a great blow up with Sandfield and Holton about Bell's rumoured appointment. He is not to go into the cabinet—indeed, I doubt if he ever intended going in—and the government, whatever he does, will have a majority on the address. Now that the fuss is over, matters are all serene between us, and I doubt not they are heartily glad that I put an impassable bar in the way of the proposal. Our friends in the House are heartily thankful for the escape they have had. I have been writing this by fits and starts, while the debate has been going on about the address to the Prince of Wales.

QUEBEC, February 29, 1864.

I cannot tell you how I hate this parliamentary work, because it keeps me away. I think what a fool I am to be here ; and then come thoughts of the country and public duty, and the newspaper, and so I give a great sigh and turn away from the subject. What I would give to be able to set out for Toronto this afternoon, never to return ! And yet, what hinders me? Are the reasons sufficient? Ought I not break through the meshes and be off?

QUEBEC, March 1, 1864.

Rose has just risen to speak, and he has said the only sensible thing that has yet been uttered in the debate ; he hoped the debate would now be brought to a close without further waste of time, and that we may get to the business of the country. Would you believe it ? Cartier commenced on Thursday at 4 o'clock and spoke till 6 ; he resumed at 8.30 and spoke till 11.15; resumed yesterday at 3 o'clock and spoke till 6 ; resumed at 7.15 and spoke till 1.15—thirteen hours in one speech. They used to charge me with being long-winded, but Cartier outdoes all the world, past, present or to come.

It is not at all unlikely that a crisis may be brought on this week—and it may come any day, and we may all get home much sooner than any of us anticipate. There is very little party spirit throughout the House—most of the members on both sides want to get on with the business, and how a crisis may end no one can predict.

QUEBEC, March 2, 1864.

I have delivered your message to Her Majesty's loyal opposition, and I am desired to say in reply that they entirely endorse your sentiments. They consider it highly improper that "L'Honorab memb de Sout Oxford," as Monsieur Cartier hath it, should absent himself from his duty ; they are convinced that whistling to little Maddie is the very thing he is cut out for, and are most willing to spare him for that purpose. Mr. Sandfield and his section of ministerialists heartily reciprocate for once the views of -the opposition ; and, in fact, since the idea was propounded, peace reigns in political circles.

It is very tantalizing of you to write such things about our little darling. Tell —— that George, the father of Maddie, would rather be quietly at home than "President of the United States," and that he regards the "premiership of Canada" with supreme indifference ; it would not be modest to use a stronger word.

I fully expect there will be a ministerial crisis before many days elapse; but to say the truth, they are all very wavering of purpose. Foley made a set speech last night, and came out strong and loudly for all the views I had been urging for years. McKellar followed in reply, and then Mowat, who did exceedingly well. His speech was manly, straightforward, and judicious ; but some passages caused Sandfield to make wry faces.

QUEBEC, March 3, 1864.

I expect to introduce my motion for an agricultural committee to-night, and will say something in introducing it. I was very much tempted to make a speech on the address in reply to Galt, but refrained from fear of doing harm. A crisis will evidently come, and it would have been a pity to say a word calculated to do harm when it does come. I am very industrious these days; never go out till the House meets, and work like a beaver at letters and all sorts of things. I have a very comfortable room indeed, with a glorious view of the St. Charles; and I read a little, write a good deal, look out a little, and think and muse about home. It is very doubtful if there are many people in the world who have so much to be thankful for as I have. I sometimes tremble; and strive to pray: Lord, make me to know and feel from whom all this comes. Make me humble; teach me how to serve Thee; teach me how to use all these blessings aright.

The liberal government resigned before the close of the session, and were succeeded by a conservative cabinet. The following letters were written after this change:

QUEBEC, May 13, 1864.

I can scarcely tell you how matters stand here. When I got here, I found the party in an uproar—dissatisfied with the conduct of the leading men, and urgent for a test vote. I did not think this prudent; but urged that continual incidental votes should be recorded against them until all confidence was taken from them. The caucus had determined, however, before I got down, to take a direct test vote, and it was thought best to humour the rank and file, so a vote is to be taken on the canal toll question.

QUEBEC, May 16, 1864.

Our vote of want of confidence has commenced and will be continued to-night. What the result may be is still uncertain, but I expect we will be beaten by from 1 to 3 votes. Things here are very unsatisfactory. No one sees his way out of the mess—and there is no way but my way—representation by population. There is great talk to-day of a coalition; and, what do you think? Why, that in order to make the coalition successful, the Imperial government are to offer me the governorship of one of the British colonies! I have been gravely asked to-day by several if it is true, and whether I would accept!! My reply was, I would rather be proprietor of the *Globe* newspaper for a few years than be governor-general of Canada, much less a trumpery little province. But I need hardly tell you the thing has no foundation, beyond sounding what could be done to put me out of the way, and let mischief go on. But we won't be bought at any price, shall we?

QUEBEC, May 17, 1864.

We are in the middle of the debate on the vote of want of confidence. Heretofore, the speaking has been but ordinary—except Holton's speech of last night, which was very good—but this afternoon the debate has opened up much better. Scatcherd commenced with a very good speech, and Dr. Parker followed with a very able one from his point of view. I say from *his* point of view, for he went the whole figure for a coalition—a most dangerous and demoralizing resort of weak men. I shall probably speak to-night, but at no great length.

QUEBEC, May 18, 1864.

I brought on my motion for constitutional changes this afternoon, and we had a capital debate upon it—the best debate on the question we ever had in parliament—calm, temperate, and to the point. I really believe there is a chance of my motion being carried—not a great chance, but still a chance. I am writing at 7 o'clock, just after dinner. The debate begins again at 7.30, and I must be at my post, so I have only a few minutes to spare. I feel a very great desire to carry the motion. It would be the first vote ever carried in parliament in favour of constitutional change, and even that would be some satisfaction after my long fight for it. But I have taken care not to set my mind on success, and so if I don't succeed I won't break my heart about it.

Don't say another word about giving up parliamentary life; that is all settled. I have announced it to friends and enemies here distinctly and beyond recall.

QUEBEC, May 20, 1864.

It was indeed a great success, and took Cartier, Macdonald, &c., by intense surprise. They had no conception that there was a probability of my motion being carried. It has excited great discussion this morning, and my committee had its first meeting at noon to-day. Sixteen members of the committee were present, and we had a very useful and harmonious discussion. Much that is directly practical may not flow from the committee; but it is an enormous gain to have the acknowledgment on our journals that a great evil exists, and that some remedy must be found.

QUEBEC, June 11, 1864.

Saturday morning, 1.30 a. m.—The ministry have just announced that they intend putting through the whole supplies before they adjourn, and that certainly will not be before daylight. There is no prospect of an immediate termination to the session. It will probably not close before two or three weeks.

Ministers are very weak, and dare hardly make a motion; but there is an unwillingness among the opposition to push things to extremities, and the probability is that ministers will go through the session without a defeat.

QUEBEC, June 18, 1864.

Past 1 in the morning.—We have had great times since I wrote you. On Tuesday we defeated the government by a majority of 2. They asked the Governor-General to dissolve parliament, and he consented; but before acting on it, at the Governor's suggestion they applied to me to aid them in reconstructing the government, *on the basis of settling the constitutional difficulties between Upper and Lower Canada.* I refused to accept office, but agreed to help them earnestly and sincerely in the matter they proposed. Negotiations were thereupon commenced, and are still going on, with considerable hope of finding a satisfactory solution of our trouble. The facts were announced to the House to-day by John A. Macdonald, amid tremendous cheering from both sides of the House. You never saw such a scene; but you will have it all in the papers, so I need not repeat. Both sides are extremely urgent that I should accept a place in the government, were it only for a week; but I will not do this, unless it is absolutely needful to the success of the negotiations. A more agreeable proposal is that I should go to England to arrange the new constitution with the Imperial government; but as the whole thing may fail, we will not count our chickens just yet.

QUEBEC, June 20, 1864.

I intended writing you a long letter, but the negotiations have occupied

every moment since 5 in the morning, and I fear that I may not have
the opportunity of doing so. It is now 5.30 and the mail closes at 6
o'clock ; and I am waiting in the Governor-General's office for his Excellency, who has sent for me to meet him. If he is brief in his discussion,
I will write you ; if he is lengthy, I will not be able to do so. But meantime, I may say that I have closed the negotiations for the construction of
a new government, pledged to carry constitutional changes, and that I
have the offer of office for myself and others to be named by me. I call
a meeting of the party to-night to accept or reject this offer, and I must
abide by its determination. I am deeply distressed at having this matter
thrust on me now, but dare not refuse the responsibility, with such vast
interests at stake. I shall try to do my duty to the country. So far I
have received the approval of the best men on both sides.

QUEBEC, June 20, 1864.

I wrote you half an hour ago, just before going in to see His Excellency. I have now a few minutes to spare before meeting the deputation
from the Executive Council, and I shall try to use it in explaining, as well
as I can, the position of matters at this moment. Cartier and all his
party, by the compulsion of circumstances, have been driven into the
necessity of taking up the representation question openly and vigorously.
They have asked me to enter the cabinet with two friends : to conduct
the negotiations with the Lower Provinces for a union of all British North
America, and to conduct the negotiations in London with the Imperial
government. They agree to bring down a measure next session to apply
the federation principle to Canada alone, with population as the basis of
representation, and with provision for the admission of the Maritime
Provinces and the great North-West gradually into the union.

I reject the proposal to go into the cabinet, but offer all my aid outside,
The government insist on my going in, and my party insist on my going
in ; but my party insist on our getting four cabinet seats instead of three,
and the others are not willing to do so. I think the Governor-General is
with me in this controversy, and that he will urge the cabinet to give us
four seats, or at least three departments, and myself to be sworn in an
executive councillor, without a department and without a salary. Whether
they will yield to his urgent appeal I cannot say, but he is entirely
with us.

QUEBEC, June 23, 1864.

We have had great doings since I wrote you on Monday. My negotiations with the government were successfully closed on Monday night.
On Tuesday I called a meeting of the Upper Canada liberals, and submitted what I had done. You will see from the published proceedings
(which I send you) that my course was sustained almost unanimously.
You will see that the meeting passed a resolution urging me to go into
the government, but that did not influence me wholly ; private letters
from many quarters did something more, and the extreme urgency of the
Governor-General did still more. His Excellency sent a very kind letter,
urging me to go in, of which I will send you a copy. The thing that
finally determined me was the fact, ascertained by Mowat and myself,
that unless we went in the whole effort for constitutional changes
would break down, and the enormous advantages gained by our
negotiations probably be lost. Finally, at 3 o'clock yesterday, I consented to enter the cabinet "as President of the Council," with other two
seats in the cabinet at my disposal—one of which Mowat will take, and
probably McDougall the other. We consented with great reluctance, but
there was no help for it ; and it was such a temptation to have possibly
the power of settling the sectional troubles of Canada for ever. The

announcement was made in the House yesterday, and the excitement, as over the province, is intense. I send you an official copy of the proceedings during the negotiations, from which you will see the whole story. By next mail I intend to send you some extracts from the newspapers. The unanimity of sentiment is without example in this country; and were it not that I know at their exact value the worth of newspaper laudations, I might be puffed up a little in my own conceit. After the explanations by ministers I had to make a speech, but was so excited and nervous at the events of the last few days that I nearly broke down. However, after a little I got over it, and made (as Mowat alleges) the most telling speech I ever made. There was great cheering when I sat down, and many members from both sides crowded round me to congratulate me. In short, the whole movement is a grand success, and I really believe will have an immense influence on the future destinies of Canada. We are to be sworn into office on Monday. Immediately after I go up to Toronto for my re-election and to arrange matters; then return here for a week or two; then back to Toronto for a week or two; then go to Prince Edward's Island as one of the representatives of Canada in the Convention of Provinces; and from there to England as a delegate from Canada to the Imperial government.

We got home at 2.30. The House met this morning at 11, and we have been hard at work ever since trying to close up the business of the session. It is 1 o'clock in the morning, and the boat which is to take this letter sails six hours hence. The weather is fearfully hot.

I send you the Governor-General's letter and the formal statement of the late negotiations. I also send you a few extracts from some of the newspapers. They are not selected extracts, but simply a few that I picked up round the House; scarcely one of the papers friendly to me is among them.

Uxbridge, July 20, 1864.

On Monday at noon I left Bothwell for home and reached there in the evening. Next morning (yesterday) I left again by the early train for Whitby, took carriage there with Mowat and Edwards, and arrived here in time for the North Ontario nomination at 10 o'clock. There was an immense crowd present; McDougall and Cameron, his opponent, made good speeches, and I followed at no great length. We had the show of hands, and Cameron demanded a poll. In the evening I addressed a meeting here in the Town Hall; it was densely crowded, and I succeeded in converting a good few and strengthening others; Cameron was present, but did not venture to reply. This evening I speak in Scott, to-morrow at Wick, on Friday at Manchester, and on Saturday at Beaverton. I propose remaining there over Sunday, and on Monday returning to Toronto. On Wednesday or Thursday I go back north. I think the election is safe, but we must not leave a stone unturned to secure success.

I am staying with Joseph Gould, the old member for this county, in a splendid house.

The drought continues here to a most alarming extent, and fires are going on in the woods and fields over the country; while I write I can see three fires burning in the fields, looking from two windows. Fire in so dry a season catches very easily, from the ashes of a pipe or cigar, or the slightest cause.

This is a very thriving little town, with a stream running through it, driving various mills and factories. The population is about 1,500 to 2,000, and Mr. Gould owns a great part of the village. He is one of the self-made men of this wooden country, who go ahead in defiance of all difficulties.

TORONTO, July 28, 1864.

On Wednesday, after writing you, I held a meeting in the township of Scott; on Thursday at Manchester, in the township of Reach; on Friday at Wick, in the township of Brock; and on Saturday I spoke at Manilla and at Cannington, and held a monster meeting at night in Beaverton. The meetings were all largely attended, and very enthusiastic for Mowat and me, but very cold for McDougall. I never had such up-hill work; I never met such personal hostility against anybody as against McDougall. Had it not been for these meetings he would have been awfully beaten; but as it is, he has lost the race by a minority of 100. This result does not matter a great deal; McDougall will get another county, and the wheels will roll on. We did all we could for him, and it is to be hoped he has had a lesson that will do him good. I stayed at Beaverton over Sunday, and heard two capital sermons—no, one capital, and the other very fair for a young beginner.

UTICA, N.Y., August 1, 1864.

When I wrote on Thursday I expected to go down to Quebec the following day, but a telegram from Quebec rendered this unnecessary, the Governor-General's absence preventing any Council being held till the day after to-morrow. I can therefore utilize the interval by seeing after my dairy. I left Toronto on Saturday at noon, got to the Bridge at 5 o'clock, to Rochester at 8 o'clock, and here at midnight. I am now writing on Monday morning. Yesterday was a fearfully hot day, close on 100°, and not a breath of wind blowing. I hardly ventured across the door the heat was so fearful, but lay upon the sofa and imbibed iced lemonade! This morning I am up betimes. It is now 5.30. A carriage is to be at the door at 6 o'clock to drive me round the celebrated cheese factories in this locality. I mean to visit Whitesboro', Vernon, Rome, etc., if I can overtake them all in time, then at 4.20 this evening take the train at Rome for Ogdensburg (150 miles), cross the St. Lawrence to Prescott, catch the Grand Trunk train through the night, reach Montreal in time for breakfast to-morrow morning, leave by the steamer at night, and be in Quebec on Wednesday morning. Pretty good work this hot weather; but it must be done so, or not at all.

QUEBEC, August 5, 1864.

After closing my letter to you on Monday, I started off in a carriage for Whitesboro' and a number of other places, and got complete insight into the working of the new dairy system. It is very profitable, and well calculated for adoption in Canada. I think, however, that very great improvements can be made on their mode of management.

I got to Rome at 4 p.m., got dinner, and off by the train to Ogdensburg, where we arrived at midnight. Took a wherry and crossed the St. Lawrence to Prescott, a thunder-storm going on at the time—a very splendid sight. Lay down for an hour, and at 2 o'clock in the morning went to the Grand Trunk Railway station to catch the Montreal train. Table time 2.30. Waited till 3 o'clock—no train; till 3.30—no train; till 4 o'clock—no train. Thought it time to kick up a row, and found a freight train had run off the track above Kingston, and stopped the way. Could not tell when the obstruction would be removed. Got back to hotel at 4 o'clock; lay down and slept till 8—no word of train; got breakfast, recrossed the St. Lawrence to Ogdensburg, and took passage by steamer *Lord Elgin* to Montreal. Had a fine run down the rapids. Telegraphed Quebec steamer to wait for us, which was kindly done, and so got on board at once on arrival at Montreal, and steamed down here on Wednesday morning. There now, you have the whole of my pilgrimage. Have taken possession of my official quarters; read up all the business; prepared

15

matter for council, and laid regular siege to my pile of unanswered letters. Been very industrious, and got through quite a lot of matters. I hope to-day or to-morrow to know when I shall sail for Liverpool. The meeting of provincial delegates is to be held on the 10th of September, at Charlottetown, Prince Edward's Island, and we will either go direct from there to England, or return here first, and start for Liverpool early in October.

QUEBEC, August 8, 1864.

I am writing on Monday afternoon at 5 o'clock, and as the post closes at 6, and I have been in council for five hours, and the heat is very oppressive and sciatica very troublesome, I am sure you will pardon for this time only a short note.

I am so glad you approve of all I have done ; at least I have a clear conscience in the premises, and if I have erred it has been the judgment and not the heart. It was a bitter pill to swallow going into the government, and nothing but a sense of duty could have forced me into it. It is very gratifying to see, however, that the public, not only here but in the United States and Britain, have given me full credit for patriotic motives.

We have been hard at work in council ever since I last wrote, and have got through a vast amount of detail business. I am happy to tell you that all fear of our compact not being carried out in good faith has pretty well passed from my mind, and I now feel very confident that we will satisfactorily and harmoniously accomplish our great purpose. Taché, Cartier, and their colleagues, have behaved very well, and show no inclination to swerve from their bargain. Cartier, John A., Galt and I are deputed to go to Charlottetown for the provincial conference, to be held there on the 10th of September. The seat of government is positively to be removed to Ottawa in October. It will be a great comfort to be within a few hours of Toronto.

TORONTO, August 15, 1864.

I left Quebec by the steamer on Thursday afternoon, and arrived at Montreal at 6 o'clock in the morning ; took the train to Lachine at 7, and spent the day in ascending the Ottawa river. It is a most beautiful river ; I think, considering its size and length, the most picturesque river I have ever seen. Reached Ottawa at 6 o'clock ; went at once to the Parliament buildings, and went all over them. They are really very magnificent, fit for the British, French, and Russian empires, were they all confederated ! A hundred years hence the people will fancy the men of these days were giants in imagination, if not in ability. The architecture is something like the Toronto University, but not the same style. The work is beautiful, and seems of the most substantial character. There is one main pile for the legislative departments, and two enormous side-piles for the departmental buildings. The three piles form three sides of a grand square. The whole will cover about twenty-three acres ! The centre is to be laid out in ornamental grounds, fountains, and so forth. The whole stands on a high promontory 160 feet above the river, and is seen all around for a great distance, and amid scenery nowhere surpassed except in Quebec, if even there. We were all anxious to remove from Quebec this fall, but it seems to me impossible to have the buildings ready in time.

QUEBEC, August 26, 1864.

I have a piece of news for you to-day, the day on which we propose sailing for Liverpool ! If all goes well, Galt and I leave by the *Persia* from New York on Wednesday the 6th October, and I hope to be in Edinburgh on Monday the 17th.

We have been hard at work with our constitutional discussion for two days, and everything goes as well as we could possibly hope for. I do believe we will succeed. The discussion to-day lasted from 12 o'clock till 5.45, and from first to last it was highly interesting, most deeply interesting. For perhaps the first time in my political life I indulged in a regular chuckle of gratified pride (no higher sentiment) at the thought of my presiding over such a discussion by such men, there not being one man at the table who had not openly derided the idea of such a scene ever occurring in our lifetime. I could not help recalling many furious scenes in which several of those around me had bitterly denounced me for even proposing the consideration of the very subject they were then engaged in settling under my presidency ! It will be an immense thing if we accomplish it. I don't believe any of us appreciate in its true importance the immensity of the work we are engaged in. But there is one thing peculiar about our position. There is no other instance on record of a colony peacefully remodelling its own constitution, such changes having been always the work of the parent state and not of the colonists themselves. Canada is rightly setting the example of a new and better state of things.

HALIFAX, Sept. 12, 1864.

Now for my travels. We sailed down the St. Lawrence in the good steamer *Queen Victoria* on Monday night, 29th August ; had fine weather all the way, and enjoyed ourselves greatly. On Wednesday morning we reached Gaspé, and went into that beautiful little fishing town amid firing of cannon and all sorts of rejoicings. So far our negotiations have gone most favourably. We are all in favour of federation, if we can agree on conditions, and we have good hopes that we can do so.

QUEBEC, Sept. 19, 1864.

We left Halifax for St. John, N. B., *via* Windsor. After a pleasant run by rail and boat, we got safely to our destination the same evening. St. John is a pleasant city of 40,000 people, the most thriving place in the Maritime Provinces. On the night of our arrival we had a grand entertainment by the citizens, at which we all made speeches. The affair went off splendidly, and we made quite a good impression. Next morning we took steamer for Fredericton, the capital of the province, 84 miles from St. John, up the St. John river. This a noble stream, very picturesque ; hills rising on both sides high above it, and gradually sloping down to its level. On our arrival we found the Governor's carriage waiting for Cartier, Galt and myself, he having invited us to be his guests during our stay at Fredericton. He is a son of Lord Aberdeen, who was a few years ago prime minister of Great Britain. Next day we returned to St. John ; the same night took a special train for Shediac, where our steamer was awaiting us. We got safely on board at midnight on Friday, set sail for Quebec, and had a delightful run up the St. Lawrence. Our expedition has been all and more than we could have hoped.

QUEBEC, Sept. 23, 1864.

I sat down at 9 o'clock to write you a long letter, but before I had made a commencement the correspondent of the New York *Herald* came in to ask some hints on the subject of federation. He consumed an hour and more. While he was still with me in came Mr. Philips Day, a freshly arrived commissioner from the London *Herald* and *Standard*—" Mother Gamp" and " Mrs. Harris," as *Punch* delights to designate them—on the same errand as the New York *Herald* man. I could not turn them out, so it was 12 before they went, and then came my messenger boy by appointment to take my letters and papers to the post office. Neither were begun, so I set him to put up a lot of papers with my Halifax speech, and I addressed them to friends in Scotland and England. He is just gone, and is to come early in the morning for this. I have been up to the ears morning, noon and night since I wrote you, drawing up reports for council, framing minutes, and all sorts of things. My correspondence is fearfully in arrears.

I am happy to tell you that we won't have to sail from Liverpool until December. It will rejoice you to know that business claims will entirely harmonize with comfort, and that the first week in December will be our time of sailing. I intend, if all goes well, to sail by the *China* from New York on the 19th October.

I mark your crowing over the fine Arran weather, but cannot help noting the cautious wording, "Not a day lost!" Nothing about half days, and umbrellas and great-coats. What would the aboriginals of Arran think of ten weeks without a drop of rain or a cloud on the sky, night or day? That is a climate for you! The blessings we enjoy in Canada are unspeakable; though it must be confessed that such charming weather is hardly the thing for turnips!

I dined at the Governor-General's on Wednesday evening to meet Lord Lyons, the British ambassador at Washington. And whom else do you think I met! Why, the Earl of Airlie, the descendant of the lady of *my* song. I told him I had a great admiration for his great-great-great-grandmother, whom "the fause Argyle" entreated to "come doon and kiss me fairlie," or he would burn up the bonnie house o' Airlie—the unmannerly Covenanter that he was!

I enclose a confidential paper showing the outline of our federation scheme—it is for F. T.'s perusal. It will be published next week in the Canadian papers, to elicit criticism, without official sanction. It is, however, an accurate sketch of our scheme.

QUEBEC, Oct. 17, 1864.

For the first time since my return to Quebec, I have a quiet moment. Last week the council met at 9 o'clock, and sat till 11; the conference from 11 o'clock to 4. Council again from 4 o'clock to 6 or later, and after dinner came letter writing, resolutions, drafting, till all hours in the morning. This week we have council from 9 to 10 o'clock; conference from 10 to 2; council from 2 to 6; and conference from 7.30 as long as we like to sit.

The conference proceedings get along very well, considering we were very near broken up on the question of the distribution of members in the Upper Chamber of the federal legislature, but fortunately we have this morning got the matter amicably compromised, after a loss of three days in discussing it. We have eight or ten other points of great difficulty yet to be got over, and it is impossible to say when we will get through. If the conference lasts all next week, I am distressed to say that I must delay my departure till the 9th November. I hope and believe that this will not be necessary; but I know that you would not wish me to imperil all my work, and ruin myself with my political friends throughout the country, by abandoning this great scheme at the very moment when a firm hand was most needful.

QUEBEC, Oct. 15, 1864.

I have just come from a grand ball given by the Executive Council to the Maritime delegates in the parliament buildings. It went off very well; but I have come to my quarters weary and worn, and with a shocking headache. We have had such a week of it. Council from 9 o'clock to 11, conference from 11 o'clock to 4; council again from 4 o'clock to 6, and sometimes till 7 every day, and then letters and orders in council to write at night. It has been very hard work; however, the deliberations of the council go on harmoniously, and there is no appearance yet of any insurmountable obstacle. We progress very slowly, however, and how soon some difficulty may show itself no one can tell. The probability is that at least another week will be consumed, which will forbid the possibility of my leaving before the *Scotia* sails—the 2nd November, my poor dear mother's birthday. It cannot be helped, and we must not repine at doing our duty.

QUEBEC, October 21, 1864.

Since writing I have received a whole batch of letters from you, and I am delighted to hear that you are well and enjoying yourself so very much, and that baby is not only able to say pa-pa, but to stand up in the corner with a little help. It is no little deprivation to have lost all the pleasure of watching her progress to such an advanced stage of babyhood; in fact, the little darling will have ceased to be a baby before I get over.

The conference is still sitting, and I am sorry to say there is no hope of our rising before the middle of next week. We have had pretty hard work to settle a number of knotty points, and have not done with them yet. We have settled the constitution of the federal executive, the federal senate, and the federal House of Commons; we have also settled the form of the local legislature and governments, but we have yet to determine the whole of the money questions, the school question, and the powers and functions of both general and local governments. There is yet plenty to do, and quite enough to split us up should we disagree. It is quite possible this may be the result, but we shall try to avoid it.

The position of matters is such that I cannot leave the conference at this moment. I must stick to the ship until the breakers are passed, and I see no hope of this being accomplished in time to let me off by the *Scotia*. It is quite possible that such a turn of affairs may occur as will render it necessary for me to see at once my parliamentary friends before finally assenting to the new constitution. It will therefore be safe to say that I cannot leave before the 9th November. I am more distressed than I can tell you, but it cannot be helped; I must do my duty in the position I have assumed. Nothing could save my reputation—more important still, nothing could ever restore peace of mind and self-respect to me—were this great movement to fail in consequence of my absence at the critical moment. The very moment I dare leave I will be off. We shall finish this business up, and retire, at least in the consciousness of having tried to do our duty.

TORONTO, Oct. 31, 1864.

We got through our work at Quebec very well. The constitution is not exactly to my mind in all its details; but as a whole, it is wonderful— really wonderful. When one thinks of all the fighting we have had for fifteen years, and finds the very men who fought us every inch now going far beyond what we asked, I am amazed, and sometimes alarmed lest it all goes to pieces yet. We have yet to pass the ordeal of public opinion in the several provinces, and sad indeed will it be if the measure is not adopted by acclamation in them all. For Upper Canada, we may well rejoice the day it becomes law. Nearly all our past difficulties are ended by it, whatever new ones may arise.

I think I wrote you about the entertainments at Quebec—the ball given by the Executive Council, the drawing room held by the Governor-General, the ball given by the bachelors of Quebec, and the endless dinners and feastings in honour of our guests. The same sort of thing is now to go off in Montreal, Ottawa, and Toronto. On Friday they go on to the Falls, and home by New York and Boston. From the day they left home till the day they get back, the whole of the delegates, and the ladies accompanying them, are the guests of Canada. I am hard at work preparing for my departure, and there is much to do. I send you photographs of a number of the members of our conference. I will get the balance of them on Thursday, and send them to you this day week. We must keep them as a memento of the great occasion. If we live twenty years, we will prize them much as recalling stirring times—that is, provided the federation goes on.

TORONTO, Nov. 7, 1864.

I am very sorry for all the disappointments you have had from week to week, but indeed it could not be helped, and they will soon end now. One week from the day you receive this letter I shall be with you, if all is well. I am writing before breakfast on Monday morning. The mail goes to-day at 11.30, and this is my last day in Toronto. I go to Quebec to-morrow morning; reach there on Wednesday; leave for Montreal on Saturday; leave Montreal for New York on Monday; reach New York on Tuesday; and sail by the *Persia* on Wednesday.

We have had great times in Toronto this week. The delegates arrived on Wednesday night, and only left for Montreal on Saturday. The *déjeûner* and ball went off splendidly; I only looked in at the ball for ten minutes, having urgent business requiring my attention at the office that night. I send you a copy of the *Globe* with the speeches at the *déjeûner*. People are making a fuss about my speech, which they say was the best I ever made, but that is stuff. This was the first time that the confederation scheme was really laid open to the public. No doubt —— was right in saying that the French Canadians were restive about the scheme, but the feeling in favour of it is all but unanimous here, and I think there is a good chance of carrying it. At any rate, come what may, I can now get out of the affair, and out of public life, with honour, for I have had placed on record a scheme that would bring to an end all the grievances of which Upper Canada has so long complained.

QUEBEC, Nov. 11, 1864.

I left Toronto on Tuesday morning, and got here safely the next morning. Before leaving, among other things I bought a wall paper for dear little Maddie's room—a bright, lively pattern for the little darling to wonder at, and a pretty border round it.

LONDON, Dec. 5, 1864.

The government here has given a "most gracious" answer to our constitutional scheme. Nothing could be more laudatory. It outdoes anything that ever went to any British colony—praises our statesmanship, discretion, loyalty, and so on.

LONDON, Dec. 6, 1864.

I went to see Gladstone last evening, and had an hour and a half with him—a most delightful talk, frank, able, clear-headed, and most straightforward. I was glad to find we agreed in almost everything, and I was able to put him right on many points that he had not clearly understood about Canada. From his kind manner one does feel he is a tremendous length beyond all others intellectually, as he has really shown himself to be. I had been an hour and a half with the ablest man in England, and though (as he remarked) we had been discussing the highest questions of statesmanship, he did not drag me by any means out of my depth. He was immensely civil; regretted he was going out of town to-morrow, but hoped to have the pleasure of seeing me again before I left England, and urged me to look in on him at any time: and so on.

LONDON, Dec. 8, 1864.

About that little bit of my letter concerning Gladstone, I thought it quite natural that you should read it aloud, as another proof of Dundreary's profound enunciation that "every perthon maketh an ath of himthelf at times."

I am glad to hear that baby was very wild yesterday. Kiss her dear little fingers for tearing my letter; it was a proof of her agricultural tastes. She knew the letter was from Captain Taylor, and she was luxuriating in the rambles she is to have with papa through the woods of Bothwell, and wanted to know how matters were proceeding for her reception. Oh, the day when that shall come!

QUEBEC, Feb. 7, 1865.

John A. opened the confederation debate last night. Cartier is now addressing his countrymen in English, and he is to do it in French afterwards. I was to have followed him, but as I am not yet ready, and as there will not be time enough left for me after Cartier closes, Galt has kindly agreed to follow Cartier, and leave me all to-morrow (after 7.30) to myself. If I am in the right frame, I will make a vigorous speech! It is in my mind, if I can get it out; so look out for Thursday morning's *Globe.*

QUEBEC, Feb. 9, 1865.

I commenced my speech at eight o'clock, and spoke till 12.30. The House was well filled the whole time, and I was listened to throughout with earnest attention. I suspect it was pretty successful, and between you and me, the argument in favour of the scheme is perfectly irresistible. When I closed, the members of all sides came round me, warmly congratulating me on the speech. They say it was far the best speech I ever delivered; but of that I am not certain. Kisses dear for little Maddie.

QUEBEC, February 24, 1865.

The confederation debate goes slowly on. We have heretofore commenced it at 7.30 every night, but hereafter we propose to begin the debate every day at 3 o'clock until it is closed. We don't expect that over 30 will vote against the measure.

The weather is beautiful. I am wearying to be away, and looking out for another farm to which the select portion of the Bothwell flocks and herds may be carried.

Write all about little darling's daily doings. You cannot tell how much I enjoy all you say about her; kiss her for papa a thousand times.

QUEBEC, March 6, 1865.

It does pain me somewhat to part with Bothwell; I feel a blank. It supplied relaxation when I wanted to escape from the pressure of thought about things around me. I believe thinking of Bothwell has been of essential service to my mind, and the working it out was most enjoyable. I could readily, to-morrow, without regret or hesitation, give up politics and the press and go on a large farm. I might tire of it, of course, but I don't think I would.

We are to have a great scene in the House to-day, and I am writing this before going down to it. The government of New Brunswick appealed to the people on confederation by a general election, and have got beaten. This puts a serious obstacle in the way of our scheme, and we mean to act promptly and decidedly upon it. At 3 o'clock we are to announce the necessity of carrying the resolutions for confederation at once, sending home a deputation to England, and proroguing parliament without any unnecessary delay—say in a week. Three o'clock is just at hand, and I must be off to the House, but I will not close this letter until I can tell you the effect of our announcement.

6 p.m.—We have had a stirring debate. Our proposals have all been accepted most favourably by the House; so the House will soon rise. I cannot say who will go to England, but I will not go as one unless there is an imperative necessity.

Quebec, March 7, 1865.

Our announcement was received yesterday favourably by the House. Our friends are greatly encouraged, and are anxious to have the business of the session brought to an immediate close. We have just made a second move that will probably shorten the session still more. We have moved the previous question, which prevents any amendment being moved, and will bring the debate much more speedily to a close.

I see everybody is expecting that I will be one of the delegates to England, and some members of the liberal party have spoken to me strongly on the subject, from learning that I would refuse to go; but that does not alter my purpose, and unless an absolute necessity arises, I will not go.

Quebec, March 8, 1865.

The affair in New Brunswick does not discourage us; we shall go on just as we have been going, and push the matter to a termination. If it fails after all legitimate means have been used, we will go on with our scheme for Canada alone. We expect that 38 or 40 will vote against confederation.

Quebec, March 9, 1865.

The confederation debate keeps wagging along, but there is some hope of its coming to a termination to-night. The division will be very much as I wrote you yesterday—from 35 to 40 against the measure, and all the rest for it. Amendments will be moved afterwards, however, on which our majority will not be so large. We are in some hope that the House may rise on Tuesday or Wednesday next, but we cannot of course be sure. A dead set has been made on me to go as one of the deputies to England, but I have decidedly refused; John A. refuses also, and there is a grave difficulty before us.

Quebec, March 13, 1865.

The confederation debate was kept up till 4.30 on Saturday morning, and it was 5.30 before I got to bed. I was at council from 1 to 3 o'clock, and then, feeling unfit for anything else, Fergusson Blair and I set off for a drive to Cape Rouge.

Quebec, March 14, 1865.

This morning at 2.30 we got through finally with our address to the Queen by increased majorities; and so is accomplished one of the grandest political revolutions ever peacefully accomplished in any country. Whatever happens now, my honour is safe in going into the coalition, and my fifteen years' labour is amply recompensed by the consent, recorded beyond recall, of a large majority of both sections in favour of representation by population. I feel now quite relieved of all uneasiness as to what may hereafter happen. Come what may, I have placed the question on such a basis as must secure its early settlement. I could not possibly have abandoned the trust that has gradually grown up and now rests upon me.

Would you not like that darling little Maddie should be able, twenty years hence, when we may be gone, to look back with satisfaction to the share her father had in these great events? for great they are, and history will tell the tale of them. I have been writing this while the defence debate proceeds, for I dare not leave my seat.

QUEBEC, March 15, 1865.

I am so glad you will allow me to get the bird for baby. What shall it be—a parrot, or a parrot and some canaries? I am glad she likes animals. By and by we shall have rabbits for her, and pigeons, and a pony, and all sorts of things to make her kind and gentle. Do you know, I think the care of little creatures has a most softening effect on all children. I recollect how I petted my rabbits, and ever since I have been unable to see, without extreme horror, even any rough usage of dumb creatures.

Since writing the above we have had a vote of want of confidence, and the government has been sustained by a majority of 93 to 23. We are now on the second motion. Rose has just spoken, and Street is firing away on the defence question, and I must close and take part in the debate.

Don't for a moment fancy that what I am now doing will unfit me for a quiet settled life. On the contrary, every day makes me more anxious to get quit of politics forever. I don't like it, and would with all my whole heart abandon it finally to-morrow.

QUEBEC, March 21, 1865.

I have been in council on special business from 11 o'clock till 1, and from 1 to 6 o'clock we have been in full conclave in regard to the English mission. It is 6 o'clock, and we are still discussing. It has been the gravest discussion I ever took part in, and I look forward to the result of the English negotiations with considerable apprehension. But of all this when I get up.

QUEBEC, March 22, 1865.

We have been closeted in solemn council since 12 o'clock, and it is now near 6. Our discussions are very grave. We are at it yet; and it is impossible to say what will be the result; possibly a break up.

6.15.—A solution of our difficulties seems to have been found since I commenced writing this note. I really believe it will harmonize everything, and is so simple, that it is amazing none of us thought of it before. I think we shall get through to-morrow.

ON BOARD THE "CHINA,"
April 21, 1865.

We are fairly off; the day is splendid; the wind fair, and the ship spanking along splendidly.

April 28, 1865,
240 miles from Queenstown.

You have crossed the Atlantic in the *China*, and will consequently understand why letters written on board of her cannot be models of penmanship.

We have had a very pleasant passage so far—not one storm. The wind has blown steadily from the east the whole way; we have not had sail up once except occasionally for an hour or so to steady her. But then the waves have not been high, and we have gone steadily on, making about twelve miles an hour all the way. We have had a very pleasant party—have had throwing large balls, sword exercise, tig, seances, balls and concerts. I never saw a ship's company so full of life and good humour.

When we reached the Mersey the yellow flag was hoisted, a case of yellow fever having occurred on board during the voyage. We were detained several hours in consequence.

Macdonald and I left for London by the midnight mail, and here we are at the Westminster Palace Hotel.

Yes, I do regret being so much separated from wee Maddie in her baby days, but I must only try to make up for it by being great friends hereafter. What fun I promise myself, romping with her! What a life it will be when we have cut politics and settled down to quiet home and happiness.

BOTHWELL, October 13, 1865.

Bothwell village lots are in great demand, and selling from hand to hand at constantly increasing prices, and persons who bought from me ten years ago, and from whom I never expected to hear again, are coming in every hour, demanding what they owe and ready to pay up. You have no idea what a stir there is here, houses and stores and churches running up all round, as if by magic. People are absolutely sleeping in stables, and paying any sum for the privilege. And if another good well or two should happen to flow soon, the excitement will be prodigious. As it is, the streets are crowded with people, and money is flying about in thonsands. The fifth part of a lot I sold a few mouths ago for $200 was sold to-day for $1,500 in gold.

TORONTO, June 8, 1871.

It gave me a sore heart to see you all sailing away from me, but I did not feel what it really was to have lost you till I got back to our home yesterday forenoon and found no one expecting me—no one in the drawing-room—no Maddie nor Oda to run out and meet me on the landing, and no little fellow to make his "Ba!" resound through the house. I wandered through the rooms and scanned all the little remembrances of the absent ones, and felt very disconsolate and woe-begone. But never mind; the few weeks will soon roll by, and then we will be all together again, never to have the ocean rolling between us any more, I fervently hope.

BOW PARK, June 25, 1871.

This place is looking magnificent at present. I cannot give you even an idea of the beauty of the woods and wilds. You have only seen them in the fall, but now they are out in all their spring glory. The wild grapes and the Virginia creepers, the clematis, the raspberries and nut trees, are all out in overwhelming abundance of foliage.

Coming up in the train last night there were two little girls of about the same age as Maddie and Oda. I tried to fancy a resemblance, and could glady have kissed them and made of them for our pets' sakes.

TORONTO, July 2, 1871.

What a solitary house this is without you and our little romps; it is painful to live in it. There is a feeling constantly of something amiss: you hear the tick of the clock at mid-day, and speak under your breath. I am wearying to be off to you and have you all back.

Toronto, August 22, 1872.

I have been so overwhelmed with business of all kinds that really I have not had even a moment to write to you. I have had to go down early, return late to dinner, and go back again to the office as quickly as possible, and stay till all hours. But I have had my reward. The elections have gone splendidly, and the final result does not now seem doubtful. I was unprepared for the grand triumph in South Brant. Evidently the people took the money and voted against Mr. H——; there is no other way of accounting for the result. The struggle in Centre Toronto yesterday was the keenest and bitterest I ever knew. To-morrow is our grand day! Ten elections come off all in one day; we feel sure of seven, pretty confident of eight, hope for nine, and won't be astonished if we get all ten.

Toronto, August 29, 1872.

I telegraphed you half an hour ago the result of to-day's polling so far. We had a glorious victory yesterday, and to-day's will come fast on its heels. I think we have carried 14 out of the 16, and have a good chance for both of the other two. But no one can tell certainly about any election until the last vote has been polled. There is a great crowd round the office, and strong excitement throughout the country. The office is to be illuminated to-night in grand style, and Ginney and "the children" shall have the Chinese lamps for the harvest home.

Steamer "Algeria," August 1, 1873,
200 miles from Queenstown.

I have found the rest and the sea air very beneficial already. The pain is very much less, and I feel more vigorous. I intended writing letters to Maddie, Oda and Ginney, but I feel hardly equal to it to-day. Tell them that I look at their photographs many times each day, and think about what they are doing. Tell them that papa would rather be back at Bow Park with them than have all the enjoyments of Europe.

Ottawa, March 12, 1875.

My speech [on reciprocity treaty] is over and went off well enough, but it was an awful job. The senate is so quiet, and I had such a lot of facts and figures to arrange; and I had both sides of the line to satisfy, and had to be so careful of my words, that it was a very grave affair. The attendance of members of the Upper House and strangers in the gallery was a complete novelty. My speech would read well enough, I daresay, but it required great fortitude to sit it out as so many did. I spoke two and a half hours, and was very tired.

Moville, Aug. 27, 1875.

I had only a moment to get my letter on board the tender, but it went; and a telegram I wrote after it was gone I threw on board the tender, with a shilling wrapped in it, in hope of its reaching you; and just as this was done, I found that a small boat was still hanging to the ship for the purpose of being towed down to the mouth of the bay; and as that will take ten minutes more, I seize the opportunity of sending a line to say how vexed beyond belief I am at having missed sending you and all our darlings parting letters. Tell each of them it was not from want of will I have not written them, for I was eager to do it, and was looking forward to it as a delightful close to my day's work.

(*Toronto, Sept. 12.*)—I cabled you from Father Point, informing you of the safe arrival of the *Moravian* in the St. Lawrence, but I said nothing of the accident that happened to us on our voyage. I enclose slips of a despatch I have sent to the *Globe* from Father Point. This slip, I need hardly say, puts the affair in its most modest light. In truth, every soul on board escaped death by a hair's-breadth. The iceberg was a very large one, and we ran straight at it ; but fortunately it was washed away below, and *had no ice protruding from it under the water ;* and better still, the *Moravian's* cutwater extends out very far and her bows are immensely strong, and she has an enormous bowsprit, stretching far out. Consequently the bowsprit struck the iceberg squarely, smashing it into splinters, forcing it from its strong socket, and crushing a number of the iron plates from the bow. We struck the iceberg just as the bell struck midnight. I had gone to bed fifteen minutes before, and was asleep, but the lurch instantly awoke me, and I knew at once what had happened. I jumped out of bed, and as I did so the vessel fell over on her side, all but on her beam ends, and I was thrown over against the settee, and all the things in the berth with me. The conviction flashed on me that this was the effect of the water pouring into the ship, and that we were fast settling. A million things rushed through the mind in these few dreadful seconds, but the feeling of joy and thankfulness overtopped all other thoughts that you and our darlings were safe and away in the coming struggle for life. It soon appeared, however, that this rolling over of the ship was caused by her sheering off from the iceberg, and she righted herself in a few long moments. I rushed on deck, and found myself the first passenger who had scrambled up stairs. I went at once on the bridge; learned the exact position from the captain ; saw how promptly every step for emergencies was being taken ; observed the perfect discipline among the men ; and then went astern to aid in maintaining composure among the passengers. The forward compartment of the ship was at once closed off from the other compartments ; the pumps were set to work to bail out the water that was rushing in ; the cargo was moved from the forward hold, and the leaks stopped up as well as possible—the *debris* of the bowsprit and fore-rigging was cut off and thrown overboard—and by 10 o'clock peace and thankfulness reigned throughout the ship.

I have seen far more flutter on a railway train from a shrill whistle of "down-breaks," because a cow had got on the track, than there was among the 400 people on board. Some passengers were seen busy getting on swimming jackets and getting floating mattresses ready, and gathering things suited for the boats ; but not a creature showed craven fear, or even manifest loss of self-control. Not a soul went into a boat, except the men at work getting them out; there was not even any eagerness displayed to get into them or keep near them. Captain Wylie and his officers are entirely blameless in the matter. From the moment we left Moville until we arrived, the anxious care and caution of them all could not have been surpassed. . . .

Tell Maddie, Oda, and Ginney that I found the rabbits at Bow Park all right and the pigeons and the chickens, but I did not see one cat or kitten about the place ; they must have emigrated to greener pastures. Tell them I gave Lady Thorne and Dexter three apples each (St. Lawrences). I explained to them as I did it—"There, Dexter, that's from Maddie, and that's from Oda, and that's from Ginney ;" and "they are very sorry they can't be here and at Oban too, to give it yon themselves." And the same to Lady Thorne. They quite understood what I said, and bobbed their heads, meaning, no doubt, "All right."

Business is very good. It is very hard work night and day, but I like it immensely and enjoy it. I have a capital set of fellows in the office now, and the work is thoroughly well done.

OTTAWA, March 19, 1878.

I am very sorry to be absent on Oda's birthday, but it cannot be helped. I have telegraphed her, wishing her all happy things for the coming year, and I shall try and find some nice present for her, and bring it with me.

OTTAWA, March 21, 1878.

Tell Oda I got her dear little letter, and if I have time to-night I will answer it : if not, she will have it in person. I am writing in my place in the senate, and may have to speak any moment, and in that case may not be able to write to-night. I avail myself of the chance to have a few lines ready. I am all ready to speak, and have got myself pretty well up on the whole question. Tell Oda that I will telegraph her as soon as I know certainly, and that a royal proclamation must be issued postponing the great event and ordering preparations for the happy day. I was very sorry I was not at home when Oda's birthday came, and still more that I forgot a little love gift for her ; but I will supplement your offering when I get home.

OTTAWA, May 9, 1879.

We are having busy times at last. The government is bringing down daily some new surprise for us. One day it was a list of supplementary estimates that called for over a million of money ; the day following it was their Pacific Railway bill of fare, demanding no less than a hundred million of acres in addition to the fifty million of acres already granted, and thirty millions of cash ; and last night the climax was capped by a demand for two million dollars to buy up and rebuild the piece of the Grand Trunk Railway below Quebec, that never has paid and never will pay a farthing ! All these vast sums to be sanctioned at once, without the possibility of inquiry.

TORONTO, July 4, 1879.

I am awfully sorry, but I cannot possibly help it. It is half-past two o'clock, and I see that with all my striving I dare not leave town to-day. There is not a creature here to see to the paper. Just this moment too comes a cable announcing that the Letellier matter has been referred back to the Canadian government, and something must be said about it ; so I must forego my pleasure for another day, and work at the oar. I will come by the first boat I can escape by to-morrow morning, and we shall have a fishing bout to-morrow evening in the old spot (Niagara).

TORONTO, July 31, 1879.

I went off to Bow Park at 7 o'clock yesterday morning ; met ——— there, and had a most satisfactory day with him ; sat up half the night to regulate Bow Park affairs ; got up at 5.30 this morning ; went round the herd ; had breakfast at 6.30, and off to the train that leaves Brantford at 7.30 ; got here at 10.10. Met ———, and went round for St. Andrew's subscriptions (for a ball to the Princess Louise) ; got $550 more, completing our $3,000 guarantee, before getting half through with our leading members. At 10 o'clock got off to business—last day of the month—and hard at it till 3 o'clock. Then to the seedsmen ; turnip and rape seeds wanted urgently at Bow Park ; got it; down to the express office, and made bargain to have it off at 3.20, and delivered at Brantford to-night ; made it out without one moment to spare ; and now, here I am writing to you, and then off home.

It is mentioned elsewhere that Mr. Brown was, when from home, in the constant habit of corresponding daily with his family. As soon as his children were able to make them out, they too received letters regularly—many of the earliest being written as if printed, somewhat similar to those written by Dr. Norman McLeod to his children. A few of these, in which, as in preceding letters, the "pet" names given to the children in their babyhood have been retained, are inserted here.

STEAMER SCOTIA,
QUEENSTOWN, Dec. 15, 1867.

MY DARLING MADDIE,—I am off on my voyage "over the hea"—away to New York and Toronto and Bow Park, and will soon see Bronte, and the Bow Park peacocks, and little calves and sheep. Won't that be nice? And I will tell them all about Maddie and baby, and Mena, and how nicely you are all getting on. And after a few weeks papa will be back again to dear mamma, and his own little Maddie and baby. Won't that be nice? And will Maddie think of papa sometimes while he is gone? and be glad when he returns? and will she be a good little girl all the while?—kind and loving to little sister and everybody, and trying hard to do all that dear mamma and grandmamma tell her? I am sure she will. And papa expects that Maddie will know all her letters, when he gets back, from A to Z. Maddie is getting a big girl now, and ought to know her letters. Good-by, my little darling; give baby ten kisses from papa, and tell her all that is in this letter.

YOUR LOVING PAPA.

OAK LODGE, Jan. 13, 1868.

MY DARLING LITTLE MADDIE,—I have received your two letters of the 19th and 26th December, and it was very kind of you to send them. Papa was greatly delighted to get a letter from his little pet, and is very sorry to be away from mamma and Maddie and baby so long; but he thinks of them all very often, and wonders what they are doing, and earnestly longs to be with them again. I am glad you enjoyed yourself so much at Christmas, and got such pretty things from the tree. What a good girl my little Maddie should strive to be, when mamma and grandmamma, and the aunties are all so kind and generous to her. Don't you think so? and won't you do so? Yesterday was my little Maddie's birthday. It was Sunday, and papa took dinner all by himself; but he did not forget whose birthday it was, and he drank Maddie's health and many happy returns of the day to his little pet. If papa had been in Edinburgh he would have made Maddie a nice little present on the occasion, but no doubt dear mamma remembered to do it.

Papa gave Maddie's message to Bronte, and Bronte wagged his tail and seemed very much pleased. Bronte is very lively at present, for there is a little boy at Oak Lodge who plays with him and has great romps with him.

Papa has not been at Bow Park yet, but will go soon, and write to his little Maddie about the peacock and the little lammies and the calvies and the mouies! Good-by, dear wee Maddie; go straight to baby and give her three kisses from papa, and tell her to be very good, for you mean to love her very much.

YOUR OWN PAPA.

OTTAWA, March 18, 1875.

MY DEAR LITTLE ODA,—Many happy returns of the day to you! that is, of the day this is intended to reach you, the ninth anniversary of your birthday !

I am very, very sorry that I cannot get home to-morrow, to be with dear mamma and you all at the rejoicings, and to find all those sixpences in the big cake tumbling out, for everybody, just as they are wanted ! I tried very hard, indeed, to get off to-night, but was compelled to remain to vote to-morrow on an important question. I am very sure you will feel certain that papa would have come if he possibly could, for he loves his little daughter very dearly. . . . Papa would have liked very, very much to have been at home to-morrow.

But never mind, Oda dear ; I will be up, if all goes well, on the day after this reaches you ; and we shall have such a time, shall we not ? You must keep a large piece of the cake for papa.

I wished to buy a little present for my Oda on her birthday, but could not accomplish it this morning ; so I enclose a bank bill, with which Oda must buy something for herself from papa.

Tell mamma that the senate refused to sit after dinner, as a number of the members wished to go to the Governor-General's party, and that I had consequently to postpone leaving until Friday night.

Good-by, dear Oda. Make Maddie and Ginney kind little speeches from papa, and accompany them with dear little kisses on each cheek from

YOUR LOVING PAPA.

LONDON, Aug. 18, 1875.

MY DEAR LITTLE ODA,—I got your two dear letters at the *Globe* office yesterday morning, and was delighted to do so. I read them joyfully ; and though your name was not signed to them, I knew very well the little hand that wrote them.

Yes, the little dog, with the other fellow's head, was very glad to see us at Abden House, and barked and frisked about at a great rate, and so did Bronte and the little hounds. I hope you enjoyed your visit to Scammadale very much, and that Freddy killed a great lot of grouse for you, and that Uncle James caught lots of salmon and trout for you and Mena and Ginney.

I am glad you are enjoying the bathing so much. You should bathe every day, for it will make you strong and vigorous. The weather here is very warm, and I would like to have a plunge in the sea off Oban rocks very much.

I expect to be in London all this week, and go to the North of England on Saturday night or Monday morning. I shall be in Edinburgh on Tuesday night probably, but will leave again on Wednesday morning ; and on Thursday will sail for Canada by the *Moravian*.

I am very sorry to part with mamma and you, and Maddie and Ginney, and it will be very lonely at Wellington Street ; but the weeks will soon run round, and we shall be all together again. Won't that be delightful ?

Give my loving regards to grandmamma and Auntie Jessie, and say how sorry I am not to have been with them longer, but that I trust we will meet again ere long.

Good-by, my own dear little Oda. Give Ginney six kisses from papa, and think of me always as your own fondly loving

PAPA.

Toronto, September 20th, 1875.

My Dear Wee Boy,—I received your letter that Auntie Jessie was so kind as to write for you, but which you signed with your own very hand, and was delighted to get it.

That must have been a very fine silver haddie you caught at Kerrera : next time you go you might catch one or two more, and send them over by the captain of the *Polynesian*. Eh ! that little hint about Edie's pony was nicely brought in. We shall see about it when the wee girls and boys that have run away from their papa get home.

Good-by. Love to mamma and grandmamma, and all the uncles and aunties and cousins, and all the good little girls and boys, and all the rest of the people, from your much-loving

Papa.

Toronto, March 26th, 1877.

My Dear Ginney,—Your letter came safe to hand and made me very happy. It was a great pleasure to receive a real letter, in the very own handwriting of my big boy. I mean to keep it carefully, and by comparing it with the letters I hope to get often from you hereafter, be able to judge of the progress you make in writing and composition ; and I am very anxious that my Ginney shall strive hard to make rapid progress in these accomplishments. . . .

Ottawa, May 7th, 1879.

My Dear Boy,—I was very much pleased to get your funny little letter an hour ago, and as the debate is going on upon the Coteau Bridge Bill, I scrawl off this line to say so to you. I am so glad you have been getting up in your classes again, though I confess I have found it very difficult to make out the figures. What does "Latin 5, 6.50" mean? What does "Reading 9, 6.75" mean? What does "Grammar 6, 7.18" mean? What does "History 12, 12.50" mean? I quite comprehend "1 in Geography"; that is the right sort of marking—so is "Head in Latin," and "1 up in History and Reading." Suppose you send me another letter explaining these mysteries?

The debate is just finished and the House about to rise, so I must close, or the gas will be put out and papa left in the dark. Good night, my dearest little Ginney. Give papa's love to Maddie and Oda, and three cheers for Hanlan !

Your Loving Papa.

SPEECHES.

ANTI-CLERGY RESERVE MEETING.

This speech was delivered at the anniversary meeting of the "Anti-Clergy Reserve Association," held in St. Lawrence Hall, Toronto, on the 26th of July, 1851. An opposition meeting was called by the conservatives in the Lower Market at the same hour. A large portion of the rougher element left the Tory gathering and proceeded to St. Lawrence Hall, and caused a serious disturbance. Missiles were thrown, and the windows were partially smashed, causing great alarm in the audience. Finally the military were called out, and the Riot Act was read, when the mob dispersed. Mr. Brown moved the following resolution: *Resolved,*—"That without enunciating any abstract principles on these subjects, we unanimously reiterate our deliberate and full conviction, that state endowments of religion are utterly inexpedient in a community like ours, leading, as they have hitherto done, to an indiscriminate and pernicious countenancing of error along with truth, and fostering among us religious alienation and civil discord."

He said: When the committee asked me to speak to the resolution which I have just read, I was instructed that the saving clause introduced into it for the benefit of those who do not condemn the abstract principle of state endowments, while they are opposed to its practical adoption in Canada, was intended to apply to the *voting* and not to the *speaking;* and that the speakers were quite at liberty to support the resolution by any arguments they chose. I take advantage of that liberty to say at the outset that no such saving clause was necessary for me; that I hold the principle and practice of establishments to be alike bad; that I view the payment of religious teachers by the state injurious to the cause of Christ, injurious to the pastors, injurious to the people, and injurious to the state. I hold that that church which cannot be maintained by the voluntary contributions of the Christian people is not worth supporting. It is true that learned ecclesiastics have showed from holy writ that kings were to be nursing fathers and queens nursing mothers to the church, and that by the nicest arguments they have attempted to establish on this foundation a whole fabric of priestcraft. But I confess that when

I read the history of the human race, and trace the dark record of wars and carnage, of tyranny, robbery, and injustice in every shape, which have been the fruits of state-churchism in every age ; when I observe the degenerating effect which it has ever had on the purity and simplicity of the gospel of Christ, turning men's minds from its great truths, as a religion of the heart, to the mere outward tinsel, to the forms and ceremonies on which priestcraft flourishes ; when I see that in all times it has been made the instrument of the rich and powerful in oppressing the poor and weak, I cannot but reject it utterly as in direct hostility to the whole spirit of the gospel, to that glorious system which teaches men to set not their hearts on this world, to walk humbly before God, and do justly by all men.   There is one argument which is perfectly insuperable in my mind, and that is, that if there never had been any connection between church and state, there never could have been persecution for conscience sake. True, churches might have persecuting principles, but without the state alliance they could not have carried them out.   But had I any scruple left on my mind as to the scriptural argument on the question of establishments, every vestige of it had been removed within the last few days by an able defence of the voluntary principle which has recently appeared.   The authority of the document is unquestionable—it comes to us with all the authority of apostolical succession in the true and veritable line, from one who has spent his life and rent his country with strife and excitement for a quarter of a century in opposing that very principle of which he is now the eulogist.   You may be astonished when I say that this combatant for the voluntary principle is Dr. John Strachan, by divine permission Church of England Bishop of Toronto.   I hold in my hand the charge of the Bishop, delivered to his clergy in May of this year—it is fresh from the church mint —there is no doubt of its genuineness, and I pray you to listen to a few extracts.   "But with or without its (the reserves) aid," says the Bishop, "*there is nothing of moment left for us but the voluntary principle.*"   Sad case !   "I am not here," he adds, apologetically, "to advocate the voluntary system in itself, for I consider it exposed to the gravest objections, but "—ah ! that *but*—"*but the necessity is upon us: there is now no alternative.*"   The case is indeed a lamentable one, but it is truly gratifying to see the new light which this fell necessity has thrown into the Bishop's mind. Now that it is "upon us," the ungodly, the infidel aspect of the thing disappears, and the voluntary principle begins to be clothed in all the beauty of apostolic antiquity !   Hear the Bishop : "It (the voluntary principle) is, as all must confess, *of high antiquity.   It began to be acted upon* in the days of the apostles."   Nay, sir, he goes further ; the results of the voluntary principle have been, he declares, "*of infinite importance* in preserving the church, her ordinances and teaching among the people," and he is quite certain that its full adoption in Canada "*God will bless.*"   If God will bless the voluntary principle to John Toronto, nobody will need to fear its being blessed to us.   It was astonishing how people progressed when they once got hold of a right principle : the Bishop, a convert of yesterday, puts his finger on the very mainspring of the voluntary principle, and warns his brethren

that "*according to the zeal and exertions of the clergy*, the voluntary principle
has produced very different results." No doubt of it; and in that sentence
he utterly condemns establishments, for they release the pastor from the
necessity of exertion.

The first risings of priestcraft in the Christian church were seen at
Rome. There was no state-churchism in the preaching or practice of our
Saviour or his apostles. The church at Rome, from its position and strength,
had early much influence over the churches beyond the city, and was frequently consulted; from giving advice the Roman bishops gradually assumed
a position of superiority, and as priestcraft felt its weight, divine authority
over all the churches was claimed. In the third century the doctrine of
unity of faith began to be strongly pressed, and the scriptural doctrine of
unity of spirit became gradually corrupted by designing men into unity of
external faith or form. In apostolic times, those who had the spirit were
members of the church, but this was now reversed, and those who were
members of the church were held to have the spirit. The admission of this
doctrine created a necessity for a church framework, and enabled ambitious
priests to work themselves in between man and his maker, and to use their
usurped authority for their own base purposes. From that time we have
had the same principle showing itself in various shapes all over the world,
according to the intelligence of the people. Mankind have made a great
advance on this point of late years, however; but even in this age, we have
not a little of it still at work. We don't burn people nowadays, but in
Spain, the other day, we passed new laws to force all men to worship at one
shrine; in Tuscany, two months ago, we put men in prison for reading the
Gospel of St. John; in England, we merely treat those not of the true
church as an inferior race, made of inferior clay, and we force them to bolt
thirty-nine articles; and in Scotland, we send men to gaol for not paying
the annuity tax. In Canada, we have had state-churchism in many phases,
but latterly it has become quite subdued; it only takes our money, stops a
Christian minister from preaching the gospel because he goes "without
bands" into the presence of his "diocesan!" or, mayhap, cuts off a faithful pastor because he "encouraged schism" by going to a Methodist chapel.
The demands of the state-churchmen are wonderfully lowered in Canada.
They are perfectly willing to extend tolerance in religion to all; all they
ask is that the state shall do its duty in maintaining the worship of God
and established truth. Only give the clergy cash, and they ask no more.

Now, admitting for argument sake that it is the duty of the state to
do this, how shall we, in a population made up of twenty sects, get at
truth? There is no standard for truth. We cannot even agree on the
meaning of words. How then shall we agree on this momentous point?
Oh, we are told, use the means—read—seek divine guidance. If twenty
conscientious men, of as many sects, honestly used every means possible to
find this truth, can any one doubt their arriving at the conclusion that there
are just twenty truths? But if eleven of the twenty agreed on one faith,
the establishment principle would entitle them, nay, make it their duty, to
force it down the throats of the others according to the majority of each

country went. So truth would be, and we would have the world covered with different truths, all under authority of the Bible. It is clear that truth in Canada would be Roman Catholicism. Setting aside the injustice of forcing men even to pay money for the support of what they deem religious error, it is most dangerous to admit that the magistrate is to decide for God—for that is the plain meaning of the establishment principle. Once admit that principle, and no curb can be set upon its operation. Who shall restrict what God has appointed? And thus the extent to which the conscience of men may be constrained, or persecution for truth's sake carried, depends entirely on the ignorance or enlightenment of the civil magistrate. There is no safety out of the principle that religion is a matter entirely between man and his God, and that the whole duty of the magistrate is to secure every one in the peaceful observance of it; anything else leads to oppression and injustice, but this never can lead to either. And here let me say that while we admire Bishop Strachan's new ideas on the voluntary question, and allow him a little reasonable grumbling, for the sake of decency, in swallowing the pill, I cannot agree with his statement that the voluntary principle "has never succeeded, in any place or country, in bringing the gospel to every creature, as the national establishments of Christian kingdoms and countries have effected." I think it will not be difficult to show that the very contrary is the fact. I contend, first, that the voluntary principle brings a purer gospel to mankind than national establishments. It matters not whether you regard the connection of church and state under the pomp of prelacy or the less pernicious form of clerical stipendiarism, the system raises a barrier between the pastor and his people. Clothe any set of men with office, and make them independent for life so long as their outward walk is pure, however negligent their services, and you will surely make them lazy ; you give them pride where there should be humility ; you unfit them for association with the outcasts of social life, you draw them from high aims, and fix their hearts on the world. Establishments make religion a matter of party politics—the church becomes the source of endless discord—and, perhaps, more infidels are produced by the exhibition of Christian pastors scrambling for the loaves and fishes, while they are preaching their worthlessness, than from any other cause. The very preaching of an established church is cold and lifeless; it has a sad lack of that "zeal and unction" of which the Bishop speaks.

But I contend further, that even if state-churchism secured the preaching of the gospel as pure as the voluntary principle, it does not supply the necessary labourers as well as the other, and church statistics show this beyond a doubt. In England, Noel states there are connected with the establishment 16,010 clergymen ; but of these 247 are heads of colleges, and 3,037 "do nothing ;" so that the actual number of working pastors is 12,923. These are expected to carry the gospel to the whole population ; and there being, by the census of 1841, 16,000,000 of people in England, it follows that there is one Church of England minister to every 1,238 persons. Now, how is it with the dissenters? The Congregationalists have 1,840 ministers, the Baptists 1,741, the Methodists 4,239, the Presbyterians

113, and the Moravians 17 ; total, 7,950. The numerical strength of these bodies has been found to be about 4,000,000 ; so that the voluntary principle in England furnishes one minister for every 500 people, looking to it for instruction. While *the* church, with its immense endowment, gives 1 to 1,238 of the whole population, the voluntary contributions of one-fourth of the community provide one to every 2,025—a very short way behind. In Scotland, a still more satisfactory result is obtained. The established church provides 1,100 ministers for the whole population of 2,600,000, being one for every 2,363—or, calculating the adherents of the establishment at nearly one-half of the population—

Dr. BURNS : It is only one-third.

Mr. BROWN continued : McCulloch states the dissenters, before the disruption, at 650,000, and the secession of the Free Church about double them ; so that the establishment would still have nearly one-half to provide for. Dr. Burns may, however, be correct, but on this calculation the establishment, with her state endowments, supplies but one minister to 1,100 of her own people, while the dissenters, on the voluntary principle, supply 1 to 900, their total number of ministers being upward of 1,500. And in the United States the superiority of the voluntary principle is fully established. The four great evangelical churches provide 14,931 ministers —being one for 925 of their own people, or one for 1,133 of the whole population—a most satisfactory result. Endowments in England provide but one in 1,238 ; the voluntary principle in America one in 1,133. And in Canada we have the same result. On the basis of the census just taken, and the numerical strength of the clergy of each denomination, the following results are obtained ·

	ADHERENTS.	MINISTERS.	BEING ONE TO EVERY
Church of England	197,000	146	1,350
" " Scotland	68,000	51	1,350
" " Rome	140,000	82	1,700
Presbyterians	105,000	110	1,000
Methodists	160,000	325	500
Baptists	33,000	119	300
Congregationalists	6,172	35	180

Here we find beyond the possibility of a doubt the result of endowments. The churches of England and Scotland, which have had all the public plunder nearly to themselves, supply but one minister to 1,350 of their people, while the evangelical bodies, that have had none, supply on an average one for every 517—an insuperable fact, quite destructive of Bishop Strachan's position. But I contend further, that even if national establishments supplied as pure a gospel and as large a corps of labourers as the voluntary principle, they do not occupy the destitute sections of the country so well as the voluntary churches, but seek the rich places of the earth for their abode. By the official returns, it is shown that there are four dioceses in England, viz. : Chester, Lichfield, London, and York, with a population of 6,148,662, and only 2,644 livings, while in 19 other dioceses, to a population of 5,753,559, there are no fewer than 6,718 livings. In the one there is 1 to every 856 people, and in the other 1 to every 2,325. In the four dioceses of Lincoln, Norwich, Oxford and Peterborough, there are 2,862 livings to 1,924,645 of the population, and in the four we have already named there are but 2,644 to over three times that population. In London, Lancashire, and Yorkshire, there are 1,298 clergy to 4,066,513 of the population, and in Huntingdon, Norfolk, and Suffolk, there are 1,297 to but 739,563 people. Of the 12,923 working clergy, 6,681 have flocks under 300, and the 6,242 others have all the rest of the population—one-half have two millions of people to teach, and the other half fourteen millions. In the sections where spiritual labour is most wanted, we find the dissenters far surpass the establishment in their efforts. In the great manufacturing districts of Lancashire and Yorkshire, the church has provided 357,984 sittings ; the dissenters, 586,135. And just so it is in Scotland, and everywhere else. The established church is the fashionable church, not the church of the people. The same thing may be seen in Canada. The churches of England and Scotland, though they get the reserves to sustain them, seek not the outposts of civilization, but may be found thickly studded in the cities and large towns. Of the 146 ministers of the Church of England, 38 are planted in 17 cities and incorporated towns, with a population of 81,000, and 42 are planted in ten incorporated towns containing about 20,000 people ; so that 100,000 of the population have 50 Episcopal clergyman, and the remaining 623,000 have but 96. But I go further than this, and say that not only do establishments fail to preach so pure a gospel as the voluntary churches—fail to provide so many men, and fail to plant their men in the destitute places—they do not produce as much cash as the voluntary principle, and this, at any rate, is an argument to reach the hearts of "churchmen." Let us first look at England. The income of the English establishment is £3,439,769, which, if equally divided, would yield a good stipend to all the clergy. But very different is the policy of state churches—the drones get the honey, the bees get little more than the labour : of this large annual revenue the cathedral clergy swallow £150,280 ; 28 ministers get £146,700, or £5,000 a piece ; 1,461 get from £500 to £3,000 : and 4,135 get from £200 to £500. The remainder of the beneficed clergy, 4,882 in number, Mr. Noel calculates, receive on an average £150 a year ! and the unfortunate 5,230 curates average but £81. There are therefore 10,112 of the established clergy of England receiving an average of £114 per annum, and the conclusion is irresistible that if that number of qualified persons can be had for that sum, any necessary number can be had. It is estimated by Mr. Conder that the average stipend of dissenting ministers in England is £110, raised entirely by voluntary contribution, and costing the contributors 4s. yearly per head. Now, with all their riches and boasting, we will not ask the establishment to do more than dissenters, but if they would only give as much, the eight millions of Episcopalians might supply over 15,000 ministers at the same salary as the state now gives to 10,112 of her pastors ! two thousand working clergymen more than they do at present with their immense endowments. And in Scotland the cash argument is still more conclusive. Before the disruption, the whole sum provided by the state for religious teaching was under

£250,000 a year, divided among 1,100 ministers. The Free Church has been but eight years in existence, but already has the voluntary principle placed her revenue far above that of the establishment. In the year just closed, her contributions for all purposes were not less than £303,480, and in the eight years she has received the enormous sum of £2,475,616. Notwithstanding the heavy load laid on her people for building and other purposes, which future years will remove, the Free Church ministers each receive £123 from the general fund, and many of them large supplements in addition, but all £9 more than ten thousand Anglican ministers receive. Already she has 728 ministers, and no one will dispute their equality with the establishment in piety, learning and zeal. And it is highly interesting to observe that the heavy drafts on the Free Churchmen have not closed their hearts to the claims of benevolence and missionary effort, but, on the contrary, have taught them to extend their subscriptions with unexampled munificence. When the church was united, and the people had no ministers to support or churches to build, the total voluntary contributions for the schemes of the church were as follows : 1834, two schemes, £3,551 ; 1835, three schemes, £5,128 ; 1836, four schemes, £7,941 ; 1837, four schemes, £10,070; 1838, four schemes, £13,800; 1839, four schemes, £14,353 ; 1840, five schemes, £16,156 ; 1841, five schemes, £17,588 ; 1842, five schemes, 20,191 ; making a total, for nine years before the disruption, of £108,778. There has since been contributed by the Free Church for the schemes, in 1843-4, £23,874 ; 1844-5, £35,526 ; 1845-6, £43,310 ; 1846-7, £43,327 ; 1847-8, £47,568 ; 1848-9, £49,214 ; making a total, for six years since the disruption, of £242,819.

In France there are 400,000 clergymen paid by the state, and they get but an average of £34 per annum. And the same results are found in Canada even in more striking contrast. The Church of England here gets a large annual sum from the reserves ; she has a large sum from the London Society for the Propagation of Christian Knowledge, and she has 21,000 acres of the choicest land as rectories. Her ministers get their support almost entirely from those sources ; her people have not the burden of supporting their clergy ; and if any church, therefore, is in a position to aid the cause of missions and benevolent enterprise, it is the Church of England in this province. But what is the fact ? She has a Diocesan Society for promoting these objects, and all the churches in the diocese send in their contributions to it. I hold in my hand the report for 1850, and I find that for home and foreign missions, for widows and orphans, and for theological students, the whole contributions of the 197,000 Episcopalians was in that year but £3,693 10s. 7d.—just three pence one farthing for each of them. The Wesleyan Methodist Church, on the other hand, with 90,000 people, maintaining as she does more than twice the number of clergy, according to her numerical strength, and paying them salaries little if at all under those of the churchmen, contributed in 1850 £3,393 10s. 6d. for such purposes, or 9d. per head. The Free Church, but seven years established, and with new churches to build all over the country, has already 63 ministers and 45 divinity students ; and though she has but 62,000 adherents, she pays her ministers an average of £110, and contributes £2,000 a year to the schemes of the church, or eightpence per head.   But on this part of the argument Bishop Strachan comes to my assistance with tremendous effect.   He tells us in his charge that his people have the impression "that ample provision has been made for the sustenance of religion by government," and that "although the true state of the matter is quite the reverse, there is no getting the unwilling to believe it."   "They do not perceive the necessity of making any efforts, and if pressed too frequently, refuse even the smallest assistance." Nothing could be more condemnatory of state pay than this.   It is clear then that the connection between church and state is evil in every way— is injurious to whatever is affected by it ; and it is clearly the duty of every man who loves his country, who seeks peace and the advancement of Christ's cause, to lend his most earnest assistance in rooting out so great an evil from the institutions of our country.

In Canada, the evil is to be found in six different shapes.   Two of these have been already discussed—the reserves and the rectories ; but in regard to two others I desire to say something.   And first, as to our educational system—the most dangerous ground, in my opinion, on which priestcraft shows itself.   I hold that it is the duty of the state to place a sound practical education within the reach of every child in the province; and already have the Canadian people, to their lasting honour, done much towards this end.   We have a noble common school system, the beginning of an excellent grammar school system, and a well endowed national university.   No country has done so much as Canada, considering her age and strength, for the cause of education among the masses.   In these schools all are on a footing, and the religious faith of every one is protected from the spirit of proselytism.   We are asked to break up this noble system which has already produced such good fruits, which promises so much more, and why ?   Because we are told it is godless, it is infidel in its tendency, and already, on this fiendish pretext of priestcraft, has the sectarian wedge been thrust into it, and the whole fabric is threatened with destruction.   Tell me that it has an infidel tendency to teach a child to read and write ?   Tell me that literature and science make men ungodly !   I cannot reason with such men.   If the demand of the priests, Roman and Anglican, was that the Bible should be more taught in the schools, and that the teachers should invariably be pious men, I might believe their professed anxiety for the cause of religion.   But when I see that they have the power now to get any number of pious teachers appointed ; that they themselves, in conjunction with the parents, and not the secular teachers, are the legitimate religious instructors of our youth ; and when I see that they make no exertion to fulfil their own responsibility, I come to the irresistible conclusion that this cry is the offspring of the most miserable sectarianism—a new effort of priestcraft to grasp in its hands the moulding of the youthful mind of our country . I can conceive nothing more unprincipled than a scheme to array the youth of the province in sectarian bands—to teach them, from the cradle up, to know each other as Methodist boys, and Presbyterian boys, and Episcopal boys. Surely, surely, we have enough of this most wretched sectarianism in our churches without carrying it further! But we have a new argument recently started on this question. A very learned gentleman has just arrived from England to enlighten us on high churchism—a gentleman who, at our former meeting, proved his zeal for religion—I mean the already famous Mr. Dartnell, secretary of the Church Union. This gentleman made a speech at a church meeting lately, in which he avowed the doctrine that secular education is the fostering parent of crime, and he called on his brother churchmen to resist the schoolmaster as they would the "foul fiend." I hold in my hand the report of his speech, and I find he used these words : "It was discovered that ignorance and treason were far more expensive than religion, and efforts were made to check the evil. Had they resorted to the increase of the ministers of the gospel they might have succeeded, but the remedy applied was secular education. We have 25 years' experience of it in England, and what are the results? It has been aided by voluntaryism, and, with the two combined, the results have been that crime and pauperism have increased in a ratio almost incredible. The committals to gaol in 1813 were 7,164 ; in 1836 they amounted to 20,984, and in 1842, to 31,909. Thus, with secular education crime has increased in 30 years over 400 per cent. This year the increase has been 500 per cent. Here it is palpable that secular education has not checked the progress of crime, but rather accelerated it. And yet we are asked to introduce it into Canada." We are asked to throw open the field to secular education, and then would come crime, pauperism, and destitution. The opposite of all this is the fact—not secular education, but the want of it, has increased crime.

The people of England have been shamefully dead to the importance of education—the established church has lain almost dormant in regard to it, and now, when she comes alive, it is not to foster it, but to stop its progress as the grand leveller of priestcraft. In 1848, I find from the sessional papers of the House of Commons, that the whole amount given for that year for the support of common school education in England was but £125,000 for sixteen millions of people, though £111,547 was given for the extension of the British Museum! Why, in Upper Canada we contribute more from public funds for common school education than they do in all England. It is monstrous, therefore, to assert that education has increased crime, for there has been no national education. Indeed, the assertion is proved to be totally destitute of truth by the criminal statistics. I find that in Scotland in 1846 there were 17,855 prisoners, and that 4,210 of them could not read ; 8,374 could read with difficulty; and 5,273 could read well ; 9,551 of them could not write, 2,122 could merely sign their names, 4,715 could write with difficulty, 1,237 could write well, and but 282 had learned more; a tremendous argument in favour of secular education. In England and Wales I find the argument still stronger. Of 65,922 prisoners in 1846, 22,315 could not read or write ; 13,907 could only read ; 27,037 could read or write imperfectly ; 2,473 could read and write well, and 261 knew more than that! There is no getting over this. And as regards Canada, I have reason to know that of the 400 prisoners in the penitentiary, not six are well educated. But the sectarianism of the godless education cry is not its only evil—it proposes a new system which it is is impossible to carry out, and which, if extended much further, will destroy the whole fabric without substituting another in its place. All the sects are now combined, with the exception of about 100 schools; and yet we can only keep open 3,209 schools for an average of 9½ months in the year. In 1849 there were 138,465 children on the roll, but of these there was only an average attendance of 72,204 in summer, of 78,466 in winter, and 100,000 children of school age were not on the roll at all. If we remain united, therefore, it is clear that to cover the whole ground we want 5,000 teachers. We pay our teachers now £107,713 a year, but then we should have to pay at least £150,000. Now, the Roman Catholics have separate schools already—

A GENTLEMAN : And so has the English Church.

Mr. BROWN : Yes, they have a few, but not so many as the Roman Catholics, and if the evil is allowed to go on, it will spread to other sects. At the least calculation, under the separate system, there would be wanted 15,000 teachers, instead of 5,000—a sad waste of labour—12,000 school houses would have to be built, at a cost of some £300,000 ; and nearly half a million of pounds, or the whole revenue of the province, would be required annually to pay the teachers. It is impossible to carry out such a scheme, and it is therefore doubly unprincipled to urge it.

Our common schools are doing admirably now, and if we have any patriotism we will sternly maintain its integrity. Look at its effects in Lower Canada. In 1789, while sectarian teaching was in full bloom there, and the church munificently endowed to that end, evidence was laid before the government that in many parishes there were not six persons who could read or write. How is it under the national system? In the first half-year of 1849, 68,822 scholars were in attendance, and in the latter half 54,758.

And now a few words in regard to ecclesiastical corporations, and I have done. I cannot but express my astonishment at the indifference with which the statesmen of our country regard the progress of these injurious institutions ; for he is little versed in the history of his race who does not know the monstrous evils which they have everywhere entailed, and how often they have had to be put down at the demand of the public voice. These corporations never die ; their property cannot be alienated ; it goes on increasing with great rapidity. One would think that a glance at the alarming amount of property already at stake on this state-church question would rouse men to its importance. In " Smith's History of Canada," it is stated that the land owned at the conquest by

	ACRES.
Roman Catholic institutions was	2,115,178
Lower Canada Reserves	903,433
Upper Canada Reserves	2,395,687
Rectories	21,638
Carried forward	5,435,936

	ACRES.
Brought forward	5,435,936
School grant	546,000
New school grant...	1,000,000
Clergymen, Church of England.........................	29,200
" " " Rome	4,700
" Presbyterian Church	3,000
Total...................................	7,018,836

This immense quantity of land is at stake in the state-church question ; for, though part has been sold, the proceeds remain, and might be invested ; and if the priests had their will, every acre of the above would be transferred to their control.   But this is not all.   In addition, we have 54 religious, educational, or charitable corporations established since the union, holding property to an unknown extent ; and how many more I know not established previous to the union : 48 of the 54 are authorized to hold property to the annual value of £79,333 6s. 8d., and six of them are unlimited.   How much land they now hold I know not ; but if they had the revenue permitted them, and their property yielded the same returns as the reserves, it is an alarming statement but I believe a correct one, that they might hold six or seven millions of acres and not transgress their charters.   But the fact is, the limit to the amount of property is no limit at all.   How is it to be made to operate ?   There is no return made of the property held, and' if there were, the limit could easily be evaded.   I am utterly opposed to these sectarian corporations. I would give them every necessary power to organize themselves ; but I would enforce on all a stringent law of mortmain.

I must apologise for detaining the audience so long ; but I cannot conclude without urging on every one who hears me the deep importance of all these questions on the future well-being of our country.   There is no ground for us to take but that of a resolute determination to uproot the whole fabric—to leave not a vestige of it in existence.   A long and a fierce contest, I grieve to think, is yet before us ; our opponents are rousing themselves with fresh vigour to the struggle ; and if we are to succeed, it must be by united and energetic action.   Let us vow that we never shall give up the battle until victory has been fully accomplished, and let us keep ever before us as the goal we must reach—no reserves ! no rectories ! no sectarian education ! no ecclesiastical corporations ! no sectarian money grants ! no sectarian preferences whatever !

ANTI-SLAVERY DEMONSTRATION.

The following speech was delivered in Toronto at the annual meeting of the Anti-Slavery Association, on the 24th of March, 1852, on which occasion Mr. Brown moved the following resolution: "That while we would gratefully record our thanks to those clergymen and others in the United States who have so nobly exposed the atrocities of the Fugitive Slave Law, we deplore the indifference of some and the unrighteous approbation of others, whose duty it is to vindicate the gospel of Christ from the aspersions of those who represent it as a shield for cruelty and injustice." The subject of slavery at that time caused no little excitement in Canada on account of its hideous features being constantly brought before the public by the poor fugitives, and the necessity which existed for aiding them when they reached the free soil of Canada, and also in defending them in the courts when bogus criminal charges were brought against them to procure their extradition.

MR. BROWN said : I recollect when I was a very young man, I used to think that if I had ever to speak before such an audience as this, I would choose African slavery as my theme, in preference to any other topic. The subject seemed to afford the widest scope for rhetoric, and for fervid appeals to the best of human sympathies. These thoughts arose far from here, while slavery was a thing at a distance, while the horrors of the system were unrealized, while the mind received it as a tale and discussed it as a principle. But when you have mingled with the thing itself ; when you have encountered the atrocities of the system ; when you have seen three millions of human beings held as chattels by their Christian countrymen ; when you have seen the free institutions, the free press, and the free pulpit of America linked in the unrighteous task of upholding the traffic ; when you have realized the manacle, and the lash, and the slot-hound, you think no more of rhetoric ; the mind stands appalled at the monstrous iniquity ; mere words lose their meaning ; and facts, cold facts, are felt to be the only fit arguments. In regard to the resolution I have read, this is especially the case. I am to speak of the Fugitive Slave Bill of 1851, and if we search the statute books of the world, I know not where we shall find its parallel. Every one knows how this bill came into existence. The slaves of the south were daily escaping into the northern states, and once there, they were almost beyond reach of their masters. True, there was a law usually constructed to enable the slave-holder to recover his *property* in any part of the union ; but it had to be effected by due process of law, and public feeling in the north was rapidly becoming sensitive to the degradation of permitting the slave-catcher to drag men into life bondage from the farms of the north. A party had also arisen calling themselves free-soilers, who took up the position that the slave-holders had no right to follow the refugee into the free states, that the moment a slave put his foot on the free north, his shackles fell from his limbs. They said to the south, we respect your state rights, but you must respect ours ; you may keep slavery on your own grounds, but you must not bring it here. It was a bold movement and a noble one, and had it been firmly carried out throughout the northern states, slavery would soon have fallen before it.

But the south was aroused ; the "peculiar institution" was in danger, the cotton interest in the north was alarmed ; new and more stringent laws for the protection of the slave-owner and in aid of the slave-catcher were demanded from congress, under the penalty of a disruption of the union. Northern merchants quailed before the ire of the south, *dough-face* politicians trembled for their party alliances, aspirants for the presidency pandered for southern votes ; and the Fugitive Slave Bill was passed as a "compromise measure," to the lasting disgrace of republican America.

Let me recite the provisions of this infamous enactment. In the first place, it enabled the slave-holder or his agent to seize his "chattel" wherever he found him, *without any warrant*. You cannot arrest a criminal of the deepest dye without a warrant, but a man who is guilty of no crime but his colour can be seized at any moment without any form of law. In the next place, this law forbids the freeman of the north from showing charity to the refugee. Any one knowingly aiding a fugitive slave is subjected to a fine of $1,000 and six months' imprisonment in the common gaol, and to a civil suit for damages of $1,000. What a mockery of liberty ! Punish a man as a criminal, in the American republic, because he sympathizes with the bondsman and helps him to be free !

Another remarkable feature of this bill is, that the carrying out of its provisions was taken from the state authority and handed over to the federal officers. The slave-holders felt that their only safety was in placing the trust in the hands of men looking to Washington for their orders. The United States marshals were made the chief man-catchers of their respective districts—the United States commissioners the judges in all cases arising under the bill. And these functionaries are bound by the severest penalties to carry out the law. The marshal is made personally responsible in the sum of $1,000 for the escape of any slave committed to his care, however efficiently he may have acted. In all other cases, civil or criminal, sheriffs and other public officers are only held responsible for their fidelity and diligence ; it was left for the Fugitive Bill to punish a man for that which he did not do and could not avert.

Then, again, the bill compels the free northerners to turn out at the bidding of any southern miscreant who claims a coloured person for his property, and to aid in hunting him down like a beast of prey, and send him back to bondage.   Let not northerners speak of their *free* states after this : they have no free states.   Theirs is the most degrading of slavery. Professing to abjure the atrocious system, for the sake of their dollars they permit the south to put its insulting foot upon their necks, they allow their free homesteads to be made the hunting ground of the man-stealer.   The bold villainy of the south is not half so revolting as the despicable subserviency of the north.   But another provision of the Fugitive Bill is, that it suspends the *habeas corpus*, not towards all fugitives, but in regard to all men *claimed* as fugitives, be they bond or free, and it forbids them the right of trial by jury.   Certain commissioners are named the judges, and they must decide "summarily."   In a suit of ten dollars, one must have due notice and time to prepare for trial, and may demand the decision of twelve impartial jurors, but a man in the model republic is sent into life bondage by the summary fiat of one individual, and he too chosen under the full influence of the slave power, and holding his emoluments under its favour.

Let it be well understood that the boasted institutions of the United States demand the greatest care and ceremony about the ownership of a horse or cow, but make the fate of a human being a matter of "summary" decision; that there is far more difficulty in sending a hog to its sty than in tearing a man, unsuspected of crime, from the home of his children and making him a slave for life.   But even a worse feature of the bill is, that the witnesses are not required to be put into the witness-box in open court and cross-examined, so that perjury may be discovered ; this would be necessary in the pettiest suit for dollars, but for the enslaving of a man the proceedings may he held in the privacy of a commissioner's room, and the issue may be decided on paper affidavits, taken *ex parte*, thousands of miles away.   Nay, more than this, not content with securing every facility for catching the poor stricken fugitive ; not content with selecting the most sure tools to carry out the law ; not content with setting aside every legal and constitutional protection for individual rights, this infamous bill absolutely provides, as far as the law can provide, for a decision favourable to the man-catcher.   The southerners knew the weak point of the north, and they appealed to it; they knew the class of men who were to be the commissioners, and they provided that when one of these functionaries decided for the slave he should get a fee of $5, but when he decided for the slave-holder he should have $10. Could legislation be more infamous than this !   And the best of all is, that the expenses of the slave-catching operation come from the public treasury. In the recovery of things—ay, even in the defence of personal rights secured by law—the suitor must pay the costs ; but the model republic stands so firmly for human bondage that for it there is an exception, and the slave-holder's victim may be taken to his place of torture at the public cost.   Free northerners are made man-catchers, northern laws are suspended, northern judges are bribed to convict at five dollars a man, northern marshals are made slave-gaolers, northern constables carry home the victim, and northern taxation pays the cost of the process.   Tell me

no more of your free northern states. Did the true spirit of liberty exist
an enactment such as this would be laughed to scorn, and an attempt to
carry it out rouse a feeling at the north which would shake the foundations of the " peculiar institution." No, the full guilt of the law rests
upon the north. In the House of Representatives, which adopted it, there
were 141 northern members and only 91 from the south. There was a
sufficient number of absentees, of skulking voters on the final division to
have upset the bill. And the assent of the first branch of the legislature
was given to it by a northern president, by a citizen of Buffalo.

But let me speak of the fruits of the bill. Scarcely had it passed when
the south was awake ; affidavits were duly prepared, and the man-thief
on the track of the fugitive. Advertisements for runaways were widely
published. Let me read you a sample. [Mr. Brown here read an advertise-
ment entitled, " Catch the minister ! $250 for any one who will catch a
Methodist preacher !" and which went on to describe the party in the most
minute manner.] And it was not long ere a victim was found. A coloured
man named Hamlet, who had resided in New York for three years, a member of the Methodist church, having a wife and family, sober, industrious,
and faithful to his employers, was seized on the affidavit of a Mrs. Brown,
of Baltimore, that he was her property. This woman was not able to
write, but signed her mark. She could not of course know of her own
knowledge what the writing contained which she signed ; but yet, on that
affidavit, with the additional evidence of her son and son-in-law—who, it is
believed, were the only parties to be benefited by the result—Hamlet was
torn from his family and sent into slavery. He was the first victim, and
the north was not yet accustomed to its fetters, so the price of the chattel
was subscribed. Mrs. Brown got her eight hundred dollars, and Hamlet
came back a man.

Very soon after this a coloured person named Adam Gibson was arrested
in Philadelphia as the slave Emery Rice. The New York *Commercial
Advertiser*, a pro-slavery paper, tells us that the case came before Commissioner Ingraham ; that the prisoner's counsel demanded time to obtain
witnesses to prove that Gibson was a free man, but that Ingraham "refused the application, and ordered a summary hearing." The case proceeded, and one Price was called as a witness. The *Advertiser* tells us he
swore he knew the prisoner to be Rice " by his familiar looks," but that
he only inferred him to be Knight's slave because he rode Mr. Knight's
horse, and had seen him work for him. Mr. Commissioner Ingraham ruled
that when a coloured person worked for a slave-holder in Maryland the
presumption was that he was a slave—though the witness admitted that
many free coloured men were thus employed. Price admitted also that
he himself was bound over from the sessions on a charge of kidnapping ;
and this man was the only witness who identified the prisoner. An hour's
delay was asked, but refused by Mr. Commissioner Ingraham, although
informed that the prisoner had been kept in ignorance of the real cause of
his arrest until he appeared in court. Here was a scene ! Two witnesses,

coloured, were however obtained—men of good character—who testified respectively that the prisoner's name was Adam Gibson, and that he was formerly a slave of a Dr. Davis, who liberated all his slaves by his will. The commissioner, nevertheless, had "no doubt of the identity of the prisoner with Emery Rice," and ordered him to be returned to Mr. Knight. This was in a free state of the American union, in the land of William Penn, in the city of Brotherly Love! A human being condemned into slavery for life, on the oath of a professional man-stealer that he had once seen him on Mr. Knight's horse! Behold a republican spectacle of the year 1851. Well, what was the *finale* of this transaction? Ingraham got his ten dollars, the *posse comitatus* was called out to enforce the law, northern men took the victim to the claimant, and presented him as his chattel; but the slave-dealer had not villainy enough to receive him. He acknowledged that they had brought the wrong man—that Mr. Commissioner Ingraham's victim was not Emery Rice. What a picture was this! Northern justice prostituted, a judge of a free state, a northern marshal, the free citizens of Pennsylvania, all crouching before southern despotism, rolling in the mire of their own debasement, urging the slave-holder to take a victim, and the dealer in human flesh shrinking from the judicial award!

After this came the case of Henry Long, in the city of New York. He was brought before a sham commissioner, and kept before him until arrested under a valid authority; he was tried and condemned, and sent to Virginia —and he was sold there with the special condition that northern benevolence should never reach him, that he was never to be transferred to a northern owner. Rapidly after this came a scene of blood in the state of Pennsylvania. The Philadelphia *Bulletin* tells us that "deputy marshal Hatzel, constable Agen, and four or five other men, proceeded to Chester county to hunt up a chattel. They arrived at the house where the fugitive was supposed to be secreted, and knocked at the door. A coloured woman opened the window to know their business, when she was informed that they had broken the traces of their waggon and wished a light to mend them. She came down stairs and admitted the party in waiting. They thus effected an entrance, and were proceeding up stairs, when they were met by two coloured men and two coloured women. The women and one of the men were armed with axes, and the other had a gun. The marshal told them that they were in search of a fugitive slave; but they refused to let him or any of his men enter the room. The gun was taken from the man, and the party endeavoured to disarm the man with the axe. A pistol was fired at him, the ball of which must have entered his breast, but he still maintained his resistance. The fight continued until the southern *gentleman* (so says the *Bulletin*) who was with the party advised the marshal to withdraw, remarking that he would not have one of them killed for all the negroes in Pennsylvania. The party retired, firing several shots as they went, and more than one coloured person is supposed to have been shot. One was seen to fall as the officers were leaving. None of the marshal's party were injured." Here was a spectacle in Christian America!

Northern officials acting as slot-hounds on the track of human beings charged with no crime!—decoying the poor victims from their lair by appeals to their benevolence!—shooting them down like beasts of prey because they loved liberty! And mark the cowardice of the transaction. A posse of seven men and a southern *gentleman*, all armed to the teeth, driven off by two women and a man with axes and another man disarmed. Show me a tyrant, and I will find you a coward. They had not the courage to go forward, they turned and ran from the poor slaves; but when beyond the reach of the axe, they fired their guns at the victors with the full intent of murder.

After this we had the case of the Crafts, who are now happily in a land where no slave can live. They were closely hunted in the city of Boston, but they escaped to England.

Then came the case of Shadrach, who was seized and brought before a Massachusett's judge; but, somehow or other, there arose an excitement in the court-room, the marshal was jostled and the constables hemmed in, the law was trampled under foot, but the chattel escaped, and is now a free man in free Canada.

Shortly after came the famous Sims case, also in the city of Boston; but let us admit that the state of Massachusetts is a redeeming feature in the whole case; there are true men there yet; the blood of their ancestors yet beats in their veins. When Sims was arrested, Boston was roused to excitement; the court-house was surrounded with thronging thousands, and to preserve the sanctity of the law, an iron chain had to be carried round the court-house, and a large police force ranged within it to keep off the mob. When the judges entered their court they had to crouch under the iron chain! Of old the conquered had to pass under the yoke as an admittal of their conquest; and was it not a fitting emblem of northern servitude to their southern masters, that the judges of New England had to pass under an iron chain ere they could ascend the bench! Sims was convicted of being a chattel, and he was ordered to be sent back to Georgia. Boston men did the deed; a Boston marshal caught the victim; a Boston judge condemned him; Boston men were his gaolers and carried him into slavery. What a picture of degradation!

[Mr. Brown detailed other cases which arose under the operation of the Fugitive Law, and proceeded]—Had these occurred in Algiers, or among the savage tribes of Africa, the whole world would have been roused to indignation, but as they are daily occurrences in Christian America, in the free northern states of America, in the land of Sabbaths and churches, and schools, and missionary societies, no man must ope his mouth to its iniquity. Where in the wide world could such transactions as these be openly practised but in this boasted land of liberty? [A VOICE: In Hungary!] In Hungary, does the gentleman say? I thank him for the allusion. To their eternal disgrace, the Austrians flogged women in Hungary, but they brought down on their heads the denunciations of the whole civilized world. And what comparison is there between the cases? Despot Austria flogs a woman, but free America sells her into life bondage under all the penalties to which woman can be subject. Many a noble woman would submit to be flogged as a martyr to the cause of liberty, but what true woman would dare to live under all the unspeakable atrocities of American slavery? I have said that there are true men, noble spirits in the northern states who did not witness these things unmoved; but that the full guilt of he iniquity rests on the north, no man can doubt. When a feeling of resistance to the Fugitive Bill began to show itself, who were the men most forward to crush it? Northern merchants, northern editors, northern politicians—ay, northern ministers of Christ. The cry of the "Union in danger" was got up; the American constitution was openly declared to have higher claims to obedience than God's moral law, and popular meetings were held throughout the union to pronounce in favour of the fugitive atrocity. A mass meeting was held in the city of New York, and the great Daniel Webster, the "God-like Daniel," as he was once styled, was brought there for the occasion. In his speech to the New Yorkers Mr. Webster, while considering the cry for the repeal of the Fugitive Bill, told hem the President "considered the settlement as final," and he would 'carry it into effect." Mr. Webster continued thus: "This is the subject, gentlemen, on which the moral sense of the country ought to receive tone and tension. There ought to be a stern rebuke by public opinion, of all who would reopen this agitating question—who would break this truce, as they call it—who would arm again and renew the war." The New York papers tell us this was received by the audience with "applause and cheers." Think of northern men applauding when told that that is a "final settlement" which makes them the slave-catchers of the "southern chivalry." It is often said that slavery cannot be so bad a thing, for that slaves who have escaped are glad to get back to bondage. If such cases do ever occur, it presents one of the most startling features of the vile system, that it actually degrades men so low that they know not the difference between slavery and freedom. But these New York people bring us new testimony to the demoralizing influence of slavery; they show that it blunts all the nobler feelings in those who are but indirectly connected with it; that men born and reared in the free north can rejoice to pass under the yoke of the south, and give "loud cheers" when they are told by the man who subjugated them that their degradation is to be perpetual.

But the great guilt of slavery lies at the door of American churches. Truly did Albert Barnes say: "There is no power out of the church that could sustain slavery one hour if it were not sustained in it." But nearly all the churches of the union are steeped in its iniquities; ministers, office-bearers and people are alike its upholders. In every shape you can find it, from the smooth-tongued parson who preaches that slavery is "not a sin *per se*," down to the bold denunciator of the "fanatic abolitionist," with stipend paid him from the toil of the poor slave. How can the state of the American church be better described than by the fact that Dr. Spring, an eminent light of the Presbyterian church, and minister of a large congregation in New York, publicly made this declaration: "If by

one prayer I could free every slave in the world, I could not offer it."
Laboured arguments are constantly coming from evangelical northern
pulpits palliating the system—nice criticisms on God's law in regard to it;
but for my part, I cannot listen to such arguments; I sweep aside all such
theological humbug, and find a solution of the whole question in the grand
Christian rule, "Do unto others as you would be done unto."

It is much to be regretted that Christian men in Great Britain are so
slow to comprehend the position of the American church on this question
—that with it rests the fate of the traffic. It is said that Methodist
church ministers and members hold 219,563 slaves; Presbyterians, 77,000;
Baptists, 125,000; Campbellites, 101,000; Episcopalians, 88,000; and other
denominations, 50,000; total slaves held by professing Christians,
660,563. Let these churches declare slavery a heinous sin in the sight of
God; let them compel the man-stealer to choose between God and mam-
mon, and how long would slavery exist? And yet we find such fine-
weather anti-slavery men as the Rev. Mr. Chickering—men who make
smooth, cautious speeches and *do* nothing—passing in England as thorough
abolitionists, and eulogized as such by editors who should know better.
Mr. Roaf has alluded to the case of Mr. Chickering and the *British Banner*,
and all true friends of the slave must regret to see the course that excellent paper has taken in the matter. There never was a cause in which the
position, "He that is not for us is against us," was so imperative as in
that of abolition. Not to move is more fatal than to move backwards—it
is the sleep of death to the slave. Mr. Chickering is one of those hidden
abolitionists, whose lights burn brightly in England, but who cannot face
the task of keeping them alive under the penalties to be incurred on this
side the Atlantic. How different the man whom the *Banner* has ventured
to attack so severely! Did the editor at all understand the case, he would
take the word of Mr. Lewis Tappan on any question of abolition before a
thousand Mr. Chickerings. The names of Arthur and Lewis Tappan will
be enrolled as Christian patriots in the annals of their country; and when
all the Chickerings have gone down to the dust and been forgotten, the
Tappans will be remembered with enthusiasm as amongst the noblest and
most self-denying of the pioneers of abolition. Mr. Chickering has ventured to say there are no black pews in the American churches—

A Voice: He says he never *saw* any.

Mr. Brown: Ah! yes; he never *saw* any—that was the word. If so,
I venture to say he is the only church-going man in the States who can
make the same declaration. For my part, I have seen them often. The
first time I ever entered an American church was in the city of New
York—a Presbyterian church. A friend who was with me went into one
pew and I entered another. Immediately I noticed several persons
staring at him in a particular manner, and at last a gentleman rose, went
to one of the office-bearers, whispered, and pointed to my friend. The
second gentleman left his pew, went to my friend, and most politely conducted him to another seat. Both of us attributed the circumstance a

first to courtesy, but we soon learnt that we had got into the black pew, in which no white man should be degraded to worship his Maker. The thing is too common to be denied ; also at the sacramental table the black Christian must sit apart from his white brother worm.

I must apologize for detaining the audience so long, but one word more, and I have done. The question is often put, What have we in Canada to do with American slavery? We have everything to do with it. It is a question of humanity, and no man has a right to refuse his aid, whatever it may be, in ameliorating the woes of his fellow-men. It is a question of Christianity ; and no Christian can have a pure conscience who hesitates to lift his voice against a system which, under the sanction of a Christian altar, sets at defiance every principle of Christianity. We have to do with it on the score of self-protection. The leprosy of the atrocious system affects all around it ; it leavens the thoughts, the feel-ings, the institutions of the people who touch it. It is a barrier to the spread of liberal principles. Who can talk gravely of liberty and equality in the States while slavery exists ? Every intelligent American who pro-fesses to be a Christian, and upholds slavery, is committed to a glaring infidelity, which must lead him continually astray in trying to square with it his every-day conduct. We are alongside of this great evil ; our people mingle with it; we are affected by it now, and every day enhances the evil. In self-protection, then, we are bound to use every effort for its abolition, that our people may not be contaminated by its withering and debasing influences. And there is another reason why we have to do with slavery. We are in the habit of calling the people of the United States "the Americans ;" but we too are Americans ; on us, as well as on them, lies the duty of preserving the honour of the continent. On us, as on them, rests the noble trust of shielding free institutions from the reproach of modern tyrants. Who that looks at Europe given over to the despots, and with but one little island yet left to uphold the flag of freedom, can reflect without emotion that the great republic of this continent nurtures a despotism more base than them all. How crushingly the upholders of tyranny in other lands must turn on the friends of liberty ! "Behold your free institutions," they must say. "Look at the American republic, pro-claiming all men to be born free and equal, and keeping nearly four millions of slaves in the most cruel bondage !"

The people of Canada are truly free ; we have no slaves ; all men are alike in the eye of justice. Long may it be so ; and it is our duty to raise our voices as free men against a system which brings so foul a blot on the cause of popular liberty. Our neighbours are wont to boast that monarchy will be swept from this continent ; let our effort be that slavery shall be driven from it, that tyranny shall not find a foot-hold. But how shall we proceed—what shall we do? Speak against it ; write against it ; agitate against it ; when you get hold of a Yankee, drive it home to him ; tell him his country is disgraced ; wound his pride ; tell him his pure institutions are a grand sham ; send him home thoroughly ashamed of the black blot on his country's escutcheon. In steamboat, or railroad, or wherever you are, hunt up a Yankee and speak to him faithfully ; there is no other man so sensitive as to what others think of him. You will find strange arguments to meet, but every man of them will be "*as much opposed to slavery in the abstract as you.*" It's a great evil, they will say ; but what's to be done with it ? Tell them that slavery is not an evil but a sin, a breach of every commandment in the decalogue, and that there is no choice but immediate emancipation. Tell them there was once a tea tax attempted to be imposed on them, and there was no word of "what's to be done" then ; they flung the tea into Boston harbour, and they must send slavery after it. They'll say with the deepest sympathy that "the poor creatures could not take care of themselves," but you can tell them that we have thirty thousand of them in Canada ; that they all seem to get along, and that the men whom the colonizations wish to make missionaries to the heathen may be safely left to find for themselves food and clothing. They will presently get angry, and assert that but for the violence of the abolitionists slavery would have been done away with long ago ; but you can tell them that the cry of every despot since the world began has been : "Oh, these pests, that turn the world upside down!" and it is a wretched argument from a free American. *Then* they will come down on you with their grand reserve : "Don't you Britishers talk of slavery ; you have plenty slaves in Great Britain and Ireland, a thousand times worse off than the negroes of America!" Alas ! that the sufferings of our countrymen should be a cause of reproach, but it is the misfortune of Britain far more than her crime. But go to the veriest den of pauper misery in England —go to the bleakest of Scotland's wild rocks—go to the most barren wilderness of Ireland—and ask the famished native, if you can find him, to exchange his starving liberty for well-fed slavery, and observe his answer. He will resent your offer with indignation, and tell you that you may feed him, but so you do your horses, and they are horses still ; and that liberty to a Briton, poor and hungry though he be, is liberty still.

REPRESENTATION BY POPULATION.

This condensed speech, delivered during the session of 1857, on the question of representation by population, is selected for publication chiefly because the case is clearly put on its merits, without any admixture of other current political topics; and partly because it fairly represents the line of argument invariably adopted by Mr. Brown on what was then the burning political question in Upper Canada.

Mr. Brown said : At the risk of bringing down on myself the denunciations of the Provincial Secretary, I am about to present to the House another " abstract principle." I am quite sure that if the hon. gentlemen of the treasury benches, with regard to the resolution I have just had the honour of submitting, were under the necessity of yielding to the proposition it enunciated, there is much stronger reason why they should agree to the principle of this. I think that the resolution I am about to place in the Speaker's hands will be acknowledged by every member of this House to be sound in principle. They will say that they approve of it in the abstract, but they do not approve of it when brought into practical operation. This is the main difficulty we encounter in bringing forward this subject, that we are not met fairly by hon. members. They will not say it is wrong abstractly that all persons in the province, whether in Upper or Lower Canada, should be placed on the same level with respect to representation and political rights, but they raise objections to the carrying out of the principle which are far from being just or tenable.

The first' objection is that when, at the time of the union, Upper and Lower Canada were brought together, it was arranged that the two sections should have equal representation in the House of Assembly. But I apprehend that in framing that provision of the Union Act, it was not intended to be for all time. I apprehend that the whole extent of the meaning was, that that arrangement should prevail until the people of Canada desired to change it. It is absurd to say that a time was never to come when a change should be made. No one can say that because the people of Canada at one time formed two separate countries, having now been brought together, they are never to become one, and that the same institutions are not to be applied to the whole country. It must be a mere question of time. Supposing that either section should ever come to have three or four times the population of the other, the most extreme partisan could not assert that it would be just to continue allowing the same representation to each. No one would venture to say so for a moment. If, then,

it is a mere question of time, I am prepared to meet hon. gentlemen opposite on that ground, and to say that that time has now arrived. Hon.
gentlemen say that at the time of the union Lower Canada had a much
larger population than Upper Canada, that a change the other way has
only recently taken place, and that it is exceedingly sharp for Upper
Canada, so soon as she has a preponderance of population, to ask for a
change in the representation. They say that for years, with an inferior
population, we enjoyed the benefits of equal representation, and that the
moment the system works against us, we turn round and demand a change.
I am prepared to show that that argument is not a sound one. Though it
is true that Lower Canada at the time of the union had a population greater
than that of Upper Canada by 170,000, that has been much more than made
up since. And if Lower Canada suffered for a number of years by the
arrangement, Upper Canada has suffered by it a greater number of years,
since the change in the proportions of the respective populations of the two
sections. But the following were the numbers in each year when the census was taken. In Lower Canada, in 1836, the population was 572,827 ; in
1844, 690,782 ; in 1848, 770,000 ; in 1852, 890,262. In Upper Canada, in
1842, the population was 486,055 ; in 1848, 723,292 ; in 1855, 952,002.
From a comparison of these figures, it will be seen that Lower Canada
doubles her population once in twenty-five years, while in Upper Canada
it doubles once in ten years.

Mr. LORANGER : By emigration.

Mr. BROWN : No doubt emigration helps, but whatever be the cause,
the fact is as I have stated it. We have had no census since January, 1852.
Upwards of five years have elapsed since that period, but if we suppose
that the population in each section has progressed in the same ratio of
increase since 1852 as previously, the figures will now stand thus. The
population will be in Lower Canada, 1,068,314 ; in Upper Canada, 1,428,006 ;
showing a preponderance in favour of Upper Canada of 259,792—that is, if
the ratio of increase during the last five years has been the same as during
the previous years.

Hon. Mr. CARTIER : In the same way as Toronto was supposed to have
60,000 inhabitants.

Mr. BROWN : This is no fanciful calculation, like that which assigned
Toronto a population of 60,000. At the census of 1852 the population ot
Toronto was 30,750. If it had last year been 60,000, that would have
indicated an increase of 250 per cent. in ten years. But I stated that the
population of Upper Canada doubled in ten years, which in four years
would give Toronto an addition of about 12,000 inhabitants, as the census
shows to be under the actual fact. I believe, however, that at this time
Toronto has a population of 50,000, or about 8,000 more than I give it by
this calculation. But hon. gentlemen will perhaps say, the ratio of increase
in Upper Canada may have been very great in those previous years, but it
may not have been so great in the last five years. I apprehend that is an
altogether unsound position. We have reason to believe that the ratio of

increase has been greater. Large tracts of the country have been rapidly filled up, and in almost every part of Upper Canada there has been a great increase by immigration and otherwise. But let us suppose that the ratio of increase has not been so great. Let us suppose that we have obtained not more than the actual numbers of the increase the previous years. Even on that supposition we are ahead of Lower Canada to the extent of more than 200,000. Let us take the actual numbers of increase in any one year, say between 1848 and 1849, or between 1849 and 1850, and apply those to the five years which have elapsed since a census was taken, and we will find that the population of Upper Canada exceeds that of Lower Canada by over 200,000 souls. But I apprehend the other mode of calculation was the true way to arrive at the correct result. And there is another view which may be taken. At the time of the union the population of Lower Canada was 175,239 greater than that of Upper Canada. In 1849 the preponderance of population turned to be in favour of Upper Canada, so that if Lower Canada had the disadvantage for seven years, Upper Canada has already had the disadvantage for eight years. And Lower Canada had a disadvantage at worst measured by 175,000, while ours is measured by 359,000. But still further. Suppose we carried this resolution, and a bill founded on it were put in operation as rapidly as possible, other two years must elapse before the equitable system could be introduced, and in the meantime the population of Upper Canada will have grown to be half a million greater than that of Lower Canada. I apprehend, therefore, that as regards population the argument is as clear as it possibly can be, that it is most unjust to the people of Upper Canada that they should be allowed no greater representation than the people of Lower Canada. And I do think that, if ever this country is to occupy the position it ought to hold as a united and homogeneous people, the first step towards obtaining that end is to place the whole people on a like level in the eye of the law. We cannot hope to obtain harmony and good feeling among the people of the whole country until we in Upper Canada feel that we enjoy the same privileges as are possessed by other portions of the community.

There is another argument equally striking with that derived from numbers. I allude to the financial argument. While we are looked upon as two peoples, in respect to the equal division of power between us, it is not so with the money we contribute. The people of Upper Canada are not required to put the same amount exactly into the public coffers as the people of Lower Canada. Their contributions to the public revenue are enormously greater. I have not had time to go over the public accounts recently brought down, with this view, but have prepared an analysis of those of the previous year, which will fully bear out what I have stated. The total sum contributed to the customs revenue in 1855 was £813,819 11s. 3d. Of this there were collected at the ports of Upper Canada £446,968 15s. 7d.; and at those of Lower Canada £366,850 15s. 8d.—nearly £100,000 less. It is quite clear that all the goods entered at Upper Canada ports were for the consumption of Upper Canada; no goods are entered here and sent down for consumption below. But it is not so with regard to the goods entered at the ports of Lower Canada. A large part of the duties collected in Lower Canada is paid by the people of Upper Canada. A great many of our merchants enter their imports at Lower Canada custom houses. And in addition to that, a large number of our merchants all over Upper Canada obtain their goods from below. There are large sections of Upper Canada which are entirely supplied from Quebec and Montreal. A very large portion, then, of the goods on which duties are paid at Montreal and Quebec are for Upper Canada. I have taken considerable pains, by inquiries of leading wholesale houses in Montreal, to discover what proportion of their goods comes to Upper Canada, and have concluded that they send us two-thirds, if not three-fourths, of their whole sales. The whole of the Ottawa district, the Prescott district, the Kingston district—the whole of Upper Canada, in fact, as far as Cobourg—is almost entirely supplied from Montreal and Quebec. And all over Upper Canada, as far west as Hamilton, and London, and Sarnia, you will find Montreal merchants established and supplied with goods on which duty has been paid in Montreal, and which is charged, of course, to those who buy them in Upper Canada. If, then, I take the amount of goods sent to Upper Canada, but entered at Lower Canada ports, at one-half of the whole—I know that I am below the fact, but take it at a half—and we obtain this result with reference to the customs revenue of 1855, that £630,394 was contributed by the people of Upper Canada, and only £183,425 by the people of Lower Canada. I aver that no merchant will deny that this is a fair estimate, that one-half of the duties collected in Lower Canada is paid on goods con-sumed in Upper Canada.

MR. HOLTON : They are purchased in bond.

MR. BROWN : I am quite aware that that is partially the case now, to a greater extent than formerly, but it cannot be questioned that a large proportion of the goods sold wholesale in Quebec and Montreal are sent to the Upper Canada market.

MR. HOLTON : A considerable proportion.

MR. BROWN : I am quite sure that I am below the mark when I say that one-half of the duties collected in Lower Canada are paid by the people of Upper Canada.

MR. HOLTON : I doubt it.

MR. BROWN : If we only said three-eighths, or one-third, we would still find that the proportion contributed by Upper Canada is enormous as compared with the contributions of Lower Canada. Taking it at one-half, however, it will be found that Upper Canada contributes £630,594, and Lower Canada only £183,425; that for every £1 contributed by Lower Canada, Upper Canada contributes £3 8s. 9d.; that the amount per head contributed by Lower Canada is 4s. 1d., and in Upper Canada 13s. 3d. It is often urged by honourable gentlemen opposite—who feel that the injustice we complain of is undeniable, but must find some excuse for the vote they intend to give in this way—we cannot tell what the numbers may be ; it may turn out by the census that the position of the two countries has altogether changed ; that Upper Canada has become the slow country and Lower Canada the progressive one ; we know that at the last census the population exceeded that of Lower Canada by only 62,000 ; let us see a little further, and wait till another census is taken before we make a change. Now, Mr. Speaker, I apprehend that if we seek to make the union permanent, we must adopt representation by population before the disproportion is very great, and not afterwards. It is clear that if we take the view of those hon. gentlemen, and wait till a census is taken, we cannot hope to carry representation by population ; but so sure as you wait till that time, you will have a dissolution of the union. But we may carry the measure now, dependent on a census hereafter to be taken ; we may adopt the principle, and legislate upon it. But if we wait till hon. gentlemen opposite have a census taken in 1862, which will be printed in 1864 —any bill founded on it coming into operation in 1866, nearly ten years hence—I apprehend the population of Upper Canada will be then three millions, and that of Lower Canada little over a million and a half ; the population of Upper Canada to that of Lower Canada will be as two to one. And if the House was then for the first time asked to pass a bill to give Upper Canada a representation double that of Lower Canada, it would be next to impossible to carry it. I believe it is only now, before the disproportion is very great, that we can hope to carry out this measure with any degree of harmony. But every hon. member must see that the change is going on so rapidly that it is high time the difficulty were faced. Every day you put it off you increase the evil. Hon. gentlemen from Lower Canada cannot expect that the people of Upper Canada will always be content to remain in this position. Were they in this position, having 350,000 of a population greater than ours, would they consent to having only the same number of representatives? And if they paid three-fourths of the whole taxation, while Upper Canada only contributed one-fourth, would they not feel the grievance to be still more intolerable? How then can they expect that our people, placed in those circumstances, can submit to have only the same amount of representation? It is clear that the people of Upper Canada cannot allow the matter to rest in its present position. The demand is one of such obvious justice that it is astonishing that any one can refuse it. But I am bound to say that I have never heard a member from Lower Canada getting up and saying that the present system is just. Unfortunately, it has been from Upper Canada members that we have heard the strongest objections to the measure. I can understand Lower Canada members saying, Oh ! we have the advantage, we do not feel there is any occasion for a change, and you will only get it by forcing it upon us. But I am sure no Lower Canadian member will rise and say that if his constituents were placed in that position he would submit to such a state of things.

Mr. Loranger : We did submit to it for a long time.

Mr. Brown : If the hon. gentleman will consider, he will see that

Lower Canada never submitted to the same degree of injustice as is now inflicted upon Upper Canada. They started at the union with an excess of population of 175,000, but it took a very few years to turn the preponderance the other way, and now Upper Canada has an excess of population of 359,000. I put this as a demand of simple justice to the people of Upper Canada. If we were to demand representation in proportion to what we contribute to the revenue, as we pay £3 to £1 that Lower Canada pays, we would have three representatives to their one. But all we ask is that we stand on the same footing, man for man. We ask no more than representation strictly according to population, man for man. How can we expect to go on harmoniously—how can we hope to have the people of this country grow up a vigorous, enlightened, self-governed nation, with institutions such as will do credit to a great people, if we are ever to maintain these distinctions between the two sections of the province? Is it not clear that, if ever this country is to take that position which it ought to do among the nations of the world, it must be by our legislation being for the whole people as one, and by sweeping away those absurd distinctions which thrust themselves into every matter of legislation? We have one government for Upper Canada and another for Lower Canada. Our division of the public money is made on the same principle. So it is with the measures of the government. One day they bring forward something to please Lower Canada, on another day something to please Upper Canada. Instead of our getting quit of those prejudices and sectional feelings, every year is strengthening them more and more. We are asking at the present moment to have a vast new territory added to our borders. Are we to carry out the same principle in reference to this? Are we to say that one half of it shall be for Upper Canada and one half for Lower Canada? Is not this the time when we ought to make our institutions such as will adapt themselves to any future position in which we may be placed? With a view to those great intercolonial questions which are coming up, and those important changes that are being mooted, should we not see that we are prepared for them by having a constitution founded on principles of justice, and fitted to build up a great and prosperous people? Every day furnishes additional proof of the necessity of our adopting this reform without any delay ; and I shall therefore put my resolution into your hands, in the hope that it will be fairly met, and that in dealing with it honourable members will not suffer themselves to be influenced by sectional feelings and prejudices, whether pertaining to Upper or Lower Canada. I move that it be " *Resolved*—That in the opinion of this House the representation of the people in parliament should be based upon population, without regard to a separating line between Upper and Lower Canada."

POLICY OF THE BROWN-DORION ADMINISTRATION.

The following speech was delivered at a public meeting in Toronto a few days after the consummation of the political trick known as the "Double Shuffle," whereby Mr. Brown and his colleagues were obliged to resign, after a four days' incumbency. It is one of a series delivered during that exciting period, and gives on the whole not only a good idea of the then political situation, but also a fair specimen of Mr. Brown's political oratory. The speech deals with the whole political position of Mr. Brown, his colleagues, and his party, as well as with the ministerial ground.

Mr. Brown said : I have very often had occasion to meet my fellow-citizens in such assemblages as this, but I never came to any similar meeting with so clear a conviction as I have this night, that I am entitled to look my countrymen fearlessly in the face, and claim their full approval for every public act I have performed, for every position I have taken since I was returned by you last winter triumphantly to parliament. If there is one single act of my life above all others for which I am prepared to claim credit at the hands of the people of Canada, it is the part I have taken in the startling transactions of the last few days—it is for the bold stand I and my colleagues have just made in attempting to resist what I shall frankly characterize as a deliberate plot against the liberties of the people. I have come before you to-night in order that no time may be lost in placing the whole facts connected with the construction and fall of my administration clearly before the people, and that the taunts and injurious insinuations which have been directed against the conduct of myself and my colleagues may at once receive that complete and conclusive denial which we are able to give them.

But before proceeding to narrate recent transactions as they occurred, I desire to carry the minds of the audience back to the time of the general election, and to trace up events from that date to the present, that it may be clearly seen how the recent ministerial crisis arose, and the manner in which it was met. When I had the honour to be returned as the senior representative of the city of Toronto at the last general election, you will recollect that the invitation to me to become a candidate was the spontaneous act of the electors, and that the requisition bore an array of names far exceeding in numbers and influence any that had ever appeared attached to a similar document in this city. This strong expression of confidence from my fellow-citizens was undoubtedly in a great measure intended to strengthen the hands of the opposition—was intended as a protest against the administration of the day, against their denial of representation by population, their extension of sectarian schools, their extravagance and corruption, against the enormous additions to the public debt, and the alarming increase of taxation. You will also well recollect that the opposition contended that the cure for these evils was to find some common basis of legislative and administrative action on which the affairs of the country could be carried on, without those constant appeals to sectarian and sectional feelings which had been the rule up to this time. And you will recollect that we contended that unless some such common basis were soon found, national bankruptcy must be the inevitable result. We showed that by the existing see-saw system of setting one section against the other and governing through their divisions, our public men were being demoralized, and losing the confidence of their constituents; the men in power for the time being regularly betook themselves to corruption, to a reckless use of the Crown patronage, to an extravagant and corrupt expenditure of the public money to buy up supporters in parliament and to mollify people out of parliament, and all for the noble end of keeping themselves in office. One more trouble was this, that in regard to our school system we were threatened with its complete destruction by the growth of separate sectarian institutions grafted on the system—an evil which struck at the root of national education, and which it was feared would go on from year to year, till at last, by its wasteful expense and its weakening effect, the overthrow of the whole national school system would result. In common with my party, I urged that the only cure was to sweep away those sectarian schools altogether, and have one system which would be accessible to all classes alike, which would respect the religious feelings of all, and would do equal justice to all. You will recollect that, in addition to these views, we of the opposition demanded that a system of thorough retrenchment should be applied to the public finances; that the enormous expenditure should be cut down; that the hoards of public employees, brought into the public service for no other reason than that they were the dependants or relatives of the men in power, should be thinned, their salaries reduced to a proper scale of remuneration, and that stringent economy should be applied to every other part of the public service. On these and many other questions I raised distinct issues, and you endorsed my position by triumphantly electing me your representative.

The same feeling manifested in Toronto swept over Upper Canada. Few candidates dared to go to the polls with a doubtful sound on any of these questions. Three cabinet ministers who made the attempt lost their elections; and when the House met, the majority of the Upper Canada representatives were found firmly associated together in opposition, demanding a fair and final settlement of the differences between Upper and Lower Canada; while many on the treasury benches were found very heartily with us in their consciences, but unhappily willing to let principle rest rather than risk the loss of office for their party. Notwithstanding their defeat in their own section of the province, Mr. John A. Macdonald and his colleagues proceeded to carry on the executive and legislative business of Upper Canada by his large majority of Lower Canadian representatives, but in direct defiance of the recorded votes of the Upper Canada majority. To have men in power dispensing the patronage of the Crown, controlling the executive machinery, and guiding the legislation of Upper Canada—men whose conduct had been condemned at the polls by the people they pretended to govern—was a new and strange spectacle in our legislature, and one that created much dissatisfaction in both sections of the province.

In general legislation we had the same absence of principle, the same wasteful legislation, the same tying up of the members on the part of the administration as in the previous parliament. They were supported by a large majority from Lower Canada, and on that majority their tenure of office depended. But in opposition we had arranged a small but noble band from Lower Canada, with my valued friend, Mr. Dorion, at their head, who stood out against wrong and injustice in every shape. Many of you, I have no doubt, have been within the halls of the legislature, and you must, I think, be ready to acknowledge that the opposition at least did their duty to the country ; that if the administration did succeed in carrying many bad Acts, it was not without vigilant watching and earnest protest across the House. True, it has been charged against us that we wasted the public time ; but I confidently affirm that not an hour was thrown away, and that the whole unnecessary delay which took place arose from the utter incapacity of the administration, from their knowledge that the moral strength was with us, and their dread to face the ordeal which all their measures had to pass. Though they were in office for years, I think it was the 42nd day of the session before one of the measures mentioned in the speech from the throne was laid on the table of the House. Only a few came then, and it was 50, 60, 80, 100, and even 110 days after the opening of the session before some of the government bills named in the speech from the throne were introduced. Indeed, one of the most important of them, the Crown Lands Bill, had not received a second reading at the end of five months.

It was entirely with the administration that the delay took place, and not with us. We might, however, have gone on for some time without being able to shake the solid phalanx of Lower Canadians that sustained the administration ; but disclosures, in the recollection of you all, were made early in the session that not only shocked the people out of doors, but even touched the members of the House. I allude to the startling frauds that had been perpetrated by ministerial candidates at the general election. It was dragged to light that the poll books in many constituencies had been falsified ; that large numbers of names had been fraudulently recorded after the polls were closed ; that a cabinet minister and two other gentlemen were returned for one constituency by 15,000 false votes fraudulently recorded, and that not fewer than 32 seats were claimed from the sitting members on the grounds of fraud, violence or corruption. A partisan Speaker, entrusted with dangerous powers by the election law, and an unscrupulous majority, enabled the administration and their supporters speedily to dismiss nearly the whole of the petitions against the seats of their friends. The petition of the electors of Montreal against the return of Solicitor-General Rose, and the petition of the electors of Verchères against the return of Attorney-General Cartier, and many similar petitions, were at once disposed of by the Speaker, on some frivolous objection to the wording of a recognizance, and all the parties continued in their seats. Mr. Fellowes was declared duly elected by 320 false names of professed citizens of Rome, Albany and Troy, in the state of New York, fraudulently recorded, though with all these votes counted he had but 14 of a majority over his opponent. And the three members for Quebec have been allowed to this hour to discharge the full duties of representatives of the people by virtue of 15,000 false votes. Public confidence in the administration received a rude shock by these proceedings ; and the disclosures of the Public Accounts Committee following immediately on the back, destroyed the last lingering confidence of every independent man. It was elicited that £500,000 of provincial debentures had been sold in England by government at 99¼, when the quotation of the Stock Exchange was 105 @ 107, by which the province was wronged to the extent of £50,000. It was elicited that a member of parliament supporting the government, sold to the government £20,000 of Hamilton debentures at 97¼ that were only worth 80 in the market, by which he pocketed £3,500 without advancing a shilling. It was elicited that large sums were habitually drawn from the public chest and lent to railway companies, or spent on services for which no previous sanction of parliament had been obtained. It was elicited that in the published annual statement of the provincial finances, entries appeared of large sums as disbursed, which were not actually paid for many months after the date of entry, thereby giving a false impression of the state of the public exchequer. It was elicited that notwithstanding the large additions made by them to the customs duties, the ministry had been unable to meet their extravagant expenditures from taxation, and had gone back on obsolete Acts—Acts authorizing the issue of bonds for certain public works, but which works were paid many years ago from surplus revenue, and issued on their strength debentures in one year to the enormous extent of $3,400,000. It was proved that in their short term of four years ministers had doubled the national debt, and had increased the ordinary expenditures from £1,040,000 to £2,350,000. And not only was it proved that the shrievalty of the county of Norfolk had been sold as a piece of merchandise for £500 down, and a secured income of £300 a year, but the scandalous transaction was openly justified in parliament by the Prime Minister and his reckless partisans. The result of these and many similar disclosures was to take from the ministry what little confidence yet remained to them in the country, and even to shatter perceptibly their control over their Lower Canada adherents in the House of Assembly.

The strength of the opposition gradually increased, until at last ministers were defeated on an important part of their financial scheme for the year. They did not resign in consequence of that vote, but a few days later came a blow they could not evade. They had been trying to equivocate on the subject of the seat of government. One member of the cabinet said they were going to Quebec; another said they were going to Montreal; and a third said they were going to Ottawa; and you could not find what really was the policy of the government, if they had any. But at last they came out and stated definitely that they intended to carry the public departments permanently to Bytown; that Bytown should be the future seat of government of united Canada. I held then, as I hold now, that until the great constitutional questions of this union were decided; until we knew distinctly whether the difficulties between Upper and Lower Canada could be overcome; until we saw what was to be the permanent future constitution of this country, it was not expedient to incur the enormous expense of a million of dollars and more for public buildings at a place to which we might never go. At a meeting last night, Mr. Hillyard Cameron stated that I had insulted Her Majesty because I had voted that Bytown should not be the seat of government. Do you think Her Majesty cares a straw where the seat of government of Canada is fixed? People prate about our insulting the Crown because we speak out what nine-tenths of the whole people think; but do you ever hear from such people anything about insulting the people? If ever an insult was given to a people it was when the legislature and government of Canada declared that the Canadian people were unable to settle for themselves where their seat of government ought to be, and that they must go to a colonial minister three thousand miles off, who never had his foot on Canadian soil, to settle it for them under back stairs advice. I voted against that reference; I used every influence to prevent so ungracious a task being thrown on the Imperial government; I urged that they should not act upon the reference; I declared that the people would not abide by their decision if the place selected were unacceptable; and I unhesitatingly voted against Bytown because I felt that the permanent establishment of the government there, and especially at this moment, would be consonant neither with the wishes of the people nor the welfare of the country. The first thing in my consideration was the interests of the whole people of Canada, and not servility to Mr. Labouchere or any other colonial minister. I yield to no man for a single moment in loyalty to the Crown of England, and in humble respect and admiration of Her Majesty. But what has this purely Canadian question to do with loyalty? It is a most dangerous and ungracious thing to couple the name of Her Majesty with an affair so entirely local, and one as to which the sectional feelings of the people are so excited.

Well, the government were defeated on their declared policy of carrying the government to Bytown, and well knowing that a more damaging vote awaited them the following day, Mr. Macdonald and his colleagues placed their resignation in the hands of the Governor-General, who was pleased to accept the same. Immediately on the resignation of his advisers, His Excellency tendered to me, he was pleased to say, as "the most prominent member of the parliamentary opposition." the duty of forming a new administration. I am free to say now, as I have said always, that elevated and honourable—far beyond any merits or expectations of mine—as is the office of Prime Minister of this great country, it is a position I have never sought, and would most joyously have declined when tendered to me. I came into parliament, after eight years of public life, with a full knowledge of the constitutional and social difficulties that marred the harmonious working of the union. I was thoroughly convinced that unless a basis of legislative and administrative action could be found, just to both sections of the province, but removing from the political arena those fertile sources of sectional and sectarian strife that separated the two races and the two provinces, our national animosities would increase from year to year, until at last the national fabric would be rudely rent asunder ; and I entered parliament with a settled determination to grapple with those great evils, and devote my whole energies to their removal. From the first moment I proposed those remedial measures, which I have never ceased to urge up to this very moment, I defy all my opponents to show that for one day, or in one vote, or in one speech, I have swerved from the point at which I aimed. And to those who demur to the bold manner in which I pursued my purpose, and the strong language I have been at times compelled to use, I would simply urge in palliation that a desperate disease needs vigorous treatment ; and that when you have bands of violent opponents, and your views are held to be utterly out of reason, you must speak freely and boldly if you mean not to be crushed. I might have announced general principles, and spoken in soft language to the end of time, and made no progress, but when I went straight to the mark and said to the evil doer, " Thou art the man," then progress was made ; and painful to me, deeply painful, as have been many of the scenes through which I have had to pass, I hold all as repaid, all as justified, by this one fact, that in five years I have been able to construct the strongest administration ever offered to the country, and that administration pledged to settle finally the great questions of sectional strife for the removal of which alone I entered parliament. In carrying on the struggle I never thought of personal advancement ; I cared nothing as to who should settle the vexed questions ; all I sought was to urge their settlement on the public mind until somebody must do it ; and it was little to me that, in urging the cause forward, by my bold tone I left behind me men personally inimical to myself, though compelled to acknowledge my policy. The constant taunt, therefore, of the last two or three years—" He can't form a ministry"—was no taunt to me at all. I did not desire to form a ministry, or to be part of any ministry, but to see the great disturbing questions of my country settled, and then retire to private life. It was not that I doubted my ability to succeed if the opportunity was offered, but much rather would I have seen some other gentleman of the same principles called in my place, and right heartily would I have laboured outside to aid him in his work. But this I could not conceal from myself, that those who had influenced my being called in to form a government were under the fullest conviction that I could no more undertake the task than any gentleman in this room. They had not the slightest doubt that, within an hour of the time when I might make the attempt, I would break down, and that the old set of incapables would be brought back at once with flying colours. That was the undoubted expectation; it was in the mouth of every man on the other side of the House of Assembly. Had I then stated to His Excellency that I would not undertake the task, corruption would have been fixed in power more sturdily than ever, and my opponents would never have ceased to throw my failure in my teeth. They would have said, and said with plausibility: "You profess that your views are the only correct ones; you have all along claimed that if your party only had the chance of forming a government you could carry out your principles; you have now had a chance; you have not succeeded; give up your position; no longer continue to do dog-in-the-manger policy, neither doing the work yourself nor letting us do it."

The case was clear; no alternative was open to me but to accept the task, if I was able to accomplish it. I did undertake the task. I told the Governor-General I would see my friends immediately, and consult them on the subject. I called a meeting of my friends from Upper Canada in the House of Assembly and the Legislative Council, and with one accord, without a dissenting voice, they, with a kindness I will never forget, gave me their cordial and generous support, assuring me that they would stand heartily by me whatever might ensue, in the full conviction that I would stand by my principles and never desert them. The next step was to invite Mr. Dorion to aid me, as leader for Lower Canada. For four years I had acted with that gentleman in the ranks of the opposition, had learned to value most highly the uprightness of his character, the liberality of his opinions, and the firmness with which he carried out his convictions. On most questions of general public policy we heartily agreed, and regularly voted together; on the questions that have divided all Upper Canadians from all Lower Canadians, alone we differed, and on these we had held many earnest consultations from year to year with a view to their removal, and not without arriving at the conviction that when we had the opportunity we could find the mode. Mr. Dorion met me with that frankness I anticipated from him. He at once expressed his willingness to aid me, provided we could come to an understanding on the old points of difference. Mutual friends were called in, grave deliberations were held, and at last we arrived at a groundwork on which we considered we could mutually uphold our principles honourably and consistently, and accept the task of forming a government pledged to the settlement of those great grievances which had for so many years distracted the province. What, then, was the basis of our argument? I will tell you; there is no secret about it, none whatever; and, as you will see, all the statements that we have given up our principles are utterly without foundation. Mr. Dorion's first question to me was, "What are to be the principles of the administration?" I said to him, "Mr. Dorion, you can understand that I can form no administration in which the question of representation by population is not directly meant." Mr. Dorion replied, "I have always admitted, and no person can deny, that population is the only just basis of representation in a popular government, but," he added, "this country is peculiarly situated; we are two races; we have two languages; and my countrymen in Lower Canada are very much alarmed that if representation by population were adopted, Upper Canada might obtain an overwhelming preponderance of representation over them; that the whole of our institutions would be swept away, and the people of Upper Canada would rule us with a rod of iron. For myself," he continued, "I do not participate in these alarms. I think we French Canadians will always be able to hold our own under equal advantages with our British fellow-subjects. I admit, moreover, that the large votes which have been recorded by the representatives of Upper Canada in favour of representation by population compel us to meet the question, or run the risk of evils coming upon the country far greater than we now endure. I admit that we cannot have peace till this question is settled, and I am prepared to meet it fairly and endeavour to settle it. But then," he went on, "to guard my people in Lower Canada, constitutional checks, constitutional protections, must be granted for our local institutions, in some such manner as under the Union Act." I said at once, "I am perfectly willing to agree to any reasonable protections for local interests; the people of Upper Canada desire no advantage over the people of Lower Canada. All we ask is justice; all we ask is that the province shall not be one for purposes of taxation and two for representation; our whole demand is that the same number of electors in Upper Canada and Lower Canada respectively shall return a representative to parliament. We want no advantage whatever over Lower Canada, but we will not submit to the unfair disadvantage now existing. Give us representation by population, and let it by all means be accompanied by every reasonable protection for your local interests and for ours." Earnest discussions followed as to the character of the desired protections and the mode of securing them, whether by a written constitution proceeding direct from the people, or by a Canadian Bill of Rights, guaranteed by Imperial statute, or by the adoption of a federal union, with provincial rights guaranteed, in place of the legislative union that now exists. We had little time to arrange details, and if we had, out of office as we now are, it would be unreasonable to expect that we should disclose them for the benefit of our opponents. It is sufficient that I say to you that we found the strongest reason to believe that we could mature a measure, acknowledging population as the basis of representation, that would be acceptable to both sections of the province; and this measure we pledged ourselves to lay before parliament at its next assembling, and to stand or fall by it as a government.

The next question that came up was that of the seat of government. I said then, as I say now, that the seat of government should be a ministerial question, and should not be left a matter of local contention. I stated to Mr. Dorion that I was willing, along with our measure to settle the vital constitutional questions to which I have referred, to bring down a bill for the settlement of the permanent seat of government as a ministerial question, and to stand or fall by it as part of our policy.

The next question that came up was that of education. Mr. Dorion asked, "What do you propose upon that?" I said, "I want of course that the common school system of Upper Canada shall be made entirely uniform, and that all the children, of whatever denomination, shall come into the same school-room, sit at the same desks, grow up hand in hand, and forget those sectarian animosities that now form the greatest obstacle in the way of our progress as a people." And what was Mr. Dorion's reply? He said, "Undoubtedly, Mr. Brown, these are most desirable ends; but we cannot conceal this from ourselves, that the catholics are a very large and influential portion of the people of Upper Canada; that they now number greatly over two hundred thousand : that they hold that religion should be the basis of all education ; and that they contend that the present national system does not admit of that." I endeavoured to show that our Upper Canada system was based upon the broad principles of revealed religion and morality, and I claimed that we, as protestants, held as strongly as men could hold that religion was the true foundation of education and of every man's act. "But," I went on to argue, "there is this difference between us ; we of Upper Canada hold that while it is desirable that religious truth should be instilled into the child, that religious instruction should go along with secular, we hold also with equal firmness that the state should not give that instruction, and, amid the endless sectarian divisions among us, could not give it—could not step beyond the elements of religious truth, without getting into a sea of sectarian differences utterly inconsistent, and assuming a right in matters of conscience that in no manner pertains to it. We hold that the state should only give secular instruction, and that the parent and the church should give religious instruction." I went on to contend that separatism for one church could not exist without separatism for all churches, and that, with separatism for all, the national system must be broken up, and ignorance prevail among the masses. But, I continued, it is of the utmost importance that in making the system uniform, it should be rendered as acceptable as possible to all denominations ; and if you can show any way in which, without deviating from principle, facilities can be given to the clergy of all denominations for the religious instruction of the children, I am prepared to agree to it. I am prepared to give every possible guarantee that the religious feelings of no child should be interfered with by the teacher, or in the contents of the school books, and if the clergy are willing to give religious instruction to the children of their several flocks, a certain number of hours on so many days of the week, or a certain day in each week, might be fixed on which the children should be discharged from school, and instructed to attend the religious instruction of their pastors. Another suggestion was made. Why, it was suggested, should not a settlement of this fertile cause of discord be found by engrafting on our school system some of the modifications of the Irish national schools? That system, it was urged, was recognized by protestant and catholic alike

to be admirably adapted for a mixed population, because, while it acknowledged the primary principles of Christianity, no sectarian dogmas were
allowed to intrude. These schools were now attended by many hundred
thousand children of all denominations ; and if, by the adoption of the best
portion of that system, it might reconcile all differences, and entirely do
away with the desire for separate schools, why should it not be done ?
My reply was, "I am not intimately acquainted with the details of the
Irish system, but I know that the Presbyterians of Ulster, and the Church
of England in Ireland, and the Roman Catholic hierarchy, do unite in sustaining that system ; we know also that the great mass of the south of
Ireland, Roman Catholic and protestant, are being educated under it ;
every one acquainted with the modern history of Ireland admits the satisfactory results which have flowed from it. And I am prepared, therefore,
to say that I will go with you into a full and generous consideration of that
system, with a view to the introduction here of such modifications from
it as will bring in all denominations in hearty support of the national
schools of Upper Canada ; this investigation to proceed forthwith, and the
bill founded upon it to be a government measure, by which we should stand
or fall."

But one other sectional problem remained to be solved—the final settlement of the seigniorial tenure question of Lower Canada. My friends
Mr. Dorion and Mr. Drummond contended that the government and legislature of Canada were pledged to complete the abolition of the tenure,
and bound to find the means declared by their own statute to be necessary
to that end. I demurred ; I contended that this was a local matter, with
which we in Upper Canada had nothing to do. But let me say frankly,
that I would have been ill-content that the limited sum alleged to be
required should stand in the way of the final removal of sectional strifes,
which are entailing on the country every year, in corruption and extravagance, vastly more than the whole demands of the *censitaires.* Fortunately,
that option was not required. We considered earnestly how the money
could be obtained, and I am happy to say several modes were found by
which the end could be attained without injustice to Upper Canada. We
were prepared to grapple with that question satisfactorily so soon as it
presented itself.

Now, I have put before you the whole story from beginning to end, without evasion, without varnish ; and I fearlessly ask you, did I abandon my
principles ? I appeal to you if the measures here traced in outline, if carefully matured, would not have removed, in a great measure, the animosities
between the two sections of the province, would not have infinitely lessened
the grave difficulties which have distracted our country ; and whether on
this platform all could not have united, Upper and Lower Canadian, French
and British, protestant and catholic ? But let it not be thought that our
whole policy ended here. Coupled with these measures, we were prepared
to initiate a system of rigid economy ; we proposed to reorganize the public
departments, and to set ourselves with earnest determination to consoli-

date the public debt, collect the public arrears, and reduce the burdens of the people. We were prepared to consider anxiously by what means reciprocity could be extended with the United States, and the markets and the ports of the great republic be thrown open to our manufacturers and our ships. At the time of the last election, I had no idea of the state in which the public finances were ; I had no idea that the extravagance was so monstrous, or that the danger to our public credit was so alarming as it is. To bring the finances into a proper state was a task from which the boldest might have shrunk ; but it was one to which, from the very outset, we were prepared to apply ourselves.

The principles and measures of the administration thus satisfactorily arranged, we soon found that the difficulty was not to find gentlemen from Lower Canada prepared to enter a cabinet with that dreadful George Brown in it, but the difficulty was to make room for the capable men whom we desired to have with us, and who were willing to come ; and if the vote which followed our inauguration was joined in by not a few we were unprepared to find in it, we have reason to attribute that fact to other reasons than hostility to our principles. In a very short space of time the cabinet was completed ; and I hesitate not to repeat that, for talent and business capacity, and political influence in the country, it has not been surpassed, if it has ever been equalled, by any government in the history of Canada. I need say nothing of the Upper Canada section. Our fiercest opponents have not dared to question the capacity of a ministry which included the names of Messrs. Sandfield Macdonald, Mowat, Connor, Foley, and Morris. The only cause of regret—and of deep regret to me—was that I was forced to omit from the list the names of several firm friends who were entitled equally with ourselves, by their ability and long service in the cause, to be included in the arrangements ; and I shall remember to the end of my life the kindness and generosity with which those friends voluntarily requested me to forget all personal considerations, and to think only of what would conduce to the best interests of the country. As regards Lower Canada, the *personnel* of the government was to the full as satisfactory. My opponents have indeed preferred the charge, that my alliance with the gentlemen of Lower Canada was but one of these unworthy coalitions that I have so strongly denounced in others ; that all our opinions were antagonistic ; that office was our sole bond of union. I utterly deny the charge ; nothing could be more unjust. On the contrary, I say that never were twelve leading politicians brought together under such circumstances, so naturally and consistently, as were the gentlemen who formed the late cabinet. For five sessions of parliament Mr. Dorion, as the leader of the Lower Canada opposition, and myself as a prominent member of the Upper Canada opposition, had sat side by side, working cordially together so far as sectional differences would permit, and not concealing these, but attempting to remove them. Rarely did I draw a motion which was not shown to him first for his advice, and as uniformly I think did he the same to me. We never rose to vote without knowing beforehand how the other should go, and striving if possible to be on the same side. We had a perfect knowledge of each other's views on all political questions, and the journals of the House will show that for every division in which we stood apart, there were many in which we were found together, and in all the time never did one harsh word pass between us.   On the general policy of the country, on measures affecting the whole province, on questions of commerce, of finance, of retrenchment, of departmental organization, and on all questions of reform and progress, you who witnessed the debates from the galleries must have seen that Mr. Dorion and myself almost entirely agreed, and with a unanimity rarely witnessed in opposition.   The only questions on which we disagreed, as I have said, were those on which all Upper Canadians differ from all Lower Canadians.

Then as regards Mr. Holton.   He was in an admirable position for entering such a government, and the very man to grapple with the augean stable of the Board of Works.   A native of Upper Canada, but entirely identified as a leading merchant of Lower Canada—having long represented Montreal in parliament, and only deprived of his seat for that city by the prevalent election frauds—he was in a position to make his great abilities and experience most serviceable to the government in the task before them. His political opinions have always been those of the advanced liberals of the province, and the policy of the new cabinet was altogether consistent with his often declared opinions.

Mr. Laberge, one of the most talented and eloquent of the Lower Canadian representatives—a gentleman warmly esteemed by every man in the House of Assembly—was also the right man in the right place.   In last parliament as well as in this, he was a firm friend of Mr. Dorion, and went thoroughly with the liberal party led by that gentleman in opposition.

The only three gentlemen to whom the plea of inconsistency could even for a moment be raised, were my friends Messrs. Drummond, Lemieux and Thibaudeau ; and as regards them it is utterly untenable.

And first of Mr. Drummond.   This gentleman for fifteen years has held a foremost place in the political world of Lower Canada.   He was Solicitor-General under Mr. Lafontaine, Attorney-General with Mr. Hincks, and leader of the House for many years ; and though I have often differed *toto cœlo* from the acts of the government with which he was connected, I am bound to admit that in his personal views Mr. Drummond is a genuine liberal.   I think he was the first Lower Canadian in the last parliament who admitted that the demand for representation by population must be met ; and if I recollect rightly he ventured to throw out some such solution for it as that which the late government was prepared to undertake. When the sectarian clause was forced into Mr. Hincks' School Bill of 1850, I well recollect that Mr. Drummond earnestly contended against it, and only yielded when his friends from Lower Canada forced the matter to extremities.   He enjoys the distinguished honour of having been the leader in overthrowing the feudal tenure, and endeavouring to replace it by land tenure more suited to the age ; and he has been the warm advocate of progressive assimilation of the laws and institutions of Upper and Lower

Canada. No man could be in a better position—by his talent, his high standing, his eloquence, his old services, though yet a young man, and especially by his firmness—to stand forward and say to his countrymen that a crisis has arrived in public affairs, and that a bold effort must be made, now or never, to settle the constitutional differences betwen Upper and Lower Canada. I considered it a very great advantage to have the aid of Mr. Drummond.

Then as regards Mr. Lemieux. This gentleman for very many years has held a prominent position in the Quebec district and in parliament. He entered public life with the advanced section of the liberal party, and held strong views on the subject of the feudal tenure. He has never been an extreme man, and his influence in the Quebec district rendered his accession to the ministry of the highest importance. He was a member of Mr. Hincks' cabinet, and of that which succeeded it; and though it is not for me to palliate the acts of those administrations for a moment, still I am bound in candour to say that Mr. Lemieux's personal integrity was never for a moment called in question, and that no man would rejoice more over the introduction of a purer and healthier departmental system than would that gentleman.

One word as to my friend Mr. Thibaudeau. He was a member of the last parliament, as well as of the present; and a more independent, clear-headed, energetic man was not to be found among his compatriots. Mr. Thibaudeau was the first French Canadian on the treasury side of the House who had the courage to get up and assail the government for making George Brown a buga-boo with his countrymen to serve their own petty ends. He told them that the sole difference he found between Mr. Brown and his friends, and Mr. John A. Macdonald and his friends, was, that the former boldly spoke what everybody in Upper Canada thought, while the latter had not the courage to avow their thoughts for fear of losing office. Mr. Thibaudeau holds an excellent position in the Quebec district, and we gladly welcomed his assistance.

A cabinet better fitted to do the work it had undertaken could not possibly have been imagined, and its thorough capacity was undoubtedly the very thing that so aroused the dire alarm of the old place-holders, and drove them to those fierce measures of hostility which will live on record to their disgrace.

Now, gentlemen, I have told you how we got into office; let me tell you next how we got out. On Saturday morning I waited on the Governor-General, and informed him that, having consulted with my friends, and having obtained the aid of Mr. Dorion, I was prepared to undertake the task of forming a new administration. I have no doubt that up to this moment every person connected with the late government, outside and within, felt absolutely certain that I must fail, and that I and my friends must return to our seats and become the butts for their wit during the remainder of the parliament. But in proportion to the confidence of their anticipations, was their indignation and disappointment when they found out their mistake. During the day negotiations went on, and when Saturday night arrived the success was established—the government was formed. On Saturday night I parted with Mr. Dorion, with the understanding that the new government should meet on Monday morning, and on Sunday it was known over town who were to compose the new ministry. At nine o'clock on Sunday night, learning that Mr. Dorion was ill, I went to see him at his apartments at the Rossin House, and while with him the Governor's secretary entered and handed me a despatch. No sooner did I see the outside of the document than I understood it all. I felt at once that the whole corruptionist camp had been in commotion at the prospect of the whole of the public departments being subjected to the investigations of such a second Public Accounts Committee. I comprehended at once that the transmission of such a despatch at such an hour could have but the one intention, of raising an obstacle in the way of the new cabinet taking office, and I was not mistaken. The contents of Sir Edmund's memorandum are before the country, and I will venture to assert that the document is without a parallel—that nothing so indefensible was ever directed by the representative of the Crown to one charged with the formation of a responsible cabinet under a British parliamentary constitution. We have all heard of Sir Francis Bond Head's high-handed proceedings ; but in his days there was no pretension to responsible government—the system was an oligarchy. We have heard, too, of Sir Charles Metcalfe's doings ; how, to carry his personal point, he dismissed his cabinet while commanding large majorities in both Houses of Parliament ; but I apprehend there was nothing in Sir Charles Metcalfe's first movement at all approaching in wrongful assumption, or in danger to the rights of the people, this attempt of Sir Edmund Head to lay down conditions precedent, to enforce a stipulation as the price of office on men constitutionally summoned to advise the Crown. His Excellency is the representative of Her Majesty in this province, and it is my duty as a subject of Her Majesty to speak of her representative with all due respect ; but I would not be true to you or to the cause I represent did I hesitate to explain the whole transaction, and to show you that throughout it all my colleagues and I sought only to maintain the rights and liberties of the people, and that the course we took was the only course open to us. What right had the Governor-General to lay down conditions, on which only I would be allowed to assume office ? What right had he to settle beforehand the measures that must be taken up or laid aside ? Why insult us by inviting us to become the constitutional advisers of the Crown, if we were only to execute his mandates ? And why lead us to believe that we had his whole confidence, that we should enjoy all the influence to which men in our position were entitled, and then at the close of four days' negotiations, on the very eve of being sworn in, throw this missile of war at our heads ? From the moment I read His Excellency's despatch, I felt that I would be a traitor to my own position and to the rights of the people, if I submitted to enter office shackled by any stipulations whatever imposed upon me by the Crown. I felt that I could only accept office with the full powers of Prime Minister, or not accept it at all. I felt that my submission in this case might be a precedent for worse concessions by other ministers hereafter. I felt that I ought not to go into office shackled by any conditions : that after going in, it was my duty to advise His Excellency on all public affairs, and if he refused my advice, at once to retire. I resolved that the Governor-General's memorandum must be met at once and by myself, without reference to my colleagues, and very early on Monday morning I sent this note to His Excellency : "Mr. Brown has the honour to acknowledge receipt of His Excellency the Governor-General's note of last night, with accompanying memorandum. Before receiving His Excellency's note Mr. Brown had successfully fulfilled the duty entrusted to him by the Governor-General, and will be prepared, at the appointed hour this morning, to submit for His Excellency's approval the names of the gentlemen whom he proposes to be associated with himself in the new government. Mr. Brown respectfully submits that, until they have assumed the functions of constitutional advisers of the Crown, he and his proposed colleagues will not be in a position to discuss the important measures and questions of public policy referred to in His Excellency's memorandum." This was the only manner in which I could meet His Excellency's memorandum, and it was for him now to break off the negotiations if he had not entire confidence, and was not prepared to give us all the support that other men in our position had at all times received. He gave no such intimation—he admitted that the position I had taken was the truly constitutional one. At half-past nine on Monday morning I met my colleagues and read to them His Excellency's memorandum and my answer to it. With one voice they said I had taken the only course open to me with honour, and they cordially endorsed what I had done. We then sat down deliberately to consider what was the object in sending such a document at such a moment, and what course it was our duty to pursue. We came unanimously to the conclusion that it was written purposely to raise a bar in the way of our accepting office, and that the paragraph in regard to dissolution was the one on which issue was expected to be raised. It ran thus : "The Governor-General gives no pledge or promise, express or implied, with reference to dissolving parliament. When advice is tendered to His Excellency on this subject he will make up his mind according to the circumstances then existing and the reasons then laid before him." Now, what need was there for this instruction ? Whoever thought of demanding any such pledge ? It was time enough when the necessity arose for us to demand a dissolution, and for His Excellency to assent to or refuse our demand. Clearly the expectation was, that the moment we read that warning sentence we would get alarmed and post down to Government House and demand a promise that if we could not command a majority in the present House we should have an immediate dissolution. And why did you not do so? asked Mr. John A. Macdonald yesterday in the House of Assembly. Well he knew why ; well he knew that such a demand would have been utterly unconstitutional ; and well he knew that he was standing ready to raise the cry of "The prerogative in danger !" the moment we should do it.

Let us suppose that before being sworn in we had gone to the Governor-General and demanded a dissolution, what would his answer have been? He would of course have answered in the words of his letter, "I cannot pledge myself; when the case arises I will hear your arguments, and judge from them." And then suppose we had answered, "That will not do; we must either have a distinct pledge or we won't accept office." What then? Only this, that we would have been out of pain at once, and we must have risen that night in the House and declared that we were called to form a government—that we did form one and a powerful one—but that the Governor-General would not pledge himself to a dissolution, and we therefore declined to be sworn in. Only fancy then the triumph with which Mr. John A. Macdonald would have risen! "What!" he would have exclaimed, "not content with your great powers as advisers of the Crown, would nothing serve but to tear from His Excellency's hands the prerogative of his royal mistress? You would not consent to be sworn in, forsooth, until you bound the Governor-General hand and foot to dissolve parliament! Before the necessity had arisen—without the facts before him, without any knowledge of what changes might arise in the meanwhile—he must pledge himself, at all hazards and in all events, to dissolve the legislature at your bidding! Did he not promise you his whole confidence, the entire authority of men in your position? Did he not promise to receive and consider your advice when the necessity for dissolution arose? Ah! it is clear you felt your government impossible, and you took this means of evading the task you have always been telling us you were prepared to undertake!"

No, gentlemen, we knew our position better than to make such a mistake as this; we were not willing that the Governor-General should encroach on our domain, but we were quite as unwilling to encroach on his. And besides our general knowledge of what our proper course should be, there was one notable circumstance that prevented our falling into this particular snare. In 1843, precisely the same trap was set by the astute hand of Mr. Wm. H. Draper for Messrs. Baldwin and Lafontaine; and in consequence of its success, the liberal party were kept five years out of power. It was rather too much to expect that such a game could be played twice with effect; no one but the original author of the device could possibly have fancied so.

Let me state the case of 1843. Messrs. Baldwin and Lafontaine learned by accident that Sir Charles Metcalfe had made an important appointment without consulting them. They properly deemed this in direct hostility to constitutional government; and they waited forthwith on the Governor-General and told him so. He refused to yield, and they declared they could not retain office without a change in this matter. They resigned; Sir Charles called Mr. Draper to his counsels, and raised the cry of the prerogative. In his explanation to the House of Assembly, the Governor-General thus stated the case: "On Friday Mr. Lafontaine and Mr. Baldwin came to the Government House, and after some other business, and some preliminary remarks as to the cause of their proceeding, demanded of the Governor-General that he should agree to make no appointment, and no offer of an appointment, without previously taking the advice of his council." . . . In other words, that the patronage of the Crown should be surrendered to the council. . . . The Governor-General replied that he would not make any such stipulation, and could not degrade the character of his office, nor violate his duty, by such a surrender of the prerogative of the Crown. Gentlemen, we had those words fresh in our memories, and we perfectly understood how they could be made to apply to us, if we asked a pledge of a dissolution. We had a salutary recollection of the long years of misrule that resulted from the trick of 1843, and we were willing to risk our being turned out of office within twenty-four hours, but we were not willing to place ourselves constitutionally in a false position. We distinctly contemplated all that Sir Edmund Head could do and that he has done ; and we concluded that it was our duty to accept office, and throw on the Governor-General the responsibility of denying us the support we were entitled to, and which he had extended so abundantly to our predecessors. True, we might have declined office without an explanation, but we all felt, I believe, that this would have been very injurious to our position before the country, and that no option was left, consistent with our dignity and the interests of the public, but to be sworn in.

I need not tell you that we had not taken possession of the council chamber an hour, when the war commenced against us. The late ministers had telegraphed all over the country for their friends ; a special train was run on Sunday over the Grand Trunk to bring them up in time ; and the Governor-General's name was freely used in assuring certain members that if the new government were voted down from the start there would be no dissolution of parliament, but let them get over the session, and that dread alarm of such a House, a dissolution, was inevitable. With the ten ministers absent from the House, and many of our friends away unsuspicious of so unprecedented a proceeding, a vote of want of confidence in the new government was immediately moved at the instigation of the late ministers, and sustained, I need hardly remind you, by these gallant gentlemen with dastardly assaults, false and fierce, against absent men. No doubt we will live to repay them, but I trust in more manly fashion. The following morning the cabinet advised a dissolution. His Excellency demanded reasons in writing. They were furnished ; our advice was refused, and we instantly resigned. Not in a hundred and fifty years of English history, nor in the whole history of Canada, can a single case be found in which men in our position were refused a dissolution. When His Excellency called on me to form a government, well he knew that I was in the minority of the House, and that I had so assailed the electoral frauds by which so many of the members were returned, that it was next to impossible to proceed without a general election. Why then expose us to the mockery of a hollow invitation? And why not say frankly at once that he would not grant a dissolution? Mr. Hincks went to the country in 1851 ; at the opening of his second session he was defeated, but the Governor-General came down suddenly and prorogued the House, and gave him one more chance for life. The McNab government followed in September, 1854 ; in 1855 three members retired, and His Excellency consented to a reconstruction ; in 1856 the government was beaten twice and twice resigned ; but His Excellency would not accept, and Ross, Drummond and Cauchon, nay, the Premier himself, were all driven out, but still a reconstruction was allowed, with Colonel Taché at the head. In 1857 Lemieux, Territt, Ross, and the Premier were all driven away ; but another reconstruction was at once granted, with Mr. Macdonald as Prime Minister. Unable to fill up the vacant offices, suddenly and inconveniently, in the middle of the financial crisis, Mr. Macdonald demanded a general election, and at once he obtained it. And though three ministers were beaten in Upper Canada, still His Excellency permitted the thing to go on by the aid of irresponsible members of the Upper House, and an office left vacant from pure inability to fill it up. He permitted a session of five months to be wasted by the utter incapacity of his advisers ; he submitted to all their departmental blundering and mismanagement ; but he refused to the opposition the only favour they asked, a fair appeal to the people against the misdeeds of his late ministers. If a designed intention had existed to get the leaders of the opposition out of the House, and then pass the numerous obnoxious bills before parliament, no more direct way could have been taken than that followed by His Excellency.

And to cap the climax of the affair, on dismissing our government, he sent for a gentleman—and he a Lower Canadian—to form a new one who had not and never had one follower in the House, and who was only known to public life as the author of the famous Grand Trunk prospectus, offering $11\frac{1}{2}$ per cent. dividend to all who were fortunate enough to get shares ! I submit to you that a grievous wrong has been done throughout this matter, and I ask you if you will not show your condemnation of such work by returning me again with an overwhelming majority ? I ask you if the government I formed ought not to have had a fair trial ; that at least we should have had time to appear in our seats to vindicate our policy : and if so, I urge you to put all your hands to work, and we will get another and better opportunity ere many months elapse. In one way this strange crisis has done great good ; we have found a method of settling the differences between Upper and Lower Canada ; we have formed a strong party in opposition, in both sections, on the basis laid down by the late government ; and when parliament meets a few months hence, the effect will soon be shown.

Gentlemen, I had a great deal more to say, but I am exhausted with heat and recent indisposition, and I can proceed no further. I shall address you many times in the course of the election contest, and it only now remains for me to thank you very cordially for your kind attention.

ANTI-SLAVERY.

The following speech was delivered by Mr. Brown, at Toronto, on the evening of February 3rd, 1863, in moving the second resolution. Its delivery was frequently interrupted by the hearty plaudits of the large and enthusiastic audience.

MR. BROWN said : I have frequently enjoyed the privilege of addressing my fellow-citizens in the public halls of our city, but I say sincerely that I never before experienced such heartfelt pleasure in appearing on a public platform as I do on this occasion. The Anti-Slavery Society of Canada has been many years in existence, but I see around me not a few who, long before its establishment, were the earnest and untiring friends of the down-trodden slave. For twenty-five years many of us have striven together to promote the cause of emancipation, and long, long years we laboured almost without hope to arouse our neighbours to the frightful position they occupied in the eyes of the Christian world, and to goad them on, if possible, to some vigorous efforts towards the suppression of the inhuman traffic that disgraced their land. How earnestly did we watch every passing event in the republic that promised some little amelioration to the condition of the slave, or some additional influence to the friends of emancipation. Sad, hopeless work it appeared to be for many, many years. But at last light broke in upon the scene, and now what a change has passed over the whole picture ! What man among us ten years ago, ay, five years ago, ever hoped to live to see the day when the cause of emancipation would occupy the position it does at this moment in the American republic.

For several years it has happened that I have not been able to be present at the annual meetings of this society ; but well do I recollect the work we had on hand at the last meeting I attended. Our work then was to mark and deplore the increasing power of the slave interest over the federal government, to denounce the infamous Fugitive Slave Law as a disgrace to civilization, and to express our hearty sympathy with the noble but inconsiderable band of true men throughout the republic who were standing firm for the cause of liberty. That was a very short time ago ; but what an entire revolution have these few brief years witnessed. Now we have an anti-slavery president of the United States. Now we have an anti-slavery government at Washington. Now we have an anti-slavery congress at Washington. Already slavery has been abolished in the District of Columbia. At last a genuine treaty for the suppression of the slave trade has been signed at Washington with the government of Great Britain, and for the first time in her history the penalty of death has been enforced in the republic for the crime of man-stealing. Then, the black republics of Hayti and Liberia have been recognized by the United States as independent powers ; and, even more important still, the vast territories of the United States have been prohibited by law from entering the republic except as free states. And the climax was reached a month ago when Abraham Lincoln, as President of the United States, proclaimed that from that moment every slave in the rebel states was absolutely free, and that the republic was prepared to pay for the freedom of all the slaves in the loyal states. The freely elected government and legislature of the United States have proclaimed that not with their consent shall one slave remain within the republic.

Was I not right, then, when I said that we ought to rejoice together to-night? I congratulate you, Mr. Chairman (Rev. Dr. Willis), on the issue of your forty years' contest here and on the other side of the Atlantic on behalf of the American slave. I congratulate the venerable mover of the first resolution (Rev. Dr. Burns), who for even a longer period has been the unflinching friend of freedom. I congratulate the tried friends of emancipation around me on the platform, and the no less zealous friends of the cause throughout the hall, whose well-remembered faces have been ever present when a word of sympathy was to be uttered for the downtrodden and oppressed. Who among us ever hoped to see such a day as this? And does it not well become us to meet as we are now doing to proclaim anew our earnest sympathy with the friends of freedom in the republic, our hearty gratification at the great results that have been accomplished, and our gratitude to the men who have staked life and fortune on the effort to strike shackles from the bondman. I care not to pry narrowly into the motives of all those who have contributed to bring about this great change in the republic. I care not to examine critically the precise mode by which it has been brought about. I care not to discuss the arguments by which it has been promoted or defended in the republic. What to us signifies all this? We see before us the great fact that the chains have already fallen from the hands of tens of thousands of human chattels ; we see that if the policy of the present government at Washington prevails, the curse of human slavery will be swept from the continent for ever ; and our hearts go up with earnest petitions to the God of battles that He will strengthen the hands of Abraham Lincoln and give wisdom to his councils.

But we have yet another duty to perform. In the face of all the wonderful progress that the anti-slavery cause has made in the United States —in defiance of the decided emancipation measures of Mr. Lincoln's government—it is the fact, the strange and startling fact, that professing abolitionists—nay, genuine abolitionists, men who have done much for the cause of negro emancipation—are to be found, both here and in Great Britain, who not only refuse their sympathy to Mr. Lincoln, but regard the slave-trafficking government of Jefferson Davis with something very much akin to sympathy and good-will.

As you are aware, I have recently returned from a visit to Great Britain, and I am bound to say that I was astonished and grieved at the feeling with which I found the contest now waging in the United States generally regarded. In my six months' journeyings through England and Scotland I had opportunities of conversing with a very large number of persons in all positions of life, and I am sorry so say that, while there were many marked exceptions among men of thought and influence, the general sympathy was very decidedly on the side of the south. I entirely agree with you, that this feeling has not originated from any change in the popular mind of Great Britain on the subject of African slavery; on the contrary, I believe that the hatred of slavery, and the desire for emancipation all over the world, are nearly as strong as ever. In almost every one of the hundreds of discussions in which I was a participator, it was again and again repeated by all that, could they believe African slavery to be the cause of the civil war, and that Mr. Lincoln was sincerely desirous of bringing the horrid traffic to an end, they would promptly and heartily give their sympathy to his cause. But the truth is, that the systematic misrepresentation of the London *Times* and other journals, commenced shortly after the outbreak of the civil war and diligently kept up ever since, has perverted the public mind of Great Britain, and the most amazing misconceptions as to the true nature of the struggle are everywhere met with, and that even among the most candid and generous-minded men.

I have said, that to this general state of feeling there are many eminent exceptions—that there are many men in Britain who perfectly comprehend the whole merits of the contest, and pre-eminent among them, I believe, stand the members of the British cabinet. I entirely agree with you, that the whole policy and conduct of the British government throughout the war has been worthy of all praise; and I do think it is much to be regretted that our neighbours across the lines have not viewed aright the wise course it has pursued, but have permitted their journals and some of their public speakers to indulge in accusations as groundless as impolitic. When the impartial history of this civil war shall be written, that page of it which will record the part taken in it by the British government—its dignified disregard of contumely, its patient endurance of commercial distress and individual suffering and destitution directly resulting from the war, its firm persistent resistance of the seductions of other powers to intrude unasked in the domestic feuds of the republic—will, I am persuaded, stand out as an imperishable monument to the wisdom and justice of the men who held the helm. Whatever misconceptions may exist among the people, there have been no misconceptions on the part of the British government; firmly and discreetly it has pursued the only course open to it, that of scrupulous neutrality. That the sympathies of the people of England have not been with the north in the present struggle—that those who urged the American people to throw off the disgrace of slavery have not acted up to their own principles when their advice was followed and the contest came —that aid and encouragement have been largely given to the slaveocracy by the subjects of Great Britain—we are forced to concede and to deplore ; but the British people are a free people—over these things their govern. ment has little or no control—and what has been done by the British government as a government has been all that any just American could demand.

Now, I humbly conceive that in all this we, the anti-slavery men of Canada, have an important duty to discharge. We who have stood here on the borders of the republic for quarter of a century protesting against slavery as the "sum of all human villainies"—we who have closely watched every turn of the question—we who have for years acted and sympathized with the good men of the republic in their efforts for the freedom of their country—we who have a practical knowledge of the atrocities of the "peculiar institution," learnt from the lips of the panting refugee upon our shores—we who have in our ranks men well known on the other side of the Atlantic as life-long abolitionists—we, I say, are in a position to speak with confidence to the anti-slavery men of Great Britain—to tell them that they have not rightly understood this matter—to tell them that slavery is the one great cause of the American rebellion, and that the success of the north is the death-knell of slavery. Strange, after all that has passed, that a doubt of this should remain! The north declares that it was the determination to perpetuate and extend slavery that caused the south to appeal to arms; the south declares that the determination of the north to abolish slavery caused the election of Mr. Lincoln, and that this is the great end and aim of his government; the whole thirty millions of the American people unite in declaring slavery to be the one great issue of the war ; but these good people, thousands of miles off, who never had their foot on American soil, are satisfied that they know better, and that slavery has no concern in the matter! Tens of thousands of lives have been lost, hundreds of millions of treasure have been spent, the peace and happiness of every family in the land has been broken up; but it seems the combatants are in entire ignorance of the cause of quarrel ; the whole contest is a mere strife for power !

Now, we who have watched the struggle from the commencement, and from day to day, almost from hour to hour, well know how erroneous all this is. We can look back on the time when the abolitionists of the states were a small and feeble party ; we can recollect when James G. Birney, the abolition candidate for the presidency, received no more than six thousand votes in the whole republic; we can recollect when noble old John Quincy Adams stood almost alone battling in congress for the first right of freedom—the sacred right of petition ; we can remember how completely and how ruthlessly the slave influence dominated over the whole affairs of the republic : and well can we remember when the first ray of hope broke in upon us when the slaveocracy, growing insolent in their day of power, rushed to their own destruction by the repeal of the Missouri compromise that laid down the line of demarcation between slavery and freedom. That act did more for the cause of emancipation than tongue can tell. The fierce contests fought in Kansas and Nebraska between freedom and slavery added immensely to the strength of the friends of freedom ; and the atrocious Fugitive Slave Law, compelling the freemen of the north to become slot-hounds on their own farms after the human chattels of the slave-holders of the south, roused a feeling deep and strong throughout the free states. It was soon apparent that the time had come when the issue between freedom and slavery for supremacy in the republic must be fought and won. That feeling increased and strengthened until it became overwhelming in the northern states ; and under its influence the great republican party was formed, and Abraham Lincoln selected as their standard-bearer in the presidential contest.

Now, let it be well remembered that Mr. Lincoln was not elected as an abolitionist in the sense ordinarily applied to that term. He did not openly avow that slavery was an outrage on all law, human and divine, and that every law or constitution framed to legalize and establish it should be treated with contempt, and the vile traffic swept away. Mr. Lincoln and the party who elected him did not go that length. They said, we want nothing more than the constitution gives us; we wish to abolish slavery wherever we have control under the constitution ; we wish to restrict slavery within its present domain, so far as the constitution permits us to do ; we wish to exercise our constitutional right to prevent the extension of slavery over the territories of the republic not yet admitted as states of the union. That was the sum and substance of the republican demand ; they stood by the constitution. And when it is asked why the northern men have always averred that they were fighting for the union and the constitution, and not for abolition, it should be borne in mind that the constitution gave them all the power that they could possibly desire. Well did they know, and well did the southerners know, that any anti-slavery president and congress, by their direct power of legislation, by their control of the public patronage, and by their application of the public moneys, could not only restrict slavery within its present boundaries, but could secure its ultimate abolition. The south perfectly comprehended that Mr. Lincoln, if elected, might keep within the letter of the constitution and yet sap the foundation of the whole slave system.. And they acted accordingly. A great and final effort was resolved on by the slave power for the mastery of the union ; and it was insolently proclaimed that if the northern electors dared to elect Mr. Lincoln to the presidential chair, the south would secede from the union, and enforce their secession by an appeal to arms. The present rebellion then was conceived and planned, not only before Mr. Lincoln appeared at Washington, but previous to his election ; it was his determination to restrict the limits of slavery so far as he had the power under the constitution, and no further. Well, the north was not intimidated by the threats of the south, and Mr. Lincoln was elected. From that day actual revolution began. Months before he was sworn in, the southerners, with the connivance of a weak democratic president, commenced their preparations for revolt. Arms and supplies were distributed over the south, and before Mr. Lincoln reached Washington, the tocsin of civil war had been sounded. The first blow was struck by the southerners—it was struck at Fort Sumter—although Mr. Lincoln had not yet taken the slightest step in the direction of emancipation. The preservation and perpetuation of slavery was the one cause why that blow was struck ; and, had any doubt on that point existed, the speech of Mr. Stephens, Vice-President of the confederate states, delivered at Savannah in March last, would have effectually removed it. He said :

" Last, not least, the new constitution has put at rest *for ever* all the agitating questions relating to our peculiar institution—African slavery as it exists among us, the proper status of the negro in our form of civilization. This was the immediate cause of the late rupture and present revolution. Jefferson, in his forecast, had anticipated this as the ' rock upon which the old union would split.' He was right. What was conjecture with him is now a realized fact. But whether he fully comprehended the great truth upon which that rock stood and stands may be doubted. The prevailing ideas entertained by him and most of the leading statesmen at the time of the formation of the old constitution were that the enslavement of the African was in violation of the laws of nature, that it was wrong in principle, socially, morally and politically. . . . Those ideas, however, were fundamentally wrong. They rested upon the assumption of the equality of races. This was an error. It was a sandy foundation ; and the idea of a government built upon it—when ' the storm came and the wind blew, it fell.' Our new government is founded upon exactly the opposite ideas ; its foundations are laid, its corner stone rests, upon the great truth that the negro is not equal to the white man; that slavery subordination to the superior race is his natural and moral condition. This, our new government, is the first in the history of the world based upon this great physical, philosophical and moral truth."

Here the issue between north and south is clearly and frankly stated, and those who sympathize with the south can see very plainly what it is they are aiding to establish. But the question is constantly put, Why, when Mr. Lincoln and his government saw that the southern states were determined to leave the union, did they not let them go in peace, and save the fearful effusion of blood that has been witnessed ? To this I think it might be enough for an American to reply, Why did not England let the thirteen states go? Why did not Britain let Ireland go? Why did not Austria let Hungary go ? Why does not the Pope let the people of Rome go ? We have often heard of parts or sections of states desiring to secede, sometimes with reason and sometimes without, but who ever heard the central authority of any country patiently acquiescing in the dismemberment of their land ? Such a concession is not in human nature, however reasonable the demand for it. But it is contended the south had the right to secede ; the republic was but a collection of independent states surrendering for a while their sovereignty, but holding the right to reassume it at any moment. Now, I do not think it worth while to waste

time in discussing this point. I have failed to meet with any proof that
the federation was assented to for a limited time. The argument appears
to rest simply on the plea that as the states freely chose to enter the
union, so may they freely choose to depart. Well, Scotland freely entered
into union with England ; but does that prove that Scotland can separate
when she chooses? Ireland entered the union with Great Britain, not
over-willingly ; but does that prove that she can leave it when she chooses?
No doubt the southern states, like Scotland or Ireland, may break the
compact and go—*if they have the power*—but success would be revolution,
and failure rebellion. Governments exist for the good of the whole people.
We once had a glorious revolution in England ; and assuredly, when the
government of any country ceases to be administered for the essential
benefit of the people, a revolution is the sound and politic remedy. The
world no longer believes in the divine right of either kings or presidents to
govern wrong ; but those who seek to change an established government
by force of arms assume a fearful responsibility—a responsibility which
nothing but the clearest and most intolerable injustice will acquit them
for assuming. The southern states plead as their excuse for revolution
that Abraham Lincoln was duly and constitutionally elected president of
the republic, and that the permanency of slavery was thereby placed in
danger. Is that a plea to be accepted by the civilized world in the second
half of the nineteenth century? Revolutions were wont to be efforts of
the oppressed to deliver themselves from bondage ; but here is a revolution to perpetuate slavery, to fasten more hopelessly than ever the chains
of servitude on the limbs of four millions of human beings. Is it with that
Christian England can sympathize? Ought not an outburst of indignation
at such a spectacle be heard from every land? There is no justice, no
right, in the case of the southern slave-holders—it is simply a question of
might. If they have the power to go, assuredly they will go. But
whether they go or stay is now of comparatively little moment. What
does concern us, and what must rejoice every true-hearted man in Chris-
tendom is, that go when they may, they will go without their slaves. We
owe that much at any rate to Abraham Lincoln and his friends.

But let us return to the question, Why did not Mr. Lincoln let the
slave states go? And before proceeding to examine that question from an
anti-slavery point of view, will you permit me to make a digression, and,
speaking for myself and not for any other, to give an answer with which I
am persuaded every true British heart ought to sympathize. We all know
the prejudice at this moment against the United States in Great Britain
and Canada ; we know well all that is said, and that unfortunately can be
said with too much truth, as to the statesmanship of the republic, as to the
tone assumed by the Americans towards foreign nations, as to the defects
in their political system, and as to the conduct of the civil war ; but were
all that is alleged on these scores true—were vastly more than is averred
true—I do think that no man who loves human freedom and desires the
elevation of mankind could contemplate without the deepest regret a failure

of that great experiment of self-government across the lines. Had Mr. Lincoln consented to the secession of the southern states, had he admitted that each state could at any moment and on any plea take its departure from the union, he would simply have given his consent to the complete rupture of the federation. The southern states and the border states would have gone—the western states might soon have followed—the states on the Pacific would not have been long behind—and where the practice of secession, once commenced, might have ended, would be difficult to say. Petty republics would have covered the continent ; each would have had its standing army and its standing feuds ; and we too, in Canada, were it only in self-defence, must have been compelled to arm. I for one cannot look back on the history of the American republic without feeling that all this would be a world-wide misfortune. How can we ever forget that the United States territory has, for nearly a century, been an ever open asylum for the poor and persecuted of every land. Millions have fled from suffering and destitution in every corner of Europe to find happy homes and over-flowing prosperity in the republic ; and I confess I know no more wonderful or more delightful spectacle than to pass, as you easily can, for thousands of miles along the high-roads of the republic, and witness the wonderful material success that has been achieved by men who, a few short years ago, landed on the American shore, for the most part without means and without education. Is there a human being who could rejoice that all this should be ended ? And who could fail bitterly to regret the effect of such a catastrophe on the polities of Europe ? Who can tell how much influence the great American republic has exerted on the liberties of the world ? Circumstances have caused me to search deeply and often into the debates of the British parliament, and I confess I have been frequently struck by the constant references, in the speeches of our greatest statesmen for nearly a century past, to American practices, American precedents, and American institutions. These may not have been copied by the mother country, but it is impossible to doubt that on many important questions the free theories and the free examples of America have greatly influenced for good the legislation of Great Britain. And if this has been the case under the good government of Britain, what influence may not have been exerted upon the despotic systems of the European continent ? Can the hosts of Frenchmen, Austrians, Prussians, Italians, and other Europeans, who found homes in the United States, have failed to waft across the Atlantic, or to carry back with them to their native lands, the new ideas of popular rights acquired in the land of their adoption ? And would it not be sad indeed if the echo of these ideas, so often heard on the continent in the shape of demands for extended popular rights and free constitutions, could be met by the despotic rulers of Europe with the taunt to look at America and learn how free constitutions and popular rights ended in disruption and anarchy ? Who can deny that the American constitution, as framed by the fathers of the revolution of '76, was one of the noblest conceptions that ever emanated from the human mind ? And if one must regret that the fruit of late years has not been worthy of the tree, who shall say how much of that we are compelled to deprecate may not be directly traced to the cankerworm of slavery?

With a free constitution, the United States has not been a free country. One half has been entirely surrendered to slavery, and the other half has been subject to the same malign influence. The southern states have been knit together by one common bond—touch the slave interest, and the whole south was in a flame and drawn together as one man. The northern states, on the contrary, had no such universal interest to bind them together, and through their divisions as Whigs and democrats, liberals and conservatives, the south always continued to hold the balance of power and control the national policy of the union. The south has had entire sway at Washington. No man could be successful in public life, no man could hope to rise to eminence in the administration of affairs, unless he knelt at the southern shrine, and maintained with his whole strength the peculiar institution. Nothing could be more corrupting, more utterly demoralizing, to the public men of the north than the choice constantly presented to them—adhere to your northern principles, and ruin your career; abandon your principles and bow your neck to slavery, and the gates of the White House are open to you. Nor was the slave influence confined to the public arena—it permeated every walk of life. The vast cotton trade and the supplying of goods to the slave-holder extended their ramifications all over the union; their influence was felt in the store, the work-shop, the lecture room, the press—ay, even in the pulpit. Every one was made to feel the potency of cotton; and a style of argumentation in defence or palliation of slavery was heard everywhere from men who, on any other question, would have scorned to advance such miserable sophistries. The whole union was debauched by the cotton influence; and it does appear to me that it would be unreasonable and unjust to test the American constitution by its working while controlled by influences so malign and injurious. Let the friends of freedom rejoice that at least the hope of a better state of things begins to dawn, and that, freed from the curse of human slavery, the American people may yet show themselves worthy of their high origin, and take their right place among the free nations of the world.

We in Upper Canada cannot help having some sympathy with the northerners in their peculiar position; for although we have no south we have an eastern influence to contend with—an eastern minority that rules the western majority, that controls our public affairs, and dictates terms to our public men as the price and the penalty of official success. None know better than the people of Upper Canada the demoralizing scenes that may be witnessed in the public arena under an influence like this. Let it not be imagined for a moment, from my speaking thus, that I am a republican either in theory or practice. I am persuaded that no one can have studied closely and impartially the republican system of the United States, and compared it with the limited monarchy of Great Britain, without coming to the conclusion that the practical results obtained from our own form of government are infinitely more satisfactory than those secured under the system of our neighbours. But let us not forget that we are apt to judge of monarchy by the monarchy of Queen Victoria—the best, the wisest sovereign that ever ascended a throne. Let us not forget, too, that there have been, and are still, very different monarchies in the world from that of our own beloved Queen; and assuredly there are not so many free governments on earth that we should hesitate earnestly to desire the success of that one nearest to our own, modelled from our own, and founded by men of our own race. I do most heartily rejoice, for the cause of liberty, that Mr. Lincoln did not patiently acquiesce in the dismemberment of the republic.

But let us turn from this long digression, and examine the question from an anti-slavery point of view—*Why not let them go?* No honest anti-slavery man can hesitate in answering, Because it would have been wrong to do so, because it would have built up a great slave republic that no moral influence could have reached. Had the extreme slave states been allowed to secede without a blow, there is every reason to believe that all the border states would have gone with them, and a large portion of the unadmitted territories of the union would have been added to the slave domain. Such a confederacy would have overawed the free northern states; the slave trade would have been at once thrown open, and no foreign government would have ventured to interfere. It has been said that if that were attempted, France and England would enforce by arms a treaty against the inhuman traffic. I do not believe anything of the kind. If England could have been induced to go to war about the slave trade, she would have gone to war with Spain long ago. She paid money to Spain to give up the shameless traffic, and yet Spain carries it on to this day, and England has not gone to war to compel her to desist. No, if this confederacy had been formed, with slavery and the slave trade as its beautiful corner-stones, no European government would have interfered; and we should have on this continent, under the protection of a regularly organized government, the most monstrous outrage of humanity that has disgraced the present age. Had Mr. Lincoln passively permitted all this to be done—had he permitted the southern states to go, and such a government to be formed without a blow—he would have brought enduring contempt upon his name, and the people of England would have been the first to have risen up and reproached him for his monstrous imbecility. "Why," they would have demanded, "did you allow the whole of that vast country to pass under the rule of slavery without one effort to prevent it? How came it that you struck not a single blow to avert such a frightful evil? Had you only stood firm, the attempt would have broken down, and even if it had not, you might have fearlessly looked to us for sympathy, and at once we would have aided you!"

Mr. Lincoln and his government did their duty in resisting the establishment on this continent of so infamous a government; they are striving to do it now; but unfortunately the sympathies of a large portion of the British people are wrongfully withheld from them, if not indeed given to their opponents. And yet I believe most sincerely that if they had allowed the south to go, if they had permitted a vast slave republic to be built up and the slave trade to be declared legal, there are few men in England or France who would not have expressed bitter indignation at such lamentable imbecility ; and foremost among them, I do not doubt, would have been the very men who now cry, Why not let them go? Mr. Lincoln and his friends would have disgraced themselves forever had they consented to let the south go, with a knowledge of what would happen. And come what may hereafter, already has enough been achieved to justify their refusal. Slavery has been abolished by law in the District of Columbia ; half of Virginia has declared for freedom; the great state of Missouri has resolved to accept indemnification and manumit its bondsmen ; and there can be very little doubt that Delaware, Maryland and Kentucky, come what may, will now cast in their lot with the free northern states. Tens of thousands of slaves have been actually set free—the law has declared every slave in the rebel states free, and were the south to achieve its freedom to-morrow, it is hard to see how the chattels can be held in bondage. These great results have not been obtained without prodigious sacrifices ; but assuredly for what has been done the hearty thanks of the civilized world are due to the government at Washington.

But there is another question constantly heard, and it is this : Why did not Mr. Lincoly openly, frankly, and from the first declare the overthrow of slavery to be his object in the civil war? Now, I could understand such a question as this coming from a pro-slavery man, for we have become used to the twistings and windings of that class of disputants, but I confess I do not comprehend such a question coming from the lips of a true emancipationist. Mr. Lincoln was not elected by the whole north, but only by a portion of the northern electors ; Mr. Lincoln's views on the slave question were not held by the whole north, but, on the contrary, a large portion of the north approved of slavery and denounced Mr. Lincoln's policy upon it. Mr. Lincoln had a divided north to fight with against a united south ; and yet these professing abolitionists would have had him come out with an unnecessary declaration which would have split up his supporters, and given the south the uncontrolled mastery of the union. No ; Mr. Lincoln knew better what he was about. He simply declared for the maintenance of the union. And why? Because he knew that men would come in to fight with him for the maintenance of the union, whose political antecedents forbade them from fighting for the overthrow of slavery. He desired to get a united north as against a united south, and he could only get them united on the ground of the maintenance of the union. But well he knew that if the union were maintained, and he himself remained president of the union, his end would be accomplished. One can fancy Mr. Lincoln reasoning thus : "If I am president, I have power to abolish slavery in the District of Columbia ; I will have power to prevent its entrance into the territories ; I will be able to offer money to induce each state to abolish slavery ; I will have a right to put men loving freedom in all public offices of the south ; and by these and other means I shall confine slavery within so narrow a compass that it will soon come to an end." By this course he kept his great object in view, and prevented open division in the north at the commencement of the struggle. Time did its work; many of the democratic party, in the heat of strife, forgot their political antecedents, and gradually saw and admitted the necessity of waging war against slavery; and Mr. Lincoln was enabled to venture on measures that dared not have been breathed at the beginning of the struggle.

But we are told that if the north and south separated, and the north became an independent state, the most friendly relations would spring up between the south and Great Britain, and an immense trade would be thereby secured to the mother country. Now, I apprehend that we here very well understand what all this amounts to. If there is a body of men on the face of the earth who hate Great Britain with undying hatred, it is the slave-holders of the southern states. They hate the very name of Britain, because they know that the British people love freedom, and are the genuine enemies of slavery throughout the world. To serve present purposes they may profess to be friendly for the moment, but as soon as their ends are obtained they will speedily be seen in their true colours as the bitter enemies of Great Britain. The most violent attacks on Great Britain, the most insulting language has almost invariably proceeded from southern lips and southern pens. But, it is said, "the north has the same feelings; the north has no love for Great Britain; and the moment the present civil war is ended, the northerners will cross over to Canada, conquer us in a week, and annex our country to their dominions." I fancy that we in Canada understand the eccentricities of our American neighbours much better than our friends in the mother country, and can place a truer value on the vauntings of their press, and the boastful language of their orators. We have lived at peace with them for fifty years, and notwithstanding all that is come and gone, we hope to live at peace with them for fifty more. We have large commercial relations, mutually profitable relations, with them; we have no cause of quarrel with them, and except as oratorical flourishes, the idea of attacking Canada, I am persuaded, never entered their conception. Were the civil strife ended to-morrow, our neighbours will have had quite enough of war to last them for many years to come; but assuredly should they be mad enough gratuitously to attack us, we are vastly more able now to defend our soil than we were fifty years ago; and what we did in 1812 we would unflinchingly do again. It is not by such petty bugbears that honest Britons will be prevented from candidly examining the true merits of the American civil war, and praying earnestly that God may uphold the right.

There is one fact that I conceive ought to be perfectly conclusive with every sincere emancipationist, whether in Britain or in Canada, as to the side on which their sympathy should be cast. There have been for many years in the United States noble men fighting for freedom—the Tappans, the Jays, the Adams, the Beechers, the Garrisons, the Gerrit Smiths, and a host of other patriots, whose names will one day have a high rank in the annals of their country. Those men have justly enjoyed the confidence and esteem of the British public, and they have never done anything to forfeit it. Now, it is a fact, an instructive fact, that there is not one such man, not one man who ever stood high in English estimation for moral worth and sterling patriotism, who is not found ranged on the side of the north in the present struggle—there is not one such man who is not found on the side of Mr. Lincoln and heartily supporting him. Every one of them perfectly comprehends, and we anti-slavery men of Canada perfectly comprehend, that the whole hope of thorough and immediate emancipation, rests on the success of Abraham Lincoln's administration.

I must apologize for detaining the meeting to so unreasonable a length ; but I felt that it was a duty we owed to ourselves, to our neighbours across the line, and to our friends in Great Britain, that the true merits of this great struggle should be clearly stated from our position of advantage, and from an anti-slavery point of view. I am well assured that those of us who may be spared some years hence to look back upon this civil war in America, will never have cause to repent that they took part in the proceedings of this night, but will remember with pride and pleasure that we did what we could to uphold the right. For myself, whatever may be the result of the present strife, I shall always feel the highest satisfaction in recollecting that with the sin of sympathizing with slavery or secession my hands are not defiled; but that from the commencement of the struggle my earnest aspirations have gone with the friends of freedom.

CONFEDERATION RESOLUTIONS.

The following speech was delivered on February 8th, 1865, immediately after the reading of the Order of the Day for resuming the debate on the resolution for a union of the British North American colonies. Its delivery was frequently interrupted by the hearty cheers of the House, and at its conclusion Mr. Brown resumed his seat amid loud and continued applause.

HON. GEORGE BROWN rose and said : It is with no ordinary gratification I rise to address the House on this occasion. I cannot help feeling that the struggle of half a lifetime for constitutional reform—the agitations in the country, and the fierce contests in this chamber—the strife, and the discord and the abuse of many years—are all compensated by the great scheme of reform which is now in your hands. The Attorney-General for Upper Canada, as well as the Attorney-General for Lower Canada, in addressing the House last night, were anxious to have it understood that this scheme for uniting British America under one government is something different from " representation by population "—is something different from " joint authority "—but is in fact the very scheme of the government of which they were members in 1838. Now, it is all very well that my honourable friends should receive credit for the large share they have contributed towards maturing the measure before the House ; but I could not help reflecting while they spoke, that if this was their very scheme in 1858, they succeeded wonderfully in bottling it up from all the world except themselves, and I could not help regretting that we had to wait till 1864 until this mysterious plant of 1858 was forced to fruition. For myself, I care not who gets the credit of this scheme—I believe it contains the best features of all the suggestions that have been made in the last ten years for the settlement of our troubles ; and the whole feeling in my mind now is one of joy and thankfulness that there were found men of position and influence in Canada who, at a moment of serious crisis, had nerve and patriotism enough to cast aside political partisanship, to banish personal considerations, and unite for the accomplishment of a measure so fraught with advantage to their common country. It was a bold step in the then existing state of public feeling for many members of the House to vote for the constitutional committee moved for by me last session—it was a very bold step for many of the members of that committee to speak and vote candidly upon it—it was a still bolder thing for many to place their names to the report that emanated from that committee—but it was an infinitely bolder step for the gentlemen who now occupy these treasury benches, to brave the misconceptions and suspicions that would certainly attach to the act, and enter the same government.   And it is not to be denied that such a coalition demanded no ordinary justification.   But who does not feel that every one of us has to-day ample justification and reward for all we did in the document now under discussion ?   But seven short months have passed away since the coalition government was formed, yet already are we submitting a scheme well-weighed and matured, for the erection of a future empire—a scheme which has been received at home and abroad with almost universal approval.

Hon. Mr. Holton (ironically): Hear, hear !

Hon. Mr. Brown : My honourable friend dissents from that, but is it possible truthfully to deny it ?   Has it not been approved and endorsed by the governments of five separate colonies ?   Has it not received the all but unanimous approval of the press of Canada ?   Has it not been heartily and unequivocally endorsed by the electors of Canada ?   My honourable friend opposite cries "No, no," but I say "Yes, yes."   Since the coalition was formed, and its policy of federal union announced, there have been no fewer than twenty-five parliamentary elections—fourteen for members of the Upper House, and eleven for members of the Lower House.   At the fourteen Upper House contests, but three candidates dared to show them-selves before the people in opposition to the government scheme ; and of these, two were rejected, and one—only one—succeeded in finding a seat. At the eleven contests for the Lower House, but one candidate on either side of politics ventured to oppose the scheme, and I hope that even he will yet cast his vote in favour of confederation.   Of these twenty-five electoral contests, fourteen were in Upper Canada, but not at one of them did a candidate appear in opposition to our scheme.   And let it be observed how large a portion of the country these twenty-five electoral districts embraced.   It is true that the eleven Lower House elections only included that number of counties, but the fourteen Upper House elections embraced no fewer than forty counties.   Of the 130 constituencies, therefore, into which Canada is divided for representation in this chamber, not fewer than fifty have been called on since our scheme was announced to pro-nounce at the polls their verdict upon it, and at the whole of them but four candidates on both sides of politics ventured to give it opposition.

Was I not right then in asserting that the electors of Canada had, in the most marked manner, pronounced in favour of the scheme ?   And will honourable gentlemen deny that the people and press of Great Britain have received it with acclamations of approval ?—that the government of England has cordially endorsed and accepted it?—ay, that even the press and the public men of the United States have spoken of it with a degree of respect they never before accorded to any colonial movement ?   I venture to assert that no scheme of equal magnitude, ever placed before the world, .was received with higher eulogiums, with more universal approbation, than the measure we have now the pleasure of submitting for the acceptance of the Canadian parliament.   And no higher eulogy could, I think, be pro-nounced than that I heard a few weeks ago from the lips of one of the foremost of British statesmen, that the system of government we proposed seemed to him a happy compound of the best features of the British and American constitutions. And well might our present attitude in Canada arrest the earnest attention of other countries. Here is a people composed of two distinct races, speaking different languages, with religious and social and municipal and educational institutions totally different ; with sectional hostilities of such a character as to render government for many years well nigh impossible ; with a constitution so unjust in the view of one section as to justify any resort to enforce a remedy. And yet, here we sit, patiently and temperately discussing how these great evils and hostilities may justly and amicably be swept away forever. We are endeavouring to adjust harmoniously greater difficulties than have plunged other countries into all the horrors of civil war. We are striving to do peacefully and satisfactorily what Holland and Belgium, after years of strife, were unable to accomplish. We are seeking by calm discussion to settle questions that Austria and Hungary, that Denmark and Germany, that Russia and Poland, could only crush by the iron heel of armed force. We are seeking to do without foreign intervention that which deluged in blood the sunny plains of Italy. We are striving to settle forever issues hardly less momentous than those that have rent the neighbouring republic and are now exposing it to all the horrors of civil war. Have we not then great cause of thankfulness that we have found a better way for the solution of our troubles than that which has entailed on other countries such deplorable results? And should not every one of us endeavour to rise to the magnitude of the occasion, and earnestly seek to deal with this question to the end in the same candid and conciliatory spirit in which, so far, it has been discussed ?

The scene presented by this chamber at this moment, I venture to affirm, has few parallels in history. One hundred years have passed away since these provinces became by conquest part of the British Empire. I speak in no boastful spirit—I desire not for a moment to excite a painful thought—what was then the fortune of war of the brave French nation, might have been ours on that well-fought field. I recall those olden times merely to mark the fact that here sit to-day the descendants of the victors and the vanquished in the fight of 1759, with all the differences of language, religion, civil law and social habit, nearly as distinctly marked as they were a century ago. Here we sit to-day seeking amicably to find a remedy for constitutional evils and injustice complained of—by the vanquished ? No, but complained of by the conquerors ! Here sit the representatives of the British population claiming justice—only justice ; and here sit the representatives of the French population, discussing in the French tongue whether we shall have it. One hundred years have passed away since the conquest of Quebec, but here sit the children of the victor and the vanquished, all avowing hearty attachment to the British Crown— all earnestly deliberating how we shall best extend the blessings of British institutions—how a great people may be established on this continent in close and hearty connection with Great Britain Where, in the page of history, shall we find a parallel to this ? Will it not stand as an imperishable monument to the generosity of British rule?

And it is not in Canada alone that this scene is being witnessed. Four other colonies are at this moment occupied as we are—declaring their hearty love for the parent state, and deliberating with us how they may best discharge the great duty entrusted to their hands, and give their aid in developing the teeming resources of these vast possessions. And well may the work we have unitedly proposed rouse the ambition and energy of every true man in British America. Look at the map of the continent of America, and mark that island (Newfoundland) commanding the mouth of the noble river that almost cuts our continent in twain. Well, that island is equal in extent to the kingdom of Portugal. Cross the straits to the mainland, and you touch the hospitable shores of Nova Scotia, a country quite as large as the kingdom of Greece. Then mark the sister province of New Brunswick—equal in extent to Denmark and Switzerland combined. Pass up the River St. Lawrence to Lower Canada— a country as large as France. Pass on to Upper Canada, twenty thousand square miles larger than Great Britain and Ireland put together. Cross over the continent to the shores of the Pacific, and you are in British Columbia, the land of golden promise—equal in extent to the Austrian empire. I speak not now of the vast Indian territories that lie between— greater in extent than the whole soil of Russia—and that will ere long, I trust, be opened up to civilization under the auspices of the British American confederation. Well, the bold scheme in your hands is nothing less than to gather all these countries into one—to organize them all under one government, with the protection of the British flag, and in heartiest sympathy and affection with our fellow-subjects in the land that gave us birth. Our scheme is to establish a government that will seek to turn the tide of European emigration into this northern half of the American continent—that will strive to develop its great natural resources—and that will endeavour to maintain liberty, and justice, and Christianity throughout the land.

MR. T. C. WALLBRIDGE : When ?

HON. MR. CARTIER : Very soon !

HON. MR. BROWN : The honourable member for North Hastings asks when all this can be done? The whole great ends of this confederation may not be realized in the lifetime of many who now hear me. We imagine not that such a structure can be built in a month or in a year. What we propose now is but to lay the foundations of the structure—to set in motion the governmental machinery that will one day, we trust, extend from the Atlantic to the Pacific. And we take special credit to ourselves that the system we have devised, while admirably adapted to our present situation, is capable of gradual and efficient expansion in future years to meet all the great purposes contemplated by our scheme. But if the honourable gentleman will only recall to mind that when the United States seceded from the mother country, and for many years afterwards, their population was not nearly equal to ours at this moment—that their internal improvements did not then approach to what we have already attained, and that their trade and commerce was not then a third of what ours has already reached—I think that he will see that the fulfilment of our hopes may not be so very remote as at first sight might be imagined. And he will be strengthened in that conviction if he remembers that what we propose to do is to be done with the cordial sympathy and assistance of that great power of which it is our happiness to form a part.

Such are the objects of attainment to which the British American Conference pledged itself in October. And said I not rightly that such a scheme is well fitted to fire the ambition and rouse the energies of every member of this House? Does it not lift us above the petty politics of the past, and present to us high purposes and great interests that may well call forth all the intellectual ability and all the energy and enterprise to be found among us? I readily admit all the gravity of the question, and that it ought to be considered cautiously and thoroughly before adoption. Far be it from me to deprecate the closest criticism, or to doubt for a moment the sincerity or patriotism of those who feel it their duty to oppose the measure. But in considering a question on which hangs the future destiny of half a continent, ought not the spirit of mere fault-finding to be hushed?—ought not the voice of partisanship to be banished from our debates?—ought we not sit down and discuss the arguments presented in the earnest and candid spirit of men bound by the same interests, seeking a common end, and loving the same country? Some honourable gentlemen seem to imagine that the members of government have a deeper interest in this scheme than others—but what possible interest can any of us have except that which we share with every citizen of the land? What risk does any one run from this measure in which all of us do not fully participate? What possible inducement could we have to urge this scheme, except our earnest and heartfelt conviction that it will inure to the solid and lasting advantage of our country?

There is one consideration that cannot be banished from this discussion, and that ought, I think, to be remembered in every word we utter; it is that the constitutional system of Canada cannot remain as it is now. Something must be done. We cannot stand still. We cannot go back to chronic, sectional hostility and discord—to a state of perpetual ministerial crises. The events of the last eight months cannot be obliterated; the solemn admissions of men of all parties can never be erased. The claims of Upper Canada for justice must be met, and met now. I say, then, that every one who raises his voice in hostility to this measure is bound to keep before him, when he speaks, all the perilous consequences of its rejection; I say that no man who has a true regard for the well-being of Canada can give a vote against this scheme, unless he is prepared to offer, in amendment, some better remedy for the evils and injustice that have so long threatened the peace of our country. And not only must the scheme proposed in amendment be a better scheme—it must be something that can be carried.

I see an honourable friend now before me, for whose opinions I have the very highest respect, who says to me : " Mr. Brown, you should not have settled this part of the plan as you have done ; here is the way you should have framed it." "Well, my dear sir," is my reply, "I perfectly agree with you, but it could not be done. Whether we ask for parliamentary reform for Canada alone or in union with the Maritime Provinces, the views of French Canadians must be consulted as well as ours. This scheme can be carried, and no scheme can be that has not the support of both sections of the province."

Hon. Mr. Cartier : There is the question.

Hon. Mr. Brown : Yes, that is the question and the whole question. No constitution ever framed was without defect ; no act of human wisdom was ever free from imperfection ; no amount of talent and wisdom and integrity combined in preparing such a scheme could have placed it beyond the reach of criticism. And the framers of this scheme had immense special difficulties to overcome. We had the prejudices of race and language and religion to deal with ; and we had to encounter all the rivalries of trade and commerce, and all the jealousies of diversified local interests. To assert, then, that our scheme is without fault, would be folly. It was necessarily the work of concession ; not one of the thirty-three framers but had, on some points, to yield his opinions ; and, for myself, I freely admit that I struggled earnestly, for days together, to have portions of the scheme amended. But admitting all this—admitting all the difficulties that beset us—admitting frankly that defects in the measure exist—I say that, taking the scheme as a whole, it has my cordial, enthusiastic support, without hesitation or reservation. I believe it will accomplish all, and more than all, that we, who have so long fought the battle of parliamentary reform, ever hoped to see accomplished. I believe that, while granting security for local interests, it will give free scope for carrying out the will of the whole people in general matters—that it will draw closer the bonds that unite us to Great Britain—and that it will lay the foundations deep and strong of a powerful and prosperous people.

And if the House will allow me to trespass to a somewhat unusual degree on its indulgence. I am satisfied that I can clearly establish that such are the results fairly to be anticipated from the measure. There are two views in which this scheme may be regarded, namely, the existing evils it will remedy, and the new advantages it will secure for us as a people. Let us begin by examining its remedial provisions. First, then, it applies a complete and satisfactory remedy to the injustice of the existing system of parliamentary representation. The people of Upper Canada have bitterly complained that though they numbered four hundred thousand souls more than the population of Lower Canada, and though they have contributed three or four pounds to the general revenue for every pound contributed by the sister province, yet the Lower Canadians send to parliament as many representatives as they do. Now, the measure in your hands brings this injustice to an end ; it sweeps away the line of demarcation between the two sections on all matters common to the whole province ; it gives representation according to numbers wherever found in the House of Assembly ; and it provides a simple and convenient system for readjusting the representation after each decennial census. To this proposed constitution of the Lower Chamber, I have heard only two objections. It has been alleged that until after the census of 1871, the number of members is to remain as at present ; but this is a mistake. Upper Canada is to receive from the start eighty-two representatives, and Lower Canada sixty-five ; and whatever increase the census of 1871 may establish will be then adjusted. It has also been objected that though the resolutions provide that the existing parliament of Canada shall establish the electoral divisions for the first organization of the federal parliament, they do not determine in whose hands the duty of distributing any additional members is to be vested. No doubt on this head need exist ; the federal parliament will of course have full power to regulate all arrangements for the election of its own members. But I am told by Upper Canadians—the constitution of the Lower House is all well enough, it is in the Upper House arrangements that the scheme is objectionable. And first, it is said that Upper Canada should have had in the legislative council a greater number of members than Lower Canada.

Mr. T. C. WALLBRIDGE : Hear, hear !

Hon. Mr. Brown : The honourable member for North Hastings is of that opinion ; but that gentleman is in favour of a legislative union, and had we been forming a legislative union, there might have been some force in the demand. But the very essence of our compact is that the union shall be federal and not legislative. Our Lower Canada friends have agreed to give us representation by population in the Lower House, on the express condition that they shall have equality in the Upper House. On no other condition could we have advanced a step ; and for my part, I am quite willing that they should have it. In maintaining the existing sectional boundaries and handing over the control of local matters to local bodies, we recognize, to a certain extent, a diversity of interests ; and it was quite natural that the protection for those interests, by equality in the Upper Chamber, should be demanded by the less numerous provinces. Honourable gentlemen may say that it will erect a barrier in the Upper House against the just influence that Upper Canada will exercise, by her numbers, in the Lower House, over the general legislation of the country. That may be true to a certain extent, but honourable gentlemen will bear in mind that that barrier, be it more or less, will not affect money bills. Hitherto we have been paying a vast proportion of the taxes, with little or no control over the expenditure. But, under this plan, by our just influence in the Lower Chamber, we shall hold the purse strings. If, from this concession of equality in the Upper Chamber, we are restrained from forcing through measures which our friends of Lower Canada may consider injurious to their interests, we shall, at any rate, have power, which we never had before, to prevent them from forcing through whatever we may deem unjust to us. I think the compromise a fair one, and am persuaded that it will work easily and satisfactorily. But it has been said that the members of the Upper House ought not to be appointed by the Crown, but should continue to be elected by the people at large. On that question my views have been often expressed. I have always been opposed to a second elective chamber, and I am so still, from the conviction that two elective houses are inconsistent with the right working of the British parliamentary system. I voted, almost alone, against the change when the council was made elective, but I have lived to see a vast majority of those who did the deed wish it had not been done. It is quite true, and I am glad to acknowledge it, that many evils anticipated from the change when the measure was adopted have not been realized. I readily admit that men of the highest character and position have been brought into the council by the elective system, but it is equally true that the system of appointment brought into it men of the highest character and position. Whether appointed by the Crown or elected by the people, since the introduction of parliamentary government, the men who have composed the Upper House of this legislature have been men who would have done honour to any legislature in the world. But what we most feared was, that the legislative councillors would be elected under party responsibility; that a partisan spirit would soon show itself in the chamber; and that the right would soon be asserted to an equal control with this House over money bills. That fear has not been realized to any dangerous extent. But is it not possible that such a claim might ere long be asserted? Do we not hear, even now, mutterings of a coming demand for it? Nor can we forget that the elected members came into that chamber gradually; that the large number of old appointed members exercised much influence in maintaining the old forms of the House, the old style of debate, and the old barriers against encroachment on the privileges of the Commons. But the appointed members of the council are gradually passing away, and when the elective element becomes supreme, who will venture to affirm that the council would not claim that power over money bills which this House claims as of right belonging to itself? Could they not justly say that they represent the people as well as we do, and that the control of the purse strings ought, therefore, to belong to them as much as to us? It is said they have not the power. But what is to prevent them from enforcing it? Suppose we had a conservative majority here, and a reform majority above—or a conservative majority above and a reform majority here—all elected under party obligations—what is to prevent a dead-lock between the chambers? It may be called unconstitutional—but what is to prevent the councillors (especially if they feel that in the dispute of the hour they have the country at their back) from practically exercising all the powers that belong to us? They might amend our money bills, they might throw out all our bills if they liked, and bring to a stop the whole machinery of government. And what could we do to prevent them? But, even supposing this were not the case, and that the elective Upper House continued to be guided by that discretion which has heretofore actuated its proceedings, still, I think, we must all feel that the election of members for such enormous districts as form the constituencies of the Upper House has become a great practical inconvenience. I say this from personal experience, having long taken an active interest in the electoral contests in Upper Canada. We have found greater difficulty in inducing candidates to offer for seats in the Upper House, than in getting ten times the number for the Lower House. The constituencies are so vast, that it is difficult to find gentlemen who have the will to incur the labour of such a contest, who are sufficiently known and popular enough throughout districts so wide, and who have money enough to pay the enormous bills, not incurred in any corrupt way—do not fancy that I mean that for a moment—but the bills that are sent in after the contest is over, and which the candidates are compelled to pay if they ever hope to present themselves for re-election.

But honourable gentlemen say, " This may be all very well, but you are taking an important power out of the hands of the people, which they now possess." Now, this is a mistake. We do not propose to do anything of the sort. What we propose is, that the Upper House shall be appointed from the best men of the country by those holding the confidence of the representatives of the people in this chamber. It is proposed that the government of the day, which only lives by the approval of this chamber, shall make the appointments, and be responsible to the people for the selections they shall make. Not a single appointment could be made, with regard to which the government would not be open to censure, and which the representatives of the people, in this House, would not have an opportunity of condemning. For myself, I have maintained the appointment principle, as in opposition to the elective, ever since I came into public life, and have never hesitated, when before the people, to state my opinions in the broadest manner ; and yet not in a single instance have I ever found a constituency in Upper Canada, or a public meeting, declaring its disapproval of appointment by the Crown and its desire for election by the people at large. When the change was made in 1855 there was not a single petition from the people asking for it—it was in a manner forced on the legislature. The real reason for the change was, that before responsible government was introduced into this country, while the old oligarchical system existed, the Upper House continuously and systematically was at war with the popular branch, and threw out every measure of a liberal tendency. The result was, that in the famous ninety-two resolutions the introduction of the elective principle into the Upper House was declared to be indispensable. So long as Mr. Robert Baldwin remained in public life, the thing could not be done ; but when he left the deed was consummated. But it is said that if the members are to be appointed for life, the number should be unlimited—that, in the event of a dead-lock arising between that chamber and this, there should be power to overcome the difficulty by the appointment of more members. Well, under the British system, in the case of a legislative union, that might be a legitimate provision. But honourable gentlemen must see that the limitation of the numbers in the Upper House lies at the base of the whole compact on which this scheme rests. It is perfectly clear, as was contended by those who represented Lower Canada in the conference, that if the number of legislative councillors was made capable of increase, you would thereby sweep away the whole protection they had from the Upper Chamber. But it has been said that, though you may not give the power to the executive to increase the numbers of the Upper House in the event of a dead-lock, you might limit the term for which the members are appointed. I was myself in favour of that proposition. I thought it would be well to provide for a more frequent change in the composition of the Upper House, and lessen the danger of the chamber being largely composed of gentlemen whose advanced years might forbid the punctual and vigorous discharge of their public duties. Still, the objection made to this was very strong. It was said : "Suppose you appoint them for nine years, what will be the effect? For the last three or four years of their term they would be anticipating its expiry, and anxiously looking to the administration of the day for reappointment ; and the consequence would be that a third of the members would be under the influence of the executive." The desire was to render the Upper House a thoroughly independent body —one that would be in the best position to canvass dispassionately the measures of this House, and stand up for the public interests in opposition to hasty or partisan legislation. It was contended that there is no fear of a dead-lock. We were reminded how the system of appointing for life had worked in past years, since responsible government was introduced; we were told that the complaint was not then that the Upper Chamber had been too obstructive a body—not that it had sought to restrain the popular will, but that it had too faithfully reflected the popular will. Undoubtedly that was the complaint formerly pressed upon us, and I readily admit that if ever there was a body to whom we could safely entrust the power which by this measure we propose to confer on the members of the Upper Chamber, it is the body of gentlemen who at this moment compose the legislative council of Canada. The forty-eight councillors for Canada are to be chosen from the present chamber. There are now thirty-four members from the one section, and thirty-five from the other. I believe that of the sixty-nine, some will not desire to make their appearance here again; others, unhappily, from years and infirmity, may not have strength to do so ; and there may be others who will not desire to qualify under the statute. It is quite clear that when twenty-four are selected for Upper Canada and twenty-four for Lower Canada, very few indeed of the present House will be excluded from the federal chamber ; and I confess I am not without hope that there may be some way yet found of providing, for all who desire it, an honourable position in the legislature of the country. And after all, is it not an imaginary fear—that of a deadlock? Is it at all probable that any body of gentlemen who may compose the Upper House, appointed as they will be for life, acting as they will do on personal and not party responsibility, possessing as they must a deep stake in the welfare of the country, and desirous as they must

be of holding the esteem of their fellow-subjects, would take so unreasonable a course as to imperil the whole political fabric? The British House
of Peers itself does not venture, *à l'outrance*, to resist the popular will, and
can it be anticipated that our Upper Chamber would set itself rashly
against the popular will? If any fear is to be entertained in the matter, is
it not rather that the councillors will be found too thoroughly in harmony
with the popular feeling of the day? And we have this satisfaction at any
rate, that so far as its first formation is concerned, so far as the present
question is concerned, we shall have a body of gentlemen in whom every
confidence may be placed.

But it is objected that in the constitution of the Upper House, so far
as Lower Canada is concerned, the existing electoral divisions are to be
maintained, while, as regards Upper Canada, they are to be abolished—
that the members from Lower Canada are to sit as representing the divisions in which they reside or have their property qualification ; while in
Upper Canada there is no such arrangement. Undoubtedly this is the
fact ; it has been so arranged to suit the peculiar position of this section of
the province. Our Lower Canada friends felt that they had French Canadian interests and British interests to be protected, and they conceived
that the existing system of electoral divisions would give protection to
these separate interests. We in Upper Canada, on the other hand, were
quite content that they should settle that among themselves, and maintain
their existing divisions if they chose. But, so far as we in the west were
concerned, we had no such separate interests to protect—we had no diver-
sities of origin or language to reconcile—and we felt that the true interest
of Upper Canada was that her very best men should be sent to the legislative council, wherever they might happen to reside or wherever their
property was located. If there is one evil in the American system which
in my mind stands out as pre-eminently its greatest defect, except universal suffrage, it is that under that constitution the representatives of the
people must reside in the constituencies for which they sit. The result is
that a public man, no matter what his talent or what his position, no
matter how necessary it may be for the interest of the country that he
should be in public life, unless he happens to belong to the political party
popular for the time being in the constituency where he resides, cannot
possibly find a seat in congress. And over and over again have we seen
the very best men of the republic, the most illustrious names recorded in
its political annals, driven out of the legislature of their country, simply
because the majority in the electoral division in which they lived was of a
different political party from them. I do think the British system infinitely better than that, securing as it does that public men may be trained
to public life, with the assured conviction that if they prove themselves
worthy of public confidence, and gain a position in the country, constituencies will always be found to avail themselves of their services, whatever
be the political party to which they may adhere. You may make politicians by the other, but assuredly this is the way that statesmen are produced.

But it is further objected that the property qualification of the members of the Upper House from Prince Edward Island and Newfoundland may be either real or personal estate, while in the others it is to be real estate alone. This is correct; but I fancy it matters little to us upon what species of property our friends in Prince Edward Island or in Newfoundland base their qualification. In Canada real estate is abundant; every one can obtain it; and it is admitted by all to be the best qualification, if it be advisable to have any property qualification at all. But in Newfoundland it would be exceedingly inconvenient to enforce such a rule. The public lands there are not even surveyed to any considerable extent; the people are almost entirely engaged in fishing and commercial pursuits, and to require a real estate qualification would be practically to exclude some of its best public men from the legislative council. Then in Prince Edward Island a large portion of the island is held in extensive tracts by absentee proprietors and leased to the settlers. A feud of long standing has been the result, and there would be some difficulty in finding landed proprietors who would be acceptable to the people as members of the Upper House. This also must be remembered, that it will be a very different thing for a member from Newfoundland or Prince Edward Island to attend the legislature at Ottawa from what it is for one of ourselves to go there. He must give up not only his time, but the comfort and convenience of being near home; and it is desirable to throw no unnecessary obstacle in the way of our getting the very best men from these provinces.

But it is further objected that these resolutions do not define how the legislative councillors are to be chosen at first. I apprehend, however, there is no doubt whatever as regards that. Clause 14 says: "The first selection of the members to constitute the federal legislative council shall be made from the members of the now existing legislative councils, by the Crown, at the recommendation of the general executive government, upon the nomination of the respective local governments." The clear meaning of this clause simply is, that the present governments of the several provinces are to choose out of the existing bodies—so far as they can find gentlemen willing and qualified to serve—the members who shall at starting compose the federal legislative council; that they are to present the names so selected to the executive council of British America when constituted—and on the advice of that body the councillors will be appointed by the Crown. And such has been the spirit shown from first to last in carrying out the compact of July last by all the parties to it, that I for one have no apprehension whatever that full justice will not be done to the party which may be a minority in the government, but it is certainly not in a minority either in the country or in this House. I speak not only of Upper Canada but of Lower Canada as well—

Hon. Mr. Dorion: Ha! ha!

Hon. Mr. Brown: My honourable friend laughs, but I assure him, and he will not say I do so for the purpose of deceiving him, that having been present in conference and in council, having heard all the discussions and well ascertained the feelings of all associated with me, I have not a shadow of a doubt on my mind that full justice will be done in the selection of the first federal councillors, not only to those who may have been in the habit of acting with me, but also to those who have acted with my honourable friend, the member for Hochelaga.

Now, I believe I have answered every objection that has come from any quarter against the proposed constitution of the federal legislature. I am persuaded there is not one well-founded objection that can be urged against it. It is just to all parties ; it remedies the gross injustice of the existing system ; and I am convinced it will not only work easily and safely, but be entirely satisfactory to the great mass of our people. But I go further ; I say that were all the objections urged against this scheme sound and cogent, they sink into utter insignificance in view of all the miseries this scheme will relieve us from—in view of all the difficulties that must surround any measure of parliamentary reform for Canada that could possibly be devised. Will honourable gentlemen who spend their energies in hunting out blemishes in this scheme remember for a moment the utter injustice of the one we have at present? Public opinion has made rapid strides in the last six months on the representation question,— but think what it was a week before the present coalition was formed ! Remember how short a time has elapsed since the member for Peel (Hon. Mr. J. Hillyard Cameron) proposed to grant one additional member to Upper Canada, and could not carry even that. Remember that but a few weeks ago the hon. member for Hochelaga (Hon. Mr. Dorion), who now leads the crusade against this measure, publicly declared that five or six additional members was all Upper Canada was entitled to, and that with these the Upper Canadians would be content for many years to come. And when he has reflected on all this, let the man who is disposed to carp at this great measure of representative reform justify his conduct if he can, to the thousands of disfranchised freeholders of Upper Canada demanding justice at our hands. For myself, I unhesitatingly say, that the complete justice which this measure secures to the people of Upper Canada in the vital matter of parliamentary representation alone, renders all the blemishes averred against it utterly contemptible in the balance.

But the second feature of this scheme as a remedial measure is, that it removes to a large extent the injustice of which Upper Canada has complained in financial matters. We in Upper Canada have complained that though we paid into the public treasury more than three-fourths of the whole revenue, we had less control over the system of taxation and the expenditure of the public moneys than the people of Lower Canada. Well, the scheme in the Speaker's hand remedies that. The absurd line of separation between the provinces is swept away for general matters ; we are to have seventeen additional members in the House that holds the purse ; and the taxpayers of the country, wherever they reside, will have their just share of influence over revenue and expenditure. We have also complained that immense sums of public money have been systematically taken from the public chest for local purposes of Lower Canada, in which the people of

Upper Canada had no interest whatever, though compelled to contribute three-fourths of the cash. Well, this scheme remedies that. All local matters are to be banished from the general legislature ; local governments are to have control over local affairs, and if our friends in Lower Canada choose to be extravagant they will have to bear the burden of it themselves. No longer shall we have to complain that one section pays the cash while the other spends it ; hereafter, they who pay will spend, and they who spend more than they ought will have to bear the brunt. It was a great thing to accomplish this, if we had accomplished nothing more, for if we look back on our doings of the last fifteen years I think it will be acknowledged that the greatest jobs perpetrated were of a local character, that our fiercest contests were about local matters that stirred up sectional jealousies and indignation to its deepest depth. We have further complained that if a sum was properly demanded for some legitimate local purpose in one section, an equivalent sum had to be appropriated to the other as an offset, thereby entailing prodigal expenditure, and unnecessarily increasing the public debt. Well, this scheme puts an end to that. Each province is to determine for itself its own wants, and to find the money to meet them from its own resources. But I am told that though true it is that local matters are to be separated and the burden of local expenditure placed upon local shoulders, we have made an exception from that principle in providing that a subsidy of eighty cents per head shall be taken from the federal chest and granted to the local governments for local purposes. Undoubtedly this is the fact, and I do not hesitate to admit that it would have been better if this had been otherwise. I trust I commit no breach of discretion in stating that in conference I was one of the strongest advocates for defraying the whole of the local expenditures of the local governments by means of direct taxation, and that there were liberal men in all sections of the provinces who would gladly have had it so arranged. But there was one difficulty in the way—a difficulty which has often before been encountered in this world—and that difficulty was simply this, it could not be done. We could neither have carried it in conference nor yet in any one of the existing provincial legislatures. Our friends in Lower Canada, I am afraid, have a constitutional disinclination to direct taxation, and it was obvious that if the confederation scheme had had attached to it a provision for the imposition of such a system of taxation, my honourable friends opposite would have had a much better chance of success in blowing the bellows of agitation than they now have. The objection, moreover, was not confined to Lower Canada—all the lower provinces stood in exactly the same position. They have not a municipal system such as we have, discharging many of the functions of government ; but their general government performs all the duties which in Upper Canada devolve upon our municipal councils, as well as upon parliament. If, then, the lower provinces had been asked to maintain their customs duties for federal purposes, and to impose on themselves by the same Act direct taxation for all their local purposes, the chances of carrying the scheme of union would have been greatly lessened.

But I apprehend that if we did not succeed in putting this matter on the footing that would have been the best, at least we did the next best thing. Two courses were open to us—either to surrender to the local governments some source of indirect revenue, some tax which the general government proposed to retain, or collect the money by the federal machinery, and distribute it to the local governments for local purposes. And we decided in favour of the latter. We asked the representatives of the different governments to estimate how much they would require after the inauguration of the federal system to carry on their local machinery. As at first presented to us, the annual sum required for all the provinces was something like five millions of dollars—an amount that could not possibly have been allotted. The great trouble was that some of the governments are vastly more expensive than others—extensive countries, with sparse populations, necessarily requiring more money per head for local government than countries more densly populated. But as any grant given from the common chest, for local purposes, to one province, must be extended to all, on the basis of population, it follows that for every $1,000 given, for example, to New Brunswick, we must give over $1,300 to Nova Scotia, $4,000 to Lower Canada, and $6,000 to Upper Canada, thereby drawing from the federal exchequer much larger sums than these provinces needed for local purposes. The course we adopted then was this : We formed a committee of finance ministers, and made each of them go over his list of expenditures, lopping off all unnecessary services and cutting down every item to the lowest possible figure. By this means we succeeded in reducing the total annual subsidy required for local government to the sum of $2,630,000—of which Lower Canada will receive annually $880,000, and Upper Canada $1,120,000. But it is said that in addition to her eighty cents per head under this arrangement, New Brunswick is to receive an extra grant from the federal chest of $63,000 annually for ten years. Well, this is perfectly true. After cutting down as I have explained the local expenditures to the lowest mark, it was found that New Brunswick and Newfoundland could not possibly carry on their local governments with the sum per head that would suffice for all the rest. New Brunswick imperatively required $63,000 per annum beyond her share, and we had either to find that sum for her or give up the hope of union. The question then arose, would it not be better to give New Brunswick a special grant of $63,000 for a limited number of years, so that her local revenues might have time to be developed, rather than increase the subsidy to all the local governments, thereby placing an additional burden on the federal exchequer of over eight hundred thousand dollars per annum ? We came unanimously to the conclusion that the extra sum needed by New Brunswick was too small to be allowed to stand in the way of union—we also determined that it would be the height of absurdity to impose a permanent burden on the country of $800,000 a year, simply to escape a payment of $63,000 for ten years—and so it came about that New Brunswick got this extra grant—an arrangement which received, and receives now, my hearty approval. It is only right to say, however, that New Brunswick may possibly be in a position to do without this money. The House is aware that the federal government is to assume the debts of the several provinces, each province being entitled to throw upon it a debt of $25 per head of its population. Should the debt of any province exceed $25 per head, it is to pay interest on the excess to the federal treasury; but should it fall below $25 per head, it is to receive interest from the federal treasury on the difference between its actual debt and the debt to which it is entitled. Now, it so happens that the existing debt of New Brunswick is much less than it is entitled to throw on the federal government. It is, however, under liability for certain works, which if proceeded with would bring its debt up to the mark of $25 a head. But if these works are not proceeded with, New Brunswick will be entitled to a large amount of annual interest from the federal chest, and that money is to be applied to the reduction of the $63,000 extra grant. And this, moreover, is not to be forgotten as regards New Brunswick, that she brings into the union extensive railways now in profitable operation, the revenues from which are to go into the federal chest. A similar arrangement was found necessary as regards the island of Newfoundland—it, too, being a vast country with a sparse population. It was found absolutely essential that an additional grant beyond eighty cents per head should be made to enable her local government to be properly carried on. But, in consideration of this extra allowance, Newfoundland is to cede to the federal government her crown lands and minerals—and assuredly, if the reports of geologists are well founded, this arrangement will be as advantageous to us as it will be to the inhabitants of Newfoundland.

I am persuaded, then, that the House will feel with me that we in Canada have very little to complain of in regard to the subsidies for local government. But if a doubt yet remains on the mind of any honourable member, let him examine the trade returns of the several provinces, and he will see that, from the large quantity of dutiable goods consumed in the Maritime Provinces, they have received no undue advantage under the arrangement. Let this too ever be kept in mind, that the $2,630,000 to be distributed to the local governments from the federal chest is to be in full and final extinguishment of all claims hereafter for local purposes; and that if this from any cause does not suffice, the local governments must supply all deficiencies from a direct tax on their own localities. And let honourable members from Upper Canada who carp at this annual subsidy, remember for a moment what we pay now, and they will cease their grumbling. Of all the money raised by the general government for local purposes in Canada, the tax-payers of Upper Canada now pay more than three-fourths; but far from getting back in proportion to what they contribute, or even in proportion to their population, they do not get one-half of the money spent for local purposes. But how different will it be under federation! Nine hundred thousand people will come into the union, who will contribute to the revenue quite as much, man for man, as the Upper Canadians, and in the distribution of the local subsidy we will receive our share on the basis of population—a very different arrangement from that we now endure. I confess that one of the strongest arguments in my mind for confederation is the economical ideas of the people of these Maritime Provinces, and the conviction that the influence of their public men in our legislative halls will be most salutary in all financial matters. A more economical people it would be difficult to find ; their prime ministers and their chief justices get but £600 a year, Halifax currency, and the rest of their civil list is in much the same proportion.

But there is another great evil in our existing system that this scheme remedies ; it secures to the people of each province full control over the administration of their own internal affairs. We in Upper Canada have complained that the minority of our representatives, the party defeated at the polls of Upper Canada, have been, year after year, kept in office by Lower Canada votes, and that all the local patronage of our section has been dispensed by those who did not possess the confidence of the people. Well, this scheme remedies that. The local patronage will be under local control, and the wishes of the majority in each section will be carried out in all local matters. We have complained that the land system was not according to the views of our western people; that free lands for actual settlers was the right policy for us; that the price of a piece of land squeezed out of an immigrant was no consideration in comparison with the settlement among us of a hardy and industrious family ; and that the colonization road system was far from satisfactory. Well, this scheme remedies that. Each province is to have control of its own crown lands, crown timber and crown minerals, and will be free to take such steps for developing them as each deems best. We have complained that local works of various kinds— roads, bridges and landing piers, court houses, gaols and other structures —have been erected in an inequitable and improvident manner. Well, this scheme remedies that ; all local works are to be constructed by the localities and defrayed from local funds. And so on through the whole extensive details of internal local administration will this reform extend. The people of Upper Canada will have the entire control of their local matters, and will no longer have to betake themselves to Quebec for leave to open a road, to select a county town, or appoint a coroner. But I am told that to this general principle of placing all local matters under local control, an exception has been made in regard to the common schools. The clause complained of is as follows : "6. Education ; saving the rights and privileges which the protestant or catholic minority in both Canadas may possess as to their denominational schools at the time when the union goes into operation." Now, I need hardly remind the House that I have always opposed and continue to oppose the system of sectarian education, so far as the public chest is concerned. I have never had any hesitation on that point. I have never been able to see why all the people of the province, to whatever sect they may belong, should not send their children to the same common schools to receive the ordinary branches of instruction. I regard the parent and the pastor as the best religious instructors—and so long as the religious faith of the children is uninterfered with, and ample opportunity afforded to the clergy to give religious instruction to the children of their flocks, I cannot conceive any sound objection to mixed schools. But while in the conference and elsewhere I have always maintained this view, and always given my vote against sectarian public schools, I am bound to admit, as I have always admitted, that the sectarian system, carried to the limited extent it has yet been in Upper Canada, and confined as it chiefly is to cities and towns, has not been a very great practical injury. The real cause of alarm was that the admission of the sectarian principle was there, and that at any moment it might be extended to such a degree as to split up our school system altogether. There are but a hundred separate schools in Upper Canada, out of some four thousand, and all Roman Catholic. But if the Roman Catholics are entitled to separate schools and to go on extending their operations, so are the members of the Church of England, the Presbyterians, the Methodists, and all other sects. No candid Roman Catholic will deny this for a moment; and there lay the great danger to our educational fabric, that the separate system might gradually extend itself until the whole country was studded with nurseries of sectarianism, most hurtful to the best interests of the province, and entailing an enormous expense to sustain the hosts of teachers that so prodigal a system of public instruction must inevitably entail.

Now, it is known to every honourable member of this House that an Act was passed in 1863, as a final settlement of this sectarian controversy. I was not in Quebec at the time, but if I had been here I would have voted against that bill, because it extended the facilities for establishing separate schools. It had, however, this good feature, that it was accepted by the Roman Catholic authorities, and carried through parliament as a final compromise of the question in Upper Canada. When, therefore, it was proposed that a provision should be inserted in the confederation scheme to bind that compact of 1863 and declare it a final settlement, so that we should not be compelled, as we have been since 1849, to stand constantly to our arms, awaiting fresh attacks upon our common school system, the proposition seemed to me one that was not rashly to be rejected. I admit that, from my point of view, this is a blot on the scheme before the House; it is, confessedly, one of the concessions from our side that had to be made to secure this great measure of reform. But assuredly, I for one have not the slightest hesitation in accepting it as a necessary condition of the scheme of union, and doubly acceptable must it be in the eyes of honourable gentlemen opposite, who were the authors of the bill of 1863. But it was urged that though this arrangement might perhaps be fair as regards Upper Canada, it was not so as regards Lower Canada, for there were matters of which the British population have long complained, and some amendments to the existing School Act were required to secure them equal justice. Well, when this point was raised, gentlemen of all parties in Lower Canada at once expressed themselves prepared to treat it in a frank and conciliatory manner, with a view to removing any injustice that might be shown to exist; and on this understanding the educational clause was adopted by the conference.

Mr. T. C. WALLBRIDGE : That destroys the power of the local legislatures to legislate upon the subject.

Hon. Mr. Brown : I would like to know how much "power" the
honourable gentleman has now to legislate upon it ? Let him introduce a
bill to-day to annul the compact of 1863 and repeal all the sectarian School
Acts of Upper Canada, and how many votes would he get for it ? Would
twenty members vote for it out of the one hundred and thirty who compose this House ? If the honourable gentleman had been struggling for
fifteen years, as I have been, to save the school system of Upper Canada
from further extension of the sectarian element, he would have found
precious little diminution of power over it in this very moderate compromise. And what says the honourable gentleman to leaving the British
population of Lower Canada in the unrestricted power of the local legislature ? The common schools of Lower Canada are not as in Upper Canada—
they are almost entirely non-sectarian Roman Catholic schools. Does the
honourable gentleman, then, desire to compel the protestants of Lower
Canada to avail themselves of Roman Catholic institutions, or leave their
children without instruction ? I am further in favour of this scheme because it will bring to an end the sectional discord between Upper and
Lower Canada. It sweeps away the boundary line between the provinces
so far as regards matters common to the whole people—it places all on an
equal level—and the members of the federal legislature will meet at last
as citizens of a common country. The questions that used to excite the
most hostile feelings among us have been taken away from the general
legislature, and placed under the control of the local bodies. No man need
hereafter be debarred from success in public life because his views, however popular in his own section, are unpopular in the other, for he will
not have to deal with sectional questions ; and the temptation to the
government of the day to make capital out of local prejudices will be
greatly lessened, if not altogether at an end. What has rendered prominent public men in one section utterly unpopular in the other in past years ?
Has it been our views on trade and commerce—immigration—land settlement—the canal system—the tariff—or any other of the great questions of
national interest ? No ; it was from our views as to the applying of public
money to local purposes—the allotment of public lands to local purposes—
the building of local roads, bridges, and landing-piers with public funds—
the chartering of ecclesiastical institutions—the granting of public money
for sectarian purposes—the interference with our school system—and similar matters, that the hot feuds between Upper and Lower Canada have
chiefly arisen, and caused our public men, the more faithful they were to
the opinions and wishes of one section, to be the more unpopular in the
other. A most happy day will it be for Canada when this bill goes into
effect, and all these subjects of discord are swept from the discussion of our
legislature.

I am further in favour of this scheme as a remedial measure, because
it brings to an end the doubt that has so long hung over our position, and

gives a stability to our future in the eyes of the world that could not
otherwise have been attained.

HON. MR. HOLTON : Hear, hear !

MR. BROWN : The hon. member for Chateauguay cries "hear, hear" in a
very credulous tone; but the hon. member should be one of the very last
to express doubts on this point. Has he not, for many years, admitted
the absolute necessity of constitutional changes, ere peace and prosperity
could be established in our land ? Has he not taken part in the contests
to obtain those changes? Has he not experienced the harsh and hostile
feelings that have pervaded this House and the whole country? And did he
not sign the report of my committee last session, declaring a federal union
to be the true solution of our troubles, political and constitutional? And
does the honourable member think these matters were not well known in
the United States, and that the hope of our annexation to the republic was
not kept alive by them from year to year ? Does he fancy that our dis-
cords and discontent were not well known in Great Britain, and that the
capitalist and the emigrant were not influenced by our distractions ? Does
he fancy that people abroad, as well as at home, did not perfectly understand that Upper Canada would not much longer submit to the injustice
from which she suffered ; and that until the future relations of the two
sections were adjusted, no one could predict safely what our future position might be ? But when the measure before us has been adopted—when
justice has been done to both sections—when all are placed on an equal
footing—when the sectional matters that rent us have been handed over to
sectional control—when sectional expenditure shall be placed on sectional
shoulders—will not a sense of security and stability be inspired which we
never before enjoyed, and never could have enjoyed under existing circumstances? Viewed then from a merely Canadian stand-point—viewed solely
as a remedial measure—I fearlessly assert that the scheme in the Speaker's
hands is a just and satisfactory remedy for the evils and injustice that have
so long distracted the province ; and so strongly do I feel this, that were
every word of objection urged against our union with the Maritime Provinces just and true to the very letter, I would not hesitate to adopt the
union as the price of a measure of constitutional reform in Canada so just
and so complete as now proposed. So far from the objections urged against
union with the Maritime Provinces being sound, so far from union with
them being a drawback to this measure, I regard it as the crowning advantage of the whole scheme. I make no pretension to having been in past
years an advocate of the immediate union of the British American colonies.
I always felt and always said that no statesman could doubt that such was
the best and almost the certain future destiny of those colonies ; but I
doubted greatly whether the right time for the movement had yet arrived.
I knew little of the Maritime Provinces or the feelings of their people ; the
negotiations for a union were likely to be difficult and long protracted ; and
I was unwilling to accept the hope of a measure so remote and so uncertain
in lieu of the practical remedy for practical evils in Canada which we were

earnestly seeking to obtain, and which our own legislature had the power immediately to grant. But of late all this has been changed. The circumstances are entirely altered. A revolution has occurred in Great Britain on the subject of colonial relations to the parent state—the government of the United States has become a great warlike power—our commercial relations with the republic are seriously threatened—and every man in British America has now placed before him for solution the practical question, What shall be done in view of the changed relations on which we are about to enter? Shall we continue to struggle along as isolated communities, or shall we unite cordially together to extend our commerce, to develop the resources of our country, and to defend our soil? But more than this: many of us have learned, since we last met here, far more of the Maritime Provinces than we ever did before. We have visited the Maritime Provinces—we have seen the country—we have met the people and marked their intelligence, their industry and their frugality—we have investigated their public affairs and found them satisfactory—we have discussed terms of union with their statesmen, and found that no insuperable obstacle to union exists, and no necessity for long delay. We come to the consideration of the question to-day in a totally different position from what we ever did before ; and if the House will grant me its indulgence, I think I can present unanswerable arguments to show that this union of all British America should be heartily and promptly accepted by all the provinces.

I am in favour of a union of the British American colonies, first, because it will raise us from the attitude of a number of inconsiderable colonies into a great and powerful people. The united population of Canada, Nova Scotia, New Brunswick, Newfoundland and Prince Edward Island, is at this moment very close on four millions of souls. Now, there are in Europe forty-eight sovereign states, and out of that number there are only eleven having a greater population than these colonies united, while three of the eleven are so little ahead of us that before the next census is taken, in 1871, we shall stand equal in population to the ninth sovereign state of Europe. Then the public revenues of the united provinces for 1864 were $13,260,000, and their expenditures summed up to $12,507,000. And large as these sums may appear, it is satisfactory to know that the taxation of British America—were there no reduction from present burdens, which I am sure there will be—will be one-third less per head than the taxation of England or France. There are only five or six countries in Europe in which the taxation is less than ours will be, and these, moreover, are either petty principalities or states which do not enjoy a very high degree of civilization.

Then, as regards the imports and exports of the united provinces, they summed up in 1863 to the following dimensions : Imports, $70,600,963 ; exports, $66,846,604 : total trade, $137,447,567. Now, I should like honourable gentlemen to notice this fact, that in 1793—long after the United States had achieved their independence and established a settled government—their exports and imports did not amount to one-third what ours do at this moment. There are few states in Europe, and those with a vastly greater population than ours, that can boast of anything like the extent of foreign commerce that now passes through our hands.

Then, as to our agricultural resources, I find that 45,638,854 acres have passed from the governments of these colonies into private hands, of which only 13,128,229 are yet tilled, and 32,510,625 acres have still to be brought into cultivation. The whole of these forty-five millions are picked lands —most of them selected by the early settlers in this country ; and if our annual agricultural products are so great now, what will they be when the thirty-two millions yet to pass under the plough have been brought into cultivation? and what will they not be when the vast tracts still held by government are peopled with hardy settlers ? According to the census of 1861, the value of the agricultural productions of the previous year in the united provinces of British America was $120,000,000 ; and if we add to that the garden products, and the improvements made on new lands by the agricultural labourers of the provinces, it will be found that the actual product of the industry of our farmers in that year was $150,000,000. The assessed value of our farms—which is always greatly less than the real value—was $350,000,000 in the year 1861.

Then, in regard to the minerals of the united provinces ; what vast fields of profitable industry will we have in the great coal beds of Nova Scotia, in the iron deposits found all over the provinces, in the exhaustless copper regions of Lakes Huron and Superior and the eastern townships of Lower Canada, and in the gold mines of the Chaudière and Nova Scotia. And if the mind stretches from the western bounds of civilization through those great north-western regions, which we hope ere long will be ours, to the eastern slope of the Rocky Mountains, what vast sources of wealth to the fur trader, the miner, the gold hunter and the agriculturist, lie there ready to be developed.

Nor can another source of wealth be altogether forgotten. The President of the United States is said recently to have declared that the produce of the petroleum wells of the United States will in half a dozen years pay off the whole national debt of the republic. Well, we too have "struck oil," and every day brings us intelligence of fresh discoveries, and if the enormous debt of our neighbours may possibly be met by the oily stream, may we not hope that some material addition to our annual industrial revenue may flow from our petroleum regions ?

. Another vast branch of British American industry is the timber and lumber trade. In the year 1862 our saw-mills turned out not less than 772,000,000 feet of manufactured lumber, and our whole timber exports summed up to the value of $15,000,000.

The manufacturing interests of the provinces, too, are fast rising into importance ; agricultural implement works, woollen factories and cotton mills, tanneries and shoe factories, iron works and rolling mills, flax works and paper mills, and many other extensive and profitable mechanical establishments are springing up among us, and rapidly extending their operations. And to add to all, we have already 2,500 miles of railway, 4,000 miles of electric telegraph, and the noblest canal system in the world, but which, I hope, will soon be infinitely improved.

These are some examples of the industrial spectacle British America will present after the union has been accomplished; and I ask any member of this House to say whether we will not, when thus united, occupy a position in the eyes of the world, and command a degree of respect and influence, that we never can enjoy as separate provinces? Must it not affect the decision of many an intending emigrant, when he is told not of the fishing and mining pursuits of Nova Scotia, or of the ship-building of New Brunswick, or of the timber trade of Lower Canada, or of the agriculture of Upper Canada, but when he is shown all these in one view, as the collective industrial pursuits of British America? I am persuaded that this union will inspire new confidence in our stability, and exercise the most beneficial influence on all our affairs. I believe it will raise the value of our public securities, that it will draw capital to our shores, and secure the prosecution of all legitimate enterprises; and what I saw while in England, a few weeks ago, would alone have convinced me of this. Wherever you went you encountered the most marked evidence of the gratification with which the confederation scheme was received by all classes of the people, and the deep interest taken in its success. Let me state one fact in illustration. For some time previous to November last our securities had gone very low down in the market, in consequence, as my honourable friend the Finance Minister explained the other night, of the war raging on our borders, the uncertainty which hung over the future of this province, and the fear that we might be involved in trouble with our neighbours. Our five per cent. debentures went down in the market so low as 71, but they recovered from 71 to 75, I think, upon the day the resolutions for confederation, which we are now discussing, reached London. Well, the resolutions were published in the London papers, with eulogistic editorial articles, and the immediate effect of the scheme upon the public mind was such that our five per cents. rose from 75 to 92.

Hon. Mr. Holton: What has put them down since?

Hon. Mr. Brown: I will presently tell the honourable gentleman what has put them down since. But I say that, if anything could show more clearly than another the effect this union is to have on our position over the world, it is a fact like this, that our securities went up 17 per cent. in consequence of the publication of the details of our scheme. The honourable member for Chateauguay asks, "What put them down again?" I will tell him. They remained at 91 or 92 until the news came that a raid had been made from Canada into the United States, that the raiders had been arrested and brought before a Canadian court, and that upon technical legal grounds, not only had they been set free, but the money of which they had robbed the banks had been handed over to the robbers. The effect of this news, coupled with General Dix's order, was to drive down our securities 11 per cent. almost in one day. But, as my honourable friend the Finance Minister suggests, this is but an additional proof of the accuracy of the argument I have been sustaining—for this would not have happened, at all events to the same extent, if all the provinces had been united and prepared, as we are now proposing, not only for purposes of commerce but for purposes of defence.

Secondly, I go heartily for the union, because it will throw down the barriers of trade and give us the control of a market of four millions of people. What one thing has contributed so much to the wondrous material progress of the United States as the free passage of their products from one state to another? What has tended so much to the rapid advance of all branches of their industry as the vast extent of their home market, creating an unlimited demand for all the commodities of daily use, and stimulating the energy and ingenuity of producers? I confess that in my mind this one view of the union—the addition of nearly a million of people to our home consumers—sweeps aside all the petty objections that are averred against the scheme. What, in comparison with this great gain to our farmers and manufacturers, are the fallacious money objections which the imaginations of honourable gentlemen opposite have summoned up? All over the world we find nations eagerly longing to extend their domains, spending large sums and waging protracted wars to possess themselves of more territory, untilled and uninhabited. Other countries offer large inducements to foreigners to emigrate to their shores—free passages, free lands, and free food and implements to start them in the world. We ourselves support costly establishments to attract immigrants to our country, and are satisfied when our annual outlay brings us fifteen or twenty thousand souls. But here is a proposal which is to add, in one day, nearly a million souls to our population—to add valuable territories to our domain, and secure to us all the advantages of a large and profitable commerce now existing. And because some of us would have liked certain of the little details otherwise arranged, we are to hesitate in accepting this alliance! Have honourable gentlemen forgotten that the United States gladly paid twenty millions in hard cash to have Louisiana incorporated in the republic? But what was Louisiana then to the Americans in comparison with what the Maritime Provinces are at this moment to Canada? I put it to honourable gentlemen opposite—if the United States were now to offer us the state of Maine, what possible sum could be named within the compass of our ability that we would not be prepared to pay for that addition to our country? If we were offered Michigan, Iowa or Minnesota, I would like to know what sum, within the compass of Canada, we would not be prepared to pay? These states are portions of a foreign country, but here is a people owning the same allegiance as ourselves, loving the same old sod, enjoying the same laws and institutions, actuated by the same impulses and social customs; and yet when it is proposed that they shall unite with us for purposes of commerce, for the defence of our common country, and to develop the vast natural resources of our united domains, we hesitate to adopt it! If a Canadian goes now to Nova Scotia or New Brunswick, or if a citizen of these provinces comes here, it is like going to a foreign country. The customs officer meets you at the frontier, arrests your progress, and levies his imposts on your effects. But the proposal now before us is to throw down all barriers between the provinces—to make a citizen of one, citizen of the whole; the proposal is that our farmers, and manufacturers and mechanics, shall carry their wares unquestioned into every village of the Maritime Provinces, and that they shall with equal freedom bring their fish, and their coal, and their West India produce to our three millions of inhabitants. The proposal is, that the law courts, and the schools, and the professional and industrial walks of life, throughout all the provinces, shall be thrown equally open to us all.

Thirdly, I am in favour of a union of the provinces because—and I call the attention of honourable gentlemen opposite to it—because it will make us the third maritime state of the world. When this union is accomplished, but two countries in the world will be superior in maritime influence to British America, and those are Great Britain and the United States. In 1863, no fewer than 628 vessels were built in British America, of which the aggregate tonnage was not less than 230,312 tons. There were built in Canada, 158 vessels, with 67,209 tons ; Nova Scotia, 207 vessels, with 46,862 tons; New Brunswick, 137 vessels, with 85,250 tons ; Prince Edward Island, 100 vessels, with 24,991 tons ; Newfoundland, 26 vessels, with 6,000 tons ; total, 628 vessels, with 230,312 tons. Now, in 1861—the year preceding the outbreak of the civil war—all the vessels built in the United States, with their vast seaboard and thirty millions of people, were in the aggregate but 233,193 tons—only three thousand tons in excess of the British American Provinces. And I hesitate not to affirm that if the people of British America unite cordially together in utilizing the singular facilities we unitedly possess for the extension of the shipping and shipbuilding interests, many years will not elapse before we greatly surpass our neighbours in this lucrative branch of industry.

Hon. Mr. Holton : How much of the shipping built in that year do we own now ?

Hon. Mr. Brown : How much of what the Americans built in 1861 do they own now ? Why is my honourable friend so anxious to decry the industry of his country ? If we have not the ships it is because we sold them, and the money is in our pockets, and we are ready to build more. In 1863 we sold ships built by our mechanics to the large amount of $9,000,000 in gold. But if my honourable friend from Chateauguay will permit me, I am going on to indoctrinate him upon the point of the ownership of vessels—

Hon. Mr. Holton : Don't !

Hon. Mr. Brown : Ah ! my honourable friend does not require to be instructed ; well, will he tell us how many tons of shipping are now owned by British America?

Hon. Mr. Holton : I am aware that most of the vessels my honourable friend speaks of, and the building of which he cites as a proof that we will be a great maritime power, were sold abroad. Building ships is a good thing, and selling them is a better, but that does not prove us to be a great maritime power.

Hon. Mr. Brown : My honourable friend cannot eat his cake and have it too. If we got $9,000,000 for a portion of the ships we built in 1863, it is clear we cannot own them also. It did not require a man of great wisdom to find out that. But I was going on to show the amount of shipping that was owned in these provinces. I hold in my hand a statement of the vessels owned and registered in British America, made up to the latest dates, and I find that the provinces unitedly own not fewer than 8,530 vessels, with an aggregate tonnage of not less than 952,246 tons.

Hon. Mr. Holton : Sea-going ?

Hon. Mr. Brown : Sea-going and inland.

Hon. Mr. Holton (ironically) : Hear, hear !

Hon. Mr. Brown : Why is my honourable friend so anxious to depreciate ? Is it then so deplorable a thing to own inland vessels ? None knows better than my honourable friend when to buy and when to sell—and yet, I greatly mistake if there was not a time when my honourable friend thought it not so bad a thing to be the owner of ships and steamers on our inland seas. Am I wrong in believing that my honourable friend laid the foundation of his well-merited fortune in the carrying trade of the lakes ? and is it for him, from momentary partisanship, to depreciate such an important branch of national industry ? What matters where the ship floats, if she is a good and a sound ship ?—and the inland tonnage includes so many steamers, that in value it will compare favourably with that of the sea-going. On the 31st December, 1864, Canada owned 2,311 vessels, of 287,187 tons ; in 1863, Nova Scotia owned 3,539 vessels, of 309,554 tons ; New Brunswick, 891 vessels, of 211,680 tons ; Prince Edward Island, 360 vessels, of 34,222 tons ; Newfoundland, 1,429 vessels, of 89,603 tons ; total, 8,530 vessels, of 932,246 tons. Now, it is quite true that the United States have a much larger commercial navy than this, and Great Britain a vastly larger one ; but it is equally true that the country next to them in importance is France, and that notwithstanding her thirty-five millions of people, large foreign trade, and extensive sea-coast, she owns but 60,000 tons of shipping more than British America. In 1860, the aggregate commercial navy of France was but 996,124 tons. I say, then, that even as ship-owners the British American confederacy will occupy from the first a proud place among the maritime states of the world, and that when her ships hoist a distinctive flag alongside the Cross of Red, there will be few seas in which it will not be unfurled. And let me here mention a fact which came under my notice while recently in the Lower Provinces—a fact of great importance, and from which, I think, we, who are more inland, may well profit. I learned that, as in the British isles, a system of joint-stock ship-building has been spreading over many parts of the Maritime

Provinces. Ships are built and owned in small shares—say in sixteenth, thirty-second, or sixty-fourth parts, and all classes of the people are taking small ventures in the trade. Most of the ships so built are sold, but a portion, and an increasing portion every year, are sailed, and sailed with profit, by the original joint-stock holders. I was delighted to be told that some of those clipper vessels which we often hear of as making wonderful trips from China and India and Australia to British ports, are vessels built and owned in New Brunswick, under this joint-stock system. So much for the building and ownership of ships ; now let me show you what will be the strength of the united provinces in seafaring men. By the census of 1861, it appears that the number of sailors and fishermen then in Canada was 5,958; in Nova Scotia, 19,637; in New Brunswick, 2,765; in Prince Edward Island, 2,318; in Newfoundland, 38,578; total, 69,256. Whether regarded merely as a lucrative branch of industry, or as affecting our maritime position before the world, or as a bulwark of defence in time of need, this one fact that British America will have a combined force of 70,000 seamen, appears to me an immense argument in favour of the union. And let us look at the products of the labour of a portion of these men—the fishermen. From the latest returns I have been able to meet with, I find the joint products of our sea-coasts and inland lakes were, in the years named, estimated at the following values : Upper Canada (1859), \$380,000 ; Lower Canada (1862), \$703,895 ; Nova Scotia (1861), \$2,072,081 ; New Brunswick (1861), \$518,530 ; Newfoundland (1861), \$6,347,730 ; total, \$10,022,236. I was unable to find any estimate as regards Prince Edward Island, but fancy the amount there must be about \$200,000. But be this as it may, so valuable a fishing trade as this of the united provinces does not exist in any part of the world. And no doubt these estimates are far under the fact, as a large portion of the delicious food drawn by our people from the sea and inland waters could not possibly be included in the returns of the fishery inspectors. And let us observe, for a moment, the important part played by this fishing industry in the foreign commerce of the provinces. The exports of products of the sea in the year 1863 were as follows : From Canada, \$789,913; Nova Scotia, \$2,390,661; New Brunswick (1862), \$303,477; Newfoundland, \$4,090,970; Prince Edward Island, \$121,000; total exports, \$7,696,021. Add to this, \$9,000,000 received in the same year for new ships, and we have \$16,696,021 as one year's foreign exports of our ship-building and fishing interests. With such facts before us as the result of only a partially developed traffic, may we not fearlessly look forward to the future in the confident hope of still more gratifying results, when, by combined and energetic action, a new impetus has been given to these valuable branches of industry?

But there remains a still more singular comparison to be made. I refer to the statement of ships annually entering and leaving our ports. Of course every one comprehends that a large amount of the tonnage entering and leaving ports on the upper lakes is repeated in the returns over and over again. This is the case, for instance, with the ferry boats between the American and Canadian shores, that carry passengers and a small quantity of goods. It would be unfair to put down the tonnage of such boats, every time they enter or leave a port, as foreign commerce. Still there is a large amount of valuable shipping engaged in the inland trade, and a vast amount of freight is carried between the countries ; and the only just plan is to state separately that which is sea-going shipping and that which is inland. Acting on this plan, I find that in 1863, the tonnage between Canada and foreign ports was as follows:

	Inwards.	Outwards.	Total.
Canada	1,041,309	1,091,895	2,133,204
Nova Scotia	712,939	719,915	1,432,854
New Brunswick	639,258	727,727	1,386,985
P. E. Island (1862)	69,080	81,208	150,288
Newfoundland	156,578	148,610	305,188
	2,639,164	2,769,355	5,408,519
Inland Navigation.			
Canada	3,538,701	3,368,432	6,907,133
Total tons	6,177,865	6,137,787	12,315,652

Now, the United States are in the same position as we are in respect to this inland traffic, and they include it in their returns as is done here. And what do you think is the difference between their tonnage and ours? Why, ours is over twelve millions and theirs is but sixteen millions. There are not four millions of tons of difference between the two. And let it be recollected that the United States have had seventy years start of us. As regards France, the whole amount of shipping that entered and left the ports of that great country in one year was but 8,456,734 tons—four millions of tons less than that of the British American Provinces. May we not then, when this union is accomplished, fairly claim to be the third maritime state of the world ; and may we not even entertain the hope that, at some future day, a still higher position is not beyond our reach, when the days of puberty have been passed and the strength of manhood has been reached? I ask honourable gentlemen, in looking at these figures, to consider what the effect must be when they are set down thus collectively, side by side, in official commercial returns, in comparison with the commerce of all the great maritime states? Will it not strengthen our position abroad? will it not give us a degree of influence and importance to have it known that British America wields so large a share of the world's commerce? And if honourable gentlemen will still further consider the deep importance to Canada, in her inland position, of exercising her just influence in the control of so valuable a maritime interest, I think they will come to the conclusion that all the objections urged against this union are, in the balance of its advantages, utterly contemptible.

In the fourth place, I go for a union of the provinces, because it will give a new start to immigration into our country. It will bring us out anew prominently before the world—it will turn earnest attention to our resources, and bring to our shores a stream of immigration greater, and of a better class, than we ever had before. I was in England when the first public announcement of this scheme was made, and witnessed, with pleasure, the marked impression it produced. You could not go abroad, you could not enter into any company, in any class of society, where Canada or the British American Provinces were mentioned, but you heard this union movement spoken of almost with enthusiasm. And I say that it is desirable that this scheme should not be delayed, but be carried through promptly and vigorously. I hesitate not to say that it should be accomplished with a vigorous effort to give a new impetus to our industrial enterprises, to open up fresh lands for settlement, and to cheapen the transport of our produce to the sea-board. With the consummation of this union, I trust we will have a new immigration and a new land settlement policy—that we will ascertain every lot of land we actually own, so that a printed list may be placed in the hands of every immigrant—that the petty price we have been heretofore exacting will no longer be exacted, but that to actual settlers, who come among us to hew out for themselves and their children homes in the forest, no burthen or condition will be demanded, beyond resident occupation for a certain number of years, and a fixed amount of improvement on the land.

Hon. Mr. Holton : Unfortunately for your argument, the lands will be in the hands of the local governments.

Hon. Mr. Brown : So much the better. My honourable friend can manage his public lands in Lower Canada as he likes, and we will manage ours. And, speaking for the western section, I am bound to say there are very few shrewd men in Upper Canada who do not feel that far more public benefit is to be gained from the industry of a hardy actual settler upon 100 acres of land given to him free, than the trumpery $150 that can be squeezed out of him as its price, the payment of which keeps him in trouble perhaps for years, and retards the progress of the country. On this question of immigration turns, in my opinion, the whole future success of this great scheme which we are now discussing. Why, there is hardly a political and financial or social problem suggested by this union that does not find its best solution in a large influx of immigration. The larger our population, the greater will be our productions, the more valuable our exports, and the greater our ability to develop the resources of our country. The greater the number of tax-payers, and the more densely they are settled, the more lightly will the burden of taxation fall upon us all. And in this question of immigration is found the only true solution of the problem of defence. Fill up our vacant lands, double our population, and we will at once be in a position to meet promptly and effectually any invader who may put his foot with hostile intent upon our soil.

And this question of immigration naturally brings me to the great subject of the North-West Territories. The resolutions before us recognize the immediate necessity of those great territories being brought within the confederation and opened up for settlement. But I am told that, while the Intercolonial Railroad has been made an absolute condition of the compact, the opening up of the great west and the enlargement of our canals

have been left in doubt. Now, nothing can be more unjust than this.
Let me read the resolutions :

"The general government shall secure, without delay, the completion
of the Intercolonial Railway from Riviere du Loup, through New Brunswick to Truro, in Nova Scotia.

"The communications with the North-Western Territory, and the improvements required for the development of the trade of the great west
with the seaboard, are regarded by this conference as subjects of the highest importance to the federated provinces, and shall be prosecuted at the
earliest possible period that the state of the finances will permit."

The confederation is, therefore, clearly committed to the carrying out
of both these enterprises. I doubt if there was a member of the conference who did not consider that the opening up of the north-west and the
improvement of our canal system were not as clearly for the advantage of
the Lower Provinces as for the interests of Upper Canada. Indeed, one
gentleman held that the Lower Provinces were more interested—they
wished to get their products into the west, they wanted a back country
as much as we did, they wanted to be the carriers for that great country
—and they were, therefore, to say the least, as much interested in these
questions as we were. But honourable gentlemen lay stress upon the
point that, while the one enterprise is to be undertaken at once, the other
is not to be commenced until the state of the finances will permit. No
doubt this is correct, and the reason for it is simply this : The money has
already been found for the Intercolonial Railway. They must be well
aware that the late government (the Macdonald-Sicotte administration)
agreed to build the Intercolonial Railway. and obtained from the Imperial
government a guarantee of the debentures for building it, so that that
money is ready, at a very low rate of interest, whenever required. We
know where to find the money for one enterprise at a rate we are able to bear,
and can thus at once go on with a work which must be gone on with if this
union is to be consummated. But we don't know this of the other great
work ; and we all felt that it would be exceedingly indiscreet—I, myself,
as the special advocate of opening up the great west and of the enlargement of our canals, felt that I could not put my name to a document which
declared that at all hazards, while our five per cent. debentures were
quoted at 75 or 80 per cent. in the money market, we would commence at
once, without an hour's delay, any great public work whatever. Honourable gentlemen opposite must not imagine that they have to do with a set
of tricksters in the thirty-three gentlemen who composed that conference.
What we have said in our resolutions was deliberately adopted, in the
honest sense of the words employed, and not for purposes of deception.
Both works are to go on at the earliest possible moment our finances will
permit, and honourable gentlemen will find the members of the cabinet,
from Lower as well as from Upper Canada, actuated by the hearty desire
to have this whole scheme carried out in its fair meaning.

When recently in England, I was charged to negotiate with the Imperial government for the opening up of the North-West Territories. In a few days the papers will be laid before the House, and it will then be seen whether or not this government is in earnest in that matter. The gentlemen who formed the conference at Quebec did not enter upon their work with the miserable idea of getting the advantage of each other, but with a due sense of the greatness of the work they had on hand, with an earnest desire to do justice to all, and keeping always in mind that what would benefit one section in such a union must necessarily benefit the whole. It has always appeared to me that the opening up of the north-west ought to be one of the most cherished projects of my honourable friends from Lower Canada. During the discussion on the question for some years back I had occasion to dip deep in north-west lore—into those singularly interesting narratives of life and travels in the north-west in the olden time, and into the history of the struggles for commercial dominancy in the great fur-bearing regions ; and it has always struck me that the French Canadian people have cause to look back with pride to the bold and successful part they played in the adventures of those days. Nothing perhaps has tended more to create their present national character than the vigorous habits, the power of endurance, the aptitude for out-door life, acquired in their prosecution of the north-west fur trade. Well may they look forward with anxiety to the realization of this part of our scheme, in confident hope that the great north-western traffic shall be once more opened up to the hardy French Canadian traders and *voyageurs*. Last year furs to the value of £280,000 stg. ($1,400,000) were carried from that territory by the Hudson's Bay Company—smuggled off through the ice-bound regions of James' Bay—that the pretence of the barrenness of the country, and the difficulty of conveying merchandise by the natural route of the St. Lawrence, may be kept up a little longer. The carrying of merchandise into that country, and bringing down the bales of pelts ought to be ours, and must ere long be ours, as in the days of yore ; and when the fertile plains of that great Saskatchewan territory are opened up for settlement and cultivation, I am confident that it will not only add immensely to our annual agricultural products, but bring us sources of mineral and other wealth on which at present we do not reckon.

While speaking on this question of immigration, I would remind the House, and it is impossible to urge it too strongly, that these provinces are now presented to the world in a very disadvantageous aspect, as different communities. When a party in Europe thinks of emigrating here, he has to ascertain separately all about New Brunswick, and Prince Edward Island, and Nova Scotia, and Upper and Lower Canada, and if by chance he meets a party from some one of these provinces, he has to listen to a picture of the merits of that one section in high contrast to the demerits of all the rest, and the result is the poor man's ideas about us become a mass of confusion. On the other hand, if he seeks to know the inducements for emigration to New South Wales or New Zealand, he gets it in one picture— in an official form—and the offer is made to pay his passage to these lands of hope.   A large amount of emigration, and of money which the emigrant takes with him, are thus carried off to a much more distant land than this, and one that does not offer equal inducements to the settler.   But how different will all this be when these provinces stand united, and present to emigrants a combination of so many branches of profitable industry?   In turning over some United States statistics, I recently fell upon a very curious official calculation, made by the United States government, as to the value of immigration.   By the census of 1861 the population of the United States was over thirty millions; and this calculation was to ascertain what the population would have been had there been no immigration into the country, but the population had been left to advance solely by its own natural increase.   And what do you think was the result?   Why, it is shown that if the United States had received all the immigrants that came to them up to 1820, and then stopped receiving them, the population, at this moment, instead of 30,000,000, would have been but 14,601,485.   It is shown that if immigration had gone on until 1810, and stopped then, the population now would have been only 12,678,562.   Had it stopped in 1800, the population now would have been 10,462,944; and had it stopped in 1790, the population now, instead of 30,000,000, would have been but 8,789,969.   These are most valuable facts, which should be impressed on the mind of every public man in British America.   If we wish our country to progress, we should not leave a single stone unturned to attract the tide of emigration in this direction; and I know no better method of securing that result, than the gathering into one of these five provinces, and presenting ourselves to the world in the advantageous light which, when united, we would occupy.

Fifthly, I am in favour of a union of these provinces, because it will enable us to meet, without alarm, the abrogation of the American reciprocity treaty, in case the United States should insist on its abolition. I do not believe that the American government is so insane as to repeal that treaty.   But it is always well to be prepared for contingencies; and I have no hesitation in saying that if they do repeal it, should this union of British America go on, a fresh outlet for our commerce will be opened up to us quite as advantageous as the American trade has ever been.   I have never heretofore ventured to make this assertion, for I know well what a serious task it is to change, in one day, the commercial relations of such a country as this.   When the traffic of a country has passed for a lengthened period through a particular channel, any serious change of that channel tends, for a time, to the embarrassment of business men, and causes serious injury to individuals, if not the whole community. Such a change we in Canada had in 1847.   But as it was in 1847, so it will be in 1866, if the reciprocity treaty is abolished.   Our agricultural interest had been built up on the protective legislation of Great Britain, and in 1847 it was suddenly brought to an end.   We suffered severely, in consequence, for some years; but by degrees new channels for our trade opened up—the reciprocity treaty was negotiated—and we have been more prosperous since 1847 than we ever were before.   And so, I have not a doubt, will it be in the event of the reciprocity treaty being abolished. Profitable as that treaty has unquestionably been to us—and it has been more profitable to the Americans—still, were it brought to an end to-morrow, though we would suffer a while from the change, I am convinced the ultimate result would be that other foreign markets would be opened to us quite as profitable, and that we would speedily build up our trade on a sounder basis than at present. A close examination of the working of the reciprocity treaty discloses facts of vital importance to the merits of the question, to which you never hear the slightest allusion made by American speakers or writers. Our neighbours, in speaking of the treaty, keep constantly telling us of the Canadian trade—what they take from Canada and what Canada takes from them. Their whole story is about the buying and selling of commodities in Canada. Not a whisper do you ever hear from them about their buying and selling with the Maritime Provinces— not a word about the enormous carrying trade for all the provinces which they monopolize—not a word of the large sums drawn from us for our vast traffic over their railways and canals—and not a whisper as to their immense profits from fishing in our waters, secured to them by the treaty. No; all we hear of is the exports and imports of Canada—all is silence as to other parts of the treaty. But it must not be forgotten that if the treaty is abolished and this union is accomplished, an abolition of reciprocity with Canada means abolition of reciprocity with all the British American provinces—means bringing to an end the right of the Americans to fish in our waters ; their right to use our canals ; their right to the navigation of the St. Lawrence ; and that it also implies the taking out of their hands the vast and lucrative carrying trade they now have from us. It must be always kept in mind that though the United States purchase from Canada a large amount of agricultural products, a great portion of what they purchase does not go into consumption in the states, but is merely purchased for transmission to Great Britain and the West India markets. They merely act as commission agents and carriers in such transactions, and splendid profits they make out of the business. But beyond this, another large portion of these produce purchases, for which they take so much credit to themselves, they buy in the same manner for export to the Maritime Provinces of British America, reaping all the benefit of the sea-going as well as the inland freight—charges and commissions. The commercial returns of the Lower Provinces show not only that the Americans send a large quantity of their own farm products to those provinces, but a considerable amount of what they (the Americans) receive from us, thereby gaining the double advantage of the carrying trade through the United States to the seaboard, and then by sea to the Lower Provinces. I hold in my hand a return of the articles purchased by the Maritime Provinces from the United States in 1863, which Canada could have supplied. I will not detain the House by reading it, but any member who desires can have it for examination. I may state, however, in brief, that in that year the breadstuffs alone bought by the Lower Provinces amounted to no less than $4,447,207; that the import of meats, fresh and cured, amounted to

$659,917; and that the total value of products which the Lower Provinces might have bought more advantageously from us, summed up to over seven millions of dollars. The Americans must therefore bear in mind, that if they abolish the reciprocity treaty, they will not only lose that seven millions which they now receive for their products, but the carrying trade which goes with it. But, on the other hand, when we have this union, these products will, as they naturally should, go down the St. Lawrence, not only for the advantage of our farmers, but swelling the volume of our own shipping interests. The Americans hitherto have had a large portion of our carrying trade; they have brought us our goods—even our European goods—and taken our produce not only to Europe but even to the Lower Provinces; and I say one of the best features of this union is, that if in our commercial relations with the United States we are compelled by them to meet fire with fire, it will enable us to stop this improvidence, and turn the current of our own trade into our own waters. Far be it from me to say I am an advocate of a coercive commercial policy; on the contrary, entire freedom of trade, in my opinion, is what we in this country should strive for. Without hesitation, I would, to-morrow, throw open the whole of our trade and the whole of our waters to the United States, if they did the same to us. But if they tell us, in the face of all the advantages they get by reciprocity, that they are determined to put a stop to it, and if this is done through a hostile feeling to us—deeply as I should regret that this should be the first use made by the northern states of their new-found liberty—then, I say, we have a policy, and a good policy, of our own to fall back upon. And let me say a word as to the effect of the repeal of reciprocity on the American fishing interest. The Americans, in 1851, had engaged in the cod and mackerel fishing, in our waters, shipping to the extent of 129,014 tons; but under the influence of the reciprocity treaty it rose, in 1861, to 192,662—an increase, in ten years, of upwards of 63,000 tons, or fifty per cent. The repeal of reciprocity will give us back all this increase, and more, for it will be a very different thing in the future from what it was formerly to poach on our fishing grounds, when these provinces are united and determined to protect the fisheries of the gulf. This fishing interest is one which may be cultivated to an extent difficult, perhaps, for many of us to conceive. But we have only to look at the amount of fish taken from our waters by the Americans and other nations, and the advantages we possess, to perceive that if we apply ourselves, as a united people, to foster that trade, we can vastly increase the great traffic we now enjoy. On the whole, then, I come firmly to the conclusion that, in view of the possible stoppage of the American reciprocity treaty, and our being compelled to find new channels for our trade, this union presents to us advantages, in comparison with which any objection that has been offered, or can be offered to it, is utterly insignificant.

Sixthly, I am in favour of the union of the provinces, because, in the event of war, it will enable all the colonies to defend themselves better, and give more efficient aid to the empire, than they could do separately. I am not one of those who ever had the war-fever; I have not believed in getting up large armaments in this country ; I have never doubted that a military spirit, to a certain extent, did necessarily form part of the character of a great people ; but I felt that Canada had not yet reached that stage in her progress when she could safely assume the duty of defence ; and that, so long as peace continued and the mother country threw her shield around us, it was well for us to cultivate our fields and grow in numbers and material strength, until we could look our enemies fearlessly in the face. But it must be admitted—and there is no use of closing our eyes to the fact—that this question of defence has been placed, within the last two years, in a totally different position from what it ever occupied before. The time has come—it matters not what political party may be in power in England—when Britain will insist on a reconsideration of the military relations which a great colony, such as Canada, ought to hold to the empire. And I am free to admit that it is a fair and just demand. We may doubt whether some of the demands that have been made upon us, without regard to our peculiar position at the moment, and without any attempt to discuss the question with us in all its breadth, were either just or well considered. But of this I think there can be no doubt, that when the time comes in the history of any colony that it has overcome the burdens and embarrassments of early settlement, and has entered on a career of permanent progress and prosperity, it is only fair and right that it should contribute its quota to the defence of the empire. What that quota ought to be, I think, is a matter for grave deliberation and discussion, as well as the measure of assistance the colony may look for, in time of war, from the parent state ; and assuredly, it is in this spirit that the present Imperial government is desirous of approaching the question. I am persuaded that nothing more than that which is fairly due at our hands will be demanded from us, and anything less than this, I am sure, the people of Canada do not desire. In the conversations I had, while in England, with public men of different politics, while I found many who considered that the connection between Canada and England involved the mother country in some danger of war with the powerful state upon our borders, and that the colonial system devolved heavy and unreasonable burdens upon the mother country, and while a still larger number thought we had not acted as cordially and energetically as we ought in organizing our militia for the defence of the province, still I did not meet one public man, of any stripe of politics, who did not readily and heartily declare that, in case of the invasion of Canada, the honour of Great Britain would be at stake, and the whole strength of the empire would be unhesitatingly marshalled in our defence. But, coupled with this, was the invariable and most reasonable declaration that a share of the burden of defence, in peace and in war, we must contribute. And this stipulation applies not only to Canada, but to every one of the colonies. Already the Indian empire has been made to pay the whole expense of her military establishment. The Australian colonies have agreed to pay £40 sterling per man for every soldier sent there. This system is being gradually extended; and, union or no union, assuredly every one of these British American colonies will be called upon to bear her fair share towards the defence of the empire. And who will deny that it is a just demand, and that great colonies such as these should be proud to meet it in a frank and earnest spirit. Nothing, I am persuaded, could be more foreign to the ideas of the people of Canada, than that the people of England should be unfairly taxed for service rendered to this province. Now, the question presented to us is simply this: Will these contributions which Canada and the other provinces must hereafter make to the defence of the empire, be better rendered by a hardy, energetic population, acting as one people, than as five or six separate communities? There is no doubt about it. But not only do our changed relations towards the mother country call on us to assume the new duty of military defence —our changed relations towards the neighbouring republic compel us to do so. For myself, I have no belief that the Americans have the slightest thought of attacking us. I cannot believe that the first use of their new-found liberty will be the invasion, totally unprovoked, of a peaceful province. I fancy that they have had quite enough of war for a good many years to come, and that such a war as one with England would certainly be is the last they are likely to provoke. There is no better mode of warding off war when it is threatened than to be prepared for it if it comes. The Americans are now a warlike people. They have large armies, a powerful navy, an unlimited supply of warlike munitions, and the carnage of war has to them been stript of its horrors. The American side of our lines already bristles with works of defence, and unless we are willing to live at the mercy of our neighbours, we too must put our country in a state of efficient preparation. War or no war, the necessity of placing these provinces in a thorough state of defence can no longer be postponed. Our country is coming to be regarded as undefended and indefensible—the capitalist is alarmed, and the immigrant is afraid to come among us. Were it merely as a measure of commercial advantage, every one of these colonies must meet the question of military defence promptly and energetically. And how can we do this so efficiently and economically as by the union now proposed? I have already shown that union would give us a body of 70,000 hardy seamen ready and able to defend our sea-coasts and inland lakes; let us now see what would be the military strength of the confederation. By the last census (1861) it appears that the men (from 20 to 60 years of age) capable of bearing arms in British America, were as follows: Upper Canada, 308,955; Lower Canada, 225,620; Nova Scotia, 67,367; New Brunswick, 51,625; Newfoundland, 25,532; Prince Edward Island (from 21 to 60 years of age), 14,819; total, 693,918. With the body of efficient soldiers that might be obtained from this vast array of men, the erection of defensive works at salient points, and the force of British troops that would soon come to our aid, who can doubt that the invasion of our country would be successfully resisted?

Seventhly, I am in favour of this union because it will give us a sea-board at all seasons of the year. It is not to be denied that the position of Canada, shut off as she is from the sea-board during the winter months, is far from satisfactory; and should the United States carry out their insane threat of abolishing the bonding system, by which our merchandise passes free through their territory, it would be still more embarrassing. The Maritime Provinces are equally cut off from communication inland. Now, this embarrassment will be ended by colonial union. The Intercolonial Railway will give us at all times access to the Atlantic through British territory. As a commercial enterprise, the Intercolonial Railway has not, I apprehend, any considerable merit; as a work of defence it has, however, many advocates; but if the union of the provinces is to go on, it is an absolute necessity; and as the price of union, were there no other argument in its favour, I heartily go for it. The advantage it will confer on the Maritime Provinces can hardly be overrated. It will make Halifax and St. John the Atlantic sea-ports of half a continent; it will insure to Halifax, ere long, the establishment of a line of powerful steamers running in six days from her wharves to some near point on the west coast of Ireland; and it will bring a constant stream of passengers and immigrants through those lower provinces that never otherwise would come near them.

I could go on for many hours piling up arguments in favour of this scheme, but already I have detained the House too long, and must draw to a close. But I think I have given reasons enough to satisfy every candid man who desires the advancement of his country, why this House should go unanimously and enthusiastically for "the union, the whole union, and nothing but the union!" Before sitting down, however, there are one or two general objections urged against the scheme which I am desirous of meeting, and I will try to do so as briefly as possible. And first, I am told that we should have made the union legislative and not federal. Undoubtedly this is a point on which different opinions may be honestly held by men sincerely seeking the same ends; but, speaking my own views, I think we came to a most wise conclusion. Had we continued the present legislative union, we must have continued with it the unjust system of taxation for local purposes that now exists, and the sectional bickering would have gone on as before. And can any honourable gentleman really believe that it would have been possible for a body of men sitting at Ottawa to administer efficiently and wisely the parish business of Red River and Newfoundland and all the country between? Only think of bringing suitors and witnesses such distances to promote a bill for closing a side-line or incorporating a club! And if such a thing were desirable, would it be possible for any body of men to go through such a mass of work? Why, the Imperial parliament, with 650 members, sits for eight months in the year, and even our parliament sits three or four months; how then would it be possible for the legislature of all the provinces, with a thousand or twelve hundred bills before it, to accomplish it all? The whole year would not suffice for it—and who in these colonies is able to sacrifice his whole time to the duties of public life? But there is another reason why the union was not made legislative—it could not be carried. We had either to take the federal union or drop the negotiation. Not only were our friends from Lower

Canada against it, but so were most of the delegates from the Maritime Provinces. There was but one choice open to us—federal union or nothing. But, in truth, the scheme now before us has all the advantages of a legislative union and a federal one as well. We have thrown over on the localities all the questions which experience has shown lead directly to local jealousy and discord, and we have retained in the hands of the general government all the powers necessary to secure a strong and efficient administration of public affairs. By placing the appointment of the judges in the hands of the general government, and the establishment of a central court of appeal, we have secured uniformity of justice over the whole land. By vesting the appointment of the lieutenant-governors in the general government, and giving a veto for all local measures, we have secured that no injustice shall be done without appeal in local legislation. For all dealings with the Imperial government and foreign countries, we have clothed the general government with the most ample powers. And finally, all matters of trade and commerce, banking and currency, and all questions common to the whole people, we have vested fully and unrestrictedly in the general government. The measure, in fact, shuns the faults of the federal and legislative systems and adopts the best parts of both, and I am well persuaded it will work efficiently and satisfactorily.

I am told that the cost of working this federation scheme will be enormous. Now, it would be a very rash thing for me, or any other person, to assert that the expense will not be great ; for we all know that any system of government may be made either economical or extravagant precisely according to the discretion of those who administer it. But this I am confident of, that with ordinary discretion, far from being more costly than the existing system, a very considerable reduction may be readily effected ; and one thing is quite certain, that no ingenuity could make it a more costly or extravagant system than the one we have now. Undoubtedly the mode in which the local governments shall be constructed will very much affect the cost of the whole scheme ; but if we adopt (as I earnestly hope we will) simple and inexpensive machinery for local purposes, I am quite satisfied that there will be a reduction to the people of Canada on the amount they now contribute. I have great confidence in the economical effect of placing local expenditures on local shoulders, and in the salutary influence, in the same direction, of the representatives of the Maritime Provinces when they come among us.

Hon. Mr. Holton : The trouble is that they will spend our money—not theirs.

Hon. Mr. Brown : The honourable gentleman is entirely wrong, and I am amazed at his making such a statement. There is no portion of the community that will pay more money, per head, to the revenue, than the people of the Maritime Provinces. If the honourable gentleman had turned up the commercial returns of those lower provinces and calculated the effect of our tariff, if applied to them—or even a tariff less than ours, for our tariff must be reduced—he would have known that they will bear their full proportion of the national burdens.

I am told that the arrangement as to the debt is unfair—that we have thrown on the federal exchequer the whole of the debts of the Maritime Provinces, but only a portion of the debt of Canada. There is not a particle of force in this objection. The whole debt of Canada is $67,500,000, but five millions of this is due to our own people, to meet which there are certain local funds. Now, if we had thrown the whole $67,500,000 on the federal treasury, we must also have handed over to it the local revenues, which, so far as these five millions are concerned, would have been precisely the same thing. But, as regards the public debt with which the federal government would start, it would not have been the same thing. By restricting the debt of Canada to $62,500,000, we restricted the debt of the Maritime Provinces to the same proportion, or $25 per head of their population ; but had we thrown our whole debt of sixty-seven and a half millions on the confederation, the proportion of debt for the several Maritime Provinces must have been increased, and the whole debt very greatly augmented. But in throwing these five millions on the local governments of Upper and Lower Canada, do we impose a burden on them they are unable to bear? Quite the contrary ; for with the debt, we give them the corresponding sources of revenue from which to meet it. The local governments of Upper and Lower Canada will severally not only have funds, from the subsidy and other sources, to meet all expenditure, but a large surplus besides. I am told that this federation scheme may be all very right—it may be just, and the very thing the country needs—but this government had no authority from parliament to negotiate it. The honourable member for Cornwall (Hon. John S. Macdonald) particularly pressed this objection, and I am sorry he is not in his seat.

Hon. Mr. Holton : It is quite true.

Hon. Mr. Cartier : No, the reverse is true.

Hon. Mr. Brown : I am astonished to hear such a statement repeated. No one knows better than the honourable member for Chateauguay and the honourable member for Cornwall that in the ministerial explanations brought down to this House at the time of the formation of this government, it was distinctly declared that the government was formed for the special purpose of maturing a scheme of federal union, and that it would take means, during the recess, for opening negotiations with the Maritime Provinces, to bring about such a union.

Hon. Mr. Holton : But not to conclude them.

Hon. Mr. Brown : What we have done is entirely subject to the approval of parliament. The honourable member for Cornwall is the very last man who should have raised such an objection, for he attended a caucus of the liberal members of the assembly, heard the whole plans of the government explained, precisely as they have been carried out, and he was the very person who moved that I should go into the government to give them effect.

MR. DUNKIN : And I heard something more said—that nothing should be done which did not leave the House perfectly free.

HON. MR. BROWN : I can assure my honourable friend that, as far as that goes, he never was more free in his life than now. We do not pretend to say that anything we have done binds this House ; any member may object if he pleases : but I do say we received the approval of the House for opening negotiations, and it is a miserable pretence to say anything to the contrary. We did no more than has been done by every government, under the British system, that ever existed. We have but made a compact, subject to the approval of parliament. So far as this government is concerned, we are firmly committed to the scheme ; but so far as the members of the legislature are concerned, they are as free as air; but I am confident that this House will almost unanimously accept it—and not with changes and amendments, but as a whole—as the very best compromise arrangement that can be obtained.

HON. MR. HOLTON : We have not the treaty-making power.

HON. MR. BROWN : I remember a government formed from that side of the House, and the honourable member for Hochelaga (Hon. Mr. Dorion) will remember it too, which made a treaty respecting the building of the Intercolonial Railroad. The honourable member for Cornwall was premier of that government, and it does not lie in his mouth now to object to what he himself did. But the honourable gentleman is entirely wrong when he says we had no power to make this compact with the Maritime Provinces. We had full power, express instructions to enter into it.

HON. MR. HOLTON : Did the Parliament of England give you that power?

HON. MR. BROWN : No ; the honourable gentleman ought to know that the treaty-making power is in the Crown—the Crown authorized us specially to make this compact, and it has heartily approved of what we did.

I am told that the people of Canada have not considered this scheme, and that we ought not to pass it without appealing to the electors for their approval. Now a statement more incorrect than this, or more injurious to the people of Canada, could not be made. They not only have considered this scheme—for fifteen years they have been earnestly considering it—but they perfectly comprehend it. If ever question was thoroughly debated in any country, the whole subject of constitutional change has been in Canada. There is not a light in which it could be placed that has not been thoroughly canvassed ; and if the House will permit me, I will show from our historical record how totally absurd this objection is. The question of a federal union was agitated thirty years ago, and here is the resolution adopted by both Houses of the Imperial parliament so far back as 1837:

"That great inconvenience has been sustained by His Majesty's subjects inhabiting the provinces of Lower Canada and Upper Canada, from the want of some adequate means for regulating and adjusting questions respecting the trade and commerce of the said provinces, and divers other questions wherein the said provinces have a common interest ; and it is expedient that the legislatures of the said provinces respectively be authorized to make provision for the joint regulation and adjustment of such their common interests."

In the instructions given to Lord Durham by the Imperial government in 1838, this passage occurs :

"It is clear that some plan must be devised to meet the just demands of Upper Canada. It will be for your Lordship, in conjunction with the committee, to consider if this should not be done by constituting some joint legislative authority, which should preside over all questions of common interest to the two provinces, and which might be appealed to in extraordinary cases, to arbitrate between contending parties in either ; preserving, however, to each province its distinct legislature, with authority in all matters of an exclusively domestic concern. If this should be your opinion, you will have further time to consider what should be the nature and limits of such authority, and all the particulars which ought to be comprehended in any scheme for its establishment."

In Lord Durham's admirable report of 1839, I find this passage :

"The bill should contain provisions by which any or all of the other North American colonies may, on the application of the legislature, be, with the consent of the two Canadas or their united legislature, admitted into the union on such terms as may be agreed on between them. As the mere amalgamation of the Houses of Assembly of the two provinces would not be advisable, or give at all a due representation to each, a parliamentary commission should be appointed for the purpose of forming the electoral divisions and determining the number of members to be returned on the principle of giving representation as near as may be in proportion to population. The same commission should form a plan of local government by elective bodies, subordinate to the general legislature, and exercising a complete control over such local affairs as do not come within the province of general legislation. The plan so framed should be made an Act of the Imperial parliament, so as to prevent the general legislature from encroaching on the powers of the local bodies. A general executive on an improved principle should be established, together with the supreme court of appeal for all the North American colonies."

And here is the statement of Lord John Russell, in 1839, while introducing the original bill founded on Lord Durham's report :

"The bill provides for the establishment of a central district at Montreal and its neighbourhood, at which the government shall be carried on, and where the assembly shall meet. The other parts of Upper and of Lower Canada are each to be divided into two districts. It is proposed that these districts should be formed for the purpose of becoming municipal districts, for the imposition of taxes and rates for all local purposes."

My next quotation shall be from the proceedings of a body of gentlemen who made a great commotion in their day and generation—the British American League. I hold in my hand the proceedings of the league of 3rd November, 1849, and among other names mentioned I find those of the Hon. George Moffatt, Thomas Wilson, the Hon. Geo. Crawford, the Hon. Asa A. Burnham, John W. Gamble, Mr. Aikman, of Barton, Ogle R. Gowan, John Duggan, the Hon. Col. Fraser, George Benjamin, the Hon. P. M. Vankoughnet, and last, though not least, the Hon. John A. Macdonald—of whom, however, I find it recorded that he spoke in a very jocose manner. Here is the resolution of the league :

"That whether protection or reciprocity shall be conceded or withheld, it is essential to the welfare of this colony, and its future good government, that a constitution should be framed in unison with the wishes of the people, and suited to the growing importance and intelligence of the country, and that such constitution should embrace a union of the British North American Provinces on mutually advantageous and fairly arranged terms, with the concession from the mother country of enlarged powers of self-government."

I pass on to 1856, when we had the motion and speech of my honourable friend the Minister of Finance (Hon. Mr. Galt) in favour of a union of all the British American Provinces, but, as the whole House is familiar with it, I shall not read the document. But in the Votes and Proceedings of this House, of 25th April, 1856, I find a very remarkable document. It is a notice of motion to be made in this House, and its contents are as follows :

" *Resolved,*—1. That the inconveniences arising from the Legislative Union between Upper and Lower Canada, render desirable the dissolution of that Union.

" 2. That a committee be appointed to inquire into the means which should be adopted to form a new political and legislative organization of the heretofore provinces of Upper and Lower Canada, either by the establishment of their former territorial divisions, or by a division of each province so as to form a confederation having a federal government and a local legislature for each one of the new provinces, and to deliberate as to the course which should be adopted to regulate the affairs of united Canada in a manner which would be equitable to the different sections of the province."

Hon. Mr. Cartier: Whose notice was that?

Hon. Mr. Brown: This notice of motion was given by my honourable friend the member for Hochelaga (Hon. Mr. Dorion).

Hon. Mr. Dorion: It was in amendment of that of the honourable member for Sherbrooke, which I did not exactly like.

Hon. Mr. Holton: And which that honourable gentleman did not venture to move, so that the House did not pronounce upon it.

Hon. Mr. Brown : But my honourable friend (Hon. Mr. Dorion) made a speech which I perfectly remember. He held this motion in his hand while he spoke.

Hon. Mr. Dorion : I made a speech on the motion of the honourable member for Haldimand, Mr. Mackenzie, not on my own.

Hon. Mr. Brown : That does not signify. I seek not to fasten down my honourable friend to the views he then held. Much light has been thrown on the whole subject since 1856, and I trust we will all act on our conscientious convictions of what is best for the country now, without regard to any opinions we may at other times have held. But when my honourable friend and others allege that there never has been in Canada an agitation in favour of a federal system, and that the people have never considered such a proposition, I think it directly in point to prove the contrary by my honourable friend's own proceedings. The next step in the constitutional agitation of the country was the formation of the Brown-Dorion administration. That was in 1858 ; and to show how serious my honourable friend opposite (Hon. Mr. Dorion) and myself and our ten colleagues viewed the position of the country from the denial of constitutional reform, I will read the official statement of the basis on which the government was formed. I read from the Journals of the Legislative Council for 1858 :

"For some years past, sectional feelings have risen in this country, which, especially during the present session, have seriously impeded the carrying on of the administrative and legislative functions of the government. The late administration made no attempt to meet these difficulties or to suggest a remedy for them, and thereby the evil has been greatly aggravated. His Excellency's present advisers have entered the government with the fixed determination to propose constitutional measures for the establishment of that harmony between Upper and Lower Canada which is essential to the prosperity of the province. They respectfully submit that they have a right to claim all the support which His Excellency can constitutionally extend to them in the prosecution of this all-important object."

Here was a government formed seven years ago for the express purpose of doing that which we are now engaged in—a government distinctly telling the Governor-General that the peace and prosperity of the country were endangered because constitutional remedies were deferred ; and yet my honourable friends opposite, who with me were responsible for that document, tell us that we are not now in a fit position to legislate upon this question. But I come next to the famous despatch to the Colonial Minister, signed in 1858 by my honourable friend the Minister of Finance, the Attorney-General (east), and the Hon. John Ross. It stated that "very grave difficulties now present themselves in conducting the government of Canada ;" that "the progress of population has been more rapid in the western section, and claims are now made on behalf of its inhabitants for giving them representation in the legislature in proportion to their numbers ;" that "the result is shown by an agitation fraught with great danger to the peaceful and harmonious working of our constitutional system, and, consequently, detrimental to the progress of the province;" that "this state of things is yearly becoming worse;" and that "the Canadian government were impressed with the necessity of seeking for such a mode of dealing with those difficulties as may for ever remove them." What must have been the state of public feeling when the conservative government of 1858 ventured to use such language as this?—and how can any one pretend that the people do not comprehend this question, when seven years of agitation have passed since that document was penned?

I come now to a still more important document—one that goes into the details and the merits of just such a scheme as that before the House. I refer to the manifesto issued, in 1859, by the Lower Canada members of the liberal party in this House. It is very long, and I will only read from it a few extracts:

"Your committee are impressed with the conviction that whether we consider the present needs or the probable future condition of the country, the true, the statesmanlike solution is to be sought in the substitution of a purely federative for the present so-called legislative union ; the former, it is believed, would enable us to escape all the evils, and to retain all the advantages, appertaining to the existing union.   .   .   .   .   .

"The proposition to federalize the Canadian union is not new. On the contrary, it has been frequently mooted in parliament and in the press during the last few years. It was, no doubt, suggested by the example of the neighbouring states, where the admirable adaptation of the federal system to the government of an extensive territory, inhabited by people of divers origins, creeds, laws and customs, has been amply demonstrated; but shape and consistency were first imparted to it in 1856, when it was formally submitted to parliament by the Lower Canada opposition, as offering, in their judgment, the true corrective of the abuses generated under the present system.   .   .   .   .

"By this division of power the general government would be relieved from those questions of a purely local and sectional character, which, under our present system, have led to much strife and ill-will.   .   .   .

" The committee believe that it is clearly demonstrable that the direct cost of maintaining both the federal and local governments need not exceed that of our present system, while its enormous indirect cost would, in consequence of the additional checks on expenditure involved in the new system, and the more direct responsibility of public servants in the province to the people immediately affected by such expenditure, be entirely obviated.   .   .   .

"The proposed system could in no way diminish the importance of the colony, or impair its credit, while it presents the advantage of being susceptible, without any disturbance of the federal economy, of such territorial extension as circumstances may hereafter render desirable."

Now, who were the signers of the address ?—on whose special responsibility was this manifesto sent forth to the world? Why, it was signed by my honourable friend opposite, Hon. A. A. Dorion, Hon. T. D. McGee, Hon. L. T. Drummond, and Hon. L. A. Dessaulles, four of the most able and most popular leaders of the Lower Canada liberal party—the party now virulently opposing the resolutions before the chair. So my honourable friend opposite (Hon. Mr. Dorion) not only agitated the country for constitutional changes, but insisted that it should take the shape of a federal union, because of the cheapness of that system and the facility it afforded for bringing within the federation the other British American Provinces; and yet, six years after the promulgation of this document, my honourable friend gets up and repudiates a federal union because of its frightful cost, and because it does bring within the federation the other British American Provinces!

Mr. Powell : Who wrote that document?

Hon. Mr. Brown : I cannot exactly say who did the composition; but will not my honourable friend from Chateauguay (Hon. Mr. Holton) permit me to ask if his hand is not discoverable in it? If so, he well may be proud of it, for it is a masterly exposition.

Hon. Mr. Holton : Will my honourable friend accept it as an amendment to his scheme?

Hon. Mr. Galt : No; ours is better than that !

Hon. Mr. Brown : I come now to the great meeting of the reformers of Upper Canada, known as the Toronto convention of 1859, and at which 570 delegates were present from all parts of the western province. Here are the two chief resolutions :

"5. *Resolved,*—That in the opinion of this assembly, the best practicable remedy for the evils now encountered in the government of Canada is to be found in the formation of two or more local governments, to which shall be committed the control of all matters of a local or sectional character, and some joint authority charged with such matters as are necessarily common to both sections of the province.

"6. *Resolved,*—That while the details of the changes proposed in the last resolution are necessarily subject for future arrangement, yet this assembly deems it imperative to declare that no government would be satisfactory to the people of Upper Canada which is not based on the principle of representation by population."

Here we have the very essence of the measure now before us for adoption—deliberately approved of by the largest body of representative men ever assembled in Upper Canada for a political purpose; and yet we are to be told that our people do not understand the question, and we must go to them and explain it, letter by letter, at an immense cost to the country, and at the risk of losing the whole scheme? But let us see what followed. A general election was ordered in 1861—there was a fierce contest at the polls—and the main question at every hustings was the demand for constitutional changes. The result of that contest was the overthrow of the Cartier-Macdonald ministry and the formation of the Macdonald-Sicotte administration in its room. But so bitter had been the struggle for and against constitutional changes, and so clearly defined were party lines upon it, that it was found impossible to construct that government without a distinct pledge that it would resist every motion made upon the subject—

Hon. Mr. Holton : Did you recognize the propriety of that course ?

Hon. Mr. Brown : No, indeed, I did not. I but cite the fact to show how thoroughly the whole question has been agitated, and how perfectly its bearings have, for years past, been understood. Well, mark what followed. One short year had not passed over the heads of the Macdonald-Sicotte ministry before they tottered to their fall; and so repugnant to the House and to the country was their conduct on the constitutional question, that they dared not appeal to the country until they had changed their avowed policy upon it, and replaced the men who had forced upon them the narrow policy of the year before, by gentlemen understood to be more in favour of constitutional changes. The government (Macdonald-Dorion), so reconstructed, went to the country in 1863, but in the year following, it too fell in its turn, simply because it did not deal boldly with the constitutional question—

Hon. Mr. Dorion : We had the support of all who were in favour of the question.

Hon. Mr. Brown : Indeed, you had not.

Hon. Mr. Holton : We should have fallen if we had attempted to deal with it.

Hon. Mr. Brown : I entirely deny that ; had you pursued a bold policy upon it you might have been in office up to this hour. Well, the Macdonald-Dorion made away for the Taché-Macdonald administration, but it too soon fell by a majority of two, simply because it did not deal with the constitutional question—

A Voice : Oh, oh !

Hon. Mr. Brown : My honourable friend cries "Oh, oh," and I am perfectly amazed at his doing so. I am about to offer my honourable friend the most complete proof of the correctness of my statement—proof so conclusive that if he does not accept of it as such, I do not know how he can be convinced of anything. In one single day the Taché-Macdonald administration, by taking up the constitutional question boldly, turned their minority of two into a majority of seventy. Could anything prove more unanswerably than this the deep hold this question has on the public mind, and the assured confidence of the members of this House that their constituents understand its whole merits, when, in one day, such a startling political revolution was brought about ? Was it, think you, a doubtful consideration that could have induced the Upper Canada opposition, almost as one man, to cast down their party intrenchments and make

common cause with their opponents? Could there have been the slightest
doubt as to the sentiments of our people and the imperative necessity of
immediate action, when such men as now sit on the treasury benches were
forced, by their supporters, to unite for the settlement of this question?
And could there be a more conclusive proof of the ripeness of public opinion
than the unanimous and cordial manner in which our so uniting has been
sustained by the press of all parties, and by the electors at the polls?
Never, I venture to assert, was any great measure so thoroughly understood, and so cordially endorsed by the people of Canada, as this measure
now under consideration. The British government approves of it, the
legislative council approves of it, this House almost unanimously approves
of it, the press of all parties approves of it; and though the scheme has
already been directly submitted to fifty out of the one hundred constituencies into which Canada is divided, only four candidates ventured to appear
at the hustings in opposition to it—all of them in Lower Canada—and but
two of them were elected.

And yet we are to be told that we are stealing a march upon the
country; that it is not understood by the people; and that we must dissolve the House upon it, at a vast cost to the exchequer, and at the risk of
allowing political partisanship to dash the fruit from our hands at the very
moment we are about to grasp it! I have no fears whatever of an appeal
to the people. I cannot pretend to speak as to the popular feeling in
Lower Canada, but I think I thoroughly understand the popular mind of
the western province, and I hesitate not to say that there are not five
gentlemen in this chamber (if so many) who could go before their constituents in Upper Canada in opposition to this scheme, with the slightest
chance of being returned. It is because I thoroughly comprehend the
feelings of the people upon it, that I urge the adoption of this measure at
the earliest possible moment. The most gross injustice is to be rectified
by it; the tax-payer is to be clothed with his rightful influence by it;
new commercial relations are to be opened up by it; a new impulse to
the industrial pursuits of the country will be given by it; and I for
one would feel myself false to the cause I have so long sustained, and
false to the best interests of my constituents, if I permitted one hour unnecessarily to pass without bringing it to a final issue. It was only by the
concurrence of most propitious circumstances that the wonderful progress
this movement has made could have been accomplished. Most peculiar
were the circumstances that enabled such a coalition to be formed as that
now existing for the settlement of this question; and who shall say at what
hour it may not be rent asunder? And yet, who will venture to affirm
that if party spirit in all its fierceness were once more to be let loose
amongst us, there would be the slightest hope that this great question
could be approached with that candour and harmony necessary to its satisfactory solution?

Then, at the very moment we resolved to deal with this question of
constitutional change, the Maritime Provinces were about to assemble in

joint conference to consider whether they ought not to form a union among themselves ; and the way was thus most propitiously opened up for the consideration of a union of all British America. The civil war too in the neighbouring republic ; the possibility of war between Great Britain and the United States ; the threatened repeal of the reciprocity treaty ; the threatened abolition of the American bonding system for goods *in transitu* to and from these provinces ; the unsettled position of the Hudson's Bay Company ; and the changed feeling of England as to the relations of great colonies to the parent state ; all combine at this moment to arrest earnest attention to the gravity of the situation, and unite us all in one vigorous effort to meet the emergency like men.

The interests to be affected by this scheme of union are very large and varied ; but the pressure of circumstances upon all the colonies is so serious at this moment, that if we cannot now banish partisanship and sectionalism and petty objections, and look at the matter on its broad intrinsic merits, what hope is there of our ever being able to do so? An appeal to the people of Canada on this measure simply means postponement of the question for a year ; and who can tell how changed ere then may be the circumstances surrounding us ? The man who strives for the postponement of this measure on any ground, is doing what he can to kill it almost as effectually as if he voted against it. Let there be no mistake as to the manner in which the government presents this measure to the House. We do not present it as free from fault, but we do present it as a measure so advantageous to the people of Canada, that all the blemishes, real or imaginary, averred against it, sink into utter insignificance in presence of its merits. We present it, not in the precise shape we in Canada would desire it, but as in the best shape the five colonies to be united could agree upon it. We present it in the form in which the five governments have severally adopted it—in the form the Imperial government has endorsed it—and in the form in which we believe all the legislatures of the provinces will accept it. We ask the House to pass it in the exact form in which we have presented it, for we know not how alterations may affect its safety in other places; and the process of alteration once commenced in four different legislatures, who could tell where that would end? Every member of this House is free as air to criticise it if he so wills, and amend it if he is able ; but we warn him of the danger of amendment, and throw on him all responsibility of the consequences. We feel confident of carrying this scheme as it stands, but we cannot tell what we can do if it be amended. Let not honourable gentlemen approach this measure as a sharp critic deals with an abstract question, striving to point out blemishes and display his ingenuity ; but let us approach it as men having but one consideration before us—the establishment of the future peace and prosperity of our country. Let us look at it in the light of a few months back —in the light of the evils and injustice to which it applies a remedy—in the light of the years of discord and strife we have spent in seeking for that remedy—in the light with which the people of Canada would regard this measure were it to be lost, and all the evils of past years to be brought back upon us again. Let honourable gentlemen look at the question in this view, and what one of them will take the responsibility of casting his vote against the measure ? The future destiny of these great provinces may be affected by the decision we are about to give to an extent which at this moment we may be unable to estimate, but assuredly the welfare for many years of four millions of people hangs on our decision. Shall we then rise equal to the occasion?—shall we approach this discussion without partisanship, and free from every personal feeling but the earnest resolution to discharge conscientiously the duty which an overruling Providence has placed upon us ? It may be that some among us will live to see the day when, as the result of this measure, a great and powerful people may have grown up on these lands—when the boundless forests all around us shall have given way to smiling fields and thriving towns—and when one united government, under the British flag, shall extend from shore to shore ; but who would desire to see that day, if he could not recall with satisfaction the part he took in this discussion ?

I have done. I leave the subject to the conscientious judgment of the House, in the confident expectation and belief that the decision it will render will be worthy of the parliament of Canada.

THE RECIPROCITY NEGOTIATIONS.

The following speech was delivered in the senate during the session of 1875, being the one immediately following the reciprocity negotiations at Washington in 1874, and was intended to be a semi-official account of these negotiations—conducted by Sir Edward Thornton and Mr. Brown as joint plenipotentiaries—and also a general review of the whole trade relations of Canada with the United States, and a history of the former negotiations, including the Washington treaty of 1871. The speech also contains many statistical statements which Mr. Brown had prepared for his work at Washington.

Mr. Brown said : In rising to make the motion of which I have given notice, I am sure you will all feel that it is right and fitting, and will be expected by the country, that I should take this earliest opportunity of laying before the House such a statement of the recent negotiations between the United States government and Great Britain in regard to commercial reciprocity between the United States and Canada, as may be in the public interest and befitting my position. I have the more pleasure in doing so because I feel that in dealing with this matter before the senate, I shall be sustained by the honourable gentlemen who compose this body in taking an enlarged view of the whole question, in leaving aside many frivolous criticisms that have been made by political partisans, and in contending that because a commercial treaty is very advantageous for one party it does not follow that it may not be equally good for the other. It is very easy to fancy things that might advantageously have been included or omitted in any such arrangement, but it must be always borne in mind that when two parties sit down to make a bargain the result arrived at cannot be what each desires to obtain, but what both will consent to. The merit or demerit of every such compact must therefore be tested by looking at it in its bearings as a whole, and not by minute dissection of minor points.

I shall not waste time by entering into any elaborate argument as to the advantages which must flow from throwing down the barriers in the way of international commerce between two countries so contiguous to each other as are the United States and this Dominion. We have ample proof of this in the commercial history of Great Britain since the union of the three kingdoms. We have it still more markedly in the great material results directly flowing from the free interchange of products between the several states of the neighbouring republic. And nowhere can be found a more gratifying illustration of the grand results that flow from commercial freedom than we have in the progress of our own Dominion since the accomplishment of confederation. Though the customs barriers against intertraffic between the British North American provinces have only been removed since July, 1867, the united foreign commerce of the provinces has risen from an annual average, for thirteen years before confederation, of $115,000,000, to the enormous amount, in the seventh year after it, of $240,000,000. Twenty-five years ago the subject of commercial reciprocity was, I believe, quite as well if not better understood by the people of Canada than it is now. It is twenty-one years since the treaty of 1854 went into operation ; but it took six years to negotiate it, and during that time the people of the provinces became thoroughly conversant with the various advantages which flow from such arrangements ; and if the statesmen who conducted the negotiations of those years were present to-day they would hear with astonishment that any member of this chamber entertained a doubt as to the enormous advantage which must accrue to both countries from the consummation of such a treaty as that which has been recently discussed. It is only nine years since the old treaty of 1854 was brought to a close by the action of the United States government. The wonderful success which attended that treaty is shown by the fact that the interchange of traffic between the United States and the British North American provinces, during the thirteen years of its continuance, increased from $33,000,000 in the year immediately preceding that in which the treaty went into operation, to no less than $84,000,000 in 1866—the year in which it was repealed. Since 1866 there have been several negotiations with the United States for the renewal of the old treaty.

I will briefly refer to each of them, not for the purpose of drawing invidious comparisons—for I hope nothing will cross my lips to-day to excite party feeling—but simply for the purpose of showing clearly the past history and present position of the reciprocity question. Such questions as this should, I think, be regarded from a higher point than that of mere partisanship. We are all alike concerned in the prosperity of our foreign commerce, and in securing good relations with our powerful neighbours, and to these ends we should all heartily contribute, whatever party may be in power, or charged with the negotiations. In the negotiations of 1865-6 for a renewal of the treaty, offers were made to the American government by our then Finance Minister, Sir A. T. Galt, which in my opinion ought not to have been made. The government then existing in Canada was the coalition government formed in 1864 for the special purpose of carrying confederation of the whole British North American provinces. I was a member of that government and, as is well known, it was in consequence of the policy adopted by my colleagues in the conduct of the reciprocity negotiation that I felt compelled to resign my position as President of the Executive Council. I resigned because I felt very strongly that though we in Canada derived great advantage from the treaty of 1854, the American people derived still greater advantage from it. I had no objection to that, and was quite ready to renew the old treaty, or even to extend it largely on fair terms of reciprocity. But I was not willing to ask for renewal as a favour to Canada ; I was not willing to offer special inducements for renewal without fair concessions in return ; I was not willing that the canals and inland waters of Canada should be made the joint property of the United States and Canada, and be maintained at their joint expense ; I was not willing that the customs and excise duties of Canada should be assimilated to the prohibitory rates of the United States ; and very especially was I unwilling that any such arrangement should be entered into with the United States, dependent on the frail tenure of reciprocal legislation, repealable at any moment at the caprice of either party. I firmly believed that good as the reciprocity treaty had been for Canada, in the event of repeal, we had a commercial policy of our own open to us for adoption not greatly inferior to that we would be deprived of ; and unless we got a treaty for a definite term of years, and conditions of fair reciprocity, without such embarrassing entanglements as were proposed, I was willing that the treaty of 1854 should be repealed, and each country left to follow its own course. My colleagues determined to proceed in the manner I deprecated ; I could not be responsible for such a policy ; and to avoid responsibility for it, I resigned office. The government sent deputies to Washington to obtain, if possible, legislative reciprocity—they did all they could to obtain it, but without success, and the treaty of 1854 came to an end on the 17th of March, 1866. I have not changed my opinions from what they were in December, 1865. I still believe that Canada largely profited by the treaty of 1854, but that the Americans profited by it still more ; and we all know now—for we have tested it—that Canada has a commercial policy of her own but little if at all inferior to that she was deprived of in 1866. Notwithstanding this I am still strongly in favour of a commercial treaty with the United States for a definite number of years ; and so long as it was just and profitable to Canada, I should be all the better pleased the more profitable it proved to our American friends. It is always well to have two strings to one's bow ; it cannot possibly be injurious to secure access to a market of forty millions of people at the price of permitting our own people to buy some of their wares from them free from customs duties. Treaties of the comprehensive character of that proposed with the United States ought not to be—cannot be—adjusted by ounce scales. By the removal of all artificial barriers in the way of a fair exchange of the products of industry, both parties must benefit. No man sells unless he benefits by doing so, and no one buys unless he finds advantage in it. And who shall tell, when two countries throw open their respective markets to each other, which of them derives most advantage from the arrangement? It takes years of practical experience to obtain *data* for such a comparison ; and the ramifications of commercial interchanges are so far-reaching, and so various and complicated, that it is hardly possible to judge with accuracy on which side the balance turns.

More than one effort was made by the late government for the renewal of the old treaty between 1866 and 1869. In 1869 formal negotiations were entered into with the American government, and the *projet* of a treaty was presented for discussion. The negotiations continued from July, 1869, to March, 1870. This *projet* included the cession for a term of years of our fisheries to the United States; the enlargement and enjoyment of our canals; the free enjoyment of the navigation of the St. Lawrence River; the assimilation of our customs and excise duties; the concession of an import duty equal to the internal revenue taxes of the United States; and the free admission into either country of certain manufactures of the other. This negotiation ended abruptly in March, 1870, but it is instructive to observe—and I refer to it for the purpose of pointing out that, from the repeal of the old treaty in 1866 up to the recent negotiations, the government of Canada has always held the most liberal views as to the considerations that might be included in a treaty with the United States.

The negotiation of 1870 was soon followed by the high joint commission, nominally for the adjustment of our fishery disputes, but in reality for the settlement of the *Alabama* embroglio. We all know what was the cost to Canada of that negotiation. The fisheries of the St. Lawrence went from us for twelve years; the navigation of the St. Lawrence was presented to the United States in perpetuity; the use of our canals was ceded to them for twelve years. And to show exactly the position to which the relations of the two countries were then reduced, it will not be deemed unfitting that I should read a few short extracts from the official protocols of the high joint commissioners. And first as to our invaluable sea-coast fisheries.

The question of the fisheries was discussed at the conference of the 6th of March, 1871, when the British commissioners stated that "they considered that the reciprocity treaty of the 5th of June, 1854, should be restored in principle. The American commissioners declined to assent to a renewal of the former reciprocity treaty." They said, "That that treaty had proved unsatisfactory to the people of the United States, and consequently had been terminated by notice from the government of the United States, in pursuance of its provisions. Its renewal was not in their interest, and would not be in accordance with the sentiments of their people."

At conferences held on the 7th, 20th, 22nd and 25th of March, the American commissioners stated: "That if the value of the inshore fisheries could be ascertained, the United States might prefer to purchase, for a sum of money, the rights to enjoy in perpetuity the use of these inshore fisheries in common with British fishermen, and mentioned $1,000,000 as the sum they were prepared to offer. The British commissioners replied that this offer was, they thought, wholly inadequate, and that no arrangement would be acceptable of which the admission into the United States, free of duty, of fish the produce of the British fisheries, did not form a part; adding that any arrangement for the acquisition by purchase of the inshore fisheries in perpetuity was open to grave objections." . . . . During these discussions the British commissioners contended that these inshore fisheries were of great value, and that the most satisfactory arrangement for their use would be a reciprocal tariff arrangement and reciprocity in the coasting trade.   The American commissioners replied that their value was overestimated ; that the United States desired to secure their enjoyment not for their commercial or intrinsic value, but for the purpose of removing a source of irritation, and that they could hold out no hope that the congress of the United States would give its consent to such a tariff arrangement as was proposed, or to any extended plan of reciprocal free admission of the products of the two countries.   But that inasmuch as one branch of congress had recently more than once expressed itself in favour of the abolition of duties on coal and salt, they would propose that coal, salt and fish be reciprocally admitted free, and that . . . they would further propose that lumber be admitted free from duty, from and after the 1st of July, 1874."   The British commissioners, on the 17th of April, stated that this offer was "regarded as inadequate ; that H. M. government considered that free lumber should be granted at once, and that the proposed tariff concessions should be supplemented by a money payment.   The American commissioners then stated that they withdrew the proposal which they had previously made of the'reciprocal free admission of coal, salt and fish, and of lumber, after July 1st, 1874." . . . They expressed their willingness " to concede free fish and fish oil as an equivalent for the use of the inshore fisheries, and to make the arrangement for a term of years ; that they were of opinion that free fish and fish oil would be more than an equivalent for those fisheries ; but that they were also willing to agree to a reference to determine that question and the amount of any money payment that might be found necessary to complete an equivalent."   The British commissioners on 18th April accepted this proposal, and Articles XVIII. to XXV. thereanent were agreed to.

"The British commissioners proposed to take into consideration the question of opening the coasting trade of the lakes reciprocally to each party—which was declined."

" The British commissioners proposed to take into consideration the reciprocal registration of vessels as between the Dominion of Canada and the United States—which was declined."

At the conference on the 23rd March, the American commissioners stated : " That unless the Welland Canal should be enlarged so as to accommodate the present course of trade, they should not be disposed to make any concessions, &c. . . ."   At the conference on the 27th March, the " proposed enlargement of the Canadian canals was further discussed.   It was stated on the part of the British commissioners that the Canadian government were now considering the expediency of enlarging the capacity of the canals on the River St. Lawrence, and had already provided for the enlargement of the Welland Canal, which would be undertaken without delay."

It would be seen by these extracts from the official records of the high joint commissioners how very humble a position in the eyes of the commissioners Canada held as a negotiator with the United States for reciprocal commercial advantages ; and to show the effects of the concessions made by that commission, I will now read from a speech made by Sir A. T. Galt, in the Canadian House of Commons, on 24th February, 1871, in reference to the appointment of that commission, and the great danger that serious injury might be done by it to Canadian interests. Sir Alex. Galt used the following language :

"The fisheries were of paramount importance to us. They meant an important source of employment and trade to us, and a field for the training up of seamen. They have intrinsic merits also. They constitute valuable means of commercial exchange with the United States—means of securing useful trading equivalents from our neighbours. It was the way we dealt with the fisheries and navigation of the St. Lawrence, upon which depended our future advantage and superiority with the United States, in negotiating any commercial convention. If we made an improper use of them, if we lost those advantages, we should be placed in a position of inferiority, having nothing to offer for enviable opportunities."

Sir Alexander Galt wound up his speech by moving the following as one of a series of resolutions, earnestly deprecating interference by the commission with the territorial rights of the people of Canada :

"That this House has always been, and now is, prepared to concede the most free and unrestricted use of the fisheries and inland navigation to the United States, upon receiving as an equivalent therefor complete compensation in the modification of the United States' commercial system, directed to the more free and liberal interchange of the products of labour in the two countries. That the concession to the United States of the freedom of the fisheries and of the St. Lawrence, without compensation, would place Canada in a most disadvantageous position for future negotiations, by depriving her of the means of offering any adequate equivalent for those concessions she is desirous of obtaining from that nation."

Other negotiations took place after the treaty of Washington was signed, but to these it is not now necessary to refer. Such then was the position of the reciprocity question when Sir John Macdonald's government resigned and the present administration came into power. And to show the light in which the right honourable gentleman who leads the opposition in the House of Commons then regarded the situation, I will now read from a speech of that gentleman, made in the other chamber in March, 1874, when the announcement was made to parliament that I had been associated with Sir Edward Thornton in the renewal of negotiations:

"His honourable friend from West Toronto had thrown out a remark which would discourage the negotiation at Washington, because he had stated that the old reciprocity treaty, if they obtained that, would not give satisfaction to the country, as something more was wanted. Now, if they were only to be consulted in making such a treaty, they could put in what they thought proper ; but there were two sides to the question, and what our negotiator had to think of was, not whether we should get all we required, but to get as much as possible. He should be very glad to see Canada get the old reciprocity treaty; he had no hopes that he would succeed in getting it in its entirety, but if the honourable gentleman made an approximation to it he should be exceedingly glad. If they could protect the salt, wool, and timber interests, so much the better; and if they could open the market still more, so much the greater gain for Canada. They should not scan too much the concessions made on the part of the United States, so long as our concessions were not too great on the other side."

The right honourable gentleman, at the very moment when the men who had relieved him of the cares of office were about opening negotiations at Washington, might well have omitted so inconsiderate a statement as that even a small portion of the old treaty would be acceptable to Canada in exchange for what he (Sir John A. Macdonald) had left it in our power to offer to the United States. I cannot but think it was exceedingly wrong that such a statement should have been made with the certain knowledge that it would be carried to Washington, and be used there in depreciating the value of our concessions to the Americans. While agreeing with both of the honourable gentlemen from whose speeches I have read, as to the injurious influence of the Washington treaty concessions on our position as negotiators with the republic, I entirely dissent from them in their assumption that, apart from the use of our great sea fisheries and the free navigation of the St. Lawrence, we have not commercial advantages to offer to the Americans quite equal in value to any we seek from them. I venture to think that this error has tinged all their negotiations at Washington, and that a close inquiry as to the value to the United States of the commercial traffic alone between the republic and the British provinces for a long series of years past would show it to have greatly surpassed in importance and profit any other branch of their foreign commerce, except their direct trade with the British Isles. I have never doubted that our neighbours, if they did not already recognize this fact, would come ere long to acknowledge it, and that the value of the vast carrying-trade they derive from us, of the great saving in cost of transportation realized from the free use of our internal navigation, and of their lucrative enjoyment of our Atlantic coast fisheries, would come home to them more clearly as the settlement loomed nearer in the distance that must be made, and cannot be evaded some seven or eight years hence, when the concessions of the high joint commissioners shall come to an end. It was in this belief that the present Canadian government reopened negotiations at Washington—not, as has been diligently asserted by their political opponents, with hat in hand, but in the frank, independent attitude of men who ask no favours, but believed they had ample equivalents to offer for all they sought to obtain. The time of their going to Washington was not of their selection—they had to go. Articles XXII. and XXIII. of the Washington treaty rendered it absolutely necessary that they should do so. Let me read the words :

"ARTICLE XXII.—Inasmuch as it is asserted by the government of Her Britannic Majesty that the privileges accorded to the citizens of the United States under Article XVIII. of this treaty are of greater value than those accorded by Articles XIX. and XXI. of this treaty to the subjects of Her Britannic Majesty, and this assertion is not admitted by the government of the United States : it is further agreed that commissioners shall be appointed to determine, having regard to the privileges accorded by the United States to the subjects of Her Britannic Majesty, as stated in Articles XIX. and XXI. of this treaty, the amount of any compensation which, in their opinion, ought to be paid by the government of the United States to the government of Her Britannic Majesty in return for the privileges accorded to the citizens of the United States under Article XVIII. of this treaty; and that any sum of money which the said commissioners may so award shall be paid by the United States government, in a gross sum, within twelve months after such award shall have been given.

"ARTICLE XXIII.—The commissioners referred to in the preceding article shall be appointed in the following manner, that is to say : One commissioner shall be named by Her Britannic Majesty, one by the President of the United States, and a third by Her Britannic Majesty and the President of the United States conjointly ; and in case the third commissioner shall not have been so named within a period of three months from the date when this article shall take effect, then the third commissioner shall be named by the representative at London of His Majesty the Emperor of Austria and King of Hungary. In case of the death, absence, or incapacity of any commissioner, or in the event of any commissioner omitting or ceasing to act, the vacancy shall be filled in the manner hereinbefore provided for making the original appointment, the period of three months in case of such substitution being calculated from the date of the happening of the vacancy.

" The commissioners so named shall meet in the city of Halifax, in the province of Nova Scotia, at the earliest convenient period after they have been respectively named, and shall, before proceeding to any business, make and subscribe a solemn declaration that they will impartially and carefully examine and decide the matters referred to them to the best of their judgment, and according to justice and equity; and such declaration shall be entered on the record of their proceedings.

"Each of the high contracting parties shall also name one person to attend the commission as its agent, to represent it generally in all matters connected with the commission."

Mr. Rothery, a distinguished English jurisconsult, and registrar of the High Court of Admiralty, arrived in Canada shortly before the late government left office in 1873, as the duly appointed agent of the British government to get up the case for Canada in the fishery arbitration provided for by these articles. I know nothing of what passed between either the late or the present government and Mr. Rothery while he was at Ottawa; but in passing through Toronto on his way to Washington, Mr. Rothery saw several prominent public men, with a view to acquiring information as to the value of our sea-coast fisheries, and the best mode of collecting evidence to sustain our claim, and among them I had the honour to be included. I availed myself of the opportunity to express to Mr. Rothery my strong conviction that the submission to any three arbitrators of the power to place a cash value on our great sea fisheries was exceedingly distasteful to the great mass of the Canadian people. I reminded him that Canada in 1854 conceded these fisheries to the United States for a term of years as part of a commercial arrangement between the two countries, and I ventured to suggest how much better it would be were the same thing repeated now, and the concession of the fisheries merged in a general treaty of commercial reciprocity for a term of years and on a mutually advantageous basis. I expressed my belief to Mr. Rothery that if he could succeed in bringing this about he would confer a great benefit on both countries, and establish good relations between them for years to come, and that probably he might find the United States government not disinclined to entertain the proposition. Who that owns a property of enormous value would voluntarily consent to dispose of it for a price to be determined by three persons, of whose very names he was ignorant? Would he not say: "Let us dispense with arbitrators; tell me the compensation you propose, and then I will tell you if I will dispose of it?" Who can tell what view may be taken of our fisheries by the umpire selected by the Austrian ambassador? Would the Americans be satisfied if he gave an award equal to the great estimate we place upon them? And what would be the feeling of our people if he named a sum much under their expectation? Nay, in view of the vast annual value now drawn from the St. Lawrence fisheries—the exhaustless character of those fisheries—the rapidly increasing population of this continent dependent on them for daily supplies of fish, and the fact that there is no other fishery in the world to enter into competition with them—what greater folly could be imagined than to have a money value placed upon them at all?

Mr. Rothery went on to Washington, and some weeks after I had the pleasure of learning from him that he had suggested the substitution of a general commercial treaty for the fishery arbitration, and there was some hope of its being favourably entertained. But meantime, the Canadian government had been moving in the matter, and in February of last year I was informed by them that there was some movement at Washington in favour of a renewal of the old reciprocity treaty, and they were anxious that I should visit that city unofficially, and ascertain what were the prospects of success. I went immediately to Washington, and had the advantage of discussing the whole subject with many of the prominent public men of the republic.   I heard a very general desire expressed for the establishment of better commercial relations with Canada, if terms could be arranged to the satisfaction of both parties; this I communicated to the government on my return home.   Of the official action that followed I have no personal knowledge, but on the 17th of March a commission was issued, under the great seal of Great Britain, appointing Sir Edward Thornton and myself joint plenipotentiaries on the part of Her Majesty to negotiate a treaty of fisheries, commerce, and navigation with the government of the United States.   On the 28th March the negotiation was formally opened, and I will now read, from the official record, an extract showing the position held in the matter by the Canadian government:

"When Her Majesty's advisers invite the government of the United States to reconsider the whole commercial relations of the republic and the Dominion, with a view to place them on a friendly and durable basis of reciprocal advantage, the question naturally presents itself, how it comes that, having prospered so well since the repeal of the reciprocity treaty of 1854, Canada now seeks for its restoration.   The answer is as natural as the question.   The population of the United States is forty millions, and that of the Dominion is but four millions.   The boundary between them is for the most part but a surveyor's line, often unknown even to those who live beside it; and it is of the utmost importance to Canada that common interests and mutual good-will should exist between the two countries. And what so conducive to this end as commercial intercourse, generously carried on and mutually profitable?   The people of Canada are not ignorant that a market near at hand is better than a distant one; and good as their present markets are, they would gladly have the old one in addition.   They comprehend the barrier that custom house restrictions throw in the way even of the existing traffic; and they seek to have these withdrawn.   They are proud of their own St. Lawrence route, and intend to improve it to the uttermost for the benefit of the great west and Canadian traffic, but would gladly use the ocean ports and other channels of commerce of the republic, when freights and fares and friendly reciprocity draw them in that direction.   And very great as have been the advantages always accruing to the United States from reciprocity, the Canadians can find only cause of rejoicing at that so long as they themselves continue to enjoy that moderate degree of prosperity with which Providence has blessed them.   There is no mystery in their desire that the commercial relations of the republic and the Dominion should be placed on the most kindly and unfettered and mutually advantageous basis consistent with their respective existing obligations, and with that connection with Great Britain which the Dominion so happily enjoys.

"It was with these views, and in this spirit, that the Canadian administration availed itself of the opportunity presented by the twenty-second article of the treaty of Washington to represent to Her Majesty's government the advantage that would accrue to both countries by the substitution of a satisfactory commercial treaty in lieu of the money compensation to be paid (under arbitration) by the United States, for twelve years' enjoyment of the coast fisheries of the Dominion. It was felt that if the large value placed by the Canadian people on their fisheries were not reasonably compensated by the results of the arbitration, a feeling of dissatisfaction might be engendered in the provinces not conducive to international harmony; and that if, on the other hand, an award were made equal to the confident anticipations of the provinces, the good feeling restored in the United States by the treaty of Washington might be sensibly impaired. To merge the matter in a general measure of mutual commercial concessions, for the mutual advantage of both parties, and with injury or injustice to neither, seemed the fitting conclusion to be arrived at by the governments of two great nations. Her Majesty's ministers were pleased to adopt the suggestion of the Canadian government, and the matter having been brought under the attention of the Secretary of State, and through him to the notice of the President of the United States, a friendly response was at once received, and the necessary measures instituted for opening formal negotiations."

Gentlemen may therefore dismiss from their minds the false impression that the initiation of this negotiation by the gentlemen on the treasury benches was in the slightest degree improper or undignified. And I take this opportunity of expressing my regret that heated partisans outside the walls of parliament should have spoken of the attitude held by the United States government in these negotiations as if it had been intended to delude or overreach. Nothing could be more unfounded or unjust. The President of the United States, the Secretary of State, and all the other distinguished persons who took an interest in the negotiations, with hardly an exception, showed the most friendly feeling towards Canada, and a sincere desire to bring about more satisfactory commercial relations. True, they naturally enough looked at the question from their own point of view, and sought to get an advantageous arrangement for their country; but they never concealed or undervalued the difficulties that stood in the way of success; and to the unsettled condition of the country, and the financial difficulties now pressing for adjustment, may, in a great measure, be attributed the unfavourable advice in the matter recently given to the President by the senate of the United States.

And now let me call attention to the manner in which the negotiations proceeded, and especially to the fact that all that was sought by the British plenipotentiaries was simply the renewal, for a term of years, of the old reciprocity treaty, and the concurrent abandonment of the fishery arbitration. From the American government came the suggestion of an enlargement of the scope of the old treaty. Mr. Fish suggested the enlargement of our canals, and he was at once informed that the Canadian government was ready to treat for their enlargement. Mr. Fish suggested the addition of manufactures to the free list of the proposed treaty, and here is the reply that was made as officially recorded:

"In regard to the addition of certain classes of manufactures to the free list under the old treaty, we reminded Mr. Fish that the revenue of the Canadian Dominion was largely obtained from a fifteen per cent. *ad valorem* duty on manufactured goods, and that any articles made free in Canada under agreement with any foreign country must be made free to Great Britain. But we added that the government of Canada was desirous to afford every facility for the encouragement of extended commercial relations between the republic and the Dominion, in the belief that nothing could tend more to their mutual advantage, not only in a pecuniary sense, but as tending to foster and strengthen those friendly feelings that ought eminently to prevail between two peoples mainly derived from the same origin, speaking the same language, and occupying the geographic position towards each other of the United States and Canada. We conveyed to Mr. Fish the assurance of the Canadian government, that acting in this spirit, and in the confidence that we would be met in the same spirit by the government of the republic, the assent of Canada will be heartily given to any measure calculated to promote the free and fair interchange of commodities, to reduce the cost of transportation, or conduce to the joint advantage of the two countries, so that it be not seriously prejudicial to existing industrial interests of the Canadian people."

It was then suggested that a *projet* of a treaty should be prepared, to form the basis of discussion. That was agreed to, and a *projet* was accordingly prepared and presented to the American government by the British commissioners. It suggested : 1.—That the duration of the treaty should be 21 years. 2.—That all the conditions of the old treaty of 1854 should be renewed. 3.—That the following additional articles should be added to the free list of the old treaty : Agricultural implements to be defined ; bark, extracts of, for tanning purposes ; bath bricks ; bricks for building purposes ; earth ochres, ground or unground ; hay ; lime ; malt ; manufactures of iron and steel—to be defined ; manufactures of iron or steel, and wood jointly—to be defined ; manufactures of wood—to be defined ; mineral and other oils ; plaster, raw or calcined ; salt ; straw ; stone, marble, or granite, partly or wholly cut, or wrought. 4.—That the fishery arbitration provision of the Washington treaty should be abandoned. 5.—That the entire coasting trade of the United States and Canada should be thrown open to the shipping of both countries. 6.—That the Welland and St. Lawrence Canals should be enlarged forthwith, so as to admit of the passage of vessels 260 feet long, 45 feet beam, and a depth equal to that of the lake harbours. 7.—That the Canadian, New York, and Michigan Canals should be thrown open to the vessels of both countries on terms of complete equality, and with full power to tranship cargo at the entrance or outlet of any of the said canals. 8.—That the free navigation of Lake Michigan should be conceded forever to Great Britain, as the free navigation of the St. Lawrence River had been conceded to the United States by the high joint commission in 1871. 9.—That vessels of all kinds built in the United States or Canada should be entitled to registry in either country with all the advantages pertaining to home-built vessels. 10.—That a joint commission should be formed and continued, charged with the deepening and maintaining in efficient condition the navigation of the St. Clair and Detroit Rivers and Lake St. Clair. 11.—That a similar joint commission should be formed and maintained for securing the erection and proper regulation of lighthouses on the great lakes. 12.—That a similar joint commission should be formed and maintained to promote the protection and propagation of fish in the inland waters common to both countries. 13.—That the citizens of either country should be entitled to letters patent for new discoveries in the other country on the same terms as the citizens of that country enjoyed. 14.—That joint action for the prevention of smuggling along the lines should be a subject of consideration and co-operation by the custom authorities of the two countries.

Time was of course needed for consideration of these suggestions, and for inquiry and discussion in regard to them, and it very soon became manifest that the absence of exact knowledge as to the intertraffic between the republic and the provinces in past years, as to the actual operation of the treaty of 1854 during the thirteen years it was in force, and as to the advantage to be gained by our neighbours from access to our markets in our improved position, stood greatly in the way of successful negotiations.

The misapprehensions found to exist as to the condition of Canada, her revenue, her foreign commerce, her shipping, her railway system, and the extent and prosperity of her various industrial avocations, was truly marvellous. On every hand, and from very unexpected quarters, you heard it alleged as beyond question that the commerce between the countries in bygone years had been of little account to them, but always in our favour; that our neighbours bought from us pretty much all we had to sell, while we bought little or nothing from them; that the reciprocity treaty made the matter much worse, and enriched us at their expense ; and that the abolition of the treaty of 1854 had brought us well nigh to our wits end. I do not mean to say that such mistakes as these were found among many of the prominent statesmen at Washington, but with a very large proportion of the politicians congregating at the capital such ideas were sincerely entertained and unhesitatingly affirmed. Let me give you an example. I had the good fortune to meet a well-known statesman, equally remarkable for his ability, high personal character and kindness of heart, as for the extreme nature of his protectionist opinions. The subject of the proposed treaty came up, and I ventured to express the hope that it would receive a more friendly reception from him than had been accorded to a previous one. "What possible good," was his exclamation, "can we get from a treaty with Canada! When the last treaty existed we took everything from you that you had to sell, and you took nothing from us." "Surely," I replied, "you are not stating this seriously." "Of course I am," said he; "surely you don't deny that it was so?" My reply was that I not only denied it, but was prepared to show, beyond the shadow of a doubt, and from the official returns of the United States, that from 1820 up to 1864 the inhabitants of the British provinces had bought from the

United States merchandise and produce to the extent of over $150,000,000 in excess of what the United States had bought from them in the same years. I said I had no faith myself in what was termed "the balance of trade," but if there was any truth in it, the traffic of the United States with the provinces must be all that could be desired, for up to the third year before the treaty was repealed it always showed a large annual balance against Canada. He was utterly incredulous—indignantly incredulous—though my statement was strictly accurate. "But," said I, "let us suppose that you are correct—let us suppose that during all these past years you bought a vast amount from Canada and we bought very little from you—was that a very great disadvantage to you? Do you think your merchants and traders would have flocked over as they did to the lumber mills and farm-yards, and factories and fishing ports, of the provinces to buy our stuff, to the extent of many millions per annum, unless they got profit by it? They might have done it once or twice with a loss, but would they have done it for fifty years in succession, steadily and largely increasing the amount of their purchases from year to year? And apart from the great profits that must have been realized by the resale of the goods, was there not great gains to the United States from the transportation of all that stuff overland to your ocean ports, and in shipping it from them in your sea-going vessels to foreign countries?"

I made very little impression on my protectionist friend, and his case is but one out of a great many similar to it. Indeed, it is hardly to be wondered at that very great misapprehension should exist in the United States as to our traffic with that country. Until the B. N. A. colonies were confederated in 1867, all the provinces were isolated from each other, their public accounts and trade and navigation returns were published separately, if published formally at all; their customs and excise duties were entirely different; and their shipping returns were made up separately, if made up at all. No clear statement of the united traffic of all the provinces with the American republic in past years was ever compiled until last year—we ourselves in Canada were ignorant of its vast extent—and the absence of reliable data left us open to the misrepresentations of our protectionist opponents in the republic. Put our traffic together in one account, and hardly could a branch of trade in the United States be named which did not profit by it; but take the traffic of the several provinces apart, and there was hardly a branch of trade that could not be shown, from the example of some one province, to buy nothing of that sort. Upper Canada was shown to send wheat and flour to the United States every year to great amounts—and the attention of western farmers was pointed earnestly to the fact—but it was carefully omitted to be told at the same time that Nova Scotia, New Brunswick, Newfoundland and Prince Edward Island took much more of these commodities from the United States than the States took from Upper Canada. Cape Breton and Nova Scotia were shown to send a few hundred thousand tons of coal to the Boston and New York markets—and the indignant protests of Pennsylvania were hurled against such an iniquity—but it was carefully omitted to be told that Upper and Lower Canada took four or five times the quantity of coal from Pennsylvania that Cape Breton and Nova Scotia sent into the States. Just so was it with a very large portion of the commodities we sold to our American friends. Yet it was by such weapons that the false impression was implanted deep on the public mind of the United States that the traffic with the provinces was utterly unprofitable to the republic.

It soon, as I have said, became perfectly manifest that these false impressions so created must be removed if satisfactory progress was to be made in the reciprocity negotiations. Reliable returns of the traffic for a long series of years between the countries must be compiled, balances struck, comparisons with other countries exhibited. All this was done— every figure having been taken from the official returns of the United States, and a memorandum on the commercial relations of the two countries was prepared, which is now, I believe, in the hands of hon. gentlemen. How entirely erroneous were the impressions of our neighbours as to our traffic with them in past years, is shown beyond cavil in that document. It shows that the British North American provinces, in the 34 years from 1820 to 1854, bought merchandise from the United States to the extent of $167,000,000; that the United States bought from us in the same period goods to the extent of $67,000,000; and that the so-called "balance of trade" was, therefore, $100,000,000 against the provinces. It shows that from 1854 to 1866—being the thirteen years during which the treaty of 1854 was in operation—according to the United States returns (for there is a great discrepancy between their returns and ours) the balance was $20,000,000, and according to the Canadian returns, $95,000,000 against us and in favour of the republic. A large portion of this discrepancy occurred during the last two years of the treaty's existence, and no doubt arose in large degree from the loose valuations at the custom houses on the lines during these years. The memorandum shows further that the gross traffic between the United States and the British provinces, rose, in the eight years immediately before the treaty went into operation, from eight millions of dollars in 1845, to nine millions in 1846; to ten millions in 1847; to twelve millions in 1848; to fifteen millions in 1850; to eighteen millions in 1851; and to twenty millions in 1853. In 1854 the reciprocity treaty went into operation, and at one jump the traffic went up in that year to no less than thirty-three millions of dollars. In the following year it went to forty-two millions; in 1857 to forty-six millions; in 1859 to forty-eight millions; in 1863 to fifty-five millions; in 1864 to sixty-seven millions; in 1865 to seventy-one millions; and in 1866 (when the treaty came to an end) to no less than eighty-four millions of dollars. The gross amount of traffic between the countries during the thirteen years of the treaty's operation amounted, according to the United States returns, to no less than $671,000,000, and according to the Canadian returns, to $630,000,000— either of them a sum which, considering all the circumstances, must be admitted to be marvellously great. I know not where, in the history of commerce, a parallel of success to this can be found, if we keep in mind that one of the parties to the treaty had at the time but three millions of population.

The memorandum shows also that the purchases from the United States by the British American provinces during the thirteen years of the treaty's operations were greater than the purchases from them of China, Brazil, Italy, Hayti, Russia and her possessions, Venezuela, Austria, the Argentine Republic, Denmark and her possessions, Turkey, Portugal and her possessions, the Sandwich Islands, the Central American States, and Japan, in the same years, all put together. It shows further, that our purchases during the existence of the treaty were of the most valuable character, there having been no less than $150,000,000 of farm products, $8,500,000 of timber, $24,000,000 of miscellaneous, and no less than $151,000,000 of general merchandise—a sum to which no other country approached in these years. The memorandum shows also that, in addition to these great commercial exchanges between the countries, an enormous transportation traffic was carried over United States railways and canals between the provinces and Atlantic ports, and *vice versa*. Accurate returns of this traffic do not appear to have been kept until very lately, but in the six years—namely, from 1868 to 1873—for which we have returns, it appears that the merchandise transported for the British American colonies over American lines was of the total value of $162,000,000. The memorandum brings out, moreover, from the official statements of United States commissioners, that our shore fisheries are not of the slight value to the United States that they were placed at in the protocols of the high joint commissioners, but that, on the contrary, they had in the year 1862 over 203,000 tons of shipping engaged in the St. Lawrence fisheries, and 28,000 seamen ; that the returns that year considerably exceeded $14,000,000 ; that at least 5,000 new seamen are annually broken in for the United States marine service ; that 600 sail have in one season fished for mackerel in the Gulf of St. Lawrence, and taken fish to the value of $4,500,000 ; and that from 40,000 to 50,000 tons of the United States fishing fleet, worth from $5,000,000 to $7,000,000, annually fish near the three-mile line of the provinces. It shows that three years from the repeal of the reciprocity treaty, which deprived United States fishermen of the shore privileges enjoyed under the treaty, the United States tonnage in the trade had fallen from 203,000 tons in the year 1862 to 62,000 tons in 1869, a falling off of seventy per cent.; that the reconcession of these shore privileges under the Washington treaty doubled the tonnage of the American fishing fleet from what it was in 1869, and that it will soon exceed the tonnage of 1862. The memorandum shows yet further that the foreign trade of Canada was not seriously injured, as seems to have been supposed across the lines, by the abrogation of the treaty ; but that, on the contrary, while from 1854 to 1862 our foreign traffic had averaged but $113,000,000 per annum, it had in the year immediately following the abrogation risen to $142,000,000, in 1869 to $145,000,000, in 1870 to $165,000,000, in 1871 to \$189,000,000, in 1872 to \$214,000,000, and in 1873, the seventh year of the repeal, to no less than \$240,000,000.

But the memorandum brings out another fact worthy of note—that though the repeal of the treaty did not for an hour stay the increase of our foreign trade, it greatly lessened the proportion of it done with the United States. During the existence of the treaty the aggregate exchange of commodities with the republic gradually rose, until in the year of its repeal it amounted to $52\frac{1}{2}$ per cent. of our whole foreign traffic. But in the first year after repeal it fell to 42 per cent.; in 1868 to 41 per cent.; in 1869 to 40 per cent.; in 1872 to 36 per cent.; and in 1873 to 35 per cent. And the memorandum discloses another most important fact—that a great change in the character of the traffic between the countries resulted from the repeal of the treaty. For example, that the price of lumber has gone up so much, and the demand has continued so good, that while we sold to the United States people but five millions of dollars worth in the year before the expiry of the treaty, and an annual average of but three millions during its whole continuance, we sold in the single year of 1873 over eleven million dollars worth. Again, that in regard to wheat, flour, provisions, and other like commodities, of which both countries have a surplus, the effect of the prohibitory duties of the United States has simply been to send the Canadian surplus of these products to compete successfully with the American article in foreign markets where they formerly held sole possession. And still further, it shows that Canada has become a large purchaser of American products in the Chicago and Milwaukee markets, which it carries by the St. Lawrence route for consumption in foreign countries— that this trade only commenced with the repeal of the treaty, but in the six years following that event aggregated the large amount of \$46,583,312. And strange enough, in regard to the much abused "balance of trade," it shows that since the repeal of the treaty the balance had gone so systematically against the republic, and so steadily in favour of the provinces, that, in the seven years following repeal, a balance of nearly \$52,000,000 had to be settled with our people by the United States. Nay, it is clearly shown that in spite of all the discouragement that has been thrown in the way of our traffic by high customs duties and custom house barriers, our annual purchases from the United States are still large enough to keep us in the front rank of their foreign customers ; and that with the exception of the British Isles, no country takes as large an amount from them as we do. This memorandum was completed on the 27th of April, and was immediately communicated to Mr. Fish. It was referred to the treasury department for examination, and remained in its hands for several weeks. Its facts and figures were closely examined, and their accuracy acknowledged fully and frankly. From that time there was a manifest improvement in the impressions, as to the character of Canadian commerce, of such persons as took the trouble to read the memorandum, and these were not a few ; and the progress of the negotiations was sensibly accelerated. The attention of the United States public press was aroused to the importance of the question—the merits of the proposed treaty were thoroughly canvassed, and, though severely criticised by the ultra-protectionist organs, I have no recollection of any similar measure being received with such general favour by the leading papers of the republic as was accorded to our *projet*. In New York, the *Tribune, Herald, Times, World, Evening Post, Express, Journal of Commerce, Graphic, Mail*, and many other leading exponents of public opinion, all declared in favour of a new treaty; and in Boston, Chicago, St. Louis, Cincinnati, and other great cities, the unanimity of opinion among the leading journals was equally remarkable.

I cannot pass from this part of the subject without referring to a charge that originated in Philadelphia, and was echoed far and wide over the continent—ay, even in Canadian journals—that this unanimity of the press was obtained by the corrupt use of Canadian public money. The charge is utterly without foundation—it has not a vestige of truth to palliate its concoction. Not one shilling has been spent illegitimately to promote the negotiation, and a final answer to this and all similar charges is found in the fact that the entire cost of the negotiation to the people of Canada, including all necessary disbursements, will amount to little more than $4,000. The negotiation now went on from day to day; the several clauses of the *projet* were discussed, alterations suggested, modifications adopted, the draught treaty as it now stands submitted for the approval of the three governments, and all that remained to make it ready for signature was the clear definition for custom house purposes of some articles in the free lists, and the correction of an appearance of ambiguity in the wording of one or two passages. It had been understood that congress would be unable to adjourn before the end of July, but unexpectedly the determination was arrived at to adjourn on the 22nd of June, and that day was near at hand. The Secretary of State suggested that the draft treaty, as it then stood, should be sent down by the President of the United States to the senate for advice, and if favourably entertained by that body, the necessary correction of language could be made and the treaty formally executed. It was of course for the United States government to judge as to the mode of obtaining the sanction of the senate, and the plan suggested was adopted. The draft treaty only reached the senate two days before the adjournment of congress, when it was quite impossible to discuss and decide so large and complicated a question as its adoption involved, and the consideration of it was accordingly adjourned to the next ensuing session.

We come now to the consideration of the several provisions embraced in the draft treaty, as transmitted to the senate by the President of the United States. And let me say very frankly that I do not stand here to-day to contend that the conditions of this bargain are more favourable to Canada than to the United States. On the contrary, I believe that in a commercial treaty between a people of forty million souls and one of four million, it is almost in the nature of the thing that to the larger country the largest advantage must accrue. But greatly advantageous as this treaty—if it ever goes into operation—must be to our friends across the lines, there is enough in it, I venture fearlessly to assert, to set the wheels of industry in motion on this side the lines, and to give such an impetus to the development of our great natural resources as would amply compensate us for all the concessions we are pledged to in the agreement. I acknowledge the force of all that is said as to the immense advantage possessed by the American people in a contest with a colony of one-tenth their population, and hardly yet past the first stages of forest settlement. I admit the larger means, the vastly greater experience, and the eminent business sagacity they would carry into the contest; but I have faith enough in the industry, the energy, the enterprise, and the indomitable perseverance of my countrymen, and in the cool blood of our northern clime, to believe that in the long run, and with a fair field, Canada would hold her own under all these disadvantages.

As you are aware, the draft treaty embraces ten propositions: 1.—The concession to the United States of our fisheries for twenty-one years, and the abandonment of the Washington treaty arbitration. 2.—The admission, duty free, into both countries of certain natural products therein named. 3.—The admission, duty free, of certain manufactured articles therein named. 4.—The enlargement of our Welland and St. Lawrence Canals. 5.—The construction of the Caughnawaga and Whitehall Canals. 6.—The throwing open to each other, reciprocally by both countries, the coasting trade of the great inland lakes, and of the St. Lawrence River. 7.—The concession to each other on equal terms of the use of the Canadian, New York, and Michigan Canals. 8.—The reciprocal admission of vessels built in either country to all the advantages of registry in the other. 9.—The formation of a joint commission to secure the efficient lighting of the great inland waters common to both countries. 10.—The formation of a joint commission to promote the protection and propagation of fish on the great inland waters common to both countries.

Now then, let us examine these propositions *seriatim*. The first, second and seventh of them go naturally together, and they need no comment. They embrace simply the conditions of the old treaty of 1854, which operated so favourably for us, and so much more favourably for the United States. The third proposition—as to manufactures—is the only item that has met with bitter opposition, and that, strangely enough, from all three countries. I will leave it for the present and return to it again. The fourth proposition—for the enlargement of our existing canals—is one eminently for the advantage of the United States, and involves a very large expenditure on our part. It is impossible to estimate the enormous annual gains that must result to the farmers of the western states when vessels of 1,000 or 1,200 tons shall be able to load in the upper lake ports and sail direct to Liverpool—free from transhipment expenses, brokers' commissions, way-harbour dues and ocean port charges, and return direct to the prairies with hardy immigrants and cargoes of European merchandise. Canada, no doubt, would have her share of benefit from all this—

but it could not be compared for a moment with that of the great north-western and some of the middle states. The fifth proposition—for the construction of the Caughnawaga canal—would be also an immense boon to the United States. It would open up to the dense manufacturing population of New England, for the first time, a direct water communication of their own with the great west : it would enable them to load ships of 1,000 tons at their Lake Champlain ports with merchandise for the prairie states, and bring them back freighted with farm produce ; and when the White-hall Canal should be enlarged to Troy, and the improvements of the Upper Hudson completed to deep water, where in the wide world could be found so grand a system of internal water navigation as that, stretching, as it then would, in one continuous ship channel from New York on the Atlantic to the west end of Lake Superior, and possibly, ere long, to the eastern base of the Rocky Mountains? Canada, too, would have her share of profit in all this. Her great lumber interests on the Ottawa and its branches would find full advantage from it, and the enterprising farmers of the middle and eastern counties of Ontario would have the New England market, with its three and a half millions of manufacturing population, opened to their traffic. The sixth proposition is the concession to each other of the inland coasting trade, and nothing could be done more sensible or more profitable to both parties. Our season of navigation on the lakes is short—the pressure for vessels in particular trades at special times is very great on both sides of the lakes, and freights advance to unreasonable rates. Cheap transportation is a foremost question in this western industrial world, and what can be conceived more absurd than to see, as is often seen, large quantities of produce lying unshipped for want of vessels, because foreign bottoms cannot take freight from one port to another in the same country? What the United States could fear from the competition of our limited marine, with the 5,570 vessels of all kinds, and an aggregate tonnage of 783,000 tons, it is difficult to imagine. The eighth proposition—for the reciprocal admission of vessels built in either country to registry in the other—is generally regarded as highly advantageous to this country, and no doubt such is the fact. But I confess I cannot see why it ought not to be regarded as infinitely more advantageous to the United States. During the civil war the merchant vessels of the republic were sold in large numbers to foreign owners, and acquired foreign registers ; and notwith-standing that ship-building had almost disappeared from the United States in consequence of an extreme protectionist policy, the law absolutely forbade their being brought back or vessels of foreign build being purchased in their room. The consequence is, that at this moment nearly the entire passenger traffic of the Atlantic is in the hands of foreigners—a vast proportion of the freight of merchandise from and to foreign countries is also in the hands of foreigners—and only two months ago we had the startling statement made officially by Mr. Bristow, the very able secretary of the United States treasury, that no less a sum than one hundred millions of dollars is paid annually by the people of the United States to foreign ship-owners for freights and fares. Now, a large portion of these ships, which the people of the United States require so urgently, can be as well built in St. John and Halifax and Quebec, and at less cost than in any other country. Why then deprive American citizens of the privilege of buying them from us, and sailing them as their own? We are told that American ship-building is reviving, but were it to revive with all the rapidity the most sanguine could desire, it could not keep pace with the wear and tear of the present reduced marine and the annually increasing demand, much less begin to supply the vacuum created since the war. The ninth and tenth proposals are for the appointment of joint commissions for the care of the lighthouses and the fisheries of the inland waters common to both countries; but as to these there is no difference of opinion, and no doubt of the great mutual advantage that might flow from the proposed concerted action in regard to them.

These, then, are the whole of the items ; and now let us return to the one we passed by—the list of manufactures.

I shall not allege for one moment that there is no ground whatever for the loud outcries we have heard from protectionist manufacturers against the admission of their wares to the free list of the treaty. That some would have suffered by the competition it would have entailed I readily admit, for in all avocations there are men whose want of experience, or want of energy, or deficiency of capital, unfit them for such a contest. But while all our sympathies must have gone heartily with such men in these circumstances, had the treaty been consummated, I cannot think that this great measure, affecting advantageously as it would have done so large a proportion of our industrial population, ought to have been given up simply because some among us might have suffered from its provisions. Are there not always sufferers by every new measure of taxation, by every change of the tariff, by every new municipal assessment scheme ? And yet who dreams of rejecting a great measure of public policy because such individual hardships unfortunately attend them? I cannot, however, help thinking that many of the gentlemen who have been complaining most loudly of their threatened ruin would have been more frightened than hurt had it gone into effect. It cannot be an unmixed evil to exchange a market of four millions of buyers for one of forty millions, and I know some shrewd manufacturers among us who heard with deep regret of the action of the American senate. It is not to be doubted, however, that a great deal of the alarm which has been professed in reference to this section of the scheme has arisen from the parties not knowing exactly what the treaty proposed. I have myself met many persons who supposed that they would be most injuriously affected by it, but who found on a little inquiry that their articles were not in the slightest degree affected. A curious instance of this was seen in the exciting meeting of New York druggists to denounce the injurious influence of the treaty on their trade, though not an article in their business was touched by its provisions. Only within the last few days I met a most intelligent gentleman who was positive that his business was to be very much injured, if not destroyed ;

but it turned out, after a little conversation, that the article he mainly manufactured was not at all affected by the treaty. And there have been many such cases among those loudest in their protestations. A great deal of the indignation, too, and a great deal of the eloquence has proceeded from parties who were angry, not because their wares were included in the scheme, but because they were excluded from it.

But I am ready to meet all objections to this part of the proposed treaty on higher and broader grounds. I contend that there is not one article contained in the schedules that is a fit object of taxation ; not one that ought not to be totally free of duty, either in Canada or the United States, in the interest of the public. I contend that the finance minister of Canada who—treaty or no treaty with the United States—was able to announce the repeal of all customs duties on the entire list of articles in schedules A, B and C—even though the lost revenue was but shifted to articles of luxury—would carry with him the hearty gratitude of the country. I call the attention of the senate earnestly to this fact, that nearly every article in the entire list of manufactures is either of daily consumption and necessity among all classes of our population, or an implement of trade, or enters largely into the economical prosecution of the main industries of the Dominion. Let me read to you the whole list : Agricultural implements, all kinds ; axles, of all kinds ; boots and shoes, of leather ; boots and shoemaking machines ; buffalo robes, dressed and trimmed ; cotton grain bags ; cotton denims ; cotton jeans, unbleached ; cotton drillings, unbleached ; cotton plaids ; cotton ticking ; cottonades, unbleached ; cabinet-ware and furniture, or parts thereof ; carriages, carts, waggons, and other wheeled vehicles and sleighs, or parts thereof ; fire-engines, or parts thereof ; felt covering for boilers ; gutta percha belting and tubing : iron—bar, hoop, pig, puddled, rod, sheet, or scrap ; iron nails, spikes, bolts, tacks, brads, or springs ; iron castings ; india rubber belting and tubing ; locomotives for railways, or parts thereof ; lead, sheet or pig ; leather, sole or upper ; leather, harness and saddlery ; mill or factory or steamboat fixed engines and machines, or parts thereof ; manufactures of marble, stone, slate, or granite ; manufactures of wood solely, or of wood nailed, bound, hinged, or locked with metal materials ; mangles, washing machines, wringing machines, and drying machines, or parts thereof ; printing paper for newspapers ; paper making machines, or parts thereof ; printing type, presses and folders, paper cutters, ruling machines, page numbering machines, and stereotyping and electrotyping apparatus, or parts thereof ; refrigerators, or parts thereof ; railroad cars, carriages, and trucks, or parts thereof ; satinets of wool and cotton ; steam engines, or parts thereof ; steel, wrought or cast, and steel plates and rails ; tin-tubes and piping ; tweeds, of wool solely ; water-wheel machines and apparatus, or parts thereof. These articles were selected with a triple object. The first was, as I have already stated, that they should be articles of common daily use among the people or affecting the prosecution of our leading industries ; the second was that they should be of such a character as to be difficult to smuggle across the lines, and easy of identification as the genuine production of Canada or the States ; and the third was that they should be as far as possible the production of branches of industry natural to Canada or the United States, and in which a considerable intertraffic between the two countries might reasonably be expected.   And if the list is carefully examined, I think it will be admitted that the articles fairly fulfil these three conditions.   Could anything be more impolitic than the imposition of customs duties on such articles as these?   Time was in Canada when the imposition of duty on any article was regarded as a misfortune, and the slightest addition to an existing duty was resented by the people.   But increasing debt brought new burdens ; the deceptive cry of "incidental protection" got a footing in the land ; and from that the step has been easy to the bold demand now set up by a few favoured industries, that all the rest of the community ought to be, and should rejoice to be, taxed 17½ per cent. to keep them in existence.   And it is remarkable how small a portion of the community are concerned in the maintenance of this injustice.   I hold in my hand an accurate return of the men, women and children personally employed in all the industries that could possibly have been affected either advantageously or injuriously by the treaty had it gone into operation, and it appears that the entire number is 68,813.   Of these, a considerable number would practically not be affected at all, for they have no protection now and do not want any ; a large number would only be affected in a small part of their business ; and a very large number would be advantageously affected by the treaty.   The number who could honestly declare that "ruin" to them would be the result would be small indeed. And it is not unworthy of note how very small are the contributions of the industries that might be affected by the treaty to the foreign exports of the country.   In the year ending 30th of June, 1874, the exports of domestic products were as follows :

```
Products of the farm ............................................... ..$34,269,311
Products of the forest... ................................  ............ 26,817,715
Products of the fisheries........... ........  .............  ............  5,292,368
Products of the mine........................ .................... ..  ........ ...  3,977,216
New ships................................... ............. .......  ..............  796,675
Miscellaneous......... ........  ....................................  ............  419,800
                                                                            ──────────
                                                                            $71,573,085
Manufactures................................... ............ ........................  2,353,663
                                                                            ──────────
       Total....................... ..........................  ...............$73,926,748
```

The amount of manufactures imported that year was, therefore, a little over two millions of dollars ; but I hold in my hand a return of the articles that made up this amount, and I find that several hundred thousand dollars of it could not fairly be classed as manufactures at all ; that more than half of the remaining amount is made up of articles not protected now ; and that the contributors who are protected now and could injuriously be affected by the treaty, are few in number and very small exporters.   And now let us place in contrast with this the great agricultural interest with its half million of hardy workers, which has no protection, which feeds the whole people, and contributes besides annually to the foreign exports of the Dominion commodities to the value of thirty-four millions of dollars. I hold in my hand a return of the customs duties levied on agricultural products going into the United States; and to show the advantage that would have accrued to our farmers from the operation of the treaty, I will now read some of the items : Animals, 20 per cent.; beef, 1c. per lb.; butter, 4c. per lb.; cheese, 4c. per lb.; honey, 20c. per gallon ; lard, 2c. per lb.; meats smoked, &c.), 35 per cent.; pelts, 10 per cent.; pork, 1c. per lb.; sheepskins, 3 per cent.; tallow, 1c. per lb.; wool (worth 32c. and under), 10c. per lb. and 11 per cent.; wool (worth over 32c.), 12c. per lb. and 10 per cent.; barley, 15c. per bushel ; beans, 10 per cent.; bran, 20 per cent.; flax (undressed), $5 per ton ; flax (dressed), $20 per ton ; flax-seed, 20c. per bushel ; flour, 20 per cent.; fruit (green), 10 per cent.; hay, 20 per cent.; hops, 5c. per lb.; Indian corn, 10 per cent.; malt, 20 per cent.; maple sugar, 20 per cent.; meal (oat), ½c. per lb.; meal (corn), 10 per cent.; oats, 10c. per bushel; peas (seed), 20 per cent.; peas (vegetable), 10 per cent.; peas (split), 20 per cent.; rye, 15c. per bushel ; seeds, 20 per cent.; tobacco, 35c. per lb.; vegetables, 10c. per lb.; wheat, 20c. per bushel. All these duties would have been swept away, and the American market thrown freely open for all farm products. The great lumber interest, too—in which 100,000 men are said to be engaged—which has no protection, which not only supplies our home market, but sends twenty-seven millions of dollars worth of lumber annually to foreign countries, and employs a large fleet of vessels in its traffic—how would it have been affected by the operation of the treaty ? Why, it would have swept away an average duty of 20 per cent. from the entire exportations to the States. And just so would it have been with our great mineral interest. Seventy-five cents per ton now levied on Cape Breton and Pictou coal would have been abolished, and the New England markets would have been freely opened to our coal trade. Twenty per cent. on iron ore and one and a half cents per lb. on lead ore would also have disappeared. The great coast fishery interest would also have been largely benefited, for the American market would have been secured to it for twenty-four years to come. On the whole, therefore, I think it will be safe to come to the conclusion that however a portion of our manufacturing interests might have been affected by the treaty, the result on the large industries of the Dominion could not have failed to be beneficial.

I come now to the objections which have been urged against the treaty from such quarters as entitle them to a formal answer. The first of these is the allegation that the treaty discriminated against Great Britain in favour of the United States. Nothing could be more unfounded than this. It was perfectly understood from the opening of the negotiations that no article could be free from duty in regard to the United States that was not also free with regard to Great Britain, and nothing else was ever contemplated for a moment.

The other objections which have been made I find so clearly formulated in a memorial of the Dominion Board of Trade, and clothed in such unusually temperate language, that I shall answer them *seriatim.* And I venture to believe that a very cursory examination will show how very little force is contained in the whole of them.

The first objection of the board is in regard to what has been styled "the sliding scale," and about which we have heard a very great deal for many months past. In the first place, then, I have to say that the gradual reduction of the existing customs duties was not part of the treaty, but merely a mode of putting the treaty in operation as easily as possible for all parties concerned. It was suggested merely as a means of overcoming two difficulties found to exist, not only in the United States but in Canada as well. It was supposed to be not undesirable to give manufacturers some time of preparation for the change by gradually reducing the existing duties on foreign goods. Moreover, had the duties gone off in one day the revenues of both countries would have been seriously affected, and the simultaneous imposition of new taxes to replace the loss of revenue might have been a difficult task. But, in truth, the importance of this matter has been absurdly exaggerated. It has been totally ignored that though the duties of the United States on fine manufactured goods are enormously high, on the articles we send them the average is only about 24 per cent. Now, one-third of this coming off would have made their rate for the first year 16 per cent. while ours would have been nearly 12, and for the second year their rate would have been 8 per cent. against our 6 ; and at the end of the second year all the duty would have come off in both countries. Moreover, the important fact seems to have been forgotten or concealed, that we would have had some compensation for that small sliding scale disadvantage, in the fact that the coasting trade and ship registry clauses would have gone at once into operation, while the enlargement of our canals could not have become available before 1880. And to sum up the matter, it is by no means certain that the sliding scale might not have been dispensed with altogether ; for in the Customs Acts giving effect to the treaty, clauses would no doubt have been inserted giving the two governments power by proclamation to put the whole treaty in force at any earlier moment they might mutually find convenient.

The second objection of the Board of Trade is the danger they see in a promise to complete the canal works by 1880. I dare say the Canadian government carefully considered this matter before they committed themselves to it, and had the best advice upon the point that skilled engineers could afford them ; and I venture to believe that my honourable friend in the other chamber, who so admirably presides over the public works department, was as competent to judge of what was fitting to be done in the premises as any man in Canada.

The third objection is that in the opinion of the Board of Trade the entire ocean coasting trade of the United States should have been conceded to Canada.   No doubt; but probably the other party had something to say to that.

The fourth objection of the board is that the right of obtaining United States registry for Canadian ships cannot be regarded as a valuable concession, seeing that Canadians, instead of keeping their ships and sailing them, might be seduced into selling them, and thereby transfer to the Americans the great profits of the carrying trade.   I venture to think this objection is not worthy of a reply.

The fifth objection of the board is, that the Caughnawaga Canal should not have been stipulated to be built until the construction of the Whitehall Canal was absolutely secured.   The Canadian government thought otherwise, and I venture to believe they were right in what they did.   The chief interest of the United States may be " in the opening up of a new route to the ocean ;" but a very important interest in Canada is to open up a new water route from New England to the West.

The sixth objection of the board is, that the right of re-entry of goods into the country of their production should have been provided for, but was not.   All goods placed in bond can now be re-entered in the country from whence they came.   Surely the board cannot mean that broken packages of goods should be returned?

The seventh objection of the board is, that it cannot tell whether goods manufactured in either country must be composed entirely of native materials.   Certainly not.

The eighth and last objection is, that all consular fees and certificates should have been abolished by the treaty, but were not.   It is by no means clear that this would have been an advantage.

With regard to the recent action of the United States senate on the draft treaty, and its return to the president with the advice that it was inexpedient to proceed with it, I may state he explained that the proceedings of the senate were taken in executive session, and therefore strictly secret, but the probability is that no full discussion of the matter had taken place in consequence of the shortness of the session, the absorbing interests of the questions now agitated, and the large financial deficit that had to be met by the imposition of new taxes.   The fate of the negotiation is, however, settled for the present, but the agreement that resulted from it is on record, and no doubt will yet make its appearance again, and form the basis of a new and more successful negotiation.   It took six years to conclude the negotiation for the treaty of 1854, and not a few delays and rejections occurred in that time.   I totally misconstrue the present temper of the American public mind if a great change on the subject of protection and finance and foreign trade is not approaching; and when that day arrives, the large and practical scheme embraced in the draft treaty will hardly be forgotten.   But be that as it may, it is not for the people of Canada to be influenced by any such anticipation.   They have shown their ability to open new markets for themselves when the American market was closed against them, and the clear path for them is to follow up, with redoubled energy and perseverance, the policy on which they have entered. Let the Americans load their industries with customs duties as they choose; be it the firm policy of Canada to remove every barrier in the way of commercial extension, to repeal all duties on raw materials, on articles used in manufacturing, and on the common necessities of daily life, and to replace the revenue lost, if needed, by a wiser and cheaper system of taxation; let them seek to develop their great national industries, and especially the agricultural, shipping, fishing, mineral, and lumber industries; let them open up new markets adapted to their traffic; and let the Canadian flag be found floating on every sea.

INDEX.